Deepwater

❧ ❧ ❧ CAPE OF FEAR ❧ ❧ ❧

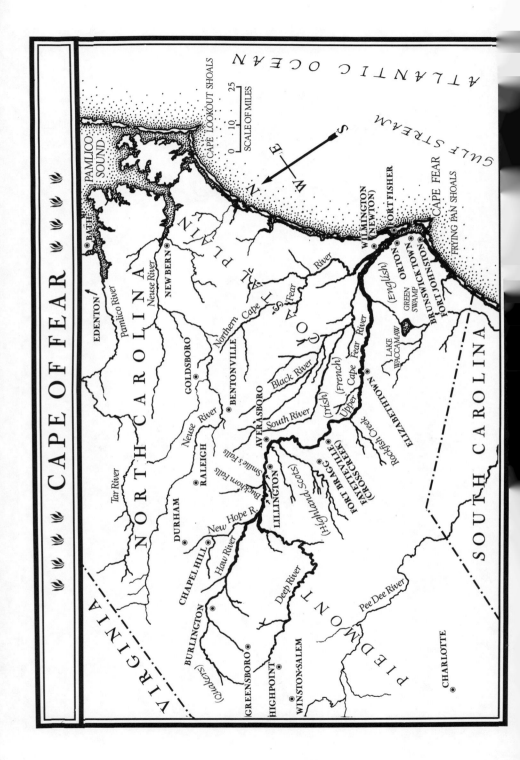

PAMELA JEKEL

*A
Novel
of the
Carolinas*

Deepwater

KENSINGTON BOOKS

KENSINGTON BOOKS are published by

Kensington Publishing Corp.
475 Park Avenue South
New York, NY 10016

Library of Congress Catalog Card Number: 93-080435
ISBN 0-8217-4485-2

First Printing: March, 1994

Printed in the United States of America

For my father, William Dale Jekel:

Hands that could tease out a splinter
And never retreat when I flinched.
Hands that held family reins lightly,
Easing them well when they pinched.

Hands that turned color to tableau
With a wave of a sable wand,
Hands like my own, long-fingered,
With a mind made to correspond.

My father's hands, my father's voice,
Are the roots of my writing life,
My father's heart heard my becomings,
My stories of daughter, woman, wife.

Though other hands balance my three-wheeler now,
I'm not so flawless as I was then,
And I doubt few will ever hear me
With such rapt attention again.

PREFACE

❦ ❦ ❦

There is a place in the middle of the East Coast of America, a three-hundred-mile sweep of sand and water, where the Gulf Stream meets the Labrador Current quite close to land. There the cold gray and warm blue waters clash and surge to make the stormiest place on the continental coastline, forming a great underwater quicksand nearly the size of Rhode Island and of an unknown depth. These are the Outer Banks of the Carolinas, long curves of shoal, sound, and island that sweep down from Virginia in a series of graceful, thin silver arcs and capes, the most famous barrier islands in the world.

Starting at the Currituck Sound, crossing the Albemarle, bounding the Pamlico, the Ocracocke, the Roanoke, the Core, Bogue, and Croatan, the Banks end north of the jut of land where the region's largest river runs to the sea: the Cape Fear.

Here, the fragrances of honeysuckle, jasmine, wild grape, and loblolly pines drift far out over the water as though to entice land-hungry mariners like the songs of mermaids. Here, ancient stands of cedar, live oak, and cypress enfold one of the densest swamps in America—the Great Dismal—and some of the richest salt marshes on the continent. And here, the wild sea winds blow constantly, often rising to great storms in the autumn, which crash out of the Caribbean and batter the Banks, taking a toll of ships and lives and earning these hungry shoals the epithet, the Graveyard of the Atlantic.

The Cape of Feare, early explorers called it from dread experience, but they returned again and again to its mountain-high dunes, its wild landscape of wax myrtle, yaupon, bayberry, and Spanish bayonet, to its dramas of legend and loss and dreams that did and did not come true. A place of wild beauty and solitude, this coast is also a place where time seems to stop, as it so often does by the sea. The waves surge in and out like the very rhythm of blood in the heart; the boundaries between watcher and water melt in the sun like sand under the high tide, and the only sound is the boom of distant waves and the endless rattle of sea oats in the wind.

Once the land was young, and breaker and undertow carried sand and made inlets where none now exists. Old maps show more than two dozen passageways to the mainland, though only six presently remain. The Atlantic rose and at the close of the Mesozoic, the Age of Dinosaurs, the coastline began where the cities of Rocky Mount, Raleigh, and Rockingham now stand. The glaciers advanced, the Atlantic fell, and the shoreline pushed fifty miles further east than it does today. Where the Blue Ridge mountains rise, a vast sea once ebbed and surged. To the east of this gulf, a great spine of mountains climbed out of the ocean bed, buckling and thrusting higher than the Swiss Alps, finally eroding down to the Smoky Mountains. This ancient Ocoee Range was a shoulder of old and dying mountains when the Rockies and the Andes were born. Across the Ocoees walked mammoths and mastodons, camels and great sloths, giant cave bear and woods bison. Following the game, the first tribes came across the land bridge from Asia to the Carolinas more than ten thousand years ago.

Man found there a paradise—but a paradise which sometimes, with small warning, extracted a high price for its pleasures. The Indians were well evolved by the time they reached the eastern shore of the continent, and more than thirty separate tribes claimed lands for their own. The Algonquin peoples lived mostly on the coast; the Tuscaroras or "Hemp-Gatherers" ruled the coastal plain. The Sioux tribes lived in the Piedmont region, and the Cherokee occupied the Blue Ridge Mountains. Whatever land they claimed, the people understood, at the deepest level, that they did not own the earth, that it belonged to the rain and wind and sun. The land was theirs only so long as they cared for it. Nature was always waiting to take it back.

But in the time of harvest, these lands offered rich bounty. Almost anything could be planted and would thrive, for the sandy loam was fertile, and the rivers flooded each season, refreshing the soil. Quartz and copper and clay were plentiful for tools and bowls, food was abundant in the rivers and the sea, and the winters were mild. Carolina, more than anyplace in the Americas, was Nature's sample case. There was something of everything . . . and something for everyone.

Coastal tribes like the Hatteras and the Croatoans found life more easy than most. As the pumpkins ripened, the people moved inland to their fields to harvest their crops and escape the winter storms. The dogs yapped as the hunters returned from the nearby woodlands shouldering white-tailed deer and wild turkey. Laughter and singing came from the women as they worked the wooden pestles, pounding corn and acorns that would be stored in the people's elevated bins for all to use. Then the corn dances began, and the old stories wove through the wattle-and-daub houses, tales of Owl and Turkey, Panther, and Wolf, and most of all, of Rabbit the Trickster. The children grew fat as young bear cubs. The priests led the men in ceremonies of purification, and the warriors shared the "black drink" from conch-shell cups, tea made from the holly bush for strength and wisdom. Over the fires, every hand turned to the carving of peak, or wampum from the conch shells, in preparation for the trade feasts with distant tribes. Life was easy, so long as they listened to the winds and watched for the coming of the storms.

But where life is easy, the land soon becomes crowded. As more generations thrived, game trails were trespassed, crops were stolen, and war shattered the peace. The Tuscarora, bolder and more numerous than the Croatoans, attacked by dawn, killing many warriors and abducting women and children as slaves. The Croatoans, in turn, raided the smaller Pamlico villages, taking away what spoils they could carry, including enslaved captives to serve in stead of those lost. In time, each man carried a war club when he left the protection of his walled village, and all about the palisades, the severed heads of enemies looked down to remind him to be vigilant against attack.

By the year 1524, when Florentine navigator Giovanni da Verrazano set foot on American soil, it was these native Carolinians who greeted him at the lower Cape Fear. His journals report that he and his men walked the land until they "became conscious of a murmuring in the silence of the night as if people were near, and proceeding a little farther, saw lights and heard the barking of dogs, the crying of children, and the chatter of men and women." They found the village of Necoes of the Waccamaw tribe, where one day the English city of Wilmington would stand. These coastal people were lords of an agricultural empire with communal fields, well-tended orchards, and a rich trade economy. They were also well acquainted with war. Canny and vigorous, they were not to be bought with a few trade blankets and brightly colored beads.

Later English explorers found these tribes harvesting crops they had never seen before like tobacco, corn, squash, pumpkin, and sunflower. They witnessed rivers choked with fish, wild turkey flocks of more than five hundred, parakeets in clouds so dense they blotted out the sun, and vast bays, tidal creeks, and grasslands, which were the nurseries for oysters, clams, scallops, crabs, turtles, and a thousand species of fish and birds. Schools of bluefish and porpoise crowded the waters just below the surface, and gulls, pelicans, terns, and skimmers wheeled and hovered overhead. They thought it "the goodliest paradise," this sweet-scented edge of a massive continent.

At first welcomed by the Indians and offered food and fish, the English took the offerings and laid claim to all they saw. They had found a fierce old coast, the oldest in America in terms of habitation, a place of windblown legend. They had found a people who knew far more than they about paradise. And they had found the Cape of Feare, where the only warnings of foul weather were the mare's tail clouds that drifted across the moon like tresses of silver hair, mermaid hair, outriders of the storm.

Cape Feare

❧ ❧ ❧

"It is the playground of billows and tempests, the kingdom of silence and awe, disturbed by no sound save the sea gull's shriek and the breaker's roar. Its whole aspect is suggestive, not of repose and beauty, but of desolation and terror. There it stands today, bleak and threatening and pitiless, as it stood three hundred years ago when Grenville and White came near unto death upon its sands. And there it will stand bleak and threatening and pitiless until the earth and sea give up their dead. And as its nature, so its name is now, always has been, and always will be the Cape of Fear."

George Davis, *South Atlantic Magazine,* 1879

PROLOGUE

❧ ❧ ❧

Roanoke Island, 1587

The August heat could do little to quell the women's delight at finding their feet on dry land once more. Even encumbered with heavy woolen skirts and laced bodices, they skipped as they went in and out of their huts carrying the trenchers and bowls, noggins and knives, platters of roast fowl and greens and meat pies. Calling to one another gaily like so many water birds, they soon had the long boards laden with enough good bounty to make a man's mouth water with gratitude, even if it might be the last decent meal they'd have in their lives.

John White watched them with deep satisfaction. He stood aside with the men, only half listening to their worrisome complaints. He knew the men must unburden themselves; he also knew he could do little to satisfy them. What did they expect, after all? The land was paradise, any fool could see it. Yes, the stores were scant, the heat unremitting, and the savages less hospitable than he had hoped, but he had brought these men safely to land, which was well worth some sacrifice, and he was weary of their fears. Their wives were more practical. They were arrived safe in the New World, they could prepare victuals and set them down on a table that did not threaten to tilt with every passing wave, and for now, they were content simply to feed their own.

In the line of women coming and going, he spied the taller head of his daughter moving gracefully toward the long table, heard her happy laugh above the chatter of the others, and he dropped all pretense of attention to the men at his elbow. "Even now," he said to Ananias Dare, his son-in-law by his side, "her step is as light as her heart." He smiled with unabashed pride. Eleanor White Dare, his only child and all he had left of his old life in England, was more lovely than any of the goodwives here. And also more pregnant.

"She has her father's spirit," Ananias murmured dutifully.

John White's smile turned slightly sour. Ananias Dare, assistant to Lord Raleigh, had been Margaret White's first choice for her daughter, despite the man's unctuous court manners and the fact that Eleanor was a full head taller besides. Now Margaret lay in the family crypt at Oakcroft, Eleanor carried the man's child, and White must endure this oily earwig across the heartless Atlantic and aye, even to the New World.

Eleanor lifted one slender arm then and waved to them both, gesturing them forward to the table. "Come and partake now, gentlemen, or we call the savages to board in your stead!" The women laughed as the men hurried to fill their trenchers, all their fears and discomforts forgotten for the moment.

John White took up his plate, filled it with good roast duck and sat a bit apart from his colonists where he might keep one eye on Fernandes's ship anchored beyond the farthest reef. Soon the ship would sail, leaving them here with no escape.

Flocks of waterfowl lay in the lee of the closest shoal, bobbing lightly on the blue-green sea, and he could feel the heat finally abating. It had been another relentlessly hot and humid day like the one before. The island felt so desolate now; a whole continent from which to choose and here they were stuck, surrounded by the mocking sea. Eleanor would give birth far from the feather beds and cunning hands of her women at Oakcroft; here in a mud-wattled hut, by the light of a guttering candle, on an island off the edge of the wilderness, she must bring forth the first Christian child in the New World.

He chewed more vigorously, pushing his doubts from his mind. Of them all, he must stand most firm in his faith. Raleigh did not choose him Governor so that he might babble of his fears aloud as the others did, nay, he did not have that luxury.

Eleanor left Ananias's side then and came to drop heavily alongside her father. She pinched off a bit of her meatpasty and slipped it in his mouth. "Do you think so long as you watch him, Fernandes cannot slip away on the next tide?" She smiled pertly, teasing him as always.

"I think even if God watches him, he'll do as he pleases," White said bitterly. "Got rot his avaricious soul."

"And may the West Indian pirates loose it swiftly from his breast," Eleanor murmured softly. She called gaily to Goody Cooper and added, "we're down to scant meal and water, Father. This will be the last pasty we'll see—"

"I know that well enough." White patted her hand gently. "But the fowl are plentiful, and the seas are rich with bounty."

"Some say we should make our way to Virginia as planned. Overland, if we must."

White was silent. Ninety-three men, seventeen women, and nine boys. How many would survive such a trek? How many would the savages leave alive?

They'd been a month at sea before White realized that Captain Fernandes's first priority was plunder, not the passengers in his care. He refused to stop for water and provisions, so hurried was he to reach the richer sea lanes of the Caribbean. Once there, he wasted precious weeks preying on small Spanish sloops. By the time they lay at anchor off Roanoke Island, intending only to return their two Indian passengers, stores were already light. White almost came to blows with the man, but no threat he might offer was as compelling as the lure of Spanish gold. It was always thus. Plunder pulled a man's soul astray.

The Bay of the Chesapeake had been their destination, but Fernandes refused to take them further. He set their goods onboard the landing ships, and they had no choice but to follow. Now here they were on Raleigh's old beachhead, a dilapidated military outpost on a windswept barrier island.

With Raleigh's blessing and the queen's command, they were to found "the City of Raleigh." He was governor. It was his duty to lead his people toward hope, since they had no choice but to stay. In the two weeks they'd been ashore, he already could see that they would need much of that commodity, since they had precious little of anything else.

As though she could read his thoughts Eleanor said, "Was my Lord Raleigh so blinded by ambition that he forgot the simple progression of the seasons? Mild though the climate might be, it surely will not grow vegetables in the depths of winter."

" 'Tis not his fault Fernandes tarried too long fishing for fat

Spanish flounder," White said wearily. He would not tolerate criticism of Lord Raleigh, not even from Eleanor.

"It does seem the height of arrogance to suppose that a single ship might carry everything a hundred and quarter emigrants might need to survive," she said mildly, following his gaze out to the calm water. "Nary a pulse will grow in this sand and not a stalk of maize."

Her father looked down at the ground, knowing what she said was true. The soil was more than half sand, and the hills at their back could nourish only scrub palmetto and sea oats. There were scant game trails on the island, and they'd be sick to death of fish inside the month. They must get to the mainland and soon. And then, he thought dispiritedly, then they could contend with the murderous savages as well as the killing land—

"Pipes!" John White suddenly called to the company still clustered around the long table. He rose to his feet, setting aside his trencher, ignoring Eleanor's start of surprise. "We must have a song of celebration!"

In answer, Goodman Cooper plucked his wooden flute from his pocket and started a bouncing tune. His wife quickly executed a clumsy jig, a slice of meatpasty still balanced on her open palm. A few of the bolder fellows stepped forward then to form a quadrille, pulling their goodwives into the dance, ignoring their happy protests. White saw that even Ananias Dare stooped to clap approvingly at their antics, and he helped Eleanor to her feet. "Go and dance with your husband then, mistress," he said to her, pushing her gently in his direction. "I can stand any discouragement but yours."

Eleanor glanced at him, a poignant look of understanding, and then she dimpled obediently and took her husband's arm in the quadrille, whirling away from her father as lightly as her bulk would allow.

🌿 🌿 🌿

Five days hence, John White's prayers were answered. Eleanor White Dare was delivered safely of a baby girl, named Virginia for her queen, Elizabeth of the House of Tudor.

The christening had to be delayed four days until the scouting party returned. White had sent six of his strongest men to walk the island, searching among the wax myrtles, palms, and live oaks for arable land to plant. They came back to report that the dunes were inhabited only by ghost crabs and clams up to where the sea oats and grasses turned to broom sedge, wild lettuce, and pennywort. What forest they found was a wild tangle of vines, Spanish moss, and stunted trees tortured by salt spray and storms. The soil was either sand or so soft and peaty that it could not support proper crops. It had taken them three days and two nights to hack their way through the brush, only to find less than two acres of decent soil for their efforts and a single small buck to carry back to too many mouths.

Fear spread through the colony, and eyes turned often toward Fernandes's ship, still anchored in the bay. John White was grateful for those few voices who joined him to counsel faith and patience, but in the empty places of his belly, his own doubt grew.

Had he been a fool to think he could succeed where others had failed? The first expedition made landfall safely and returned with favorable reports and the two savages, Manteo and Wanchese, the finest of their breed, with ample trade goods. The Indian chief and his brother were the darlings of court and a spectacle whenever they walked about the streets of London in their capes of feathers and fur. The queen was pleased, Raleigh got his knighthood, and Elizabeth laid claim to a continent, naming the lands Virginia in her honor.

The second expedition was not so fortunate. Seven ships and a hundred soldiers left behind at what was now Fort Raleigh—but they soon had to give up and sail back to England because no supplies arrived.

The third expedition was even worse. This time the men left behind at the run-down fort could not even secure passage home, and they were never found again. All they left as evidence of their courage were the ramshackle mud-and-wattle huts, which White's colonists now occupied.

Perhaps, after all, those who were afraid were the wise ones. They had trusted him, John White, appointed governor with Raleigh's blessing and at the queen's command, to bring them to the New World. Had he brought them, good Englishmen and gentlewomen all, to their doom instead?

White stayed up late into the night recording his thoughts in his logbook by a wavering candle. Raleigh had insisted that this time was different: with women along to firmly root the colony, they could not fail. And they would not be abandoned. White only prayed that Raleigh was still in favor at court, or they would be erased as surely as their footprints in the sand.

ⅲ   ⅲ   ⅲ

On Sunday next, John White led his company in celebration once more as they gathered to christen his granddaughter. He stood proudly in the makeshift chapel as men, wives, and boys wearing the finest clothes they could unearth from their trunks trooped in. Even in this heat, they paid him the honor of woolen doublets, sleeves tied in place, and full ruffed collars. Eleanor arrived on Ananias's arm, the baby swathed carefully in the christening linen brought all the way from England. As though Virginia Dare were a child of their own collective loins, the men and women voiced their approval in fond murmurs and exclamations of joy.

White used the opportunity to remind the company of their arduous journey, of their hopes, of the vast potential of the land about them, and then he turned to his daughter and nodded. She carefully drew the lace swaddling back from the baby's brow, smiling when the people leaned forward as with one pair of eyes to see this infant with such obvious pleasure.

White said, "In the name of the English church, the English queen, and English sovereignty, I christen thee Virginia Margaret Dare, the first Christian child born in the Virginia Territory. The first English child in the New World. And I commend thy Christian soul to God."

He held out the silver chalice brought all the way from Oakcroft and sprinkled the requisite drops on the baby's brow. Virginia awoke out of a sound slumber with that start, which only an infant can make—as if the earth itself had suddenly called its name. Without a cry, she swiveled her eyes about the company until she settled on the gleaming chalice. The silver flared and fired in the light of the candles and danced in her eyes. She stared—and suddenly sneezed.

Her mother laughed softly and recovered her head. "Such a welcome sound in the wilderness."

"Amen," echoed Ananias then, and the company repeated the benediction.

White took from his vest pocket a small packet and unwrapped the silk covering. He held up a gleaming filigree locket of gold on a heavily worked chain. It was distinctively marked with the White crest and the inscription, "The Year of Our Lord, 1565." He placed it gently over the baby's head so that the locket hung down over his daughter's hands.

"I gave this to Margaret White on the day of our marriage," he murmured. "And she never took it off for twenty years."

Eleanor's eyes welled up suddenly, and John White felt his own eyes instantly water in response. Always, had it been so. As a child, if she wailed, he felt her pain. Now, he felt her sorrow and joy, all mingled as the currents of the bay. He cleared his throat, raised his voice then and said to the company, "Let us toast my daughter and my granddaughter!"

Spontaneously, Goody Cooper threw her apron over her head and sobbed, and the rest of the company broke into loud and vigorous hurrahs, crowding forward to press hands and pat the child and take from the moment whatever comfort they could, as though they realized well enough that these victories might be few and far between.

🌿 🌿 🌿

Each day that passed saw the *Faire Wind* lighter and lighter of their goods and heavier and heavier with wood and water for its return sail. The men had cursed the ship with vigor when confined in her sweating, heaving belly. Now, like a lover taking her final farewell, she never looked more seductive. Emigrants no longer, they would have to become colonists at last.

After much discussion, they agreed that they could make it to late winter, perhaps early spring, with no new supplies. But past that, they'd be begging stores from the savages. Someone had to return with Fernandes to bring more hands and supplies. And no one had the power to approach Raleigh and the queen save John White, governor.

At first, he refused to leave his people. His duty was to them, he vowed; Raleigh had not appointed him governor that he would abandon them no sooner than they landed. And he could not leave his daughter and granddaughter!

But there was no one else who could accomplish what he might, and when Eleanor herself asked him to make the voyage and hurry back to them, he finally consented. They promised him that if they moved the settlement they would leave clear word of their destination and would protect his goods until he returned.

And now he stood on the beach bidding goodbye to those one hundred and twenty souls he had sworn to protect in the New World. Could anything have prepared him for this moment? he wondered. For shoals of shifting sands that could sunder the mightiest ships, which made landing itself as perilous as three months at sea? For winds so heavy and storms so violent that they left the very trees themselves as twisted and stunted as a Newgate beggar? He had the strong sense that just beyond the island lay paradise. Manteo had told him on the voyage of flocks of pigeons so thick that they snapped the branches off the trees, of doves, mallards, swans, and geese so plentiful that a man could swamp his boat with them, of oysters more than a foot across and shrimp the size of a man's fist. Yet they were clumsy in the face of this bounty, and starvation now threatened on this tiny strip of land.

Behind him rolled the pounding waves and the vast indifferent seas. As he shook hands and embraced comrades, a red-winged blackbird chortled from the waving marsh grass, swaying precariously in the wind. A quarreling mass of myrtle warblers fought over the scrub bayberries. Nothing in the land had been changed by his arrival, he saw, and nothing would be altered by his departure.

Will Claxton clapped him on the back heartily and said, "Don't let England forget us, Governor!" He was turning to shake his hand when the murmur came through the crowd, "Manteo is here, the chief is here. Let him speak; let him by."

From the edge of the company strode the chief of the Croatoan tribe, Manteo, newly christened and made Lord of Roanoke and of Dasemunkepeuc, his village, as ordered by Sir Raleigh, himself. They had seen little of the man since their arrival on the island, for he had been with his own people down the coast.

John White watched him approach, and he marveled at all the man's eyes had witnessed: the landing of the first English ships, the *Tyger* and the *Admirall*, the trade goods they brought, the vast

Atlantic from the deck of an English ship, the streets of London, and even the Queen.

Manteo was dressed in the clothes he had received from Raleigh, with a full panoply of armor, bombast-padded breeches, and a steel morion with full crest, despite the heat. His intricate black tattoos were visible down his arms, and his hair, black with white at the edges of his crown, was shaven except for his greased and painted scalplock. The colonists fell away from him quietly to let him pass.

John White bowed to him as if he were still at court. "King Manteo, Lord of Roanoke, I'm honored you come to say farewell."

The chief held up his hands in the gesture of friendship, and White saw that his nails were nearly as long again as his fingers. He remembered then how the savage had mocked the sailors of Fernandes's crew for cutting off from the body something that was so obviously intended for defense.

"I would not let John White leave without my words. We have been comrades for too long."

"I shall return before the corn goes in the ground again," White said. "We shall speak of all we have seen in my absence over a pipe, and you shall tell me which of your wives has given you another son."

Manteo smiled. "You will see the Queen?" He lifted up the silver medal he wore that Raleigh had presented to him in Elizabeth's name. "Tell her I wear her gift, yes?"

"I will tell her."

Manteo took White's arm and turned him gently away from the company. "And now I tell you what I came to say, but we will walk by the waves so only your ears and the sea will listen."

White glanced back at the colonists but patiently followed Manteo where he walked. Out beyond the breakers, the *Faire Wind* and Fernandes waited. He must go soon.

"I come to you as friend, not as king," Manteo was saying gently, "to say a truth before you take your leave. I was there on the beach five summers ago when the first white men came to our lands. I saw the sun flash on their helmets, I saw their great ship. I stood and greeted them with a speech of welcome, and then I went to my canoe and paddled out to catch fish. They took the fish and then claimed the beach as theirs. But still, we made them welcome."

"And you have been a good friend," White said patiently. "All who know Manteo know him as friend."

"This is also a truth. And so as friend I say to you, you must take your family with you."

White turned from where he had been gazing back at his daughter then, all his attention riveted on Manteo's face and words. "Why? You must tell me. Is there danger?"

Manteo shrugged. "I cannot say. But your people do not belong here. They will destroy themselves as the waves beat to nothing on the rocks. I have watched, and I have seen that the land does not want you on it. You cannot make it give up its goodness to you, my brother." He glanced up as a flock of black skimmers swooped in over the waves and out toward the reef, veering off from the crowd in a panic. "Even the birds fly from you in fear. It is a wonder to me you whites do not go out of this world, so uneasy are you in it. You say you have discovered the New World. But you are not first. And it is not new."

White felt anger rise in him, but he stifled it. "That may be, my friend, but we are here and here we stay. Now I must ask you this boon. Protect my daughter and her child. Keep them from harm while I am gone."

Manteo hesitated again, gazing out at the ship near the horizon. "I cannot do this. Your Raleigh may call me 'king,' but these lands know no king. Neither do the Tuscaroras or the Chowanoc or the Secotan. But I will say that no danger shall come to your daughter and her child from the hands of *my* people. That much, I will promise."

White dropped his head and considered. There was little else to say. He took the man's hand and clasped it firmly. "Thank you for your words, Chief Manteo, Lord of Roanoke. I shall give your greeting to the Queen, and I shall see your face again soon."

Manteo inclined his head slightly as a monarch learns to do, in that peculiar bow, which was less bow than dismissal. Then he walked down the beach, away from the waiting colonists.

John White hurried back to embrace his daughter, sweeping the savage's words from his mind with fierce will. "I will be back before the child can walk," he murmured in her hair. She kissed him tenderly on each eyelid, slowly, as though in benediction. She put her mouth in the fold of his neck, pressing the infant between them. He held the child's head softly in his hand, fondled the gold filigree locket she wore dangling round her neck, and then raised his eyes to his daughter.

"In the spring," she said softly, her voice level and clear. He noted with reluctant pride that she was able to make her farewell with a minimum of sadness, that not a single tear marred Eleanor's lovely cheeks as she stood waving, waving, still waving stoically as he was rowed past the first line of breakers, to where her figure was nothing more than a dark column on the sand.

🌿 🌿 🌿

And so John White sailed away from what Raleigh had called "the goodliest land" in the New World, tracing his way back through the Outer Banks, past treacherous currents and deadly rips where waves seemed to have no trough nor predictable path of travel. As Fernandes cursed and hauled and shoved the *Faire Wind* around unrelenting sandy shoals and shallow traps, the water leaped up in pointed seamounts, just beyond the islands, as if pushed up by monsters underneath.

When White finally saw open sea before him, he knew both great relief and inutterable sadness. Likely, he was safe, for the most dangerous part of the journey was behind him. But he could see no point of land now that gave him the illusion that Eleanor was still near. That he might ever hold his tiny granddaughter again. Ahead of him lay only the vast Atlantic.

🌿 🌿 🌿

On a warm night in early August when the tide was high, a massive shape rose from the waves and lumbered slowly up the sand. Even with the moonlight, her dark shell was difficult to spot, for she was low to the ground and kept her head in the water as long as she could. She stopped just up the beach and waited, listening intently for sounds of peril, waiting for the vibration of the sand, which would mean an enemy approached. When all seemed clear, she moved as quickly as she could in the direction of the softer sand, up to the dunes.

She was a female loggerhead turtle, almost five feet from nose to tail, covered all over her brown scaly back with barnacles that attested to her age and the watery world she had just reluctantly left. If the moonlight caught her right, the pattern of her red-brown scales on her head would be plainly visible, like the interlockings of mosaic tile. Her webbed front flippers helped her wriggle through the sand, but it was mostly her strong hind claws that propelled her out of and into danger.

Her heart-shaped shell distinguished her as a loggerhead, one of the largest of the six ocean turtles. Nearly a thousand pounds in weight, she feared little in the sea. But there was much to fear on land. Man. More fearsome even than the jaws of the shark. But even without man, she could perish easily enough. Simply falling over a rotted log or a sliding dune could leave her on her back, baking and exposed to the sun, the crabs, and the gulls, which would come in droves with the dawn.

Again, she stopped, watched, and waited, as though expecting a sudden noise or alarm. Again, she bent her head and struggled to hurry up to the dunes, propelled by a force from some dim recess of her brain that told her what she was soon to do was likely worth her own death, should it come to that.

Finally, she made it to a sheltered rise in the soft sand, turned and faced the sea, and began to dig rhythmically. In short time, she had excavated a wide hole with her hind feet, down to the place where the sand was more firm and almost damp. She backed up over the hole with a strong sense of relief and began to lay her eggs, one at a time, slowly and without stopping. She strained, her neck tautened and her mouth gaped as if to shriek silently, but there was no sound. All the while, tears streamed from her great eyes, while her lacrimal glands helped her get rid of her excess salt. Spasmodically, she forced out eggs between pauses, until she had deposited one hundred and forty-eight leathery spheres in the deep nest. Packed together like cells of a honeycomb, the eggs shone dully in the moonlight.

The loggerhead then methodically covered the eggs with sand, kicking slowly and determinedly with her hind feet. When the nest was covered, she raised herself as high as she could on her short, stubby legs and then let herself drop with a dull thud. Over and over, she smashed her belly on the sand until it was compacted, smooth, and betrayed no trace of her nest. Without a backward glance, she then made her way back to the sheltering waves and disappeared into the Pamlico Sound.

Ten weeks later the loggerhead's nest, long-since erased by the wind and the rain, began to erupt from the inside out.

Within hours, soft-shelled hatchlings, no more than two inches in length but perfectly formed, pulled themselves out of the sand under the bright light of dawn, and turned instinctively toward the reflection of the sun on the water. It was the brightness that called them. Had a fiery torch been waved before them in that instant, they would have hurried to it instead. But the sun was strong, the water beckoned, and so barely hesitating long enough to try their untaught flippers, they each raced frantically toward the safety of the sea. A hundred tiny turtles, leathery slate-gray bits, sprinted in clumsy fashion, leaving individual trails in the sand behind them.

From the dunes, gulls and vultures rose as if to a silent signal. They circled, then plummeted down; in winged fury, they sparred and screeched over the infant turtles. Some of the hatchlings were neatly decapitated by scissors-sharp beaks. Some were knocked on their backs, churning the sand desperately to right themselves. Some were plucked up by their tiny, waving flippers and dropped on the rocks below to be devoured quickly. Some merely stopped, exhausted and unable to continue, the weakest of the brood and doomed to die from their first breath. Others trundled on, never hesitating.

Now came the ghost crabs by the thousands, like a living, moving mat, waving their pinchers and descending on the turtles, eating them alive, even as they struggled to keep moving. Plovers and skimmers swooped in and picked them off methodically.

A pounding of bare feet then, and the noise of human voices. Two Croatoan fishermen casually walked among the turtles, collecting many in their nets, following the trail back to the erupted nest to gather the rest of the yet unhatched eggs. They then walked the dunes, poking with a long stick until it came up yellow. Quickly, they unearthed three more turtle nests.

Still, the remaining turtles kept moving to the water. Less than half of their number remained, and most of those would fall to the sharks, groupers, seals, and other predators waiting just beyond the surf line. A few, a tiny minority numbering less than two dozen would swim past the surf to find shelter at the ocean bottom and perhaps survive.

For seven years, the loggerhead hatchlings would never leave the sea and so would evade man, their most rapacious enemy. In those seven years of growing and feeding, each turtle would learn to escape the worst of threats—except the one that walked on two legs on every nesting beach.

Of the thirty-four turtle infants that made the long trip to the sea that morning, eighteen were female. Each one, if she bested seven years of tremendous odds, would come once more to this narrow Carolina coast, to almost the exact spot she first entered the waves, to meet with a male of her species to mate. Then she would trundle up the same beach to lay her eggs as turtles had done since the melting of the glaciers, never once looking back to see which survived.

🌿　🌿　🌿

Three years passed before two large merchant ships, the Moon-light and the Hopewell attempted to get close enough to the barrier islands to drop off one small boat to cross the shoals. John White stood on the deck of the Hopewell, anxiously scanning the distant shore for signs of life with the captain's glass. He held himself steady against the rolling of the ship with braced knees, but his heart was as tumultuous as the seas around them.

How could it be that any benevolent God could have allowed such ill luck? Three years since he sailed from Roanoke! Three years he had tried to return, but always, always, his efforts were mocked and plagued with misfortune. He no sooner arrived back to Plymouth, but the damned Spanish threatened the seas. By the time the Spanish were defeated, the sea lanes were infested with pirates. Then the hurricane season, the Spanish again attacked, and finally, finally, he sailed with a captain whose skill at the helm was as rigorous as his sense of duty. And now, after five months at sea, White could just make out the inlet past the sandy bars where he had last seen his family. But as he trained his glass over the land carefully, peering through the mist, he could see no sign of any life.

And then, just to the north up the hazy coast, John White saw a wisp of smoke trailing up from the trees. "Captain!" he shouted, "A signal fire! They've seen us!"

Captain Spicer strode forward, taking the glass from White.

"Might be the heathens. Or a woods fire. Might be anything at all."
After peering a long moment where John White pointed, he said,
"I'll send two boats only, sir, and then only with men I can spare.
We've lost too much time already, and the storm season'll be on
us in a few weeks." He nodded firmly. "Ye have three days to find
them, that's all."

The next day, the seas were heavy and the tide was strong.
Captain almost foreswore his promise, but he resignedly gave orders for two small landing boats and a dozen men to row John
White to shore in the direction of the feeble plume of smoke. They
were tortured in heavy breakers as they tried to cross the bar and
one ship was swamped, tossing four sailors into the waters. White
watched in horror from the other boat as, shouting and flailing,
they drowned before his eyes and were carried out to sea in the
strong undertow.

It was dusk when a second landing party finally struggled to
sand, rowing for the light of a fire they saw through the woods.
They anchored and offered prayers for the souls of their fellow
sailors lost in the waves. John White sadly wondered if he would
be saying still more prayers the next day. But he persuaded the men
to join him in his efforts, and they sounded the trumpet, sang
familiar English songs as loud as they could manage, and called out
to whomever might be listening that they came as friends. The only
answer was the soft lap of waves against the hulls of the beached
craft.

With morning light, John White led the landing party toward
Fort Raleigh. It was August 18, 1590, as fate would have it, exactly
the date of the third birthday of his granddaughter, Virginia Dare.

As he walked the low, sandy shore, he was flooded with memories and smitten by the familiar scent of the land with its ripe
grasses and scrubwoods of cypress, cedar, and fragrant pine. What
a lush Eden this had seemed at first landing! Images taunted him as
he passed the place in the sand where he had stood and waved
farewell to the company. The place where he'd last seen Manteo,
the Croatoan chief. He could still hear the strange and winsome
sound the man could make—most exactly like the call of an abandoned fawn—by rolling a leaf together in his mouth and gently
blowing. A trusted ally. A man worthy of the honors Raleigh had
bestowed on him.

Behind him, the men struggled in the sand, their heavy armor and swords making their progress slow and clumsy. White cast his eyes about at the damp sand closer to the water without letting them see his obvious search. Then he saw what he sought: bare footprints. "Look there." He pointed to them, gesturing to the pilot who hurried up to stare. "Those are no more than a few hours' old." The news quickly rustled down the line of men, and White saw them shoulder their weapons, assuming new caution.

At the rise of the hill before the fort, they stopped. Below them, the high palisade encircled all that was left of the City of Raleigh. The weeds and vines had overrun the walls, and no sign of life disturbed the silence. A leaden fear settled over White. He raised his eyes to a tree at the edge of the sand. His eyes narrowed suddenly. Something was carved in the bark. He hurried over and bent down to touch the plain letters, "CRO" etched deeply in the bark.

"See here!" he called, as the men rushed to look. "We had agreed on just this! If they left this place, they were to carve on a tree where they had taken themselves. It means the Croatoans! But look, it has no sign of distress about it. We had agreed, if they were in trouble, they were to make the sign of the cross above their message. No cross is here, lads!"

"Perhaps whoever started it was stopped in midcut," a sailor said, peering closer.

White ignored him and hurried to the fort, the pilot right behind. Nearer to the walls, they found another tree, this one stripped of its bark in a wide semicircle round about, as though to clearly mark its message. "CROATOAN" was carved in the tree's girdle, deep and dark. The pilot bent and fingered the letters. "Been here a season at least," he murmured. "The sap is long dry, and the edges are curled and brown. No cross."

"They have gone in peace to the Croatoans, to stay with our friend and ally, Manteo. I am sure of it," White said triumphantly.

The men pushed aside the vines that tumbled about the front gate of the fort and assembled inside the high walls. Some of the sailors gingerly laid aside their weapons; others kept them by their sides. John White's triumph quickly dissolved as he stood and gazed at the destruction around them.

All the houses within the fort walls were torn down, some of them obviously ripped apart by violent hands. Doors were cast aside and splintered, chests pulled out on the ground and scattered, and over it all, the noxious, rank weeds poked and prodded and smothered the remains. As White went from one house to another, his alarm and sadness grew. Finally, he found his own chest of possessions, maps and papers, weapons and armor he had left in the care of his son-in-law until his return.

It, too, was rent and split open, the maps torn and rotted from rain, the armor rusted and ruined.

White straightened, passing one hand over his eyes in despair. Wherever Ananias and Eleanor had fled, they had done so in a state of peril. Nothing else, he knew, would make his daughter so abandon his possessions like this. He bent and picked up his breast-shield. Almost eaten through with rust. How long would it take to so defile such metal in this damp climate? Strange that whatever hands had so disturbed the armor had not stolen it outright—

"Master White!" the pilot called. "Come and see this, sir!"

White went to where the pilot and a few sailors were searching the remains of one of the few standing houses. A sailor's stricken face told him to expect the worst before he even saw it in the man's hand: a sword, only slightly rusted, protected as it had been by the light cloth wrapped about it. The sword was encrusted with a dark, tarlike substance.

" 'Tis blood," the sailor said grimly. "Likely a woman's blood, as that be a woman's linen."

White steeled himself to speak with the calmest voice he could muster. "No proof of that, man. Might not be blood at all, and if so, no proof it's even human."

"It's human, all right," called a sailor from behind him, "but the likes of him who shed it weren't!"

The pilot said quietly, "Sir, looks clear enough to me that the owner of that sword left it in a hurry, and likely not willingly. No man would, unless he could no longer hold it upright. I'm mustering us back to the ship."

White turned on him, appalled. "But we've hardly searched! What about the light from the woods? The smoke?"

"Likely the same savages who ravaged this place. Anyway, I'll not send men to their deaths chasing phantom fires and spirit smokes." The pilot turned to his second and gave the order to assemble outside the fort walls.

White grabbed his arm. "Women and children were left here, man, *English* women and children. We must rescue them!"

"English women and children should stay on English shores," the pilot said. "I'll not risk more men on these shores after nightfall." He pulled his arm away gently. "I lost four, and that's enough."

As the boats struggled back to where the *Hopewell* lay at anchor, White stared at the receding coastline. Hope was all he had left, and so he would cling to it as ivy clings to brick in the blasts of winter. It came to John White in that moment, gazing at the coastline that seemed to promise so much and had taken away so many, that in every life there is likely one large error, that one misstep that makes a man realize that all his previous mistakes have been mere deviations, and negligible. Coming to the Americas had not been that mistake. Leaving had been. Leaving his family—all that was left of his family—to return to England, even for rescue, leaving them to their fate, to be suffered without him. That was the most grievous error.

He resolved to himself that he would never stop searching for his daughter and his grandchild, not so long as he could put one foot before the other.

But when he asked to be put ashore farther south that he might try to find Manteo or his people, Captain Spicer refused. "Look, sir, ye can see my difficulty here. The storms will soon be on us, the coast is more treacherous than any I've sailed, and we chase phantoms with a crew who has seen a blooded sword and fears a massacre at every inlet. I risk mutiny if I sail south and anchor; I risk disaster for my vessel each time I move closer to shore. I'll not do it, sir, not for you nor the poor souls ye wish to save, and neither would my masters *have* me do it."

"But I know they are there! We cannot leave them!"

"I agreed to put ye off at Roanoke to search, I did not agree to survey the whole god-rotted coast looking for a castoff score of fools who may or may not be dead for their pains!"

Though White protested, Spicer would hear no more. When White threatened to jump overboard and swim for the coast, Spicer had him tied, his feet shackled, and bundled him belowdecks. From a tiny porthole, White watched as the shore of America receded in the distance. As the *Hopewell* struggled desperately against high seas and a hard gale to turn away from the bar, he turned his back on the view, put his bound hands to his face, and wept for a world and a family he knew was lost to him forever.

❧ ❧ ❧

John White never saw his people again. Some later settlers heard rumors that a Spanish warship came on them and killed most, enslaving the rest. Other explorers reported that they had been massacred by hostiles; some suggested that they might have tried the perilous journey back to England in their small boat and been lost at sea.

John White continued to believe, however, that his people went south with Manteo, lived with the tribe for years, and eventually emigrated inland with the rest of the Croatoans. For years, White pressed Raleigh to send rescue, to let him go again to the treacherous coast to find his family and the other families he'd abandoned. But Raleigh had lost influence at court and could no longer help him. When White went himself to beg favor, he could gain no audience. When he tried to hire a ship himself, no captain would take him on.

Rumors plagued White until he was no longer himself in his mind. He wrote to the relatives of those colonists, back and forth incessantly, trying to discover what could be done. The last rumor that reached him was the most bitter.

Captain John Smith's men reported that south of the James, they were told that there were whites dwelling among the Chowanoc who lived in high houses, wore clothing like Smith's men, and owned much brass. Most of them had been slaughtered by Powhatan's warriors, but a few had escaped . . . four men, two boys, and one young maid. These lone survivors had taken refuge with the Chowanoc who protected them. Powatan, chief of all the Chesapeake tribes, a man who would one day play a major role in the history of Jamestown, had been told by his shamans that if the English were not destroyed, they would ultimately bring an end to his empire.

The king gave instructions to the Jamestown colonists to try to find any survivors of the lost colony. Two men sailed down to Roanoke Island, but they could find no trace.

John White eventually settled on one of Raleigh's estates in County Cork, Ireland, for his own lands had been sold or bartered to Fernandes, to other captains, to those at court to buy favor. He wrote one letter to Richard Hakluyt that spoke of "The Lost Colony" of 1587 and said that he believed they had survived, but he never referred to it again.

❦ ❦ ❦

For long years, the coastal tribes were little bothered by the white men in their sailing ships. The bright tin dishes the English left behind soon brought more than twenty skins, for once hung about the neck, they made good defense against the arrows of enemies. Their copper kettles were worth more than fifty skins, and their hatchets, axes, and knives eagerly disappeared among the tribes as quickly as summer rain onto the parched land, dispersed along the trade routes as far to the west as the mountains of the Cherokee.

Across the vast sea, the Queen whose hand had placed the silver medal around Manteo's neck died an old woman, still a virgin by all reports. Her favorite, Raleigh, was beheaded by her successor, James I, but the news did not reach the shores of what King Charles II then called "Carolana," nor if it had, would it have made a difference.

And so, for half a century, the tribes of the coast saw no more sailing ships bringing white men to their shores, and the faraway rumors of a city of English in the largest bay to the north, Powatan's Chesapeake, were too distant to be repeated around the fires with any but the most scant interest.

In the fall of the year 1654, a young man from Jamestown in a boat laden with furs landed at Roanoke. The chief received him cordially and showed him the ruins of the palisade walls and the ancient leaning walls of the colonists' houses. He showed the visitor some remnants of rusted armor and brittle linens they had left behind, but no, he could not say where they had gone.

A few years later, more English began to drift south from Powatan's territory, following the Chowan River, which flowed past the Chowanoc village, down the Blackwater River, and finally to the Albemarle Sound. As they moved among the tribes, they saw that the lands were clear, wide, and fertile, for they had been worked for generations. Because the Indians rotated fields, not crops, large areas appeared to the newly arrived settlers as abandoned land, open for use.

The elders cautioned that the settlers must be driven out, and the warriors were eager to try, but so many of them were weak from the new sicknesses that swamped the villages that they were unable to muster enough for war. The shaking disease and the painted sickness came round regular as the seasons now, and with each new plague, the warriors were fewer. Meanwhile, more and more settlers moved over the cornfields and set their walls across the game trails.

In 1700, more English came to Manteo's old village of Croatoan, along the narrow strip of sandbank that the tribe had been able to hold, largely because it was useless land. The people there now called themselves Hatteras, but they greeted the whites eagerly as long-lost kin, saying that some of their ancestors were white as they were and could talk in a book. Three elders tried to tell the English the old tales, but the visitors only pointed to their gray eyes and spoke among themselves.

When Voyaook, the old woman, came before the fire, she wore her metal buckle in her red hair and her skirts, each one over the other, as her mother had taught her. She tried to tell the English one of her people's favorite stories, of how the first white children learned the words of the Croatoan by listening to the gulls—but the men were rude to her and did not stop their speech for her tale. She had planned to show them her most valuable treasures, the chain of yellow metal with the tiny round yellow clamshell that opened and the paper with talking pictures that her mother had given her, but since they did not seem to show interest, she shrugged and went back to her own fire.

Part One

❦ ❦ ❦

1711—1750

"I find these colonists to be extremely ignorant, insuffer-
ably proud, and consequently ungovernable. In addition,
they are fractious, mutinous, and domineering."

An Anglican missionary sent by
King Charles II to the Carolinas

❦ ❦ ❦

Of all the colonies, North Carolina had the most unsatisfactory relationship with the Crown. Because of its isolation—largely a matter of geography—and the spirit of its people—largely a matter of those who sought isolation—this southern region was early marked "the Colony Different" by those who would attempt to rule it.

In 1677, John Culpepper, a Carolinian who had been "invited to leave" Charles Town because he liked a good fight, arrived in the Albemarle and found the unstable conditions there much to his liking. He organized a defiance against the king's new Duty Acts and Navigation Acts, which resulted in the first popular uprising in any of the colonies against the Crown a full hundred years before the infamous Boston rebellion. So it was in North Carolina, not Massachusetts, that the Revolution began. And it was not over tea, but tobacco.

Yet while the colony was simmering in rebellion, and the Indians and settlers bartered, stole, and quarreled over the inland coastal plains, the land that essentially defined and isolated the Carolinas—the sweeping coastline—remained largely undisturbed. The unique combination of impenetrable sandbars, shallow estuaries, vast inland swamps, and river bottomland forest dramatically shaped the lives of the Indians, the voyages of discovery, the settlements of the colonists, and even the course of the Revolution.

Virginians were irreversibly committed to tobacco, and every year, hundreds of indentured servants shipped to the Chesapeake to toil in the fields. But when they completed their terms of service and became freedmen, they wanted their own tobacco land—and even in 1700, there was little to be had.

They moved south. Because they could not approach from the sea, the settlers had to travel by land among and finally past the Indians. This infiltration and eventual encroachment was to make a crucial difference for the fate of the tribes. Soon, the towns of Roanoke, Bath, and Beaufort grew like spring mushrooms, often displacing dwindling native villages. One settlement, New Bern, was founded at the juncture of the Trent and Neuse rivers, where the Indian palisades of Chattoka once stood. By the year 1710, the Chowanoc and Weapemeocs had to abandon their hunting trails and cornfields to English settlements and cattle. Those who escaped enslavement fled south, where they joined the larger and more fierce Tuscarora tribes.

Never a people to tolerate trespass for long, the Tuscaroras were the most numerous tribe in the Carolinas, with fifteen villages and over twelve hundred warriors. Famous for their boldness and brutality in battle, they were the last strong native people on the coast. By the year 1710, they had lost so many game trails and so many of their women and children had been stolen into slavery by the white traders, that they appealed to the government to move them to a far region where they might live unmolested. While an answer to their petiton was delayed, settlers continued to ply them with rum, cheat them in trade, and force them off their lands.

By late summer in 1711, the fury of the Tuscarora warriors could no longer be controlled by the elders and shamans who still sought peace.

🌿 🌿 🌿

The heat of that September had improved little but the corn harvest. In the village of New Bern on the river Neuse, as the temperatures rose past ninety with humidity hovering almost as high, Leah Hancock pinned up her skirt and left off her bodice and sleeves. It was simply too hot to bear the layers modesty prescribed. The slaves already were nearly naked, and all of the matrons in town were weary of trying to keep them clothed decently. Like trying to keep the flies from the victuals this summer, it was a losing battle.

She left the turn of the meal grinder to Mistress Schoen, hoping that her stout German arm could make short work of the task. She excused herself from the dozen women working together and walked quickly to the shade of the live oak to stand, dabbing at her brow and tucking stray ends of damp hair up under her cap.

The river was hazy and listless in the heat, as though it could not tell itself from the edges of the air. In the distance, Leah could see the ocean, sense it actually, as she always could, at the farthest reach of her horizons. Often, it seemed to call to her in a voice like mermaids, and she would walk down the Neuse toward the Pamlico, to where the river was more salt than fresh, to where the low, scrubby vegetation gave way to sea oats and white sand. Far, far in the distance, she always felt the low hollow boom of the waves, sensed them in her skin and muscles. James always told her she was imagining it, you couldn't hear the ocean from the riverbank, he said, but she could. More, she could see the waters clearly in her mind's eye, the combers marching in one after the other, perfect and powerful all the way across the tossing blueness, all the way from England. She could almost hear, she thought, in the hush-sh-sh of the waves and the catcalls of the gulls, the hum and cackle of London streets, translated by all those miles of water and time. Likely, she knew, this translation would be all she would ever hear of England again.

Most here never gave England a thought, she supposed. When the Baron de Graffeneried secured this land from the savages, he filled it first with his Swiss and German compatriots, and they were so grateful to leave the Continent, she doubted they ever gave home a backward glance. But to those few English in New Bern, those several allowed small tracts among the good *herrs und fraus*, England sang to them across even the great Atlantic.

Leah glanced around to the women working, hoping she had not yet been missed. Lord, but these Germans loved labor! In the three months since she and James had moved to New Bern, she had seen no rest taken except on the Sabbath—and then, only scant hours from noon to dusk for services.

But James had only praise for his new neighbors, and so she stifled her own despair at their condition and tried to appear as grateful as he was for the free land and the opportunity. Certainly, it was better here than in Bath, he said, where every garden plot was taken and every eye watched to see that none trespassed the boundaries of taste and culture. Bath had far too many, James said, of the three greatest scourges of mankind: priests, lawyers, and physicians.

She sighed and closed her eyes for a moment. Bath was as close to England as the colony could provide, she guessed, and she would miss it till the day she was old and fat as Mistress Schoen.

She turned from the river and gazed upward. The men were about half through with the cottage shingle roof. No more thatch! James would be pleased to see it done at last before the fall-of-the-leaf. Lord knows, he had helped raise his neighbors' roofs often enough; it was more than their turn. She watched for a moment as her husband and the other men clambered about on the eaves, working together as a small army of ants might assemble a sand castle, grain by grain.

The sound of a child's voice raised in pert demand reminded her instantly that she had not checked her own two in the last half hour. She walked over to where the slaves were shucking the corn and saw with wry amusement that her Tess and Glory were right where she saw them last—hunkered down at Whypin's knees, listening to one of her interminable stories.

The two little heads, baby Glory's red hair bright against Tess's larger brown thatch, both of them bent close to Whypin's black head, did not smite her heart with the same misgivings such a scene might have raised in the hearts of so many mothers in the settlement. I am fortunate, she told herself as she did often, to have such a dependable servant. She is no more infidel than I, she thought, then realized what response such a reflection would get from most of her neighbors.

Leah Hancock much preferred the native slaves to the redemptioners who had come over on recent ships. Let her neighbors take that flotsam on, she told James in bed at night. Let them try to get five years' work out of them and then have to pay their freedom dues of fifty-some acres, seed, clothing, and tools. Let them try to teach the debris of London streets a decent trade. Most of them were poor orphans or bastards, the meaner sort of people. No, she told her husband, I will take a savage to my hearth any day over an indentured servant.

But few of her neighbors had been so lucky in their choice of slave as Leah, and that she could not deny. No wonder little was on their lips these days but the treachery of the heathens. They were like vipers they had nursed to their collective bosom, they said, sly and barbaric, capable of godless cruelties and torture, which they would inflict with no warning. Yet there they sat, twenty of the settlement's thirty slaves, patiently shucking the settlement's corn, while the children ran to and fro as gleefully innocent as colts.

"Tess!" she called to her eldest. Tess stood obediently and caught up her young sister's hand. Leah Hancock smiled down at her daughters as they came running. One was good and one was lovely, and so they would do well in the world. "Leave Whypin to her work, chicks," she said to the girls. "She'll run out of stories if you keep plaguing her for them."

"Well then, if she runs out she can tell them all over again," Glory said with her habitual flounce of hip as they walked away. " 'Twon't hurt her to say them twice."

"Maybe it would make her weary," Tess said to her sister. She was two years older and had grown a maternal voice that she used exclusively with Glory. "Maybe we should let her rest a bit before we make her tell another."

Glory considered that for a moment, her fair mouth pursed up into a melon-colored bow. Leah Hancock was at once alarmed and amused to see that her daughter at five years had well refined most of the blandishments of a maid thrice her age. "We should tell John and Daniel not to plague her then, they're too old for stories, and she doesn't belong to them, anyway. That way, she won't get weary too much."

"And what makes you think, miss," Leah said lightly, taking both girls by the hands and leading them to where she could watch them at the grinding, "that John and Daniel'll do your bidding?"

"Oh they will," Tess confided to her mother. "They'll do anything for Glory." And she smiled proudly at her younger sister as though she, too, could understand that two grown boys of the village, their closest neighbors, would also be devoted to Gloriana, youngest and most lovely daughter of the Hancock house.

Whypin raised her head briefly and watched the Hancock woman walk her daughters away.

"You look at them as though they were your own," Ooka said to her. "You who will never have a cradleboard on your back." She yanked the corn husk angrily, and the ripping noise it made matched the venom of her words.

"I do not," Whypin said calmly. "But it is not hard to feel affection for the young of any creature."

"Why do you say she will never have her own children?" Una asked beside them. She kept her head down, but her words floated far over all of them with a high voice much like a skimmer's call. "After the English are swept from the land, we will all be returned to our people. We will take husbands and we will carry our own cradleboards."

Ooka laughed spitefully. "Even after all the English are dead and their bones are scattered to the seas, our people will not welcome us. We are slaves! For you to be slave, one must sell and one must buy, neh? Your own people betrayed you."

"Our people did not sell us," Whypin said patiently. "Why do you speak such hatred? One tribe fights another, captives are traded, it has always been this way. We were unlucky, that's all. But once the English are gone, we will go back to our people—"

"If there are any men to go back to. Once war starts, the English will fight like the bear in the season of berries."

"We will never be able to kill them all," Kenta said. "They have too many guns."

"We are already killing them, even as we speak," Ooka said softly.

"What news do you have?" Whypin asked. Eyes were kept down, hands still moved on the corn, but all breaths stopped and held fast for Ooka's words.

"The war has started," Ooka whispered. "My people took two English and their black slaves this dawn as they came up the river. They are in my village even now. They took John Lawson, the one who measures and marks the trees of the forest. They tied him to a tree and stuck him full of small splinters of wood like the bristles of a hog. Then they set him slowly on fire. When he was nearly dead, they cut his throat. The other white man is not dead yet, but he will never leave Catechna alive."

Whypin gasped. Ooka was stolen from her village of Catechna, from her Tuscarora people, by slave sellers from the place the whites called Charles Town to the south. From there, she had come by one of the big ships to New Bern on the Neuse. Almost, was she home again, for her people lived no more than a dozen miles upriver.

"Now the whites will fight to the death," Una said fretfully. "Before, they might have gone away if we wearied them enough."

"They will never go away," Whypin said. "They will be killed.

So will our people. That is the way it happened before, and that is the way it will happen again.''

"But here, we are more than they," Ooka said. "This village, at least, will be ours. And when the war is over, those who tried to make the peace will likely be dead as well." She looked pointedly at Whypin. "It has begun. When the warriors attack, you will kill your mistress, neh?"

Whypin picked up a final ear of corn and pulled the husks from it defiantly. "If my people fight, then I will fight."

"You will kill her hatchlings, that they will not live to build nests of their own?"

"I will do what I must," Whypin answered.

Kenta sighed and signaled the oldest child of her mistress to come and bear away her large pile of shucked corn. As the child came, bundled the corn into her basket, smiled and ran away again, the woman said sadly to Ooka, "Still it must be admitted that they do make pretty children."

"So does the snake. But would you hold one to your breast?"

🌾 🌾 🌾

That night it was still so stifling, even with a slight breeze from the river, that Leah was reluctant to fire more than the two betty lamps, though James needed the light to make his journal entries and she herself had more than her usual mending to do. Glory was growing so fast, so heedless of her shifts, she might take an hour every evening and still not keep up with the child's rents and tears. And cloth so dear! The supply ships from England came only every three or four months; the ones from Amsterdam came more often, but their prices were higher—five pounds of the best leaf tobacco for a decent bolt of Holland! Almost better to wait for the London ships, even if one did take the chance of importing the plague along with the cloth.

She gazed about to let her eyes rest for a moment, letting them fall on her pewter dishes so carefully arranged in her cupboard, diligently polished with wood ashes and oil. A wedding gift from her mother, they were her fondest possession, for they seemed to promise that eventually, she might have again around her tolerable quantities of plate and furnishings as she had hoped to have when

James Hancock asked for her hand. For now, she must be content with her Turkey-work chairs, her cedar chest with the brass lock and key, and her best silver saltcellar and cruet, all brought at no small trouble across the wide sea and from there, across the river from Bath. Now that solid shingles replaced the thatched roof, she at least would no longer need to trouble herself over rain leaks onto her table rugs.

Leah glanced over to the corner of the two-room cottage where Whypin was showing the girls how to make a corn-shuck doll. She was using silk grass, what the savages called bear grass, for thread to bind the doll. Soon, Leah herself would have to use the grass instead of worsted, if the supply ships were late again. The girls were intent on Whypin's hands, her words, and their voices, low murmurs that scarcely rose above the hot silence, wove and piped one over the other like a trio of birds, one low, the other two high and questioning.

The smells from the lamps, of burning hog fat, left her feeling slightly ill in the heat. She hoped the chandler would come to New Bern soon. Candles were so dear for the settlement had too few sheep for tallow as yet, but James said by next year, perhaps they would have a pair of lambs of their own.

James's head looked heavier now over his papers than a half hour before. The poor man was so weary these nights, Leah sighed to herself, straightening stiffly to relieve the ache in her back. Too many worries, too little to do about them.

"Girls," she called softly across the room, "say your prayers now, it's time for bed."

"Oh Mother!—" Glory began her perennial protest.

"Not tonight, daughter," James said roughly, rousing himself and shaking his head like a sun-dazed dog.

"Whypin," Leah said over her shoulder as she supervised the scrubbing of Glory's face, "I want you to pull your pallet closer to the door tonight, hear? In case I should need you, I don't want to call over half the woods to find you."

Whypin murmured her usual response. "As you say, missus."

"No," James said quickly. "You will bring your pallet inside the door tonight." He gestured to a corner farthest from the two sleeping cots. "Over there, put it."

Leah looked at him questioningly. The slaves of the settlement generally slept outside together like a pack of hounds. They preferred it that way, especially in this heat. James returned her glance and shook his head, and so she said nothing.

Whypin, with the slave's practiced talent to turn away unwanted notice, simply dropped her head in obedience. She rose and went to the door. Her silent movement was the only one that caused Lion, James's hunting hound, to raise his head and watch. James observed the dog carefully as Whypin went to the door, unlatched the leather strop, stepped outside the light of the lamps and then came back again in a few moments, carrying her worn blanket. She had slept on nothing else since she had come to the Hancocks, though Leah once had offered her a shuckstuffed pallet, much like the one on the girls' cot.

Leah quickly washed herself, unlaced her skirt, hung her linen on the wall peg, and slid under the thin oznaburg sheet on the cot. Even the touch of that worn, soft fabric seemed too heavy in this heat. She longed to throw off the cover, toss away her shift, and run to the door and feel even the smallest breeze from the river, stand there naked and exposed to the black, warm air. But she only turned restlessly, once, twice, then moved aside for James as he settled beside her.

A decade, they'd been wed. James had been the most promising young man in her village of Maidstone, in west Kent, with dreams of a fortune to be made in the colonies. Once Tess was born, they sailed to Bath where James hoped that tobacco land would be cheap and plentiful. But land was scarce, so with Glory in arms, they turned their wagon south to the village of New Bern.

She tried to ignore the heat and relax her weary legs. In the darkness, she waited for sleep. As it did not come, she listened to the light, shallow breathing of her daughters. How dear they were. How she envied them their easy descent into each night's rest. She held her breath and listened for Whypin's breathing. It seemed to her to be, too, the natural slow rhythms of sleep.

But James was wakeful beside her. He lay still, but she knew he did not rest. Finally she whispered, very close to his ear, "What is it, my heart?"

He sighed, and she knew that whatever he carried, he longed to let down.

"You must tell me," she added. "I can't be ready for what comes unless you tell me."

"It's only rumors."

"Tell me, James."

He rolled so that he could see Whypin on her pallet. Still unmoved against the wall, she appeared to be fast asleep. He rolled closer to her, his mouth up against her temple. "Lawson and his party didn't return to the settlement tonight. They were expected, but no one's seen them. At least not by darkfall."

"Perhaps they came in late," she whispered after a moment. "And you'll hear in the morning."

"They're saying he's been taken."

"Who?"

"Crenshaw, Newton, a few others. They say no surveyor general would lose his way and stay in the woods beyond his expectations. They say the savages have him." His arm crept round her and lay gently on her breast. "If that's so, war is upon us."

"Surely, they won't be so foolish again. Last time they rose against us, we drove them down. They lost how many warriors? Most of fifty? And their whole harvest, and their lands. That was eight years past, and their elders have sued for peace—"

"I'm only saying what I heard," he whispered, faltering now at the vehemence of her denial. "Perhaps I should have said nothing."

"No, you were right to tell me. I must be ready for whatever comes." She glanced over once more at her sleeping daughters. "Tomorrow, we'll go to Goody White's cottage for the day. The girls can play, and I owe her a call. She's closer to the village center, and her house is stouter. We will wait for news from you there." She stroked the arm that lay across her breast. "Surely all will be well."

"Take Lion with you and leave the slave behind," he whispered.

"But the girls will ask for her—"

"I don't want the savage near you tomorrow."

"Yes, James."

He was silent so long that she thought he had finally slipped into sleep. But then he said, "Perhaps it was a grave mistake, bringing you to this wilderness. Perhaps the mistake of my life."

"Hush," she said quietly, rolling over now so that she fitted easily into the curve of his body, her back to his front as a fist and a hand together. " 'Twas no mistake. The morrow will come, and with it news of Surveyor Lawson. The brutes dare not bring down such trouble on their heads again."

As her husband's breathing settled finally into rhythms she recognized, Leah lay awake, her eyes burning into the darkness. Burning into the dark shape that was Whypin, lying on the dirt floor against the chinked cabin wall. She saw that in the dark, Lion had crept so that he lay close to the slave without touching her. Likely the coolest place, she thought to herself, as she drifted into dreams of shadowed woods, faraway blue horizons, and the distant sound of rushing water.

💮 💮 💮

Whypin knew why the woman left her behind. As she washed the linens, wrenched them, and hung them to dry, she saw once more the way the woman's eyes did not meet hers, and she knew.

The missus was wary. For the first time in the three seasons since the white woman had bought her from the slave traders, she was regretting her purchase; Whypin could feel it coming from her skin like a sweat. She was plumped with suspicion, this mother, like a broody hen with eggs.

Whypin worked more slowly at her chores once they left her behind, for she knew that she could not possibly finish all that had been left for her to do, even if she tried.

Water must be carried, bucket after bucket, so that the linens could be washed with the stinging lye soap in the kettle and then twisted and twisted, finally to drip from the line strung across the side porch. The yard must be wet down and swept, the smokehouse cleaned, the vegetable rows weeded, and the fowls plucked, salted, and hung. She must round up the hogs that were running loose in the lower fields and lock them in the pen for fattening. And finally, the most hated work of all—the dried corn must be pounded in the samp mortar. This alone could take half a day, she knew; most of the white women set their slaves to this chore before any other, for it was the most tedious. Pound, pound, pound! These seasons, the steady thumping of the stamp mortars was the first sound heard from a white village, from a mile away across the water. That was how her people marked how close they were to New Bern when the fogs came in.

Her people. Whypin sensed them coming like a storm rising up from the sea. As she kneeled in the pumpkin rows, rooting out the weeds with her digger, she listened to the earth as though it were a great heart beating beneath her body. As if she could hear the thunder rolling, not from the sky, but from the ground itself.

And so she was not surprised when the missus came back, hurrying with her skirt flying, pulling the children behind her, their eyes wide with alarm. But she was startled when the woman called to her, "Whypin! Whypin! Come here at once!", and without thinking, she dropped her digger and went to her, even though a voice in her head told her to run in the other direction, away toward the woods.

Leah Hancock met her on the porch, holding Tess and Glory by each hand. "Is there to be war?" she asked Whypin quickly, her eyes searching Whypin's face. Her voice was hurried but calm.

Whypin immediately dropped her head, silent.

"You must tell me," she pleaded softly, "if you know. It is one thing for our men to fight each other, it is quite another for them to kill our children. Please, tell me!"

Whypin glanced at Tess, who stared at her with wide, frightened eyes. "I have heard it told," she answered finally.

"When?"

No response.

"When will they come!"

For answer, Whypin looked past the cottage toward the village where she saw a small band of her people going to the door of the White cottage. As they did every morning, they went to doors for food and meal. But this time, there were more than a score of beggars, all of them men.

Leah followed her glance, gasped once, only once, and then set her face firmly. "Well, then. You must take the girls and hide them in the cold cave. Stay with them, Whypin, and keep them silent and safe."

Glory cried out, "Mother!", and Tess's face was very pale.

Whypin gazed down at Tess, speaking more to her than to the missus. "I cannot."

"You must!"

"My people come."

"I don't ask you to shoulder a musket, I ask you to save the children. Now, take them and hurry!" Leah begged, thrusting the girls' hands into Whypin's own.

She took their small fingers into hers. "You would trust me with your babies?" she asked softly, wonderingly.

"I have no choice," Leah said.

Still more savages threaded down between the cottages; more Indians than she had ever seen in one place. And in this heat, they still wore their capes about their bodies. . . .

"Go now!" she cried out, pushing Whypin away from her, as she saw James hurrying down toward their cottage. Lion loped at his side, his tongue hanging out foolishly as though he, too, smelled peril in the humid air.

Without another word, Whypin turned and pulled the girls behind her, Glory now weeping softly, Tess silent as stone. She bent low and hurried them around the corner of the cottage, past the cookhouse, the smokehouse, the necessary building, back through the fields, and toward a small hill that rose at the rear of the Hancock plot. There, the mister had dug a shallow cave in the earth to keep the pumpkins and the potatoes cool. It was empty now, waiting for the harvest. Whypin moved the brush and rocks that had been set before the opening to keep out the dogs and quickly slipped inside, pulling the girls after her. Then she pulled the brush over the opening so that some light entered, but they could not be seen easily from the cottage.

Now Glory began to wail in earnest. Without hesitation, Whypin sharply slapped her small lips, and she gasped and stuttered into shocked silence. "You will be still," Whypin said gently, "or you will be killed."

Tess moaned, low and keening as a rabbit in a trap. "Will they kill my mother?" she asked, the tears running freely down her cheeks.

"I do not know," Whypin answered. "We must wait and see."

"They will kill everyone!" Glory hissed. "The savages will kill Papa!"

Tess snatched Glory's hand and squeezed it so tight that the young girl cried out softly. "Don't say that," Tess said, her voice suddenly stronger. "Be very still and don't say that again."

Glory subsided, pulling her hand away and rubbing at her eyes.

A sudden shot of musket fire and the sound of yells came from down the hill and across the fields. Whypin stiffened and moved so that she could spy through the brush cover to a small window of pumpkins and cornstalks and beyond to the cottage. Smoke was rising from another cottage farther away, and she could hear the running of many feet coming closer.

Tess parted the brush just enough so that she could see, but Whypin pulled her hands down and turned her head away. "There is nothing you can help by watching," she said.

But then the screams came to them over the tops of the corn-stalks, and all three of them pressed to the edge of the cave in horror, unable to pull their eyes away from the small slits of light and sight through the brush. Lion came racing round the corner of the cottage with three warriors fast behind him. They had thrown off their capes, and Whypin could see they were painted for battle. Without stopping, they took aim, arrows flew at the dog's head and haunches, and he tumbled and rolled, trying to bite at his flanks in desperate pain. One Indian clubbed him brutally in passing, stretching the dog out in a long, unmoving line of yellow fur, bristling with arrows. Then the warriors turned to the cottage, where James Hancock bravely met them in the open doorway, his musket raised before him. He shot down one, turned to aim for a second, when four more warriors rounded the cottage and fell on him. His body disappeared beneath their rising arms.

Tess was sobbing audibly now, but she did not move her eyes away. Glory sank to the ground, covering her head and eyes with her sister's skirt, and Whypin could hear her retching and weeping all at once.

Beyond the cottage, flames were consuming one building after another, and the shouts and yelps of the oncoming battle were louder still. Musket fire answered the shouts, rapidly at first and then less and less as the fight moved through the village. From the smell of the smoke, Whypin could tell that her people were burning the fields as well as the buildings, and when she saw another cluster of warriors running toward the cottage, her eyes widened in amazement. One of the men was her brother, she was certain, though she'd not seen him in more than two years. He was markedly taller, stouter, and painted with the black and red stripes of war. He raced past the cottage with a burning torch in his hand, and she lost him in the moving throngs of warriors who were circling the cabin now. Smoke began to rise from the back of the Hancock place, and Whypin could smell the quick incineration of the master's baled corn shucks, which he had stored in the back.

Two warriors jumped on the newly-shingled roof and began to

set it ablaze at two corners; three more tossed burning torches inside the door and the two small windows to the rear.

"Mother," Tess whispered, half moan, half sob. As if her call were an incantation, a woman's scream shivered across the fields toward the cave.

"That was not your mother," Whypin said quickly.

"No!" Tess cried, "that wasn't her!"

Glory pushed herself up again and forced her head next to Tess's, still weeping. The smoke was boiling off the cabin now, and it was hard to see much of anything except when the occasional breeze moved the gray haze aside as if by a languid hand. In that instant, Whypin heard the shouts of the warriors increase, and she looked to see Leah Hancock rush from the burning cottage, holding a blanket over her head and beating at her smoldering skirts. She was instantly surrounded by a pack of warriors and yanked away from the flames, beyond the cottage to where Whypin could see her no more.

She glanced at Tess and Glory. They had seen their mother taken as well. Both girls slid down from their vantage points then, holding each other and weeping, rocking to and fro for all the world like two old women just widowed. There was nothing she could say to comfort them. She put a single hand on Tess's shoulder and silently pressed her hard to warn her of silence. Tess started, stared at Whypin's hand as though it were completely alien to her, and then convulsively gripped it. She continued to weep, more quietly now, and rock her sister back and forth.

It was hard to see much of anything for the smoke, but it did seem to Whypin that the shouts and tumult of war were fading somewhat as the endless moments crept by in the cave. She had no idea how long they had been hidden there, but she could tell by the slant of the light that some time had passed and that the long shadows of early dusk would come soon. The battle had taken most of the day, and the night was still to come.

Glory finally ceased her sobbing and sat quiet and stunned, her face white and stricken, her eyes closed as though she never wanted to see again. Tess leaned back against the cool wall of the cave, her hands empty on her lap and her eyes wide and unseeing. Whypin wondered what visions the girls watched behind those closed or vacant eyes. There was a noise again, this time from fairly close. Tess roused herself to look as Whypin did the same.

Across the smoking field, three warriors were searching for something on the ground. They bent and moved the weeds aside with their lances, murmuring to each other, occasionally stopping to pick up this or that bit of wood or metal and examine it.

"What do they look for?" Tess asked.

"I do not know," Whypin whispered, cautioning her to silence. "The metal nails, perhaps."

The warriors came nearer to the cave then and stood scanning the destruction around them. The cornfield and the pumpkin patch had been burned nearly entirely away. From where Whypin sat, it looked as if many cottages were destroyed. Smoke still hung heavy over the village, but when it parted, she could see some of the bodies of the English, many of them in tortured positions of desperate pain or flight. Many were partially stripped of their clothing, and small bands of warriors came and went from what was left of the bodies and the cottages, bearing war trophies away in their arms. Whypin wondered what spoils her brother had borne away and who waited for him to return in her village. Did he now have a wife? Perhaps a child of his own? Did he ever wonder what became of her?

"Is everyone dead?" Tess murmured.

"I do not know," Whypin whispered, with a glance to Glory. "Perhaps many fled in their boats."

"What will we do?" In her anxiety, Tess's voice raised above a whisper.

Whypin swiftly placed her palm over the girl's mouth, never taking her eyes from the men in the field. One had turned toward the hill where the cave was hidden, scanning his eyes over the rubble and brush suspiciously.

Tess and Whypin watched in fear as one warrior called another toward the cave; the two began to climb the hill while the third bent to pull something from the ground. Tess glanced at Glory, ready to clap her hand over the young girl's mouth instantly should she open her eyes. But Glory's face was slack, her mouth open with shallow breathing as though she slept fitfully. Whypin held her own breath, watching as the men came nearer, then nearer still. They poked about with their lances in the brush, and she heard one of them say, "See, the English are stupid about corn as well. They did not even know enough to keep the brush from the edge of their fields. By the time of sowing seed next season, this would be overrun—" and they moved closer still to the clump of brush that hid the cave, probing with their lances as they came, less than ten feet away.

Just as Whypin thought they would surely be discovered, a shout came from the Hancock cottage, and the two men turned to see what had been found. A warrior came out of the smoldering ruins, rolling before him a large cask. Whypin recognized it as a barrel that had supported one end of Leah Hancock's trestle table. The man stood the cask on end and hit it hard with his club. A spout of liquid shot forth, and the warriors who stood no more than a body's length away from her laughed and ran down the hill to join their comrades in dispatching the barrel.

"Papa's rum," Tess said sorrowfully. "He was saving it to trade for a horse when the next ship came." The girl searched Whypin's face for an answer or at least some comfort. What she saw there made her move closer, burrowing her face in the slave's breast. Whypin let Tess nestle against her, leaned back against the wall of the cave, and watched silently as her people finished off the cask, rounded up the rest of their plunder, and finally straggled away through the fields toward the river.

By nightfall, the village was silent and empty. Whypin quietly woke Tess and Glory, cautioning them to be as still as wary deer. Glory was moving as though she still dreamed, but Tess seemed to have taken some stolid strength from her brief sleep, and she followed Whypin's commands without question.

They moved aside the brush and crept from the cave to stand above what was left of the cornfield. No movement in the fields; no movement at the Hancock cabin.

"Wait here," Whypin whispered, and she lowered herself to a smaller silhouette, creeping down through the blackened cornstalks and across the smoking earth. The Hancock cottage was still partially standing, with a piece of the roof yet intact. Two walls were undamaged, and the chimney rose like a ghostly spire in the shadows.

Whypin stepped on the wooden porch, which creaked familiarly under her bare feet. Perhaps, she said to herself, this is the last time I will ever go inside such a place so long as I live. She sniffed the air for the smell of death, of blood, of terror. Except for the strong stench of smoke and the odor of rum where it had splashed over the wood, she could smell nothing unusual. Though she had seen James Hancock killed almost where she stood, she could not feel the blood beneath her feet. Idly, she wondered where he lay— but then she pushed the thought from her mind and went inside.

The cabin itself was ransacked, the beds pulled apart, the cooking tools gone, the chairs upended. James Hancock's wooden chest was hacked open, its papers spilled out and strewn across the floor, mixed with dried corn husks from the split bedding. The missus' cherished metal plates were gone, and the cupboard doors torn from their hinges. Charred timbers had fallen haphazardly, and the dim light from the open evening sky fell upon the open floorboards in strange patterns of black shadows.

Whypin saw a glimmer of something under a blackened blanket, and she bent to pick it up. The missus' keys—a shiny band of metal with three keys attached, to open the storage shed and the closet where the master kept his heavy leather shoes. As Whypin straightened, she heard the creak of the wooden porch behind her and she whirled suddenly in alarm.

Tess and Glory stood in the open doorway, framed by the night behind them. Glory's eyes were still huge, wide, and stark with uncomprehending bewilderment. Tess's mouth was set more firmly, and she held her sister by the hand. "Where's Mama?" she asked quietly.

Whypin shook her head. "I told you to stay."

"I was afraid. Where's Mama?"

Whypin heard the thin edge of hysteria in Tess's voice, and she knew that the girl was a hairbreadth from collapse, no matter the set of her jaw. She left the debris at her feet and went to Tess, taking her by the shoulder and turning her around. "She is not here. The roof is falling in. We will go and find her."

The girl followed Whypin without question, Glory trailing behind linked only by Tess's clutching hand to the moment. The three walked out beyond the cabin door, out into the open yard before the edge of the field, just as the moon rose hugely above the trees. It was a hot night again, and the swamp frogs cried harshly from the river grass in the distance. Whypin started down the path toward the nearest cabin, grateful that the dark hid the worst details of the raid. There, no more than a dozen steps from the path, the stretched body of Lion made mute testament to the day's deaths. But Tess only glanced at him once. Glory never glanced at a thing.

A sound came from the rear of the cabin as they passed, and

Whypin turned reluctantly, wondering what new horror they must witness now. She stared into the dark and from the cornfield, just at the edge where the kitchen rows began, she saw an arm, lighter than the ground around it, rising up from the dirt and the fallen stalks. She walked toward the sound, which repeated, a high whine of pain and pleading.

Leah Hancock lay in a tangled heap in the field, her head pitched back and held upright by charred cornstalks. Evidently, she had seen them cross the open space of the pathway with the moon behind them. Whypin bent to the woman, heedless of Tess and Glory who followed right behind her, stricken dumb.

The missus had an arrow stuck in her right breast and another in her left side. One leg thrust out at a frightening angle, her skirt up and over her lap exposed her bare skin, and the other leg stretched out white and stained by blood. Whypin knelt at her side, scarcely hearing Tess who began to weep again quietly. The girl sat down a few feet from her mother, pulling her sister down alongside her, unwilling to come closer.

"Have they gone?" Leah whispered hoarsely. Her voice was as broken as her body.

Whypin nodded. "The mister is dead," she said calmly.

"I saw it." Leah painfully extended a hand to Tess. "Come here, daughter."

At the sound of her call, Tess flung herself to her mother's side and put her head in her lap. Leah cried out at the movement, but her one hand dropped to rest on Tess's head. "Are you harmed?" she asked weakly.

"No, Mother, they never caught us." Tess caught her breath in a sob. "Are you going to die?"

"Where's my Glory?" Leah answered fitfully, trying to move her head around as though the child might be behind her.

At the sound of her name, Glory started as from a sleep and threw herself past Whypin onto her mother, screaming in terror as though the savages were attacking all over again. Whypin deftly plucked her off, shook her gently, and said, "Sit now and be still. Your mother is alive."

Tess took Glory's arms and held her down, away from their mother, murmuring to her over and over again, "Glory, Mama is here, Mama is here, be a good girl now, Mama is here."

Whypin saw that Leah Hancock had fainted, and that Glory's

assault had started the bleeding again from the arrow in her side. She stood and looked down at the three at her feet in sudden weariness. There was every chance that the missus would die, if not soon then before the next night came. There was strong chance, too, that more English might come to punish her people for making war. Tess and Glory would likely perish if left alone, and if she took them as prisoners to the village of her people, she might be punished for saving their lives.

She passed a hand over her eyes, listening to the sounds of the night. The English village was silent, but there might be others who lived, as the missus did.

Walk away, her heart said to her plainly. Turn and disappear into the forest as the doe slides into shadow, soundlessly and safe. Turn and walk away from the English woman and her blood and her cries and her children.

But then Tess grasped Whypin about her bare ankle, looking up into her face. "Please help her," the girl asked, and her voice sounded as old and inevitable as the river. "You can't let her die."

"I am no longer your slave," Whypin said gently.

Tess moaned, "I know that, but please!"

Whypin almost said aloud, you English. You think if you say "please" and "thank you" that anything will be granted or forgiven. She turned away from the girl.

"She would do the same for you, wouldn't she?" Tess asked then.

The logic of the girl's question struck Whypin fully in that moment and without having ever made a decision to stay or to leave, she simply bent to Leah Hancock and began to examine her wounds to see what could be done.

🌿 🌿 🌿

For three days and three nights, Whypin nursed Leah Hancock, staving off death as best she could. She made pallets for the girls on the porch of the cabin under a small section of roof that had not burned. She cut the arrows from the missus' breast and side, set her broken leg with green saplings, and bound her wounds after cleansing them with turpentine. Frightened of the village pump that was surrounded with stinking corpses, she made the long walk to bring back cool water, turning her head away from the vultures as they fought and screeched over the bodies, searching out a deer path to the deeper pools, which were hidden from the opposite side of the river.

Every day and night, she watched for her people to return, but they did not. Perhaps, she thought, they feared more English would come to punish them for war; perhaps they had already left for the lands to the north, taking with them their spoils.

She left the woman's side only to bring back water and whatever foodstuffs she could collect from the ravaged cabins. She tried not to smell the bodies of the English, tried to look past the destruction and the death around her, and concentrated only on imagining where the women of the village would have stored what they wished to save. In that way, thinking as she guessed a white woman would think, she found much that had not been lost.

In the night, when the howls of the wolves collected closer to the village, she told Tess and Glory stories she recalled of the animals, of the bears and the bobcats, of the otters of the river and the birds of the air, the tales the old ones told around the fires in the times of the winter moons.

But every morning, as the sun rose, her spirits sank as she woke to remember where she was. By the end of ten mornings, she had ransacked more than half the houses left standing. Once Tess tried to follow her in her foraging, but she angrily commanded the girl to return to her own cabin, and Tess obeyed instantly. Glory spent the long hours nestled next to her mother, telling her small stories and singing snatches of song. Sometimes the child seemed as damaged in her mind as her mother was in her body. In other moments, she was her old self again, fretting about the heat and demanding cool water.

The trek to the river was Whypin's only respite from the woman and the children, and each time she made the walk, she longed to throw herself in the water and float to the sea. By now, the bodies were so swollen and torn, so covered with flies and debris that they scarcely resembled anything human. It was easier to avert her eyes, to step around them, to see them as only part of the landscape. It was harder and harder to return to the missus and her wounds. But each night, she found herself again tending the woman and her children. And when the wolves who worried the corpses came too close to the cabin, she shouted at them, and they slunk away.

Finally, Leah Hancock began to rouse from her fitful and fevered state, and Whypin knew she would live. The woman looked much older than she had in June. For that matter, so did her children.

One morning, she asked to be propped against the cabin so that she might gaze out over the fields. She was strong enough to hold the tin dish of corn bread to feed herself. "They're not coming back," she said to Whypin.

"No, missus," she answered. "You need not fear them again."

"I mean *my* people, not yours," Leah said weakly. "They're not coming back for us. Those who escaped believe all here are dead. They've probably gone to Bath, on the Pamlico. If I'm going to get to Bath with my children, I must do it alone."

Tess was listening intently. With each day that had passed, with each bit of strength her mother gathered, she had grown stronger, too. It seemed to Whypin now that the missus and Tess were more sisters than mother and daughter . . . and both of them were mother to little Glory.

Glory asked then, "What about Papa?"

Leah Hancock gazed at her youngest thoughtfully, as if assessing what truth she could bear. "Papa is dead," she answered finally. "You know that, Glory. I could not even find his body. They took him away, I guess, because I searched everywhere before I fell down where you found me. I looked for him, but he's gone. We must go to where we will be safe. To Bath, that's a good town, he would want that for us." Gasping now with her exertion, the missus slumped back again, shaking her head. "I am so tired," she murmured. "I want to go home. Tess, do you remember Bath? Glory never saw it but you must remember, don't you?"

"Some, I remember," Tess said, though she remembered nothing. "Rest now," she murmured, leaning up against her mother to help support her weight. "Don't talk anymore."

That day, when Whypin went to get the water, Tess went along and would not be sent back. She only shook her head firmly when Whypin ordered her away, fell in step with the slave, and marched along resolutely, averting her head from the masses of buzzing flies.

"How far is Bath?" she asked Whypin.

"Three, perhaps four days walk to the north."

"How far by boat?"

"Four or five. It is easier by water but longer. But there are no boats. I have looked, and they are gone."

"You searched the whole village? What happened to them all?"

Whypin shrugged. "Perhaps the English sailed away in them."

"And the savages took the rest," Tess said calmly, unselfconsciously, as though she even still did not comprehend Whypin's place in her world. "We must get to Bath," she added. "Mother can walk, I think, and we have to go where they can help us."

Whypin turned to the girl and gazed at her. Somehow she had grown years in the last few days, but the child in her still did not grasp the horror of what had occurred. "Your mother cannot walk so far. To try will kill her. And if they are making war all over the land, they will kill you as you journey."

"Maybe in a few days—"

"No. Not even in a few moons. And what of Glory? She is not strong enough for such a journey—"

"Glory will do what I tell her. We must get to where there are white people. Are you sure you looked all over the village? There must be a boat left somewhere."

Whypin turned and continued to walk down to the river. If the missus were well enough, she could leave them without remorse. If the missus were dead, she could take the children to her people, perhaps, or leave them at another English settlement. But until the missus was either well enough or dead, she could not walk away into the woods and leave the three alone. Perhaps she should kill the woman herself and take the girls back as slaves. Were her people making war with the English everywhere or only here? Were the English, even now, ransacking her village in retribution? Angry at herself, Whypin savagely struck out at the brush on either side with her water bucket. She suddenly could not abide Tess following her so closely.

"Go back and watch your mother," she snapped.

"She'll be all right for now. I'll help get the water," Tess answered.

Whypin turned once more, glaring at her. "Go back, I said. I do not need your help."

"No," Tess said, "I need yours. If you're going to leave us, I have to know where to get water by myself." She dropped her head.

Whypin felt the heat of her anger sweep out of her as though pushed by a cool river breeze. She bent and touched the girl's head briefly but did not let her eyes linger on Tess's eyes, for the pain there was too hard to see. She drew from her buckskin bodice a slender golden chain and locket.

"Where did you get that?" Tess asked wonderingly.

"My mother gave it to me. Many years ago. But I want nothing more of the whites about my body. You take it."

Tess took the locket carefully, as though in a dream. She slipped it in her pocket.

"I belong with my people," Whypin said. She turned and walked away from the girl hurriedly, leaving her there alone on the path to the river. When she saw that she was not being followed, Whypin turned back over her shoulder. Tess lifted one hand in a bewildered farewell. Whypin walked into the dark and shadowed woods without once again looking back.

🌱 🌱 🌱

It was early October before Leah Hancock finally brought her daughters to the Pamlico River, forded it, and refuged in Bath, the largest English settlement on the Carolina coast. A week of exhausted walking, hiding during the night from feared attacks by roaming war parties, and losing their way several times in the forest almost killed Leah.

Glory's mind seemed to have receded to babyhood, and she prattled to herself aimlessly as she walked. Tess forged ahead as best she could, but usually by midday, no one could go further, particularly as the small trunk they carried with all they could salvage seemed to get more leaden with each hour. A few items of clothing for each, two pairs of shoes, the small cache of silver coins Leah had hidden behind a loose chimney brick, and a leather-bound Bible were all they could find.

Leah walked for a few hours on her own, carrying one end of the trunk, then leaning on a stick of oak she carried, then finally a bit more, half leaning on Tess, and then, exhausted, she would sleep away the rest of the day and into the night. Sometimes she wept softly as she walked; sometimes she did not answer when Tess spoke to her, but only plodded along as mindlessly as Glory.

The September heat had shriveled most of the berries, but the wild grapes, peaches, and apples were still plentiful. Sometimes they ventured on unfenced fields of corn, which they knew must belong to the savages. Only the English fenced their fields to keep the cattle and hogs from ransacking the rows. The Indians preferred to fence their livestock instead. This had been a source of resentment, James said, for the English hogs often strayed into the Indian fields.

One trouble among many, which had led them to this trail they followed now. Tess tried not to think of him, but images of her father floated up before her constantly. She could only imagine how torturous it must be for her mother. When she could find some, Tess picked up the stray ears left behind from the harvest, and they gnawed them as they walked. Their cornmeal ran out on the third day, but since they were too fearful to make a fire anyway, it seemed a small loss.

Leah said, so long as they traveled north, they could not miss the Pamlico. They might come out of the forest long or short of Bath, but at least once they sighted the river, they should be able to find people. So Tess tried to use the trees as Whypin had told her, traveling always in the direction that the moss grew, watching the sun as it moved from her right shoulder to her left. Still, they lost their way many times. Often, they made small headway, for the brambles and undergrowth were dense. Often, too, they had to divert around steep ravines or streams, taking hours of precious daylight and strength to find their way again.

And always, the fear of the savages and the beasts shadowed their steps. Twice, they found evidence of campfires, but they hurried away, expecting to be attacked at any moment.

Once, they blundered upon a large female bear and her cubs. Tess was ahead on the trail and she saw the creature first. Quickly, she hushed Glory behind her and waved to her mother, her finger over her lips. They watched the great, brown beast digging grubs for her cubs, who climbed over her whining with eagerness for her teats. She finally sat square on her bottom with her back against a tall cedar and a paw on the back of each cub. To Tess, she looked for all the world like Goody White, as she pointed her nose straight up and slowly rotated her head as if to loosen a stiff neck. The cubs thrust hard with their feet and shuddered and grunted with satisfaction at what she gave them. Her touch seemed tender, but Leah hurried them carefully off, back the way they had come, before the bear could catch their scent. They did not stop that day until they had put a wide stream between them.

Just about the time that Tess thought they might not make it at all, they came to the banks of the Pamlico. Up and down they searched the side of the river for some sign of habitation, but they saw only piles of white shells and fishing weirs abandoned by the savages. Walking toward the rising sun, they finally came to a place where the river widened and there, they found a ferryman who took them across to Bath.

To secure passage, Leah Hancock gave him her wedding ring and the cameo brooch James had given her the day Tess was born. Tess had pinned the gold locket deep within her pocket, and she did not offer to trade. They might need it more later on, she told herself, and her mother seemed to have forgotten it altogether.

In Bath, Glory's spunk began to come back again, and the constant bustle of people coming and going lifted Leah's spirits, too. They lodged in a keep down by the docks, and when people heard of their ordeal, they attained small celebrity overnight. The Tuscaroras had waged war all over the territory, devastating some settlements and scarcely bothering others, but affecting all men with a mingled fear and wrath. Few Englishwomen, however, had survived what Leah Hancock had endured, and so she was called upon to tell and retell her story, only to be commended and comforted again and again by horrified wives and outraged husbands.

Bath, itself, had been briefly attacked, and the town was in chaos. The land was wasted, stores were ruined, and winter would be sure starvation now. Colonists were leaving on any ship for safer ports, and Leah was finally able to secure passage for the three of them on a small, fat-bottomed trader bound for the Cape of Feare. Captain Joseph Innes, a broad Scots with a pipe and a thatch of red beard streaked with gray, took one look at Leah Hancock and welcomed her cordially aboard the *Portsmouth Lady*, taking most of her silver and her arm in his as he escorted the three of them to their quarters.

🌿 🌿 🌿

The Cape of Feare loomed out of a bank of fog, rearing up in white, ghostly dunes like high, spume-topped waves as the *Ports-mouth Lady* made her way past the shoals and into the skirling mouth of the river. Tess leaned far over the rail, concentrating on easing her tortured stomach, which had been in rebellion ever since Captain Innes turned away from the docks at Bath.

Glory clung to the rail beside her, cheeks glowing in the salt air, her bright hair fanning about her face like a scarlet flag. She took to the motion of the ship like an old tar, with nary a bilious moment, and Tess envied her with a swift, stinging hatred that she felt so pert.

"Mama says, once we get past the breakers, the river'll be calm and then you'll both feel better," Glory said to Tess. "Just a little while more, and it'll be over."

Leah Hancock had not fared much better on the four days from Bath to the Cape Feare, walking the ship up and down with the white face and the shrunken form of a woman barely holding onto the meager broth she'd been able to keep down. She rallied only when Captain Joseph walked with her, attempting then to push herself to some slight conversation. But Tess could see her relief when the man left her alone again, and she could cling to the rail, gazing out to sea, willing herself to survive the ordeal.

The waves were steeper now, as if they wanted one last chance at the ship before she slipped away into the refuge of the river. The *Lady* rocked and heeled violently from one side to the next, almost rolling on her ribs, it seemed to Tess, as she was thrown hard into Glory, and the two of them hung on the rail as though it were suspended above their heads. Then suddenly, the ship righted herself, slid through a pass in the rocks, and the waters were calmer.

There was a flurry of activity above their heads, as the tars let go of ropes and sails dropped, sagged, and were furled quickly to slow the ship. With now a single huge sail bellied open and pushing them onward, they glided past the two spits of land on either side of them, fully into the Cape of Feare.

Captain Joseph left the wheel where he'd been shouting orders to all and sundry and came up beside Tess and Glory. "Now, ye be more easy, lass," he said to Tess. "We'll stop at New Town just long enough for me to pass my papers, then two more days, and we'll be up Cross Creek, with nary a wave 'twixt here and there."

Tess already felt better, simply to have the ship beneath her knees more steady. Still, she longed for nothing more than to abandon the *Lady* the moment they touched land.

"What's Cross Creek like?" Glory asked, pushing under his arm as though she belonged there.

"Well, 'tis no Bath, God be blessed! Just a tiny hidey-hole where a nest o' Scots have carved out a little place in the sun. But they're running timber through, the best loblollys on the river, more'n seven hundred board feet a day. And white oak, the finest for topside planking, and black oak, which keeps the worms off the hull in the warmer waters, why ye can't find better anywhere on the coast. They pay a pretty penny for it across the water, too, and so the lot of us are making a fortune on the forests of this land."

"What're Scots?" Tess asked, leaning against him.

Captain Joseph started as though he'd just seen her nestled close. "Why, the lass lives! Lives and breathes and graces the very air!"

"Are ye feeling better, Tessie?" Glory asked, unconsciously aping the captain's brogue.

"A little. What're Scots?"

"Highland Scots, the best and only kind o' man to be, to my mind. Clans came over from Scotland; they speak the old tongue and bend their knees to the old God. After bonny King Charles run afield, they hoisted their claymores and came to seek their fortune. And find it they have at Cross Creek."

"Why did they build their sawmill all the way upriver?" a voice came from behind them.

Tess saw the man's face change as he turned to greet her mother. Moving aside at the rail for her, he smiled and lost some of his natural swagger, almost as though he were about to bow but held it contained. He shifted his pipe from one side to another, then took it out of his mouth altogether, damping it and pocketing it in one sure motion. "That's where the best trees be, mistress. A sawmill's a dear thing to build, so it need be where it's worth the most investment. The saws must be brought over from England, the masons to build the foundation, the carpenters to make the waterwheels—and the risks are high. A hard winter with heavy ice can tear it down, a spring freshet can wash it out, a summer drought leave it high and dry, takes men like Highland Scots to wrest it away from the river and keep it going strong."

"Why do they call it the Cape of Feare?" Glory piped up.

"Because these waters are the roughest along the whole of the coast, and plenty of wrecks lie beneath the waves to attest to that, lass." He glanced quickly at the woman standing next to him who seemed to be only partially listening, so intent was she on watching the banks of the river move past them. "It takes a sure eye and a deft touch to get a ship past these shoals safe, and those who stood outside and couldn't get past 'em named the barrier after their own lack of courage, to my mind. They might well have called the place 'cape of persevere,' for that's what it takes to learn her ins and outs."

Leah turned to smile at him enchantingly for his small wit, and Tess felt her stomach turn in that moment. As though someone had showed her a picture in a book, she knew now what was going to happen. Part of her felt enormous sorrow; part of her heart felt strong relief. Her mother would marry this man, and they would be safe again.

She eyed him carefully while he continued to entertain Glory and Leah with tales of the river, the Scots, and Cross Creek. He was a solid fellow, a gruff walrus of a man, but he'd likely take good care of what he thought belonged to him. Her mother could do much worse, and so far as Tess could see, Captain Joseph could scarcely do much better. She closed her eyes and sent a silent plea to her father in much the same voice she might have addressed God, Himself. *If that is your will, Papa, then let her find him pleasing. Let him find her comely. Let us be at rest somewhere, soon.*

"You feeling poorly still?" Glory whispered at her side.

Tess shook her head. "Let's go see what the river looks like from the backside of the ship." She pulled Glory away as the captain said, "Stern, lass, stern! Every part's got a name, every name's got a reason—" and Tess heard her mother's silvery laugh behind her as the two sisters hurried off to watch the Atlantic disappear in a froth.

🌿 🌿 🌿

New Town or Newton, as the newcomers were calling it, was a small port town on the north bank of the Cape Feare, spread out haphazardly with little of the planned charm of the streets of Bath.

Tess knew as soon as she stepped onto the docks that this was a place to pass through quickly.

There were no fine houses facing the water, only a few patched and random cottages that seemed barely able to hold themselves upright. A pair of spotted dogs rested in the shadows, and a pig stalked determinedly up a dusty path toward a deserted, dry corn-field. All the noise and life of New Town centered on a single cabin with an open door and within, Tess could hear the sounds of men drinking and carousing. The keep sported a lone, bedraggled Union Jack, the only vestige of English order as far as she could see.

Tess turned as Glory and Leah came from behind her, their mother walking unsteadily on legs that waited for the dock to rise to meet them. " 'Tis a relief to feel land again," Leah said, tying her bonnet strings with shaking fingers. Her face was still unnaturally pale, but her eyes were less dull, Tess noticed, as though she were going to consider life a possibility once more.

In that moment, Captain Joseph emerged from the keep where he'd gone to do his business, a laughing gentleman at his side. Or rather, Tess noted, no gentleman at all. The man was dressed like a French jack-a-dandy, but when you looked closer, she saw, his cuffs were torn and soiled and his trousers were badly frayed. He shook Captain Joseph's hand and cuffed him roundly on the shoul-der, then turned to gaze appraisingly at Leah Hancock, whose pale yellow bonnet shone brightly in the sun.

Tess moved closer to her mother and took her hand. Captain followed the man's gaze and quickly moved toward them, taking Leah's arm and turning her aside. "You don't want to go up there," he murmured low, still smiling at the man. " 'Tis a nest of pirates and buccaneers, the whole town swarms with them."

"Why did we stop here then?" Tess asked indignantly.

"Because if I don't pay their customs, they'll stop *us* soon enough somewhere upriver. Every ship that crosses these shoals pays the price o' doing business or they know the reason why. And they're not men to be trifled with," he added, glancing at Leah nervously.

"I think," she said wearily, "we better stay onboard the *Lady* then. Though I did so look forward to walking round a bit—"

"We can walk onboard, Mother," Tess said, pulling her gently in the direction of the docks again. "We should heed Captain Joseph's advice."

Both her mother and the captain looked down at Tess suddenly with surprise, as though she had just assumed the air of a grown woman with those few words. But her mother docilely let herself be directed back aboard the ship with no other complaint. It was Glory, of course, who must be maneuvered with more skill.

"I want to see the pirates," she said to Tess later that evening. "I'm going to go look at them through the windows; they won't see me, for I'm too short."

"You'll do no such thing," Tess said firmly, "or I'll tell Mama."

"Tell her, then," Glory said as she made to walk down the plank. "She'll only scold me, and at least I'll get to see what the scoundrels look like for myself. I wager they look like sin in hard skin!"

Tess was hard-pressed not to laugh aloud as her red-haired sister screwed up her face in what she hoped was a good imitation of true deviltry. But she did not let her smile show. "If you dare step off this ship, I'll tell Captain Joseph 'twas you ate all the oranges he was saving for his trip back to England."

She turned, frowning. "I didn't! 'Twas Robin and John Dawes who ate them all, and the rest of the crew, they—"

"No," Tess said calmly, "that's what he thinks, but I'll tell him the truth. I'll tell him that you ate them and hid the peelings under your linens."

"Oh, Tess, you wouldn't tell!" Her frown dissolved suddenly into alarm and sorrow. "I meant to only eat a few, but they seemed to settle my belly and keep me from getting bilious like you and Mama—"

"No spying on the pirates."

Glory kicked at a coiled rope defiantly. "I shall see a score of them one day, and up close, too."

"Why would you want to?"

Glory's eyes danced. "Tessie, didn't you hear Captain talking about them? Why, they slip in and out of the tiniest hiding place with their fast ships, and nobody can catch them, and they bring in the most wondrous stuff, all sorts of riches and gold and pretty frocks from France and the West Indies, and Spain, and everyplace! And they go wherever they want, nobody can stop them, and when they walk down the street, men move aside or seek them out, and the ladies bow—"

"Not all of the ladies. Decent ladies wouldn't receive pirates in their homes."

"Ho, that's all that you know! Captain says that's the only way they get the goods they want without paying customs, and they're only too happy to seat a pirate at their table if he'll bring in the finest wines and silver and plate without the king's ransom in taxes."

"You're besotted." Tess turned away in scorn. "Anything Captain tells you, you believe."

She looked suddenly bewildered. "Why, Tessie, don't you? I think he's a fine man of parts, Mama thinks so, too." She peered at her older sister. "He likes you awful well. You thought him nice enough in Bath."

Tess sighed hugely. "And so I still do. But you needn't take his every word as writ by the king, himself, Glory. He's just a man."

Glory grinned at her impishly. "You're just jealous 'cause he likes me and Mama. If you be nice to him, he'll like you, too." And she skipped off to see what stir she could cause belowdecks.

They sailed out of New Town that afternoon and two days later were far upriver, expecting to see Cross Creek by noon the next day. That night, Leah pulled Tess and Glory into her small cot and asked, "Do you like the good captain well enough?"

"Well enough for what, Mother?" Tess asked.

Leah hesitated, lightly separating the tangles out of Glory's hair with her fingers. "Well. I mean, do you like him well enough to—say, well enough to perhaps consider him as a second father?"

Glory's eyes opened wide, and her mouth followed suit.

"Has he asked you, then?" Tess casually looked away to give her mother time to recover.

"No, but—"

"He will," she finished Leah's sentence calmly. She sighed, a sadness suddenly flooding her heart. This is what she had guessed, had even wished for, but now that it was here, she felt the ache of loss.

"Likely," her mother said gently. "So. What would you think, should I say aye to the man?"

"Yes," Tess said promptly. "I like him well enough. If he asks, you should tell him yes."

"Tess!" Glory exploded. "What about Papa!"

Their mother looked down at Glory fondly and said, "Child,

no one is saying that you'll ever forget your father, or that I'll ever love another man as I did him. But the world is a wide and dangerous place for women and children alone. And Captain Joseph is a good man, a kind man. We could take good care of him, I think, and he could help us care for each other." She put Glory briskly off her lap and hugged them both. There seemed nothing else to say on the matter at all.

🌿 🌿 🌿

The land along the Cape Feare changed as they moved upriver, so that by the time the *Portsmouth Lady* reached Cross Creek, Tess scarcely recognized this swift river as the same lazy water that had flowed into the angry sea at its mouth, two days before. This was the Piedmont, Captain said, an altogether different territory from the Tidewater flats of Bath and the coastal plain of New Bern.

Tall pine forests lined the river, mixed with oak, hickory, and blueberry bushes tall as a man. The woods were higher, deeper, and more dense than any Tess had ever seen, thicker than those they'd traversed in their flight from the savages north to Bath. Even the birds this far upriver were different. Here, there were none of the gulls, terns, and skimmers she had grown to know and love so near the sea. Here, no pelicans and oystercatchers plied for fish and clams, for the river had taken away the beaches and the waters had a clean sparkle, which was completely foreign to her. Above her head, new birds called and darted with bright colors and strange songs.

Captain called them woodpeckers and warblers, kingfishers and thrushes—"There's a beast called a beaver in these parts that I wager you've not seen before," he said solemnly to Tess. "The finest builder of any four-footed creature in all God's world. They make great dams across the widest rivers—"

"Are they fierce?"

"No, lass, if you take them young, they follow you like a pup. But they get mischievous when they get loose in the orchards, for they cut down the saplings and block up your door at night with the sticks and wood they haul in."

Tess laughed aloud. "That's a pretty tale!"

" 'Tis a true one!"

"Bears?" Glory asked. "Are there bears in Cross Creek?"

"Aye, they live right in the very houses with the Scots, lass," he teased her, "and they get along like pease and pie."

Where the *Portsmouth Lady* had been the smallest ship at the docks in Bath, now she seemed suddenly too large on the river, crowded on both sides by tall trees and rocky banks. Indeed, it took the captain most of an hour to gingerly bring her to anchor in a tiny, sheltered cove. From there, they took landing boats and rowed upriver farther until they finally saw the sparse cluster of cottages and the sawmill that was Cross Creek.

The settlement sat in a clearing of dappled sunlight with a smoke haze hanging over roofs of no more than a dozen buildings. The screech of the sawmill drowned out all birdsong and the barking of the dogs that rushed to greet them as they disembarked.

Tess pulled her skirt to one side as a large hound reared up and pawed her, a happy, muddy tail whisking to and fro. Captain cuffed him soundly when Leah and Glory edged up to his side, but he only yelped and turned his attentions to his comrades who fell to wrangling at their feet. At Captain Joseph's call, two men, then three, then six came running, all of them bearded with long, matted hair pulled back into tangled tails. The tearing, splitting scream of the sawmill suddenly ceased, and now Tess could see women, too, come out of their cottages, wiping their hands and smoothing their hair under their bonnets. She did not see an unsmiling face amongst them.

Captain Joseph shook hands all round, even embraced a few men and women, too, and the sounds of gaiety and welcome grew almost as deafening as the sawmill had been. Captain's tars were embraced as eagerly as the captain, himself, handed from one to another like long-lost kin. The strange Scots burr rang in Tess's ears, making some of the speech almost unintelligible, and she glanced up at her mother anxiously. To her surprise, Leah Hancock was accepting the clasping hands eagerly, her face a wreath of smiles. Glory peeped from behind her mother's skirts until a young girl about her age spied her and fell on her, crowing over her bright hair. Won over, she let go Leah's hand then and ventured over nearer to the men, reaching up to touch Captain Joseph's sleeve as though for reassurance.

He swept her up into his arms and called out, "This time, I bring more precious cargo than ever before, lads!"—and the small crowd cheered eagerly, sweeping them inside the nearest cottage before Tess could catch her breath.

The cabin was rough and dark within and quickly crowded with too many shoulders and feet. A large man commanded, "Let our guests take a seat at the board, mistress above the salt, the wee lasses below, and all take a seat or standing room as ye may!"

Captain Joseph sat Leah down in one of the few chairs in the room near the head of the table, a wide planked board set on trestles with a large saltcellar set in the center. The women bustled about setting out wooden trenchers, far too few for so many, Tess thought, and crude leather noggins for drink. Wood spoons were tossed in a heap for all to reach, but there were no forks, no knives, no plate, and no pewter. Two more men rolled in a small cask that was immediately split to a chorus of cheerful toasts, and noggins were passed all round.

Someone put a noggin in Tess's hand and gestured she was to share it with Glory. She hesitantly put it to her mouth and found the mead to be sweet, strong, and thick as porridge. No wonder the spoons!

The toasts were still ringing in the strange, liquid language of the settlers, when a woman bustled the children outside the cabin so that there would be more room for the men to sit. The next few hours were a whirl of exotic speech and fanciful images that left Tess feeling she had landed on a different continent than America, after all. The men all looked so large and odd, with their long hair, their colorful tartan skirts, and their legs showing bare at the knees. The women, few as they were, were comely enough, but they, too, wore the bright capes of the same woolen that matched the men's skirts.

Glory was quickly taken up into a game of scotch-hoppers, and Tess repaired to a quieter corner where she might still hear the men within the cottage. Soon, her mother came and collected them, taking them to another cabin where they were to spend the night, the owners having kindly vacated it for their convenience.

Once alone, Leah sat them down and said, "We must speak of our plans. Captain Joseph has asked me to wed."

Tess gaped at her. Though she was not surprised, the baldness of her mother's statement, the total calm with which she announced it left her numb.

"I like him, Mother," Glory said promptly.

"I know you do, sweet." Leah smiled, pulling them both a little closer. "And you, Tess? Can you countenance this marriage in your heart?"

Tess nodded miserably. Now that it was actually here, she felt bereft.

"Good. Then give me a kiss for good luck."

Tess dutifully kissed her smooth cheek.

"Now, Captain Joseph has had his *own* good luck, and 'twill be ours as well, I believe. The good men of Cross Creek have offered him partnership in the mill, in exchange for his share of the *Portsmouth Lady.* There are handsome profits to be made in timber, he says, and by the looks of his welcome here, he's a man of parts who knows his business. 'Twill mean a change of plans, though, for us. What would you say to making our home here?"

Tess thought for a moment. A woman's place was with her husband, that much Tess knew. And Captain Joseph was not the sort of man to brook interference with his plans.

"Glory, what do you say to all this?"

"If you marry him, will he be our papa?"

"No," Tess answered quickly, "you have only one papa, and he's dead. He'll be our stepfather. Sort of like an uncle."

Leah gazed at her solemnly. She let out a little sigh, a sound that Tess had heard constantly since New Bern and even before. It seemed to her, in fact, that it was the most constant thing about her mother, that sigh. That sound seemed to say that if things could only be different, as they once were, as they should become, she might be content. "That's true," she finally said, "he won't be your papa. But he will be my husband. And perhaps that is enough, after all."

The next morning, Tess and Glory stood by solemnly and watched as the large man in charge of the toasts the day before joined their mother and Captain Joseph Innes as man and wife. The man was the chief of the clan and had the power to act as liege, as lord, as king in Cross Creek, should he choose to do so. Since no minister and no church graced the settlement, he said the words over Leah and Joseph as every villager looked on.

It was over so quickly that later, Tess could barely recall the details of how her mother looked or spoke. As though in a dream, she saw her become Mistress Innes, Mistress Hancock no more. Some vestige of James Hancock was forever erased with that moment and those words, and she could find little to be glad for that. But when she saw her mother's shy smile as the captain bent and kissed her cheek before all, she grew more content.

Tess and Glory were moved to another cabin for two nights, that her mother and the captain might have the privacy of their own bed. The village set about with a great bustle and flurry to build a small cottage for them, as though its tangible presence in the clearing would make the marriage fast. Glory threw herself into her new friendships with abandon, and Leah became quite busy setting up housekeeping and exchanging murmured confidences with the good wives in neighboring cabins.

It seemed to Tess that she was the only one who felt the bright, cold ache of abandonment. Each face she saw looked as though it belonged to a family, which did not include her. Even to their clothes, these Scots were kin. Their speech, their food and drink, their songs, even their prayers were to Tess as foreign as though she'd been set down in China. How could her mother and Glory accept Cross Creek and these strangers as home?

For a day and two nights, Tess could not be reconciled to any of her circumstances. She wished herself unstepfathered, unmothered, and unsistered and anywhere at all save this clearing in the Scottish wilderness.

But then she saw that Glory and her mother were content with their lot. So content, in fact, that she was in danger of losing the little family she still had left. The next morning, she shyly joined Glory's friends at their games, tagging along behind her younger sister as though she, not Glory, was the baby.

Whatever else, she told herself, we must stay together.

🌿 🌿 🌿

The woods around Cross Creek were still as wild and dense as they had been before man ever set foot on the river. Though the Saponis and the Pedees and the Tuscaroras had traipsed a tangle of trails through the forest, they were no more an intrusion on the land than those made by the deer, the wild boar, and the wolves.

In a vast tract that lay north of the Cape Feare, roughly bounded by what white men would come to call the Little River and the Rocky River, a large tan wolf moved down a ravine, crushing the brown leaves of fall under his huge forepaws as he climbed. He was following a scent he had picked up two days before while stalking a red squirrel, and he had followed it carefully.

He was a young male who had seen only three summers, and so he was bewildered at the inner stirrings the strange scent aroused in him. He came out of the ravine into an open field and before him, he saw another wolf. A female. She was moving quickly over the level ground, loping in that long wolf stride that eats up miles effortlessly.

He moved to cut her off in a wide circle across the meadow, much as he would have swung to intersect a running herd of deer. He saw soon that she had slowed. She was aware of his presence. She was timing herself so as not to outpace him. She ran smoothly, fluidly, with her tail held high in the easy, undulating manner of a female in the prime of her life, ready to mate and full of confidence.

Manners of the pack dictated that every wolf who encounters a stranger has a duty to let that stranger know at once if his or her presence will be welcome. In that way, battles were rarely to the death. A wolf will make such a decision quickly and communicate it without hesitancy, so there is no doubt.

The gray female turned to look at the male fully for an instant, so that he would know he was seen. Then she dropped down in the grass, wagged her tail rapidly, and rolled over from side to side, her forepaws held tightly against her chest. As was proper for the male, he crouched down a few paces from her and watched her welcoming display, his jaw slightly open in a wolf grin.

She rolled over and back, again and again, only occasionally meeting his eyes until he could stand the tension no more. He began to inch forward on his belly, closer and closer, his head low, until finally her last roll brought her neck under his chin. She bared her throat to him, whining softly. He rested his chin on her throat for a long few moments, feeling the pulse of her life strengthen and quicken and then, with a soft whining and mutual humming, they got up and trotted off shoulder to shoulder. Like the rest of their kind, they were therefore mated for life.

They traveled together across the Piedmont territory, crossing and recrossing the rivers, chasing game, sleeping wrapped together in each other's tails under whatever fallen brush or cover they could find. Winter widened their range, and they sometimes found themselves within the boundaries of other wolves, but they kept to themselves and were rarely confronted, even as they trespassed.

In late winter, the male became aware of a change in his mate. Her body was becoming richer, more swollen, more full of life than she had been before. The stirrings to be near to her made him eager for even more physical closeness, and they licked each other far past the need for mutual grooming, nuzzling, and nipping each other gently about the muzzle. Now he bit harder, held on a little longer. Her response altered as well. Those small pains of affection had before caused her to give him a slight, warning growl. Now as he bit and held, she only whined and moved closer, throwing a foreleg over his neck until they rolled over and over each other in a gentle agony that summoned up an ache within them both.

Her odor changed, and his longings grew. Sometimes he was alternately irritated with her and yet could not get her close enough, so he would erupt in wild displays of puppy romps, leaping like a deer about her, nipping and enticing her to play until they were lathered with exertion.

One night, the gray wolf stopped in an open clearing by the river and refused to follow him further. She stood, watching and waiting, gazing at him unflinchingly. The tan male hurried up the embankment above the river and stared down at her, willing her to follow. She did not. He whined, he barked, he knelt on all fours and rolled to beseech her. Still, she would not move. Finally, he sat down on his haunches and put his muzzle to the sky, sending a long wailing into the night sky. His howls rang over the embankment, among the trees and over the river, startling a thousand small ears on all sides. Two deer burst from cover nearby and thrashed away to safety. He did not notice. A raccoon bolted from the riverbed and raced up a tree to safety, chirring his alarm and anger. The wolves never turned their heads. A great owl took wing and swept away from the noise, but the tan only called again and again, the cry of his painful desire and the end of a part of his youth, while she waited silently watching and listening by the river.

His song ended, he retraced his steps, bounding down into the shadows where she stood, nuzzled her quickly, and mounted her for the first time. She stood and accepted him as though she had known for a lifetime that it would be he.

❦ ❦ ❦

Five years passed quickly on the river, and Tess was thirteen when Leah Hancock Innes had a second son for Captain Joseph. This one, Daniel, was as robust and demanding as his brother, Samuel, had been before him. Tess tended her mother's labor with Glory's help, and the women of Cross Creek marveled at the closeness of the sisters, saying that Mistress Innes was fortunate, indeed, to have her own clan in the making.

The village had grown like the spring morels in the meadows, but still, midwives and priests had not easily found their way so far upriver. The ninety miles from New Town up the Cape Fear were no longer passable by larger ships, for the river had changed its course as subtly as it had its name so that now, rivulets and side streamlets diminished its depth. The mill was larger, though, and through the efforts of every man at Cross Creek, still produced board feet as fast as they could sell it to the steady traffic of canoes and other river rafts that transported it downriver again.

A small market now marked the spot where the two streets of Cross Creek came together, and more than a dozen houses had been built in the five years Tess had known the town. The neighbors of Cross Creek were determined that the village would be a beacon in the wilderness to draw more settlers from the great Wagon Road that was leading people from the north into the Carolinas, and so they divided the duties of town life among them. Each man was responsible for clearing and draining a certain portion of common property, and any male above the age of twelve years must devote five days a year to clearing and repairing streets and digging drainage ditches, for as the horses pulled the logs to and from the mill they tore up the cobblestones and left deep trenches in the dirt. Tess and Glory had the duty of cleaning the street in front of their house, as did every woman in the village.

Fire was a constant danger at Cross Creek, for the piles of dust and debris that the mill produced were deadly fodder for any errant spark. One year, the chief of the village even forbade his clansmen to smoke their pipes, so fearful was he of a devastating blaze. But there rose such a hue and cry from the wives from the increased irascibility of their menfolk that the ban was soon lifted and pipes reemerged. However, the chief made each man pay up a portion of his mill profits to send to Bath for an alarm bell, ladders, leather buckets, and rope to fight fires, and each agreed. Better a loss of profits than pipes.

After five years, Tess no longer felt herself such an outcast among strangers, yet she never found the easy comfort with these Scots that Glory seemed to enjoy. The whole town loved Glory. At eleven, she had become the lovely girl that the child had promised. With her long bright curls and her impish smile, she was rarely without companions.

Tess wondered sometimes if Glory never wearied of the attention and pettings of her playmates, if she never wished for a quiet hour to wander the woods and dream her own dreams. But Glory had the "nervous skittums," as their stepfather called it, and she could not keep still for more than a few moments at a time. Like the water in the river, she must stay moving or grow somber and stagnant.

As unalike as they seemed, however, Tess and Glory were alike in their fidelity to each other. In whatever pantheon of gods Glory believed, she had most faith in Tess. And though Tess often found Glory an annoying responsibility, she also knew that no one would ever love her as her sister would. So when the town seemed a closed coven to Tess, she turned to her younger sister. Glory stuck out her small chin and attached to Tess in those moments like a cockleburr, daring her friends to oust them both. With a love-me-love-my-dog loyalty, which scorched any who might not find Tess as fine a companion as she did, she pushed her sister into groups of children who normally would have found her too old, too quiet, too staid and standoffish for their play. Thus, whatever small acceptance Tess found among the Scots of Cross Creek, she found mostly through Glory.

Leah Hancock Innes was far too busy with her new husband and her sons to concern herself overmuch with two daughters who seemed to find ample comfort in each other. When Tess would moon around the little cottage, dismal and cranky for want of someone her own age for companionship, her mother shooed her outside quickly enough or, worse yet, handed her a baby to tend.

Joseph Innes had even less patience with his stepdaughter's loneliness. A perpetually busy man with an energy second only to Glory's, his was the task of clearing out the wilderness for his family and making a large fortune in the process. When Tess would

wander to the mill in search of him, perhaps only to hear his voice
or watch him order about his work crew, he had for her always a
quick smile and a pat on her head, but then he turned back to his
business at hand: running the mill at such a pace that Cross Creek
would soon outstrip New Town at the sea as a place for profits to
be made.

And visitors to the little village said it was so. New Town was
still a nest of thieving pirates and dock workers, while Cross Creek
had the smell of civilization about it, even if it was planted in the
middle of the wilderness.

On one memorable evening, Cross Creek seemed suddenly
much closer to the debauch of New Town than anyone would have
imagined. A small ship anchored in the cove, a shallow-drafted
vessel that looked as though it could ride on the dew alone. It was
sleek and narrow as a floating tern, and it nosed up to the village
dock with a certain sure arrogance.

The men in the village rushed to greet the newcomer, and the
women, Tess noticed, took a while longer to move forward to the
dock, but when they came, their skirts were smoothed, their bonnets neatened. Captain Stede Bonnet had come to Cross Creek.

A pirate, it was whispered, a brigand, a rascal, a renegade, said
some. No, others staunchly argued, a skilled blockader, a trader, a
man of parts much needed on Carolina's coast. Leah tried to keep
Tess and Glory within the cabin when Bonnet arrived, but it was
impossible, when the whole town turned out to see him, to deny
Glory's clamor to join her comrades. Reluctantly, then, Leah put
on her bonnet with the wide, starched wings, that her face might be
more hidden, and walked with her girls down to where the crowds
had gathered.

Bonnet's craft flew a double jack with the King's flag at the
highest mast. Now that he had a Letter of Marque and Reprisal
from Governor Eden at Bath and also from the governor of the
Island of St. Thomas, he was a legal privateer, they said. And if
anyone could get Cross Creek timber through the intricacies of
customs cheap, it was Captain Bonnet. Less taxes meant more
profits for all, and so Tess was not really surprised to see that
Captain Joseph was at the front of the crowd to hail the newcomer
as he approached. Stede Bonnet strutted up the street with men
clustered about him as closely as the ruffled collar about his leath-
ered neck.

In no time, the privateer and his pilot were seated at the chief's board, crowded about by women hastening to serve the men their best, and Tess was put to work filling the pitchers with warm rum, the finest Cross Creek had to offer.

The grumbles of the men rose as the fumes of the mead and rum filled the cabin, and Tess heard her stepfather's familiar tirade against "home government and the poxed, money-hungry Whigs," a common complaint on the river. England was harrowing the colonies with taxes, folks said, just as she'd repressed Ireland and Scotland before. By the King's navigation laws, all goods bound for the colonies must be first sent to the mother country, taxed, and then shipped back to America, an enormous waste of time and trouble. Likewise, good Cross Creek timber must be first sent to London, taxed, and then sent to the West Indies where it was bound in the first place. No detours were allowed, by law, for the King would have his due. And at village tables, talk of taxes and the cost of allegiance to the King was as frequent as talk of crops.

Bonnet looked like a pirate should look, to Tess's eyes. He was a tall man, swarthy but suave. His belly was large enough to proclaim his success, and his fine frock coat with full lace jabot and Dutch linen at his cuffs only underscored his prestige. His pilot, on the other hand, was a vulgar ship's rat of a man, already red-faced from rum, with scarlet breeches and a single gold hoop in one dark ear.

Bonnet said, "The Brethren are hastening their own demise about Hatteras and Ocracoke, and 'fore long, Blackbeard will bring the King's navy down on all of our necks. He's deviling Charles Town and blocking the harbor till the citizens give in to his demands—"

"And what are those?" a man asked eagerly.

At that instant, Tess was leaning closer to the board, filling the glass of Bonnet's pilot as cautiously as she could. Not a drop spilled, not a clank to draw the eye—at that instant, he turned and glanced at her appraisingly, and Tess felt the rake of his gaze.

"Enough wenches to sink his *Revenge*, I trow," the pilot said silkily, his eyes still on her. The men laughed uneasily; a few saw the direction of his stare.

Tess shrank back, blushing, her stomach suddenly hollow with fear and chagrin. Instantly, her mother was at her side, moving her away smoothly, taking the pitcher from her hand. The man turned his head away, and the conversations went on about her in a numbing buzz as she hurried from the cabin, out to where Glory and the younger girls were discussing the cut of Stede Bonnet's fine coat.

For a moment, she stood in the lowering shadows, feeling her heart pound and willing her stomach to silence. Never before had a man looked at her in that way. Never had she seen so swift a message that only her body seemed to translate, no matter what her mind might acknowledge. A part of her was filled with humiliation and disgust. The man was a sweating, dark lout with no grace and little honor, as savage as the brutes of the forest. But another part of her savored his glance and the residual feeling it left in her body, now that the quick surge of shame had softened to only a small excitement. She vowed that she would never put herself in such a position again. Nay, not unless she wished such feelings and such a glance would she welcome them.

Captain Stede Bonnet left Cross Creek the next morning with a pledge by the clan to provide as much board feet of white oak, the most sought-after timber in the Indies, as the privateer could carry. In return, he contracted to take their cargo direct to those who would pay the best prices, eluding English taxes in the bargain. There were some in the village who argued that they were loyal to King George, taxes or no, and that those who bedded with Bonnet were no better than pirates themselves.

But there were others, and theirs were the strongest voices in the settlement, who said that King George had granted them the same rights as any Englishman in the mother country. Taxes without council, they argued, went against every right they'd been promised. Let the King's navy come up the Cape Fear and anchor where Bonnet had anchored, and they'd pay taxes with pleasure. And with them, let them bring proper clergy and soldiers to help defend the village against the savages, so that they might have the same protection any Englishman should have. Until then, let King George plow his own field, they said, and they'd plow theirs.

🌿 🌿 🌿

Tess was sitting outside the cabin in the lazy sunshine of June, feeding Daniel. Her half-brother was just a year old, big for his age, and a handful to try to keep attentive to his porridge. Tess had found that if she moved him outside to the rough-hewn bench by the door, he was more content to sit and watch the world pass by as she spooned the gruel into him as quickly as she could. "Do take this last, Danny," she coaxed him fondly, "and then you can dig in the garden." The boy had a new spade, shiny metal with a red wood handle, and it was his delight and his mother's torment. If he could not be kept from the corn rows, they'd have less meal than they needed by September.

From the clearing that emptied out into the wagon road heading north, a dust cloud was rising. Tess finished with Daniel, put him to his play, and stood to shade her eyes from the sun, watching to see what came. Now, she could hear the low rumble of oncoming hooves, moving slowly across the meadow.

Another wagon. They were more and more frequent these months, as settlers moved down from the Old Dominion and William Penn's colony. Though the village was still a place of Highland Scots, there were now strangers among them, newcomers who built their cabins on the edge of the settlement and mingled among the clans. Tess felt drawn to these new people, sensing that they must feel some of the same strangeness and isolation that she had felt when she first came to Cross Creek.

One new family had recently moved in from the Shenandoah Valley of Virginia, Ulster Scots from Ireland, Presbyterians with no love for the English who had driven them from their home, a small clan of five who quickly put up a cottage on the edge of the farthest meadow.

Glory didn't like the Garlands. She said they were a cold bunch, haughty and stiff and standoffish. But Tess liked them well enough and the oldest boy, Arthur, seemed to her to be the best of his kin. A tall lad with nut-red hair and sober eyes, she often saw him tending the apple trees his father had planted the first month of their arrival. He kept the small orchard immaculate, grubbing out the weeds at the base of each sapling as though it were fruit, not corn, which would take his family through the winter. He shaped the tender branches in such a way that they barely touched in a lacy canopy, and Tess often walked that way, taking pleasure from the sense of order the Garland apple trees had brought to the clearing.

But this new wagon approaching did not seem as promising as some. The groan of the creaking wheels and shifting load as it pulled up by the Innes cottage told Tess that in another five miles, it likely would have fallen apart. The man driving the worn two-mule team had the haggard stare of a driver too long at the reins with no respite, and the woman clutching the rickety seat beside him wore a bonnet that might once have been yellow but now was faded to a sickly jaundice color. From the inside of the wagon, Tess could clearly hear a whimpering as from a pack of half-grown mongrel pups.

"Good day to you, sir," Tess said as the man pulled up the team. "Where do you come from?" It was the standard question at any crossroads, she knew, a safe thing to ask even if a man did not wish to give his name to a stranger. She wondered idly if she should go and get her mother who was visiting Mistress Darby up the road, but changed her mind. Daniel was digging furiously at the edge of the potato patch, the sun was high, and a new wagon at Cross Creek was scarcely reason to fetch her.

He wrenched off his brown-brimmed hat and ran his forearm roughly over his brow. "Suffolk," he said shortly, "fortnight back."

Virginia folk, Tess thought, and not so far down the road as she'd thought by the look of the team and the wagon. He must have driven hard. At the sound of his voice, the whimpering from the wagon rose in volume. The woman turned back to whatever lay inside, and Tess saw her face clearly then behind the edges of her bonnet. She looked worse than the man, more exhausted than the team, and there was a stricken, vacant look to her eye that startled Tess and made her instantly uneasy.

"This Cross Creek?" the man asked suddenly, his voice stronger, as if to divert Tess from his wife.

"Yes, sir, you'll want to go to the largest cottage near the dock yonder," she said, pointing to McDonald's cabin, "and see the chief of the clan. He'll tell you where you can stop." She hesitated a moment. She knew right well what her mother would have done. "Can I get you some cool water? Perhaps your children would want—"

"Got plenty, thanks," he said shortly, turning the team toward the expanse of clearing that stretched back to the north, away from the dock. Without another word, the wagon trundled slowly, creaking and groaning in protest, back up the road and then stopped so that it was as far from the edge of the village as possible, without actually leaving sight of the houses nearby. Tess went back

indoors, but she watched them over the next hour while he unhitched, set up camp, and the woman tended the children within
the shambled wagon. They never emerged, though she could no
longer hear their whimpers.

As the afternoon lengthened, she went out to the woodblock
to chop kindling for the supper fire. The wagon looked deserted.
They were all within, she supposed, and she kept one eye on their
distant camp as she chopped the wood and resharpened the ax
blade on the whetstone. Nothing Joseph hated more than a dull ax
when he took a hand to it.

By suppertime, the village was well aware of the newcomers and
their unspoken refusal to present themselves for welcome. Though
none wanted to run them away, Joseph said, not a few men demanded to know more about them than simply their origin.
"There's land enough for all," the captain said firmly, his brow
wrinkling in consternation, "so that's not the point. But those who
are here have a right to say who shall join them, it seems to me.
McDonald'll see to it by the morrow, I'm thinking. If he don't,
others will soon enough."

"Seems a pity," Leah said gently, "to make them feel unwelcome over such a point of courtesy. Perhaps in Suffolk, 'tisn't
necessary to gain permission to make a home."

"God's gullet, wife!" Captain scoffed good-naturedly. "Even
the savages ask a tithe or two to let strangers onto their lands. A
man could be killed for such in New Town, I wager. The least they
can do is come and doff their caps and ape respect for those who
govern, even if they don't mean it a whit. Nay, something's likely
akimbo with that lot, mark me, and McDonald'll sniff it out soon
enough." He forked another potato. "I'll not see him raise his roof
that close to mine, that much is sure. Let him clear out a patch
upriver. If he's so wary o' Scots, we'll not miss the pleasure of his
company."

Sure enough, two mornings later, a committee of men made
their way to the makeshift campsite. Tess saw them coming and
took up her seat on the bench to watch the proceedings, bringing
a bowl of peas to be shelled lest she seem to spy. Anyone observing
the six men—McDonald, his two assistants, one of the elders, and
two bosses from the mill—would have thought them out only for
a small amble in the sunlight, so unhurried did they seem.

But the man in the wagon did not read the same indifference in their stance, and he hurried to meet them, cap in hand, some distance from the wagon where his wife and brood were still within. She could not hear their words, of course, but after some conversation, the men approached the wagon, and Tess saw plainly enough that the master of the camp did not wish their approach.

McDonald and his crew stood at the tongue of the wagon for a time, evidently speaking to the woman inside. As though by a signal, they then left suddenly, and their progress back past her cottage, back to the village was decidedly different from their approach. They hurried as though their dignity was no longer important.

The news came to the cottages by the noon hour: Smallpox, the men told their wives angrily, a contagion they've brought in our midst, by God! Did you go near the wagon? Did the child? Did the hound stray near their mules? They must be driven away and swiftly, before the whole village is stricken!

Tess heard Joseph tell Leah the terrifying news, and she paled, glancing over toward Daniel playing quietly at the corner of the hearth. The boy hadn't gone near enough, she thought, to catch the disease—but I did! I stood alongside the man and the woman, close enough to hear the whimpers of the children inside. I offered them a jug of cool water!

Leah turned to her daughter in horror when her husband said the word "smallpox."

"Did you touch the wagon, Tess?" she asked her anxiously. "Did you touch the newcomers at all? How close did they come to you? My God, did they speak to Daniel or touch him?"

"I didn't," Tess murmured, shaking her head. "Truly, Mother, I barely spoke two words to them, and the mister never got down off the wagon at all. Daniel never came close."

Leah took the girls aside then, where Captain Joseph could not hear them. "Smallpox is not so terrible as they say," she said to them quietly, "not so frightening as your stepfather believes it to be. In Scotland, in parts of Ireland, I suppose, they die of it there, but they die of many things that do not kill others so easily. There was a time when the smallpox killed thousands, but now, it's mostly the very young and the very old. Not that it's anything to scoff at, and you must stay far away from that wagon and the newcomers, but we must show charity to the stricken as well. It's the children who will suffer the most. Daniel and Samuel must be watched, Tess, and Glory, you should be especially careful, for the pox would scar your face. But it's not as dangerous as they say."

"Will they be driven away?" Glory asked.

"Likely they will be, if the men have their way," Leah said, her voice a little harder. "They have enough trouble countenancing strangers in their midst."

Their mother was right, of course, and by noon of the next day, the dilapidated wagon had trundled slowly out of the clearing back up the road it had come. Tess pitied the man, the team, the poor woman perched alongside him. But most of all, she wondered after the invisible children within the lurching wagon. It was hard enough to make a home in the shelter of some settlement, among those who could lend a hand. It was nigh impossible, she had to guess, to do so all alone with nothing but an ailing wife and who-knows-how-many sick babies to tend.

For two nights after their departure, she dreamed the wagon came back once more, the woman's eyes burning under her bonnet wings from fever, the whimpers of the children risen to shrieks of torment. And each time they approached, she was so stricken, she could not move from the cottage door. She could not go inside and slam it; she could not run away. She had to stand and watch them come, slowly, painfully, knowing that they would come to an unsteady halt right before her, and she would ask them to step down to rest themselves.

Two weeks later, the mystery of where the outcast wagon had sheltered was at least partially solved. The savages in the nearby tribes began to drift into Cross Creek, shivering and clutching their soiled blankets about them, their faces and hands masses of red and white pustules. The smallpox had, like the Virgin Mary, been denied refuge at the inn and had therefore flourished in the stables.

At first, only the Peedee came to their doors, begging help and some white medicine to heal the scourge. They rarely wandered into Cross Creek these days, for though they were peaceful enough, the good Scots wives usually turned cool cheeks to their begging. Now, their desperation drove them back to cottages they had been driven from in better times. And the reception was immediate and sharp at most doors.

And yet, it was impossible to ignore the pitiful wretches who had allowed the man from Suffolk to stop his wagon in their midst. There was the constant danger that those savages not stricken might well rise in revenge for their sickened kin and wipe out all whites in the region, thinking that the settlers were somehow responsible for their torment.

The women gathered together what blankets, food, and tonics they could spare and left them in a pile in the middle of the clearing, hoping that those offerings would appease the Peedees. But then the Saponi began to drift into the village as well, and it seemed to Tess that within a short week, they were under siege. Sick Indians hovered at the fringes of the village, hoping for help, moaning in their pain. Some, near death, wrapped themselves in their blankets and lay down in the shallows of the river, not far from the dock. More leaned against the sides of the cottages, begging for comfort and help from whomever went in and out.

Before the pustules erupted, their fevers soared, and they trembled so hard they could scarcely stand, alternately wrapping themselves in what blankets they could find and then stumbling desperately to the river to cool their tortured skin. Once the smallpox began to blister and ooze from their faces, hands, shoulders, all over their torsos, even on their palms and the bottoms of their bare feet, they simply lay on the ground moaning, half unconscious in their suffering. At that time, if someone passed, they might reach up and beg for water, clutching at a skirt, but mostly they simply died. Every morning, new corpses dotted the clearing, and now no one could turn a deaf ear or refuse a hand to help.

The men selected burial parties by random lots; the women drew lots as well to see which wives would distribute what medicines, meal, and water they could. Tess could not abide the poor wretches at her door, nor could she find it in her heart to callously turn them away with nothing. Since their cottage was so close to the road, it seemed that most made Joseph Innes's door their first stop. For a few, it was their last.

Leah and Glory took Samuel and Daniel to the back of the cottage and would not allow them outside or even within touching distance of the door or windows. It took both of them to subdue the boys and keep them from tearing down the walls of the cabin with four restless hands. Joseph stayed long hours at the mill, where the Indians did not go, for they feared the huge saws and hated the shriek of the splitting wood. Coming home only to eat and sleep, he managed to avoid the worst sights round his door, but Tess could not.

Finally, of course, she had used what meal and medicines her mother would let her offer, and every spare blanket was gone. With only water to offer, she still could not simply ignore the soft scratching the sick Indians made at the door, the walls, the windows, as they peered within to see who would come. The days passed, and those who stopped were more horribly stricken than the first beseechers, their faces almost unrecognizable as human beneath the swollen pustules, their skin sticking in great oozing patches to their blankets, their clothing, even their own hair. They held their brows in anguish, trying to relieve the pounding headaches, and they walked as though they felt pain in every bone. Finally, she began to weep as she opened the door, and then Leah banished her to the back of the cabin with Glory to tend the two boys, answering the scratches herself.

A horrid week passed, the worst the village could remember and finally, the Indians began to drift away again. The weak, the old, the very young had perished with the contagion. The few survivors struggled back to their feet and up the road, terribly scarred but alive.

Two nights after most of the savages had disappeared, Leah took to her bed with a high fever, complaining of a pain in her head. Captain Joseph came home for his meal to find her wrapped in one of their few remaining blankets, her face turned to the wall. He paled visibly, sitting down beside her gingerly and reaching out to touch her hair. "Is it the contagion?" he asked her in a horrified whisper.

"Nay," she reassured him calmly. " 'Tis only a chill. I likely tired myself tending the boys. By morning, I'll be fit."

He ate a silent supper and would not be diverted as usual by the boys' antics, Glory's animated chatter, and Tess's effort to slip the choicest morsels on his plate.

By morning, however, Leah was weaker still. Where she had been willing to take broth the night before, now she refused anything but cool water, and she could not keep still on her bed, but tossed and turned restlessly, occasionally stopping only to ask Tess a question about Samuel or the bread or perhaps a bit of gossip that had happened weeks before and been long forgotten.

As the hours passed, Tess knew that her answers were not being heard, not truly, for Leah asked again and again, her voice growing more plaintive. When Tess asked her why she could not lie still, she whispered that her legs hurt her, her arms hurt her, her back ached unendurably.

Tess sent Glory and the boys to Mistress Darby's cottage, ignoring Glory's protests that she was not a child to be bundled off with the boys. Joseph came home from the mill early to find Leah weaker and sent a message that he'd not be at work until she was up and about. Together, then, Tess and her stepfather began a worse siege than they'd endured with the savages.

By night, they knew it was the smallpox. Leah's fever rose alarmingly, her body was drenched with sweat, and her palms and feet were clammy as a corpse. The blisters multiplied on her skin by the hour, and an angry purple mottling discolored her neck and shoulders. Within hours, the papules covered every bit of skin that Tess could see.

Now, Leah did not know them nor was she aware of their efforts to help her, for she sometimes begged for water as though Tess withheld it and alternately refused it completely, turning away in desperate anger as though she might force her to drink.

Joseph could do little, yet he would not leave the cottage. They took turns bathing her brow, trying to keep the fever down, turning the cloths again and again and wrenching them in fresh water. Then, when her chills made her shiver so hard that she cried out in terror, he banked her body with what blankets they had, heated bricks in the hearth for her feet, and finally lay down beside her to add his warmth to hers.

"Is there no medicine for the disease?" he asked Tess repeatedly. "If I could find a physician, could he help her, do you think?"

"Mayhap, he could," she said, sighing with fatigue. Leah was sleeping now, so they kept their voices low. "But where would you go to find one?"

"I couldn't get to Bath and back again fast enough to save her. By the time I could get a doctor upriver, she'd likely be cured."

Or dead, the unspoken words hovered between them.

Of a sudden, Joseph's mood slanted precariously, and he was instantly angry. "You couldn't turn them away, could you?" he glowered at her. "Every damn savage for ten miles square, most of them reeking with contagion, you had to open the door to every heathen face!"

She bowed her head in anguish. Even if she had known a defense, she knew it was useless to speak it. In his present mood, with nothing and no one in the cottage to blame save her, with the constant pressure of Leah's twisted face confronting him, he could not forgive her.

She could scarcely forgive herself, in fact. It was true that she had been weak, had not been able to turn away the heathen, and perhaps it was after all—

"God's punishment on us, is what it is! Ye brought it on the house, ye brought it on your mother!" he shouted.

She glanced to her mother, but she slept heavily, noisily, her lungs thick and ropy with the sickness. He followed her eyes and lowered his voice to a harsh whisper. " 'Ye must turn from the heathen,' the Lord said, but ye embraced them!"

The surprise of hearing her stepfather mention the word of God, something he had never done in her memory, startled her into her first defense. "I didn't embrace them," she murmured. "I only gave them what we could spare."

"You gave them your mother!" he hissed at her. "Can we spare *her*, then?"

She winced as if struck. At that moment, Leah moaned and turned, and Joseph went instantly to her, his voice suddenly gentle, his hands replacing the warm cloths with fresh, cool ones. Tess saw that the blisters were beginning to ooze, were fiery red, and had dimpled the skin all round them.

But Captain showed no disgust. Finally he said, this time in a voice that might have been announcing the change of the seasons, "If the boys and Glory aren't stricken, 'twill be a miracle we don't deserve. Jesus, she's hotter than she was an hour hence." He turned back to Tess, and she saw that his face was collapsed in anguish and grief. She forgave him completely, and immediately for his attack. "She'll likely lose the babe," he whispered.

A third shock. But she kept her face still. Another child! She said only, "She's very strong, Father. And we don't get the contagion as bad as the savages. She told me herself, it's often not so dangerous as people think."

He turned away from her, and Tess rose quickly to bring more cool water, anything, anything to avoid the accusing pain in his eyes.

That night, Leah's fever rose even further, and together, they struggled her into a bath of tepid water to try to bring it down. She fought them weakly, striking out at Joseph and Tess, and in her delirium, she called for James over and over, begging him to help her. Now, the blisters covered her face so badly that Tess could see, if she lived, she would never be lovely again. It was hard enough for Tess to hear her; she knew that it must be a rare torture for Joseph, for Leah looked at him with stark fear as though he were the devil himself come for her.

Once she was partially submerged in the small washtub Joseph had dragged into the cottage, her fever fell and she slept fitfully. Four hours later, Tess found her bleeding badly from her female parts and still in a stupor. Though she packed her mother tightly with what linens she could find, she could not halt the flow. By the clotting, Tess feared that she had lost the child, yet she did not stir once as it left her. That was the only time that Joseph left the cottage, left her alone to tend what seemed to be a corpse bearing another corpse, but Tess was almost grateful that he left her, for she was then free to weep as she cleansed her mother, taking away all evidence of the lost babe that no one else might see its pitiful remains.

Sometime in the early dawn, Joseph returned and woke Tess. She had fallen asleep at her mother's side, leaning over her hip with one arm stretched out, a cloth still in her hand.

"She's gone, lass," he said as she came to wakefulness.

"No!" she wailed, falling next to her mother and trying to pull her body into her arms. "Her fever was down!" But she could see that the waxen face before her, composed and blank, had nothing of her mother in it. Even the fiery pustules had faded. Her mother's face shocked her to silence, but the tears ran freely down her cheeks.

"Sometimes it happens like that," he said dismally. "They get better right before the end. I remember, when I was a boy." He wiped his own eyes and tried to gently pull her away.

"Leave me alone! If I'm going to take sick, I'm going to," she wept, pulling her arms away and nestling down again beside her mother. She put one arm round her shoulders as if they were two confidants whispering secrets. "Now what will we do? Oh, Glory! Oh, God—"

Joseph said dully, "She died without either of us there for her." His face was a constricted mix of grief and reproach.

Something in her rose above her own pain and wild sense of abandonment, and her voice had the firmness of anger when she answered. "I *was* there for her. So were you, even if you weren't here at the momen*t*, she knew we were there. Don't say she had no one!"

Her stepfather lifted his head in surprise at her tone, and he gazed at her long and appraisingly, as though he saw her for the first time. "Then I'll chide you no more, lass. You'll miss her much as any. Mayhap, more." He rose unsteadily, averting his eyes from Leah's tranquil, empty face. "Well, I'll get the men to help me. And you must tell your sister and brothers that she's gone. Go tell Mistress Darby to come and ready her."

"No," she said quickly, "I'll wash her myself. Then I'll go to Glory." She wiped her face stolidly on her mother's linen and moved to pick up the basin and the damp cloths.

He watched her the while, silently. Finally he said, "Keep far from the others until ye see if ye take it. Don't kiss them, don't touch the boys. But ye must tell them, for I cannot. Ye must be mother to them all now, lass. Let that be your burden, then." He bent and gently kissed Leah's cheek, then turned and left the cottage. She knew without asking that he'd not be back that night.

Slowly, Tess uncovered her mother's body, observing as from a high, distant place what a lovely woman she was, even in death. She saw the fine, blue tracery on her white legs, a map of all the miles she had walked in her life. She noticed, with a calm absence of emotion, the way her breasts lay on her rib cage, her nipples darkening with the coming child. She saw that her hands were darker than her upper arms, for having been revealed to the sun and the wind and the garden. Except for the fading pustules, she was a woman of grace and finely made. Her hands, particularly, drew Tess's eyes. Hands that had held her, nursed her, bathed and dosed her through a score of childhood ailments. Hands, too, that had rocked her, caressed her with love.

Now her mother's hands lay partially open, collapsed upon themselves like two small, limp animals of the woods. They were not cold and stiff, but only cool and dry, like the petals of spotted lilies, happened upon in a shaded glen. Weeping now, Tess washed each part of her mother's body carefully but quickly. She did not want Glory to come upon them together. She wanted her mother to herself this once, whoever might take her away soon.

This was the body that bore me, she told herself as she laved and dried the limbs, the hands, the neck and shoulders, the belly, the back, and the feet. This was my mother, this flesh, this set of hands and eyes and ears. And now, I must be mother to them all.

Before Glory could intrude, Tess withdrew her housewife from her apron pocket and closed the small shears upon a dark lock of her mother's hair, snipping a tendril gently. She opened the locket that lay hidden under her bodice, the locket she never took off, and she gently pressed the dark hairs within. At least she could save this much of her mother and keep it close to her.

🌿 🌿 🌿

Tess was sitting, exhausted and light-headed, staring bleakly at her mother's body. Leah was washed and dressed in her finest bodice, her new damask-sprigged skirt tied about her waist, her white stockings neat and straight, her hair brushed and coiffed within her bonnet. When she entered heaven, Tess thought dimly, James would know her in a moment. In that space of silence, Glory burst into the room, sobbing.

"I heard Papa talking! He told Mistress Darby Mama was dead—!" She stopped in her flight to the bed and gasped, her hands to her mouth. "Oh, Tessie!" she wailed then, throwing herself onto Leah's figure and gripping her tightly about the hips. Tess remembered, as if in a dream, the same way Glory had thrown herself at her mother after the savages attacked. She had almost killed her then. Now, she could do no harm. Except to herself.

She rose wearily and went to Glory, taking her gently off Leah and holding her tightly. "She died sometime this morning," she said brokenly. "She never woke up. You mustn't get close, else you might get it." She stroked Glory's bright hair to comfort her. That always soothed her sister.

But Glory pushed her away violently. "You got to be with her, at least! You sent me away!"

Tess ignored her flailing arms and embraced her again. "She never woke up, I told you. She didn't know me, she didn't know Captain."

"She would have waked up for me!" Glory sobbed, twisting in Tess's arms.

Her sister let her go. "Mayhap she would have," Tess said

wearily. "But Captain said you had to go with the boys. He didn't want you to catch the contagion, Glory."

She slumped down beside her mother, resting her cheek against Leah's flank. Her wails began to subside. "She is ugly!" she whimpered. "Those awful things all over her face!"

"That's the pox," Tess murmured. "They'll fade soon enough."

After long moments, Glory sat up and moved away across the room to their own small bed and curled up on it, pulling the blanket up about her head as though she might never come out again. "What will we do now, Tessie?" she asked in a small voice, hiccoughing softly between the hitches of her fading sobs.

"We'll do what we've always done," Tess said, curling up beside her and pulling the covers so that she was covered as well. "We'll take care of each other, I guess. And Samuel and Daniel and Captain."

"Mama would want that," Glory ventured.

Tess pushed her stepfather's warning out of her mind resolutely. If the contagion wanted her—wanted Glory, too—then it would have them both. But it would not take one of them alone, nor would it keep them apart. She embraced her sister, pulling her close so that they might weep together, softly into each other's hair.

That is how Joseph Innes found his two stepdaughters when he returned with Mistress Darby and Mistress Russell to help him prepare his wife. Both of them, side by side in their bed, nestled together like two exhausted pups in a welter of bed linen and clothes, Glory's bright head resting on Tess's arm.

The village of Cross Creek did not waste time laying Leah Hancock Innes to rest. The fear of contagion would have dictated haste, even if custom did not. By nightfall, most of the clan was gathered at the edge of the small clearing to the west of the settlement, which served as a burial ground, hemmed by tall pines and within sight of the river. Chief McDonald said the words over the grave, and the goodwives placed the pine boughs over the mound to keep her spirit within.

Joseph stood staunchly beside his chief, his two young sons in his arms. Samuel and Daniel looked fearful and bewildered, Tess thought, as she stood with Glory on the other side of the grave. Flanked by all members of her family, Leah was surrendered forever into the soil of a new land she scarcely wanted to visit, much less be a part of for eternity, Tess realized dimly. She could remember her mother, it seemed now so many years ago, weeping as they came across on the great ship from England. Weeping again as they left Bath. Always, she was being moved about from one place to another by the whim of some man.

In this way, at least, she vowed as she watched the men do what had to be done about the grave, I will not be like my mother. Glory will follow some man, no doubt, through all of her life from one place to another, but I will not. If I find a husband at all, he will live where I wish to live.

If I ever find such a place, she added, wondering if her mother could hear her now. But wherever I go, I won't forget where you are, Mother. Some part of me will be here, too, forever.

Glory was weeping loudly now, as the women set a sprig of flowers on the pine boughs. Tess helped her bend and put a sheaf of lavender, her mother's favorite, at the head of the mound. Once the grave was smoothed, covered, and spoken over, there was little left to do but go back to the silent cottage.

Suddenly, the thought of returning to their home empty-handed and empty-hearted smote Tess with the strength of a physical slap. Back to the cottage where Leah would be nevermore. Back to her chair, her bed, her board, her kitchen pots and servers where she would never sit, never move to and fro, never speak, never pick up and put down again. Tess felt sick, and the light-headedness that had come and gone for a day now swept over her with a wash of despair; she almost staggered with it. Her head ached, and her back wrenched as though it cried out from within. She could no longer endure the sound of Glory's weeping, could no longer bear another moment of standing. With a small sound of bewildered pain, she slid senseless to the ground, and the blackness that had been hovering at the edges of her sight for hours completely engulfed her at last.

For seven days, Tess wandered in and out of herself, and she was only dimly aware that somewhere, voices called to her, hands touched her. At some point during that time, she knew with sureness that she was very ill. At another time, she felt that she was likely dead, for her mother and her father were with her, as real and close as though they had never left her side at all. She wept with joy to see her father and wept again quietly when she knew that he was not really with her and would never be, so long as she lived.

Mostly, she dreamed a hundred feverish and disjointed dreams in which Glory and Captain Joseph and Samuel and Daniel and her mother and father and the man from the wagon and the pirate, Stede Bonnet, and Chief McDonald, and Mistress Darby, and a score of others came and went, to and fro, cluttering her mind with voices and antics and scoldings.

When she finally woke, she found Glory seated in the small chair beside their bed, knitting dutifully on a pale gray shawl. Her shoulders looked shrunken, older somehow, as though Tess had been gone for a very long time. That was how she realized that she must have been very ill, indeed—Glory was knitting. Nothing else would have made the child sit still long enough, nothing else would have kept her busy fingers to such a tedious task. She meant to speak but found she could only sigh.

Glory looked up instantly and set aside her knitting, rising to lean over her. "Tessie, you're awake," she murmured. "Thank God!"

Tess tried to say, of course I'm awake and whatever has ailed me, but all she could manage was a hoarse squeak. Finally, she croaked, "I'm sick."

"Yes, you've been very sick, but you're better now. Captain got a doctor all the way from New Town to look at you, such good fortune he happened to dock not a day after you were took—"

"With what?" She struggled to rise but could hardly lift her head.

"With the smallpox, of course, and no one was surprised, either, but you're stronger than Mama, you licked it. You broke the fever last night, and now you're going to get better, Mistress Darby said." Glory peered at her carefully. "The ones on your face aren't too awful, really."

"How long have I been here?"

"Seven days, since Mama's burial." She sighed sadly and sat down beside Tess, moving her over, making room for herself unconsciously, as she always did. "It's been a fearsome time."

"My face?" Tess asked weakly.

She glanced at her sister and then glanced away. "It's not so bad, really, Tessie, I told you. Mistress Darby says, she's seen a lot worse who had nary a pox when they finally healed." She smiled brightly. "You're lucky, really."

Tess moaned and closed her eyes. Lucky? From the time the man pulled up the wagon, nay from the time the savages overran New Bern, she'd had no luck that she could see. And now, she was likely scarred for the rest of her life. "Bring me the glass," she whispered.

Glory shook her head adamantly. "Mistress Darby said you would ask for it, they always do, she said, but you're not to see the glass until you're stronger. Papa said—"

"He's not my papa!" she shouted. "Bring me the glass!"

"I won't do it." Glory pulled herself up to her full height and set her jaw. " 'Twill only make you sad and you need all your strength to get better. Time enough to worry later, now you just worry about getting well. You're alive, anyway. Give thanks for that and don't ask me again."

"I'll get it myself!" Tess angrily tried to rise up on one elbow and throw off her linens, but she only struggled herself into exhaustion in an instant. She slid back down, confused and beaten.

"See?" Glory smiled gently.

Tess suddenly could not keep her eyes open another moment, and she moved back into the blackness, willing aside her despair.

It was another full fortnight before Tess was able to get to her glass herself. By the time she stood and gazed at her face in her mother's old silvered mirror, she felt as though she looked at a stranger's face, not her own. She was pocked on both cheeks, badly on her forehead, a smattering of pocks on her chin, and little on her neck or upper shoulders. Like erratic, misshapen dimples, the small craters dappled her skin, leaving interesting patterns where none had been before.

She had expected to feel horror, but she felt only small, resigned relief. Well, it was over, at any rate. She would never be beautiful, never even be comely. If she had ever wondered, now that decision was made forever. Forevermore, she would make her way in life knowing that her face would not help her. Neither need it be a cause for despair. Others had larger burdens to shoulder, and if this was the worst life would hand her, she might consider herself blessed.

But blessed she did not feel. She sat down wearily at the table, put her face on her arms, and wept in a way she had not wept for years. For her father, for her mother, for her own loss of innocence, she wept until she could weep no more, thankful only that the cottage was empty and that she need not stifle her pain.

When she finally wept away every tear she could summon, she rose and wiped her eyes resolutely. The boys and Glory would be back soon, and dinner must be prepared. She moved to her mother's hearth, lifted her largest kettle out over the smoldering coals, and began the preparation.

❧ ❧ ❧

It was three years before Tess could look in the glass and almost not see the scars from that terrible time. Not that they weren't there. The pocks she would carry always, but she no longer noticed them. They were obvious enough, just like her blue eyes and her pink lips. But she was nigh seventeen, and her days were too full of busy duties to moon before a mirror. No one else seemed to care for her looks so, she determined, she wouldn't either.

That spring of 1720, news came upriver that they had hanged Stede Bonnet and others of his Brethren in Charles Town, the bustling seaport in the colony of South Carolina, not so far away. The notorious Blackbeard, a pirate said to be worse than any score of his peers, was caught and killed near Ocracoke Inlet, and his head was hung high in the rigging when the British warship sailed into Bath. New Town, lately named Wilmington by those who wanted it to sound better than it should be, was also cleaned out, they said, and no pirate dared show his face on the streets. Tess wondered how many streets they actually had, these days, since she could scarcely picture more than one in the squalid nest of thieves she remembered.

But Cross Creek was still far from the governments at Bath and Charles Town, and the Cape Fear River a useful artery for those who wished to escape both. Further, it was growing larger every season, with shiploads of Scots coming over, following their relations, and newcomers coming steadily down the wagon road from the north. No town on the river produced more ships, stores of tar and turpentine; no mill more than Captain Innes's cut more board feet. The ships needed the wood and the naval stores, and the Scots made good trade, for every soul turned to work. Samuel and Daniel worked in the mill longside their father now, and even Glory, the grasshopper amidst the ants, was able to be persuaded that she could learn to bake Captain's favorite apple pie. Cross Creek was a community that wasted nothing, certainly not a pair of hands.

That spring, a score of new ships made their way up to the settlement to trade with the prosperous Scots, but most attracted little notice. Once, however, in mid-April when the freshets were full, a sleek, shallow-hulled ship anchored outside the docks, and within a few days, the name of Jack Dobbs had been spoken at every board in the village.

Tess saw him first at Chief McDonald's table, for she was asked to come and help serve when his crew took their welcome. She knew that Master Dobbs must be a man of parts—or at least a man who could turn a profit on them—for Chief McDonald no longer took the trouble to welcome every newcomer to port. Indeed, she had only to see Jack Dobbs for herself to know that he was worth the flurry of attention he had claimed.

He sat down the table from McDonald, his pilot to his right hand. Tall and swarthy, he smelled of the open sea and fresh winds. When she passed by his left side, she saw that his black hair, cut close to his head with a small tail behind, was graying slightly at the temples. Older than he seems, she thought, or mayhap the sea does this to a man.

He paid her no mind, of course, and the conversation that moved easily about the table, though light and flexed with courtesy, showed the man to be about his business uppermost. The word "privateer" was never spoken, but it was quickly apparent that this Dobbs was willing to forgo the name to continue the trade. "The old ways and the old scoundrels are dead," he said easily, "and good riddance, I say. A man with wit and connections can pass through customs without drawing his purse and can cross the English sea lanes without drawing a sword."

"Your reputation precedes you, man," McDonald said solemnly. "Your last shipment from Bath paid no taxes at all, I'm told."

"Most gossip, as the bard said, is weary, flat, stale, and unprofitable," Captain Dobbs replied smoothly, "and I'd not insult your table with idle tales."

"But if the tales are not idle?" McDonald pressed.

Dobbs shrugged amiably. "Taxes are the last resort of a king who cannot fill his hands with friends." He looked about the table. "Fortunately, I have never lacked for that commodity. I hope I never shall."

An understanding seemed to have been reached, Tess saw, with little of substance actually being said. The men bent their heads to earnest discussion, and Jack Dobbs put questions to Captain Joseph that were pertinent and to the point. Moreover, he listened carefully to the answers. Tess sensed that her stepfather was as taken with the man as some of the women behind her, for he leaned over closer to Captain Dobbs in a confidential manner and tried to engage him in talk of the sea, though he'd been landlocked for most of eight years. To her surprise, she overheard him ask Dobbs to the cottage for supper the next night.

What could Joseph be thinking? They were no longer prepared for guests in that manner, not with her mother gone and only her hands and Glory's to attend. It couldn't be proper for the man to be in a house with two grown daughters and no mother—what if he brought his crew!

In that moment, as if feeling her alarm, Dobbs glanced at her, and Tess flurried to the back of the room, suddenly unable to maintain her dignity. She felt a rush of heat up her neck and face as shame and confusion swept over her. Resentment, too, rode her heart with bright spurs of pride. Well, and if the man came, she would teach Captain Joseph a lesson he'd not soon forget. The meal would be at the board, but 'twould scarcely be fit to eat. Likely they'd be in their cups by the time the roast hit the trencher anyway, so let it be tough, unsavory, and salty as Jack Dobbs's wit.

Sure enough, the next morning as he left for the mill, Captain Joseph announced that Jack Dobbs would join them for the evening meal. "Just himself, lass," he threw over his shoulder, "still make it a grand feast. The man has a taste for the best, I wager!"

Does he, indeed? Tess fumed to herself as she mixed the biscuits and threw them in the pan. She set Glory to work in a whirlwind of testy commands, cleaning and dusting and stowing the boys' clutter in their trunks, pounding the roast, chopping the onions, paring the apples. Glory hastened to obey, casting long looks at her sister over her shoulder, uncharacteristically docile.

And a good thing, too, Tess frowned to herself, she's as much daughter as I am, so let her step to his bidding. More, if the truth

be known! I'm more scullery maid and cook than kin, and if Jack
Dobbs thinks he can strut in here like a cock o' the walk—

"Tessie," Glory suddenly interrupted her timidly, "you seem
mighty wroth this day."

"Father had no business asking the man here!" she exploded
with an anger that startled her. "He's nothing but a privateer, and
'tis unseemly to have such a man here now that Mother's gone.
And how am I to feed him properly on the small change Captain
gives me to feed us all? This roast was meant to last us for three,
mayhap four nights, and now 'twill be gone down some scoundrel's
gullet in one meal!"

Glory sat quietly, one foot tucked up under her chair, a bowl
of apples and parings in her lap. "Why, Tessie, whatever do you
mean? Unseemly? Papa will be right here, so will Samuel and Daniel
and likely two or three goodwives will drop in, they always do.
And as for not enough food, you know that Papa gives us whatever
we need. If you want another roast, I wager he'll buy one soon
enough." As always, Glory went right to the core of the fruit.
"Seems to me," she said softly, "that something else is pricking
you, Tessie. Seems to me it's the man, not the meal."

Tess turned to Glory, aflame with indignation. "What nonsense!"

" 'Tisn't, I expect," her sister said idly, continuing to pare the
apples as though they discussed Goody Russell's new scarlet bodice with the aubergine ribbons. "They say he's a bonny man with
a jaunty eye. Mayhap, you noticed."

"Who says!"

Glory looked up innocently, "Why, most every lass who
served him. They say you thought so, too, or must have, for you
fled to the farthest corner of the board the minute he gave you an
eye."

"I didn't!" Tess sputtered. "He never looked at me once! But
I was amazed when Captain asked him to dinner, without even a by
your leave, and I—"

"Since when does Papa ask your leave to bring a newcomer to
table?"

Tess saw in that moment that Glory had grown quickly in the
past year. Now past fourteen, she was no longer a child. No longer
simply her sister. The roundness of her face had changed to a more

womanly curve of cheek and lip, and her eyes held a certain sure knowledge.

Glory smiled softly. "Ah, Tessie, ye worked yourself in a dither." She laughed, aping Joseph's burr. "Jack Dobbs will come, he'll eat your good roast, and he'll be gone again by the time ye got the trenchers scrubbed."

"Good," Tess said stoutly. "And as for his jaunty eye, miss, you better keep out from under it, yourself. Just because you've got your womanlies now, doesn't mean you are one."

Glory shook her head indulgently. "And what would such a rogue want with the likes of me?" She looked up and grinned. "Jack Dobbs, be damned."

That startled a laugh out of Tess, and she went to her work again with an easier heart. But as they labored together, she watched her sister with a new eye. Glory was changing. Both of them were, truth be known.

That evening, Tess set a fine table. Samuel and Daniel sat on one side, Glory and Tess on the other, Captain Joseph in his usual place at the head, and Master Jack Dobbs of the *Happy Delivery* took the seat of honor at the other end of the board. Between them spread a bounty of roast beef swamped in beer and apples, hearty oat cakes, fried potatoes and onions, Glory's apple pie, and a frosty pitcher of buttermilk to wash it all down. Captain swiftly put the pitcher before the boys and called for his best ale.

Tess had guessed as much. She had the jug readied and full to the brim on the sideboard.

"Is this the infamous Scots' brew I've heard of, sir?" Dobbs asked the captain. "In Newton, they say it whitens the teeth, perfumes the breath, and makes childbirth a pleasure." He grinned toward Tess, who ignored him pointedly.

"Ay, 'tis the same!" laughed Joseph eagerly. "It does all that and tastes like two cats fighting in your mouth in the bargain."

"Does it improve with age?"

"I canna say, for I never keep it long enough to find out!"

The men had no more than filled their plates when the boys called for stories of pirates and battles at sea. Tess half expected Captain Joseph to quell such talk, for she remembered he showed no love for the Brethren when they stopped at New Town so long ago. But to her surprise, he, too, called on his guest to regale them with his adventures, after once glancing nervously at Glory to see if she paid close attention.

But Glory, as always, seemed to be half at table, half in her own world, and she scarcely took notice of Jack Dobbs.

"So it's skirmishes you want to hear of?" the man asked wryly, one eyebrow cocked at the boys. "Tales of smoking pistols and gore?"

"Ay!" the boys chorused at once, gleeful at Tess's frown.

"Well, I've seen my share." Captain Dobbs grinned. "Back when the Brethren ruled every sea lane from Norfolk to Charles Town and the Indies, besides, I sailed with Teach aboard the *Revenge*, out of Topsail Inlet. He was the worst o' the lot, boys, and no mistake. You've heard his name, no doubt."

"Blackbeard," hissed Samuel. He turned to Danny, both of their mouths agape, their eyes wide in the candlelight.

Tess settled back, her chin high, her arms crossed over her breasts. Glory was methodically making neat, narrow rows of her fried potatoes.

"Ay, Blackbeard. The blackest heart, too, on all the seas. He put his own men to torture; took prisoners and made them walk the plank if they displeased him. Once, I was aboard when we were becalmed west of Antigua. Not a whisper of a breeze moved the sails. The men were maggoty-headed and spoiling for a fight. They broke out the rum, and Blackbeard got drunk as David's sow."

"And that's very drunk indeed," Captain Joseph murmured, glancing nervously at Tess, who only rolled her eyes and looked away. But the boys hung on every word. Dobbs darted his eyes to Tess, to Glory for a long moment, then dropped his voice conspiratorially.

"Ay. Well, he was staggering about the decks, swinging his killing sword round his shoulders, when he said, 'Come on, men! Let's make a Hell of our own and see who can stand it the longest!' Well, three besotted fools accepted the devil's challenge, and they went down to the hold with him." He leaned closer to the boys and hissed, "Unarmed."

Samuel and Daniel goggled at him, struck silent.

"Down in the hold, we kept big rocks to ballast the ship, and Teach called for pots of brimstone to be lowered down. He bade the boys sit like at a fancy tea party and set those pots afire. He called out, 'Close the hatches, lads, and lock 'em!' And we stood uptop, watching as the smoke came billowing up out of the hold like a mill going up in flames! You should have heard those poor beggers scream! All but Teach.''

"The man sounds a fool,'' Glory said mildly, her voice sliding through the tense silence like an eel through an eddy.

Jack Dobbs sat back and laughed, a bark of surprised delight. "But did they all burn up?'' gasped Samuel.

He shook his head ruefully. "The men begged to be let out soon enough, but ol' Blackbeard, he stayed down the longest, just to prove he was captain by rights and best man, to boot. We opened the hatch, and they scrambled out, weeping and cursing and wiping their eyes. And when Captain came up, he said, 'Next time, we play at gallows, to see who can swing longest without being throttled!' ''

Dobbs looked to Glory, to see if she cared to add another comment. She asked, "Did you never wish to be a farmer then, sir?''

He chuckled ruefully. "My mother's second husband was that, mistress, on a piece of land so poor it would scarcely raise hell, much less a living. Nay, that life's not for me.''

She smiled at him indulgently, as one would smile on a small boy who has just done a difficult trick, and dropped her gaze again. Tess saw the small exchange between them and rose swiftly to her feet, her stomach suddenly queer and uneasy. "Well, 'tis well those evil days of pirates are gone for good,'' she said briskly, reaching for the pewter coffee urn. "Captain, will you take another cup before you go?''

He held up the cup to her without looking. "Ay, lass, I thankee. Joseph, the market for spars'll be good this season, for the mills are down in Bath, from the floods. What do ye say to running a thousand more board feet of white pine—?''

As the talk moved abruptly to business, the boys eased from the table swiftly, whispering to each other of pirates and planks and swordplay on the seas. Glory rose with an armful of platters and followed Tess to the washtub. "I told you he was a rogue,'' Tess murmured to her, once they were out of earshot.

"And so he is,'' Glory whispered, unconcerned. "And I told you he'd be gone by the time we wash these trenchers. Care to make a wager on it?''

"Ay, he'll be gone, but I think he'll be back,'' Tess replied meaningfully.

" 'Twont ruffle my ribbons."

Tess touched her on the arm softly. "You don't want him, then?"

Glory giggled smartly, rolling her eyes. "Now you're a bigger fool than *he* is!"

Tess glanced to the pool of light where Jack Dobbs and Joseph Innes bent their heads together, and her heart seemed to move slightly, taking away her breath. In that moment, she was filled with a fearful exhilaration. She knew now the source of her annoyance, her restlessness, her unease around the man. He was beautiful, and she was drawn to him.

🌾 🌾 🌾

That night, Tess lay in her narrow cot next to Glory who slumbered peacefully, as always, her arm across most of the pillow, her leg thrown over half the bed. But she scarcely noticed her sister beside her, so used was she to her body.

It was her own body she was infinitely, painfully aware of this night. A body she at once rejoiced in and at once hated for its betrayal. She watched Jack Dobbs over and over in her mind's eye, replaying every time she had seen him, rehearing every word he had spoken in her presence since he'd arrived. She knew, even as she lingered over the pictures, that they were unwholesome in some deep, secret way. Or if they were not unwholesome, her intense focus upon them was, somehow. She felt ashamed. But her shame did not make her cease. Nor could she turn away and welcome the blankness of sleep.

Jack Dobbs. A dark head of crisp hair, not silky like her own, she'd vow, but almost wired by the sun and the salt air. Such hair would feel coarse and springy under her hand, particularly where she touched the gray, she guessed. And the skin on his face was etched around his eyes and mouth—too much laughter, no doubt at things that should be taken seriously. And the hands, rough and sinewed, finely made at the nails and joints when he handled his fork. Quick, deft hands, which looked as though they knew how to handle most anything that came within their grasp.

She turned her head to the side as though to turn away from her visions of him, but they followed her. There was something about him that smelled of power and maleness, a certain cast to his shoulders that signaled a complete indifference to all that the world might deem seemly.

My God, am I in love with this scoundrel? Is this what such a circumstance feels like, and if so, how does one survive such a calamity? For he is nothing that I would want in a husband, nothing that any woman would need for more than a fortnight. In that moment, she yearned for her mother, even though she knew she would not have been able to speak of this to her, even if she were here. He is nothing she would want for me, likely.

Yet she remembered the bright, hot flurry of the women when he entered the chief's cottage, and she understood that they knew something of him before she did. They would know him again, in a hundred guises, every generation of him, so long as men knew women and women wanted their knowing.

And now, she was one of them. She could never be so young again.

She twisted her head back the other way and gazed at Glory sleeping, the curves of her lovely face visible in the dim light. He would want her. If he wanted anyone at all, it was Glory who would be his choice. She could see that much in the simple gaze he gave her that night. And Glory? Glory would not want him; he would have no other, and so he would go away and likely not return.

That thought, more than any, twisted her heart so that she could scarcely breathe. Then she prayed, ay, make him go away and take with him this feeling. Let me forget I ever felt this way, for I never wish to feel it again. Or if you will not make him go away, at least make me not wish him to stay quite so much.

The next morning Tess felt crochety and stiff, as though she had hoed the whole garden in one long night while the others had the privilege of blissful sleep. She snapped at the boys to hurry with their breakfast and smacked Glory's hand when she reached under her arm to take a hot cruller from the pan before she had set them down.

Joseph came back for his meal, as he always did, after he'd started the crew at the mill. As he took his seat, he called Glory to him, and she came, wiping her hands on her apron. "Daughter," he said easily, watching her as he spoke, "when did you grow pert and comely? Seems like you did it when my back was turned."

Glory smiled and slipped close to him, wrapping one arm about his neck and giving his cheek a quick kiss. "Last month, I think," she said, teasing him. " 'Twas when you were taking supper at Widow Newcombe's table and you didn't come home till cock crow."

He grinned and tugged gently at a red curl at her neck. "Ye minx. Your own mother never had such a tongue on her. Nor," he added, appraising her closely, "did she have such blue, blue eyes. Well, 'tis not hard to understand, all told, why Captain Dobbs is taken with ye."

Glory's mouth dropped open and she quickly glanced at Tess. Tess froze, her wiping cloth in her hands. Both sisters turned to stare at their stepfather.

"Ay, lass, 'tis true. Out of all the village, the man's eyes lit on ye, and he wants ye for his wedded wife."

"But she's only a child," Tess murmured without thinking.

"She's young, 'tis true, but not too young to make a bride. And for such a man as Dobbs—"

"A pirate!" Glory burst out, her fists clenched.

"Not anymore," Joseph said calmly, holding up his hand to silence her. "He's a man of trade, master of his own ship, and welcome in every port, as you've seen with your own eyes. I wager he'll clear a thousand sterling on that last load, if he clears a quid, and it's the first of many he'll ship for us." He leaned forward and put his hand on Glory's shoulder. "He's a fine man, lass, and a rich one, too. He'll take good care of you and give you a better life than I can."

"He's too old!"

Joseph laughed kindly. "He's got a bit o' gray in his hair, but that just means he's wise enough to know what he wants. He's old enough to handle you, lass, and not so old that he won't please you. Did ye not see the way the wenches flocked to his side? Not a one o' *them* thought him too old, I wager. And yet of them all, he chose you, my Glory. Shows he's a man with an eye to finer things. To my mind, it's a likely match."

"I don't want to marry anyone!" Glory cried. "I don't want to go away!"

"Ye won't be alone," Joseph continued, glancing at Tess, "for I'm sending your sister along. He's willing to take ye both."

Tess slid slowly down in the seat across from her stepfather.

"Jack Dobbs wants to marry Glory. And he's willing to take me in the bargain? Take me where?"

"Not take ye as wife, mind, we're not savages after all. He's willing to take ye on as companion to Glory, sisters together as ye should be. He sails for Wilmington in a week. There, Tess, ye can find a proper kind o' husband if ye wish or keep under his roof, high and dry, long as ye please and welcome." Joseph turned back to Glory who still stood stock-still before him, clenching her fists as if to hold onto something, anything that might offer comfort.

"You can't make me marry if I don't wish to," she said defiantly. "I'll not be made wife, just to please Jack Dobbs. I *won't* do it, no not for you, not for all the silver in the Carolinas!"

Joseph shook his head ruefully. "I told him you'd say such, lass. I warned him of your willfulness, but he won't be put off. He's coming round this evening to put his proposition to you properly—"

"Proposition!" Tess snorted. "That's a fine name for it, then! A fire sale, more like. Two for the price of one, he's getting."

"No, he's not!" Glory wailed. "I won't marry Jack Dobbs! I don't care if he's the richest man on the river!"

Joseph sighed and leaned back in his chair, his arms crossed over his chest. "Just hear him out, lass. Surely ye can do that much for me."

"Why do you want to get rid of us so quick?" Tess asked baldly, pinning him with her glare. "What has the man offered you that you want so badly?"

Her stepfather returned her glare, to her surprise. "Freedom, lass, and nothing else. I plan to wed myself, and soon as I can. The widow'll have me, and the boys are off to Bath for their education, soon as I can put them on a ship. I want to know you've both found a safe berth before I begin my own married life, and this is the best offer you'll get." He frowned defiantly. " 'Tis not for lack o' love, ye know. He's a good man, and he'll make ye a good provider. He's offered to take you, Tess, along with your sister, out of respect for ye both. He'll make a home for ye, till you find one o' your own. You'll be together, you'll be well taken care of, and—"

"I'm not even fifteen!" Glory wailed. "Tell him to go away and leave us be."

"I wish I could, lass," Joseph said softly, "but I got to think of my happiness just a little, too. I loved your mother, but she's gone.

The boys are old enough to go to school proper, and you're both old enough to be on your own. He's coming this evening, Glory. I want you to hear him out."

"Just like that," Tess replied softly. "No one asks what *I* may wish. 'Glory, hear his offer.' And I am to be included like an extra sweet in a baker's dozen."

Joseph turned to her. "Do you find him so distasteful, then?" His gaze was intent.

She did not flinch from it. "Not at all."

"Let him take Tessie, if he wants her, Papa! I don't want to marry!"

"He doesn't want Tessie," he said gently. "He wants you."

Tess turned to her sister with a bright, hard smile. "And he's only taking me to keep you happy."

"Well, I *won't* be happy!" Glory cried.

"Enough of all this caterwauling," Joseph said, standing abruptly. "You'd think I sold you to the savages, such fuss and bother. He's a good man, see if you can't find him so, both of you, when he comes round this evening. Think o' this," he urged, "if ye can find no other silver lining. He's a man of the sea, he'll be gone most of the season, and the two of you can run his house however you wish. You'll be rich, leisured lasses, wanting for nothing but the good sense to count your blessings." He turned to Tess. "And as for you, miss, you'll not have a finer offer, mark me. Do what you can to make your sister see the truth o' *that*, if ye will." He strode to the door and slammed it behind him.

Glory whirled from the chair, shrieking with frustrated rage, slapping at the table, the seats, the walls with her damp apron. "I'll run away! He can't make me do this! He's not my father! I'll kill Jack Dobbs in his sleep!" She spun finally in a dizzy stagger and fell into her chair again, her head on her arms, sobbing. "Mother wouldn't let him do this, Tessie," she moaned. "I want my mother. Don't let him!"

Tess drifted aimlessly about the table, numb to the core of her belly. She touched Glory lightly on the shoulder as she slid down beside her. She felt cold as a woman long dead. Jack Dobbs did not want her. Would never want her. Wanted her sister. As all men likely would, all of her life.

Glory did not want him.

And Joseph Innes did not want either of them.

She leaned her head on Glory's shoulder, and she listened to her sister's sobs begin to diminish. Perhaps, after all, that's what life was made up of, then. People wanting each other, not wanting each other, the tangle of yearnings and rejections that moved between them like the ebb and flood of unseen tides. If I had not opened the door to the pitiful Indians, if I had not caught the smallpox, would it have made a difference? Did all of fate distill then, at the end, to a smooth cheek and an enticing smile?

Tess stared down at Glory, who had turned her head toward her in misery. Even in the depths of despair, she could not be unlovely, Tess saw, and she could not hate her for it. By long habit, she reached over and took her sister into her arms.

"It might not be so awful," she said softly into Glory's cheek. "At least we'd be together. And Joseph's right, he'd be gone all the time. We'd have a fine house on the water, perhaps, and get out of this place forever."

"We'll never see Sam and Danny again," Glory mumbled mournfully.

"Nay, that's not true. In fact, we'll see them more than their own father will, for Bath's closer to Wilmington than Cross Creek. They have to go somewhere when school is out, and they'll likely come to us."

"I hate him." Glory pulled away slightly and wiped her cheeks. "He only cares about himself. I hope the widow gives him no pleasure and her cooking makes his belly ache."

Tess smiled ruefully. "Most people care only about themselves. It's hard, but true."

"It's not true about you, Tessie," Glory said, pulling back and gazing into her face. "You're good." She dropped her eyes. "I'm not."

"Well, being good hasn't gotten me very far, has it? It's you Captain Dobbs is coming to see, after all."

"Do you want him? You can have him, Tessie. I'll help you get him." Glory's face shone with a rare, unselfish love.

Tess looked away and rose to her feet. "Even if I did want him, I couldn't turn his face from you."

Glory thought about that for a moment. "Then we'll listen to his proposal. We likely don't have much choice, anyway." She sat up straighter, her spine stiffening with resolve. "Anyway, I won't love him. I never will."

Tess began to take out the necessaries for supper. After all, if the man was coming, he might as well be amply fed. She heard Glory's last words in her mind, but she knew the truth in her heart. Glory loved those who loved her, it was as simple as the sun rising each morning. The admiration in their eyes as they looked at her kindled a return affection in her. Sometimes Tess wondered if she could love others who did not love her first. Whether she needed to see her own reflection in their eyes before she could see them . . . but then she shook off the thought. It was a waste of needed strength to ponder such as that. Jack Dobbs would love Glory, she would return his admiration, and they would be content enough.

And she—she would no doubt be able to find contentment somewhere in all of that for herself as well, if she tried.

🌿 🌿 🌿

All in all, the coming and going of Jack Dobbs was almost unimportant, after the shock of Joseph's announcement. The man came, he spoke to Glory respectfully in the company of her stepfather, and then he took her briefly outside the cottage for a walk to the river. They were gone no more than a half hour, and when they returned, they were betrothed. He would come again to claim her in a fortnight, he said.

Before he left, he came to Tess and told her that she would be welcome under his roof all the days of her life. He smiled at her kindly, taking her hand as he might that of a maiden relation, as he told her that he hoped she would be content in the company of her sister. He said he felt himself a fortunate man and that surely the river had brought him to Cross Creek for a reason. She murmured small thanks and agreement, and then he was gone.

That night, Glory clung to Tess in her sleep as though she feared that something else would be taken from her if she relaxed her vigilance. When the morning came, the two women were calm and they spoke little of Jack Dobbs. He would come soon enough, they seemed wordlessly to agree; no sense in summoning him with their words before they must.

In a week, the flurry of preparing for the boys' departure distracted them and left the cottage in a constant state of upheaval with clothes being prepared, trunks being packed, and last-minute instructions by Tess as to their manners, dress, and attentions to their schoolmaster. Samuel and Daniel were to attend the master's school at Bath, and if they did well, would likely be sent to Charleston to the university there. They were too young for such a departure, Tess knew, and she pitied them once the excitement of leave-taking was gone. They would miss their father, their half sisters, and their childhood. But there was nothing she could do about that decision either, and so she set herself to preparing them as best she could.

The day the boys and their father sailed for Bath, Glory and the Widow Newcombe stood weeping and waving farewell at the docks. Tess waved, but she did not weep. She wondered that she did not, for she felt as though she were saying goodbye to her own children. The numbness that had possessed her for so long, that had lifted only when she first knew her feelings for Jack Dobbs, that had fallen again on her when she knew he would belong to Glory, was still in firm residence within her heart. She could not weep.

It was just as well, since Glory and the widow seemed stricken enough for three.

Another week passed, and Glory and Tess busied themselves getting their own possessions ready for transport to Wilmington. Joseph would return just in time to wave them farewell on Jack Dobbs's *Happy Delivery*. Since the widow had more plate and cutlery and linens than any two goodwives in Cross Creek, Tess was loath to leave much behind. "I'm taking this ladle, it's the best I've got," she said to Glory, passing it to be packed, "and these forks came from London, I'll not leave them behind."

"And no doubt," Glory said sourly, "they've got no forks in Wilmington."

Tess replied stoutly, "They were Mother's, and we're taking them."

Glory only shrugged and kept packing.

Later, they were hoeing in the garden, toward the end of the cabbage rows that were overrun with high grass and wild thistle. With all the commotion, Tess had neglected the garden and though she could not take it with her, she did not intend for the widow to be able to remark on its disorder.

Glory hated hoeing. She muttered as Tess put her to the row, but she bent to the task dutifully, wishing aloud that in Wilmington, they'd not have enough ground for more than a kitchen plot. As the two sisters worked the back rows, fifty feet down one end and back again, the sun came on strong and hot on their backs and they fell to rhythmic, silent hoeing, reaching down to grub out the most stubborn weeds by hand.

The only sound was a slight swishing from the firs behind the garden as the warm breeze blew in from the river. Tess's thoughts eddied in a jumble as her arms worked up and back, rooting out the weeds, and the usual contentment she felt at moving the soil did not come so readily. All of a sudden, Glory shrieked in horror, jumped up from where she'd been kneeling, and staggered backward, holding her hand.

"Snake! Snake!" she screamed, flailing at her skirts as though it were chasing her, had attached itself to her linens, holding her hand out stiffly to Tess in supplication. "It bit me!"

Tess dropped her hoe and ran to her sister, willing the panic down. She knew that whatever else, she must keep calm, must keep Glory calm, for if she let hysteria take her, she would swiftly be dead. She grabbed her sister and pulled her away from the clump of weeds where she'd been kneeling. "Glory, what was it! Let me see!"

But Glory shrieked as though her life was draining away before her eyes, holding her hand out in horror, gripping her wrist, crying, "It burns! It burns like fire!" Tess could see the fang marks, two equally spaced on the back of Glory's hand, already puffed and angry, frighteningly far apart.

Tess took a step back to the weeds, for she must know how dangerous the bite might be, and then she froze as a large diamond-back rattlesnake slid slowly out of the shadowed grasses, fat and lethargic and long as she was tall, without a glance at her, sliding slowly, slowly toward the woods at the end of the garden. So arrogant of its strength, it did not deign to rattle.

A diamondback. The only snake even the savages feared, the most deadly serpent on the river, and the largest she had seen in years. She whirled back to Glory and she could see that there was no time to scream for help, no time to think of what to do, no time to lance the bite and drain the venon, too much poison at any rate, no time, no time, Glory was down on the ground now, among the cabbage rows, her hand outstretched and swelling swiftly, mottled and evil-looking, her open, wailing mouth and fearful eyes hidden under her arm.

Tess took five steps to the woodblock, grabbed the ax, raised it over her head, and chopped off Glory's hand at the wrist before she knew what she was doing.

She hurled the ax across the rows, fell to her knees as Glory gasped and shrieked incoherently, ripping at her skirts to tie her sister's gushing wound. It was a clean cut, she saw that much, as she shouted at Glory to lie still, that she would save her, and she had the wrist tightly bound in seconds, so tight that the blood slowed to a fast seepage from a fountain almost instantly. Glory had fainted, her eyes rolled back white into her head, she saw now, and she thanked God for that. She pulled her sister's poor arm close to her, tightened the binding still more, held it against her breast and pressed so hard on the stump of the wrist and the vein at the elbow that she feared she might crack the fragile bones within, screaming as loud as she could for help.

Only when she saw people—Goodwife Russell, Master Campbell, more then behind them—only when she saw them running to help her did she allow herself to weep, and only as they quickly carried poor Glory away into the cottage did she let the panic take hold of her as, stumbling behind them, she stopped to fall on her knees and vomit into the earth, staggered back to her feet and struggled to follow, her head swirling with horror.

The wives bound Glory's hand, stitching it closed and burning it to close the nerves, ladling hot wax on the edges of the serrated flesh to keep it sealed. While Tess watched, numb and stricken, they worked over Glory like a small troop of bees, applying leeches to the red poison streaks up her arm, drawing out the oozing liquid that swelled her elbow and her armpit, keeping her arm packed in cold compresses, and dosing her with laudanum when she threatened to wake and flail about again.

For hours, Glory vomited and retched far past the time when she had anything left to expel, as her body tried to throw off the toxin. Only half conscious, she sweated so heavily that the blanket was soaked through and had to be replaced; her hand must be unclamped from its folds. Her limbs were rigid and hot, she trembled violently, but her mind seemed to have gone elsewhere into a half sleep, half death.

Finally, she seemed calmer and the wives left, saying that if she survived the night, she would likely live. Tess took over the changing of the compresses, and she was at last alone with her sister in the shadowed cottage, with only a low lamp for light. She could scarcely bear to look at the wrapped stump that was Glory's arm, neither could she stand to look at her face, so pale and twisted with pain. Tess sat close enough to her to see her, but far enough away so that she could see out of the small window that faced the river.

Exhausted and burdened with guilt, she stared out into the night. The goodwives told her she had likely done the right thing, that Glory would have died if she had not taken away the source of the poison. She might die yet, but at least she had a chance. With her hand attached to her body, with the full measure of poison the snake had delivered, she would have had no chance at all, they said.

Tess wanted to believe them. She wanted to know that she had done what had to be done, what anyone would have done, that Glory would forgive her if she lived. But each time she glanced at Glory's bandaged arm, she turned away in despair. What sort of life could her sister have with only one hand? What would she say when she awoke? What would Joseph say when he returned?

What would Jack Dobbs say?

She shoved that thought from her mind swiftly and firmly. He was not important now. All that mattered was that Glory lived. In that moment, a low moan came from the cot and Tess rose quickly to go to her. But Glory was still drugged from the laudanum. Thank God for that, for she might not have been able to stand the pain of her amputation. Tess looked closely at her arm. The red streaks seemed no worse than a few hours before. She settled wearily back into her chair before the window.

She must have slept for a few hours, but something woke her suddenly. It was very dark without and still, as if the entire planet dozed. The lamp still glowed in the corner, however, and Glory was quiet. Tess turned and looked out the window, somehow sensing that whatever woke her came from the outside, rather than from within.

A light was shining on the river, a glimmering, shadowed light, as though through waving leaves and branches the moonlight streamed and dappled itself. But she knew that from this window, there was no view of the river. In fact, there was no moon. Strangely, she was not surprised to see the river nor the light, and she kept gazing at it, half expecting to wake suddenly, as if from a dream.

A woman was washing linens at the river, bent over so that Tess could not see her face. Her hair fell down her back in a wispy stream, and she wore a gray cloak over a dark green dress. The dress was tattered and frail as the woman herself. As she washed, she sang a mournful melody, a haunting song of loss and sadness.

Tess was gripped by a sudden cold knowledge. The woman was not there; the river was not there, and no moon illuminated this scene but the one in her mind. It was the *bean-nighe*, the banshee that the old ones spoke of, who came when death waited round a house. In the Highlands, her appearance was common, but here in the New World, she came only rarely. As Tess stared, the old woman turned and gazed calmly at her, her lips moving in a doleful lament. Her eyes burned out of a pale complexion, and then with a sigh more like the wind than breath she vanished, leaving behind only cloud and darkness and the silence of night.

Tess reached inside her bodice and withdrew the locket she always wore round her neck, the locket Whypin had given her, the locket that held the talisman of her mother's hair. She gripped it tightly, closed her eyes, and vowed that what she had seen was not true. It is nothing but a Scots apparition, she told herself fervently, a superstition from the old Highland clans, and has nothing to do with me, nothing to do with Glory. We are not Scots! We are not believers! She looked back to the window. If the old woman had reappeared, she was ready to shout at her, "Go away! No one here knows you!" But the apparition did not return.

Tess rose, wavering slightly on her feet, and went to Glory's side, half expecting to find her as cold and pale as the *bean-nighe's* cheeks. To her vast relief, her sister was breathing. Faint and labored, struggling, yet she was alive. Tess sat down gently at her side and put one hand on her brow, holding her as if the pressure of her hand alone could keep her in this world. She fell asleep that way.

The next morning, it was clear that Glory would live. And in the mornings to follow, she was stronger and stronger, until she finally could weep and rage about the loss of her hand with enough vigor that everyone knew she was healing. She did not blame Tess, not once. Without being told, she accepted that Tess had saved her life.

Joseph returned from Bath, swooped Glory into his arms and

raged against fate, all serpents, and his own guilt at not being there when it happened. Tess waited for him to blame her for Glory's disfigurement, but he never said a word. She, therefore, said all the words she imagined he might have said, but silently, and only within the secret confines of her own heart.

Glory struggled to sit upright and accepted passively Tess's efforts to sew her sleeves into attractive shields for the ugly stump at her wrist. With added lace, her disfigurement was scarcely noticeable. But then the pain came over her, particularly at night, and Glory sobbed weakly in Tess's arms, as she thought of all she would never be able to do easily again. Together, they awaited the coming of Captain Dobbs.

Of course, he heard the news before he reached the cottage, yet when he came to the door, his face betrayed no emotion. Tess scanned it more earnesly than Glory did.

Glory already had a plan. To Captain Dobbs's slow bow, she offered a slight bow in return and led him to a chair. Without preamble, she asked, "You know what happened to me?"

"They told me at the docks. I am dreadfully sorry," he said.

Tess felt a slight chill at the formality in his voice. This was not the tone of a lover, she thought quickly, and then put it from her mind.

"I'm sure you'll agree that I cannot marry now," Glory went on calmly. With little fuss, she moved so that the lace covering of her mangled wrist no longer hid her stump. "I can be of little use to any man. I release you from your proposal."

He dropped his head, and Tess saw the fleeting grimace of pain about his mouth. "You are lucky to be alive," he said softly.

"So they say," Glory answered shortly. "But I daresay I don't spend much time counting my lucky stars these days. At any rate, I thank you for your concern, Captain. But I cannot marry you or anyone else." She lifted her destroyed wrist. "With this."

"But where will you and your sister go? As you know"—he hesitated, rather delicately, Tess thought, for a man of his stripe—"it will be . . . difficult."

He didn't say he loved her! Tess noticed swiftly. No word at all of persuasion, of argument, of the disappointment of his heart.

Glory smiled ruefully. She had evidently noticed, too. "I release you from your concern for us, Captain. We will manage, I'm sure. But I will not marry."

"But, I could surely—"

"I will not marry," she repeated steadfastedly.

A long moment of silence ensued, and Tess could see that the man was not to be dissuaded so easily. Without thinking much past her first words, she heard herself say, almost without her own volition, "Perhaps there is another way."

Both Glory and Jack Dobbs looked up at her in momentary confusion. Tess saw a dawning wariness in Glory's face, in the familiar set of her jaw, but she plunged on. "I could marry Captain Dobbs. Glory could accompany me, as it was planned that I would accompany her. In that way, sir, you would have a wife, Glory would have a home, and two sisters would have each other." She did not drop her head as every instinct prompted her to do. Instead, she stood behind Glory's seat, gazing down at both of them as calmly as she could manage. "After all," she added gently, "everything is all arranged. Would it be so very different if we simply changed places?"

Glory gaped at her, a half frown of anger forming on her brow. "Why, Tessie, we never spoke of this—"

"I know, but it makes perfect sense," she said smoothly. "I know I'm no beauty, Captain Dobbs, but I am a capable, honest woman who can make you a fine home. I bring you no infirmities save a plain face. Glory brings you a beautiful face, for whatever other incapacities she may suffer. Together, it seems to me that we offer more than most any one woman could by herself." She smiled, trying to keep her lips from trembling. "I realize that this is terribly forward of me, but the circumstances may, perhaps, excuse my directness. I daresay, we could make you happy."

Jack Dobbs returned her smile, half shocked, half amused. "Let me understand you, mistress. I am to wed you both?"

"Of course not," Glory snapped. "Don't be ridiculous, Tessie, this is impossible—"

"It's not at all impossible," Tess replied calmly. "It may be complicated, but only if we make it so. No, Captain, you may wed only one woman, of course, by the laws of God and man. But you may take to your hearth two women for the price of one, just as you intended to do in your original proposal. But now, because Glory won't wed, you may marry me, instead. And Glory will be my companion, if she will not be yours."

To her surprise, Jack Dobbs threw back his head in a short bark of laughter. "You amaze me, mistress." He gazed at Glory sadly, as if she were disappearing on a slow-moving ship. "And what do you say to this, my love?"

"I am not your love. I never was. If you loved me, the loss of a member would scarcely deter you. I don't love you, either, I guess that's no secret. You wanted me, for you liked the way I looked. I had as little to say about your proposal then as I have to say about Tessie's now." Glory wrapped her hand around her injured wrist, as though to comfort it. "It seems to me that pretty girls have even less say over their destiny than those who are not comely, no matter what folks say to the contrary. If you are pretty, someone is always trying to decide your fate for you."

Tess thought that Glory had rarely looked so unpretty as she did right then, her jaw was so set, her words so hard.

Jack Dobbs's eyes narrowed appraisingly. "Perhaps you are right, lass." He stood up suddenly, clasping his hands behind his back and pacing to the window.

Tess was struck instantly with how well he moved, how much in command of his body he was, even at this moment of bewilderment. She was suddenly aware that she had been holding her breath.

"Why should I strike such a bargain in the first place?" he murmured, half to himself, half aloud. "I needn't marry at all, after all. I've gone this many years without a wife, and now of a sudden, I am to take on two?"

"Not two," Tess said gently. "One wife, one sister. And I doubt you will find any one woman who will devote herself to you with such steadfastness as we shall." She drew up all her courage and went to him where he stood by the window. She touched his shoulder lightly. "You will be the happiest of men, Captain Dobbs, this I vow. You'll not find a more lovely woman than Glory, and you'll not find a more loving woman than I."

He looked down at her hand on his arm for a long moment, but he did not draw away. Finally he asked, "And you agree to this as well, Glory?"

She nodded slowly. "Tess is likely right," she said. "She always is."

He took a deep breath. In another man, Tess thought, it might be considered a sigh of resignation, but in Jack Dobbs, it was a breath of decision. "All right, then. I accept your proposal. We shall speak nothing of this to others, and I shall tell your stepfather myself. Agreed?"

The two women nodded.

"Make yourselves ready then. We'll sail as soon as my ship is loaded."

🌿 🌿 🌿

On the upper Cape Fear, even after man invaded the forests, grizzlies were common in the spring months. The large bears moved down from the Appalachians as the season warmed to fish the river for char and salmon that were then plentiful in the rivers of the Carolinas. In a small valley of lakes surrounded by low mountains that would one day be named the Bladen Lakes State Forest, a female grizzly emerged from her nesting den with her two one-year-old cubs in tow.

She was a medium-size bear for her species, yellowish-brown in color with white-tipped hairs on her back. The marked hump on her shoulders, as well as her larger size, distinguished her from the many brown and black bears in the woods. The claws on her five-toed paws were more than four inches long, and she weighed just under six hundred pounds.

Behind her romped a male cub and his sister, two who were born the year before in the winter den of the higher mountains and now faced their second spring with their mother. Like their mother, they were light brown in color, but they lacked her hump and her silver-tipped appearance. Unlike their mother, they were in the mood for play, for they had only been out of the winter den for a week and had been slowly traveling south, enjoying the warmth of the season.

The sow was disagreeable when they first emerged into the valley, and only after several hours of feeding among the spring grasses and early strawberries would she allow them to come as close to her as they liked. Her behavior was markedly different from their first spring, when she kept them near at all times, fondled and nuzzled them, and allowed them to nurse whenever they wished. Now, she was restless and irritable, yet they still followed her wherever she went and whimpered when she turned and snapped her jaws at them in annoyance.

As the weather warmed, she also seemed to warm to them, and the two cubs moved closer to her, gratefully. Once she even let them try to nurse, but when she felt their larger teeth and claws, she pushed them away abruptly, snarling softly at them. There had been little milk anyway, but they were bewildered at her rejection. The cubs ate in a trail behind her, mouthing and trying to chew whatever she ate, though she made no particular effort to guide them to the most choice foods.

For days, the family of three wandered along the river, in a seemingly aimless fashion. Twice, the sow scented another bear close by, and she called them to her for safety, but then just as quickly seemed to forget their presence and ambled along, letting them tag after her if they could. In the higher meadows, they found fields of barley; on the shores of the river, they found clumps of beach rye. As May moved slowly into June, the berries became more plentiful, and the wild grapes ripened in sporadic patches.

Once, the mother bear found a nest of ground squirrels who had foolishly made their den in the open ground. She swiftly dug it out, and and three large squirrels erupted out of the ground like a geyser of hot, sputtering water. The two cubs pranced about, trying to slap the squirrels down, but they soon had to sit quietly on their haunches, whining hungrily, while their mother dispatched and swallowed a squirrel without sharing a part of it with them.

Another time, the sow came across a partially buried owl carcass, probably hidden by a fox. She chased the cubs off with surprising anger, devouring the rank meat all by herself. They soon learned to keep away from her kill.

As July came and went, the cubs grew more and more confused. They still followed her, but always at careful distances. Her temper was shorter and shorter, and her sudden whirlings of snarl and tooth were not simply reprimands but carried a real threat.

One day, their mother wandered into a low valley and caught the scent of a nearby male grizzly. Her reaction shocked the cubs. Instead of calling them closer or sending them up the nearest tree, she turned on them violently and drove them away from her. They retreated to a faraway pile of dead brush on the side of a hill, hungry and frightened. They whined pitifully, calling to her, but the sow did not answer. The next day, the female cub urged her brother out of cover, and they hunted their mother, finally finding her trail. But when they approached her, she drove them off again even more angrily, even catching the female and giving her flank a bad bite. Again, the two cubs hid in the underbrush, hungry and miserable and whining to each other.

In the first part of August, they found her again, and once more the two cubs tried to approach her to follow. This time, she let them come a little closer, and they fed together on some bearberries near a small set of rapids. Salmon were beginning to come up the Cape Fear, and in a shallow pool, the cubs tried valiantly to catch one each. They slapped at the water and growled menacingly at the fish, but to no avail.

Their mother waded deeply into the swift river up to her shoulders and came out with a large salmon in her jaws, for the waters were alive with fish. The char or trout were coming from two directions to mix with the migrating salmon. From the bays, the trout came, following the salmon to feed on their roe, and from the streams, the two-year-old trout were migrating downstream to salt water. In between were the bears.

But the cubs could make little use of this plenty. Their mother ate her fill of the large fish she'd caught and left a quarter of it behind on the bank, where the cubs fought off the gulls for the remains. While they fed, a large male grizzly came up out of the brush to fish, snarling at the two cubs. They scuttered away in fear, panic-stricken, and in their haste, they lost her once more.

It was several days before they caught up with her again. This time, she was in the company of another male, and she drove them away with such savagery that they never followed her trail again. They were miserable and hungry for weeks, sometimes laying up under brush for days at a time as if waiting for her to return.

Finally, their hunger drove them from cover, and they began to try to hunt squirrels, to fish, and to forage for the grasses and berries they had seen her eat. Their time had come. They now would survive on what they had learned during their short infancy, or they would not. There would never be another teacher in their lives, nor would there ever again be another creature whom they would trust to care for them and ease their hunger, their fear, or their pain.

For a while, they would depend on each other. Soon, even that tie would loosen, and by the end of the summer, they would drift apart to meet whatever fate they might find.

On a morning in May 1725, the story-and-a-half house on Bay Street in Wilmington was in a welter of confusion, which was unusual, for Mistress Tess Dobbs and her sister, Glory, kept this house in a state of order the nuns at Bath might envy. But the reason for the chaos was forgiven, for Captain Dobbs was sailing for England.

Glory leaned out the casement window of her upstairs bedroom for the third time in a quarter hour to see if Captain's horse had been brought round yet. Now that Tess was so near her confinement, she could scarcely move swiftly anywhere at all, much less up the narrow stairs to see to that lazy groom.

Glory yanked her head back in the window with exasperation, answering Tess's call. "No, not yet!" she shouted, keeping her voice as pleasant as possible. Captain hated to hear what he called "fishwife squalls" in his house, so Glory saved them for when he was at sea. Fortunately, that was often enough. She privately wondered how her sister, a loving and warm woman who was quick to laugh and hug, could tolerate her spouse absent more days in the year than he was at home. Captain Dobbs sailed at least four times a year between Wilmington and London, Wilmington and the Caribbean, Wilmington and New York or Boston—and each sailing lasted two months. It didn't require much schooling to do the figures. The man slept away from his own bed more than he slept in it.

That hadn't, however, kept him from getting Tess with child quick enough, Glory winced ruefully. Thrice pregnant in five years, she'd lost all the babes early on in her confinements. Not a thing to show for five years of wedded bliss! But finally, this one had taken hold and stuck fast, and Tess was now far past the most dangerous stage of her pregnancy.

Glory almost dreaded the child's coming, for she knew how much their lives would change then. No more carefree outings to the market or the inn, no more leisurely carriage rides to farflung neighbors for afternoons of lazy gossip, and likely fewer trips down to Charleston to see Sam and Danny and take in the heady spring season. The coming child would change Tess far more surely than her marriage had, that was certain. She would be mother first and sister second. No, even that wasn't right. Tess would be mother first, wife second, and sister third. With each enrichment of her sister's life, Glory noticed, her own importance diminished. Like a star rotating farther and farther from the sun, she was growing a little colder and dimmer each year. Meanwhile, radiant with health and joy, Tess already had turned inward, away from Glory and toward the coming babe.

Glory sighed in heightened annoyance and leaned further out the window to shriek louder to that worthless slave. The smell of the sea wafted to her on a warm breeze, and she hesitated just long enough to hear, at last and finally, the sound of hooves moving rapidly down the street and here came that black scamp of a groom, yanking at General like it was the stallion's fault he was late. "He's coming!" hollered Glory, louder this time, not caring that Jack Dobbs might frown at her when she hurried down the stairs.

Tess stood at the door, the warm May sun shining in on her hair from the mullioned window, as Captain bent to give her his farewell embrace, already in his cutaway coat and short wig for travel. Glory realized with a dim pang that she had never seen the man kiss her sister. She, herself, would never have missed it, but she guessed that Tess must. And yet, there she stood, hugely pregnant with her captain's first child at last, beaming her contentment.

"Write to me from London," Tess was saying to Jack, one arm around his waist and the other reaching up toward his neck.

"I always do," he said cheerfully, half lifting her off the planked floor, despite her bulk. "And I hope to have excellent news, lass, on that new contract from Palmer-Marsh soon enough. That last shipment pleased them, one hundred barrels of tar, ninety of turpentine, ten of pitch—I hope to add to it this trip, and sixty sides of leather besides. Between Wilmington and Brunswick, we've got the English market fed and fat."

"That's wonderful, Jack. Perhaps we can add that wing soon and move the servants out from underfoot."

"Ay, soon enough. Glory," he said, looking up at her as she came down the staircase, "look after this baggage and the one she's carrying, too." He grinned at her and in that instant, she remembered the first time she saw him.

"I always do," she answered him cordially, saving her warmest smile for her sister.

They stood at the door and waved him off as he pranced away

on the roan stallion, Tess flagging her canary-yellow handkerchief at him gaily, the one he brought her last from Spain. Glory raised one hand, her good left one, and let the long lace she wore over her cuffs fall back just enough so that he could barely see the tips of her fingers in farewell. Then she turned and gently pulled Tess inside, closing the door behind them.

"It'll be a long two months." Tess sighed.

"Nonsense." Glory patted her, urging her away. "I wouldn't waste time brooding after him if I were you, that babe'll be here in a month and then you'll be so busy, the time'll fly. You'll look up when he walks in and say, 'Why, man, are you back so soon?' "

Tess glanced at her younger sister fondly. She knew well enough what she was trying to do, take her mind off him, was all. And it was on the tip of her tongue to say, 'Glory, you don't know—' but she did not. Of course, she could not understand. As virgin as the day she was born, Glory could not possibly comprehend the deep rapture and private mystery of sharing a bed with the likes of Jack Dobbs. Likely she never would. Tess wasn't about to make her feel the lack by reminding her. "You're probably right," she only said, lifting her voice to a note of determined cheer for Glory's sake. "It'll fly by."

They went about their chores then, each calling one to the other as they moved through the house, as much in rhythm as two carriage horses long in the same harness. It was a middle-size house, set back from the docks far enough to be genteel and close enough so that the tang of the salt air off the Cape made biscuits damp within two hours if they were left uncovered.

Made of solid English brick brought over in the captain's own vessels, it had four rooms downstairs and four rooms upstairs, six with fireplaces. Two privies, a laundry shed, the back kitchen, and Captain's office made up the five outbuildings, and farther from the main house clustered together the barn, the stable, the poultry yard for Glory's prize guineas, and the smokehouse. Optimistically, Captain had put in quarters for the servants back by the stable, but the only slaves they had at present were the groom, the stable boy, the cook, and the laundress, and two of those lived in the main house proper, in a small room behind the dining room.

The furnishings of Jack Dobbs's house proclaimed him master of the *Happy Delivery* and exotic ports, besides, if not possessed of the most discerning eye. Ornately carved chairs perched beside the most common sofa; wide inventories of pewter, mirrors, telescopes, globes, and a great variety of draperies and rugs crowded the room but there were few books on the tall bookshelves. Tess well remembered when she first came to his house she was struck by the ugliest coffee service that squatted next to an exquisite leaded crystal punch bowl. The very next morning, she separated the two, lest one be condemned by the other.

Like most Carolina captains, Jack Dobbs was making money too fast to keep track of his money much less what he bought with it. Wilmington had most recently been the little village of Newton, a sleepy hamlet across the Cape Fear from Brunswick Town. Now, Wilmington and Brunswick Town together made up Brunswick port, the busiest trade center in the colony. Only Charleston shipped more tonnage, and that in rice. But for naval stores of tar, pitch, turpentine, and tallow, London looked to Wilmington, and Wilmington looked to captains like Jack Dobbs, who could never turn down a chance at a profit, no matter where it might lead his ships.

But for all its hodgepodge and bustle, Captain's house was a comfortable one, and the strong wind that blew in regularly from the Cape scarcely caused the draperies to ripple when the shutters were closed. Best of all, those Tess loved most were near. She gazed fondly at the room as she moved through it, rearranging with her eye and tidying with a free hand. The house was hers now, truly, after five years of marriage. She had claimed every corner as her own. One vow she'd not forgotten, made at her mother's graveside, that she would live where she liked, and her man could come and go as he pleased or needed—this vow she had kept. Jack Dobbs came and went like the wind. We are the roots, Glory and me together, she thought peacefully, which keep this house planted firmly in Carolina soil.

She was to recall that moment of peace a few weeks later as she hurried to the kitchen to set the day's meals in motion. She had one arm curved protectively about her belly, an unconscious gesture of defense, a habit now after so many blighted pregnancies with nothing to show for her pains but an empty heart. The West Indian cook, Bonanza, stood at the oven stirring Glory's stockings in a kettle of black dye. Since Jack had brought back those lady's fashion books from London, nothing would do but Glory dress as those at Whitehall did, even if it meant turning all of her white stockings dark as Bonanza's arm.

"Bonny, when you've finished there, you must go to market and fetch what we'll be needing this week, remember the stalls'll be closed on Thursday for the holiday—"

Bonanza turned with a fierce scowl. "How come Miz Glory don' make Giffy do such as dis? She be de washer; I be de cook! Look like she forget who is who, an' I cain' be doin' more'n I be doin' already, I only got dese two hands."

Tess smiled winningly at Bonanza. Glory never did seem to understand the intricacies of dealing with the cook and the laundress, or for that matter, the groom and the stable boy. Each had his or her own domain, and woe to the housewife who forgot the slave's innate and highly developed sense of hierarchy. Glory had no patience with their pouts and small rebellions.

"I'm sure you're doing a better job than any three laundresses could do with those," Tess soothed the glowering slave. "And besides, you know you can't abide Giffy underfoot in your kitchen—"

Glory would have said, "Oh for pity's sakes, if you want to pout, go on the roof with the pigeons, Bonny!"

"That be de truff," Bonanza huffed, slightly mollified. "That no-count Giffy cain' boil water, so I guess if somethin' got to be cooked, even if that somethin' be Miz Glory's stockins, I be de one got to do it." And she heaved a huge and weary sigh as Tess gave her a consoling pat on the shoulder.

That pat, Tess knew, would last Bonanza halfway to supper, no matter how many indignities she had to endure between now and then. Sometimes she wondered if slaves were more trouble than they were worth. Still, she could scarcely do without them since every decent household in Wilmington had their "folks" to do for them. Tess could remember her mother's preferences and like her, she could not abide the redemptioners, Christian servants who worked halfheartedly for five years and then left the household in disarray. Bonny was a trial at times, but she was loyal, at least, and predictable. A fleeting memory of Whypin drifted into Tess's mind, and she absently fingered the locket she wore around her neck, under her bodice. Where had she gone? Not an Indian remained within miles of the river, Tess knew. Many were dead of disease, many more driven away to the mountains. Perhaps Whypin was an old woman, passing her last days in peace. Perhaps she had been dead and buried for years.

The acrid smell of the cooking dye suddenly made Tess's stomach queasy and she turned away from the stove and the distant memory. Reaching up to the open shelves of the crockery hutch, she began to pull down the heavy plates and cups to stack them on the kitchen work table, when she felt a stitch in her side, almost as though she had pulled a rib out of place for an instant. She gasped and dropped her hands to her waist, holding very still.

Bonanza turned a sharp eye. "You feelin' poorly, Miz Tess?" she asked instantly, her gaze running over her mistress's rounded skirts.

Tess waited a moment for her breath to return. She shook her head then, smiling weakly. "I guess I just pulled something. But it's gone now." She drew a kitchen stool over to the hutch so that she did not have to stretch her arms high over her head to reach the crockery. She felt Bonanza's eyes on her back, but she went on blithely. "Now when you get the fish today, Bonny, make that monger sink those clams in water before you take them. I'll not be paying for dead clams again, nearly a quarter of those you got last week were long gone. If they float, I don't want them, hear?"

"Yes'm," Bonanza said. She added casually, "Miz Glory be havin' company again tonight?"

Tess glanced over her shoulder at the cook, now studiously stirring the black dye as though she expected to see some portent within its depths. She knew the slaves gossiped with cheerful malice and no charity about Glory and her frequent gentleman callers, and a fierce protectiveness rose in her as she said firmly, "Whether Miss Glory has guests in to supper tonight or not is neither your concern nor any extra bother to this house, Bonanza. We shall be ready for any friends to call, as we always are, and grateful that they enjoy sharing our table. Captain wants it that way and so do I."

"Yes'm." Bonanza dropped her head sheepishly. "I get the most freshest clams, don' you worry."

Tess turned back to her work with a frown. Glory and her men friends were a certain embarrassment, it was true, but she would never let the servants see that. Poor Glory wanted attention, was all, and men were quick enough to give her plenty. Some nights, five or six gentlemen callers crowded the boards, and she bantered gaily with all of them equally. But for some reason, few of them became regular callers, and no one so far had asked for her hand. Tess's frown deepened. For that, of course, she would always feel guilt. Glory would have been married long ago, with a house and family of her own, were it not for her—her disfigurement. They never used the word between them but there it was.

For all her beauty, Glory seemed to draw and then repulse men and Tess could think only that her poor, crippled stump was the reason. As much as she wanted Glory to stay always, she knew her desire was selfish. Bad enough that I ruined her chances, the least I can do is provide her what small happiness I can, Tess thought. "And get out another bottle of Captain's good Rhenish," she added to Bonny. "I want the table especially nice tonight."

Glory burst through the kitchen doors then with her usual careless stride, almost knocking Tess off her perch. "Why, what in the world do you think you're doing?" she demanded of her sister.

"I'm moving this crockery out so that we can clean the back of this hutch," Tess said patiently. "I know it's not been dusted out for three seasons at least—"

"Let Bonny do that, you want to lose another one? Climbing up on that rickety stool, what if you fell right down—" Glory stopped suddenly when she saw a peculiar look pass swiftly over Tess's face. "What, did you hurt yourself? I told you!"

Tess shook her head, easing down off the stool with slow, wary steps. "I just felt a pain. I felt it before."

"What sort of pain?" Glory demanded.

"Could be, de babe comin'," Bonanza said quietly.

"Nonsense," Glory snapped at her. "It's a month too soon. She's just overdone, like I said. You go up right now, Tess, and get in your bed and stay there. Moving crockery in your condition, well I suppose you're satisfied now, you'll likely have to be off your feet most of the day—"

"Bonny, take that kettle off the fire," Tess said faintly.

"Dis not near set yet, Miz Tess—" the slave began to protest.

"—and go get Doctor Massie right away."

"Oh Lord, oh Lord!" Glory cried, gathering her sister in her arms. "Is it the baby, Tessie? Bonanza, run quick! Bother those stockings, just shove the kettle over and put on some fresh water to boil in case we need it fast." She gently enfolded Tess close to her and ushered her out the kitchen and toward the stairs. "Tessie, does it hurt awfully? Does it feel like the baby's trying to come?"

Tess nodded again, her face whiter this time. "Feels like a stitch in my side, like I've been running too hard." She laughed ruefully. Painfully. "I can't remember the last time I was able to run like a girl."

"You will again, Tessie, soon enough, that baby'll keep you running upstairs and down. Now lean on me and we'll get you to bed safe and sure—" she murmured and pulled and half carried her sister up the stairs, somehow holding her firmly even with only one hand, crooning to her low words of comfort and love. On the way out the door, Bonanza glanced up at the two women ascending the stairs, the one tall and red-haired and slim, the other short and dark and hugely bloated and she thought that even with those differences and from the back, no one would ever mistake the two for anything but sisters.

By the time Dr. Massie came up to Captain Dobbs's spacious bedroom on the second floor, Tess was in the throes of a cruel and relentless struggle. No amount of comforting words now from Glory could stave off the pain; no number of cool cloths at her brow and warm bricks at her back could stop her writhings. Bonanza had been sent up and down the stairs a dozen times for water, herbal tonics, cold compresses and hot rags, but Tess's labor was swiftly past the point where any kitchen remedies could help her much.

Now Dr. Massie, Wilmington's oldest and most respected surgeon, bent low over Tess's contorted form, while Glory hovered at her other side. "The baby is in some distress, Mistress Dobbs," the doctor was saying softly. "Though it's early, I believe we should take the child if we can do so. It might do better outside your body than in."

Tess began to weep quietly, the first real tears she had shed. Glory felt a bright flare of hatred for the doctor that he would say such a thing to her sister.

"What is going wrong?" Tess asked miserably between her groans. "Why is this happening to me? I promised him children at least if I couldn't give him much else. Why can't I carry a child to life?"

"I can't answer that for sure," the doctor said glumly. "Could be just bad luck—"

"Four bad lucks?" Glory asked then. "She's as healthy as a

summer sow, there must be some *reason*, even if you don't know what it is."

He shrugged politely. "Perhaps when the child is born we'll know more." He turned back to Tess. "Mistress, I can give you something for the pain, but it might make it harder on the child. Or I can simply take the child as quick as I can and have it done. With some luck"—he glanced at Glory and then away again—"you'll both come through it fine enough."

"Nothing," Tess panted through the contractions. Clearly, this child would come with or without her will. "Do nothing that will hurt this baby!"

Glory turned away, her face contorted in sympathy.

"You must understand," the doctor persisted, "that birth itself will hurt the baby, it always does. I will do my best, but I cannot promise you the child will survive."

Tess said nothing, only turned away and moaned as the pain convulsed her again. Glory wanted to reach out and shake the man, shouting, "You fool, give her hope, at least! Give her something to fight for!" but she knew that Tess needed her calm and strong now, so she held her tongue and moved closer to the doctor's side to aid him in what he must do.

The next two hours were the most gruesome either sister had ever experienced. Unfortunately, Tess was as strong as she looked, and she could not escape into unconsciousness, no matter how the pain racked her body. When her water finally broke, blood followed, and the doctor had to move quickly then to deliver the child without pausing for Tess to recover from one contraction before the next one began. In one long blur of agony, she finally gave up a boy child to his hands, hands that had reached so far inside her belly that Glory was certain he must have jarred her heart.

White with shock, Tess lay in a half stupor when Dr. Massie finally finished with her and turned his attention to the baby. Glory did not care at that moment whether the boy lived or died, but hovered over Tess like an avenging angel, trying to call her back to life. Warm cloths at her breast and belly, cold cloths at her brow, dry cloths packed between her legs to staunch the bleeding, Glory's hand moved over Tess continually in a sort of frantic prayer, all the while calling her name and exhorting her to take every breath.

"The child is healthy enough," the doctor said from the corner of the room where he tended it. "Considering what he's been through, he looks like he'll make it fine. I thought for a moment, I lost him sure, and then he shifted himself—"

"Come and tend to my sister, then," Glory interrupted him abruptly. "Can't you give her something for the pain now?"

He straightened and gazed at Glory as though from a great distance. "I should think the best medicine I could give her is the news that her son is born and will live."

Glory sensed the censure in his tone and it inflamed her. Why did every man think that a woman would be proud to die giving birth to a son? "She'll have to be able to hear the news before it'll heal her, I believe," she snapped. "Doctor, she's slipping away from us!"

Dr. Massie moved quickly to Tess's side, almost with a grimace of distaste. "Sleep is the best thing for her now, madame. Perhaps if you leave her to me, she'll find that comfort soon enough."

Glory moved to the end of the bed but no farther. "Give her something for the pain," she insisted again.

Ignoring Glory, Dr. Massie bent over Tess and called to her. "Mistress Dobbs, you have been delivered of a healthy boy, and he looks strong enough to live. You did a fine job. I could find no reason why your other babies did not survive, nor can I find any reason why your next babies will not do well. Perhaps you were simply not ready for birth, and now you are. At any rate, you are healthy, as is your son."

Tess opened her eyes and smiled wanly up at him. She moved her head slightly and sought Glory, found her, and then sighed with a great weariness. Sliding into sleep as though she knew she could now, with Glory near, she finally relaxed her white-knuckled grip on the bed linens.

Glory eased gently into the seat by the bed and began to breathe freely once more. Tess was going to live after all.

"Have you a wet nurse for the child?" the doctor asked her as he prepared to take his leave. "I doubt she'll be strong enough to nurse him properly."

"She'll be strong enough," Glory said softly. "We'll manage together."

He shrugged and went toward the door.

"Thank you, Doctor," Glory said, not rising or opening her eyes. "Thank you for my sister."

They named the boy John, after his father. Tess made the decision, though Glory argued to name him James, after their own father. "I think Jack would like to have his son named for him," Tess said to Glory. "Men make much of that sort of thing."

"All the more reason to break them of it," Glory grumped, holding the boy. "They have enough foolish ideas without being coddled in them." But she bent and nuzzled the child she held in her arms. "Well, it won't hurt him, I guess. I shall call him John, however."

"I knew you would," Tess smiled wryly. How could she protest? Her sister obviously loved the babe to distraction. She had nursed Tess with an herbal tisane and poulticed her breasts with the same mixture, and they flowed copiously as a milch cow. Thus, they could take turns feeding the child, Glory with a rag teat wrapped on a bottle and Tess offering her breasts. The baby took both eagerly and settled in her arms as easily as in his mother's. Glory tweaked his small, perfect cheek. "Papa would have been so proud."

Tess gazed lovingly at her son in her sister's arms. "So long ago it seems, doesn't it, Glory, that he died?"

"I can scarcely remember Papa now."

"I can. But I can't remember who *I* was, then."

Glory laughed low in her throat. "Oh, I remember well enough who I was, and you, too."

"Good." Tess smiled. "You be the keeper of the memories for us both, then. You protect the past, and I'll provide our future."

Glory dropped her head over the child so that Tess would not see how much that last remark, however innocent, had wounded her. It was true. She had only such future as Tess might choose to share. In that moment, the baby boy in her arms smiled up at her as though in conspiracy. He is almost as much mine as hers, she thought, or could be. The ache in her heart lessened then as she returned the baby's smile and cuddled him closer.

In the next five years, Tess gave birth as regularly as the captain's arrivals and departures, until the house on Bay Street was alive with the laughter and bustling chaos of three children. Nursemaid after nursemaid came and went, providing extra pairs of hands, but always the constant figure in and out of the nursery was Glory—after Tess, of course.

As a team, the two sisters managed the Dobbs household so efficiently that life within its four walls seemed to flow as effortlessly and regularly as the Cape Fear tides.

Life beyond its walls, however, was less easy to subdue. A relentless flow of immigrants was swelling the city: the Welsh, more Highland Scots, and some German newcomers were settling in Wilmington, and a goodly number of those must be made welcome at Captain Dobbs's table whether or not he was in port, for it was from such society that shipping contracts were often consummated.

As Scotch–Irish and more Germans began to move down from Pennsylvania and overland from Maryland and Virginia, they traveled the Great Wagon Road, what they called "the Bad Road," and arrived in need of bed and board for a night or two. Quakers, Moravians, Lutherans, Presbyterians, few homes that could house them would turn them away, and so spare rooms at the Dobbs house were usually full.

Guests relished invitations to dine, for Dobbs's table was known for offering some of the finest meals in the county. Tess would have nothing less, and Bonanza knew better than to bring back anything from Wilmington markets that would not meet her exacting standards. Clarets, Fayals, Madeiras, and Rhenish wines flowed generously; tea, coffee, and chocolate—all imported and dear—accompanied every meal.

Guests who were fortunate enough to spend the night under Dobbs's roof knew the softest Holland sheets, brass warming pans, the cleanest chamberpots, and the sweetest potpourri strewn on their pillows, for Glory ran the upstairs with equally high demands, and every dressing maid and servant was made to feel personally responsible to meet them.

When Captain came home from the sea, he found his wife, his children, and his sister-in-law lined at the door to meet him, a picture of familial harmony and pride. He did not wish to hear what was necessary to provide such a greeting, nor would Tess have

ever told him. In her heart, she sometimes felt that the real marriage
that held together the household was that between herself and
Glory—but then she swept such thoughts from her head as disloyal. When she retired behind her bedroom door with her husband, after so many months apart, the bond she felt with him was
strong enough to persuade her that this—this set of arms, this
smiling male face—this was the reality.

But when he left again, the day-to-day partnership she shared
with her sister was the strongest bond that lasted. And then Jack
Dobbs seemed only a pleasant memory, an enjoyable fantasy to
wile away whatever small leisure hours she might find, in between
the rich realities of life with Glory and the children.

There had been a time in their marriage, brief but electric, when
she could have willingly, cheerfully, almost drowned in him. It was
before the babies came, a time when he was as essential to her as
food in her belly and air in her lungs. She could recall that time
vividly, even these ten years past. Once, she remembered, they had
gone for a walk down by the river as it skirled away from the edges
of the town and moved inland, becoming more turbulent with
every turn away from the sea.

It was hot that day, and the air seemed as full of moisture as the
river at their feet. First, she drew off her bonnet and let it hang
down her back, then slipped off her shoes and tied them around
her, and then unbuttoned her bodice down to her waist until only
her light underlinen stood between her and the soft, warm breeze.
They ambled up and over the banks of the Cape Fear, talking softly
of this and that, round rocks and small beach inlets until they had
gone more than a mile from town. Jack took her hand often,
helping her up small embankments, pushing aside brush and tall
ferns that she might follow him easily, and the touch of his hand
was as welcome to her as the cool of the water on her bare feet.

They came to a shaded pool ringed by tall hemlocks and huge
sycamores, where the water was deep and quiet and dark in its
depths. Jack picked a flat rock and beckoned her to sit beside him.
"A glorious day," he murmured, "and a perfect spot."

She smiled and took her shoes from round her waist, dropping
her bonnet beside them.

"And a glorious woman beside me." He grinned at her.
"Who'd have thought that little Tessie would grow to be such a
handsome wench?"

She glanced at him sharply, blushing and ducking her head. He teased her so often, she could not say when he was petting her in earnest—she knew well enough she was not handsome, but there was no mocking in his voice. He spoke to her as though she were a sprightly tavern maid! "You've been too long at sea," she said, half taunting, half hoping, "you wouldn't know handsome unless it wore a tail and fins."

He draped a casual arm about her shoulders. "Nay, wife, there's some who are born handsome and others who come to that state of grace over time. You're one of the lucky lasses who only improve with age." He bent and kissed her softly, lingeringly. "And I, the lucky man who's got you."

She pulled away from his embrace then, teasing him with her smile. "And who's to say you've got me all that fast, Jack Dobbs?"

He slid her bodice down from her shoulders so that the tops of her breasts were bare in the dappled sun. "I do," he said, his voice growing rougher round the edges. "I say I've got you fast as a fish on a hook." Caressing her all the while, he drew her bodice down completely, pulled down her linen, and pushed her light skirts up to her waist. She was now mostly bare before him, shaded only by the close trees and the looming rocks behind them.

"This fish can swim!" She laughed, and slid off the rock easily, down into the deep pool below, kicking loose of her skirts even as she hit the water. Her hair came down around her shoulders and, nearly naked to the cool water, she paddled to the underhang of the rock and clung to a boulder. Above her, she could hear him as he, half laughing, half cursing, threw off his clothes and dove in the water after her. He found her swiftly, covered her mouth with his, and drew her close, murmuring in her neck, "You still surprise me, lass, after all these years."

She savored that memory every time he left. It was easy, she had learned, to keep that fire alive in them both, probably in no small part because he was home so little to taste of it. Over the years, of course, it was different, particularly now that the children clamored for her day and night. But still, she remembered. And she knew he remembered as well. The memory alone often conjured up enough heat to make them forget the present and disappear into one another as completely as river water joined the sea.

❧ ❧ ❧

Tess was pregnant again that September of 1738, in fact, when the third yellow fever epidemic in a decade swept Wilmington like a strong wind from the sea. She was not overly afraid, for in the past, the defenses Glory and she had erected had stood well between her family and the plague. No visitors allowed, and none of the children were permitted beyond the confines of their own fenced yard. All windows shut tight, no matter how hot the day, and all curtains drawn to keep the house as cool as possible. Each child and adult under Glory's care must take her malefic special tonic that she brewed herself in Bonny's black kettle, a sour mash of fresh herbs, roots, and fish oil, to be washed down with at least six glasses of fresh water every day.

Severn, Tess's daughter, complained mightily that she'd rather have the fever than endure her Aunt Glory's vile brew, but Tess brooked no rebellion, and Severn choked down the tonic along with her two brothers under Tess's watchful eye.

And so, the yellow fever had, so far, sailed past Captain Dobbs's house time and time again, though more than half of the nearby homes were struck and struck hard. Fewer than a third who contracted the disease survived, and death from the fever was fearsome. It was not called "the black vomit" for nothing.

On one particularly stifling day at the end of that September, Tess's two boys, John and Noah, did not come in when Bonanza called the first time from their play out in the yard. The shadows were falling fast behind the house, and Bonny called once, then forgot them for a time. When she realized that they hadn't come in as ordered, she swept outside in a flurry of angry shouts to shoo them indoors before the pestilent night breezes could infect their lungs.

"What you thinkin' of, young massers, I call you an' call you!" she scolded.

"You didn't." John scowled. "I never heard you."

"Me, neither," Noah echoed solemnly, eyeing his older brother. "Not once."

"Lyin' scamp, an' you, John, you de oldest, you know better. Even if I never call you, you got 'nuff sense to see de shadows grow long 'fore your nose. You know you not to be out so late, with de pest goin' round! De night air gots fever floatin' in it, an' you catch it, sure! Double dose o' tonic for you both dis night! Now get in here 'fore I tell your mama to whup you good.''

John and Noah clumped dutifully in behind her, wiping their boots on the kitchen mats and rolling up their sleeves to wash. Noah scratched at his neck, grumbling, "Some ol' skeeter got me good, John. You got any bites?"

John peered at his arms and hands. "Nah, I'm too tough to bite. They like that baby skin better—"

Noah leaped on him, of course, as expected, and Bonanza had to chase them out of her kitchen half washed before they upset her kettles.

Glory got the requisite two doses of her tonic down both boys' protesting throats that night, and Tess decided that was punishment enough. But sometime far past the hour when the night crier had passed the house, she heard Noah calling faintly from the room he shared with John. She rose swiftly, threw on her wrapper, and padded down the long, silent hall to the boys' room. By the low lamp that was kept lighted all night to ward off Noah's nightmares, she could see the faint sheen of sweat on John's pale face. Noah was sitting up in bed, fully awake and frightened.

"He called to me, Mama," he whimpered. "He said he felt hot all over, but he was shivering. Then he fell back asleep, I guess. Now, he won't wake up no more, and I called him, too—"

"Hush," she whispered to Noah calmly, hurrying to John's side and feeling his brow. The boy's skin was hot as a brick in the sun. She gasped and turned to Noah. "Are you feeling poorly, too, son?" She went to him and pulled him to her breast, feeling for his cheeks. Noah, too, was warm to her touch. "I guess," he moaned softly. "My head hurts, Mama. Does John got the fever?"

"I hope not, child. But he's surely got something, maybe just something he ate. Did you and John eat anything out of the garden today? Did John eat something you didn't? Maybe a mushroom or too many of those little green tomatoes?"

"No'm," Noah said mournfully. "We didn't eat nothing at all."

"Did you see anybody to speak to? Any strangers pass by and shake John's hand, maybe? Come to the fence?"

"No'm," Noah said, trying manfully not to cry. "John's got the fever, Mama. John's gonna turn black and die!"

"Hush, now, where did you hear such nonsense?"

"Bonny said folks who get it turn black in the face and curl up their toes in their sleep and die! Bonny told us—"

"Well, Bonny's wrong, child," Tess said, forcing calm into her voice though she felt none. "If your brother's got the fever, then we'll get him well, and that's all you need to know. Now, settle down and lie back in your bed—"

A tap at the door, and Glory came into the room, her wrapper half tied, her hair wild and askew. "What's wrong?" she whispered. Her eyes fell on John's pale face, blank and closed as though he had been asleep for a week, and she gasped, one hand to her bare throat. "Oh God, he's got it," she groaned.

At her words, Noah burst into frightened sobs, and Tess whirled into action. "Glory, take Noah into your room and keep him quiet and warm. Make him take water until he can't hold more, and put warm bricks at his feet to bring out the sweat."

Glory needed no other word, but turned to Noah with low words of comfort, gathering the boy, blanket and all, into her arms and hoisting him, big as he was, right out the door. Tess turned all her attentions then to John, her eldest, and it was only then that her fear rose into her throat and stopped her breath.

The child was still as death, his skin clammy and jaundiced with a peculiar odor of sourness so unlike his usual clean smell of boy turning into a young man.

"Oh my Lord," she whispered softly, "give us all strength now." She could hear Glory moving down the hall with Noah, the child's voice whining but still strong, the comforting murmur trailing away to the depths of the house. She knew Glory would care for Noah as well as she could, and she felt such a fervent gratitude to her sister in that instant that her eyes welled with hot, stinging tears. But she wiped them savagely away and turned to her eldest son, pulling up a chair swiftly by his side and drawing the blanket down from his chest.

"John!" she called to him loudly, calmly. "John, wake up now, son!" The boy did not stir. "John, it's Mama, wake up now!" She gently shook his shoulder. He moaned softly and struggled to open his eyes. Even in the lamplight, she could see they were streaked with red and sunken in his face. John always showed his sickness in his eyes, she remembered from when he was so tiny, the dark pink circles he would get when he was not well. Now his eyes were puffed and bruised-looking, matted at the corners as though he'd had the grippe for a fortnight. And yet he'd seemed so healthy at supper!

"John, tell me where it hurts, son. Can you sit up? John? John, open your eyes now!" The boy was slipping back into sleep, and she knew it was not a healthy rest he sought but oblivion. She grasped his shoulders and pulled him slightly upright, appalled at how heavy he was, how little help he seemed to give her. Oh God, it had to be the yellow fever, nothing else came on so fast!

Fear and angry defiance made Tess move swiftly now, as she pulled back the covers, ignoring John's whimpers, and removed his sodden nightshirt. For a moment, she thought perhaps he'd lost control of his bladder, he was so wet, but she realized that it was simply sweat, so heavy that he'd soaked through two layers. Now she had him naked, reaching for a dry nightshirt in the cupboard and dry blankets, blessing Glory again for running the upstairs like a well-stocked merchant ship. She stopped to cradle him for a moment, his boy's body suddenly seemed so vulnerable and young. It had been too long since she'd seen him without his clothing. When had he become such a little man?

Almost then she lost control as she remembered the fierce pleasure she took in holding him, snuggling him against her breast, kissing his little hands and feet when he was tiny. Her firstborn. Her son. The first child in her heart and, though she'd never admit it aloud, the one she'd always love best. She could not lose him now!

John did not fight her embrace as he might have when he was well and alert. Dazed and almost unconscious, he cuddled to her as for comfort, whimpering low in his throat as he did so long ago for the breast.

Stricken, she thought quickly of all the mothers she knew who had lost at least one child. Few escaped that worst of despairs. The lives of children seemed so precarious, particularly in the first year. Out of every four babies born, a family might expect to lose at least one before the age of one year, perhaps another before he was completely grown. If a woman had five children, it was as sure as the seasons that more than one would not survive, and so the mothers told themselves quietly, "don't set much by it," when the child was born, the less to mourn if he were lost. On Bay Street, she knew of one family who just last year lost two children to scarlet fever and another a few houses down who lost four little souls to a whooping cough epidemic.

Death came with the seasons. The late winter and early spring brought the lung diseases; the late summer and early fall brought intestinal grippes, the intermittent fevers of ague, and yellow fever. Ah, John, she sighed, I could have stood it better to lose you early, but not now! Not now, when you are so much grown and so much of my heart.

There was no time to waste, Tess knew, and she gently put him back down under the clean, dry linen once more, saying firmly, "John, you're going to be all right, son. Do you hear me? Don't be afraid, I'm here with you, and you're going to be all right."

Glory whisked through the door then, carrying another lamp, and the room was suddenly as bright as day. "Has he got it?" she half whispered, half demanded.

Tess nodded dismally.

"If I had to make a bet, I'd say Noah's right behind him. He's tucked into my bed, and I woke Bonny to put the kettle on and warm the bricks. Least she can do after scaring them both half to death—"

"I don't want to hear the words, not even once," Tess said then, her voice steadying as she spoke. "The boys are ill. That's all they need know. The name of the sickness will not be spoken aloud, not to me and not to them."

Glory shrugged, setting down the lamp and leaning close over John. "I don't care what you call it, let's just get rid of it fast as we can. Nobody outside need know our business anyway. The doctors are no help with this, you know, and between us, we can likely physic these boys better than any two surgeons in town, even with only *three* hands between us." She brushed the boy's hair back from his eyes and glared down at her sister. "If God wants to take one or both of these scoundrels, He'll have to come through me first."

Tess knew that Glory's brisk bravado was as always for her sake, and she hugged her swiftly, unable to speak her love. She took a terrible risk, both of them did, for the pest was infamous for its contagion. And they were not even her own children! But then Tess put that thought aside, for of course, they might as well be. She rose and Glory followed, both of them already fierce in their concentration, moving from one task to the next with scarcely any need for talk at all, and by noon the next day, the upstairs had been turned into a hospital to rival any in Wilmington.

Severn had been wakened, bundled up with enough clothes for two weeks, and sent by carriage with a servant to visit a school chum. She knew only that her brothers had some sort of influenza, and so that she did not catch it, she could have herself a holiday.

Both boys were back in their room again, but their beds were pushed wide apart now, so that two chairs for watching fit easily between them. Chamber pots were readied, four of them for each boy, and placed about the room within easy reach, as well as towels, basins for the sick cloths, and a kettle of water placed on the coal tender to steam the room. Glory kept the water filled with her herbs and roots, so that when Tess opened the door from the hall, it was like stepping into a warm, damp marsh, with the odors of vegetation and wet moss everywhere. On the table were her instruments of medicine: spoons, knives, measuring tablets and grinders, droppers, cups, drawing plasters and poultice rags, powders, lead waters, and mortification utensils and more than two dozen vials and bottles of her private concoctions.

Both boys looked more dead than alive by noon, their faces yellow with the bile so characteristic of the disease, their eyes sunken, their breath labored and shallow. Tess kept them sweating to force out the contagion; Glory kept them breathing, half by exhortation, half by the use of a bellows that she pumped round them continuously, fanning them with the mentholated air. Tess dribbled warm tisanes down their throats, urging them softly to take just a sip more, then another sip. If some came up, she praised them and urged them to try again. Glory massaged their bellies, encouraging them to move their water as often as every quarter hour, whisking away the befouled chamber pots and sliding clean ones under their bodies so smoothly that their fitful rest was scarcely disturbed.

For five days, the two sisters rarely slept and ate only in short shifts, spelling each other so that the boys were never alone. Neither of them spoke of anything but the boys' inevitable recovery; neither mentioned the disease by name or whether or not they might catch it themselves. Bonanza finally became so exhausted, simply running up and down the stairs to do their bidding, that she broke down in a weeping fit and had to be sent to her pallet. Glory then took over the kettles in the kitchen, and the nursing went on for another two days.

When seven days had passed, Tess knew her sons were going to live. She wondered if they would ever be strong again, but she did not allow her fear the reality of words. They would live, and for now, that was all she would demand of God.

At last and occasionally, they began to speak a word or two, to respond to her entreaties to take yet more broth, to cough up the thick phlegm in their throats, to roll to one side so that she might massage their kidneys and backs. On the morning that John complained loudly of her rough treatment, telling her to leave him alone, she knew he was coming round.

The next day, Tess woke to the sure knowledge that the pest had cost her a child after all. She was cramping hard and by noon began to bleed. She sat quietly in her room, gazing out her window toward the sea, feeling the life drain from her. So many times a confinement had ended thus, she could scarcely find despair in her heart. Sadness, yes, but at least she had her boys safe. She could not weep for the unborn. By dusk, she rose emptied and cleansed of all regret. The child would come again when it was ready. For now, the living needed her more.

Only when Tess was certain her boys would survive, did she let word of their illness seep from the silenced corners of the house. Severn came home and was kept as far from the sickroom as the walls would allow, but social animal that she was, the neighborhood soon knew that John and Noah had come through yellow fever and lived.

They were now minor celebrities, as were Tess and Glory, who had saved them without a single doctor's visit. Tess took little credit, telling Severn and all others who asked that it was Glory who had rescued the boys with her nursing skills. Perhaps, she thought hopefully, one of their many acquaintances might pass the gossip along to an eligible brother or cousin. . . . Soon, Glory found her stock had soared among their mutual friends and neighbors. Those who before might have viewed her as a pathetic cripple now saw that she was able to do what few surgeons could—save a child from the plague. The wives of Wilmington began to seek her out for knowledge of herbals and tisanes. Tess prayed they might continue their friendships once they came to know Glory's wry wit and her readiness to speak her mind on any subject.

"It's ironic," Tess said one evening as the two sisters sat together by the fire, "that the very contagion that can destroy neighborliness on the one hand can actually increase it once it passes. You have so many admirers these days!" She smiled lovingly at Glory. "Next they'll be asking you to hang up a shingle."

Glory took a long measured draught from her camomile tea, glancing above their heads. The boys slept peacefully in the room upstairs, the deep and profound sleep of bodies that were still healing, and she knew she would carry the habit of listening for them now for long months after their cure was complete. "We were lucky," she murmured to Tess. "We could have lost one or both just as easy as not. Some of those brews I never tried, and some I just made up in my head, and most I surely didn't know if they'd work or not. But so long as we kept them sweating, I figured they'd live to complain well enough."

"I hope you wrote them all down. You'll be called on now to save others when they're stricken."

"Only for friends. The surgeons can tend the rest."

"That scarcely eliminates a lady in a four-square area, then. It'll take you till Christmas to return all the calls."

Glory smiled, a little shyly. " 'Tis nice to be invited to so many places. But I don't suppose it'll last."

"It will," Tess said briskly, "if you cultivate the friendships with a little effort of your own, Glory." She softened her voice when she saw Glory draw away slightly. "You have a delightful sense of humor, dear," she continued gently, "when you don't use it for ridicule or impertinence."

"I thought only the very young could be impertinent," Glory said, an edge coming into her voice.

Tess reached out and covered her sister's hand with her own. "People fear that witty tongue of yours might turn on them, too, I think sometimes. Now that you are finding new friends, I hope you'll take care to nurture them." She gave Glory almost a flirtatious smile. "You know the rules, dear. The ladies likely will enjoy your wit well enough, but the gentlemen often prefer something a little . . . softer. It's their loss, of course, but there it is."

Glory was silent for a moment, gazing into the fire. But she did not pull her hand away from Tess. "You know," she said finally, "everything I have in my life that I care about, I receive from your hands."

"Why, that's not true," Tess began, "it's your own beauty and cleverness that draws people to you—"

"A place to live, children to love, a community to be a part of, the food on my plate—" She extended her slippers out to the warmth of the flames. "Even the shoes on my feet. All of it comes from you."

"You saved my sons' lives. Anything I have given you, you've repaid a hundredfold and everything this house ever provides in the future could never be payment enough."

"Still," Glory said thoughtfully, "a woman should have a life of her own."

"And so you do, judging by the calling cards left this afternoon alone. If you'll only treat them as gently as you do me."

But Glory did not return her sister's bantering smile. She sat quietly, gazing into the fire, and Tess knew better than to try to tease her further out of her reverie.

🌿 🌿 🌿

Another spring came to the house on Bay Street, and Tess and Glory sat on the new arbored porch, waiting for Captain Jack's arrival. His ship was due in that afternoon, and Tess looked forward to showing off what she had caused to be built in his absence. The new porch wrapped round the house like an embrace, with a deep, shadowed seating area canopied by wisteria and evergreen ivy, so that even in winter, some cover would remain. The veranda depths were cool and private yet from any chair, one could see the whole of the daily parade of passersby down the street. The very first full veranda in Wilmington, it was Tess's pride and had swiftly become Glory's favorite place. Now the two sisters anticipated the sight of Dobbs's horse coming from the docks.

"Severn is going to miss his homecoming," Tess remarked to Glory, leaning back and closing her eyes. The rocker was so soothing. "I can remember, seems like only last week, when she cried when he left and hopped around on one foot driving us all crazy on the day he was expected in port. Now, she can scarcely be bothered to arrange her social calendar."

"Soon enough, she'll be gone altogether," Glory murmured, matching her sister's mood. "Then John, likely, and then Noah."

"What a dispiriting thought. I best have more babies, then, for I can't stand the house so quiet."

"I think eight confinements are quite enough."

"Oh, I don't," Tess said happily.

Glory shot her sister a sharp look. "Are you pregnant *again?*" It was like Tess to make this an announcement in such a round-about way.

She smiled shyly. "Don't make me tell you until I've told Jack."

"Oh for pity's sake," Glory snorted with exasperation. "As if he cares, one way or the other. He's the last to know most everything else around here. But Tess, another baby! Must you breed like a Virginian? When are you going to put a halt to this? Don't you ever want to be free to come and go as you please without a milk stain on your bodice and a pair of sticky hands clinging to your skirt?"

Tess laughed softly. "No, not really. And listen to you talk! You love them as much as I do; you'll take to your bed when Severn leaves for good, for all your scolding and fussing at her."

"Well, she needs fussing, that one. But Tess, another baby! You've just got to stop this, you're not a young woman anymore—"

"Oh rubbish, pet, don't get yourself in a pother about something you can't do anything about. I certainly don't."

"But, Tessie, you *can* do something about it! Just tell him no. Make your bed elsewhere, if he won't respect your wishes, but tell him under no uncertain terms you'll not accommodate him further. Another baby! God, the man's going to kill you yet!"

Tess stood then, and Glory saw her face change from the soft peace of acceptance to a heightened excitement. "He's here!"

Glory stood, too, and saw that Captain Jack Dobbs's new black hunter was rounding the corner toward them at a jaunty trot. She smiled and waved as Tess was doing, adding under her voice, "Tessie, it's not as though it's all that unusual, after all. I would imagine most of the married folk on this street have arranged to sleep in separate beds by the twentieth year of their union. It's simply a convenience and a mark of respect for their wives, and I should think—"

Tess never took her eyes off her husband as he was dismounting and throwing the reins to the welcoming stable boy, moving toward the women now with the vigorous step of a man who had not spent the better part of three decades at sea. Glory was instantly annoyed with him and his exasperating good health.

"Convenience? I shouldn't find that convenient at all," Tess murmured. "No, Glory, please say no more about it. There'll be no such arrangement in Captain Dobbs's house."

With that, she was swept into his arms laughing as Jack Dobbs strode up the porch steps and enveloped her, planting a hearty kiss on both cheeks in salutation. "There's my Tess!" he shouted as though the greeting had to cross a league of sea. Over his wife's shoulder he sought Glory's eyes and winked at her, as if in conspiracy.

My sister is a matron, Glory suddenly realized with a flush of mingled confusion and delight, and I am still a beautiful woman. Despite my impairment, my face is still as it was when he first chose me. When he chose me first. While Tess has been swiftly aged by the years, her confinements, and her own steadfast resolve to be everything to everybody, I am still relatively pretty. He must notice the difference between us. He does not love her, though he cares for her, of course. He feels no passion there. Perhaps he never has. Yet it is to her bed he'll go tonight, her belly that will swell with his seed, while mine has never known a man at all—

"Lovely Glory!" Jack trumpeted then, releasing his wife and sweeping her up with the same enthusiasm. "It's so good to have the two of you waiting for me!" And he planted two fervent kisses on her cheeks as well. The man has kisses to spare, Glory thought a trifle sourly.

Tess called to him gaily, "Give my sister an extra hug, my dear one, for she deserves it mightily. She takes better care of me than any two mothers and worries more."

"Worries! What in the world have you to worry about, Gloriana?" Jack Dobbs pulled back and grinned into her face, still hugging her hard.

Glory glanced at Tess swiftly. It was so tempting to snap at him, "I'd worry a heap less, Jack Dobbs, if you'd stay home a little more and get your wife with child a little less!" but she saw the trust and love on Tess's face and she could not speak. She mock-scowled and pushed him away. "The price of decent lace, for one, Captain. Did you manage to bring any back with you this time or must we haggle with that thief, O'Flanner, at the common market for the worst stuff with the rest of the goodwives?"

And with that, Jack Dobbs sailed into the house, pulling the two in tow, to regale them with his latest adventures, bargains, coups, and near-misses, pulling small treasures out of his pockets and calling for his children at the top of his voice.

It was always thus, Glory thought later in the silence of her room, whenever Jack Dobbs returned. As though all the clocks in the house stopped when his foot crossed the threshold, life ceased its normal rhythms and a half-dozen people going in as many directions all swiveled to center and marched to his drum. This is what it is to be a man, she supposed. To be this man, at least. She both envied and resented his complete expectancy that he could be absent months at a time but once he appeared, he was central to everything, the exuberant sun around which all of them gratefully orbited.

Part of her was angry at Tess for fostering this illusion for him and part of her wanted to *be* Tess, wanted to be the hand that closed the bedroom door behind them, locked away with this sun that came into and went from their lives with such maddening ease.

Glory knew well enough what went on behind that bedroom door, and it was not that which she wished for, no not at all. But just once, she admitted sadly, she would like to know passion. She would like to belong to someone completely, as Tess did to Jack Dobbs.

🌱 🌱 🌱

As it happened this time, Captain Dobbs was in port when his second daughter was born in the early autumn. He sat in the library drinking port and smoking his Spanish cigars while Glory, as usual, helped Tess through her labor to bring another child into his house.

Always before, he had been at sea when the children were born, usually arriving soon after, bearing sumptuous gifts and high praise for his wife's success. Sometimes Glory suspected that he kept his ship offshore deliberately, just long enough to hear the word that the child had come before he dropped anchor in the river.

But this time, he paced the floor of the library and absently dropped his cigar ash on the carpets as he strode up and down before the fire, and Bonanza reported with satisfaction that "de

Captain, he say he d'ruther face a passel of pirates than to hear his wife holler like that again."

It was shortly after midnight when Glory came triumphantly down the stairs, bearing in her arms the baby girl for Jack Dobbs to see. She found him seated by the fire, the decanter of port nearly empty beside him, yet he rose instantly to his feet when she entered the room.

"You have another daughter," she said softly, drawing the blanket back from the child's face. "Tessie is fine, but she's sleeping. She says she'll see you in the morning."

He reached down and touched the child gently on the cheek. "She was at it more than six hours. But she is well, you say?"

"Just weak and worn out." Glory appraised him closely. "She's done this often enough to know what she needs." She felt more bold with the child in her arms, between them like a shield. "Too often, if you ask me. Captain, my sister shouldn't really have any more children."

He looked up from his daughter's face with some alarm. "Is something wrong?"

"No, but she's wearing herself out bearing your children year after year. Haven't you noticed, she's hardly a young girl anymore? You're making her an old woman before her time."

Jack gazed at her solemnly. "I see. And she asked you to tell me this?"

Glory shrugged and sat wearily down in the chair opposite his, cradling the child against her breast. "She doesn't need to say the words, I'm her sister. I know her heart."

"And she wants no more children from me."

"She *needs* no more, that's certain. Eight confinements and four children is enough for any woman, I should think."

"Especially," he said softly, "when some women have none."

She stiffened with hurt pride, but she kept her voice level. "It requires some sacrifice, of course, on the part of the husband—"

"On the part of the wife, too, I would think."

"But many husbands willingly make the sacrifice," she went on, taking no notice of his insinuation, "for the health of their wives. Childbirth wears women out faster than anything. And Tess is weaker and weaker with each one. Though she'd never think of complaining, of course."

He sat watching Glory carefully over the temple of his finger-tips, the smallest smile playing over his lips.

"What is it?" she asked with some annoyance. This was not the first time she wondered what in the world her sister saw in the man.

"I was just remembering you as a girl, Glory," he said gently. "Such a beauty, you were. So full of life. How did you become so—angry about things?"

"I'm not angry," she said quickly. "I just hate to see my sister worn to a frazzle by a man's selfish desires—"

"Yes, you are. You've got an edge to you, always. Waiting for someone to knock the chip off your shoulder. You speak of my selfish desires. What makes you think it's I who initiates the acts that bear such fruit as you hold in your arms?" he asked calmly, nodding to the sleeping baby. "Perhaps this is one aspect of your sister that you can't understand, Glory, any more than a nun could understand a wanton. If Tess wants separate bedrooms, it's fine by me. But she'll need to tell me that herself." He grinned at Glory and in that instant, she could see the spark of his appeal. "And, little sister, something tells me she won't."

"No, of course she won't," Glory snapped. "She's afraid of what you might do or say—"

He laughed aloud, but not unkindly. "Tess isn't afraid of any-thing, you know that as well as I do. She's completely capable of telling me what she wants and doesn't want, and she does it one way or another every time I walk up those steps. But she doesn't carry the chip that you bear, Glory. And so a man doesn't mind hearing what she wants, for she doesn't beat him over the head with it like you do."

She slumped, suddenly despondent. "Ah, Jack, I don't mean to do that. Do I truly? Carry such an ugly chip as all that, I mean?" Her face fell into sad lines, something she rarely allowed herself to do in front of someone else. "It's no wonder no man will have me, then."

He rose and went to her quickly. To her surprise, he pulled her to her feet and embraced her, with the child nestled tight between them. "My dear little Glory, you are still attractive. You're not a girl anymore, it's true, but you're a lovely woman, nonetheless. Many men have come to call—"

"But none come to stay."

"Perhaps that's because you give the impression that you are perfectly contained, completely happy living as you live, doing as you do. Do you, then, want to marry and move from this house?''

She relaxed in his arms, feeling closer to him than she had in years, perhaps ever. The sleeping baby between them only added to the tenderness she felt. This could have been our child, a part of her remembered sadly. He could have been *my* husband easily enough. If it had not been for Tess.

"Sometimes," she murmured, "sometimes I think how good it would be to have someone of my own to love. Someone who would love me."

"Well then," he said, brisk again, putting her from his arms and settling her back in the chair, "we must do our best to see that it happens."

She dropped her head miserably. "If they didn't want me when I was young and pretty," she held up her maimed wrist, letting the lace fall away in a rare display, "they surely won't want me now. You didn't."

"I was a fool," he said quickly. "Your stepfather pushed me, Tess pushed me, and I capitulated. But any man can see that one hand or two, you're more than capable of everything required of a wife. And beautiful, besides. If you'll only take that chip off your shoulder and the edge from your tongue, you'll marry fast enough, I wager."

She looked at him, her face open and searching. "Tell me the truth, Jack. Do you ever think about me . . . that way? Do you ever wonder how it would have been if it was me and not Tess?"

He did not avert his eyes. "Many times, Glory," he said softly. "Why do you ask?"

Bonanza stepped into the room then and said, "Miz Tess say she like to nurse de babe 'fore she sleep, Miz Glory, an' you to bring her up, if you please."

Glory rose, her face shining with the fire, the warmth of the baby, and the pleasure of his confession. "Thank you, Bonny," she said graciously. "Please be sure the captain's comfortable before you go to bed." And she swept gracefully from the room, leaving Bonanza staring after her.

🌿 🌿 🌿

In the next few weeks, others in the house besides Bonanza noticed the new tone in Glory's voice, the softness in her manner.

"If I didn't know better," Severn said to Bonanza, "I'd say Aunt Glory was in love." She had asked to borrow Glory's pearl choker, a request that would usually have been only very reluctantly granted after a host of warnings and a litany of exasperated head-shakings and eye-rollings. This time, Glory had said, "Of course, dear. It will be lovely on you."

"Maybe it is de baby," Bonanza said. "Sometime a new baby in de house make de woman go all tender for a piece."

"Was she like this when the others were born?"

"Never her, chile! Seem like de last one come make her mad *all* de time. Matter a fac', since Noah, she be crochety as a old she-bear."

"Well then, who could she be in love with?" Severn asked, delighted. The prospect of her Aunt Glory being smitten with a man, Aunt Glory who seemed sometimes twice as old as her mother despite her unlined and lovely face, absolutely beguiled the young girl. "Who has come to call?"

"Nobody," Bonanza said firmly. "Nobody come in or go out dis house I don' see—"

"Then she must be meeting someone outside the house," Severn said. "Mother will know."

When she next got her mother alone, Severn asked the same question. "Aunt Glory's changed lately, have you noticed?"

Tess was nursing little Caroline, and she only murmured, "Umm? Changed? How do you mean, dear?"

"Why, even Bonanza's noticed! She's all sweetness and light, these days, like butter would just melt in her mouth. Not a sharp word, not a single tease—well, she's just not herself, Mother, I can't believe you've not seen it!"

Tess gave a small, wry smile. "I have been a little preoccupied, Severn, but I'm not blind. Your aunt has always been sweet, I think, but some don't see it as readily as others."

"No," Severn said with the complete assurance of youth. "She's different. Competely. She acts like she's in love."

Tess glanced up then, appraising her eldest daughter. "In love? With whom?"

"Well, I thought *you'd* know, surely, Mother. But if you don't have a clue, she must have a secret beau. Has she been going out more than usual?"

Tess laughed then, a soft, silvery laugh that made her sound like a girl again. "Neither of us has scarcely been out since Caroline was born. I think you've been reading too many novels, Severn. People can change, you know, without there being any big mystery involved. But if you're so curious, why don't you ask your aunt yourself?"

Severn stopped in midreply, her face going more somber. "You say she hasn't been out at all?"

"Not so far as I know," Tess said mildly. "With your father home, I've been so busy, you know, I haven't been out and Glory rarely goes out alone. But you can ask her."

"Yes," Severn said slowly. "Father's been home."

Tess readjusted Caroline to her other breast and murmured to the child, "There, is that better?"

Severn said, "Well, never mind then, Mother. I suppose it's nothing after all," and she withdrew from the room, holding her skirts so that they would not rustle and disturb the baby.

🌿 🌿 🌿

Tess could not help but notice, after Severn had put the idea in her head, that indeed Glory was altered in some significant way. It was not only that she spoke more gently to the servants and the children, not only that she interrupted less and listened more—there was something about even the lines of her body. Glory usually moved through the house at top speed, often banging her elbows on corners as she rounded them, so that Jack remarked of all the footsteps down the stairs, he found Glory's most like his hunter's trot.

But now, she held her arms closer to her body, kept her skirts quiet as she moved, and the constant jangle of keys that usually accompanied her was missing.

"Glory," Tess asked, "did you wrap your keys in cotton wool? I never hear you coming anymore."

"I gave them to Bonanza," she said serenely. "Surely after all these years, the woman can be trusted that much."

Tess could not hide her surprise.

"I wanted to feel lighter, I guess," Glory added confidentially. "Free."

"Well," Tess finally managed, "perhaps I do ask too much of you, dear. I don't know what I'd do without you, heaven knows, and I suppose I've taken advantage—"

Glory laughed softly, and as she did so, Tess was struck by the notion that she had not heard her little sister laugh in that way for such a long time. It filled her with joy to hear her. "No, it's me who takes advantage, Tessie. I've let you make for me such a soft cocoon that I scarcely need to venture out of it at all. But I guess it's time for me to try to fly a little while I still can. And keys would weigh me down." She glided from the room before Tess could think of an answer.

She's not in love with a man, Tess told herself, for if she were I would surely know it. But she seems happier, more soft at the edges, and whatever has made her so is to be welcomed. Maybe someone just told her she's prettier when she smiles!

A week later, Tess woke in the night to find Jack missing from her side. She thought little of it for he sometimes had trouble sleeping in a bed that would not rock, as he put it, and often as not would sit by the library fire lost in his maps and books until she found him there asleep at dawn.

For some reason she was wakeful as well, and though she reached for sleep, it would not come. Finally she threw her wrapper about her shoulders and slipped down the stairs. It would be a good time, she thought, to speak to Jack about Severn's latest beau, and they could share a private moment before the whole house was up and about.

To her surprise, as she descended the stairs she heard the low hum of quiet conversation in the library. Jack was not alone. She drew near the door and realized that Glory was by the fire with him. She hesitated. If she put her ear to the door, she might be able to make out their words. Then thinking better of it, she knocked softly, waited an instant and went in.

Glory and Jack were sitting in two chairs, side by side, facing the fire. Both of them had turned in surprise at her knock. Tess could tell by their posture that they had been startled.

"Oh, what a bonus to find you *both* here," Tess said. "I couldn't sleep either, so I hoped for some company."

Glory rose quickly. "You two likely have much to talk about without me—"

"No, stay," Tess said to her sister, pulling her back down in the chair. She drew up a third chair to the fire and turned it so that it faced them both. "My two favorite people in the world," she murmured happily. "Glory, you look so lovely by this light. Jack, doesn't her hair shine like fire?"

Glory turned to face him, and Tess saw instantly the emotion in her eyes, her mouth, and her heart twisted hard enough to take her breath away. *Severn was right. My sister is in love.*

"Yes, indeed," Jack said mildly.

Tess looked at her husband and could not tell what he knew or what he felt. His face was as opaque to her as Glory's was transparent. Glory flushed brightly at his words and dropped her head, shamed to be so praised by him before his wife . . . and also pleased beyond measure. In that single gesture, Tess knew that whatever Glory felt for her husband had gone undeclared. If Jack sensed her feelings, he had not acknowledged them. Perhaps Glory did not know herself what she was doing or feeling. That was the most likely. And Tess resolved then to cause both of them as little pain as she could manage.

She took Jack's hand and then reached to take Glory's as well. "I can't imagine," she said softly. "what my life would be like without you two beside me."

Glory rose to her feet again, sliding her hand out from her sister's. Tess saw that tears welled in her eyes. "I should leave you two alone," she said throatily. Tess sensed that she scarcely knew what she was saying. She stood also and embraced her sister, pulling Jack to his feet. Somehow, she managed to pull both of them into her arms at once, hugging them fiercely. "We don't take the time to say this very often," she whispered, "and we should. I love you both so much."

Glory squeezed Tess once, hard, and then turned and left the library, closing the door softly behind her.

Jack settled back in his chair, facing the fire. "Well, Tess. What brought all that on?"

"Nothing much." She smiled, rewrapping her robe. "Just the hour, the fire, the dark of the night, I suppose. When hearts are most easily unburdened."

"And that's what you came down for? To unburden your heart?" His voice was teasing, but his smile was kind.

"Ah, my Jack, the years have been so good, haven't they?" she murmured.

He nodded easily. The mere presence of him close to her, even after all these years, made her feel enclosed and safe. She smiled at him, almost coyly. In all their marriage, she had rarely resorted to flirtation—indeed, had never needed to. But tonight, she felt the urge to ask a question she would not have asked before. "Have you—" She stopped, a small part of her heart commanding her to silence. But she ignored the warning. "Have you . . . do you—ever regret your choice?"

He looked up from the depths of the fire at her, as though he came back from a great distance. "My choice?"

"Your choice of—me. Rather than Glory." She tilted her head in a way to soften the question. Let him take it as a tease if he chooses, she prayed silently.

He laughed softly. "Did I have a choice? I don't remember it that way. I recall that you and Glory had it all worked out between you, and I got invited along for the ride."

She glanced down at the fire, for she could not meet his eyes. "You could have chosen neither of us," she murmured. "Did you ever wish you had?"

He reached over and took her hand and held it in both of his. "You know, I always wondered why you never asked this sort of question. The kind of thing most wives get to sooner or later. 'Would you choose me again?' 'Would you marry again if I died before you?' " He patted her hand. "It all translates to the same query, I suppose. 'Are you happy with me?' " He gazed at her softly and then back into the fire, a small smile playing over his lips. "But then you never were like most wives, I guess, and I've always counted myself lucky in that."

She waited silently. It was so like Jack to refuse to answer such a question outright. He would never be cajoled into declarations of affection. They came or they did not, but only from his heart, not from her need to hear them. She had long understood that about him, knew that if she pushed hard enough he might say what she wanted to hear—but neither of them would take much comfort in the process.

He tugged gently on her hand. She rose and went to him, and

he settled her into his lap. She leaned against his shoulder easily, inhaling the familiar fragrance of him that never failed to pleasure her. "I'm a silly fool," she whispered.

He shook his head. "Never, my dear. That is one thing you have never been." He kissed her lightly. "And in answer to your question—"

She put a finger to his lips. "Don't tell me. I'm sorry I asked."

He chuckled again. "No, you're not. No woman is ever sorry she asked unless she gets the wrong answer." He nestled her closer so that his mouth was very close to her ear. "To answer your question, you have kept your vow admirably."

She waited, slightly confused. When he did not speak again, she asked, "My vow?"

"You promised me, lo these several lifetimes ago," he teased her, "that you would make me the happiest of husbands. And you have done exactly that." He kissed her again, this time more deeply, and she felt the old familiar thrill begin at the base of her spine as she sensed his stirring ardor. "No, my dear. I have no regrets. Any other questions?"

She knew then she'd been right. Whatever love he felt for Glory had been—and likely would continue to be—contained. "I know better than to push my luck." She grinned at him. "I'm sure I have a dozen more I should ask since you're in the mood to answer, but I can't think now what they might be." She bent and kissed him, letting her lips leave a definitive promise and turned to leave him to his fire.

"I thought you couldn't sleep," he said.

"I think now I can," she murmured.

As she passed Glory's closed door on her way to her own bed, she paused to listen for a moment. As she had guessed, the sounds of soft weeping came from within. Tess stood for a moment fighting a strong urge to go inside and hold her sister, to offer what comfort she could, to tell her that she understood—but she knew that Glory had to get through this night alone. She went to her bed and waited for Jack to come to her.

She sensed that he would not be long.

The region of the Cape Fear, like much of the Tidewater, was settled by staunchly English stock, whether landed gentry, dirt-poor farmers, or redemptioners. King George's Royal Proprietors found the people to be loyal to the Crown, but only to a point.

As Wilmington grew to be one of the largest cities in the Carolinas, despite her problematic port, that point was reached sooner there than elsewhere. The Navigation Acts were the initial annoyance, for they taxed colonial goods both coming into and out of the Carolinas in "proclamation money," or currency the king had "proclaimed" as valuable: tobacco, corn, beaver or otter skins—or gold. A small farmer's crop of rice or indigo might be seized by the tax man but not accepted as proper payment, and this for goods that had a difficult enough time making it past the hindrance of the Cape Fear to far-flung markets.

To add insult to injury, King George's Privy Council did its level best to undermine the colonial legislature at every turn. If the colonials questioned a royal decree, the King merely increased the quorum necessary for their legislature to vote. If the legislature resisted, King George simply dissolved the assemblage with no notice.

Carolinians protested, reminding their King that they were Englishmen, and that their Royal Charter of 1663 had granted them "all libertys, Franchises, and Privileges" enjoyed by any other Englishman, including the protection against whimsical taxes without voting rights. In answer, Royal Governor George Burrington dismissed the colonial Assembly for another two years.

Trade in Wilmington then fermented, and captains like Jack Dobbs made fortunes from helping the colonists to evade the King's Navigation Acts with small, daring ships that might somehow maneuver past the dangerous shoals and predatory currents of the Carolina shores—as well as the Royal Navy. Protest against the royal whim was no longer considered sedition but common sense.

When the King's Privy Council stripped the colonial Assembly of voting power, Wilmington responded by incorporating and giving the vote to any man who had a house bigger than sixteen by twenty feet. Houses bloomed on Orange Street, Front Street, Dock Street, and Chestnut like dandelions, low brick houses with tabby mortar and limed with burned oyster shells, two-story framed shacks with clapboard siding, anything that would shelter and provide the franchise all at once. English traditions such as the ducking stool, the public whipping post, the stocks and the pillory were dragged away, and a public dock and market put in their place.

Meanwhile in Charleston, a series of slave revolts led to the death of hundreds and the hangings of a score of captured slaves. The next year in 1740, as though to underscore the chaos, half of that "great city-state of the South" burned to the ground in the worst fire of its history. When Charleston rebuilt, she did so with an eye to her own defense and with a style more French than English. It seemed to Charlestonians, indeed to all Carolinians, that there was little they could not do and so they grew impatient with all limitations to their destiny . . . including those imposed by their King.

🌿 🌿 🌿

For many long hours, the tricolored heron had been at the edge of the marshlands off the mouth of the Cape Fear. At dawn, he had broken away from the flock of young males and arrowed down to this brackish water to hunt and feed. Now, with the sun higher in the clear sky and the shadows scanter under the black gum trees, he leaped up to land on a moss-covered stump that rose five feet out of the water and perched motionlessly for the better part of two hours.

He was listening for a particular sound. While it did not come, he remained still, only occasionally eyeing his reflection in the dark river water. Extremely slender, he was almost three feet long, with rich slate-purple streaks on his crown, the sides of his head, along his neck, and his back and wing feathers. The long aigrette plumes of his back were dark with purple as well, curling delicately about his tail and feet. At the back of his head, a crest of shining white feathers rose and fell with his breathing, and his breast feathers also gleamed white in the sun. His black beak was dagger-sharp and more than five inches long; his eyes were brilliant scarlet. Like the rest of his fellows, his neck was nearly as long as his legs, and his body made an **S** shape when at rest.

Which he seemed to be to any who could not read the tension in his feet and legs. Twice, he detected some distant sound and spread his wings as though to fly, but then settled back down again. Finally, unmistakably, the sound he awaited came ringing across the water, muted by distance but still audible. His beak opened wide and his body hunched convulsively as he replied with an explosive croak meant to carry miles over the river.

At once he leaped high and flapped quickly up over the tallest gum trees. With his long legs trailing behind, he flew quickly toward the call that had stirred him.

He was still fifty feet from the water when he spied the female and flew directly toward her. She was perched several yards above the water in a long-dead gum tree, and she watched his coming intently. When he alighted on her branch, she bobbed her head in an approving manner.

For many long moments, there was no further movement from either of them. At length, the male shifted and turned on the branch so that he faced the same direction she did. He sidled closer to her so that his wing feathers barely touched her. She did not acknowledge his nearness.

For more than an hour, they perched thus, scarcely moving. The only clue to their courtship was the quicker rise and fall of their breast feathers and the darting of their eyes. They paid no attention to the young bullfrog that leaped from hiding on the nearby shore to snatch a damsel fly from a sprig of grass. Neither bird even cocked an eye at the small flock of mallard ducks that flew past only yards away or turned to glare at the small gray squirrel that scampered up the trunk of their tree, stared at them, and scampered back down again.

Finally after long hours, the female shook herself and dropped to another branch a foot below the male. She moved a few inches until her position was just right and then, in slow motion, tilted her head until her beak rested against his flanks.

She had accepted him. Again, they sat quietly as another hour passed. Then, although neither had seemed to signal the other, both abruptly raised their heads in unison as high as possible at the same moment and shattered the stillness of the river with harsh, grating croaks. Startled, the small team of mallards took noisy flight. Now, the herons stretched in tandem and flapped their wings, shuffling from one foot to the other as if marking time in one spot. Alternately, each croaked and ruffled and bobbed, but the male became more aggressive, stepping from limb to limb, shaking himself until his plumage quivered, raising and lowering his white crest feathers in a strange and beautiful dance.

At length, the male stopped dancing and hopped alongside the female. He reached with great delicacy and entwined his long neck with hers until they were locked in a knot. After a few moments of this, they slowly unwound themselves but continued the movement, locking themselves in the other direction. Only after they finally unlocked themselves again did the male take flight.

The female seemed to make no effort to follow, but she craned her neck to watch him rise over the gum trees and disappear toward the west. She resumed her quiet stance and waited.

The male heron flew a mile away from the sea and came to a shallow backwater of the Cape Fear. He landed in water up to his knees and stood quietly there for several moments before beginning the slow walk that was the second part of his mating. Wading purposefully through the intermingled water lily, pickerel weed and water hyacinth, a movement caught his eye and he froze.

A large bullfrog lay camouflaged in the thick growth, submerged except for his eyes and nostrils, waiting for some insect or smaller frog to pass by. The heron did not appear to move at all, but if you had watched closely, you would have seen that very gradually, his position was changing. The bullfrog made the mistake of watching his great enemy very closely.

Slowly, ever so slowly, the heron moved to within striking distance, and his neck imperceptibly compressed until it was tight as a spring. To the barest fraction of an inch, the bird knew his own reach and when he was within range, he leaned forward gradually until he was soon so overbalanced it seemed he must fall on the frog in the mud.

With blinding speed, the stiletto beak shot forward and down, and even though the frog saw death coming, he could not kick fast enough to evade it. The heron drove his beak through the frog's body and lifted his head, opening his beak slightly so that the frog's struggles would not allow him to escape. In a few moments, the frog weakened and ceased kicking. With a practiced maneuver, the heron bobbed his head, flipped the frog in the air, and snatched it again in his open beak, gulped, and most of the frog disappeared down his throat. One more gulp and the frog was gone. Two more gulps, and the large swelling in the heron's throat moved downward and disappeared. It was good hunting.

Immediately, the heron moved on down the river, taking three more frogs in the same manner, a dragonfly, two shiny beetles, and many dragonfly nymphs. He heard a faint sound near the shore, pinpointed its origin, and spotted a young red-bellied snake moving slowly through the waving grasses. It was no more than a foot in length.

The heron could see by its color, faded and ghostly, that the snake was shedding. Its forked tongue flicked in and out more rapidly to make up for the fact that its vision was clouded by the shedding process. Without compressing his neck or stalking, the heron darted forward and snatched up the snake right behind its head. Shaking his beak sharply, the heron whipped the snake's body until he heard an audible crack, indicating that the snake's spine was snapped. Still not satisfied, the bird placed one foot on the snake's body and jerked the snake upward roughly five times. Now the snake waved back and forth from the heron's beak limply, and the bird bobbed, gulped, and in seconds had maneuvered the snake down his throat.

Though he was not yet sated, the heron abruptly stopped his hunting then, and a sigh seemed to shiver through the amphibious creatures of the riverbank as they sensed his abatement. He now searched the bank, his head cocked to one side as if looking for something special.

He stopped several times to pick up first one branch and then another, dropping each in confusion. Finally, he selected a dried limb more than twenty inches long and almost a half inch in diameter. He turned it over and over in his feet and bill, inspecting it thoroughly. When he was quite satisfied with it, he grasped it firmly in the middle and flew off.

The female heron heard him coming before she saw him and she straightened somewhat from her crouched position. She had not moved since his departure. He coasted in and settled beside her so that his feet were placed exactly where he had them before. After several minutes, he stretched his head out toward her and she gravely accepted the branch from him, bobbing her head up and down as if thanking him for the gift. She now moved to a crotch of the tree and positioned the branch within the dead limbs. A dozen times she picked it up and replaced it, but finally she found a position for it that she seemed to find satisfactory and she wedged it into place with her bill. Without another glance at her mate, she took off. Now, it was he who remained motionless until her return.

Just before dusk, he heard her slow flapping and he froze as she landed gently on the branch beside him. Shyly, she extended her neck and offered to him the branch she carried, one she had carefully selected in the same way he had his. He took it from her, bobbed his head in thanks, and fumbled it into the crotch of the tree, placing and replacing it over and over until at last he had it firmly interlocked with both the first branch and the dead tree limb. As the last of the daylight faded, the female resumed her position on the branch slightly lower than the male's and again she rested her head against his flank.

In this position, guarding their rudimentary nest site, they went to sleep for the night.

🌿 🌿 🌿

The town of Charleston to the south was a magnet for all Carolinians, no matter which state they called their own. Charleston belonged, they felt, to all of them, a special city with a seductive languor and accompanying excitement that made them proud. What Charleston decreed, others did. What Charleston thought this season, others thought the next.

Each year, Glory nagged Tess until she finally succumbed and a trip was arranged. The stated excuse was to see Sam and Danny, for both brothers lived in the city and welcomed their visits. When Joseph Innes had died at Cross Creek, leaving most of his fortune and lands to the Widow Newcombe, the small bequest he left to his sons was barely enough to start them on their lives. But Tess persuaded Jack to lend the boys a stake to buy a quarter partnership in a sawmill on the Ashley River, and now they lived in Charleston, tending their affairs and edging up on prosperity. Neither of Joseph's sons had married, despite Tess's teasing and frequent offers to introduce them to suitable prospects in Wilmington. Glory said she could hardly blame them. "Who would want to give up a bachelor's life in Charleston for a marriage bed in Wilmington?" she scoffed.

This spring of 1743 Tess felt that their yearly jaunt to the city was especially well-timed for Glory had been morose for a month or more. Even the blooming of the azaleas, something that always lifted her spirits as they signaled the coming warm weather, had failed to revive her.

But the sights and sounds and smells of Charleston, as their ship docked in her busy wharf, pulled Glory to the side to lean down and exclaim, "My heavens, the city's grown by half again in just a year! Tessie, do you remember that tall pink building there? No, no, over *there*." She grabbed Tess's shoulder and adjusted her properly so she could see around the high ruff of another lady passenger's collar. "There, next to the milliner's. *I* don't recall that at all, do you? It must have shot up overnight!" She wrinkled her nose ruefully. "They still haven't cleaned up this harbor, though—"

"That's the smell of money, madame," a man said next to her. The crowd jostled the rail of the ship down from Bath, Beaufort, and Wilmington, a gay and festive group anticipating the delights only Charleston could provide, and there was scarcely room to move. He grinned openly at Glory and added, "I don't think you'd want them to clean up that now, do you?"

Tess glanced at the man who had spoken so boldly to her sister, half expecting that Glory would freeze him and move aside, as she usually did when approached by a strange male in a strange place. But to her surprise, her sister dimpled and replied, "Well, I daresay no one's making a fortune on that flotsam and jetsam there, sir," pointing to a bilge of bottles, cotton packing, and broken timber floating up against the wharf, "and if I owned an establishment on the waterfront, I'd surely pitch a few pennies into the hat to clean it up." Her words were strong but the dimple saved them. Tess stared at her, openmouthed.

The stranger laughed good-naturedly, bowed as if to salute her small victory, and turned to his friend, an older man with a full and powdered white wig to say, "Well, Gaston, you heard the lady. If I provide the hat, will you provide the pennies?"

Gaston turned and appraised Glory frankly, scarcely glancing at Tess. A slow smile warmed his face, and Tess thought, my God he is a striking man. Glory barely returned his glance.

"It'll take more than pennies to clean it up," he said, bowing cordially to the two women, "but yes, I'd certainly be willing to pay my share. In the long run, every merchant in Charleston would benefit if the effort would bring such tourists to town."

"We're not tourists," Glory said quickly.

With that rejoinder, Tess could not help herself. She took Glory's elbow lightly as though to steer her away. Whatever had come over her? But Glory ignored her touch and added, "We're Carolinians, too, from Wilmington, and we visit old friends and relatives each year. Do you run an establishment here in Charleston, sir?"

"Yes, indeed," the gentleman said, and he took a card from the breast pocket of his gray linen coat. "I would be happy to be of service to you ladies at anytime."

"Why, thank you," Glory began, "perhaps—"

At that moment, the crowd began to surge toward the gangplank, and Tess gripped Glory's arm with more strength, relieved that no more conversation was likely. Glory had examined the card and carefully tucked it into her portmanteau. "Fine laces, it says he deals in, maybe we should make a point to go by his shop, just to be polite. I certainly could use a new collar on my blue velvet."

Tess said nothing. As they moved away and out of earshot, she murmured, "Gracious, Glory, I must say I'm surprised at you."

Glory turned and gazed at her sister with a look Tess could not read. "Are you? Well, don't be." And she drew her arm from Tess's hand smoothly, pushing ahead.

By the time they debarked on Water Street, hailed a carriage, and were clattering over the cobbled streets of Charleston with all their bags piled behind them, Tess had put Glory's behavior out of her mind. Well at least she's not sad anymore, she told herself, and in her eagerness to enjoy the city with her sister, she reached out and squeezed Glory's hand, happy when the squeeze was returned. It was the beginning of the high season, when the wealthier planters abandoned their fields for the cooler breezes that Charleston port could provide. The busy streets seemed to Tess as urbane and worldly as any she could imagine in London or Paris.

The Broad Hotel was one of the oldest in Charleston, a fine establishment famous for its French cuisine and impeccable service. Naturally, the maître d' recognized Tess and Glory, and ushered them to a small table near the rear of the dining room, as they usually preferred. But Glory stopped him and softly requested a table closer to the entrance.

"But of course, madame," he said smoothly, carefully taking no notice of Tess's surprise.

"I just felt like a change," Glory confided after they were seated.

The softshell crabs were excellent, as usual, and as they were finishing their sherry and deciding upon a single dessert to share,

Tess looked up and saw the two gentlemen from the ship entering the dining room behind the maître d'.

"Glory, it's him," Tess whispered, dropping her voice. "Did you tell him where we were staying?"

"Of course not," Glory said in her normal voice. She turned to gaze frankly at the two men as they took a table not far from them. They had changed their coats, Tess saw, and into more formal wigs. Their attire bespoke money that was quite accustomed to itself. Clearly, they had not come for any other reason than to dine.

"Well, I don't believe I'll have dessert after all," Tess murmured quickly. "Let's just call it an evening, shall we?"

"Nonsense," Glory said, a little more loudly. "I didn't come all this way to miss dessert. I shall have the russe Charlotte, I think; do you want to share it or not?"

At that, the gentleman called Gaston spied Glory, half rose in his seat, and tipped his hat to her in a graceful gesture. Tess all but groaned aloud.

"Do go on, if you want to, Tessie, I'll be right up."

Of course, it was out of the question. Tess could no more have left Glory alone in the dining room than she would have offered her for sale on the nearest slave block. She smiled, though, and decided to let Glory have her head. Clearly, she meant to, regardless. Sure enough, Gaston was coming over, and Tess decided she would see this out no matter how uncomfortable she felt.

Glory extended her hand to the man as though she had known him for years. "Why I do believe it's our man in laces," she said warmly, half to him and half to Tess. "Do you dine here regularly?"

Thankfully, he made no motion to join them, but only bowed over Glory's hand briefly, acknowledged Tess with a smile and a nod, and said, "I stay here whenever I'm in Charleston." He scanned the table quickly. "I'd recommend the softshell crabs, but I can see I'm too late."

"We had them and they were excellent, as always." Glory smiled. "I'm just trying to talk my sister into the russe Charlotte, but she is being balky."

"You should listen to this lovely lady," he said confidentially to Tess, "she clearly knows how to end the evening properly."

Tess was relieved to see that at least Glory had the grace to flush. She said only, "It has been such a long day—"

"Why, I'm not tired at all," Glory announced happily.

"Then perhaps you might enjoy a small entertainment the hotel provides after your dessert. I understand there's to be dancing in the ballroom this evening, and I would be honored to escort both of you."

"Oh no—" Tess demurred.

"If you don't care to dance, I can simply find you a comfortable table to watch the festivities. Some of the loveliest ball gowns in Charleston will drift through that room tonight—"

"I'm afraid that'll be impossible," Tess said gently. "But we certainly appreciate your kindness."

Glory turned and frowned at Tess slightly. "Impossible? Whyever for? Surely, it won't hurt simply to watch the dance for a moment or two. I know *I* would like to see what Charleston is calling fashion this season."

Tess's decision was made in an instant, and her smile never faltered. She rose to her feet with a slight bow in the gentleman's direction, gathered her skirts gracefully, and moved from the table.

"Oh, Tessie, don't spoil it!" Glory cried out softly, but Tess continued out the door. She had every confidence that Glory would follow fast behind her.

She was completely amazed when Glory did not come immediately to their room. She was appalled when Glory did not appear within the hour. And she was frightened when Glory did not come back to her bed before nearly ten o'clock.

She waited until the next morning to speak, for she knew that Glory would be less defiant once she had rested. She knocked softly at the door to her sleeping chamber, and when she heard Glory murmur, she went in.

Her sister was sitting up in bed, her long red hair tangled beautifully about her slender shoulders. Her good hand was visible upon the coverlet, and Tess could see, even in this dim light, that her hand was slightly clenched. She steeled herself for a confrontation.

But before she could speak, Glory asked, "When in the world did you get to be such a stick-in-the-mud? It wouldn't have hurt you to stay for a few minutes, just to see a waltz or two. The orchestra was sublime."

Sublime. Tess realized with a start that she'd never heard Glory use that word before. She must have heard it from her gentleman friend. "Glory, I'm surprised at you," she began mildly. "I've never seen you welcome advances from a stranger before, and I cannot imagine why you chose to begin here in Charleston. If you want to meet a suitable escort, there are any number of fine gentlemen Jack could introduce you to—"

"I don't need Jack to arrange my escorts, thank you," Glory said evenly, "and I don't need my sister to instruct me in proper behavior. I am a grown woman"—she laughed harshly—"a woman of certain age, as they say. And I can certainly decide for myself if a waltz or two will hurt me."

"Do you mean to say you danced with this man?" It was worse than Tess had suspected.

"Of course, I danced with him. He's a perfect gentleman and a lovely dancer." She sat straight up now and reached for her brush, yanking it through her hair defiantly. "In fact, he's calling for me this afternoon. He's going to show me Charleston."

"You've seen Charleston."

She dimpled wickedly. "Not with Gaston, I've not."

Tess sighed with exasperation and sat down heavily on the edge of Glory's bed. "What is this man's family, and where is he from? Do you know anything about him at all? Glory, you're acting like a common—"

"Don't you dare say another word!" Glory snapped, slamming her brush down on the dresser so loudly that Tess jumped a foot. "He's from a fine family here in Charleston, but he lives in Bath, he has business in both cities—"

"What is his name?" Tess asked, as evenly as she could manage.

"Garland. Monsieur Gaston Garland."

"I've never heard the name."

"Well, there's much you've not heard of," Glory replied. "But he is a fine gentleman—"

"So you keep saying. But tell me, Glory, of all the men of your acquaintance, do you know any of them who would speak to a strange woman on a ship, invite her to a ball unescorted and unchaperoned by any family at all, and then keep her out until an hour that would invite censure and gossip?" Glory lowered her head, and Tess pressed her point. "Would they treat a lady they respect as this Gaston person has treated you?" She lowered her voice. "As you have *encouraged* him to treat you?"

Glory glowered furiously and said nothing.

"Has he asked you to meet his people?"

Silence.

"Has he asked to be commended to your brother-in-law or your half brothers or sought an invitation to our home to pay his respects?"

Glory's face fell, and she looked away.

"He has only offered you a few wild waltzes and a buggy ride through the streets of Charleston." Tess allowed her voice the slightest scorn. "How very gentlemanly of him."

Glory's eyes welled, and Tess was instantly struck by pity and a sense of shame. Her words were brutal, she knew, and she already regretted them. But she knew she would have regretted not speaking even more. "My sweet sister," she said softly, "this man isn't right for you. Your own heart tells you so. There are a dozen men more right for you than this one—"

"Ah, what do you know of it?" Glory moaned. "You've had the man you wanted, you've had *everything* you've ever wanted, every day of your life!"

Tess rose and went to Glory. She put out her arms to embrace her sister, but Glory half fought her away, twisting and weeping. "You don't have any idea what loneliness is! You think you're lonely for Jack when he's away, but you don't know what it's like to have nobody at all to wait for! Nobody to look forward to seeing, not for my whole life. Sometimes I think I'll die of loneliness!"

Tess took Glory in her arms and rocked her, ignoring her rejections and refusals to be embraced. "I do know," she said. "I know you're lonely and I know how much you give up to stay with us. We've offered to help you so many times, Glory, but you've got to see that Monsieur Garland is not the answer for you. Not a man like that. You are lonely, I know, but surely you cannot think of accepting his attentions."

"What's so wrong with him?" she wailed.

"He's fast, Glory, you can see that. He's a silver-feathered hawk just looking for a bright, pretty bird like you to hunt. You deserve a man who will love you, who'll take care of you properly. If he's really serious, he'll make the effort and prove himself. But I suspect if you cancel your outing with him today, Monsieur Gaston will simply fade away like last night's sunset. Exciting and striking, but no light that lasts." She looked into Glory's face. "Do you see what I mean?"

Glory nodded in mute sadness.

"Do you think you should see him?"

She cleared her throat and sat up, moving slightly out of Tess's arms. "I suppose not. But what will I say?"

"You just leave that to me. I'll make the appropriate excuses, and he need never be insulted or hurt at all. But, Glory, promise me you won't see him again. This man isn't right for you."

"No man is!" Glory wept.

"Now that's not true at all. You know a dozen fine men at home, and if none of them pleases you, then we'll invite two dozen more new candidates to a supper party the week we return. You'll see, Glory, it'll be better. If you like, we can get out more, take more trips. I know lately I've not been a very good companion for you, but I promise I'll improve. We'll go to Savannah perhaps this autumn, would you like that? Or maybe Richmond?"

Glory nodded, her lower lip still pouting like a young girl's. She wiped the back of her hand across her eyes and said, "He was a wonderful dancer."

Tess laughed softly. "I'm quite sure he was, dear. His kind always is. But just try to imagine bringing him home to meet Jack. Could you picture yourself doing that?"

Glory did not share her laughter. "Actually, Tessie, I don't feel much like going out this morning at all. You make my excuses to monsieur, and I'll stay here and rest."

"But I'm going to Madame Carteret's to be fitted. Don't you want to come along and pick out something special?"

Glory shook her head. "You go along. I'll join you for tea at four. I just feel like being by myself, if you don't mind."

Tess patted her hand. "I don't mind at all. You rest and relax, and I'll see you in the dining room later." One last quick embrace. "You do agree with me, don't you, Glory?"

Glory slid down under the covers like an errant child. "Yes, of course, Tessie. How could I not? I'm not a fool, after all. You go on, and I'll see you later."

Tess patted her gently and withdrew.

She was to remember every nuance of Glory's last sentence a month later after their return to Wilmington. Severn came into her boudoir one evening, half breathless with excitement.

"Mother, do you remember I told you that Aunt Glory was in love? Well, I was right!"

Tess looked up from her mending and smiled at her lovely daughter, aglow with her heady news. "What do you mean, child?"

"I saw her, I saw her!" Severn cried. "An older gentleman with a handsome white wig, quite the most striking man at the inn, and he and Aunt Glory were seated together close enough to be a pair, and she looked absolutely mesmerized!"

Tess set down her mending carefully. "You're sure it was your Aunt Glory?"

"Completely. But I don't know the gentleman, Mother, do you know who he is?"

"And when did you see them together?"

"Just today! Helen and I were coming from the milliner's, and we stopped to have a sip of something cool, and in the back of the room, I saw them together. Helen saw them too, Mother, and even she said the man was stunning. She said if it weren't for his elegant dress, she'd almost think him a pirate—"

"Did your Aunt Glory see you?"

"I don't think so." Severn then peered closer at Tess's face. "What's wrong? Who is the man, Mother?"

"Probably just an old friend, perhaps he's only passing through town," Tess said quickly. "Don't tease your aunt about him, child, you know how testy she's been lately."

"Don't I know it! She's a mud wasp these days. I was glad she didn't see me, though I can't say why actually. Helen says—"

Tess rose abruptly and put aside her mending, tidying her basque and smoothing her back hairs. "You and Helen must find more to do with your time than gossip about your poor Aunt Glory. I'm sure it's nothing at all, and if you're languishing for something to do, I can certainly offer some suggestions—?" She hesitated, glancing meaningfully at the mending still to do and the pile of sewing that always, thanks to the boys, gathered faster than her fingers could move.

Severn said, "No, no, I've got plenty to do, Mother, and Helen won't say a word, I'm sure. Whatever Aunt Glory does—"

"Is her own business," Tess replied firmly.

"Completely." And Severn whisked out the door.

That night, Tess waited until the house was quiet before seeking Glory out in the privacy of her room. She knocked at her door, something she rarely did in the daylight hours, for all doors were wide open. When Glory did not answer immediately, Tess pushed the door slightly and saw her sister facedown on her bed, prostrated with weeping.

Instantly, all anger dissolved from Tess's heart, and she flew to Glory, sweeping her into her arms.

"Oh, Tessie," Glory wailed, "you were right, you were right!"

"You've been seeing him?" Tess asked, her own eyes welling in sympathy with Glory's.

"I couldn't help it! He was so persuasive! So handsome! He told me he loved me and wanted me—"

Tess felt a chill stiffen her stomach. "Glory, did he—"

"I'm with child!" Glory wept so hard she began to retch.

Tess bowed her head and wept now along with her sister. "Ah, Glory, Glory! Did you tell him? What did he say?"

Glory staggered to her feet and yanked the chamber pot up to her mouth, retching painfully, her shoulders quaking with the futile effort. When the fit of nausea passed, she slumped against the wall wearily. "He told me he loved me."

"But the child. What did he say about the child?"

Glory went to the corner of the room, clutching the pot before her absently, as though she had forgotten she held it. She paced erratically back and forth, set the pot down, turned to Tess, turned away again, her arms moving aimlessly, her one poor hand yanking through her hair. Finally, she turned to the wall, and Tess could scarcely make out her words for the sobs. "He said that a child was not—was not part of his . . . plans."

"Oh God, Glory," Tess cried.

"His *plans*!" Glory whirled on Tess, threw herself in her arms and spasmed with her weeping. "I went to his room at the inn, I wanted to tell him that whatever he wanted, I would do. I would wash it out of me if that's what he wanted, I would kill it! But he'd already left! His bags were gone!"

"Do you know where he's gone?"

She shook her head wildly, her hair all about her face and neck. "No, you don't understand! He doesn't want me. Even if I could find him, he doesn't want me. He doesn't *love* me!"

Tess held Glory as firmly as she could and rocked her then, murmuring quietly to her, words of comfort into her hair and her cheek, as Glory wept until she was exhausted. Finally, Glory could no longer hold up her head, and her hand trembled with every effort. She did not resist when Tess took off her robe and eased her under her blankets. "Sleep now," Tess said softly, "and when you are rested, we'll think what to do. Remember, there is always something that can be done, my Glory. You need not carry this burden alone. The man must be made to see his responsibilities. But now, you must sleep."

When she saw that Glory had slid into exhausted sleep, she left the room, pausing at the door to gaze at her sister. Glory's face was still swollen and contorted with grief, her hair a nest of wild despair. She was, in that moment, no longer beautiful. In fact, Tess realized with a small start, it was painful to look upon her, something that Tess thought surely had never been, could never be the case with Glory. But it was so. She was lovely no more. Desire had done this to her. Sadly, Tess closed the door to go to her own room and think on what must be done. She never missed Jack more than at that moment.

The next morning, she listened for Glory's movements within her room, but she heard nothing. She is truly exhausted, Tess thought, and let the morning hours pass. Many times, she stopped at Glory's door and listened, warning the servants and the children away, but nothing stirred within Glory's chamber. Sleep is the best antidote for her despair, she thought. If she can gain some strength from it, let her sleep the day away.

But by noon, when she still had heard nothing from Glory, Tess began to feel concern. No doubt, she had awakened in the night and likely had a terrible ordeal through the dawn hours. But still, it was unusual enough for Glory to sleep so, that she began to think of waking her after all. By one o'clock, she knocked softly at Glory's door. She still heard nothing within. She knocked again, louder this time. No sound, no movement at all. Louder still she knocked, this time turning the knob only to find it locked.

Alarmed now, she hurried downstairs, took her keys from the peg on the kitchen door, and hurried back to fumble the door open and burst inside. Glory was under the blankets, but she looked much different now. Her face was composed, her arms outside the coverlet over her breast as though in benediction, her hair smoothed as if awaiting visitors to a sickroom. Tess's heart jumped with fear as she swiftly felt for Glory's pulse at her wrist with one hand, scanning her face for signs of life. Her skin was cool to the touch and slightly damp, her pallor now unmistakable. Tess looked about wildly and saw then on the boudoir table the bottle of laudanum. She got on the bed beside Glory and pulled her to a sitting position, patting her face and calling out her name. Thank God, the children were not at home, she thought frantically, calling louder and jarring Glory from side to side, now slapping her vigorously. Finally, Glory flinched away from her slightly and moaned, and Tess laid her back down again, racing out of the room, to return with her stomach tube and her syrup of ipecac.

She fought with Glory to get the tube down her throat, fought to get the purgative into her, and then fought with her as she vomited and tried to writhe from her grip, fought her back to life as fiercely as she would have fought Death itself if it sat on the shoulders of one of her own children. The whole time, she called out her name, exhorted her to live, even cursed her angrily for her selfish, thoughtless, willful, senseless action, and finally, finally, Glory lay weak and flaccid on the pillow, a slight bit of color back in her cheeks, her breast rising and falling in weary complaint. But alive.

When Tess thought she could speak, she said, "Did you think I'd let you do such a thing, you foolish girl? Did you think I'd let you destroy my only sister in the whole world?" And then she fell on Glory's breast, weeping softly. She felt Glory's poor maimed wrist creep down and rest gently on her head, and its touch made her weep all the more.

Later, as the room grew dark with early evening shadows, Glory said weakly, "My life is so empty. I want it to end. Nothing pleases me anymore, nothing brings me pleasure at all. I don't care about anything."

Tess asked softly, "Do you care about the children?"

Glory shrugged callously.

"About your own child?"

She shook her head no.

"I know you care about me," Tess murmured, "no amount of denial from you could ever make me doubt it. And I know you care about yourself, even if you don't know it now."

"No," Glory said, "not anymore. I want it all to be over."

Tess put her face in her hands and closed her eyes in pain. She knew that if Glory wanted to destroy herself, she would. It was inevitable, no matter how she might try to stop her. The thought of living without Glory in her life was more than Tess could endure.

Glory's first response to Tess's tears was to cry out, "Stop that! Don't you dare cry for me!"

Tess could only shake her head, mute with despair.

Glory then roused herself from the bed to go to Tess and hold her, and as Tess felt her sister's arms around her, she knew that there was only one thing that would keep Glory from destroying herself. The child.

"Your baby," she managed to murmur. "What have you done to your baby?"

"What does it matter?" Glory said tiredly. "He doesn't want me *or* the child. If it weren't for the child, perhaps he might have wanted me, but now . . . maybe I should have tried to kill the child instead of myself."

Tess pulled back and slapped Glory with all her strength. "Don't ever say that! I don't want to hear that again!"

"But what good is a child to me without a man?" Glory crumpled back on the bed. "I don't want it!"

"You will, believe me," Tess said firmly. "A child is a hundred times better than any man, and this child may well be the only thing you ever have in your life that's your own. Think, Glory! Think how much you love *my* children and multiply that by a thousand. Your own child! Something that belongs to you forever."

"But if I have this child, no man will ever look at me again," Glory moaned. "I might as well die right now, for I'll never have any life except this one. I'll live forever in your house, surrounded by your things, your children. Your husband. No man will ever want to marry me with a bastard child on my hip!"

Tess knew that what she said was true. If Glory became the currency of common gossip, her chances to find happiness were decidedly diminished. No good man would want her again. She was still attractive, but she was no longer young. She had a disfigurement. A bastard child would surely doom her to spinsterhood the rest of her lonely days. Moreover, Glory would be unwelcome in most homes; few friends would stand by her in her shame. She would be outcast and alone forever, except for her immediate family, and even they would feel the sting of her shame. Severn, for example, would find some homes less hospitable to her, simply because of the infamousness of her Aunt Glory.

"Perhaps there is a way," Tess murmured, her thoughts only

half a step ahead of her words. "Perhaps I could have the child for you."

Glory looked up from her hands in bewilderment.

Tess no more than spoke the words than she knew that it would work. This was the only solution. "Think of it," she said, her words coming swiftly now. "I am often pregnant, no one would think a thing about another confinement for me. Jack will scarcely be here enough to matter. The children will accept whatever we tell them. You will be sick."

"With what?"

"I don't know, with the consumption, perhaps. Something ladylike but that will keep visitors away. Something they can all feel compassion for but it won't kill you."

"Something just a little glamorous," Glory said slowly, the plan growing in her mind, "that would keep me out of public sight for half a year or more."

"Yes. And I will have the child for you."

"But how will you fool Jack?"

"Let me worry about that. Jack'll be home in a few months, you'll scarcely be showing then, and I can pad my skirts sufficiently to fool him. With luck, before he's home once more, the baby will be born. For now, we must agree to tell everyone immediately that I'm expecting. You must be taken ill right away, and between the two announcements, that will give everyone plenty of things to worry about."

"Do you think we could do it?" Glory murmured. "It seems like such a large lie."

"Sometimes those are the ones that are believed most easily. And we will raise the child together. I'll help you with the birth, no one need ever know."

Glory thought for a moment. "It might work. If it doesn't, you'll be as humiliated as I will be."

"It'll work. We'll make it work. And you will have your child without having to live the rest of your life in shame."

"No one will know the child is not yours except you and me?"

"For now. Perhaps some day, I may have to tell Jack. But for now, no one need know."

"And if I find a man? If I am offered marriage?"

"We'll solve that problem when it comes."

"But the birth!"

"No one need know!" Tess embraced Glory, stroking her cheek lightly where she had slapped her before. "Forget him. He never existed. All that matters now is the child. And you. Do you believe me?"

"I believe you," Glory murmured obediently into Tess's hair.

❦   ❦   ❦

When Jack came home, he greeted the news of Tess's pending confinement with a graceful resignation. After all, what did one more child mean in a household already full of them? He murmured once about the possibility of Tess investigating some way of preventing further children, but when she looked aghast at the suggestion, he dropped it. Glory, meanwhile, took to her chambers with a mild case of consumption, for extended bed rest and no visitors.

The children never questioned Tess's announcement that she was expecting; the servants never gave the slightest hint that they noticed anything out of the ordinary. Visitors ceased to come to the house on Bay Street, for though consumption was not considered a contagion, no one was quite sure how the disease did spread. For a month or two, people sent notes and flowers, small boxes of candy and other delectables to tempt Glory's palate, for everyone knew that consumptives must be persuaded to eat. Then the gifts and notice tapered off, and Tess and Glory were left largely alone to get through the next few months with few questions.

Only Severn was a concern. "Mother, you're carrying this child differently than your others," she said one evening, eyeing Tess's skirt carefully.

Tess was moving about the kitchen, the horsehair pad securely tied about her waist and under her shimmy. She felt herself surreptitiously with her elbows as she carried a kettle to the table but sensed no disarray. "Oh, you think so?" she asked casually.

"Yes, this baby is riding a lot higher and flatter than Caroline did, I think."

"Well, I'm a little older each year," Tess said breezily. "Could be my muscles that are changed, rather than the baby itself."

Severn shook her head slowly, still scrutinizing Tess. "No, it's more than that. It's as though the baby is flat and wide rather than rounded. There's more baby at your hips than at your stomach."

Tess stopped herself from looking down at herself in alarm. "No doubt it's a girl, then," she said, finding an excuse to whisk herself out the door, "they always want to do things their own way."

But that night, in the privacy of her chamber, Tess discarded the horsehair pad for a cushion with more roundness to it and stayed up late to sew small buttons in place of the strings she'd used so far. Strings could come untied; buttons would lie flat and be less noticeable, she hoped.

Severn also wanted to help care for Glory, and it was getting harder and harder to keep her from her aunt's room. "But I won't get close enough to her to breathe the same air," Severn insisted to her mother, "and I miss her! Let me just go in and speak to her from a chair in the corner."

Tess could think of no real reason to keep her out, and when she spoke to Glory, both of them realized that Severn's suspicions might well be aroused more by not seeing her aunt than by seeing her.

"But you've got to keep her back from the bed," Glory said tiredly when Tess told her Severn's request. "I'll pile the pillows around me so my belly won't show under the coverlet, but make sure she doesn't get too close. She's too intelligent to be easily fooled."

Tess sighed. It was true, Severn was the weakest link in their deception. The boys scarcely noticed the details of lives other than their own; Jack was gone and likely would not notice if he were at home, but Severn, the only grown girl in the house, missed little, particularly if it had to do with appearances.

"It's a shame we can't take her into our confidence," Tess murmured. "I feel badly that I must lie to my daughter. She'd make a better ally than an adversary."

"We can't risk it," Glory said firmly. "She loves to gossip, she has a hundred friends, and she'd somehow reveal the truth, even if she didn't mean to. Promise me, Tess, you won't break down in a moment of weakness and tell her. Promise me!"

"No, no," Tess hastened to reassure Glory as she saw she was getting herself aroused. "I certainly would never tell her without your approval. This is your secret, after all, more than my own." Her face fell. "I just wish it could be different."

"Not as much as I do," Glory said fervently. "Only God knows how much I wish it."

So Severn was allowed audience in Glory's room, on the condition that she stay only a brief time so as not to weaken her, that she remain in the chair at the far side of the room, and that she not speak of anything too personal or dramatic. That last touch was Glory's. "After all, you wouldn't want to get a consumptive all excited with the most delicious gossip of the week. And if Severn can't tell me the best parts, she'll soon tire of the visits, I'm sure. Bring her in."

Severn came in almost timidly, holding her skirts so they would not rustle loudly, glanced at her mother, and then sat down gently in the chair ten feet from the foot of Glory's bed.

Glory was sitting up in bed languidly, her hair brushed out upon her shoulders, her dressing gown slightly open at the throat, awash in fat, fluffy pillows on all sides. "My dear," she said weakly, "how sweet of you to come and see me."

"I wanted to come before, but Mother wouldn't let me," Severn said, casting a severe glare to Tess.

"Really? Well my, Tess, I scarcely doubt we need be that careful of my nerves. I've missed my own Severn."

Tess rolled her eyes. They were truly two of a kind.

Severn beamed at Glory. "I told her I'd be a breath of fresh air for you, Aunt Glory. It must be so lonely just lying up here every day, all day, with nobody to talk to and nothing to do. How do you feel?"

"Some days better than others," Glory murmured.

"Well, you look just wonderful," Severn said eagerly. "I thought consumptives were supposed to look like death warmed over, but your cheeks look rosy as a girl's!"

Tess glanced at Glory warningly, but Glory only replied, with an air of some quiet pain, "Yes, I suppose it's the medicine your mother is giving me. I only hope it's helping."

"Well, it must be!" Severn went on. "And I declare, it looks to me as though you're actually putting *on* weight, Aunt Glory, instead of wasting away." She chuckled confidingly. "I wish my own breasts would look so ripe and lovely. Mother," she asked, looking up at Tess, "maybe you could give me some of that medicine, too. If it makes Aunt Glory look so good, imagine what it might do for me!"

Glory suddenly groaned and clutched at her chest.

"What is it, dear?" Tess asked in real alarm, rushing to her side.

"Oh, Tessie, I'm just so tired . . ." Glory cried. "I—I don't think I can visit any more just now." Her voice fell away in a plaintive sigh.

Severn rose immediately and backed out the door. "Oh, Aunt Glory, I'm so sorry. I'll come another time when you're feeling a little stronger." She let herself out.

Tess glared at Glory. "I left you some rice powder. Didn't you use it?"

Glory scowled.

"Your vanity just couldn't allow you to look as peaked as you're supposed to feel," Tess scolded. "And you had to show off your breasts in the process? My word, Glory, one would think you *want* to get caught."

"Yes, yes," Glory said impatiently, pulling away from Tess's smoothing hands. "Next time she comes, I'll pluck out every eyelash and brow, paint myself with whitewash, and draw blue circles under each eye."

"And cover yourself to the throat," Tess said firmly. "Don't think she won't be back, Glory, she will. Out of curiosity, if nothing else."

"I almost hope she does," Glory said. "I'm bored to death."

"Better bored than banned from every decent house in Wilmington. You've still got five months to go, Glory, you're not even halfway through this ruse."

"Ah God!" Glory screamed in frustration, muffling her mouth in the pillows packed around her. "This baby better be worth it!"

"She will," Tess said soothingly. "She'll be worth it all and more."

🌿 🌿 🌿

The next five months seemed the longest that Tess could remember, surely the most tedious of Glory's whole life. But day by day slipped away until finally, the baby was due. Severn had been sent to visit a friend in Charleston, the boys were off hunting up the Cape Fear. Tess and Glory waited for the child alone.

The morning that her pains began, low and cramping in her

back, Glory stood at the window of her upstairs room, gazing out over the rooftops to the river beyond. The wind was gusty, and the trees lashed the gutters of the house with a rhythmic rustle; the sense of movement was everywhere around her. Within her, the child was still as stone, but every muscle in her body seemed to be tensed for the impending birth.

Nothing in the evening weather had hinted at the squall to come, just as nothing in her body had warned her that the birth would be today. The rising winds brought gusts of hard rain as her water broke, and now the storm and the birth were coming together. Tess told her this morning that the ships were expecting a hard blow, and all were either safely moored or were speeding upriver to shelter as fast as they could go.

Glory gripped the windowsill, bracing herself against another pain, centered low in her back and radiating up into her shoulders. She still could not believe she carried a baby within her. She half expected Tess to tell her that she was ill, that she was dying of some ulcerous growth, not that she would soon bear a child. Sometimes, she preferred to think so.

The wind was seeping through the wood-slatted window frames of Jack Dobbs's house, rippling the light curtains. It was from the south, they said, from whence the worst blows came. At dawn, the house had been quiet, now all was a clamor. It creaked and sighed on its foundation, like a ship straining at anchor. Glory could hear the metal damper to the fireplace quiver and clang as down gusts pulled at it, the panes of glass rattled, and outside the window, the trees brushed harder and harder against the bricks as though entreating entry. Within her, the silence of pain ruled.

Glory moaned low in her throat as another pain grew to a hard knot at her back, edging round to her belly. If her labor got unbearable, likely no doctor could come in a hard storm. Bad luck, this.

A soft knock at her door, and Tess entered, carrying a tray of tea and small dishes. " 'Twould be best if you could eat something light," she said happily. "You'll need your strength soon, and likely you won't feel like eating later."

"You sound so gay," Glory said tiredly. "Should I ready my dancing slippers?"

Tess laughed lightly. "Ah, pet, I know how you feel, but you'll be dancing again soon enough. How often do the pains come now?"

"Often enough," Glory snapped, plucking up a silver cover off

a plate, grimacing at the ham slice and buttered scone, and clattering it back down again. "Where's Bonny?"

"I've sent her off for a holiday to visit her sister, and her head's
so full of glee at her new spring hat, I doubt she'll give us a thought
for days."

"What news of the storm?"

Tess shrugged lightly. "High tides, they say, and strong winds.
Nothing new, to be sure, and nothing to concern you, at any rate.
Let it do its worst, we're snug enough here."

Glory suddenly gripped her side and slid into the nearest chaise.
"Ah, God, Tessie," she whimpered when she could get her breath.

"I know, dear," Tess comforted her, settling a shawl about her
shoulders. She pushed a warm cup of tea into Glory's hands.
"Drink this now, it'll help."

Glory shook her head, her face a mask of pain.

"You must," Tess said firmly. "Truly, it will make it easier for
you to pass the next hours."

"Hours! I can't imagine it going on that long."

"Oh, it may. But then again, it may not. It's hard to tell with
your first. But you're strong and healthy; you'll be fine."

The pain ebbed and Glory let Tess guide the cup to her lips.
"And to think," she said, sighing, "you've gone through this nine
times." Her eyes widened in horror. "And some of them for nothing!"

"Not for nothing," Tess murmured. "It was never for nothing."

Another pain began to build then, and as though in answer, the
storm outside moved into a wilder phase of its own. Within hours,
Glory was crying louder than the wind, and there was little pause
in either her labor or the turmoil outside the straining windows.
Tess never left her side, but moved constantly about her, wiping
her brow, helping her to pull on the corded rope stretched across
the bed, laving her cheeks with a cool cloth in between the pains,
murmuring encouragement to her all the while.

After six long hours of painful labor, Tess's worry began to
change to a quiet fear. Outside, the wind howled incessantly, and
she knew it was unlikely to ebb before nightfall. Also unlikely that
a physician could be reached, should something go dreadfully
wrong.

Something did seem to be wrong, and she tried to explore

carefully without alerting Glory to her danger. Glory writhed away
from her hands and screeched, but Tess tried to block out her
protestations and felt her belly, moving her hand inside her sister
as best she could to determine the child's position. She could feel
nothing.

Glory gasped, "How much longer till it comes!"

Tess bathed her cheeks again, taking as long as she could to
answer. "I can't say yet, but you must have faith that you can bear
it."

"Jesus God," Glory groaned agonizingly, "is that all you can tell
me? Have faith? I can't stand this much longer!"

Tess thought quickly. The harder Glory fought to birth the
child, the more danger both were in. The wind roared outside, and
no help could be forthcoming. Her sister was strong, but how
much could she endure. How much could the child? A chill passed
through Tess as she realized that there was no real evidence the
child was still even alive—

"Give me something for the pain!" Glory cried out then, lash-
ing her wretched hand in the air in supplication.

"But it might harm the baby!" Tess cursed the storm under her
breath and poor Glory's bad luck. Why could God not have sent
her an easy labor?

"I don't care if it kills it!" Glory wept. "Give me the laudanum!"

Tess went to Glory's herbal shelves and withdrew the packet of
powder that she knew would dim the edges of her sister's agony.
Perhaps at least I can examine her properly, she told herself hurriedly, just a little rest is what she needs. The child will come, if she
can just bear it—

"Tessie!" Glory screamed over the wind.

Tess dropped a small portion of the drug into the cold tea at
Glory's bedside and held the cup to her lips. Frantically, Glory
gulped it down, gagging desperately at the bitter taste. She fell back
among the linens, weeping, her body arching as the pains rolled
through her in battering waves. Tess held down her shoulders, lest
she writhe right off the bed, tried to calm her, calling to her to try
to breathe, but Glory could no longer hear her, her body would no
longer obey her will. As the laudanum took hold, her eyes rolled
back in her head until the whites showed plainly, and her grip
finally released from the sheets. Now moaning softly, her contor-

tions relaxing, Glory slipped from consciousness away from the pain, and Tess could hear even more plainly the wild whirl of the storm outside.

She slumped against the wall for a moment. Her sister was almost still, only her limbs jerking in spasmodic response to the unfelt but ongoing labor. As exhausted as Tess was, there was no time to waste. The dose had not been enough to keep her quiet for long. Tess bent to Glory and pushed apart her legs, reaching up inside her as carefully as she could.

She gasped in horror, for the child was no closer to birth than before. She could feel what she thought was a small foot far up the birth canal, but no head was apparent, and the other foot seemed lost in the wet, close cavern of Glory's belly. If the child was stretched so grotesquely with one leg descending and the other wrapped God knows where, it likely could not be born at all. Tess began to pant in fear as she paced the room, her eyes never leaving her sister's tortured form.

At that instant, the roar from the wind reached a new high, and the tree outside Glory's room sheared away with an ugly screech, the heaviest clump of branches clattering away down the roof with a rattle and slam that made the wall shudder. The noise galvanized Tess to action. She straddled Glory now, her hand reaching once more up within her, feeling with as much gentleness as she could for the infant's lost foot, trying to shift the child lower and into a position for proper birthing. She recalled the night Joseph Innes's mare had foaled, and she heard him speak of doing much the same thing to save her, rotating the colt with his fist up the animal to his elbow, and she shuddered at the comparison but did not pull away from the task.

Glory groaned once, and Tess froze, glancing up at her face. The jaw was still slack, the eyes mercifully closed. Tess continued her work, feeling with her fingers as far as she dared and not knowing what she was feeling, only praying that she would know the infant when she encountered it. Finally she felt what she could only guess must be either an elbow or a knee, and she began to pull, turning as gently as she could at the same time. The sweat was beaded on her forehead, despite the chill of the wind outside, and she cursed for the second time that night—this time, the bastard male who had got Glory into this mess, all men, and a God who would punish the women He'd already abandoned. Glory's belly stiffened spasmodically, then in a huge contraction, and the baby eased lower. Tess moved faster now, trying to slide the child lower still. It would be breech, there was nothing she could do about that, it may well be dead, but at least it would not be torn in two, likely killing Glory in the process. Glory stiffened again and again, the contractions coming faster now, and she groaned louder, coming awake.

"Push, Glory, push!" Tess called to her sister, half lifting her shoulders off the bed. The child was coming, was coming, could not be stopped, and Tess reached again inside Glory and pulled it forth, realizing there was no more time for gentleness. The wet, white rag of flesh was delivered of Glory just as she found her consciousness and her voice, and her scream rivaled the wind's.

"It's done, it's done!" Tess cried, pulling the child away from Glory's thrashing limbs. "It's all over!"

"It tore me!" Glory wailed, and her agony seemed unabated despite her lightening. "I can't stand it!"

Tess fumbled for the laudanum again, mixed a quick draught, and poured it down Glory's throat. What harm could it do for her to remember none of this? she thought swiftly, and perhaps it will soothe the edges of her torture. Without waiting for Glory to quiet, she turned now to the soul who had bleated once, softly, at her deliverance and had been still ever since.

It was a girl child, still curled into its birth position, its eyes clenched tightly against the light and the noise as though in adamant refusal to face life at all. Tess swiftly picked it up, wiped it off roughly to start its blood moving, and cleansed out its mouth with her fingers, jiggling it up and down in her lap. "Breathe!" she called to the child, slapping its back lightly. "Breathe for me, daughter!" With a rattling gasp, the baby took a stuttering breath. Then another. Finally, its thin cry wavered through the room and Tess lifted the infant to where Glory could see her. "It's a girl!" she cried happily. But Glory was past hearing her; the laudanum had taken hold.

Through the night, Tess sat up alongside Glory and her child, only occasionally drifting into light slumber. After a difficult first few hours, the baby seemed to settle into life reluctantly. Glory bled badly after the birth, but Tess packed her with pads of herbs. She had not awakened, not even to see her child.

Sometime in the darkest hours, Tess woke suddenly with a strange feeling that someone had called her name. She glanced to the bed quickly, but Glory was still and oblivious. The child slept undisturbed. The wind was less boisterous outside the house, and she sensed that the storm was passing. She settled back into her chair, but sleep would not come. Finally, she rose and went to the window, and almost before the moon moved through the clouds, she knew what she would see.

In a patch of moonlight that wavered from the shadows of trees, a woman stood and gazed up at the house. Wrapped in light gray linens, she was tall and thin as a sapling. Her hair fell round her face, scarcely moving though the wind should have whipped it along with the trees. The long cloak fell back from her body as she swayed to and fro, and Tess gasped. It was the *bean-nighe,* come round again. The banshee of the dead.

As Tess stood transfixed at the window, the gray figure below opened her mouth wide and crooned a low, melancholy tune, her eyes never leaving the window. The song was unbearably sad, one of great loss and doleful tidings, yet not a word could Tess comprehend. The tune alone broke her heart. Tess reached quickly inside her bodice for the locket. Whypin's locket. The talisman that held her mother's hair and had turned aside the *bean-nighe* once before. She held it aloft so that the banshee could see it, calling out softly, "Go away, old one. No one wants you here."

But this time, the banshee did not fade into the rain. She stood resolutely, staring at the house, singing her song above the noise of the wind and rain. Tess felt a cold hand on her shoulder, and she whirled, her breath frozen in a startled gasp. Nothing in the room. No movement from the bed.

She hurried to Glory's side and sought the pulse at her neck. No sense of life throbbed under her fingers. She frantically pulled back the covers and reeled in horror. Under the quilt, Glory had completely soaked the linens with blood in a large circle under her and out to both edges of the bed.

"Glory!" Tess called, yanking her up at the shoulders and calling her over and over, lightly slapping her face. But Glory's skin was cool, her pallor unmistakable. While Tess had slept, her sister had quietly bled to death.

Tess whirled to the window. The banshee was gone.

Back again to the bed, lifting Glory's head into her arms, rocking her against her breasts, crying out and calling to her to no avail. After long moments with no response, Tess dimly became aware that the infant in her basket had awakened and was softly crying. As though she somehow sensed a loss, if not the magnitude.

Tess gently laid Glory back on the bed and went to her daughter, picking her up and cradling her, squeezing her eyes shut with the pain. The baby opened blue eyes and stared at Tess in abject wonder, as if she had never seen a face so close before. She locked on Tess's gaze and held it, entranced. Tess began to weep then, rocking the child close to her, easing back into the chair to sit until dawn, lost in the vision of Glory's lovely face, composed now and peaceful with death.

❦ ❦ ❦

Of course, Jack and the children had to be told the truth. Hurt and angry, he rejected the child, but Tess only said quietly, "She is all I have now of Glory. We will raise her as our own, and she will have whatever love you can give her. For my part, I will give her everything I would have given my sister." He finally subsided, but Tess knew he might never forgive her deception. Or the child.

The boys were surprised and saddened by their Aunt Glory's passing, but willingly accepted that they had a new baby sister if their mother said so. Severn stared at the child carefully and said, "She doesn't look much like Aunt Glory, I don't think. I wonder if she'll be pretty as she was." She reached out and gingerly touched the infant's soft auburn hair. "Poor orphan girl. What will you call her?"

"I've named her Della. I think Glory would have liked that."

Severn eyed her mother carefully before she spoke again. "Did she suffer much?" she asked quietly.

Tess shook her head. "She slipped away in her sleep."

"Did the father of the baby love her at all?"

Tess shrugged. "I cannot say."

Severn's eyes narrowed. "You don't know, or you can't say?"

"I don't know."

She chose her next words carefully. "Do you know who the father was?"

"No. Does it matter?"

She turned back to the infant and appraised it. Her smile was gentle, but her voice was surprisingly hard. "She looks like Caroline did at her age, I believe."

Tess glanced up at Severn in surprise. "Well. I suppose she does. She might take after our mother, after all."

Severn was quiet. Finally she said only, "Yes. I suppose that's logical."

Tess let Severn see her take the locket from round her neck and place it from the spindle of the baby's cradle so that it hung low enough for her to see. "She shall have this for good luck, at least," she murmured. "It always brought me good fortune."

Severn watched her mother carefully, a thoughtful frown on her face. Without another word, she walked away from the cradle and the sleeping infant within.

Part Two

❦ ❦ ❦

1770—1820

"There was an old lady lived over the sea,
And she was an Island Queen;
Her daughter lived off in a new country,
With an ocean of water between,
The old lady's pockets were full of gold,
But never contented was she,
So she called on her daughter to pay her a tax
Of three pence a pound on her tea
Of three pence a pound on her tea.
The tea was conveyed to her daughter's door,
All down by the ocean's side,
And the bouncing girl poured out every pound
In the dark and boiling tide.
And then she called out to the Island Queen,
'Oh Mother, dear Mother,' quoth she,
'Your tea you may have when 'tis steeped enough,
But never a tax from me.' "

a popular colonial song in 1773

🌿 🌿 🌿

The Lower Cape Fear was spangled with sails in 1770. Sleek schooners and sloops carried goods from the Caribbean, larger brigantines served New England, and three-masted ships and two-masted snows worked the Atlantic crossing. Brunswick was the center of naval stores; Wilmington the capitol of lumber production, trading wares for slaves, spices, West Indian sugar, and all the finished products from the Mother Country that every planter prized.

Jonathan Dunbibin's ready money store at the Wilmington market welcomed shoppers who came by post chaises down the Brunswick road or along the highway that now passed through the forests all the way to Bath and Edenton. For thirty miles upriver and down from Wilmington, wide plantations with names like Orton, Grovely, and Hilton spread lushly back from the water.

The French and Indian War was over, giving England twice the land and thrice the public debt. To King George III and his Parliament it seemed reasonable to expect that the colonies should help pay the costs of their defense and new real estate, but Cape Fear merchants and planters thought otherwise. They had sent militia and paid their war dues, but they saw no reason to import British Redcoats to patrol the horizons of Ohio.

The Stamp Act passed by Parliament opened the rift; Wilmington responded by refusing to land Stamped vessels in her harbor, a full ten years before the Declaration of Independence. Then the Regulators, Carolina's homegrown Sons of Liberty, began their insurrection against illegal taxes levied by local collectors, clerks, and sheriffs. A hotspur faction of farmers, they were eventually defeated by Governor William Tryon's militia in 1771 at the Battle of Alamance, a loss that only further whetted Carolinian appetitites for revolution.

All the while, English manor life thrived along the Lower Cape Fear, and huge tracts of rice, tobacco, and indigo made planters rich and the slave trade imperative.

When Parliament again tried to tax the colonists with the Townshend Acts and the Tea Act, North Carolina formed the first Committee of Correspondence and Sam Adams's "Indians" tossed a cargo of tea worth fifteen thousand pounds sterling into the Boston Harbor. Parliament retaliated by closing Boston Harbor to all English ships. The Carolinas promptly confiscated the Diana out of London and sent her cargo to Boston as a gift.

Such actions created the illusion that Carolinians were united in their revolutionary fervor, but ever stubbornly independent, they could not agree even on a common enemy. On the Lower Cape Fear, wealthy planters feared the loss of the slave trade; in the western mountains, rural settlers feared the Cherokees; and in between, the Highland Scots, the Irish, and the Germans feared each other.

But what most of the factions feared more was King George's "New Colonial Policy," and the tankards clanked hard on Wilmington tavern boards as they declared that Americans were the sons, not the bastards, of England.

🌿 🌿 🌿

Tess buttoned the black bombazine mourning frock up under her chin, wishing for the tenth time that morning that Jack could be alive again, if only for a few hours. She glanced in the glass and gave a quick swipe to her wispy hair, smoothing it flat against her temples. Della would no doubt be wearing the latest London fashion, with her hair done up in some impossibly elaborate curls—well, at twenty, that was fine.

If only her mother could see Della today, how proud she would be!

Tess sighed happily. She was very fortunate, indeed. The house and a comfortable estate would see her the rest of her days, thanks to Jack's practical turn of mind; she had Severn for company, though why the girl hadn't accepted one of her many suitors was beyond her.

Security and companionship, she smiled to herself, the two most necessary armaments for a contented old age. Tess leaned a little closer to the glass. She was in fine fettle really, given her sixty-five years, and grateful for every one of them. Her skin was actually not much more withered than Severn's, yet it was a quarter of a century older. Less color perhaps. Everything faded at this age, even smallpox scars. That was a blessing, too. She turned eagerly as Severn came into the room.

"Do you think she'll be much changed?" Tess asked her daughter, noting quickly that Severn had not chosen her newest, most fashionable frock. Well, perhaps it did not matter anyway, since they were still in mourning—

"I should say so." Severn nodded, straightening a pleat on her mother's gown with a proprietary air. "We haven't seen her since Father's funeral. From seventeen to twenty is an eon in a girl's life. I *hope* she's changed, at least. She has always been fairly badly spoiled, it's time she grew up."

"Dear, what about that sweet bonnet I brought you from Charleston last year, the one with the cutwork about the edge? It would be perfectly appropriate, I think, and—"

"Mother, I don't care a fig about impressing Della."

Tess stopped short, bewildered. "Well, I only thought that it looked so lovely on you, Severn."

"In fact, I would hope that by now Della is a little more serious about life in general. She's a grown woman now, and whether or not I wear the latest fashion in bonnets should concern her very little."

Tess glanced at her daughter and then away. Of course, Severn was jealous. It was understandable. Nearly forty, she was no longer as fresh and beautiful as she once was, though she was still a striking woman with a dignified grace, and still sought after by several excellent men of the county . . . but Della. Della was another prize altogether.

She *was* spoiled, it was true, but she was also exciting and funny and wondrously poised for her age. Della was a bird of paradise next to Severn's simple robin-brown demeanor. Tess could certainly recall what that felt like, growing up alongside Glory. She felt a quick stab of pity for Severn and then brushed it away. Her daughter would never acknowledge the need for such emotion, no matter what or from whom.

Tess picked up her skirts and moved briskly for the door. "Well, I must see to the refreshments. I know she'll be ravenous and then no doubt she'll want to rest before she receives visitors." She called back over her shoulder to Severn, "My pearl cameo would be perfect with that frock, it's in my jewel case on the top shelf—" and left her daughter to her own devices, already resigned to the almost certain fact that Severn would not in any way enhance her costume.

When Della's carriage arrived, Tess was the first to greet her, sweeping her into the house eagerly with a fond embrace. "My dear, you've grown so beautiful!" she cried, pulling her into the parlor where Severn waited. "Severn, here's our Della, home at last!"

Severn rose and embraced Della warmly, murmuring her welcome, and then added, "Child, you've shot up like a cane stalk since we saw you last."

Della extricated herself from Severn's arms and did a short pirouette before them both. "Yes, I know, I can scarcely believe it myself. Mother wasn't especially tall, was she, Aunt Tess?"

Tess shook her head, not trusting her voice. Della had become the image of her father, at least from what Tess could recall of him. In her face blended the lush beauty of Glory's features and the dark, almost leonine look of a rake of Charleston. It was a singularly arresting combination of loveliness and a certain predatory danger. Della was too young to wear it as well as she would in the years to come, Tess knew. But her body was ripe and powerful under her tight corset and the yards of expensive cherry sateen, and when she turned, she obviously enjoyed their gaze.

"No, she wasn't," Tess said, "but our father was a tall man. Perhaps you take after his side of the family."

Severn glanced at her mother curiously, but she said only, "That's a lovely frock, Della. Is that what they're wearing now in London?"

"Yes, this color's the rage this season. Of course, every woman will wear it, whether or not she has the complexion for it. 'Cerise,' they call it, and it can make a girl look stunning or half dead, as if she's not slept for a week."

"Well, it suits you perfectly," Tess soothed her, noticing that she also wore the gold filigreed locket prominently on her bosom. She led her to the chair and the platter of cakes and tarts she had waiting. "You must be hungry and tired, dear, sit and relax now—"

"I'm not the least bit tired, Aunty, and if I eat all those pretty cakes, I'll never get into my wedding dress."

Tess pulled her hand away as though she'd been stung. Severn gasped and said, "Wedding dress!"

Della laughed delightedly at their shock, a silvery trill that almost made Tess shiver, so much did it remind her of Glory. "Yes, I know it's a terrible surprise, and I'm ashamed I've not written you about it, both of you, but it's all happened so suddenly, and I knew I'd be coming soon to tell you in person—"

"Who is he?" Severn asked mildly, as though she were hardly interested at all.

"Married! Why, Della, you're hardly out of school! You've only just come home! We don't even know this man!"

Della sat down carefully, adjusting her skirts about her. "I know, Aunty, it's sudden as a hurricane, but there it is. His name is Phillip Gage," she said, with a nod to Severn, "and I met him in London while he was there on business. I was invited to dine at the home of a friend, and there he was! Imagine my surprise to discover a neighbor so far away—"

"A neighbor?" Severn asked.

"He's the master of Deepwater, a plantation just upriver."

"I know this man," Severn spoke to Tess as though Della were not in the room. "He's a rice planter, you know the place up from Grovely? His mother's people were Grenvilles." She looked then at Della. "He's a Loyalist."

"Most I met in London were," Della said, a little coolly. "Does that matter?"

"A great deal," Severn said, "if you intend to make your home here."

"A small band of treasonous farmers can scarcely be reason to forsake a vow of betrothal," Della answered with the full dignity of a woman twice her age.

"Is that what they're saying in London?" Severn laughed ruefully. "Let me assure you, dear, these are neither farmers nor small in number. Most of the most powerful men in Wilmington are Patriots, and not a few of the women." She glanced at Tess and then raised her chin a bit higher. "I'm proud to tell you that both your Aunt Tess and I count ourselves among them."

Della stared at them both for a moment and then dimpled. "Well, that's fine, I daresay! Surely there's room for a difference of opinion in any family. The king will shortly grant some sort of amnesty to those who rebelled, Parliament will repeal the taxes or whatever is offending people, and life will go on as normal. In the meantime, Phillip has asked for my hand, and I intend to give it to him."

"You can't be so ignorant," Severn said quietly, "as you pretend. Not of the situation, that is."

"Severn," Tess admonished quickly, "that's enough. Della has been in England now for three years, she can't possibly understand your feelings."

"*Our* feelings."

"Yes. Our feelings." Tess turned to her niece with what she hoped was a conciliatory smile. "Much has changed, dear, since your last visit."

"Indeed," Della said, her voice still cool and light. "My cousin hasn't changed a whit. She still is just as glad to see me as ever."

The silence hung in the room like a heavy curtain.

Tess went on bravely, "There may be some difficulty in Master Gage's political opinions, dear, for the vast majority of our friends are Patriots, of course, and—"

"And none of that has a thing to do with me," Della concluded firmly. "Phillip Gage is a gentleman of fine appearance and no small fortune, and I shall marry him within the month."

"He's a rake," Severn said clearly.

Tess almost groaned aloud, but Della scarcely acknowledged by any more than a flicker of her fixed smile that she had heard. She rose gracefully to her feet. "I find that I am a bit more weary than I thought, Aunty. I believe I'll lie down awhile, if you'll excuse me." She swept out of the room, her head high and her gaze set determinedly on the door.

The moment she was out of sight, Tess sighed and sank down into the chaise beside her daughter. "Why did you do that?" she asked Severn wearily.

"Because I feared you would not," Severn said, and she, too, rose and swept from the room to the stairs.

❦ ❦ ❦

That night, Della did not come down to supper. Tess waited as long as she felt she could and then she knocked gently on her niece's door with a tray. The long silence within made her recall Glory's locked door, and she held her breath.

When Della came at last to let her in, she was almost flustered at the girl's loveliness. Della wore a silk wrapper of black and yellow, patterned like a wasp's belly. Her dark hair tumbled down her shoulders, and her crisp black brows were high and arched against her white skin, as though she were perpetually skeptical. Tess could not read her expression, but her tone was cordial enough. She entered and set down the tray.

"Now, Della, I know you must be hungry after your long trip, and you mustn't let Severn upset you like this. She didn't mean what she said—"

"Of course she did, Aunty," Della said firmly. "Severn never says anything frivolously." She uncovered the tray and surveyed the cakes, meats, and custards Tess had crowded together for her. She took up a lemon cake, split it neatly in two, and put one-half in her mouth, gesturing with one hand full. "But she can't hurt me anymore. I'm marrying Phillip, and that's all there is to it."

"Well, of course, there's far more to it than that," Tess said gently. "There always is, dear."

"Not for me," Della said defiantly, stuffing the rest of the cake in her mouth. "Why should I listen to her anyway? All my life, she's disapproved of me. And I have no earthly idea why."

"That's not true, Della, your cousin loves you—"

"Perhaps," Della said shortly, "but love me or not love me, she hasn't liked me very much for a long time."

"Now, Della—"

"Stop it!" Della turned and shouted at Tess. "Just tell me the truth! Why does Severn look at me as though she expected me to grow horns at any moment? Is it because I'm a bastard?"

Tess looked down at her hands, dismayed.

"That is what they call my state of life, I know, Aunty," Della said contemptuously, "though no one has ever said it to my face."

"Oh, Della, that's not it," Tess said sadly.

Della picked up another cake, eyed it, then placed it back down deliberately. She crossed her arms as if to hold them still.

"I guess she's always wondered about your father," Tess began rather haltingly.

"What's to wonder?" Della said. "He came, he saw, he conquered. He left my mother with a problem and she left me with a bigger one."

"I guess she's always wondered who he was, truly."

Della's eyes narrowed. "I was always told that was unimportant."

"Well, to Severn it was important, I suppose." Tess looked up at Della reluctantly. "I think she wonders if her father was your father, too."

Della's mouth opened in surprise. "Father Dobbs?"

Tess nodded miserably. "She all but asked me several times, and I often saw the suspicion in her eyes. But it's not true."

"You never told her that?"

"She never asked."

Della's jaw firmed. "So I lived all my life with her suspicion because she never asked and you never answered?"

Tess shrugged. "I don't know for sure, of course, but I do think that's the cause of her occasional . . . ill feelings."

"Occasional! It's been all my life, Aunty!" She turned and paced the floor once. "Are you certain what she suspicions was not true after all?"

Tess turned a shocked look to Della. "As certain as I am of who your mother was, I'm that certain of who your father was *not*."

Della stared at Tess a long moment with a look of vague remembering, as though she was flipping through a mental scrapbook of her past. Finally she said, "Well, then. At least I know. The question is, did Gloriana betray her own sister? Did Father Dobbs take her to his bed in his own house?" She shook her head ruefully. "And Severn wonders if I'm her half-sister instead of her cousin. And that doubt alone is enough to make her so . . ." She snorted in fine disdain. "I should think if you were able to love and accept me, Aunt Tess, surely it's little business of hers. So that's why she hates me."

Tess stood abruptly, taking Della's hands. "That's not true at all, dear, and you know it. Think back to the times when you two have been fine friends. Never say that again, she has *never* hated you and never will. But she only sometimes feels . . . confused, I suppose."

"She is confused about a good many things, Aunty, and I'm only the least of them." Della took her hands gently from Tess, sitting down and pushing the tray away. "Let's not speak of it again, though. Severn will do as she feels best, and so will I. Regardless of her opinions, political or otherwise, I will marry Phillip at Deepwater within the month." She gave Tess a sad smile. "I would like your blessing, of course, and Severn's, too. You're the only mother I've ever had. But with or without it, I shall marry."

Tess thought in that instant how much Della looked like Glory with her jaw out and her eyes shining with determination. "I loved your mother more than anyone else in this world," Tess said quietly. "More than my own mother, more than my husband. You are all I have left of her, and so of course you have my blessing. It's little enough I can give you, child."

Della dimpled suddenly, almost impishly. She held up the locket between two delicate fingers. "You gave me luck, Aunty. Wrapped it around my throat like a benediction, so I'm told, and that's no small gift. I scarcely need much else." She stood and embraced Tess. "Except one small thing."

"Anything."

"Keep Severn away from me with her opinions about Phillip and everything else under the sun. Else I fear my tongue will run away with itself."

Tess sighed ruefully. "I have no more say over Severn's tongue than I do yours, my dear. But now tell me all about your adventures in England!"

Della laughed delightedly. "I vow, Aunt Tess, I think you enjoyed my escapades as much as I did, your letters were so filled with excitement for me—"

"I always wanted to go abroad, I can still remember my mother's yearning for London. I was born in West Kent, you know, in the village of Maidstone."

"So you never tired of telling us. You always wanted to go back, I remember you saying it. Why did you never make the voyage? Father Dobbs surely would have allowed it."

Tess shook her head. "Not in my day. Women alone, even matrons, could scarcely venture alone so far, and your uncle was unwilling to take so much time from the sea lanes. But you, my dear! To be able to go to an academy abroad! Even for just a few years—to travel to London alone!''

"Not quite alone," Della said dryly. "Who can forget the inimitable Mistress Manhollow?"

"The best chaperone in Wilmington," Tess said firmly, "and a refined gentlewoman as well."

"Refined she may have been, but Aunt Tess, the woman snored worse than Methuselah!''

Tess laughed. "Severn and I so enjoyed your descriptions of her, dear. Your letters made all the rounds, I must say. We must hope poor Mistress Manhollow never learns that half the ladies in Wilmington are intimately familiar with her sleeping habits.''

"I hope one of them asks her one day if it's true she can rattle windows at a hundred paces." Della giggled.

"Severn's right," Tess groaned, "you are simply dreadful! But now tell me, of all the sights you enjoyed, which one thrilled you the most?''

Della sighed happily. "There was one day, Aunty, which I shall remember till the day I die, I hope. We were visiting the birthplace of William Shakespeare, a lovely little village on the Avon River. Mistress Manhollow had stayed back at the keep, since the ladies of the academy were to go in a group and we numbered eight of us, all told." She closed her eyes for a moment as though feeling the memory on her skin like sunshine. "It was a warm afternoon, and the carriages were hot and dusty. We stopped outside the bard's home, and before we were taken inside to see it, we walked to the edge of the river and sat beneath a low-hanging willow in the shade. The innkeeper's woman brought us a pitcher of cool tea with mint, and the river smelled like green moss and meadow grass, and I thought then, as I sat there, that three hundred years of poets had perhaps sat where I sat and watched the waters move by." Her voice was dreamy and soft, her face as lovely as Tess had ever seen her. "In that moment, I felt so very small. And America felt so provincial and far away. England seemed like the very birthplace of everything decent and fine and good about man.''

"I envy you that memory," Tess said quietly. "It sounds like the most beautiful spot in the world."

"Oh, I saw so many wonderful things and had so many gay adventures!" Della said, the spell broken now. "I can never thank you enough for sending me abroad. I know many young women whose fathers are richer than Uncle must make do with the female academy in Jamestown, if they are schooled at all. And even Severn never crossed the Atlantic!"

"Severn never wished to," Tess said simply. "And of course, when she was your age, young women still did not travel, with or without chaperone. But you, my dear, live in fortunate times. Now," she added gently, "you must tell me all about this young man of yours."

Della blushed winningly. "You will like him, Aunt Tess. He's handsome and dashing, tall as Noah with broader shoulders, the blackest hair, and a smile that looks as though he knew a secret—a secret you've always wanted to know and never could discover."

Tess noticed that Della did not choose to speak first, as many young women might have, of the man's property or family. She smiled privately to herself, remembering the nights she had yearned for Jack Dobbs. "Is he a good man?" she asked carefully. "A kind man? For everything else will come or not come to you, child, if Fate wills it. But will he treat you well? That is the main thing."

"He loves me," Della said firmly. "And I love him."

Tess smiled. "Well, then. I can only be joyful for you. I am not so old that I cannot recall those feelings."

"Yes," Della murmured, "you loved Father Dobbs, I know. Even right before he died, I could see that in your eyes and hear it when you said his name."

The two women were silent for a moment, recalling the man who was gone. "Did Severn never feel such for a man?" Della finally asked. "I have always wondered."

"I think so, once or twice," Tess said. "But you know Severn, she keeps her own counsel."

Della nodded. "Even when we were cousins in the same house, I scarcely seemed to know her."

"Well, of course, she was a young woman when you were born—"

"Still, we were closer until Caroline died. Once she was gone, it was as though Severn would not risk investing herself in another young girl again."

"I remember wondering," Tess added sadly, "if Severn was even more heartbroken than I was when the fever took her sister. I had others to love, of course. I mourned, but I survived. But she

seemed never to be quite the same again, once Caroline was buried.''

"She was never the same to me," Della said. "I remember it,
still, more than a dozen years ago. Oh, she was kind to me, but she
never took me down to the river to play anymore, never sat and
read books with me as she used to. Caroline seemed to take most
of her heart with her when she passed.''

Tess leaned over and hugged Della fiercely. "I am so happy for
you, child,'' she whispered. "I hope you are as happy with your
Phillip as I was with my Jack. Life does not afford a woman any
keener satisfaction than that.''

Deepwater plantation spread out from the river like a green
satin fan, the lighter green of new rice flanking both sides like soft
lace. The big house, built by Phillip's father before he was killed in
a duel in Charleston, was a two-story frame building with four
chimneys, a deep overhung roof, and wide verandas, upstairs and
down, wrapping round the house and held up by six pillars. It was
not the most gracious house on the Cape Fear, Tess thought as their
ferry skiff approached the Gage dock, but it was imposing in rather
a severe way. It looked as though it could use a woman's touch.

Della will do much good here, she told herself. There was no
need to share her thoughts with Severn. She had scarcely said a
pleasant word since they left Wilmington. Ten miles upriver, she
still acted as though she'd rather be doing the washing than seeing
her little cousin married on a lovely spring evening. Tess vowed to
ignore her daughter's mood, as she usually did if allowed to do so,
and she nodded pleasantly to the black footman who helped them
alight and then put them inside one of the waiting carriages. The
dock was aswarm with skiffs and pirogues, and friends and neighbors leaned out waving and calling to one another as their boatmen
jostled for space.

Severn said, "Looks like she invited half the county," but her
eyes were curious and her mouth softer about the edges.

Tess squeezed her hand eagerly. "I doubt she did the inviting,''
she murmured. "From what I hear, I don't suppose the Gages
would let their eldest son marry without a certain amount of fan-

fare. I'm sure Madame Gage—she's still alive, you know, though I understand she rarely goes out anymore from her home in Charleston—anyway, I'm sure his mother has been received in every fine home on the river."

"He better enjoy it now," Severn said archly, making no attempt to keep her words from the driver. "Once war breaks, no Patriot will step on his land with any intention other than to arrest the man and confiscate his goods."

Tess turned on Severn sternly. "Now, I'll not have another word out of you today in that tone. This is a wedding, not a political meeting, and your little cousin deserves this chance at happiness. Goodness knows, she's had little enough of it in her life, Severn, do you begrudge her this joy? No father, no mother—"

"Yes, yes, you needn't recite the litany of Della's woes to me, Mother. Poor Della must be forgiven her selfishness and her carelessness and her willfulness—"

"And her beauty."

Severn narrowed her eyes at her mother. "Which is, of course, in the eye of the beholder. But regardless, she must be indulged and coddled because of the pathos of her birth. Well, I do hope Phillip Gage is a more clever man than he is discreet, or she will surely eat him up alive."

Tess glared fiercely at her daughter and turned to look out the window, vowing to ignore her and enjoy herself no matter what. "I believe I shall dance this evening," she finally said, low and defiantly as if to herself. "It's been too long."

Severn laughed ruefully and shook her head. "By all means, Mother. Della would certainly approve."

Della watched them alight in a flock of carriages, instantly picking out Tess and Severn among a crowd of well-dressed, merry guests. "They're here," she said to her woman, Bathsheba, pulling back from the second-story window. Now that Tess and Severn had arrived, there was no more reason to watch. No one else who was coming meant a farthing to her, and in fact, she'd be happy enough when this whole day was over and done, and she could be alone with Phillip.

Bathsheba gently pulled her to the dressing table and sat her down before the boudoir mirror, crooning that creaky old tune she always sang halfway down her throat. She handled Della like a skittish filly; Della knew it, and the deft manipulations still worked. The slave was older by half, taller by nearly a head, and had the dignity of her Biblical namesake. No one but Della got away with calling her, "Sheba," and she loved no one else in the house. It had been that way since Phillip gave her the slave the night they were engaged.

"She's yours till the day she dies," he had told Della, ushering the woman out of the darker shadows. "She'll take care of you better than your own mama would have."

Della had looked in the black woman's eyes and saw there intelligence, calm, and a certain sure knowing. This one can keep secrets, she told herself, and she accepted Phillip's betrothal gift with pleasure.

Now, Bathsheba began to comb and brush Della's hair with expert hands, plaiting and rolling and pinning the dark, heavy curls into some vision she had in her mind's eye.

"I don't want it too tall," Della said fretfully, fussing at her brows with the charcoal pencil.

"I knows how you wants it," Bathsheba said serenely, and her hands never left Della's hair.

It had taken Bathsheba three hours to bathe, anoint, perfume, paint, and dress Della for her wedding day. She did nothing twice, and she never seemed to hurry. When she finally finished with Della's hair, she led her to the glass and stood slightly behind her, smiling at her mistress.

"You never be more beautiful," she said, her black eyes glowing.

Della slowly smiled at her reflection. She wore the ivory Brussels lace lent to her by Phillip's mother, and Bathsheba had woven seed pearls through her dark hair like stars against a dark sky. Her skin looked as pale as the wedding dress, with just the faintest blush about her cheeks and temples. "I hope he thinks so."

"He make you happy, Miz Della?" the slave murmured.

Almost, it was as though her own heart asked the question rather than Bathsheba. "Supremely." Della sighed. "He makes me feel . . . powerful." She blushed then. "In a womanly sort of way, of course." And then she realized that she had been speaking far too intimately to a servant, and her voice grew more formal. "I expect it will be a good partnership."

"You goin' do de obey?" Bathsheba asked her, bending on one

quick knee to adjust the ribbon that scalloped the edge of her gown.

Della watched her, thinking. They'd all heard of a wedding last month that still had the county wits laughing behind their hands. When during the service the minister instructed the bride to repeat the promise to obey, she replied, "No obey." When a second and a third time he repeated this part of the ceremony, she answered, each time more loudly and emphatically, "No obey!" Finally the minister realized the futility of his efforts, and he nudged the bridegroom, who rolled his eyes to heaven as if for guidance. They went on with the rest of the ritual, leaving the guests murmuring for days. Della had said often enough, usually when only Bathsheba could hear, that she thought that bride had more sense than most.

"I haven't decided yet," she said finally.

Bathsheba glanced up with raised brows. "You dasn't do to Massa Phillip what dat girl do to her man. He be shamed 'for de whole county."

"I should think a man would be ashamed to ask such a thing in this day and age—"

"Dey ask, an' you answer. Up to you if you do what you say after de first babe come."

"Oh, Sheba, you're always talking like the birth of a child turns the whole marriage on its ear," Della said, a little impatiently. Would this day never be over?

"Not on de ear," the black woman said solemnly, "boot over bum, an' never walk quite right again. Leastwhys, not de same way."

Della heard Phillip's voice then, coming up the stairs closer, and she shushed Bathsheba, bade her rise, and turned to greet her bridegroom, all thoughts of rebellion gone for the moment. When he entered her chamber, Della thought to stand for a moment and let him admire her. She wanted to see the pride and pleasure in his eyes. But when she saw him, she ran to him and embraced him fiercely, wanting only his arms about her, wishing to hide her cheeks on his chest, heedless of her dignity, the watching slave, and even of the missed opportunity to be desired.

The next few hours were to become a whirl of giddy impressions in Della's memory. She curtsied to at least a hundred new people, blushed at the toasts, accepted the cool cheek kisses of a score of scented, finely dressed women, the heartfelt hug of Tess and the doleful-eyed blessing of Severn, withstood the solemn kiss of Phillip's mother, stood before the minister and spoke her vows—completely—in a clear and firm voice, then was whisked away for a round of dancing and drinking, food pressed into her hand, her flowers crushed against her waist, Phillip's arms around her briefly, then again the arms of a stranger, only to be reclaimed and released again and again.

A few times, reality threatened to intrude into the evening. When she heard an occasional snatch of conversation, it seemed to be almost all about war. But she wouldn't allow it. In any group she entered, she laughed them away from the subject, to any dancing partner, she teased them both out of harm's way and brushed aside his political opinions. Once, when she was more nervous and wearied than she'd thought, she almost cursed a man for insistently asking her new husband's thoughts on Parliament's latest folly, some stamp act or another, but she held her temper in check, dismissed him gaily, and found another partner in an instant.

A few signal instants stood out in her vision when she scrolled back her memory later that night. She remembered the feel of Phillip's shoulder as he stood next to her before the minister, in a crowded parlor with only a quarter of the guests able to squeeze inside. The heat was stifling, the weight of the dress, of her hair, of the lace, made her want to reel, but the stolid wall of him leaning into her gave her strength. She felt the solid power of his body through his wedding coat, and she wanted always to remember that.

Another instant: Tess caught her eye as she danced the first dance in her husband's arms, and she could have sworn the old woman winked at her—almost as if she knew what awaited her in her marriage bed! Della was startled and amused all at once and just for that moment, saw her Aunt Tess in a new light. She, too, had been married to a man whom others might have scorned. She, too, had chosen for herself and locked the bedroom door behind her.

A final instant: waving goodbye to the guests as their carriages departed, her arm through her husband's arm, the sun setting gold and purple behind them and upriver, then turning to go back inside . . . with the full power of the realization making her feet almost burn with triumph. These steps, these pillars, this house, these lands, they are mine. Mine to share with my beloved, but mine.

❧ ❧ ❧

The wedding trip to Charleston was Della's first inkling that her marriage might not be one of surpassing harmony. Oh, Phillip was attractive enough, that much was certain. She noticed that many women watched him behind their fans, from under their bonnets, as he strode about the ship from Wilmington down the coast, some even going so far as to speak to him gaily, letting the flush come up in their cheeks.

She could scarcely blame them. He was tall enough to satisfy most women's desire to feel protected without being clumsy. He wore his yellow coat tailored to fit his body, a torso of broad shoulders and a strong neck. His hair was black, his nose narrow, and his lips full and expressive as a young boy's. There was an air of jaunty skepticism about his smile, and Della on his arm did not seem to diminish his appeal. Yet she made certain she was on his arm whenever she could, Bathsheba trailing close behind. Della had heard enough about Charleston ladies to make her wary.

It was his temper and his moods that she noticed first, his sardonic sense of humor that both amused and pricked her concern. So long as he was laughing at *others*, she reasoned all would be well, but if he ever turned that wit to her expense . . .

When they arrived in Charleston, the carriage took them directly to their hotel, the Granville Broad overlooking the Cooper River. Once safely tucked into their suite, Della sent Bathsheba away and bounced on the wide bed like a young girl, laughing with pleasure at the luxury around them. Fine linens and colorful silk frocks were strewn about from their shopping trip, and a large box of elaborate chocolates lay open on the boudoir table. Phillip watched her bemusedly, his head cocked at an appraising angle.

"You act as though you've never been in a hotel before in your life," he said.

Della stopped instantly. There was something in his tone she had not heard before. A certain judging, the slightest condescension. She smiled, however, and rolled over so that her backside was to him, her wrapper slightly askew. "Well, certainly not with such a handsome gentleman," she purred.

"But with plenty enough who were neither handsome nor gentlemen?" he countered.

There was still that slight edge to his banter. She decided to end it here and now. "If *that* were true," she said a little coolly, "I certainly would never admit it now." But she smiled to take away the sting and patted the coverlet. "Come and lie beside me, my love."

He hesitated just a moment too long, she thought, but he finally did join her on the bed and take her in his arms. Phillip's ardor, she had already discovered, was at once passionate and calculating. He was able to lose himself in her, in her skin, her scent, her hair, and each and every bodily nook and cranny, with a sense of abandon that was powerful and contagious. At the same time, he was able to hold back his response, moving and twisting her every which way under him, never loosing his control until he decided it was time.

It was as though there were certain places he must touch, certain positions he must experience before he would allow himself that final pleasure. She admired his control, she supposed, but she also suspected it. In time, she vowed, I will teach him that he is not as in charge as he'd like to believe. But for now, she relished his touch too much to risk altering it.

He moved his mouth down on her breast slowly, deliberately torturing her with anticipation. When she squirmed and twisted, she felt his lips curve into a smile about her nipple. She reached down and trailed two soft fingers over his belly, sliding her hand inside his shirt and stroking down to his waist. His breathing changed, and she knew nothing would stop him now.

He drew back slightly and took her free hand, holding it down so that she could not tease him further with it. With his other hand, he drew a similar pattern on her skin as she drew on his. "Sometimes," he murmured, "you have to give it up, little girl. No matter how much you may not want to."

"Yes," she breathed, feeling only the sensation of his fingers on her skin.

"Sometimes," he continued, "a man must take what he wants."

"Yes." She altered the pattern of her touch now so that her fingers dropped lower, under his linen, to the side of his groin, scarcely touching him at all, grazing against him and feeling him twitch spasmodically and harden so quickly that it took her breath away.

He moved over her then and parted her legs with a skill and a confidence that she found irresistible, never allowing herself to wonder how he got so adept. As he slid only slightly within her, she moaned low in her throat, and he answered with a murmured growl, the private sound he always made for her as he took her.

Too soon, too soon, something whispered deep within her, he's inside of me too soon with too little preamble. And with a sudden shift of her hips, she dislodged him. He drew back and frowned at her.

"You didn't give me time," she murmured. "I need more time to . . . welcome you properly."

He grinned and pushed himself against her again, hesitating just outside her most delicate places. "I can wait," he said, his voice as firm and clear as though he spoke to his man across a patch of planted rice.

She chilled slightly at his arrogance and squeezed herself more tightly closed to him. She waited. He dropped his hand down to himself and began to try to slide himself within her again. Once more, she shifted her hips and kept him outside.

"Then do so," she said. This time, she moved slightly away from him so that he had to reach across the coverlet to retrieve her.

"Damn you, Della," he said suddenly, his voice coarse and graveled. But he pulled her back surely, with discernible tenderness, and held her as he stroked her into compliance.

Later, as she lay in his arms, his breath coming soft and regular, her head pillowed on his chest, she knew that she would be a worthy adversary for Phillip Gage.

And so would he be, for her.

🌿 🌿 🌿

Charleston was spoiling for war, it seemed, and managed to spoil her honeymoon trip, Della thought crossly, at every opportunity. No outing was complete without being blocked by rowdy parades of rebels and besieged by banners floating from the housetops. Strangers stopped one in the street, demanding that every man sign petitions against the king, and Phillip found it impossible to simply turn away; no, he must argue with every third solicitor about politics until she was thoroughly vexed with them all, including her husband. She finally learned to go on, Bathsheba holding her parasol over her curls, and exclaim over the nearest shop window and its delights, wondering aloud at the prices. That usually brought Phillip round quick enough.

And how the shining city-state of the South enchanted her. Proud, self-contained, and sophisticated, Charleston did not follow the rules, indeed, seemed to state that the rules did not apply within her environs. The stately houses did not face the street but their own private courtyards, like fine ladies turning a gracious shoulder to unwanted suitors. Charleston's famous promenade, the Battery, was lined with huge palms, oleander, and fragrant orange trees, so that strollers might be shaded while they watched the fleets of ships come in and out of the harbor.

With an air of the tropics rather than of London, Charleston was the richest city in all the colonies and one that took the most pleasure in shocking the prim-minded. Worshippers at St. Philip's were scarcely even surprised when their hot-tempered rector challenged another man of the cloth to a duel, but the news rocked Philadelphia, Boston, and New York.

It was the Charleston custom to have a newly-married couple visit every single friend and relation who'd been unable to attend the wedding as well as every one who had. Della found the visits entertaining and the attentions soothing, noting with satisfaction how many ladies barely masked their regret and envy that Phillip was now securely unavailable.

On the third day of visits, Phillip announced that they would be spending the morning with his brother, Stephen, who had a home on the outskirts of the city.

"Well, for heaven's sakes!" Della said, amazed. "You have a brother and I'm only just now hearing of him? Why wasn't he at the wedding? Why have we waited this long to see him?"

Phillip directed the driver to turn the carriage upriver, away from the center of Charleston. "Because he and I don't see eye to eye on much that matters, my dear."

"But still, he's your brother! Why, if I had a brother—"

"And he was as much a fool as mine, you'd never see him either."

She glared at her husband. It always annoyed her when he finished her sentences for her. "Actually," she said evenly, "fool or no, he'd always be my brother. Did you invite him to the wedding."

"I did."

"And he didn't come? Did he send his regrets?"

"He did."

"Well, then—"

"Della, just wait and meet him yourself," Phillip said with an edge of impatience. He squeezed her hand reassuringly. "You can decide what you think of him then."

The drive up the river out of Charleston soon diverted Della from all thoughts of Phillip's relations, amiable or otherwise. The land was low and somnolent, with long stretches of sand and moss-hung forests, clogged with clinging vines. When the woods opened up, she could see rice fields stretching vast and green away from the water. Lines of black slaves worked up to their knees in water among the young plants under the burning sun, and swarms of busy mosquitoes followed their carriage, as they followed anything that moved. Della tucked her veil more securely about her bosom, though she hated the scratchy thing next to her skin. Better to be scratched by netting than stung to a mottled mass.

After nearly an hour's drive, the carriage pulled down a road toward a tall house that flanked the river. Della was pleased to see that Stephen Gage had evidently not been as successful with his fields as his brother, for the house was nothing special to her eye. They descended the carriage and were greeted by an old black butler whose livery, Della thought, could have stood a good brushing. Phillip had said that his brother was not married, but a white woman opened the door to them and welcomed them eloquently, as though she were mistress of the house.

"Good afternoon!" she caroled to them, her arms open in greeting. "Welcome to Geneva!"

Della had smirked when she saw the name of the plantation on the sign out on the road and she could not restrain her smile now. Geneva, indeed. It was a good thing Bathsheba could not see this, she already put on airs aplenty.

To Phillip, she said, "Your brother is expecting you, sir, won't you and your bride please come into the parlor, and let me get you some refreshments—"

At that, a large man came round the corner, and when she heard his voice, the woman slipped away and disappeared. Stephen Gage extended his hand to his brother and bowed gracefully to Della. "I see you've met Judith. A fine woman; she takes care of me admirably."

Della flushed as she realized that she had just met Stephen's paramour. A woman who had all of the duties of wife and none of the privileges. Her heart went out to her instantly, and she had the sudden desire to pull her aside and discover her secrets. Surely, they would be asked to stay to supper—

As they exchanged pleasantries and arranged themselves comfortably in the sitting room, Della saw that Stephen Gage was very like his brother physically, no matter how they differed in their views. Stephen had the same certainty of command about him, the same gloss of manner. Almost more handsome than his brother, he smiled less easily and seemed more serious. Della glanced at her husband, stared at Stephen, and made the quick decision that Phillip was not the smartest son in the family.

The two brothers were speaking of the rice crop that year, generally bemoaning the difficulty of managing the slaves, the weather, and prices—the familiar litany that seemed to be necessary whenever two or more farmers gathered together, Della had noticed. Judith came and went with refreshments, and Della smiled at her winningly, hoping to entice her to sit down and speak, when suddenly, the tone between the two brothers altered significantly, and Della turned at the sound of anger in Phillip's voice.

"By God," he was saying to Stephen, "it's nothing but treason, man, no matter how you cloak it! Our father would have pistol-whipped a man who spoke to him as you do now to me!"

"Our father might have had good reason then, as I've good reason now. Times are different, Phillip, and you've got to open your eyes to that reality. England will never stop bleeding us out of the goodness of her heart, we're going to have to wrest our independence from her by force!"

Judith's face fell, and she scuttled out of the room so quickly that Della could not ask her to stay.

"I can see why those asses in the North want war, for their woolens and nankeens compete with London stuff, and Parliament won't stand for it. But England needs our rice, hell, welcomes it with open arms! The bounties Parliament put on shipments this year alone will make our fortunes, and now that the Spanish can't ship to London, tobacco prices'll go up, too. Let the North fight the King, if they're that big of fools in Boston, I say. The Carolinas have too much to be grateful for!''

"Grateful?" Stephen drawled silkily, his anger never more than a slow simmer. "Grateful that the bloodsuckers make us use English vessels instead of our own Carolina ships? Grateful that they stamp and tax us to death at every turn? I say, only Carolinians can tax Carolinians!''

"You sound one with the rabble in Wilmington who go about breaking windows, punching heads, and tar-and-feathering officers of the King! I had expected more from you, Stephen.''

"And I from you, Phillip," the younger man said firmly.

"Is this why you did not come to our wedding?" Della asked clearly in the silence. Both men turned to look at her as though they had only just recalled her presence.

Stephen bowed shortly. " 'Twas nothing personal, madame. I simply did not wish to seem to countenance Loyalist behavior by my presence.''

"As a matter of fact, some of the finest names in the county were there, of all political persuasions." Phillip's voice was edged with sarcasm. "I daresay, you weren't missed.''

Della gasped at her husband's rudeness, and she saw that Stephen's face whitened with controlled rage. He bowed shortly to his brother. "I shall leave you and your lovely bride now, to enjoy the refreshments Judith has prepared. She will show you out when you're ready to make your departure." He walked from the room, ignoring Phillip's angry shout, "Stephen!''

"Oh I wish you hadn't done that!" Della whispered sharply at Phillip. "It might have been fun to see the house at least!''

Her husband wasted no time getting Della bundled up, away from the refreshments and the muted apologies of Judith, bustling her out to the carriage almost roughly, giving her no chance to intercede or protest. As they drove down the long road back to the river highway, she kept angrily silent. She was wise enough to realize that any words she spoke would be as fuel to Phillip's fire, but she also knew—and vowed to remember—that her husband's temper had been just as responsible for the conflict between the brothers as their differing politics.

Phillip can be a bit of a fool, she found herself thinking as they rode silently back to Charleston. Once she was past the initial surprise of the revelation, it did not seem to her at all disloyal but rather a bit of practical self-defense to recognize such a fact about her husband.

ⓦ ⓦ ⓦ

They had not been back from their wedding trip a week but Severn came to call. Della recognized her carriage as it circled the drive slowly and called to Bathsheba to pull out her most elegant morning gown. She was laced and powdered and down to greet her cousin before she had her first cup of tea in her hand.

"Why, Severn, I'm so pleased you came by!" Della trilled as she swept into the breakfast room, noting quickly that her skirts made an agreeable susurration on the smooth mahogany floor.

Severn smiled with genuine warmth and stood to embrace Della. "Was Charleston wonderful?" she asked with what seemed to be sincere interest. "Did everyone greet you with open arms?"

Della pulled Severn down beside her and said in a confidential tone, "I can't think of a better place for a honeymoon." She was about to hint to Severn about the singular joy she and Phillip had shared when she recalled that her cousin was still a maiden. Strange to think of it, Della realized, when she seemed so matronly in her ways. Della began to tell tales about the people they had visited, the dresses she had fitted, but she gauged her words as she spoke, wondering all the while why Severn had come and when she would finally become bored enough with the chitchat to declare her mission.

When Severn at last asked, "Was there much talk of war in the city?" Della knew the reason for her call.

"Yes," she answered honestly, "Charleston does seem ready for it if it comes. But of course, few would speak of treason so openly to Phillip, knowing his sentiments."

Severn took up her cup and peered at Della over the rim, taking her time with her response. "And have you had a chance to assess those sentiments for yourself?"

Della stiffened slightly. "Do you mean, have I decided whether or not my husband is sincere?"

Severn smiled and set down her cup. "Not at all, dear. I know he's sincere. God knows, we're *all* as sincere as the plague. I mean, have you decided whether or not you can share his beliefs?"

Della shrugged. "I don't see that I have much choice, even if I wanted to. He is my husband, after all—"

"You have seen," Severn said quietly, "that even brothers do not always agree on these issues. The same may be said of husbands and wives."

Della gave a short, rueful laugh, wondering quickly how much Severn knew of Stephen and how she knew what she did. "Sounds to me as though you're advising anarchy in my own bedchamber. I should hate to poison such pleasurable pastures." Perhaps she could embarrass Severn to silence.

No such luck. Severn did not even produce the proper virgin's flush. "Della, I understand that you feel this is all rather a tempest in a teacup, but believe me, this tempest is going to draw you into the eye of the storm as surely as you sit and smile at me. Your husband is a Loyalist. The majority of his countrymen are Patriots. War *will* come, mark me well, and when it does any man who stands with the Brits will be ruined. And any woman hanging to his coattails. You have a choice, Della, at least for now. If you wait too long, you'll lose that option. You can make your sympathies to the Patriot cause public and save yourself and perhaps your husband in the bargain."

"You sound mighty sure of yourself, Severn. 'War *will* come, the rebels *will* win, and Phillip *will* be ruined.' Have you taken to reading tea leaves in your spare time?" Della did not bother to hide the disdain in her voice.

To her vast surprise, Severn only laughed. "You silly goose. I should have known better than to try and talk to you about something so serious. Stephen insisted, but I should have turned him down flat—"

"Stephen Gage?" Della felt something inside her open and turn upward, like a flower seeking light. "Stephen wanted you to talk to me? How do you know him?"

Severn shrugged. "Stephen and I have been rare friends for many years. Of late, our politics have brought us . . . closer. He was impressed by you, Della."

Della felt a flush begin up her neck, the flush that should by all rights have been creeping up Severn's neck instead. She sat up straighter. "I don't see why. I scarcely said a word the whole time we were there, scarcely had a *chance* to, the way Phillip and his brother instantly went to it, hammer and tongs."

"I doubt you'd need to say much to catch his eye," Severn murmured. "He felt you had more of substance than you were allowed to offer. But at any rate, he asked me to come to see you and tell you more about our cause than Phillip could tell you."

"In the hopes I'd betray my husband?"

"In the hopes you'd find the courage to chose justice over loyalty to a king who's long since forgotten any loyalty to you."

For the next hour, Severn spoke quietly and eloquently about the reasons sane men had finally, wrenchingly, come to act in ways that others might call treasonous. She took Della step by step, incident by incident, through the ways in which England had slowly strangled her colonies, building her case as carefully as any advocate, keeping her voice as clear of emotion as she could. Again and again, Della heard the names of men she had met in her father's house, had respected all of her life, and they all lined up on the opposite side of her husband's politics.

Finally, Della said evenly, "Well, you make a pretty case indeed. I have to say that this is not so simple as it first appears."

"Hardly anything ever is."

"I feel some sympathy, of course, to those who call for freedom." She smiled faintly. "It's always been a favorite call of mine, you know. But I feel I must be neutral, for Phillip's sake." She leaned back and crossed her arms over her bosom. "Really, Severn, what do you want from me? What can Stephen Gage expect, after all? I have no money of my own, even if I wanted to contribute to the Patriot cause. Everything I have belongs to Phillip."

"Your mind is your own, is it not? Your voice and your spirit still belong to you, no matter how married you are. We don't need money," Severn said soothingly. "We've plenty of that for now. But we may need your help later in other ways, not the least of which may be simply to save Phillip's life. If it is necessary to silence him or to get him out of the colony without his cooperation in order to protect him, can we count on you to help?"

"And Stephen sent you here for this?"

Severn nodded solemnly. "Whatever his politics, Stephen wants his brother safe."

Della sighed and put one hand over Severn's. "Tell Stephen he can count on me for that at least. If it comes to Phillip's life."

Severn leaned forward and embraced Della. "I am so happy to

hear you say this, dear. Stephen will be grateful. And I know Mother will be so relieved."

"Tess? Is Tess involved in all this conspiracy, too?" Della asked, amazed.

"Less now than before," Severn said, her voice regretful. "She's much more frail than she was, even last year. She wanted to join me today, but she wasn't strong enough for the trip."

"Aunt Tess?" Della was stricken at the sudden realization that Tess might not live forever. "But she seemed so well at the wedding—"

"Come and see her soon," Severn said firmly. "She'll be so pleased to hear of your change of heart."

"Well, of course I'll come soon, this week, in fact, but as to a change of heart, I don't know that you should tell her such a thing," Della began, but Severn stopped her with a soft hush.

"We needn't speak of these things anymore just now. You understand more about how things stand, Della. And that's all we wanted."

As Severn left that afternoon, Della stood on the wide veranda waving her farewell, a quizzical residue of bewilderment in her heart. What, exactly, had she promised to do? As she recalled Severn's words, she was unclear about much that was said. But then she shooed away her confusion. Severn had always been a bit of an old maid about life, even when she was young. Della could easily recall a dozen times when Severn attempted to be the mother she lacked, but always she became too bossy, too protective for Della to stomach her attentions for long.

And yet, she felt a strong bond to her cousin, as someone older, more fashionable, more glamorous, with all the secrets of a woman, yet still somehow a girl. Severn had a young heart before Caroline died. And then, overnight, she became a matron in a young woman's body. Della wondered for the hundredth time why Severn had never married. She could recall a score of men who buzzed about her in her youth; surely she could have had a husband if she chose.

But Severn had made the choice to walk through this world with no one clearing the path for her. Chose, too, therefore, to be without children in a society that felt no small pity for those barren wretches who could not produce as regularly as a good milch cow.

She was either very courageous, Della thought, or very cowardly. And yet she did not pale before the thought of war, even seemed to relish the chance to share in a skirmish or two.

Della firmly brushed the thought of danger from her mind. War seemed in that moment as unlikely as the possibility that Stephen Gage would ride up the long drive from the river, hail Phillip in a loving manner, and sweep her into a fond but fraternal embrace.

💢 💢 💢

In the hot summer of 1773, word came down to Wilmington that some of the Virginia legislators—among them one Thomas Jefferson and that young spitfire Patrick Henry—had formed a committee to keep in touch with other colonial legislatures. A "committee of correspondence," they called it.

"A bunch of squawking hens clogging the post with hate mail," Phillip called them and dismissed their efforts. "So long as merchants on the Cape Fear can line their pockets with British sterling, they'll look to their own larders first. What do they care for the troubles of Virginians?"

Six months later, Bostonians staged their Tea Party, dumping precious cargo into the harbor. In retaliation, British warships shut down Boston Harbor tight, and a new apprehension ran through the Carolinas. Might not Wilmington suffer the same way? Or even Charleston or Savannah?

Word came to Deepwater that a large crowd armed with sticks and pistols had chased a printer through the streets of Wilmington because his publications had enraged the radicals. In Edenton, less than a four-day ride by fast carriage, a different sort of "tea party" had been held, though the word "tea" itself was not mentioned. Fifty-one ladies of that city gathered to express their sympathies to the patriotic cause, signing an agreement to support their countrymen by whatever means they could, including refusing to wear, eat, or purchase British goods.

"Amazonians!" fumed Phillip in outrage. "Formidable idiots, next they'll be taking up spears." As he read aloud from the papers the list of women who had participated, he sputtered, "Well, the only thing I can see to prevent impending ruin is the likelihood that there are few places in America that possess so much female artillery as Edenton. Nothing but old battleaxes from stem to stern. Mrs. Johnston, I see, was the ringleader—an uglier old hag I've yet to meet—"

Della listened quietly, perusing the Wilmington papers with her usual deliberate pace. A stolid reader, she had never learned to enjoy the process, but she forced herself to move her eyes over the print nonetheless, for she knew that intelligent men were most attracted to intelligent women. When the issues of the day came up in conversation, she was determined to be able to hold her own. She glanced up at Phillip and smiled winningly at him. "It says here that they're calling for foodstuffs and relief supplies for Boston. With the harbor closed, they fear that it'll be a hard winter, indeed."

"Let the traitors starve," Phillip grumped. "They should have thought of that when they disobeyed their King."

Della set down the paper slowly and stared at him across the breakfast dishes. In that moment Phillip seemed particularly mulish. Even his jaw, a feature of his face she usually found attractive, seemed overtly loutish and stupid.

This was a side of love she had heard nothing about: that one might look at one's spouse and see a stranger. What did he see when he looked at her? she wondered. She sensed that Phillip had a vision of her that was not herself at all. Who she was in truth or who she might someday become was only clay for him to mold. He saw her as his property. Like Bathsheba, only more cherished. There was something in her, unnamed and even invisible, that defied his shaping.

But his discipline was skilled: careful scorn, the slightest of ridicules, cold aloofness—and then absence. She saw how he played the game but was, so far, unable to avoid being played.

Nonetheless, she could not be silent. "I doubt the women and children of Boston had much to say about it one way or the other," she said, "yet they'll starve right along with those who dumped the tea in the harbor. Does that seem fair to you?"

"War isn't fair, Della," Phillip said shortly. "And for all I know the women of Boston are just as bad as those in Edenton. They likely goaded their men to such foolishness—"

"Is that what we're in, then? War?"

"Damn close to it. And when it comes, every fool who sent his goods to Boston'll wish it back again thrice over. But you needn't worry your head about such stuff, Della, the King's as generous with his supporters as he is stern with his detractors. When war comes, there'll be more soldiers here at Deepwater than chickens."

"How very comforting," she said.

"Now put down those papers, dear, and stop fretting over something that shouldn't concern you. Where's that novel I brought back for you from London? It's a pretty story, the book merchant said, and far more fitting than this treasonous tripe from the pens of radicals."

Della rose and went from the room as Phillip settled back to his papers and his pipe. Treasonous tripe, indeed! How pompous he was! In that moment, she was almost relieved that she had not been able, so far, to bear him a child. How could she hope to protect her child from Phillip's repertoire of skilled sarcasm?

And yet, she must have something of her own, something to care about, or she would die.

Once upstairs, she sat down at her secretary and penned a quick note to Severn. Among other things she said, "If I can be of any assistance in the gathering of goods for the relief of Boston, please do let me know. I think it unlikely that Phillip will be able to support my beliefs, but I cannot stand by idle while American women and children starve for their country's freedom." As she sealed the note and handed it to Bathsheba to hand again to the boy who ran for the post carriage, a piece of her heart flew ahead of the message with a sense of triumph.

"Bad news, Miss Della?" Bathsheba murmured softly as she saw her writing.

" 'Twill be soon enough." Della sighed heavily.

A prompt answer came from Severn, thanking her for her offer and suggesting that they could use whatever she could spare. A week later, when Phillip was out riding with his neighbor to the east, two large flatboats tied up at Deepwater dock. Within a few hours, Della had them loaded with rice, corn, molasses, salt pork, and three casks of Phillip's best spruce beer. After they pulled away, she discovered to her dismay that she'd forgotten to include the clothing and some of the seed corn, so she wrote again to Severn.

Over the next few weeks, a wagon pulled up the long Deepwater drive almost every other day to pick up one thing or another from Della. At first nervous that Phillip might see the wagon approach or being loaded, she gradually grew incautious and finally even hoped he'd notice, for she was rather puffed with pride at her contributions. But Phillip seemed blind to the wagon, to the disappearing resources of Deepwater, and to her.

At least in the daylight hours. But at night, when he turned to her in their bed, he was blind to everything *but* her, moving his hands over her skin, pressing her body against his with a mastery that made her smile, however ruefully. Sometimes, when Phillip was kissing her, his perfect aquiline profile so close, she opened her eyes to record the moment forever. In those times, he seemed at once as much a part of her as her heart, at once so far away that he seemed a stranger. It was the stranger part of him that excited her the most and caused her to draw him closer, closer still, until he pulled her up, made her back arch, and slid inside her.

On some basic level, she understood that what they shared was largely of the body. He was often ravenous with her, and she almost as hungry for him. But she believed that what they had together was likely love, or at least what people called it, and so always, before the night was out, she would say the word or he would, thereby making holy what they did with her faith.

The nights between them, Della often reflected in the morning, were a powerful drug. But the days—ah, the days were becoming an antidote, and she was usually rid of his magic and sobered by noon.

🌿 🌿 🌿

A flurry of knocking came to Deepwater one July night, and the message was sent up through a series of nervous black hands. Phillip took the paper, read it, and passed it to Della with a bowed head. By his face and gesture, she knew it was a summons, but she was still shocked to read the words that Severn had penned hours before. "My mother has passed. Come at once."

It was like Severn to send such a missive, Della thought later in the carriage as she hurried to Wilmington with Bathsheba by her side.

My mother. Not *our* mother, ah no. And 'come at once.' As though speed somehow might alter the circumstances. She had been to visit Tess twice in the past two months and found her increasingly frail, just as Severn reported. But somehow, Della never could believe that Tess would die. Not until she read Severn's note. And then, in that moment, it seemed to her that Tess had never even been alive at all. She had disappeared in those words with the finality of the period at the end of Severn's sentence.

Della remembered as they drove quickly through the streets of Wilmington the last time she attended a funeral. A friend had lost a child, always a sad event, of course, but one that every mother expected at least once with every few births. She recalled the words of the mother: "It's not that I can't believe he's gone," she said of her three-year-old son. "But that I can scarcely believe he ever lived at all. It all seems a dream now."

And though Della could remember Tess as vividly as she recalled her own childhood, she, too, seemed only a dream now that she was gone. As much of a dream as Gloriana. Now, she could only hope, at least they were together again at last.

She sat silently, swaying in the heat, saying nothing to Bathsheba. Her heart said the name over and over. Tess. Aunt Tess. As a child, she had sometimes pretended for a moment that Tess was, in reality, her own mother and that Severn was the one bereft, not herself. Other times, she grew angry with Tess for having survived when her own mother did not. But always, whether she sought her arms or avoided them, Tess had loved her with a constant soft beam of light all of her years in that house.

And now she was gone. Whatever mother I had, I have none now, Della thought dully as she knocked at what once was a houseful of life and a bustle of children within. Captain Jack's door. Bathsheba stood quietly at her hip as though to prop her should she falter. Della murmured, "I can't believe she'll never answer my knock again," and the slave crooned a low wordless note of comfort. Then a nameless black woman let them in, and Della swept upstairs to Severn, hoping that somehow her cousin would take away the ache in her throat.

Phillip arrived later in the day as the rest of the family gathered. Tess's sons, John and Noah, had been summoned from Charleston, and they came with their wives and children in tow. Within hours, the house on Bay Street was more crowded than it had been in many Christmases.

Over them all, Severn held dignified sway. She comforted those who wept and cheered those who blamed themselves for some forgotten neglect; she kept the refreshments flowing from the kitchen and made certain that the smaller children were quietly entertained in Captain Jack's study. Della floated through the funeral as though she were as lightly bound to the earth as Tess herself, feeling a part of her heart deaden each time her aunt's name was mentioned. Only Phillip's arm round her waist kept her pinioned to the present, for her mind wanted to wander back, irresistibly back to the past. It seemed somehow safer there.

It was a quiet service, considering how many years Tess had lived in Wilmington and her large circle of friends. Because of the heat, Tess was buried with only one night of watching. When Della wondered aloud where Tess's many acquaintances were, Severn said, "It's so hard to travel now, with tensions being what they are."

Tensions? Was Deepwater that isolated that she did not feel the reality of the world beyond its long, graveled road? Della took her cousin, John, aside as they returned from the cemetery, cornering him at the edge of the parlor. "What news from Charleston?" she asked him. "Do they still speak of war?"

John nodded. "They speak of little else. I almost left Dinah and the children at home, for fear the Brits might target Charleston harbor next, but she wouldn't hear of it. Mother was with her when our last was born, you know, and Dinah thought of her as her own kin."

Della felt wrapped in cotton wool, as though she'd been buried for the last year or two. This was her family, and she scarcely knew them. These were her countrymen, and she hardly felt union with them at all. "Tess was quite involved with the cause, was she not?" she asked.

John eyed Della carefully, and she could see the wariness in his glance. "You needn't worry," she said quietly, glancing to where Phillip spoke with a neighbor in the other corner of the room. "I do not share my husband's politics." Surprised to hear herself say the words, she nonetheless did not wonder at their truth.

"Severn told me that you made generous contributions to the relief fund for Boston," John said carefully, "but she also said that you did so without his knowledge."

Della shrugged. "I doubt it'll be the last time I keep him in ignorance." She smiled to take away the sting of her words. This man might be her cousin, but he was also a man and a husband. "It only would have upset him, and for what? A few trifling bushels of rice and some odds and ends we could well afford to spare for the needy."

"Soon the stakes will be higher," John said softly. "I wonder if you'll be prepared, Della?"

"So you believe war is coming, too?" She watched his face carefully.

"I know it is. Don't you know the real reason mourners were so scarce today? Nobody has time to mourn, they're all over at the meeting at the courthouse."

"What meeting?"

"The meeting to decide whether or not there'll be a congress independent of the governor. I suspect South Carolina will follow suit soon enough, if there's general agreement. Men are coming from all over the Cape Fear today, and if they decide to go forward, I believe they'll elect a Continental Congress soon enough."

Her eyes widened. "A separate congress for the colonies? Without the King's permission? War *will* come soon, then."

He nodded. "But you didn't know of the meeting?"

"Phillip hasn't brought home the papers for days." She frowned. "At least not where I can see them."

John glanced over to Phillip and took her arm smoothly, leading her out of the parlor and toward the garden door. "We might as well speak now, Della, of your future. Of course you know that my mother thought of you always as one of her own—"

"She was so good to me," Della said simply, almost dazed by the sunlight after the cool gloom of the house.

"And she included you in her will. You will inherit, along with Severn, Noah, and myself, a small estate, once all is said and done."

She stopped and blinked at him. "Aunt Tess left me money?"

He smiled. "Did you think she would not? She always loved you, child, you know that. And I believe she wanted you to have a certain—independence in life that she did not. Gloriana would have wanted it so, and my mother loved Gloriana more, I think, than any other living soul in her life." He looked away over the garden down to the river. "Including my father. At any rate, you shall soon come into your own estate—"

She turned and faced him squarely, no longer caring that Phillip was watching them from the French doors. "How much, John?"

"I can't say for certain, but surely you can depend on at least a hundred and fifty pounds a year. Maybe a bit more."

Della's mouth opened, and she grasped her cousin's arm. "That's a fortune!"

"Not quite a fortune," John said, grinning, "but it's more than many planters make in a season on their crop. Of course you must remember that legally, it belongs to your husband, Della. All your property does—"

Della dropped his arm and turned to see Phillip gazing out at them, still in idle conversation, apparently, but watching her nonetheless. "Why does it belong to him? He was no kin to Aunt Tess—"

"It's the law. Wherever the monies come from, it's his, as your legal spouse."

She frowned, thinking for a moment. "But does he even have to know about this?"

"You mean not tell Phillip at all?"

She lowered her voice. "Why must he know about my inheritance? Why should I give it to him?"

Patiently John repeated, "Because according to the laws of the colonies, indeed, of the King, a woman cannot own property in her own name—"

"Damn the King and damn the laws," she whispered angrily, "it's not fair dealing, and I won't abide it."

"Now you're beginning to sound like a rebel—"

"I don't care what I sound like, can this be kept secret from him or not, just tell me."

John thought for a long moment, his mouth solemn. "Yes," he finally said slowly, "I think so. I'll speak with Noah about it, but I imagine there is some way to arrange for the deposit of your funds into an account in Severn's name."

"Severn's name!"

"As she is an unmarried woman, she is allowed to own property. She could keep it for you, in her name. You, being married, could not have the same freedoms."

"A maiden has more rights than a wife!"

"Exactly."

"And this is the only way?"

"Unless you wish me to consult a solicitor, Della. And then

there's always the danger that he will feel compelled to inform Phillip.''

She shook her head vehemently. "No, I will ask Severn myself. I can trust her, I think. Can I trust you, John?''

He put his hand on her shoulder. "Of course, little cousin. Now let me go back to the others before I get some questions I don't want to answer from Master Gage. I'll be in touch with you after everything's finalized. Will you come back inside?''

She stood and faced the river. "In a minute." As he turned to walk away, she called out softly, "Thank you, John. Thank you for my freedom.''

"Don't thank me," he answered. "Thank Tess Dobbs. 'Twas she who put it in your hands.''

Della stood and watched the heat shimmer up off the water for a long moment, fingering the gold filagree locket she wore always round her neck. The locket Tess had given her for luck. "Thank you," she murmured to the heated air. "I shan't waste it, Aunt Tess.''

🌿 🌿 🌿

In the months that followed, Della learned more and more about Deepwater and all that went to keep it running smoothly. At first she learned reluctantly; then, with avid interest. Phillip was absent increasingly from his fields, as his political meetings took him farther and more frequently away from the plantation. Della asked him where he went and why, but as his answers grew shorter and more impatient, she ceased to ask. She realized instinctively that it was part of his shaping of her to keep her waiting. To keep her dependent on him in some dark, subterranean way. He wanted her to need him absolutely. Once she saw the truth of that, she was free.

Soon his absence or his presence, the farewells and the reunions, stopped creating tension in her. She ceased being lifted or dropped by his arrival or his departure. No more did she watch for his horse or listen for his step. No more did she live life holding her breath, always waiting for his presence to somehow release her and give her meaning.

Deepwater gradually became, for Della, meaning enough. With

Bathsheba's help, she learned the workings of the household first. In truth, she felt vaguely ashamed that she had waited so long to do so. Bathsheba had quietly taken on her responsibilities and kept the house slaves in order, so that Della might never need to trouble herself—but once Della decided to learn, she found the intricacies of the big house amusing.

It was a large home, square and two-storied, with impressive doorways and imposing steps. The hall down the center connected the two fronts, with seventeen rooms overall. The walls were smoothly paneled with walnut, the graceful stairways with carved stepends and newel posts of rich mahogany, but all of the details of Deepwater spoke of a man's taste, not a woman's. In the first few months of her marriage, Della made few changes. By her third anniversary, however, flowered wall coverings and pretty curtains had replaced some of the dark paneling and the heavy velvet portieres of Phillip's choice.

There were keys to be carried—to the kitchen, the buttery, the dairy, and the storeroom. Della whittled them down to the storeroom and the buttery only, reasoning that nobody would steal the cows, and if a little milk was purloined by the slaves, she wouldn't miss it. As to the kitchen, she let Bathsheba carry that key, for she did not wish to be troubled early each morning so that the cook might start the breakfast fire.

Then there was the washing, the cleaning, the constant inventory of dishes and knives and spoons and tumblers, mugs, sugar pots, curets, bowls, and jugs—it was enough to make her dizzy. And the sheer number of slaves underfoot! Young Ebba did the drudgery part of the house, the fetching of wood and water, Eliza did the scouring upstairs, Nan did the scouring down, Mary Ann did the cooking, Daphne made the bread and the sausage, Moses worked in the kitchen until noon and then outdoors with the fowl, Pegg washed and milked—it all got done somehow. But after a few months, Della soon wanted no more of it. She turned her attention to the fields and the crops, letting Bathsheba take back her keys and her position as mistress over them all.

Once outside the big house, Della realized that here, at last, was something she could do better than most. The vast fields of rice that girdled Deepwater were tended by more than a hundred slaves who lived in the quarters, managed by Thomas Dublin, overseer of the plantation since Phillip had been a boy. Dublin did what he did well, but he did less and less every year. Consequently, more than a quarter of the slaves were usually, day by day, unable or unwilling to work for one reason or another, and large tracts of acreage lay fallow. Phillip had grumbled about Dublin in her hearing before, with every intention of replacing the old man as soon as he found time to do so. Now that he was gone so much, Dublin's lapses seemed even more glaring.

Della began to read all she could find in Deepwater's limited library about rice, but she was frustrated by the minimal information and the deep suspicion that even if she were able to learn how to improve the crop, Dublin could not get the slaves to work for him well enough to implement her ideas.

The more she learned about Deepwater, the more she was shocked. The world, she soon realized, should have been Phillip Gage's oyster. He had inherited vast lands made wealthy by rice, a score of slaves, and a small village of buildings to house them. He built the big house back when timber products were dirt cheap, and the threat of war made his crops worth even more on a precarious market. Why, then, was he not content?

When they had first married, Phillip was, like his neighbors, happy to seem richer than those around him, to set a heavier table, to drive a fancier carriage, to sail a larger boat—but lately, guests did not come often to Deepwater, and the carriage always looked as though it needed a good polish.

Because of his politics, Della thought with a grimace. They pulled him away from his duties here and they isolated him from his neighbors. And she could see, when she finally was able to make sense of his books, that Phillip lagged behind his friends as a rice planter as well. His crop was small overall, given the land he had at his service. She looked in vain for recent bills for fertilizer and new seed and realized that three years had passed since Dublin had put anything back into the soil. Even she knew that the land would decline rapidly if it were not enriched, and she grew increasingly angry the closer she examined the accounts.

Within a fortnight, she had hired a new overseer and sent Thomas Dublin packing. When Phillip returned, she calmly announced that the man had given notice abruptly to return to Ireland, and that the new man had some excellent ideas to improve the corn crop and to add a new orchard of fruit trees alongside the river. Further, he had sold four of their most lazy slaves, purchased three more to take their place, and put the fear of God into the rest so that for the first time, those thirty fallow acres were finally put to seed and fifty more had been cleared for the next season.

She did not tell Phillip that, in fact, these ideas had been her own and that she never felt more powerful or free than when she rode over the thriving fields and watched her people work.

🌿 🌿 🌿

At the edges of the Cape Fear as it lapped against the Deepwater dock, a certain large master of the watery world lurked and made the small region his own. He was a primitive tank of a creature nearly two feet long, who weighed over forty-five pounds and favored the soft, muddy bottom of the river as it wound close to the edge of Deepwater fields.

His powerful hooked jaws, a relatively small cross-shaped plastron or bottom shell and carapace of twelve scutes on each side marked him as the largest of all freshwater species, *Chelydra serpentina*, or snapping turtle. His size and aggression marked him the terror of that mile of river.

It was late April, and the river was swollen with spring rains. He lay in wait in the shallows, his dark brown shell slagged with algae and mud, almost indiscernible to the naked eye among the flotsam and debris left by the moving water. His tail, long as his carapace and edged with saw-toothed keels, waved gently to and fro, keeping his huge body almost motionless in the current. Anything that moved was fair game: smaller turtles, fish, snakes, muskrats, whatever was worth the trouble was worth the fight.

Slightly upriver, an inconspicuous flock of waterfowl bobbed on the surface. They were buffleheads, small ducks readying to leave the southern coasts for regions farther north. Plump and oblivious, they eddied close to the turtle, whistling and quacking to each other with unconcern.

The snapping turtle slid under the surface silently and descended to a depth of three feet, swimming swiftly toward the flock until he was directly under their churning webbed feet. Rising without hesitation, he seized a female bufflehead by the breast and yanked her under, while she flapped in panic and sent her comrades to flight with her harsh croaks. The flock scattered in protest, wheeled once over the river, and resettled again several hundred yards away. Before they had regained their formation, the turtle had already ripped her apart and swallowed her head, neck, and most of her breast. The rest, he let drift away on the current.

For the next several hours, he floated, seemingly unaware of the life that ebbed and edged around him. His massive head barely cleared the surface of the water, like some primeval reptile, more crocodile than turtle, with only his nostrils and neck tubercles exposed. He had spent the winter in an old muskrat burrow, having attacked and eaten the previous owner. Now he waited for what spring inevitably brought to the shallows of Deepwater.

A small splashing upriver caught his attention, and he turned in the water like a huge pie plate, raising his head a bit higher from the surface. A female snapper was slowly swimming in his direction. Normally, her claws would have moved through the water without a sound. Now, she deliberately made noise as she approached.

Without hesitation, he lunged at her aggressively, and any onlooker would have been unable to tell whether he intended violence or mating. She maneuvered in the water to face him, determined to inflict whatever damage she could. Like two tanks, they feinted and dodged, oaring about in circles, always facing each other with their curved beaks like carving knives.

Then she struck him, and he answered her in kind.

For most of an hour, they sliced each other savagely, the raw, red flesh of their gashed heads and necks bleeding into the water. When the female finally tired, the male swiftly grabbed her by the neck and positioned himself plastron to plastron. Locked in a fierce embrace, the two turtles then rolled over and over in the water consummating their union. For the time of mating, only the bottom turtle, upside down for a moment or two, could raise its head out of the water sufficiently to breathe.

Finally finished with their mating, the female slowly swam off to the muddy bottom of the Cape Fear and away. In two months, she would lay more than eighty spherical eggs in a cavity she would dig in the riverbank. Able to retain sperm within her body for several years, she might not mate again within her lifetime.

Her mate lay wheezing on the surface, regaining his wind. As a small cooter swam past, he reached out fiercely and snapped the smaller turtle in two, downing half of its neck and head in one gulp.

For the rest of the day and into the evening, as the sun wheeled slowly over the water, he lurked effortlessly through the gray-green shadows into darker water, pausing now and then to snorkle up without a ripple and as quietly disappear.

❦ ❦ ❦

In April of 1775, British soldiers, tormented beyond all patience by the impertinence of the colonials, fired on an unruly mob at Lexington and Concord, Massachusetts. News of the attack spread like a spring fever through the colonies, and war was no longer a probability but a reality. George Washington, in his red and blue uniform of a Virginia militia colonel, standing six feet, two inches—over the heads of most of his compatriots—was appointed commander in chief of the American forces by the Second Continental Congress.

For Washington, it would be the beginning of a long ordeal.

For the Carolinas, the revolution had all the aspects of a civil war, so divided were the people in their loyalties. Even as Wilmington readied for hostilities, a flurry of petitions expressing loyalty to King George were circulating among some of the merchants, the Anglican clergy, some elected officials, and a sprinkling of planters and shippers. In Mecklenburg County, the Committee of Safety met and drew up a set of resolves to govern themselves until the American Congress could do so. That document of independence, The Mecklenburg Resolves, was used by Thomas Jefferson, some said, when he wrote the Declaration of Independence the following June.

Parliament quickly declared all the colonies in rebellion and all ports closed—except Wilmington. The naval stores produced and shipped from the Cape Fear were far too essential for King George to allow for their loss. But Wilmington refused to be spared. Unwilling to be divided from the other colonies, North Carolina was also unwilling wholeheartedly to join them. Neighbors quarreled over loyalties and families split asunder; slaves were rebelling in the Albemarle, and a band of restless Cherokee, encouraged by British agents, were harassing Carolina settlers.

Meanwhile, British ships slipped to the mouth of the Cape Fear, ready to take Wilmington if necessary. Loyalist Highland Scots controlled the headwaters, and a band of Tories to the south of the river threatened to overrun the Piedmont. The rebels needed something signifi-

cant to pull their factions together and make them mad enough to fight, and in February 1776, they found their opportunity.

🌱 🌱 🌱

"Christmas of 1775 is going down in my books as the most cheerless on record," Della said dismally to Bathsheba.

The woman barely looked up from her efforts. She'd been trying for the past hour to brush the water stains from Della's cobalt-blue velvet gown so that she might wear it one more time before retiring it forever. By rights, it should have been replaced months ago, but Della, like so many women in town, was refusing to wear British goods, so frocks—like papers and pins and toiletries and decent stockings—were in short supply.

Of course, her refusal infuriated Phillip, but she was steadfast. Besides, how could she appear in a new gown at the holiday galas when half of her neighbors and most of her friends wore their sacrifices with pride?

"Sheba, maybe you could stitch a large white rose over the worst part or something." Della sighed as she picked up the worn blue velvet and examined it with some distaste. "Although it'll drape horribly when I dance."

"Might be, nobody be dancin' regardless," Bathsheba said smoothly, "if de war come by den."

Della said, "I wish if they're going to fight, they'd get on with it and get it done. The season's all but ruined anyway, with half the county fussing with the other half—"

A knock sounded at her bedroom door, and Della glanced at Bathsheba. Phillip. It must be important if he couldn't wait for supper. She hesitated for just an instant. Lately, they'd been barely civil to each other. There was scarcely a topic they could discuss without disagreeing, since most everything was affected by politics these days. Once he found he could not sway her to his mind, he froze her out.

Only in bed at night did he unthaw, and then backed her into the four-poster as though to claim her anew in any way he could. She remembered how recently she had asked him why he had married her, and he said wryly, his smile subtle and intriguing, "Because you were there for the taking."

She wondered if it would have made any difference if there had been a child. Bathsheba always said so. That the coming of a child turned a marriage upside down, or on its ear, or some such nonsense. Certainly, their union could stand a good shaking up.

Della signaled Bathsheba to open the door and the slave did so, backing away, her eyes down as usual when she was confronted by Phillip. He was the only person at Deepwater she would not face for Della.

"You planning to spend the rest of the evening up here?" he asked, leaning against the doorframe. He ignored Bathsheba completely.

"Why, did you need something?" Della asked, matching his tone.

His jaw hardened. "As a matter of fact, I did wish to speak to you, Della." He turned and went down the hallway toward their bedroom, assuming without looking that she would follow.

She rolled her eyes skyward at Sheba in exasperation. Taking a few pointed moments to give her woman some additional directions, she finally did trail after him, only hurrying her steps when she saw that he stood inside their bedroom door, holding it open for her. She entered, and he closed it firmly behind her.

"I'm going to Charleston tomorrow on business," he said flatly, "and I'll be gone probably until after Christmas."

Her eyes widened in surprise. Clearly his tone did not imply an invitation. "Just like that?" she asked, instantly angry at herself for such a weak reply.

He bowed. "I doubt you'll miss me much, madame. You can send off your silly bundles to the oppressed and meet with your rebel friends to your heart's content, I'll not be here to cramp your style."

So he had found out about her donations to Boston those long months ago. She tried for what usually worked in the past. Dimpling, she murmured, "Ah, dear, be sweet. I might be your next queen after the revolution rolls through."

But he wasn't having any. Without a smile he replied, "More like my executioness."

"But, Phillip, what business can you possibly do over the holiday? And to be apart for that time, of all times, why I can't imagine—"

"I've never made much over Christmas, and I'm sure you'll be swamped with enough invitations to keep you amused."

Her mouth hardened to match his. "I'm certain I will. That's not the point, of course. A husband and wife should be together during the most festive time of the year."

"A husband and wife *should* be together, that I'll grant you," he said silkily. "But since we are not, the time of the year matters little."

She rose and crossed to the window, her back to him. "And you will not take me with you." It was not a question.

His silence said more than any words might have.

She turned to face him. "I suppose you'll tell me that you're leaving me home because of the threat of hostilities."

He smirked. "I shall say exactly that."

"And you expect me to believe it?"

He shrugged. "Actually, madame, I care little whether you believe it or not. Just leave it that I go alone."

She slumped, realizing that they had come to a state of siege and she had somehow missed the first few skirmishes. A sense of helplessness overwhelmed Della in that instant, as she saw that Phillip could go, could do, could have whatever he pleased—whomever he pleased—and there was actually very little she could do to thwart him.

On the other hand, his attitude gave her certain freedoms as well. She gauged him quickly, wondering just how far to go. She decided in that moment that she would only lose power if she hesitated. "You have someone else, then," she said calmly.

He laughed low in his throat. "My dear Della, you surprise me. You have just asked the one question no proper Southern woman will ask. No matter what her suspicions, no matter how flagrant her husband's indiscretion, she will never stoop to wonder if he dares to supplant her with another. To do so would be to acknowledge that he might somehow have cause. That she was less than perfection. That he less than worshiped the ground beneath her silk slippers." He smiled, almost warmly. "This is what comes of sending young women abroad for their schooling. They forget themselves entirely."

She felt the rage rise in her as predictably as sap in the spring, but much hotter, much swifter. "You cad," she said, low and richly controlled. "You haven't even the decency to deny it."

"Since you haven't the decency to ignore it, no, I guess I shan't."

One part of her wanted to break and weep, to go to him and beg him for an answer. How had they come to this point between them, this arid, dry, and hateful place? But most of her wanted to slap that smirk right off his face. She was suddenly exhausted. Della wanted nothing more than to go back to her dressing room and burrow under the down coverlet while Bathsheba drew the shades and brought her a warm chocolate toddy. Something with a dollop of rum. She drew herself up with dignity and turned again to the window. "Well," she said. "I wish you Godspeed and a prosperous journey." She sensed his hesitation. She did not move.

A long silence. "I'll leave then tomorrow."

"You said that."

Another long silence. "Della . . ."

She heard the softer note in his voice, the almost-conciliatory beginnings of what might have been a truce. But she could not turn and face him, could not allow him entry, no, no matter how much she might wish she had later. She remained still and silent, her back a wall between them as high and wide as death.

"Della," he began again, faltering. "There was a time when you believed in me, I think. A time when my opinion was the only one that mattered. You didn't go behind my back and deliberately disobey me." He sighed. "You were lovely, then."

She thought for a moment. She could turn and extend her hand to him or she could remain aloof. Finally she said, "I had no choice. You'd have it no other way."

"What has changed, then?"

She turned and shrugged. "The world has changed, my love. I am older. Perhaps wiser."

He dropped his head. "Maybe if we had a child—"

She was instantly in pain again and angry for it. "Maybe if we shared our bed more than occasionally—"

He shook his head as if warding off blows, throwing his hands up before her words.

"Perhaps, if we shared more than our bed at all!" Her words were acid and unforgiving.

In a moment, he was on her, lifting her up and away from the window, throwing her down on the wide bed that stood, as if in witness to their pain, in the center of the room. Della felt him hovering over her, holding himself over her in that possessing way he had, all his clothes still on, hers quickly undone and rumpled by his practiced hand. He raised her wrists to the oaken bars of the headboard, held them there with one hand, and undid the knot of his cravat with the other. She felt the pressure of his buttons against her chest; the cloth of his broadloom shirt chafed her face. She breathed in his odor—the distinctive body scent that both drew and repelled her. And later, when he groaned and hissed out her name and drew a wild response from her in kind, she wondered: when he told me he was leaving, when I called him a cad, did he know he would do this even then?

🌿 🌿 🌿

Phillip had been gone more than a week when Della finally took the carriage and Bathsheba into Wilmington for a round of visits she felt were long overdue. Because of the holiday season, hospitality was relatively lavish, considering the British still had their gunboats anchored outside the Cape, and most of the homes in the city refused to serve anything remotely foreign, even if it meant raspberry leaf tea rather than English.

Severn accompanied her on some of her visits; others she and Bathsheba waded through alone. Every conversation centered on politics; every topic led inevitably to war. It was hard not to be impatient with the monotony of the subject at last, and when Della finally ordered her carriage out the river road toward home, she was wearied and relieved.

One more stop, she told Bathsheba, and then she might not budge again until the New Year. As the carriage turned down the long, graveled pathway to Geneva, past the rich fields of Stephen Gage, Bathsheba perked up and sat a little straighter. "Is we expected?" she asked.

"Of course we are," Della said, unconcerned. "His brother's complaint is with Phillip, not with me. In fact," she smiled softly, "he and I are in agreement, I'm told, about most things that matter."

Bathsheba shot her a look and subsided again. Della chose to ignore both the look and its implication.

She had long been curious about Severn's relationship with

Stephen Gage, but to all her careful, casual questions put to anyone who knew them both, the general story was the same. They were friends only, though there was a hint that many years ago they had been more to each other than allies and political compatriots.

"I believe at one time, she might have accepted him," Madam Scott whispered when Della asked the question, "but the story is that he never asked and then when he might have asked, she was not receptive to his suit."

"Star-crossed lovers caught in the turmoil of the age?" Della asked, her face bland. Madam Scott was a known fool but a fine repository for gossip of all kinds.

The old woman looked amazed. "Ye have quite a way with words, Mistress Gage," she said admiringly. "Did ye think it up yourself, then?"

Geneva looked even seedier than when she had seen it last. She could only suppose that while she had sent goods in support of the rebels, goods she and Phillip could well afford to spare, Stephen had sent what he could not. The house loomed against a backdrop of water oaks festooned with heavy Spanish moss, an almost ghostly presence in the winter fog that rose off the river at its back.

Judith answered the door, effusive with her welcome and her warmth, and Della could feel Bathsheba's fascination in the tall, tight way she held her body. The slave scanned the entry with eyes that did not miss a single detail, and Della knew that in a moment, Sheba surmised more about Master Stephen's housekeeping arrangements than any white woman ever would have. She was taken away by the maidservant to the kitchen, and Della and Judith adjourned to the parlor to wait for Stephen to come in from the fields.

"What do they say in the city about the Snow Campaign?" Judith asked the moment she had put a cup in Della's hand. "The news is so exciting!"

Della sighed inwardly. North Carolina had sent more than seven hundred men, many of them from the Cape, down to South Carolina to join the local troops in the Snow Campaign to crush the Loyalists, and their triumph had been the topic of conversation in the last three parlors she'd visited. "Well, of course, no one talks of anything else and everyone's predicting war by spring."

"Stephen says sooner," Judith said, dropping her voice to an anguished whisper. "But of course he's been preparing for it for months."

"How does one prepare for such a thing?" Della wondered aloud, taking another bite of Judith's apricot scones. Really, these were wonderful, she thought, and surely Bathsheba could train Mary Ann to duplicate them—

Judith pulled back, one hand to her bosom, her astonishment severe as the cut of her gown. "Why, my dear, do you mean to tell me that you've laid by no supplies? No ammunitions? You've not trained your people to put out a blaze, should the Redcoats fire your house?"

Della looked at her blankly as though the woman had just lost her mind. "Do you mean to tell me you've done all these things?"

"And more. The good silver's been buried for more than a month, and every slave knows the hiding place in the woods to meet if we're attacked. Della"—she put two fervent hands together as though in prayer—"you must hurry right home and prepare yourself and your people! Stephen expects hostilities within the week!"

Della decided in that moment that Judith was far less fascinating than she had originally thought. She smiled politely. Less attractive, too. In that moment, she heard heavy boots coming quickly from the foyer, and her smile warmed considerably. "There's Stephen!" she said, half turning in her chair. To her delight, he came in and patted Judith on the shoulder perfunctorily, then pulled Della to her feet, kissing her on both cheeks.

"Stephen, do you know that Phillip has made absolutely no preparations for the impending attack whatsoever?" Judith asked, almost breathless with her horror. "I've been telling Della she must get her people readied! Why, the war could start tomorrow!"

"It already has," he replied smoothly, "but it may well be a few hours before it reaches Deepwater. We'll see our little cousin refreshed first, I hope, before we turn her out to such a Herculean task." He smiled at Della. "And damn my brother for putting such a heavy responsibility on such lovely shoulders."

Della flushed and smiled, almost gratefully, at Judith. She did not dare meet Stephen's eyes.

"Honey," he said to Judith, "will you forgive me if I ask you to leave us alone for a spell? I've got some mighty presumptive favors to ask Della, and I'd rather you not see me beg, hat in hand, even if it is for a good cause."

Judith beamed at him, bustling up quickly and giving Della a quick embrace. "We'll visit later then, dear, I'll just go and see to our supper." A mock-stern glance to Stephen. "Don't take advantage of her generosity just because she's your brother's wife, Stephen. Remember, she has to live with him!" She hurried out of the room, closing the parlor door behind her.

Della felt a flood of nervousness for an instant to be alone with him, for she suddenly remembered the cool but sharp anger he had shown not too long ago in this very room. But she stilled her anxiety and watched him carefully as he poured her second cup of tea. His hands were finely tapered, strong, and surprisingly well-groomed, especially as she realized he must do far more of the labor needed around Geneva than Phillip did.

"Have you heard from Phillip?" Stephen asked, almost casually.

"Not a word. But then, I hardly expected to."

He watched her for a moment, and Della felt a strange combination of relaxation and wariness. "Do you know what he's doing in Charleston, Della?" he finally asked.

She flushed. Surely, Phillip's indiscretions could not be so brazen that even an estranged brother knew of them! "Business, of course," she said.

He set down his cup. "I thought he wouldn't tell you. Likely, he doesn't trust you not to tell Severn or someone else who could harm him, should the word get out."

"What word? What is he doing?"

"He was with the Loyalist troops outside Charleston. When they were defeated, he was arrested, retained briefly, and questioned, but when they found out he was my brother, they let him go at my word."

"Was he injured?" she gasped, her hand to her mouth.

"No, but he's in danger, nonetheless. And next time, they won't let him go, my word or no, not if he's armed against them." He pinned her hand with his own. "They could execute him, Della."

"How long have you known this?"

"Two nights. When the news came about the victory, they sent up a dispatch about the prisoners. I got him released as soon as I could."

"So he'll be coming home soon."

Stephen shrugged. "I doubt it. If he comes home now, his own side will see it as capitulation. The Loyalists aren't finished yet in South Carolina, and they'll press him to stay."

Della felt a sharp pang of panic and loss. Truly, if it were that bad, both between them and outside them, there was little hope for a reconciliation. Judith was right; she should go home right away. She set down her cup and made as if to rise, but Stephen stopped her with his hand.

"Della, this can't be easy for you. I know your sympathies lie with us, yet my brother is stubbornly blind to England's trespasses. I know I shouldn't ask more of you, but I must. War is all around us now, and soon it'll be at our doors. When it comes, we'll need every heart and every pair of hands. Lord Cornwallis, even now, is on his way at full sail from Ireland with seven regiments of regulars, and Sir Clinton's bringing two thousand more down from Boston. They mean to take the Carolinas for the King."

She gasped. So many men, all bent on violence! "How do you know this?"

"We know. We know because we have good eyes and ears in the most unlikely places. We know because good men and brave women have risked much to be sure we do know."

She knew, then, what he would ask her. But she would not make it easy for him. She wanted to see the need in his eyes.

"Della, what I'm going to ask you is wrong, I know, and it goes against all vows of fidelity between man and wife. I would not ask it if there were any other way. We need to know what the Highland Scots are going to do. We know they're loyal to the King, we know they're massing for war, and we believe they're going to march on Wilmington. If they come, we must be ready. If they join with Clinton's and Cornwallis's forces, we're doomed. Phillip will know the plans. We need to know what he knows."

She pulled her hand away from Stephen's, shocked to silence. "You want me to spy on my own husband?"

He stared at her. "Not to put too fine a face on it, yes. That's what I'm asking you to do. I'm also asking you to help save his life."

She frowned ruefully. "How will spying on him save his life, pray tell? Stephen, I believe I should be going now. Judith was right, I have dallied far too long. This is more serious than I supposed—"

"It's as serious as life and death," Stephen said. "As serious as freedom. I hate to put it like this, Della, but if you can't be counted with us, you'll be counted against us and, with Phillip, likely be arrested, tried, and exiled. Maybe worse." He bowed his head. "And I couldn't stand that. I'm begging you. Help us now and save yourself and my brother."

She almost moaned aloud. "Why me? There must be a hundred women in the county who could get you information one way or another—"

"There are, indeed, and many of them will be working alongside their men to learn what they can. You won't be the only one in the network, but think, Della, there's only one woman I know who has the two requirements we need. One, you're married to a Loyalist, yet you are sympathetic to our cause and two, you can read and write. Soon, it won't be safe for a woman to leave her home, and anyone who ventures abroad will be suspect, either by the Minutemen or the Redcoats. We need someone who can send a literate message, with a slave trustworthy enough to deliver it safely. How many women do you know who fit those criteria?"

Della thought furiously, coursing through a mental list of friends and acquaintances. A very few diverged from their husbands in their political sympathies. Of those few, not a one could sign her own name. "Oh Lord," she said, sighing, "I just don't think I can do this. Phillip and I are—estranged, Stephen, you have to know that. I doubt he'll let any information slip in my presence. He doesn't trust me." She let her eyes drop and her sadness show. "And I don't trust him."

Stephen covered her hands with his. "Yet you have been able to keep secrets from him before."

"How do you know that?" she asked sharply, looking up suddenly.

He paused. She could see him weighing his choices. "Severn," he finally said.

"What exactly is your relationship with my cousin?" Della asked, heedless of her rudeness.

He hesitated. "She has never spoken of me to you?"

"She rarely speaks to me at all."

"There was a time," Stephen said carefully, "when I suppose

Severn and I might have had something more than the fine friendship we share now. But that time was brief."

"And perhaps not as mutual as she had hoped?" Della finished
for him.

Stephen shrugged. "It is not my habit to discuss one lady with
another. May I just leave it at this, Severn and I admire each other,
and we believe in the same cause of justice. She believes, as I do,
that we must find those who feel the same and form a union for our
protection. She told me you had a small estate, but she did not tell
me the amount, Della."

"She should not have told you such a thing," Della said. "It was
not her secret to share."

"It goes no farther than me. Surely you know that I would
never do anything to risk your security. But this does tell me that
you can bring yourself, if you must, to keep yourself somewhat
independent of your husband."

He would never bring himself to risk my security? she heard
again his words in her heart. Yet if I do as he asks, I shall surely risk
more than that—and then she thought of the last time she had seen
Phillip. "I believe he has another woman," she said, her voice
almost inaudible. "In Charleston."

Stephen's face stiffened in anger, but he did not relinquish her
hands. "Then he's even more of a fool than I supposed."

She smiled at him gratefully.

"Only you can decide what loyalties you owe him now," Stephen said, barely disguising his disgust. "If what you suspect is
true, he might not be worth saving. But he's still my brother—"

"And my husband."

He did not meet her eyes. "Yes, for what it's worth. I've never
held with the common currency that a man may allow himself the
luxury of more than one woman. A good woman—a woman like
yourself . . . should be enough for any man for a lifetime. For two
lifetimes."

A flood of tenderness washed over Della then, and she put out
one hand to touch Stephen's cheek. "I cannot promise anything,"
she faltered, "but I can listen and watch. And if I learn anything,
I'll send you a message by Bathsheba. But Stephen . . ."

"Don't say anything else," he said softly. "I understand what
I'm asking of you and what it costs. You are a woman of rare

courage, Della. I admire you more than I can say." He took her two hands and pressed them to his lips.

She did not pull them away. "Stephen," she murmured, "what about Judith? Will she not—be of some help to you?"

He set down her hands. "Judith will be going home to Richmond next week. I cannot be responsible for her safety now, and she'll be better off with her own people."

"And she—agrees to this?"

He shrugged. "She is going."

"Then," she said, parroting his words and tone, "she's even more of a fool than I supposed." She smiled to soften her words. "For surely, it would be better to be with you, no matter the danger."

A small knock at the door sounded then, and they drew slightly apart. At Stephen's word, Judith peeped round the door timidly, as though she would rather expire than disturb them. "I'm so sorry to intrude," she all but whispered, "but Bathsheba seems to have been taken ill. She complains of a biliousness and asks for her mistress."

Surprised, Della called out, almost too loudly for the room and the circumstances, "Bring her to me, please."

Judith withdrew and Stephen and Della regained their previous positions, she on the sofa, he facing her in a chair, without ever having said a word. Della knew that while Judith might not notice their proximity, Bathsheba would take its measure carefully.

The slave entered then, Judith fast behind her, and Della knew the instant she saw Sheba's face that something was afoot. "Mistress," she said mournfully, "I feel mighty poorly."

Della thought swiftly but kept the concern out of her voice. With mock annoyance, she said, "It's your stomach again?"

"Yes, ma'am," Bathsheba moaned softly.

Della rose and quickly embraced Stephen, not meeting his eyes. "This is what comes of spoiling niggers, she's just like an ol' lap dog to me now, and I can't deny her a thing." To Judith she said, "I'm so sorry, dear, we had planned to stay, and I know your cook'd like to kill us, but we'll simply have to take our leave with regrets and promise to come another time soon. When Bathsheba's stomach ails her, nothing will do but Mary Ann's special broth and her own bed, you know how they are. I swear, Phillip tells me I've ruined them with my indulgences, but what can I do?"

When they reached the door, Bathsheba holding her stomach and rolling her eyes like a spaniel, Judith fussing over them both and insisting they come again just as soon as they can, Stephen said casually, "Well, I'll be by then in a few days, Della, and we can work out the details."

She smiled at him courteously, one eye on Judith, and patted his hand. "Well, you know the way, dear, and you're welcome anytime."

They bundled themselves in the carriage, and Della waited until they were almost at the end of the drive before she turned on Bathsheba. "This better be important, Sheba."

The slave nodded. "Miz Judith, she be listenin' to ever word you an' Master Stephen say. She hear it, an' I 'spect de cook hear it, too."

Della shifted uncomfortably. "What in the world are you talking about?"

"I seen her. She don' know I seen, but I do. She listen on some sort o' ear trumpet thing she got in de kitchen at de flue. She put me in de back room, an' she don' know I see her, but she listen to ever word 'tween you an' Master Stephen. I come out once, an' she stop, but soon's I go away, she start again. So I start my groans up loud enough to drown you out, but she pay me no mind till de cook, she say I maybe got de dysentary. Dat get her quick enough, an' she put down her trumpet thing an' go get you. But she hear every word 'fore dat."

Della thought quickly over all they'd said; some of it could well be dangerous. Damaging, at the least. She flushed when she realized that likely, Judith heard her call her a fool. She certainly heard her agree to spy on her own husband. Della patted the slave's hand. "Thank you, Sheba. Miss Judith's going home to Richmond next week, so I doubt she'll be any more trouble to Master Stephen. Still, he should know of her perfidy."

Bathsheba stared at Della for a moment in the dark carriage. "Yes, ma'am. I 'spect you be tellin' him."

"At the first opportunity."

🌿 🌿 🌿

The following week, as promised, Stephen rode his black mare down the long path to Deepwater. Della kept him waiting as long as she dared, while Bathsheba powdered her shoulders and arranged her hair artfully into a loose bundle on the back of her head. When she finally descended the stairs into the parlor, she was pleased to see him brighten at her approach as though the sun only now shone on his shoulders after a day of gloom.

He stood and took her hands in his, kissing her gently and properly on both cheeks. Della called for Bathsheba to bring refreshments, for she trusted no one else to see them together. "Bring the hiperion tea," she said to Sheba proudly. "We'll not serve British tea another day in this house."

They had no more than taken their seats again when Stephen said, "I have news that Phillip will be returning tomorrow." He did not look especially pleased to say so.

"How do you know this? I haven't heard a word."

"There's scarcely a move he's made in Charleston that we *don't* know about," he said.

Della kept her voice bland. "Ah, I see. Then you know, also, who he has seen and where he's gone."

Stephen put a hand on hers. "Not really, Della. I only hear those details that would concern me." He peered at her closely. "Would you really want to know any others?"

She shook her head, removed her hand gracefully from his, and poured them both the steaming tea Bathsheba brought, passing him a delicate currant tart. "Not in the least. The damage was complete once I suspected."

Stephen glanced at Bathsheba. She gave him a warm smile, bowed slightly, and withdrew. As she left the room, he murmured, "Your woman seems more clever than most. She has a real dignity about her."

"She is a gem," Della said firmly, "and I don't know what I'd do without her. I believe she'd kill for me, if I asked her."

Stephen's brows raised. "You trust her that much?"

In answer, Della rose quietly with her finger to her lips, signaling Stephen to silence. She took him by the hand and drew him to the closed door of the parlor. Without warning, she pulled it open, to find Bathsheba sitting in a hard-backed chair right outside, her mending in her hand. She glanced at them and smiled, then went back to her work. Della closed the door.

"I didn't ask her to stand guard," she said, "but I knew she would. If someone wanted to come in here, they'd have to get past Sheba first." She led him to the chaise once more. "And you should know that her loyalty has already extended to you as well, Stephen."

"To me?"

She quickly told him of Bathsheba's ruse to get her away so that Judith could not listen to their words with her "ear trumpet thing." "Likely, the woman had been spying on you for a good while, Stephen," she finished briskly. "So it's a good thing you sent her packing. If it weren't for Bathsheba, she might be eavesdropping still."

He shook his head ruefully. "She's not a slave, she's a weapon and a shield, all at once."

Della grinned mischievously. "Exactly."

They resumed their seats, and this time, Stephen sat down more comfortably, within easy reaching distance of her hand. "Have you given any more thought to what you'll do when he returns?" he asked.

"Stephen, just tell me what you want me to do," she said. "I can't make any decisions until I know exactly what it is."

He smiled. "You are the most direct woman I know, Della. That is somewhat of a relief, I must say."

"Really? Then you must know a passel of ninnies. A woman who will not ask for what she wants won't get it, in this world. Besides, we haven't time to waste if Phillip will be home tomorrow. What would you have me do?"

He took a breath as though fortifying himself. "We know that the Highlanders are on the march, more than two thousand of them. We don't know their destination, but we suspect they're going to attempt to reconnoiter with Clinton and Cornwallis at Wilmington. The city cannot possibly stand against them, and if they take the Cape Fear, they take all of the colony. Charleston is already in their grip, which means they'll have the Carolinas entire. With the Carolinas, they can control shipping over much of the South."

"So you need to stop the Highlanders before they reach the other troops."

"Yes, and that won't be easy. General Macdonald commands them, and he's a veteran of the Battle of Culloden. He's a worthy adversary and a good strategist—"

"Do they have spies, too?"

"Of course."

Her eyes widened. "I wonder if any of our Loyalist friends are spying for them? Perhaps some of the very women I visited last month!"

"It's very likely." He nodded, his voice low and confiding. "They're not above putting their women at risk to save the country for the King."

"Well," she said frankly, "neither are you, to save it for yourselves."

He looked pained as he took her hands again. "Believe me, Della, if I thought you were risking any more than your domestic harmony, I would not ask. I would never put you in actual peril."

"I'd like to believe that," she said softly. This time, she did not withdraw her hands. "Tell me what I must do."

"Nothing but listen and learn what you can. General Macdonald's troops can take one of several routes downriver. If we know their route, we can plan best where to overtake them. We can't overpower them, so we must outwit them. To do that, we need the element of surprise and the choice of position. Phillip likely will know what we need already, but if he does not, he'll surely receive visitors or messages in the next few days that will tell him what we need to know. Simply find out, if you can, and get a message to me. Will Bathsheba bring it?"

"She would if I asked her. But I'll probably bring it myself."

"No, no," he said, alarmed, "you cannot be seen coming and going from Geneva, nor can we be seen together after today. To even send your woman is a risk, but it's a risk we must take. Send her by night and on foot—"

"I cannot ask her to go so far at night! The patrols will intercept her."

"Then send her on horseback, but dress her as a white woman and send along a man to accompany her. It would be too suspicious for a woman to be out alone, and she'll be taken, sure. Can she do it, do you think?"

"There's no one else I would trust with such a task, so she'll have to."

He put his lips to her hands and kissed them one by one, and she thought, almost idly, as though they had all the time in the world, that he did that deftly, with a certain tenderness that touched her. When she did not take her hands away, he turned over her palms and kissed those as well. She felt his kiss to the bottom of her stomach. When he raised his head again, his stare was so intense that she flushed.

"You are not only beautiful," he murmured, "you are brave."

She hesitated. "Master Gage," she almost whispered, "are you making love to me?"

He dropped his eyes, and for a long moment, he did not speak. "God help me, I am," he finally said. "And to my brother's wife." He set her hands down gently and rose to stand above her. "Please forgive me, Della. I am filled with admiration for you, but that is no excuse for my conduct. I cannot be in the same room with you without being aware of your—loveliness, in every way. But I'll not trouble you further, nor will I shame us both with my grotesque desires. If you can bring yourself to help your country, I hope you will do so. But if you cannot, I shall certainly understand and say no more about it—"

"Stephen," she said gently, rising to his side, "be still." She put a finger to his lips. "There is no shame in honest emotion, and I do not find you . . . grotesque . . . in the least. I shall send Bathsheba to you with my message as soon as I am able."

He bowed over her hand but did not embrace her in farewell. Before she could recover her composure, he was gone.

Bathsheba waited a heartbeat and then gently knocked on the door, coming in before she was beckoned. "De gentleman won' be stayin' for supper?" she asked softly.

"Sheba, come in and sit down," Della said, recovering herself. It was time. She could not do this alone, and too much depended on her to risk failure. She would be chancing her marriage and her security . . . but Bathsheba might well be risking her life. "There's something you must know," she began.

❦   ❦   ❦

Phillip came home the next day, greeting her with a fond embrace and a tepid kiss. She felt every nerve in her body alert to any changes in him, and she noticed some, to be sure. He seemed older somehow, more world-weary. Though she scrutinized him, he seemed to look right through her and not really see her at all. But he was attentive at dinner, passionate in bed, and try as she might, she could sense no other woman's presence on his skin or in his heart.

That first night, lying alongside him in the darkness, Della was stricken by guilt. The man did not deserve such betrayal. Yes, he was callous at times, insensitive, even cruel in his most extreme tempers, but he was also her husband. A man she vowed to love and honor for the rest of her days. He had given her the first home she had ever known, a luxury of days with only herself to pleasure, and a certain unwavering passion, even though she sometimes wondered if it was she that excited him or only her easy availability. To spy on him! To allow his brother to make love to her, however tentatively! She imagined the shame and sorrow Tess would have expressed at such behavior, and she cringed, closing her eyes in humiliation.

Then her mind rolled into the next trough of the waves that washed over her, and she grew angry and indignant at him, as he slept soundly on. To leave her at Christmas! To taunt her with some hussy in Charleston! To go days and days without the slightest crumb of affection and tenderness, only to expect her to welcome him happily the next night in her bed—the arrogance of the man! And to join some ragtag army, some misguided band of Tory zealots, risking his life, his fortune, without even thinking of her or consulting her in any way . . . it was more than any set of vows could countenance. More than she could bear.

Della tossed back and forth in her mind, moving her body as restlessly as her thoughts. She became aware, finally, of a rhythmic rustling noise when she rolled a certain way toward the edge of the bed, and she did it again deliberately. Something was under the feather bed. Some papers, by the sound of it. Phillip had hidden something there. She slipped her hand out in the darkness and carefully felt with her fingers under the mattress. The tips of her fingers brushed paper—a rather thick bundle of it, by the feel.

Letters from a mistress, perhaps? Was there no end to the man's treason? Without really meaning to, without planning what she might do should she succeed, she dug a little deeper, gripped the papers with her smaller fingers, and eased them out from under the bed. She laid them on her breast in the darkness, staring up at the ceiling and waiting for her breathing to calm. Phillip did not stir beside her.

He was normally a light sleeper, and often, if she rose in the night, he awakened and grumbled sleepily at the disturbance. There was a chance that if she slid from the bed to read the papers, he would awaken and she would be caught with them in her hands. She could drop them on the floor, under the bed, and retrieve them in the morning when he was gone. But what if he went for them for some reason before she could return them?

She dropped her hand over the side of the bed and let the packet of letters ease to the floor. Stealthily, she moved to slide her legs outside the coverlet, keeping the mattress as steady as possible. The bed creaked abominably, and she made a promise to herself to have it oiled and tightened no later than tomorrow. She stood alongside the bed, barely breathing, watching Phillip sleep. He rolled over toward her side of the bed, murmuring something low. She froze, her toes touching the edge of the letter packet on the floor.

After long moments, he was still again. She bent, retrieved the letters, and crept to the far side of the room where moonlight streamed in from the casement window.

Now, she was at greatest risk. He had only to roll over, open his eyes, see her silhouetted against the light, and know in an instant what she did there. Her fingers trembled slightly as she drew the string off the packet. Some of the papers were older, and they crackled as she unfolded them. She frowned in concentration and peeled them apart, one by one. Six letters. She scanned the first one hurriedly, holding it to the moonlight and straining to see the dim, cursive handwriting.

"My sweetest heart—" it began, followed by a paragraph of endearments and what appeared to be a plea for an end to some quarrel. The paper was crosshatched with lines to save space, and Della had to hold it quite close to her nose to make it out. She turned it over and deciphered the barely legible signature. "Your loving, Cathleen." Turned it over again, searching for a date. None at the top, none at the bottom, perhaps in the body of the letter—

With a snort of disgust, she laid the paper down as though it were unclean.

The next page was of the same hand. She scanned again for a date, found none, and ruefully shook her head. The only reason to omit a date was to protect oneself, should the letter be found by an indignant spouse. The woman was no amateur.

The next letter, the same, and the one after that. The final letter was in a different hand, and she cast the rest away in the shadows to peer more closely at it.

"For Captain Phillip Gage," it began. Captain! "Our reports indicate that General Macdonald's Highlanders should reach the outskirts of Marlborough by the tenth of the month, assuming easy traverse of South Black fork—"

Phillip turned in the bed, groaned softly, and Della quickly dropped the paper, scooting all of them under the linen ruffle of her nightgown. Her husband rolled again, shifted his weight ominously, and called out, "Della?" half awake.

Della reached up and in a panic, wrenched the gold filigree locket off her neck where it usually nestled on her bosom. The chain parted, and she stood with it in her hand, keeping her body and gown between Phillip and the letters.

"Della?" He was more awake now, up on one elbow, peering at her in the darkness. "Where are you?"

"Here, dear," she said, scuffing the letters swiftly under the window cushion with one hand, as she walked toward him, her other hand extended. "I finally found it."

"Found what?" he inquired sleepily.

"My locket." She showed it to him plainly. "I lost it earlier, and I was frantic. But I remembered that I'd been reading in the window seat, and maybe it was there. Sure enough," she smiled tremulously, "it was in the cushion fold."

"And that couldn't wait until morning?"

She slid under the coverlet next to him, still gripping the locket. "I just couldn't rest until I searched for it. But I found it."

"I shall say a prayer of thanksgiving come the morrow," he grumbled into the pillow. "Can we have some peace and quiet now?"

"Yes," she said, feigning contentment. "Now I can sleep."

She lay quite still as he drifted back into unconsciousness, scarcely allowing herself to breathe. She had the information Stephen sought, and in the first night her husband was at home. She could send the one promised message and then stop this betrayal now, put an end to this risk to her home and her heart. Somehow, she would replace the letters before Phillip missed them, string intact, no sign of disturbance, and then she would never again put herself or him in harm's way.

She clenched the locket firmly, told herself to open her eyes at dawn well before Phillip stirred, and slid back into uneasy sleep.

※ ※ ※

"Sheba, if you don't want to do this, I won't make you," Della said earnestly. "In all conscience, slave or no, I can't send you into peril unless you're willing."

They were in Della's room, dressing Bathsheba for her midnight ride to Geneva. Della's velvet cloak covered her well, including her head, and she wore her mistress's best riding shoes, gloves, and bonnet. Pinned under the bonnet were ringlets of false curls that Della sometimes used to plump up her own coiffure. From a distance of a dozen feet, Bathsheba looked like the well-to-do mistress of some local plantation—until she turned her head.

"I be willin'," Bathsheba said calmly. "If de patrolers catch me, I break down an' weep an' say I stole my madam's clothes, an' dey bring me back for a whippin'."

"Try not to lose the mare, Phillip'd have a fit."

"I be more scared o' de horse den de patrolers."

"She's gentle as a lamb, Sheba, just keep to the river and give her her head and kick her flanks, and she'll be to Geneva's dock before the moon is gone. Thank God, Phillip's gone again, I'd hate to try to sneak you past him as well. We must lighten your skin somehow," Della muttered as she tugged at Bathsheba's curls. "It's all for naught if they see that color."

"Maybe dat rice powder?"

Della took her puff and smoothed her whitest powder over Bathsheba's cheeks and nose. To her surprise, it did help a little. "A veil," she said. "That's what we need." She reached up to a box at the top of the bureau and pulled out a short riding veil, fluffing it as she placed it over Bathsheba's head. "There, that's better. Now, what do you say if you're stopped?"

"Dat my horse pull up lame, an' I be out too long. Dat my husban', he be worrit—"

Della frowned. "Your voice will give you away, Sheba. You sound like a nigger."

The woman lifted her chin with some dignity. "Dat what I be, for truth."

"Say this. 'Sir, please let me pass.' "

"Suh, please le' me pass."

"*Sir.* Please *let* me pass."

"Suh, please *let* me pass."

Della sighed. "That's a little better. Best if you not speak at all."

"Bes' if I don' get catched at all."

"And you are to give this only to Master Stephen's hands," Della reminded her, tucking the folded message inside the hidden pocket of the mantua.

"An' I come back nex' mornin'?"

"Only if he thinks it safe. He'll tell you what to do, Sheba, you must look to Master Stephen to know what's best once you arrive."

The slave regarded Della carefully. "He a good man."

"The best," Della said briskly. "Now, Godspeed, my dear, and I'll not sleep a wink until you're safe back under this roof." She pressed a silver into Sheba's hand as they descended the stairs and out the back to the stables. "No matter what else happens, this is yours to keep, and another when you come back safely delivered."

Bathsheba's white teeth shone in the darkness in a rare smile. "Bes' give one to de mare."

Della stood by firmly as the black groom mumbled and fumbled his way round the fact that he was mounting a house slave on the master's best mare. After some initial complaint and fretting, he resigned himself to sharing in whatever punishment Bathsheba would likely garner. The fact was, Della was there and the master was not, and the jut of her jaw told him plainly enough that she would not be dissuaded.

"De whol' world gone crazy," he muttered as Bathsheba mounted, carefully adjusted Della's best habit and veil.

"You are to say not a word of this to a soul, Jacob," Della said crisply, "do you understand? No one has seen Bathsheba but you, so if gossip spreads, I'll be sure to know which tongue to twist for it."

"No'm," Jacob murmured, his head down. He wished to be anyplace at all but there.

"I wish I could carry de light along," Bathsheba said wistfully, eyeing the oil lantern at the groom's feet.

"If you keep to the path along the river, the moon off the water will be plenty of light. Also, every place along the way will have lights, so just keep the water to one side and the lights to the other, and you can't lose your way," Della reassured her.

Bathsheba touched her heels to the mare's belly gingerly and lifted the reins as Della had showed her, and the mare moved off smoothly in the direction of the path along the river. Once, Sheba glanced back at her mistress standing there and lifted her hand in a solitary wave. Della realized then that she had been holding her breath, and she let it out in a long sigh.

It would be a very long night.

🌿 🌿 🌿

Sometime before dawn, Della lay awake thinking of her past choices. She had married Phillip in a fever of something—she had assumed it was love at the time. He seemed to share the feeling, whatever it was. She realized as she remembered their courtship and early years of marriage that a certain pattern had developed. He'd insult her or hurt her in some way and then offer her something in return. Sometimes it would be a sarcastic insinuation over dinner, followed by a lovely piece of jewelry he brought back from Charleston on his next trip. Sometimes a bruise during lovemaking—which had grown increasingly rough, as she thought about it—soothed over by an offer to rub her neck the next night. If she took his offering, he believed that she had forgiven him.

But in truth, she never forgave him at all.

She recalled vividly the last time—perhaps it would truly *be* the last time—he put his hands on her neck to soothe the tension there. He began to massage her, and she should have leaned into him, but she stayed stiff and wary. She understood his touch in that moment. He would put his hands on her whether or not she wanted them, most particularly if she did not. She had tried to relax, go limp into his hands, promising herself that he would tire soon. But his fingers grew more forceful, attacking the cords of her neck with subtle ferocity. She pulled away with a wrench, stood up, and tried to move away, but he grabbed her wrist and held it, pulling her back down again, turning her and putting his hands back on her neck, now moving down over her shoulders and onto her breasts. She instantly ceased her defiance and allowed him to do what he wished. Becoming, finally, a partner to her own slavery.

This is how such things happen, she thought now. Once you accept the lie and perpetuate it, you become a part of it with him.

In the first few months she had known him, while they were beginning to fall in love, she had realized even then that he wanted to change her in some way. At first, she understood, even was thrilled that he cared enough to want to make her more perfect for him. He said she should speak a little softer, should sit up straighter, should stop touching her hair when she talked. He said he was telling her these things because he cared. For her own good. To make her even more beautiful than she already was. And she beamed at him in gratitude.

The pattern became more clear after their marriage. She would feel safe and close to him for a week, even a month at a time. Then her hopes would rise like warm, spring air, and she would think that the difficult part of their marriage was over. They would have babies now, be a family, be happy always. They would grow old together in mutual love, kindness, and respect. And then one day, the overseer would allow the slaves too long in the shade, or the rice would dry at an inopportune time, or the breakfast biscuits would be too heavy, and he would grow cold and aloof.

In moments, it seemed to her, everything she said and did was suddenly ugly and grotesque. Every word, every movement a thing to improve or correct. She was growing careless in her grooming, he would say, sniffing the air about her in an innocent manner. Or others found her just a trifle superficial. Or she should be more careful about her grammar and certainly more selective about what she said in certain company.

Her faults—and the faults of their life together—were so numerous as to submerge her. She could not keep track of it all. Why did he bother with her? she wondered aloud. Why touch her at all? she wept finally, miserably. Because he loved her, he said. Because he cared enough to want the best for both of them.

And the more aloof he grew, the more she fulfilled his slander. She *did* care less and less about her grooming, she did speak too fast about nothing, and she did, indeed, laugh indiscriminately in a vague and desperate seeking of some sort of joy, somewhere.

Della realized as she lay there that it was a lie that anger strengthened one's will. This sort of day-to-day anger only made one weary. Like a tide running always out, it depleted and exhausted rather than bolstered. And so he sought to control the ebb and flow of their days: his distance, his criticisms, her attempts to please, his coldness, her weeping, his apology. And then her final pained and cooling silence.

And what choices did she have, after all was said and done? She knew that sometimes, perhaps in New York or in Boston, married people divorced each other. Sometimes, they simply agreed to no longer occupy the same home, but they did not attempt to sever their union. To do so was almost impossible.

Not a woman she knew spoke of such. Not a marriage she saw seemed anything but harmonious. She rolled over and buried her face in her pillow. She was thirty. Perhaps she would have another forty years left of her life, if she were fortunate. More than the years she had already lived. And she would be trapped in this childless, loveless marriage until the end of those days.

As she closed her eyes against the impossibility of such a sentence, she heard the faint clopping of the hooves of the mare moving closer to the house. Bathsheba, home safe from Stephen.

Stephen. She rose rapidly, pulled her wrapper about her body, and hurried down the stairs to see her slave.

☙ ☙ ☙

The Widow Moore had a small plantation up a tributary of the South Black River, set on a coastal plain. The creek that watered her land meandered slowly, and in its marshes, Venus flytraps and swamp flowers bloomed in the shadows of the tall ferns. Just eighteen miles north of Wilmington, the creek was the last gasp of the river and here, it was more than thirty feet wide, almost as deep, with water black as the cypress roots on its banks, fordable by a lone bridge.

Brigadier General Donald Macdonald, in charge of the Highlanders Regiment, had marched from Cross Creek down the west bank of the Cape Fear for Brunswick, a hundred miles to the south. But when he heard that Colonel James Moore's first North Carolina Continentals lay in wait for him, he wisely stopped to strategize.

Most important, he must reach the coast with his troops intact. Though he might outnumber the rebels, they knew the lay of the land and had surprise in their favor. He decided to test the riffraff's resolve. Next morning, his Highlanders held a parade and rally, complete with pipes and a huzzah for the King. The only falter was the discovery that one of the companies had gone over the hill in the night, leaving a note that "*their courage was not warproof.*"

Macdonald complimented those troops left, sufficient to stop any rebel force to be sure, and sent a firm message to Colonel Moore ordering him to lay down his arms or "*suffer the fate of an enemy of the Crown.*"

The answer came back quickly enough. Moore said the Highlanders should turn and go back to their cottages or be treated as enemies of the constitutional liberties of America.

Macdonald poured over his notes and his surveys of the terrain. Moore was too strongly entrenched. Nothing for it but to go back to Cross Creek, ford the Cape Fear, and continue down the Black River, coming to Wilmington by the back door. Except for the last obstacle, Widow Moore's Creek, it was a clear shot to Wilmington and the Royal Navy's warships.

And best of all, when he turned his regiments back again, he felt sure that Colonel Moore would interpret his movements as retreat. With luck, the rebels would not discover their new route until it was too late and they were within shooting distance of Wilmington.

As he turned his regiments back, he sent a quick message to two Loyalist regiments that were forming to join him down the Cape Fear. One letter went to Captain Phillip Gage . . . and from thence to Della, to Bathsheba, and to his brother, Stephen.

Colonel Moore let him slip away. Caswell was hurrying forward with eight hundred militia and Minute Men; Ashe's rangers and Lillington's Minute Men were coming west from Wilmington. Let General Macdonald exhaust his Highlanders backtracking and fording the Cape Fear, Moore told himself. And when he turns east again, we'll be tripled in strength.

James Moore was the third of his name in America, a family known for its bold defiance. His troops were a blend of Scotch-Irish, Germans, French, and English, and not a one of them unseasoned. Already tempered by the Regulator wars, they had trained under three different colonels, and they sensed victory near. The Highlanders, they told themselves, were in for a fight.

General Macdonald marched his men confidently along the Black River, thinking they were largely unobserved. That impression was strengthened as they came closer to Moore's Creek, for they happened on a rebel camp that had evidently been left in a panic. The fires were warm and a few horses were still tethered.

The sacrifice of those horses was no accident. Long aware of the exact position of the Highlanders, Caswell had already crossed the bridge at Widow Moore's Creek, then sent a band back to weaken some trusses and grease the boards with soft soap and tallow. Colonel Lillington's Minute Men were waiting in dugout trenches a few hundred feet back from the creek. They smothered their fires and waited for General Macdonald to bring on the Scots.

Before dawn, the Highlanders reached the bridge and formed into a narrow column to cross the funnel of the small bridge. It was still too dark to tell friend from foe. As forty men went forward, a sentinel heard them coming and called out a challenge. McLean, the head of the command, answered in Gaelic, thinking that somehow some of his own men must have got in front of him.

Silence was the only response. The forty were joined by forty more, under Colonel McLeod, and now eighty Highland broadswordsmen began to cross the bridge. Half immediately fell off the greased boards into the deep, cold water; half made it across to within thirty paces of Lillington's concealed Minutemen. There, they fell under a devastating barrage. McLeod died with twenty bullet wounds, and forty-nine other Scots were massacred.

The Highlanders retreated in a panic back to the camp they'd just left, but they were chased by Caswell, Lillington, and now Moore's men, too, who had finally caught up to the others. Dispirited and panicked, they were easily taken, and in the final tally, only one rebel was killed. More than fifty Highlanders were killed or wounded, nearly nine hundred were captured, including General Macdonald. The Patriots also took plenty of ammunition, muskets, swords, wagons, medical supplies, and a chest containing more than fifteen thousand pounds sterling for their trouble.

When news of the Patriot victory reached Wilmington, the town erupted in a whoop of sheer celebration and confidence. They called it "the Lexington and Concord of the South," and they were justified, for that three-minute ambush stymied the British attempt to blockade the Carolinas at the start of the war.

But in the moment of celebration, Loyalists all over the county were hiding their valuables, collecting what they might need for a quick exodus, and loading their pistols for protection.

🌿 🌿 🌿

At Deepwater, Della waited alone with the news, wondering if Phillip was alive or dead. He had left two nights before the battle, tight-lipped and silent. She could only assume that he intended to join the fight, though she did not ask. His grim look kept her at arm's length, even had she wanted to embrace him and ask him to keep out of danger.

The isolation was the most frightening part of the wait. Della yearned to see Severn or to hear her voice, if only to know that Wilmington still was safe, that the streets were not overrun with pillaging Redcoats. Every woman had heard the horror stories of the way the British soldiers raped and brutalized the wives left alone on far-flung farms and plantations. Young girls of twelve and thirteen in Concord and Boston had been repeatedly attacked, some of them dragged out of their homes by force and into the British camps, never to be seen alive again.

Della kept the loaded pistol at her side and Bathsheba always within her sight, even after she heard the news of the Highlander defeat. Perhaps, even now, those Scots who had slipped away were moving through the dark woods back upriver, right at the edge of her rice fields.

When she heard the muffled arrival of someone at the door, the soft snorts of the horse and the distant thud of boots, she held the pistol in both hands before her as she descended the stairs, while Bathsheba stood staring, wide-eyed and frozen, at the top landing. A pounding now at the door, and Della almost screamed aloud in her fright. Then a familiar voice, "Della! Della, open the door!"

It was Stephen. She flew down the stairs, dropped the pistol in her confusion, and wrenched open the door. When she saw his face, the broadness and strength of him, she forgot herself completely and fell into his arms. "Thank God, it's you," she cried. "I've been scared half out of my wits, jumping at every noise! Are the Scots on the roads? Are they going to bring the gunboats upriver?" She realized that Bathsheba had descended the stairs behind her, and she abruptly withdrew from Stephen's embrace.

He let her go. "Haven't you heard about the victory?"

"Of course, but surely the British won't let it go at that! Phillip's gone off, to battle for all I know, and I'm here alone, and every shadow looks like a disgruntled Scotsman to me—"

He strode into the house then, tossing off his cape and hat as though taking possession with both of them. "We know where

Phillip is," he said swiftly, pulling her after him. "Bathsheba, can you bring us something hot to drink? The wind is sharp, and these hands are cold—"

Della realized then he still had ahold of her hands, and she snatched them back, following along behind him into the parlor. "You know where he is? Is he safe?"

"Safe as any other Loyalist in the county tonight. His regiment was waiting to join Macdonald six miles out of Wilmington, we had them surrounded all the time. But when Macdonald turned tail, we left them there to make their own way home."

"To fight again another day!" she gasped, appalled at the wasted opportunity.

He shook his head, reaching for the hot coffee that Bathsheba brought in. "Most of his regiment are gentlemen, planters and such just like him. They'll take the oath, soon as they see they've lost, but putting them in stockade won't help our cause or win them over any sooner. We chose to let them go and chase the firebrands instead. Highlanders would rather swing a broadsword than eat, and we needed to break them now."

"We. You were there? You saw the battle?"

"My regiment was detailed to intercept Macdonald if he got past Moore's Creek bridge. We were six miles out of Wilmington."

Her eyes widened. "You watched your own brother, then."

He nodded sadly. "Though he never knew it."

"So I might have lost you both," she murmured.

He watched her carefully over the rim of his cup and said nothing.

"When will he return?"

"Tonight, most likely."

She flinched, moving slightly away from him. "Then you must go at once. He'll be furious if he finds you here."

"It's past time for that, Della," Stephen said calmly. "Phillip's got damn few choices left, and I'm the best of what he's got. He's my brother, and I won't see him arrested or broken, like most of his political stripe will be. He's got to either take the oath or leave the Cape Fear. Maybe go east, maybe north, though they're more rabid about Tories in Boston and New York than here—maybe Canada for a while. Many are emigrating to Nova Scotia—"

"You can't mean it!" Della gasped. "Leave Deepwater? For some frozen wasteland a million miles away?"

"Not nearly so far nor nearly so frozen," Stephen said, with the smallest of smiles. "But certainly, yes, it will be a sacrifice. That's why I'm hoping to persuade him of the folly of resisting so stubbornly. We need good men, and he need only take the oath of loyalty to America, and all will be forgiven."

"He might hear it from anyone but you," she murmured, shaking her head. "But you know how he is, Stephen. He's become so . . . so angry."

Stephen watched her carefully. "Has he shown that anger to you as well, Della?"

She smiled as though to shrug off his concern. "I'm hardly the kind of wife he needs right now, am I? Naturally, he would prefer my agreement."

"You could never be the kind of woman who simply takes a stance because her husband has decreed it," he said softly. "I'm sure that's one of the reasons he loves you."

She averted her eyes. "Loved me. Perhaps. But as so often happens, what was once an intriguing piquancy is now an intolerable annoyance."

Without warning, Stephen bent toward her, hesitated an instant, looking into her eyes, and then kissed her lips softly. "I cannot imagine any man," he murmured, inches from her, "wanting to quell that spirit. Or being able to." His lips sought hers again, this time with less hesitation.

Della felt her own lips tremble under his, as though she had not been kissed for a lifetime. Indeed, in some part of her heart, she felt exactly that virgin to his touch. A distant roaring in her ears came closer and faster, and she realized she could hear her own heartbeat. It was not a graceful or an easy kiss, but one that was almost wrenched out of them both, painful and eager and full of terror. A piece of her shouted within her, Stop this, stop him! but she did not flinch away. She could not. In that instant, she needed his kiss as she needed sun on her skin and air in her lungs.

And then her mind came abruptly back to her, and she jerked herself away. "Stop this," she said in a reverie, as though she had heard it elsewhere and merely repeated it aloud. "You must stop this, Stephen."

His face was full of torment. "Must I? Tell me why, Della? You cannot love him. You say he does not love you. Perhaps he will even be banished from the Carolinas for good, and would you go with him? Yours will not be the first union that is sacrificed to the cause of freedom—"

"Oh, don't," she said, her mouth twisting with what felt dangerously close to disdain. "Don't let's tell ourselves that this is for the noble cause of liberty. At the least, we will be honest with each other."

"Yes," he said, looking slightly abashed. "You are right, of course, Della. This has less to do with politics than passion. But this isn't a base feeling I have for you, I know it."

"What then?" She stood, suddenly angry at Stephen, at Phillip, at the world, yes even at herself. "Do you propose we abandon ourselves to the general lunacy and run away to someplace where marriage vows mean as little as yesterday's hoecakes?"

He visibly winced at the harshness in her voice.

"You want me to abandon my husband? *Your* brother? To cast aside my vows and his honor and be another Judith to you? Or do you merely want to take what kisses you can and leave me less content than you found me, wishing I never laid eyes on you, Stephen Gage!" She felt a thrill of instinctive panic, a thrumming of revulsion through her, as though she had just discovered that the trapped butterfly fluttering in her hair was a bat.

He stood then and embraced her, ignoring the angry stiffness of her back and shoulders. "I love you, Della. I have from the first time I saw you. You must make of that what you will." As she twisted to release herself, he held her chin so that she must look at him. "When Phillip returns, I will come to see him and tell him that he must either take the loyalty oath or leave the county, I can't protect him further. If he chooses to join us, I'll never speak of my feelings again, Della. If he leaves the Carolinas for good, then you'll have the choice to make as well, for he cannot compel you to go with him."

"And if he chooses to stay and fight?"

"Then as a traitor to his country, he'll likely be shot."

Her eyes widened. "You would have your own brother shot?"

He shook his head slowly, as though only now seeing what could come. "No, but I will not stand between him and the bullet. Not anymore."

"And when you come to speak with your brother," she said

more softly, "will you also tell him of your feelings for his wife?"

"If you would have me do so, yes, I will." His head was high now.

Now it was her turn to shake her head, but she did so reluctantly. "Please say nothing to him at all, Stephen, save what you must to save his life." She turned away, letting the weariness show in her voice. "Now leave me, if you will. I'll be safe enough until he comes."

As though to prove her words, Bathsheba came and knocked softly at the parlor door in that moment. She peeped inside. "Do you need anythin', Miz Della?"

Della did not turn to look at the slave. "No. We're through here," she said quietly. She watched as Stephen bowed to her and took his leave with his usual unhurried grace.

When she heard the front door close behind him, she turned to Bathsheba calmly. "I want you to wash and scent my hair; and be sure my velvet dressing gown is brushed. The red one that Phillip likes. He's coming home tonight."

The slave watched her carefully, making no effort to conceal her surprise.

"Well? Did you have some question, Sheba?" Della snapped, at once full of vexation all over again.

"No'm," the woman said gently. "I go make de water ready."

Phillip did not arrive that night, though Della was prepared to greet him as she thought he might appreciate. The following night, she once again readied herself as though for the first time with her husband. *He has, after all, been in battle or close to it,* she told herself, *so he would surely appreciate some tenderness.*

He did not come to knock at her door as soon as he was in the house, and she wilted slightly, once more aware at how far apart they had grown. But she waited for him in her room, sending a message to him through Bathsheba that she was looking forward to seeing him.

Finally, his knock came at her door, and she opened to find him still in his shirtsleeves and slightly drunk. It was only eight o'clock, and by the stains on his bodice, she was sharply disappointed to realize that he must have eaten without her as well.

"My dear," she said gently, embracing him and drawing him into the room. "I'm so glad you're home safely."

"Home?" he asked, with a sardonic lilt. "Is that where I am, truly? Feels more and more like your place, Della, not mine."

"Well, if you'd stay at home more, perhaps you'd find it more to your liking," she said. Then she stopped herself with an internal rebuke. She did not want to fight him now. "Did you eat already? I had hoped we'd have a late supper together—"

"Had you?" he asked, watching her carefully. "I didn't know."

She took his hand and drew him down next to her on the chaise. "I know where you've been, Phillip," she said quietly.

He looked instantly wary. "And how do you know that?"

She took a deep breath. "Stephen told me."

"Stephen!"

"Yes," she went on swiftly, still holding onto his hand. "His regiment was in the field, he said, six miles out of Wilmington. He was ready to fight you if he had to. He was very glad it didn't come to that, and he came to tell me that you're in grave danger. We both are. And he's very worried—"

Phillip gave a sharp snort of derision. "As well he might be. It's one thing for the rebels to scatter an unruly pack of Scots, it's quite another thing to beat the King's best. When Sir Clinton gets here, the Cape will be under English rule once more."

She shook her head sadly. "That's not what Stephen says. He says you have but one chance to save your life. Take the loyalty oath or flee to Canada. Either that or be arrested. Perhaps even shot."

His laughter was ugly and sardonic. "My little brother came all the way over here to tell you this? I suppose he told you that the rebels have arms and munitions to rival the King's army and that the American gunboats can sink anything Cornwallis can put afloat."

"No," she said quietly, "but he did say they were determined."

"As are we. Well, he needn't worry about me, my pet, nor should you. Wilmington will fall to Clinton fast enough, and Charleston soon after. This 'war' will never be more than a footnote in English history. The uprising of rebel upstarts." He glared at her. "And as for my brother, I'll be sure he understands that he is not welcome in this house under the present tensions. Unless, of course, he chooses to take an oath of fealty to his King. If he comes up the drive again, Della, you will not receive him, do you understand?''

She looked down, silent.

He watched her. The silence grew between them unbearably. ''What else did my brother have to say?'' he finally asked, his voice low and ominous.

She looked up quickly and saw the suspicion in his eyes. She averted her own. ''He thinks it a shame,'' she said softly, ''that you leave me alone so much.''

''Ah, does he. Well, and I'm certain you appreciate his concern.'' Phillip's voice was arid as a cotton field in August. He stood abruptly, dropping her hand. ''It occurs to me, Della, that you have entirely too little to do around here. Of course, you can't take the carriage out, but still there must be plenty to keep you occupied at Deepwater, if you would only put your hands to it. The kitchen is a disgrace—''

''What's wrong with the kitchen?'' she asked, amazed. How did they get on this tack? ''Mary Ann is a good cook—''

''She's a monstrous cook, and the meals are presented in a slovenly manner. I am ashamed to bring gentlemen to supper, there is such a vast discrepancy between what Deepwater should offer and what it does.''

With that, she erupted in anger. ''You are never here enough to know *what* goes on at Deepwater. And if you do not bring your friends here, it's not for fault with poor Mary Ann, it's for fault with *me!* Your constant criticisms, your aloof demeanor, it's me you're ashamed of, Phillip, and don't think I don't see it clear enough!''

He regarded her long and appraisingly. Finally he said, ''You need a child, Della. You need something to occupy yourself, or you'll drive us both mad.''

She wanted to slap him, but she gripped her hands together until her nails pressed into her palms. ''A child! Yes, that would be a comfort, indeed. But to get a child, I need a husband!''

''You have a husband.''

''But he has interests elsewhere!''

''He has responsibilities elsewhere. And you, who have few responsibilities at all, could scarcely understand that.''

With all her heart, she yearned to tell him about her most recent responsibilities and how she had fulfilled them. Let him smirk at her once he discovered her role in the defeat of the Scots at Moore's Creek bridge, let him try and maintain that superior hatefulness after he learned of Bathsheba's ride in the night—but she stopped and calmed herself. The man was a fool. Remember that, she whispered. A pompous, arrogant—

"A child would calm you down, Della," he was saying.

"A child would keep me in my place, you mean," she retorted. "But well enough, get me with child. Of course, that would mean you would need to be home long enough to accomplish the task. Whether or not you can make the sacrifice remains to be seen."

"Frankly, I doubt my absence is sufficient excuse anymore. It's been too long, and we've had plenty of opportunity, I should think. Most women taken to wife are bred within the year, the rest within several at the least. You, however, remain barren."

She raised her brows. "Do you imply the fault is mine?"

He bowed low and insinuatingly. "I've never had any complaints before."

Her anger went out of her as abruptly as though someone had punched her in the stomach. She put her hands to her eyes and began to weep. "Oh, Phillip, how have we come to this sorry pass?" she murmured, the words choked and halting.

He did not touch her nor incline toward her. "The best laid plans of mice and men gang aft a-gley," he said briskly. "One cannot say, madam, that you have been poorly laid."

A great coldness settled over her heart then, and her tears dried as suddenly as they had started. "Well," she said finally, "that is as vulgar a response as I'd have expected from you, I suppose. Please leave me now, Phillip." She turned her back to him as though he were no longer in the room.

"Believe me, Della," he said amiably, "a child would do wonders for you. If you cannot have one, I can buy you one quick enough. You should reconsider the possibility."

"I am reconsidering everything, Phillip," she said as evenly as she could manage. "Everything in my life."

He stood and watched her for a moment, as though seeing her for the first time. Then he turned and left her.

❦ ❦ ❦

That night, Della slept fitfully and alone. Each time she woke, it was with the vague feeling that something was not only wrong, but was going to get worse as soon as she could fathom what it was. She lay awake for hours, listening to the even breathing of Bathsheba on the cot at her feet. She envied the woman, black as she was, slave though she be, for the freedom she had on some level that Della could never have. The woman she could never be. The liberty to have no man at all in her life, to make no decisions about her own welfare, to know, always and forever, that she had a place to sleep, food to eat, and must only please her mistress to survive. A woman alone.

In the middle of the night, Della heard a new noise from below. The sound of hoofbeats coming up the long drive and at a rapid pace. She leaned up on one elbow and listened. Bathsheba's breathing had changed also. In the darkness, Della whispered, "Sheba, do you hear that?"

"Yes'm," the slave answered. "Sound like five horse, maybe more."

Della rose quickly and threw on her wrapper. The fear in her stomach had blossomed to a cold, searching dread by the time she hurried down the stairs to the upper landing. Phillip was already at the door, and she saw him yank it open, with one hand buttoning his coat. His pistol was jammed in his pants, visible only from the rear.

She stifled a gasp as he threw open the door. Before him stood five men, all of them armed with muskets. She could hear the stamping and snorting of their horses at the picket rail, as though the animals also shared her alarm. Bathsheba stole to her side and touched her shoulder. "Best come back up, Miz Della," she said softly. Della shrugged off her hand and called out, "Phillip, what is it!"

He turned and she saw his mouth turn down in a violent curse. "Go back, Della!" he cried out hoarsely. "This doesn't concern you!"

She ignored his command, leaning down so that she could see what the intruders intended. She heard one of the men mutter in a low voice, and her husband's low rumble of anger, but she could not make out their words. In a flash, Phillip drew his pistol, and she screamed in terror, but as he raised the weapon, one of the men knocked it out of his hand, another roughly grabbed his shoulder, and he was hustled out the door, surrounded by the shadowed strangers. The door slammed, and Della raced downstairs in her bare feet, Bathsheba right behind her, imploring her to come back. As they reached the door, Bathsheba grabbed her and held her aside, gripping her shoulders so that she could not open it.

"Miz Della, he be arrested! Don' go out or dey take you, too!"

"Arrested!" Della cried, trying to wrench herself out of the slave's strong hands. "They can't do this!"

"Dey do it, an' dey take de wife, too, if she on his side!"

"How do you know such a thing? That's ridiculous!"

"Master Stephen tell me, an' he say if dey come, I to lock you in de room! If dey take you, too, you be no help to Master Phillip at all!"

Panting, Della threw off her hands and slumped against the wall. She could hear the men mounting their horses, heard the snap of rough orders, could not hear her husband's voice, and she flew to the window to look out. Phillip was up on a spare mount now, tied between two of the rebels. Two more were close behind him and a fifth led the column away from the house. The darkness quickly hid their retreat, and she was left with only the sound of their hooves rumbling away down the road. It seemed in that instant that she would never see Phillip again.

"My God, they've taken him away," she cried, gripping the sill and weeping. "I told him this would happen! Stephen told me to warn him!"

Bathsheba collected her from the window and pulled her toward the stairs. "Get dressed, Miz Della. We go to Master Stephen, an' he make it right."

"Yes," Della said in a sudden flurry, rushing up the stairs, "Stephen must do something! He'll know where they've taken him, and he'll get him free." She began to weep anew as she hurried into her clothing. "They never even gave him a chance to take the oath, perhaps he would have if they had asked him—"

"He drew his gun," Bathsheba said quietly as she helped Della into her cloak. "Dey don' talk much after that."

Sobered, Della grabbed her valise, stuffed it quickly with what she might need for a few nights of bare comfort, and called for the carriage to be brought round at once.

By the time they reached Geneva, dawn was creeping slowly over the river and a low mist obscured the house among the trees. A single light burned in the upstairs wing. Della knew that Stephen was up, might even be waiting for her arrival. She brushed past the slave at the door and hurried up the stairs, calling out to him with little regard for propriety. "Stephen! Stephen, it's Della! Stephen, they've taken Phillip!"

He appeared at the open door to his study, the light haloing his head and shoulders. He was in his dressing gown, his shirt rumpled and open at the chest. Without further explanation, she threw herself in his arms, sobbing and gripping at his shoulders. "They came and took Phillip away! Five men with muskets! You've got to save him, Stephen! Where have they taken him?"

He held her gingerly, she could feel the hesitation in him, and it frightened her even more. "You said you could save him!" she cried, pulling away and searching his face for comfort.

"No," he said painfully, "I said he could save himself." He drew her inside the room and set her gently in a chair by his mahogany desk. "I didn't think they'd move so quickly," he murmured, half to himself.

"They didn't even give him time to pack a bag! He couldn't even say goodbye!" She was no longer weeping now, the anger was rising in her as fast as her tears ebbed.

"Was he armed?"

"Yes, he pulled out his pistol—"

"Ah, God," Stephen moaned with despair, "that'll make it go harder on him."

"But they came with no warning! What else should he do, they might have been criminals!"

He shook his head. "That's the way they move. They doubtless wanted to take him before he could escape to Canada."

Something in his voice made Della pause in her weeping, and a sudden knowledge flooded her. "Did you know they were going to arrest him?"

Stephen looked away, stricken.

"You knew," she whispered. "Likely, even to the time of it."

"I told you so, didn't I?" He began to pace the room. "I told you he was in danger, that *you* were in danger. I said he had few options, and they were winnowing fast—"

"But they never even questioned him. They gave him *no* options at all! He might have taken the oath—"

"He never would have," Stephen said, almost scornfully. "You said as much yourself."

"They never gave him a chance!" Her eyes narrowed as she watched him. "*You* never gave him a chance." She stood and faced him then. "You had your own brother arrested. You told them when he would return, when they might take him. You did nothing to stop them." Her fury swept from her then and she was amazingly calm. "You did it because of me, didn't you," she added, her voice wondrously calm. "Because you wanted me for yourself."

He flushed and stopped pacing. "I told you he was in danger," he faltered. "I can't control what happens, Della. I tried to help him, to save him—"

"No," she said firmly. "You spied on him, and you got me to help you. You told his enemy how best to take him and then simply let it happen." Her heart ached as she realized how she had felt so righteous about her part in Phillip's downfall. All to help Stephen! Because, when he touched her, she felt alive again.

He stood silently, staring at the floor. He said nothing to refute her words.

"Well," she said, "I must go to him at once, of course. Where have they taken him?"

"Don't be ridiculous, Della," Stephen began, "you shouldn't even be on the roads. The British troops are everywhere, and men are being shot on mere *suspicion* of rebellion, unarmed and defenseless! The English bastards have no respect for American women. Your carriage will be stopped, your woman taken from you, and likely you'll be—"

"Are you going to get him released?"

"I can't. I don't have that kind of power. I can speak on his behalf, but I doubt they'll hear me now. He's taken up arms against the Patriots twice, and they know it. They can shoot him for treason with little ado!"

"Where have they taken him?"

"Most of the prisoners are taken to Wilmington for questioning, and thence to Bath, as soon as a ship can get out of port."

"He's in jail, then?"

He nodded reluctantly. "For now, at least."

"Ah God, Stephen, why did you not let us be?"

"Della, you needn't share his misfortune," he said. "I know where your loyalty lies! You are one of us in heart and in spirit. I tried to warn him, but he wouldn't listen, so damnably stubborn! He made his choice, and you must do the same."

"He is my husband!"

"Likely not for long," he said ominously. "He will be banished, at best, possibly executed. I know Phillip, he'll never relent. They'll have no choice but to make an example of him."

"And then what am I to do?" she asked. "Marry you, perchance?"

His face did not alter. "If I could dare hope you might accept me, Della, I would do anything to be worthy."

Her look of horror stopped him short. "I never intended for this to happen," she whispered. "I never intended for you to—to have these feelings. I will never leave Phillip."

"Never?" he asked painfully. "Despite all that has happened between you and all that may befall him?"

"Never," she murmured. "And I only just now realized it."

He tried to reach for her. "Della, don't say that now, you're not yourself. Tomorrow, we'll go together to Wilmington, and we'll see what can be done."

But she flung off his hand. "You're a selfish scoundrel, Stephen. And I have been a stupid, silly woman."

She turned and fled down the stairs, snatching at Bathsheba who waited by the door, and running to the waiting carriage.

🌿 🌿 🌿

Wilmington jail was down close to the docks, so that it might be handy for the usual occupants: drunken sailors, riffraff from the Caribbean islands, and runaway slaves awaiting exportation. In a squat stone building with few windows, patriots had jailed seven defiant Tories who would not take the oath, had not left the state, or were not in hiding. They meant to arrest a good many more.

Della's carriage pulled up a block from the jail and stopped in the shadows under a spreading magnolia tree. The stench from the docks, even at this cooler hour of the evening, was stifling, and she kept a handkerchief to her nose as she whispered to Bathsheba.

The two descended from the carriage, wrapped in cloaks against the rising fog from the bay. They walked close to the buildings as though for shelter, Bathsheba so near to Della that they appeared comrades rather than mistress and slave. Once, Della caught the back of her cloak on the rough, upraised stone of the cobbled path, and Bathsheba released it before she had time to falter or pause. They came to the heavy wooden door of the jail, charred in one corner by fire or wood smoke, and Della lifted one gloved hand to knock. Before she could, the door wrenched open, and two men shoved through the doorway, cursing and jostling each other aside. Della jumped back with a start, bumping Bathsheba. The men hurried past, one of them sliding out an impertinent remark to the other that caused them both to laugh. Della flushed to the roots of her hair, but she pushed the door open and went inside.

A burly man in a rumpled coat sat at a makeshift table within. Della strode up to him without hesitation and said, "I should like to see the constable, please."

The man stared at her as though he had not seen a woman in a decade. Peering around her at Bathsheba, he said, "He's not here."

The man's rudeness instantly annoyed Della, giving her the added courage she needed. She kept her voice low. "Be so kind as to tell me, then, when he will return."

"What do you want with him?" he asked, suddenly quite busy with the papers on his table. "Perhaps I can do for you."

Della appraised the man quickly. He was right. He would do. "I've come to see one of your prisoners, sir. I'm his sister, and I have an urgent message from our mother." She cast her eyes about the room as though in sudden despair. "Ah Lord," she murmured faintly, just loud enough for him to hear. "That our family should be brought to such shame."

"What's the message?" he asked, his eyes narrow and suspicious in the shadowed candlelight.

She lowered her head and dabbed at her eyes gently. Bathsheba swayed forward slightly as though to steady her, but she shrugged off the slave's hand. "No, I'll be all right. Better me than Mother." She lowered her voice to a whisper. "Good sir," she began, faltering slightly, "we are a family of Patriots, shamed by a treasonous brother. My mother is"—she choked back a sob—"is dying. She has a final request of her son before she departs this life."

The man's face softened slightly. "That's a damnable shame," he said, still staring at her face as though expecting to see God Himself erupt from her lips. "Who is your brother?"

"Phillip Gage," she said, wrenching the name forth as though the very syllables were a humiliation. She put her handkerchief to her mouth. "He has always been—my mother's heart."

"Ay," the man said sadly, "my own would feel the same of me, I wager."

"Your name, good sir?"

"Beechum, miss."

"Master Beechum, would it be," she began hesitatingly, "too much to ask to perhaps see my brother and give him her message?"

He shook his head ruefully. "No visitor allowed, ma'am. I'm sorry."

She stifled another sob, putting one hand to her eyes. "Ah God, I cannot go back to her deathbed and tell her I have failed. She asks for so little."

"I can give him the message for you," he said.

She shook her head in desperation. "It won't work, sir, I know him too well. This message must come from my mouth alone." She opened her veil slightly so that he could see that mouth more clearly.

The jailer's own mouth opened slightly. "What's the message?"

She tried not to show her repugnance at his rudeness. "Sir," she said softly, "I can scarcely bring myself to say it aloud." She cast a wild, despairing look at Bathsheba as though for support, and the slave murmured low words of comfort. "But I suppose I must." She wrung her hands and stared at them. "My mother's plea is that he take the vow of loyalty and rescue our family from this horrible shame. She stands ready to pledge all our lands and my dear father's fortune to the Patriot cause, if my brother will only relent and join us in our stand for liberty." She let herself weep quietly. "She—she begs him to save himself while he still can." She let her voice dwindle to a soft moan.

The jailer stood abruptly and came to the other side of the table. "You think you can turn him, then?"

"If anyone can," she said miserably.

"I cannot leave you alone with him."

"I would welcome your presence, sir," she murmured. "Perhaps it will impress upon him the desperation of his condition."

The jailer thought for a moment, then seemed to make a hard decision. "Come with me, ma'am. Your woman can stay here."

"Oh no," Della groaned, "I cannot face this alone. Please, sir, let her accompany me. If I should waver—if I should feel faint—"

"Let her come then," he said brusquely. He turned and led the way down a dark corridor to narrow stone stairs that descended into the bowels of the earth. Water seeped from the sides of the stone as though they were beneath the bay, and Della kept her gloved hands tucked tightly to her bodice, almost swaying with the stench of the mildew and the rot from all sides. They turned a dark corner, following the jailer's lamp, to a row of cells, each behind a heavy wooden door with a bar on the outside.

Della had no trouble weeping then, to think of Phillip behind one of those doors. Now, mixed with the evil brew of dampness and stagnant water, she could smell the eliminations and fear of too many men crowded into a dark space. For an instant, she wanted to bolt back up the narrow passageway, dragging Bathsheba with her, but she covered her nose and mouth against the fetid air and followed the jailer down the corridor to the last door. Without knocking, he put a key to the cumbersome lock, unbarred the door, and bowed her within. Bathsheba stood like a stone alongside the wall, withdrawn into herself and stoic.

Phillip rose off a blanket on the damp floor, blinking like an owl, groaning with stiffness. At her entry, he almost recoiled against the wall again. The jailer said sternly, "Your sister has a message for you, Gage."

"Take her away," Phillip said faintly.

Della began to weep anew, then, and turned to the jailer, gripping his hands. "Please, sir, you surely can see my brother is a man of boundless pride and a—a stubborn will! He will never hear my message so long as you are witness to his capitulation. Leave us for just a moment!"

"I cannot," he said, looking pained.

Della took out her gold locket from her bodice and held it so that the filigree shone in the lamplight. "Please, sir, for your trouble. A small trinket, but worth a good bit for the value of the gold alone—for a few moments with him alone?" She stood very close to the man, willing him to yield with her eyes. Willing Phillip, too, to be silent.

Master Beechum took the locket, feigning reluctance. "Just a moment, then. I'll be right outside the door."

"Bless you, sir," she said, catching at his hand and squeezing it warmly. "Your own mother would surely approve your kindness."

"Gage, I'll leave her to you for a few moments," he said sternly, "and I'd advise you to mark her well." He gave Della a confidential smile, set down the lamp, and closed the door behind them. Della heard the clank of the bar drop on the other side. They were locked within.

The instant the jailer left them alone, Phillip strode to her and embraced her feverishly. "How in God's name did you find me? You shouldn't have come!"

At the touch of his hands, she almost swayed into him, so violently did she remember the pleasure she had had from them once. But she steeled herself and pulled slightly away. "I made Stephen tell me where they'd taken you—" At his sudden grimace, she hurried on, "Oh, don't rage at me now, Phillip, I'm here to get you out." She went to the door and listened. She could hear the soft murmur of Bathsheba's voice without. Obviously, Beechum was engaging her in conversation, probably asking about this young miss who carried her family's shame so valiantly.

Della shrank back in the cell and withdrew from her cloak the pistol she had brought from Phillip's rack. She showed it to him, and he snatched it from her swiftly. She whispered hoarsely, "I'm your sister. Our mother is dying, and she sent me to plead with you to renounce the King and take the oath before she dies of shame."

"Who gives a damn?" he whispered back. "With this, I have no need of an alibi."

"Phillip, if you shoot a rebel, they'll hang you, sure!"

"They'll have to catch me first."

"But they will, don't you see? There are too many of them and too few Tories to hide you. You won't get north of Bath before you're captured, and this time, they'll shoot you down like a dog."

He paced the cell furiously. "Well, what do you suggest then? Why did you bring the pistol in the first place? Why did you come at all?"

"To save your life, of course," she said shortly. "Now, give me back the gun, be still, and listen to the plan."

A few moments later, Bathsheba and the jailer heard her soft knock at the door, and the man moved to unbar the cell. "He is ready to take the oath of loyalty," she murmured to the jailer mournfully. "Our mother can go to her rest in peace."

The man stepped into the cell to find Phillip on his knees in a penitent stance. "I cannot continue to go against my whole family," he said hoarsely. "Pray, swear me to loyalty, man, and let me go to my mother."

The jailer looked uncomfortable. "I'd like to do that for you, Gage, but I haven't the authority. You need to swear before a witness, sign the oath, and seal it with your mark. The constable can arrange for that just as soon as he returns, perhaps tomorrow—"

"But that will be too late!" Della cried in genuine anguish. "I understood that he had but to take the oath!"

"And that's so, miss," the jailer turned to her, "but I can't do it for him. Soon's someone with the authority comes—"

"But my mother will die without ever seeing him again!"

The jailer grimaced and then brightened. "We'll send a boy out to find the constable right away. Perhaps bring back the captain of the troops or someone else who can swear him proper."

Della glanced at Bathsheba who had come in behind the jailer, and in her eyes saw her only choice. "Very well," she said calmly to the man. "Let us go then immediately and get it done, Master Beechum. Likely, our mother will not last another day."

Turning to leave, abandoning Phillip there in the darkness again without even a lamp was the hardest thing she had to do so far, but she followed the jailer out the door, Bathsheba close behind her. He barred it carefully, and turned to go up the stairs, and she let herself begin to weep softly. Halfway up the steps, he turned to offer a word of comfort, and she pressed the pistol snout tight against his chest. "You will set him free now," she said firmly, "or I'll put a hole through your heart wide enough to whistle 'Yankee Doodle.'"

The jailer instinctively put his hands up, but then lowered them slowly, appraising her. "You won't shoot me, miss. You're a lady of quality."

In that instant, Della faltered a moment, and almost lowered the gun, but Bathsheba reached round behind her with the long hat pin she always wore and pressed the point to the man's neck. "I am not," she said calmly. "An' I kill you sure if you don' let de mister go."

Della yanked the pistol to its original position and glared at the jailer. "Move slowly now," she said, "and keep your hands up high where we can see them."

With the pressure of the gun at his breast and the sharp point of the six-inch hat pin at his throat, he stumbled down the stairs to Phillip's cell door.

"Let him out, Beechum," Della said, low and threatening.

"Your mother may not live to see him hang, but you will," the jailer said as he unlatched the bar.

"My mother died the day I drew breath," Della said shortly.

He unlocked the door, and Bathsheba pushed him inside with her free hand. "Take off your jacket," Della said, gesturing with the pistol. The jailer unshucked his jacket and Della took it from him. She handed it to Bathsheba, keeping the weapon trained on him. "Get my locket," she said. The woman pocketed the gold. "Phillip, put it on," Della ordered. He quickly donned the jailer's coat, leaving his own in the damp straw.

"They'll take you again by nightfall," the jailer said.

"De hat," Bathsheba responded, pricking him lightly with her pin. The man yanked off his hat and Phillip jammed it on his head. Now, at a quick glance, he looked enough like the jailer to pass in shadows.

"Bind his hands," Della said to Bathsheba. The slave glanced about, took up Phillip's jacket, and quickly tore off the sleeve. She hesitated an instant, then handed it to Phillip. "You best bind him, master," she said respectfully. "I keep him still." And she pressed the pin so tight against the man's neck that he gasped.

Once he was bound fast, they hurried out and shut the door behind them, barring it securely from without. They were halfway up the steps when Della said, "Sheba, you go first and see if guards are posted or if he lied."

Bathsheba moved against the wall like a sleek, black cat, sliding up the stairs silently. Her head disappeared round the corner and then her hand gestured them on. No one was in the room, to their amazement. "Outside the door?" Della whispered.

Phillip peered through the lone, high window of the jailer's room. "Two," he murmured. "One on each side of the door."

"They weren't there when we came!" Della whispered.

Bathsheba spied the jailer's cloak on a hook by the table and whisked it off and over Phillip's shoulders. "We got no choice but to go!" she hissed.

Phillip stared at the two women as though they were mad.

Della saw that he was frozen, and she fought down her own panic. "I will weep and wail about my poor brother, and you escort me to the carriage. Bathsheba, you go last, in case of trouble. Here," she said, handing Phillip the pistol. "Keep your voice low and let me make the noise."

He opened the door then, and she went out first, breaking into loud sobs and flailing her hands about in despair. The two guards flinched slightly and turned to glance at her, and Phillip followed close behind her, almost at her elbow. "Ah my God!" she wailed loud enough to raise hair on the neck. "That my brother has come to this!"

Phillip murmured something low, and directed her toward the carriage still waiting at the corner.

"Master Beechum, you have been so kind!" she cried. "The governor shall hear of this, you may be sure!"

Bathsheba saw one of the guards peer at Phillip with a beginning curiosity, and she suddenly pulled up the front of her apron at a puddle, leaving her legs bare to the knee, and wailed even more loudly than Della. The three passed unmolested, and as they approached the carriage, Della murmured to the driver, "Be ready to turn and get away fast!" Phillip helped the two women into their carriage, and Della leaned far out the window, taking Phillip's hand and pressing it as though in gratitude. She could see that the guards were still watching them. She wailed and fumbled with her purse as though to give the jailer a coin, and in that instant, Phillip hopped inside the carriage, the driver whipped the horses up, and they sped away. Della looked back to see one guard raising his musket, the other shouting to them to stop, but they rounded the corner and were out of range so quickly that she realized she was still holding her breath and they were now two blocks away.

Phillip startled her by leaning over, pushing up her veil, and kissing her fervently on the mouth, as though Bathsheba did not exist beside them. As he drew his lips away once more, she stared at him in frank wonder. His eyes glittered in the rocking carriage light, and he held her hand very tightly. It was the thrill of danger, of near-capture, of escape. She knew what awaited her once they reached Deepwater, and her stomach lurched in secret excitement.

Once alone in their room, Phillip swept her onto the bed and slid her out of her clothes as easily as though they had been oiled. Still in his trousers, he pressed against her so tightly that she feared her pelvis might crack, yet she arched her back and met his pressure, wincing at the pain and the pleasure it gave her. He kissed her eyes, her cheeks, her brow, her lips, down her neck and her shoulders, murmuring things she could not hear, and she turned her head back and forth, first to give him access and then to deny it.

She felt the tension build in her, slowly at first, and then with a solid heat that had a life of its own, which moved up and through her body, suffusing itself through her skin so that she sweated in every corner and joining of flesh. And still, his mouth roved over her, sometimes lightly, sometimes with a savage ownership that caught her and shook her into surrender.

He shucked his clothing and pulled her over him so that her breasts hung over his mouth. Circling her nipples with his tongue, he nuzzled her gently until she almost cried out at the torment, and then only finally, expertly, did he suckle her, only when he knew she was past desire and submerged in need.

This is the dark side of love, she caught herself thinking as he continued to turn and twist her body to his pleasure. This tenderness and brutality is what feeds the shadowed regions of the heart. For when he is sweetest to me, I love him the most; yet when he will not be my slave—forces me, even, to be his—that is when my desire burns hottest.

She knew that it was her surrender that allowed him to rule her, and she also knew that the longer she withheld her surrender, the more hers he would be.

She let him do his work, and then she joined him in it, and he moved over her like a secret hurricane, and she knew that when she arose from the bed, the ground would have shifted under her feet. She was swallowed up in him, and she did not remember later all the ways he took her. She realized that she scarcely saw his face, but only the dark, shadowed outline of his profile through her flickering eyelids as he kissed her again, again, again.

Later, as she lay alongside him she thought that stories of such passion were never told aloud yet were always the same in some essential way. Passion always ended in failure, at bottom, for always afterward followed the inevitable separation. And then the recurring journey toward that vital, fleeting union that each craved all over again. Always, it would be her seeking to join him; always it would be his choice to turn to meet her or turn away, for that was who she was and who she had picked for her mate. The knowledge of it made her wish to weep endlessly into the night and turn to stab him in the heart, to the death, to escape what she knew would be a lifetime of powerlessness.

But still she lay alongside him, silent, glistening with their wet-ness and replete.

He awoke and turned to her, no longer taut with desire, but now languid and full as an overfed hound. He stretched and took her into his arms, pulling her closer. She tried to find that small space between his neck and his shoulder where his collarbone did not hurt her cheek. She still said nothing. What was there to say? By noon, he would no longer love her, that much she knew. But for now, she could believe that he did.

"Let's begin again, my love," he said then, and his voice was low and haunted with feeling.

Surprised, she felt instantly wary. "What do you mean?"

"I mean our marriage. I wish us to love each other again."

The words, the very way he phrased it seemed to her to be an artifice of sorts, and yet she knew that he believed them. The tone of voice was not even his own. She said nothing.

He turned and gazed at her softly. "You amaze me, Della. Your courage, your spirit, and the depths of your passion excite me. To see you come into that cell, the light blazing about you like a goddess of hell—I wanted to kneel before you and kiss the hem of your cloak."

She held herself very still, not wanting his words to end. Had he rehearsed these phrases sometime in the night? Even while he was loving her?

"I know no woman like you. You are rare and precious to me, and I am always amazed you are my wife." He kissed her tenderly. "Sometimes you terrify me."

She knew this last was the most honest thing he had ever said to her, and still she asked, "Why?"

"Because as soon as I saw you, I knew that you had been wounded in a way that would not show on the outside. Scarred. And scarred people are hazardous. They know they can survive most other wounds as well. So they fear nothing."

"Yes," she whispered. He was speaking to some deep part of her now and it was that place that responded, not her mind.

"You will survive. I, likely, will not, but you will, and you know it. And you know you need no one to do so."

"Yes."

"And so you are dangerous for a man like me. I will spend a lifetime trying to make you need me."

She smiled gently and put her arms up over her head, listening to his words. She wanted to remember this moment forever. "It's a good thing we are wedded to each other," she murmured.

"Yes. Or we would likely kill each other."

We may, still, she thought, but she said nothing else. There was no need to add to what he said, and she wanted no interruption to his outpouring of feeling, as rare as it was.

"I want us to love each other as we did once," he said. "I want us to be faithful to one another, to raise a family, to grow old and die together. Do you think we could do that, Della?"

"Yes," she said, for that was what was needed. But she felt no conviction even as she said the words. And she knew she'd feel even less as the moment passed. Nonetheless. "We did love each other," she murmured, "and I remember those feelings well."

"If we both want it," he said, "we can have those feelings again."

"What about your woman in Charleston?" she asked calmly, amazed that she had the temerity to say the words.

He hesitated, and she felt the sharp annoyance in him rise. "I would prefer that we not speak of her again," he said.

She took a deep breath, waiting. When he said nothing more, she said, "And yet you speak of fidelity."

"I will handle that, Della," he said firmly. "We shall be true to our vows of fidelity." He said it like a litany of faith.

"What about the rebels? They will come for you soon, I'm sure. Perhaps they are even now on their way." She was rather surprised at the great calm she felt.

"I shall take the oath of loyalty," he said. "They're not going to run me off my own land, the damnable scoundrels. If I must, I'll take the oath and still defy them. But we needn't speak of that now, Della. We'll see what time brings."

That was two things they needn't speak of, Della thought, both of them having to do with vows of fidelity. She reached over and stroked Phillip's chest absently. What a very elusive man he was, she realized, even as he makes an effort to be steadfast. In that moment, she knew in her heart that they would be together always, but that they would know a lifetime of betrayal and deceit, of love and hate and passion and cold indifference. They would continue until the end, and they would often wish it would come. They were ordering their marriage with an underlying foundation of cruelty, in a way, and they would take turns being in pain. It was a deliberate design, she saw then, which would provide them with their essential drama of despair and joy, love and contempt.

"Yes," she murmured to him, reaching up and over him to cover him with her body once more. "Yes, we will love each other again."

🌿 🌿 🌿

To the right of the big house at Deepwater, a brace of flame azaleas grew alongside the porch, taller than a man and festooned with brilliant orange-red blossoms in the spring. It was there that a ruby-throated hummingbird had made her nest deep within its protective foliage. The location pleased her so much that she had not abandoned the site from the year before, but simply built on top of her old one.

Only three inches long, with a metallic green back, a dazzling white breast, and a bill like a darning needle, she could fly backward, forward, sideways, and even upside down. Now she was prepared to do exactly that as she approached, very cautiously, a large garden spider web which shared her azalea bush.

The spider sat in the middle of its nest, larger than the hummingbird by half and capable of paralyzing her with one bite. But the spider had something she needed, and the bird must take the chance. She flew to the web and hovered right before the spider, her wings beating fifty-five times a second just to stay stationary in the air. A person standing ten feet away would have heard the hum of her wings, but not the tiny squeaking sound she was making. Only the spider could hear her challenge, and hearing, raised itself off its web and held up its front legs to expose its fangs for biting and its pedipulps, the small hairy legs right beneath its jaws that could hold the hummingbird fast. The spider watched the bird with its eight eyes and waited.

The hummingbird swooped up and down before the spider, now moving her wings more than two hundred times a second. If she had been flying level, her speed would have been more than sixty miles an hour. What made her display possible were her miraculous wings, so different from other birds. Where others moved their wings freely at the shoulder, elbow, and wrist, the hummingbird's wings moved mainly at the shoulder, like little paddles in the air. She never took her eyes from the spider, but she moved closer and closer to its web. The smallest miscalculation, and she could be bitten or ensnared.

Finally, as she approached the bottom of the spider's web once more, the fearsome creature moved to strike, scuttling to the edge, and the hummingbird darted to the other edge and snatched a large piece of the web with her needle-bill, pulled it loose, and flew away, leaving the spider and its web dangling haplessly in the breeze.

The bird angled back to her own nest and there, struggling with the sticky mess, she continued the construction of her nest. It was about the size of a walnut, made of milkweed blossom, dandelions, moss, bits of bark, and finally the finishing touch, an outside webbing of spider silk to hold it all together.

She built the nest alone. In fact, she scarcely recalled the male who had visited her the week before. He had come upon her while feeding, a large male with a brilliant red throat. As she sat quietly and watched him, he made his aerial display. Rising high in the air, he swooped past her at top speed, barely missing her by inches, then rising again on the other side. All the while he darted and dove, he was careful to orient himself to the sun so as to show off his flashy colors, swinging back and forth like a pendulum until she felt quite dizzy.

As she waited, he finally dropped over her, hovering and beating the air about her head with his wings. He covered her, mated, and was gone again in a moment, leaving her alone.

Now that the nest was done, she sat within it. Two days later, she deposited two tiny white eggs within. She sat on the eggs for two weeks, leaving only to feed when she felt she must or perish. Normally, she visited more than a thousand flowers a day, taking in more than half her weight in nectar to live, refueling constantly. But she had prepared for nesting, just as she prepared for the five-hundred-mile flight over the Gulf of Mexico each spring, by adding more than fifty percent to her body weight, and all of it fat from flower sugar.

The two weeks' incubation period passed, her chicks finally hatched, and then the battle for survival began in earnest. Born blind, voracious, and smaller than bumblebees, her young must be fed more than twenty times a day. They would not grow on nectar, but needed insects and spiders to survive. The hummingbird spent every daylight moment on the hunt now, filling her crop with tiny bugs and then flying back to the nest. There, she was greeted with the two wide gaping mouths of her frantic chicks. For first one, then the other, she inserted her long bill deep into their throats and pumped food into them by regurgitating the insects she had captured and swallowed.

Two weeks later, as they left the nest, they were hummingbirds at last. Like their parents, they were nervous and irritable birds, as likely to attack and do battle with their own mother over territory as they were to fight between themselves. Less than two inches in length, they did not hesitate to drive off bumblebees or sparrows that dared to come close to their azaleas. As they flew away for the last time with not a look back to their nest or their mother, she, too, flew off across the fields of Deepwater upriver to a likely clump of lilies she had spied. But first, she stopped to investigate a red apron that flapped from the clothesline behind the big house.

Red. It was a color that always attracted her, which she could never let alone. She buzzed the garment several times and the woman who was now pinning something blue next to the red—but she saw quickly that no sugar was within that red thing, and off she flew.

🌿 🌿 🌿

For a long while, Della believed that the night of Phillip's rescue was a turning point in their marriage. She clung to that belief even as the weeks went on and he spoke no more of love, fidelity, or a family together. He was alternately loving and ardent, and once again distanced from her, yet she told herself that his ardor was warmer than before; his distance not quite so aloof.

She began to wonder if she would ever have a child. Part of her was not at all certain that such a lack would be a calamity; part of her mourned the loss as though she, herself, had died a little. She wondered if there was not something wrong with her, both in her body and her heart, that kept her from conceiving. Perhaps, she thought, my barrenness is a punishment for sin.

A scarred person. That was what Phillip had called her. Damaged. And hazardous to the hearts of others because she knew she could survive almost any wound. She knew the truth of that and also the emptiness. After all, was survival all she should hope for in this life? Phillip only knew a half-truth. Scarred souls seem dangerous because they have little compassion for the wounds of others. If they can live with the scars life inflicts, so should others.

Perhaps a woman with so little compassion does not deserve a child, she told herself.

Perhaps, she added, I am paying the price of pretending to virtue I do not have. Of virtue without real pity or love. Of passion without compassion. Of a husband not cherished, children not yearned for. The only true sin against life, after all, is refusing to love it. And if refused, it refuses one in turn and will not lodge within.

Perhaps, she said to herself until she could begin to stand it, I shall be childless after all. And if that is so, I must certainly find something to love or go mad.

Meanwhile, patriotism blossomed over the Carolinas like jewelweed in the summer. Every place she went, she was struck by the sense of universal accord she heard for fighting and freedom. It had not been fashionable to be a king's man for a year; now it was not even safe. Before, many had wanted reconciliation with England. Now, the watchword was independence. Independence by any means.

In Halifax, on the Virginia border, the rebels met as far away as they could from the forty British warships that rode at anchor in the lower Cape Fear. They called themselves the Provincial Congress, they elected a president, and they once and for all gave up the idea that the Ministry and Parliament were the source of their troubles: now they laid the responsibility directly on the sacred person of George III. They prepared the Halifax Resolves, the first official declaration of independence by any American colony, and they called for the other colonies to do the same.

Three months after the Scots fell off the bridge at Widow

Moore's Creek, the idea of these United Colonies had been spoken aloud and even put to paper. A month later, Virginia followed suit, and a month after that the Declaration of Independence was signed at Philadelphia. When the news reached Wilmington, Della was visiting friends on Royal Street. At the noise and commotion outside, they went to the door to see a hilariously happy crowd carrying homemade flags through the street.

They were American flags, with nary a stitch of England about them.

In retaliation, Lord Cornwallis and seven regiments pillaged and burned plantations up the length of the Cape Fear, set fire to Brunswick Town and St. Philips Church, then turned the sails of the British armada south to Charleston. Kendall plantation was destroyed; Orton and Russellboro and Bellfont were laid to ruin. Deepwater was left untouched.

For Loyalists, the choice was either allegiance to the new America or banishment. Most left the state for England, Canada, or the West Indies. As many Scottish Highlanders left the Cape Fear as had originally emigrated there after the Battle of Culloden. But a few staunch Loyalists stayed at home, quietly hiding out or defying the rebel majority and helping the British when they could.

Plantations up and down the Cape Fear were seized and sold, with no provision for appeal or retribution. Deepwater escaped confiscation for only two reasons: Della Gage's known rebel sympathies and the fact that Phillip Gage, under pressure from his wife, signed over his lands and title to his brother, Stephen Gage.

"The war will be over soon enough," Phillip had said to Della that night when he finally capitulated to her demands, "and if my brother does not return my holdings promptly and cheerfully when this colony regains its senses, I will personally horsewhip the two of you."

She had laughed softly to herself at his arrogance. Not only would the colony never "regain its senses" in the manner that he hoped and take back the King, but she knew he would never lay a finger on her in anger again, much less a whip. That time was passed between them, and she would never allow it to return. But she would save him from himself, and save Deepwater in the bargain. And so she had quietly promised Stephen that if he kept the lands from confiscation, when the war was over she would give him a third of his brother's property. She was not sure how she would keep that promise, but she vowed to do so.

For the next four years, the Cape Fear was largely free of the armies of either side of the Revolution. The valley was a market garden for those areas north that were ravaged by fighting. Cattle were driven up the trade routes and great droves of hogs were trotted to Virginia; fields of flax were spun into cloth, and crops were shipped to Washington's army as fast as they ripened. Wilmington privateers slipped through the Cape Fear inlets to the West Indies for small arms, gunpowder, salt, and shoes, and Patriots in North Carolina went south to help defend Charleston, west to battle the Cherokees, and north to join the army at Valley Forge.

Della helped organize a band of Wilmington ladies who went door to door collecting money for the soldiers' support. Under Severn's direction, twenty of them canvassed the city, opportuning strangers, visitors from out of state, friends and casual acquaintances, and even the servants upstairs and down, for the smallest of coins, trinkets, or currency to support the rebel cause.

Phillip all but frothed at the mouth when he discovered that Della's visits to the city were not to tend an ailing Severn, as she had claimed, but to knock on doors and beg for money. "You will not set foot outside this house!" he shouted. "I shall tell the driver to set fire to your carriage if you call for it! To think that a wife of mine would go into my agent's kitchen—the man whom I pay to bring my rice to market!—and bully his cook into giving up the coins in her apron pocket!"

"I didn't bully her," Della said calmly, "I asked, and she gave them to me freely. Just because John Larkin dare not be anything but a Tory in your employ, doesn't mean she bows to the King."

"I'll tell John Larkin to sell her south to Louisiana! They know how to deal with disloyal niggers in the bayou—"

"I doubt he will," Della said. "She makes the finest butter cake in the valley." She slid out of the room while Phillip still sputtered in rage and out to the stable. There she had the groom bridle her second-best mare and move her to a crib on the other side of the grazing pasture. If Phillip burned the carriage, even if he hobbled her best mare, then she could at least get to town without walking all the way.

But Phillip did not make good his threats. The next time she called for her carriage, the driver brought it around with nary a delay. As I suspected, she thought, he hoped to bluff me. But I won't back down from his bluffs anymore.

❧ ❧ ❧

It was a full six months by Della's counting since she had rescued Phillip from the Wilmington jail and he had announced a new and more loving beginning for them. He was still free, but little else he had promised had come to pass. They spoke together rarely now, just enough conversation to smooth them through the meals they shared. Often, he averted his gaze, as though simply to look at her was a source of some discomfort. It was an economical sort of intimacy they shared, and they did not speak of their dashed hopes and dead intentions. They honored their vows of partnership behind the closed door of their bedroom, and they took the small satisfactions from each other they were due, but they did not love.

Della tried to tell herself that she had not been somehow bilked into a bargain of pleasureless passion. This is how marriage is, she calmed herself when she felt trapped and panicked. No husband, no children, no love—! This is the truth of it, she quieted her heart. One generation keeps the secret from the next that the design is faulty and will not suffice. The marriage bond. The promises we keep that will not keep us.

One night at an early supper gathering at Severn's, Della sat talking with an animated young woman who was visiting from Roanoke. Severn was in a rare gay mood, and she presented Della to the visitor with a merry flourish. Her brother was a printer in Wilmington, she said, one of the first to publish essays of a Patriot slant, and when she said his name, Della recognized it instantly. A byline she had read a hundred times, Martin Sprull, who published a fiery broadside that frequently circulated among the more radical of her rebel friends.

As Della expressed admiration for her brother's eloquence, Jane Sprull's face brightened and she extended a hand to a man who approached from across the room. He had only just come in, and his cloak was still damp on his shoulders.

"Ah, here he is then," she said, laughing merrily to Della, "the rogue who started all the fuss!"

"Hardly," her brother replied, leaning down to kiss her cheek. "The day a few words start a revolution will be the day I shut down my press."

"Actually," Della said thoughtfully, "it usually is exactly that which starts every change for the better. A few, well-chosen words."

He turned to Della with a courteous bow. "I see my sister has been equating me with General Washington again to anyone who will listen."

Jane said, "This is Della Gage, Martin, the woman who defied her Tory husband to send rice to the Patriots in Boston. In fact, she defied him tonight by being here at all!"

Martin Sprull's eyebrows raised in polite interest. "Ah, I've heard your name before, Mistress Gage, and had hoped for an introduction someday. 'Tis said that your courage is only surpassed by your beauty." He smiled warmly. "I see that the rumors are correct."

To her surprise, Della found herself rather befuddled by his words, and she flushed slightly, turning away. "I imagine you hear all sorts of exaggerations in your trade, sir. Surely you don't believe everything you hear."

"Very little, actually," he said quickly, "but always what I see with my own eyes. They say you rode in the night to your brother-in-law's house with the information the Patriots needed to stop the Scots. They say you eluded the soldiers and the patrollers and risked your life for the cause of liberty."

There was something about his smile that she did not particularly like. It was as though he mocked himself for admiring her. "No," she said, a trifle shortly. "That was my wench, Bathsheba."

"Ah!" he smiled, his eyes glittering with interest. "That was the other story I heard, and I wondered which was the truth. Then 'tis your wench who has the courage?"

She suppressed her annoyance, aware suddenly that she was being teased.

"Martin, stop tormenting Mistress Gage!" Jane turned to Della. "You must excuse my brother, Della, he sometimes forgets himself and takes on all the charm and discretion of the Spanish Inquisitors."

Della lifted her chin, at once aware that she had misjudged this chatty child before her. Jane Sprull was no fool. She allowed herself a lilting laugh. "Not at all. I suppose a quest for truth becomes addictive in your profession, Master Sprull. Like the smell of printer's ink." She narrowed her eyes slightly, aware that he was caught in them. "And the secrets of others."

Martin Sprull leaned back slightly then, and the tension instantly dissolved. "I must apologize, Mistress Gage, for my boldness."

Boldness, Della noticed he said, not rudeness. Such an admission was no apology at all but a small, male self-applause. But she said, "And so you shall," taking his arm. "Jane, let's make your brother get us each a glass of flip. Severn's cook makes them so tart they curl your tongue into a chastened lapdog."

"Oh, that's the last thing in the world my sister would want then," Martin Sprull said deftly, and Jane caught the hint.

"You two go along," she said, waving suddenly to another woman across the crowded room. "I see Sally Carter is back from Boston with another atrocious hat!" And they were left alone.

Della took her hand from his arm and moved smoothly to the punch bowl under her own steam. She stood and waited for him to serve her. Martin selected a glass, took up the server, and ladled her a cupful of the yellow froth with nary a drop spilled. As she put it to her lips, she murmured, "Master Sprull, your hands do not give away your profession."

"You mean because they're not stained with printer's ink?" He steered her away from the punch bowl toward the doors opening onto Severn's small back garden.

"Because they look too large and strong to have the patience to set those tiny letters."

"Oh, they have the patience," he said easily. "And you'd be surprised. Printers need the strength of field hands when they're moving the presses about. So you are Severn's sister?"

"Her cousin. Our mothers were sisters."

"And you are wife to Phillip Gage, a known Tory."

"And sister-in-law to Stephen Gage, a known Patriot," she said smoothly. "Thus together, we have managed to keep my husband from ruin. He is far less vexing to the Patriots now than he was once, of course, and it is my hope that he may someday be brought to reason. After all, America is an inevitability now."

He watched her carefully. "I should truly like to know, Mistress Gage, if you would be kind enough to tell me, how you found the sand to rescue your husband from the bowels of the Wilming-ton jail. Or was that the courage of your wench as well?"

She was once again startled and discomfited by his directness. Annoyance rose in her and made her voice low and vibrant with repressed anger. "Sir, you should get out among polite society more often. You need more practice." And she turned abruptly from him to walk away.

He put a quick hand on her arm. "Please don't run away, Mistress Gage. Once more, I must apologize. 'Tis less a case of mutton-headed rudeness than an eagerness to know you. You are, without a doubt, the most fascinating woman here tonight, and I came especially with the hope of speaking with you."

At that she turned, curious. "What made you think I might attend?"

"I asked Severn. She said that Phillip Gage is in Bath on busi-ness, and that you might be here."

"You asked Severn about me? Why should Severn wish us to meet?"

He shrugged, a casual and attractive gesture. "I believe she feels that a piece about you in the paper might persuade other women to support the Patriot cause. That you might be an—example—for those who might not have the courage to speak out for what they believe."

"So you had hoped for an interview?"

"I had hoped, madame, for an introduction. Whatever else might follow I could only count my great good fortune."

She appraised him frankly. "Are you married, sir?"

"I am not."

"That explains much, then," she said. She laughed suddenly and ruefully, shaking her head. "Master Sprull, I'm afraid you give me credit for more—what did you call it? Sand? Yes, for more sand than the deserts of Araby. I am a married woman, sir, with the unfortunate dilemma of a husband who hates the cause I love. We do not share the same passions, but we must share the same life. The last thing I need is for Phillip Gage to read glowing prose about his firebrand wife in Wilmington's most radical rag. I wish you good evening, sir." She turned on her heel and abandoned the man there in the garden. With a curt bow and a small glare at Severn, she slammed her cousin's door and called for her carriage.

❦ ❦ ❦

Della did not see Martin Sprull again for more than a month, but the next time they met, she knew that he was much like Phillip in one essential characteristic: his determination.

She already knew something of him from Severn, since she had made a point to ask why in the world her cousin had encouraged his introduction in the first place.

"He's one of the finest minds in the county," Severn said calmly, "perhaps in the state."

"Why in the world would he show an interest in me, then?" Della rolled her eyes, retreating as she usually did to a feigned ignorance when she wanted information.

Severn brushed aside her comment with, "Oh, Della, let's not play these games together, shall we? We both know your mind's quick as a trap, and I pity the poor man who takes it for granted. We need more women like you, and Martin Sprull is just the man to appreciate your worth." The unspoken, "unlike Phillip Gage," hung heavily on the air between them.

Della thought for a moment. "I have no intention of being quoted in print, Severn. I'm surprised you would think me interested in that sort of public exposure."

Severn gazed at Della thoughtfully as though measuring her ability to hear the truth. "I suppose I thought you might well enjoy knowing a man such as Martin. You could do each other good."

"In what way?"

Severn did not answer that question. Not then and not later. She talked instead about the Loyalists she heard had been run out of the county, whose property had been confiscated, and which pieces were going to the block. The new government needed cash, she said, and this was as good a way as any to raise it. It was only after Della left that she realized Severn had been unusually obscure about Martin Sprull. She really knew no more about the man after their conversation than before.

The next time she met him, she saw the light of interest in his eyes once more. And surprise. Clearly, he did not expect to see her in such a place. It was the auction of the Hart house and lands, confiscated when Randall Hart fled with his family to Nova Scotia. Not a large parcel, it nonetheless adjoined a corner of Deepwater.

With Phillip unable to attend, Della felt a keen concern in the proceedings.

A goodly crowd had gathered at the courthouse square, and the mood seemed to be one of boisterous patriotism. As though Randall Hart had never been one of them, had not sat in St. Philip's every Sunday, had not married off four daughters into their midst, the people eagerly clustered about the auctioneer, hoping to profit by Hart's treason.

Della was standing to one side of the square under the spreading shade of one of the largest sassafras trees in the city. She closed her lace parasol with a snap and handed it to Bathsheba. "Bunch of vultures," she said gloomily. "Poor Cecilia Hart. She never could stand the cold. I can't imagine what she will do so far north. On the other hand, it's a good thing she can't see this motley gang today, it would break her heart. Married to Randall Hart for thirty years or more, I'd say, four grown daughters, once the toast of Cape Fear, and now banished with her husband like common scoundrels, and all her pretty things pawed over by people who used to be neighbors."

Bathsheba shook her head mournfully, as usual a mirror for Della's mood. "It all wrong."

"And I'd likely be in the same boat if I'd have dutifully taken up Phillip's point of view. Good Lord." She stopped and squinted slightly at the moving crowd. "It's that man from the paper, Martin Sprull. Pray he doesn't see us, Sheba," and she edged back slightly behind her servant, deeper into the gloom of the sassafras canopy.

"You don' like him?" Bathsheba asked, following her gaze. "Look like a comely gent, by de cut o' his cloth."

"Oh, you'd judge a horse by his blanket every time, Sheba. The man's got a tongue like a plow, cut in and turn it over, no matter what he unearths in the process." She groaned and turned her head. "He's seen me. Is he coming over?"

"Like a hound on de scent," she said placidly.

Della turned toward the crowd again with a determined smile on her lips. As Martin Sprull stepped up to them and bowed, she inclined her head and said, "Why Master Sprull, are you planning to take up planting now instead of printing?"

He grinned and turned to face the crowd, taking up his position alongside her as though he intended to stay. "Not at all. But anytime land changes hands along the Cape Fear, it's news, and Randall Hart's holdings seem most particularly significant."

"Oh?" She edged away from him slightly and kept her eyes on the crowd as though his words were only of marginal interest to her.

"Hart was once named as a candidate for governor, did you know that? Once one of the most powerful men in the county, well connected, with the ear of those at Parliament who could make him a fortune if they cared to—and now he's lost everything, all at the hands of those he and his friends would have named rabble at best." His voice was contemplative and gentle. "Lo, how the mighty hath fallen," he concluded.

Something in her softened toward him. "You sound as though you regret the confiscation."

"I regret the loss of good men, Mistress Gage, whether to war, revolution, or politics. Hart was a man of conscience, whether he could embrace the majority opinion or not." He turned toward her, his tone slightly bantering again. "And I regret the loss of good women, as well. I very much regret our last meeting, my lady, and I never intend to make such a sorry spectacle of myself again with you."

"Indeed?" Despite herself, she was intrigued.

"Yes, I was a bore."

With that, the auctioneer mounted his platform, and the dissolution of Hart's holdings began. Della said, "I don't believe I want to be any closer than this, but I suppose you need to be up where you can see the fur fly, Master Sprull."

He considered for a moment. "Actually, I would be best served by speaking with a few who are present and then relating my own impressions of the proceedings. For example, are you here to bid on Hart's lands, Mistress Gage?"

Della turned to Bathsheba as though the man were not there. "Did I not mention that Master Sprull has a gift for invasion, Sheba? Truly, Lord Cornwallis should have him on staff."

Martin Sprull laughed then, and she was moved to smile at his genuine mirth. "It's a fair question, I think, my lady. Why else would a woman attend an auction, if not for her own gain?"

"For the same reason a man might attend, of course. Natural curiosity."

"Hart's lands abut Deepwater, do they not? Reason enough for curiosity, I suppose."

"It does behoove one to know one's neighbors," she said demurely, keeping him at arm's length with her voice.

"But you do not intend to bid."

"If my husband wanted to acquire more land, he would be here himself or have sent his agent, Master Sprull. As you know, a married woman cannot own property in her own name."

"Yes, that is true," he said, "for the time being. But those laws will be changing soon."

"Not soon enough," Della murmured.

He turned to peer at her with interest. "You do intrigue me, madam. You speak your mind with a rare freedom for your sex. I shall make it a point to ride out to Deepwater one day soon, with your permission, and I hope you will favor me with your opinions on other subjects as well."

She bowed to him cordially, he returned her bow and walked away. "Blast the man," she said under her breath to Bathsheba. "He makes it difficult to refuse him, does he not?"

"He say, 'wid your permission,' but he don' act like he need it," Bathsheba agreed.

"Well, perhaps I shall not be receiving on the day Master Sprull takes it into his head to favor us with a visit, Sheba. A long ride for nothing may well do wonders for Master Sprull's manners."

Bathsheba said nothing, but she watched Martin Sprull walk up to a man in the crowd, be greeted with friendly accord, and then manage to gather a small knot of men about him who were more interested in speaking with him and each other than hearing the auction proceedings. "They 'spect him well enough," she observed.

Della snorted in disdain and took her parasol from Bathsheba's arm. "This is going to go on all afternoon," she said with sudden impatience. "We can read about it in the papers."

🌿 🌿 🌿

Not a week went by before Martin Sprull rode his bay gelding down the road to Deepwater. As usual Danny, the boy who kept the chickens out of the kitchen garden, was the first to announce the visitor, and Della heard the call come up from the downstairs wench, that a strange man was riding up to the house, but he was not a soldier.

Bathsheba hurried up the stairs to confirm it and tell her, "It dat Sprull man, Miz Della, do I tell him you not receivin'?"

Della was arranging her hair in this season's most elaborate and time-consuming fashion, a series of small and smaller curls that nested one inside the other. Once she decided how it was to go, she was determined to train Bathsheba how to duplicate her efforts. "Yes," she said shortly, around the pins in her mouth. "Tell him I'm lying down with a sick headache."

Bathsheba stood waiting for a minute.

Della turned to her in exasperation. "Well?"

"Not too 'ttractive a excuse, Miz Della."

"What do you suggest?"

The woman smiled. "Mayhap tell de gemp'man you be engaged in writin' your letters or somethin'."

Della waved her away. "Tell him whatever you wish, Sheba, and don't bother me. These damned curls are about to *give* me a sick headache, and that's for certain!" She went back to work, twisting her thick, dark hair about her fingers and trying to pin it in place. When, after a tedious three-quarters of an hour, she finally managed to get the coiffure as she thought it should look, she went to the door to call for Sheba and then listened before she called out. Strange that the wench had not come back up. All was silent below. She retied her bodice and started down the stairs, only to see Bathsheba disappear into the parlor with a tray of ice and tall glasses.

Sprull was still here! The nerve of the man. And why had Bathsheba not come up to warn her that he was waiting her out? If she called down to her, he well might hear her and come out to the foot of the stairs to importune her. Damn the wench, where was her sense? Now she would have to use the bell, and she hated to, never did, the idea of it offended her. But she went back to her room, rummaged in her boudoir for the small silver bell Phillip had given her on their first anniversary, and stood at the top of the stairs, ringing it with vexation.

She stopped and listened. She heard two things simultaneously: Bathsheba's footsteps and Martin Sprull's laughter. The latter annoyed her so that the former scarcely mollified her at all. Bathsheba hurried up the stairs and when she came in the room, Della cried, "For heaven's sakes, Sheba, where have you been? Why didn't you come back? Did you tell him I wasn't coming down?"

"No'm," the woman said, her eyes down. "I told him you doin' your letters, an' he say he wait. He say you cain' have more letters than de governor, an' he wait for him de same way. He say most important people make him wait, an' he used to it."

Della gaped at her in amazement. "So he's just going to loiter in my parlor all the day long?"

Bathsheba could not suppress her smile. "I 'spose so, Miz Della. He don' look like he goin' nowhere soon."

"Well, I guess not!" Della snapped as she threw on her gown over her stays. "After you told him what you did and now you fetching and carrying for him like he's the guest of honor at the Governor's Ball! I'm surprised you didn't ask him to stay to supper, too!"

Bathsheba dropped her head, but Della was not assuaged. She knew that Bathsheba was no more afraid of her than she was of Danny, the garden boy, and the thought of how she was being manipulated, not just by Martin Sprull but by her own slave, inflamed her out of all proportion. She slammed out of the door and down the stairs, her cheeks warm. She burst in on the man as he was taking what appeared to be the second mouthful of a piece of Mary Ann's lemon cake and despite an effort at cool disdain, her voice was up an octave and louder by half than she intended. "What in the world are you still doing here?" she asked bluntly.

The man set down the cake platter gently and turned to her with a welcoming smile. "Waiting for you, of course. Didn't your wench tell you?"

"Only just now," she said, suddenly bewildered by the warmth of his smile. The gust of anger that had propelled her down the stairs now seemed to be gone. "I really didn't want visitors today, but since you're here—"

"Why didn't you want visitors?"

She rolled her eyes. "You ask the most impertinent questions, Master Sprull! I don't believe I've ever known a man who so flouted conventional ideas of polite conversation." She picked up his piece of lemon cake and took a bite with her fingers, daring him with her eyes. "I should tell you the truth, since you're so bold to ask. Visitors wouldn't have troubled me much, but you do. I didn't want to see you again."

His eyebrows went up, but his smile did not waver. "I know that."

"Yet you came."

"Of course!" He laughed lightly. "There is something about me that makes you nervous, Madame Gage. Something about you that makes me damnably nervous, too. I won't rest until I know what it is."

"Perhaps," she said slowly, "we don't like each other much."

He laughed again. "Or perhaps we do. And we sense a danger there."

She watched him silently. Finally she said, "Yes. Perhaps."

"Why do I make you nervous?"

"I feel as though you . . . look at me," she faltered, "too deeply, somehow. Too close." He seemed to have moved nearer to her though Della knew he had not changed his position at all.

"And I feel as though you command me to look," he said, his voice suddenly softer. "As though I cannot look away to save my soul."

"You know altogether too much about women for your bachelor state, Master Sprull," she said. "It strikes me as almost obscene."

"I pride myself on being a keen observer of human nature," he said, and this time he did move closer to her subtly. A slight shift of body weight, and nothing more. "And women are, to my mind, the most interesting half of the species."

"Not an unusual conviction for a bachelor," she murmured.

"For example, shall I tell you what I find most interesting about you, Della?"

She flinched at the use of her first name.

"May I call you Della?"

She hesitated. "I suppose," she finally said reluctantly. "In private only."

He went on quickly as though her permission were a foregone conclusion. "Not only are you beautiful and intelligent, but you are one of the few women I've met who have, on some level, already decided to make her own rules for her own life." He took her hand as easily, as casually as though he had done it a dozen times before. "And in that, Della, you and I are much alike."

She did not withdraw her hand. She could not seem to muster the desire to do so.

His voice was quiet now, confidential and without guile. "I know more about you than you think I do, Della. I know that you have a fierceness of spirit that few realize." He looked into her deeply. "That likely, even your husband does not know. I know that you have a capacity for life that is rare. And I know that you are more lonely . . . more alone, than you deserve to be."

She murmured, "How do you know these things?"

"I can see them in your eyes. In the lines of your face. In the way you move your body. Tell me that I'm wrong."

She wanted to say, you are wrong, Master Sprull, and you are arrogant besides. You are not welcome here ever again. But she could not deny the truth of what he said. To her surprise, tears welled up in her eyes, and she turned her face away. His hand crept to her chin and gently turned it back again. Softly, he leaned down and kissed both her eyes, barely grazing her flesh.

"I shall come again very soon," he murmured, "unless you tell me I am forbidden in this house. I won't be able to stay away from you, Della, unless you force me to."

She could not find the will to deny him, so much was she transfixed by the feel of his lips on her skin. When he finally found her mouth with his, she turned her face up to him willingly, eagerly, and put her arms round his neck, pulling him closer.

🌿 🌿 🌿

Over the next fortnight, Della broke every marriage vow and not a few of the holy commandments, and she felt scarcely a stab of guilt. In fact, she felt more guilt about not feeling guilt than she felt for what she was doing. At first, she and Martin met only in private, several times at her home, twice at the printer's office, once at his apartments on Bay Street. Their meetings were furtive, fevered, and as brief as they could stand to make them, always worried about being seen together, and never actually allowing themselves the luxury of consummating their love affair with any sort of grace or comfort.

But very quickly, they became more selfish about their passion; brief embraces would no longer satisfy them. It seemed to them that it might be perfectly plausible that they be seen together in public, since it was common knowledge that they shared similar political views and worked on the same committees. "After all, Severn brought us together in her home," Martin reassured her, "and people will just assume that we are good comrades in a patriotic cause."

"But you're a bachelor, and I am a married woman," she protested mildly, hoping in fact to be persuaded.

"All the more reason they'll not suspect us," he vowed. "If we were both married, they'd assume adultery; if we were both single, they'd assume a romance. If I were married and you were single, they'd assume you were my mistress—so you see, this is the *only* way they'll believe us innocent."

"Which we are not," she whispered.

In reply, he held her closer and kissed her deeply. "If loving you is a sin," he said, his voice rough with emotion, "then I am willing to pay whatever penance God decrees. I cannot keep from you, Della. And you have only to give me leave, and I shall go at once to Phillip and tell him. Let him call me out, let him do his worst—"

"His worst will fall on me, not on you," she said sadly.

"What can be worse than living with a man you cannot countenance?" he asked. "Once the war is over, Gage will be ruined anyway. Come with me now, Della, and leave the man! He does not love you."

But she would not, could not think of leaving Phillip. Also, she could not bring herself to tell him the truth. And so for several tense months, she hurtled herself back and forth between her lover and her husband, feeling more estranged from her life than she thought she could survive.

On some level, she knew that Phillip sensed her betrayal. Though he would never confront her, their disagreements over all things political rose to a more dangerous edge. She was out of the house frequently now, volunteering her time and resources to the Patriot cause. The British had taken Charleston, and their presence on the Cape Fear was a powerful one. Those Loyalists left in the county now came out of hiding and began to believe that the wind might shift again in their favor. Almost overnight it seemed that British troops were everywhere in abundance.

Rebel activity did not cease, it only went underground. Secrecy became even more vital, and Della rarely spoke to Phillip at all anymore. In retaliation, he agreed to quarter six British soldiers in the outbuildings, guest quarters that were normally reserved for visitors when the big house was full over holiday seasons. Della could not leave the house these days without seeing the strangers lounging about the grounds, cleaning their muskets, or using the backwoods as a target range.

She had, of course, loudly protested when he agreed to let the soldiers on their land. "You might have some respect for my feelings!" she shouted at Phillip. "I cannot feel secure in my own home!"

"You are more secure with them here than not," he said stiffly. "If an interloper comes to Deepwater in my absence, they will protect you. Every planter up and down the river is being told to take them in, I can scarcely refuse."

"Most have! Not a single friend of mine must endure Redcoats in her own home!"

"Which friends are these? The only friends you have are treasonous scum. I'd rather have soldiers at my table any day!"

She had stormed out then, mounted her mare, and galloped down the road to town. Only one destination seemed proper refuge: Martin's arms. And from there, she did not leave until the next morning. When she returned, Phillip did not ask of her whereabouts, nor did he rage in suspicion at her. In fact, he did not speak to her at all for nearly a week.

For the next six months, Della allowed her passion for Martin to consume her as the sun consumed the water from the Cape Fear. Daily, it seemed, the air was filled with enough moisture to have depleted the river, yet every day its level stayed the same. In the same way, she wondered if she would ever tire of his embraces. She was willing now to take almost any risk to be with him, to court any shame. They were seen together often—Wilmington was a small town in attitude if not in populace—and even the news of war and skirmishes up and down the coast could not divert people completely from local scandal.

In time, of course, some well-meaning friend took it upon himself to tell Phillip Gage what he had known all along and done his best to ignore. And Della knew to the moment when he had received the disclosure, for his demeanor changed completely within the hour. From aloof courtesy, a state of frozen detachment that allowed them to live within the same walls yet never trespass each other's privacy, he was suddenly, intensely interested in her every move and feeling. Without accusation, he simply was *with* her at every opportunity.

One evening, as they walked together from a friend's supper party on Market Street—that in itself, a rare occurrence—they were drawn to the noise of a crowd round the courthouse square. Phillip unconsciously took her arm and drew her closer to him, a gesture Della found oddly touching, considering he had not touched her in any way for so many months.

The crowd seemed angry as they walked closer, and Phillip made as though to leave for her protection. "No," Della said, "let's see at least what the furor is all about. One would think, with so many soldiers in town, that they could at least keep the peace—" and her voice died away in alarm as they got nearer and saw that the crowd's focus was, in fact, a woman.

Twenty men or more ringed her, a woman whom Della did not recognize. She looked to be about thirty, perhaps, just a little younger than Della, and nearly as beautiful. Her clothes were fashionable, though conservatively cut, and her figure that of a woman of refinement. She stood on the highest step of the courthouse square, where the auctioneer usually perched, but she clearly did not wish to be there. Two bright flames of color stood high on her cheeks, and her mouth was a grim line of pain. Each time she attempted to leave the step, the men jostled her back into place. They were handling her roughly, Della could see that even from the back of the crowd, and she wondered what such a woman could possibly have done to affront so many men at once.

"She's a Tory spy," Phillip said quietly, his hand still tight on Della's arm. "Come away now, it's going to get ugly."

"No," Della murmured, unable to turn away. "How do you know her?"

"I don't," he said shortly, "but I know what she does. Her husband's lands were confiscated when he was killed at Moore's Creek. She's passed information to Cornwallis himself, 'tis said. But I suppose she got careless, and now the rebels have caught her. Come away now, Della," he said again, pulling at her arm.

"Will they kill her?" she asked, her eyes wide with alarm.

Before Phillip could answer, the current shifted through the crowd, and Della saw hands grip the woman at the bodice, the throat, the skirt—there was a flurry of confusion and a sound of ripping cloth, a cry from the woman that was muffled by the angry growl of two dozen male throats, cries of "Traitor! Spy! Kill her!"

To Della's horror, the woman was stripped of her clothes right before her eyes, crying out and holding her arms and hands over her body, attempting to cover herself. The men were relentless, and the sight of her nude body only seemed to inflame them to new anger. "Spy! Spy! Spy!" chanted the crowd, pressing closer, and someone pushed her off the steps so that she fell into their clamoring hands, her dark hair falling over their shoulders. Della screamed, and in that moment, she saw that Martin Sprull stood slightly to the side of the crowd, watching and chanting along with the others. The woman screamed once, flailing at the men's hands and trying to wrest herself from their grip, and Phillip bolted from Della's side then and roughly pushed himself to the center of the crowd, shoving men aside with both hands and cursing them loudly.

To Della's surprise, the men began to fall away from the woman, as though a single loud male voice was all it took to bring them momentarily to their senses. She stood frozen, watching the men move back sullenly, still muttering loudly. Some catcalls came from the rear, and Martin Sprull shouted something she could not make out, but Phillip ignored them all. He whipped his jacket off his shoulders, wrapped it round the weeping woman, and led her to a nearby keep.

As he approached the door, he shouted for a woman to come out and take her. The tavern keep's woman stepped outside warily, obviously frightened by the still-milling crowd. She had likely been watching the commotion from the window. She rushed forward, grabbed the naked, half-fainting woman, and pulled her inside the tavern to safety. As she disappeared within, the crowd of men outside growled once as an unruly beast with a single throat, then reluctantly began to disperse.

Della stood gripping her hands tightly together, trembling. In that moment, Martin Sprull saw her standing there and took a move in her direction, but she turned toward Phillip as he came back to her and ran into his arms. "What made you do such a courageous thing?" she cried on his breast.

He was trembling also, she could feel it through his arms and shoulders. "I—I just thought, my God, that could be my own wife. I thought of nothing else."

Della allowed Phillip to lead her away. She did not look back at Martin Sprull, stricken and white-faced there in the street.

That night, Della lay beside Phillip for the first time in months. She could not have him out of her sight. Each time she closed her eyes, she saw her lover shouting at that naked woman, his mouth open, ugly, and his arms in the air. Though he had not been part of the crowd who had stripped off her clothes, though he had not touched her in any way, Della could not escape the belief that he might have, if the fever in the crowd had been allowed to grow. And then, in her mind's eye, she saw Phillip, pushing his way through the crowd, cursing the men back, and snatching the woman away as she was crumpling into the arms of her tormenters.

Della had no doubt that Phillip would have rescued any woman so beset—Loyalist or Whig. In that moment, politics did not push him to the front of that mob, but a sense of what he could and could not allow to happen before his eyes to any woman, no matter her history.

The only victory over passion was flight, she told herself. If she allowed herself to be near Martin, she must have him. She had thought that she loved him, that he loved her. But could any man love a woman and still allow any of her sex to be so assaulted? Perhaps, after all, love was what Phillip had for her.

She beat back the doubting voice that clamored in her heart, the strident, harsh whisper that would remind her of Phillip's many callous, hurtful, neglectful times, and she simply lay beside him, feeling safe again.

Della contemplated love in that safe place, and she wondered if it could ever be defined at all while a heart was in it. She decided she knew little about love, slightly more about passion, and nothing at all about what might make her happy.

But she knew now what would not make her happy: Master Martin Sprull.

She would not answer his note the next morning nor receive him that week. And though they were to see each other infrequently again at the occasional supper party or committee meeting, she never allowed him near her again.

❦ ❦ ❦

Lord Cornwallis spent the summer of 1781 in the northern part of South Carolina, harassed by the hit-and-run warfare of Marion the Swamp Fox. In September, he crossed into Mecklenburg County, expecting loyal Tories to flock to his banner. A proclamation went out to all faithful subjects of His Majesty to join the British army and receive three guineas and a section of land once the revolution was quelled. Instead of victory, the British had one of their single most disquieting losses at King's Mountain, where in less than an hour more than six hundred Redcoats surrendered to mountain men from the Blue Ridge and Virginia.

Cornwallis fled into South Carolina to wrest what remained of his troops, but the Americans chased him there. He ran north, forced to forage for three thousand hungry Redcoats in counties that hid its cattle in the swamps and denied him supplies, recruits, or respect. By the time he marched down the Cape Fear to Wilmington, which had been held loosely in English hands by the navy for a month or two, he knew he needed to get out of the Carolinas if he was to declare them won, so he marched north to Virginia. Cornwallis left Carolinian Tories and Whigs squabbling between themselves in guerrilla surprise attacks and minor harassments, until word came that he had surrendered his army to General Washington at Yorktown.

North Carolina gave itself over to frolicking for a fortnight. It was free of the British, but not of its own civil strife.

For the next decade, general disorder claimed the Carolinas and the future looked bleak. Taxes soared, paper money became worthless, and commerce all but stopped. Thousands were reduced to poverty, schools and churches closed, and no newspaper was published for more than eight years. Political strife was intense and bitter, and North Carolina was bankrupt. Refusing to ratify the United States Constitution, it became the only state, save tiny Rhode Island, to stand outside the Union for more than a year.

When North Carolina finally joined the Union in 1789, the chaos of almost two decades began to subside.

Somehow, Deepwater had survived largely intact. When prices were good, Della quietly added land on each side. When prices dropped and taxes soared, she drained the fields and put more of them to tobacco rather than rice, reasoning that Virginians were more ravaged by the war than North Carolina planters, and their crops would be smaller and harder to get to market. She guessed right, and profits from the leaf soared, even in the midst of war but most particularly after. By the time North Carolina was a state, Deepwater was the largest tobacco plantation on the river.

Della was grateful that the land gave her something to nurture and surpassing satisfaction. Married now for almost two decades, she and Phillip had perfected their own hit-and-run war of love, disdain, and infidelity. Now certain she would never have a child, Della had gradually given over her passions to everything but her marriage.

Della had learned to run the plantation like a fine-tooled watch—at first a necessity because Phillip traveled so much and finally a preference. She was truly the mistress of Deepwater in every way. The decisions about when to plant tobacco crop, the maintenance of that profitable brown leaf, the timing of harvest, and what price to ask were nominally Phillip's, and she always made sure his advice was solicited. But the real day-to-day deliberations over which mare to breed, which slave to sell or marry off, and what to do about the hog fever in the swine pen were Della's— in actuality, most every command that went toward making Deepwater one of the finest houses on the river. This gave her deep pleasure.

Long ago, it was clear to Della that she and Phillip were too much alike to hate each other and too different to make each other content. Yet they could not seem to forsake each other. Whenever she allowed herself to love him, to truly abandon herself to the joy of intimacy with him, he began to take her love for granted. Instead of glorying in her adoration, of nurturing it, of believing that what she had to give was a gift that deserved gratitude, he seemed to think her heart small treasure once he had it. From there, he commenced to disdain her, to become aloof, and finally to punish her in small ways for being so weak as to give him her heart. As though he could not, ultimately, abide a woman who accepted him, he finally had trained her not to depend on his love at all. They were still ruthless with each other. He was alternately indifferent to her whereabouts and jealous of the most innocent friendship.

And Della knew how best to keep him engaged, even if it was at a level that simmered with violence. If her first passion was Deepwater, her second was more predictable. As was her revenge. She took a series of lovers over the years of marriage, each one carefully selected to provide the most pleasure with the least risk to her comfort and security. Each man so selected understood that she would never leave her husband, yet each came to hope that he might finally win her if he only wooed more ardently than the one who had been there before.

Della was aware that the woman she had become was as much an anomaly in the general scheme of her society as a two-headed chicken in the henhouse. She knew that she took great risks, not only with her marriage and security, but also with her reputation and the network of women friends who entertained and sustained her. But the lure of new passion was too strong for her to resist. Each time she began again with a new lover, she writhed in guilt and anxiety for days before their first consummation. But once she had finally committed herself once more to the affair, she was swept into it with giddy abandon and deep, heartfelt joy.

Bathsheba, of course, knew all. In fact, without Sheba's protection, Della could not have pursued her passion with such success. The slave not only corroborated her alibis, she sometimes invented them from whole cloth as if she, not her mistress, had the reward of freedom. And so together, the two women shaped a union that was, in many ways, more of a comfort to Della than either her marriage or her lovers could ever have been.

🌿 🌿 🌿

On a spring day in the woods behind Deepwater, the smallest of creatures lay in a bed of soft ferns, making a raspy, clinking call that seemed one of great distress. Only about five inches long with sooty gray fur, black eyes, and tiny pink hands and feet, she was completely helpless and vulnerable to any predator—indeed, to even a strong rain.

She was a baby opossum, the oldest living native mammal on the North American continent. Happily or unhappily for the creature, it had not, despite millions of years of evolution, changed its form, habits, or intelligence since it first evolved in the Cretaceous period.

But its singular sameness over millennium meant little to this little marsupial on this spring morning. What mattered was that she had somehow fallen off her mother's back the night before and still been unrescued. As she sat in the bed of ferns, trembling and chilled by the absence of a warm body to grip, a large swamp toad came hopping through the ferns. It was hunting early spring mosquitoes, but the opposum knew only that it was big, frightening, and instantly before her muzzle.

The little opposum backed away on wobbly legs, giving the toad her characteristic toothy grimace known to hunters all over the South as the "possum grin," and calling desperately for her mother. The toad, unimpressed, hopped away.

Unfortunately for the lost opposum, her mother's primeval brain made no allowance for the provision of lost babies. Once fallen from her back, they were forgotten forever. Fortunately, however, the baby opposum was at two and a half months just old enough to survive—with some luck and courage—on her own.

But she could not know such a thing. The fern leaves were wet and chilled her through her fine hair, the spring air was just cool enough to make her want to ball up into a tight knot of muscle and sleep her life away.

If the noises of the woods had allowed her any respite, she might have done exactly that. But the raucous call of a curious jay in the tree above her head caused her to start, hiss a frightening warning, and scuttle out of her nest and into the open clearing. Once there, she felt even more imperiled, and she set off her cry again to whatever might hear her. To her horror, the next creature that ambled into her clearing to investigate her noise was a large, striped skunk.

The opposum knew she could not outrun such a formidable foe, and she did not even try. Instead, she fell over on her side in a dumb faint. The skunk trotted over and sniffed at her curiously, but the opposum was still as death.

In fact, she was not pretending. Unlike some creatures that feigned a faint, the opposum truly did swoon when faced with a threat. Her mind became quickly overtaxed, threw some sort of internal switch, and she went into the oblivion of a catatonic state. Her heartbeat and breathing were barely perceptible, and if the skunk had chosen to bite her, she likely would have felt nothing. Only after the skunk ambled off, only long moments after the clearing was once more serene and empty, did the little opposum revive and scuttle off toward the smell of water.

Although she did not feel so, her body was capable of survival at this young age without her mother's nourishment. She had a remarkably short gestation period—an incredible thirteen days, compared with nine months for a human or two months for a cat. Born blind and hairless and half an inch long, she had made the journey to her mother's pouch on her own, along with her six siblings, completely unaided by her mother. Once she was in the pouch, her ordeal was still not complete. She had to locate one of her mother's thirteen pinhead-size nipples and hang on there for two months. If a nipple had not been available or she'd been unable to find it, again she would have died. And then she should have ridden on her mother's back for another week or so—but a sudden shift of her mother's weight and a grappling of claws in a shaky branch, and she had fallen below to the ferns.

Now, the smell of water led her to the edge of the wetlands within the woods girdling Deepwater. She bent and lapped at the water like a small puppy, heedless of any danger. The daylight made her blink, and she knew instinctively to seek cover until the protective darkness came. An earthworm suddenly writhed to the surface of the mud under her claws, and she snapped at it convulsively, swallowing it down in one bite. She methodically began to dig for others, finding four more within a short space.

Turning now from the water, she heard a rustle in the bushes and greeted it with her usual grin, baring all fifty of her teeth. A young fox scampered out of the brush, his ears pricked and alert, his mouth as open as her own. She instantly fell to one side, her tongue lolling out in an expert faint. But this dog fox was not to be deterred. Without hesitation, he trotted to the limp body, gripped the opossum at the head, and cracked her skull in one easy bite. She felt no pain, only a deeper blackness. And then nothing more whatsoever.

🌿   🌿   🌿

Della was nearly forty when she finally decided that she could no longer look to her lovers for the fulfillment of her passion. It had been a difficult season. The winter seemed to go on and on, in an interminable gloom of fog and chilled rain. The river droned past Deepwater with the somnolent voice of the dead, and even the birds seemed to have deserted Cape Fear forever. Her own body felt disconnected from her heart. She could feel the ebb of her beauty as distinctly as she could see it, almost daily, in her glass. Her hair did not have its usual luster, her eyes seemed veined with weariness, even if she had rested well the night before. Nothing gave her pleasure, even the wooing of an unusually ardent companion, a man she had met and enjoyed most of last summer.

"Sheba, I think I'm going through the change," she said dismally as she stared at her skin in the boudoir glass. "My face looks like an old saddle."

Bathsheba came to stand behind her, reaching out to stroke her hair. "You still like a young girl," she said comfortingly. "Not a gray hair in de bunch."

Della looked up at Bathsheba appraisingly. She was at least a decade older, likely the slave's eyesight was none too keen these days. Certainly, her hands were not as steady. She sighed restively. "I should take a trip to Charleston or maybe Savannah. Buy some new frocks." She leaned closer and frowned at what appeared to be a new wrinkle around the edge of her upper lip. "A new hat." She moaned softly. "With a heavy veil."

The sound of a rider came up above the wind from the river, and Della rose eagerly to look out the window. "My Lord, it's Jeffrey," she murmured. "What can he be thinking of, coming here?"

"He cain' wait till nex' week," Bathsheba said disapprovingly. "Dat man a storm brewin'."

"He'll think storm soon enough if Phillip comes home and finds him taking tea in the parlor. Send him away, Sheba"—she rushed to snatch up a paper and pen—"no, wait, give him this." She scrawled a quick dismissal, careful to word it gently, and pressed it in the slave's hand. "And tell him he'll catch his death out in weather like this—"

Bathsheba disappeared, and Della went to the top of the stairs, keeping out of sight. She heard him shake off his cape in the foyer, and she felt a quick impatience. Foolish man, he was adorable and a deft and sensitive lover, but if he got mud and sleet on her Aubusson, she'd scold him roundly.

"Della!" he shouted from below, and she shrank back with horror. Every slave in the house would hear him!

"Della, I'm not going away until you see me!" he shouted again, and she hissed, "Damn the man!" and whirled back into her room, snatched her wrap, and rushed down the stairs, biting her lips so they would have more color. At the bottom of the stairs, she stopped and glared at him.

"What in the world, Jeffrey?" she asked, cool and dignified.

Bathsheba glanced at them both and then disappeared through the kitchen door as smooth as marble.

"I had to see you," he said, his brow furrowed, his chest heaving.

He had never seemed less attractive to her in that moment, Della realized. Jeffrey Collins was tall, of prepossessing demeanor, with the smooth, unlined face of a man ten years his junior. She had met him at the new supper club in Brunswick, they had bantered together for months—as Della liked to draw out that part of the affair as long as she could manage—and finally, only a few months ago, she had allowed him to consummate his desire. His light hair had looked quite lovely, she thought, on the linen next to her dark curls, and she loved the way he gazed deeply into her eyes as his hands roved over her body, as if constantly monitoring her response. But now, his hair was plastered to his head by the rain, and those deft hands all but trembled. She watched him carefully, as she would a dangerous snake that had slipped under the sill and coiled at her feet.

"Come into the parlor then," she said calmly. "And see me you shall."

He crowded in behind her as though the rain still beat on his shoulders and the only shelter was within her skirts. She took his hand, trying to calm him, and led him to the chaise.

"Phillip is only visiting his brother at Geneva," she said softly, "and so, of course, you must not tarry. What is it you wished to tell me?"

Now that he was seated, his confidence had returned. "I cannot be without you another night, Della. I came to tell you this. I want you to leave the man and marry me. I've already spoken to a solicitor, it shouldn't be difficult to arrange. We'll move to Charleston, you love that city, don't you? You must tell him as soon as he returns." He took both her hands and, to her horror, slid to one knee on the Aubusson beneath her slippers. "Marry me, Della. I love you more than life, I swear it."

She did not disengage her hands, she did not allow her fear to show in her voice, she said only, "You spoke with a solicitor about us?"

He nodded eagerly. "The laws are easier now for women. The man says you need not lose all rights to your property as you would have before the war—"

"Jeffrey," she began formally, "I am honored by your proposal, and my feelings are of the utmost tenderness for you—"

"Della, don't speak to me like that," he said swiftly. "I'm not a callow boy paying court to a virgin. I'm telling you I want you for my wife."

"I already am a wife," she said firmly, gently. "Which of course you have always known."

"In name only!" he cried out desperately. "You do not love him! He disdains to even live in the same house with you three months out of every five! Della, I swear to you—"

"Do not swear to me, Jeffrey," she stopped him, a little more coldly. "And please do not tell me again of my own marriage. You had no right to speak to anyone about you and me, and I am offended that you've done so. I told you I would never leave Phillip." She squeezed his hand gently. "I have not changed my mind."

He looked at her with what seemed to her to be fear, as though he could see the future in her eyes. "You will not divorce him?"

"I will not," she said sadly. "I'm sorry that you ever thought I might."

He stood abruptly, dropping her hands. "I have no choice, then," he said. "You drive me to it. I will speak to him myself and tell him of our love. I will ask him, as a gentleman, to set you free to find happiness."

"And if you do such a thing," she said calmly, "I will never see you again. You will be as dead to me, Jeffrey, as you are dear to me now."

He looked down at her with a mixture of awe and hopelessness. "I am dead, truly," he murmured, "if I cannot have you, Della."

Nonsense, she would have said kindly, if he had given her a chance. Jeffrey, don't ruin our pleasure together, she would have softly chided him, let us be rational about our lives. . . .

But he gave her no opportunity. Before she could call him back, he strode out of the parlor, snatched his cape, and made for the front door. She hurried behind him, hoping he would not feel compelled to shout again, more fodder for the slaves to chew back and forth between them—and as she yanked open the door he had slammed, ready with a word to bind him to her again, he whirled on the steps of the house and yanked a pistol from his coat. "I have loved you as no other in your life," he said, and he put the gun to his temple—

—in a slow-motion horror that she would replay over and over for many years of her life, she saw him flinch slightly at the touch of the cold steel on his skin, heard herself cry out his name, "Jeffrey!" in a frantic, garbled screech, heard the explosion of the pistol, the sudden gaping of his mouth, his startled eyes, so white in the shadows, the instantaneous crumpling of his body into itself like a folding flower, and the awful, awful silence after, broken only by the soft hiss of the rain, a faraway cry of alarm by a slave, and the distant thunder of the storm moving closer, closer—not the storm. The sound of hoofbeats. Phillip riding down the road to Deepwater, toward her, toward her, inexorably closer, to stop finally, and slowly dismount. To face her, with that poor bleeding body between them.

🌱 🌱 🌱

Della cried out again in the darkness, and Bathsheba went to her instantly, as she had all the long hours of that night. She put her hands on her shoulders and murmured, "You all right, Miz Della. Nobody here now but me an' you."

Weeping, Della let herself be put back again to bed, but she could not stop the images that assaulted her. "He killed himself!" she cried to Bathsheba. "Killed himself for me! Right before my eyes on my own front steps!"

"I know, Miz Della," Sheba whispered.

"And Phillip! Did you see the hate in his eyes when he asked me who he was? He knew about him all along! He's known about them all, I know it!"

"Sh-sh," the slave crooned. "Likely not. Massa Phillip just shocked, like you, Miz Della. Dat not hate in his eyes, but pain. He in pain, just like you. Dat poor man musta been crazy to do such a thing, an' likely he hurt himself one day, no matter what. You not to blame."

Della threw herself facedown on the coverlet, sobbing. "Yes.

Yes, I *am* to blame, Sheba. And I deserved every word that Phillip said."

"What he say?"

Della went on as though she was scarcely aware of who listened. "Faithless. Evil. Ruination of a man's soul." Her voice broke. "Corrupt. Contemptible. A common whore."

"Nothin' common 'bout you, Miz Della," Sheba gentled her. "You a good woman, just a trifle restive. You need a husband dat stay home at night. You lonely."

"A whore, he called me!"

"How he know why Massa Jeffrey shot hisself?"

Della put her hands to her head wearily. "I told him. I couldn't think of a lie, so I just told him the truth. He knew anyway, I'm sure of it. Ah, Sheba, you should have seen his eyes. The hardness of his mouth."

"If he know, why he go out an' leave you alone so much?"

Weeping harder now. "Because he hates me! He wants me to be miserable!"

"He love you," the slave said, "an' you love him, Miz Della. But you two ain' so good at it. Seem like you torment each other near to death, all de while lovin'."

Della realized then what she had said, who held her and offered comfort, and she pulled away slightly, trying to calm herself. Nothing could be gained by letting anyone, even Bathsheba, see her in this way. But as she tried to stop weeping, the pictures of Jeffrey, of Phillip, of the parade of other lovers she had known and loved and hurt—all flooded over her, leaving her shaking and helpless. "I will surely go to hell when I die," she sobbed. "Aunt Tess would have died of shame, if she knew what I've become. Sheba, go 'way from me now. I want to be by myself."

The slave hesitated, hurt and unsure.

"I mean it, go and leave me. I must get through this by myself."

With a final small pat to her shoulders, Bathsheba let herself out of the room. Only Della and the flickering light of a single candle shared the shadows now. She moved to the window seat and sat staring out over the fields of Deepwater, bathed in moonlight. Fingering the gold locket absently at her neck, she reviewed her life.

She had married a handsome man who knew a good deal about the world but little about himself. That had been a terrible mistake. He could not make himself happy, nor could he ever hope to make her happy either. She had come to him always a step behind, and so they were never in balance. Ever competing for territory in a marriage laden with hidden traps. She had taken happiness, therefore, where she could, for she must have that sense of being cherished or die. And now, one other had died for it instead.

She turned the locket over and over. The night outside her window was wondrously beautiful and clear, as it often was after a storm. The sharp edges of her pain began to dull as she gazed over the fields. Deepwater was more her own now than it had ever been Phillip's. She had made it so. And her heart was her own as well. Likely, she would never give it away again.

Phillip will never leave me, she thought, not now. We are bound together by our common sins as much by our common need. This, too, will pass, and we will likely be stronger for it. For the unspoken secrets that we share. Poor Jeffrey, Della whispered to herself. He was too young for this.

And I, I am too old.

🌿 🌿 🌿

· One year later, long after Della believed that Phillip was no longer brooding over that scene on his front veranda, he arrived home with a secretive air, trailing a new wench behind him on a small pony. When Della came out to greet him, she saw that the slave held a bundle in her arms.

"I hope she's got milk for that child," Della said, eyeing the wench carefully. "Sissie's just weaned hers and she's dry. If you want her out in the field right away, that suckling'll have to have a wet nurse."

"She's got milk," Phillip said shortly, "and she's not a field hand, anyway."

Della frowned. He knew right well that it was her responsibility to see to the house and all its help, she certainly did not need another wench in the kitchen.

"She's the child's nurse," he said, beckoning to the slave to come closer.

Della was struck by the woman's posture. Clearly, she was afraid. But she came forward, extending the bundle to Della's arms. Eyes wide, Della automatically took the baby from the slave and unwrapped its shawl. It was a baby girl with soft, pursed lips and white-pink skin.

She stared at Phillip in amazement, but in answer, he only ushered her inside the house, the trembling slave following along behind them.

Once in their chambers, the slave dismissed for the moment, Della asked, "Whose baby is this, Phillip?" She had the child unwrapped now on the bed, her tiny limbs curled in on themselves as though still slumbering in the womb. The child had not opened her eyes, had not awakened, although Della sensed that she was remaining so still as much in self-defense as in sleep.

"She's yours," he said calmly. "You always said you wanted a child, now you have one."

"But who is this child's mother? How did you get her?"

"Don't you want her?" he asked, deliberately keeping his back to her, fussing with something in his valet drawers.

"That depends," Della said, containing her annoyance. The child was lovely, it was true, but the idea of her was somehow too overwhelming to be possible. "Whose is she, Phillip?"

He turned and faced her openly now, but his face was as closed as his shoulders had been. "I'm going to tell you this once, Della, one time only. And then I'm never going to speak of it again. The child is mine. Mine by a woman in Charleston, a woman I've known for several years. You needn't know a thing about the woman except that she was lovely—you can see that much by her child—and of some culture. She has departed for the continent and left the child to me. She is four months old, I believe. I intend to raise her as ours, if you agree. If not, I intend to raise her as mine. I wish she had been a boy, but that's my only regret. She seems a fine, healthy girl, and she will be the only heir I'll have, likely." He paused, as though to judge the quality of her silence. "I have not named her as yet. I thought perhaps you might like to do that."

Stunned, Della rose haltingly and moved from the bed to the window seat, scarcely knowing what she did or caring. The child lay still on the bed, like a package unopened. Within might lie one's heart's desire—or a lifetime trap of pain.

"Your mistress's child," she murmured. "You come to me and tell me that you have had a lover all these years and bring her child to my house? You expect me to"—she almost could not find the words—"to raise this child as my own? A child you had with another woman?"

"Let us not," he said, almost ironically, "get into the subject of lovers, Della. We both understand our weaknesses, we have both been infidels after our own fashion. But of mine, we have a chance to garner something for ourselves out of a pretty mess. Do you want her or not?"

Della deliberately did not look at the child. She knew she would be lost if she did. She turned and gazed out at the fields of Deepwater. It was summer, and the tobacco was high and rich with color, she could almost smell its pungency from within the house. Finally, the ravages of the war were over, and the county was beginning to organize itself around commerce that would sustain them all. Revolution had left them ravaged, but ultimately serene. Passion had left her own heart ravaged, too, Della thought, and she suddenly had a yearning for serenity as well.

Peace, she repeated to herself silently, peace is what we need now. Perhaps it is time to begin anew after all. I could never abandon him; perhaps it is time to embrace him.

She turned and stared at the child. "And you expect me to embrace this child and ignore her origins?"

"That's the jist of it, yes," he said firmly. "If you cannot, I shall make other arrangements for her, but I shall claim her as mine, nonetheless."

Della waited to feel a vast wave of tenderness well in her for the tiny creature who curled on the coverlet. She waited—wanted—to feel a surge of maternalism that would cause her to take the child in her arms, take it to her bosom, and be content to hold it there forever. But she felt no such wave, no surge of welcome. She felt some small compassion for the poor little thing, some awe—some—what? She could not put a name on her feelings. Fear, probably, and resentment, certainly, but something else tugged at her. A memory. A letter, several of them, signed by one Catherine? Cathleen? So many years before. Could she have been the mother? She sighed deeply. Did it matter who it was, after all?

And then the child stirred, opened her eyes, and started suddenly, as if only then feeling the softness of the blanket beneath her body. Looking around the room, the baby focused finally on the closest body to her: Della. She jerked her fists in the air convulsively and opened her mouth as if to cry out, then seemed to think better of it and subsided. Silently she stared at Della as though transfixed.

Now Della knew what the emotion was that she felt—it was curiosity. The same feeling that had led her into trouble many times before. But she could not help herself. She bent to the child and picked her up, marveling at the way the infant molded herself to her body, almost defiantly, as if daring the world to remove her now from this soft shoulder.

"She is a lovely child," she said softly, looking down at the baby. "What would you think of naming her Caroline? Since she was born in the year of our independence. After my dead cousin, Caroline. That would have made my Aunt Tess very happy."

Phillip grinned then, looking younger than she had seen him in years. "I think Caroline suits her very well." He did not say another word, did not ask her for any more commitment than that.

Della sat down on the bed with Caroline in her arms, feeling the weight of the little body, but also sensing a lightness in the room, in her heart, which had not been there before. "A new beginning, then," she said, half to herself and half to the child. "We've said it before, perhaps this time it will stick."

Phillip still said nothing, but he sat down on the bed beside her and carefully took the child's fist in his hand.

🌾 🌾 🌾

Della watched Caroline intently for the whole first two years of her life, looking for some semblance to the phantom woman who had birthed her. She held the child, rocked her, fed her the first spoonfuls of gruel, walked her round the room with two fingers when she first began to stagger upright, and she observed every gesture, every smile, every position of mouth and eye to see what the woman was whom Phillip had loved.

For loved her he certainly must have, of that much Della was certain. He refused to speak of her, but he held Caroline with such tenderness that Della almost could not bear to watch it. Surely, she thought, he must have held her mother in much the same way. But finally one day, she gave up her vigilance.

Caroline was twenty months, a fat, robust toddler with blond curls and wide-set, mischievous green eyes. She had Phillip's legs, and she learned to use them early. Della swore the child could run faster than her pony, and it was nothing to hear Caroline crow from the top of some high place or another, like the top of the larder or the roof of the sty, someplace she had climbed where no child her age should have been able—or wanted—to reach.

That morning, Della had walked with her out to the stable to see the new foal, and Caroline squealed with delight when she got close to the nickering, stomping horses. Reaching out of Della's arms, trying to touch the mare over the edge of the stall, she babbled to the animal happily, crying, "Ho! Ho!" which was her word for horse. Caroline was deft in all things physical, but slow to form words, Della had noticed. Even at nearly two, she rarely said "mama" or "papa" or "baby."

Della privately believed that on some level, Caroline sensed the confusion over her parentage and with her usual stubbornness, refused to honor a surrogate with the name of mother. Della loved her, but she kept expecting any day for someone to come to the door and say, "never mind, there's been a mistake. This child belongs someplace else." And so, she knew there was a piece of her heart she would not risk.

But that day, Caroline was particularly adorable, her smile sunny and seemingly without any source other than simply herself. If anything, she looked more like Phillip these days than she had before. Della carried her into the depths of the barn, found the foal, and knelt down with the child to show her the tiny new spindly legs. Caroline crowed and reached and then hurtled herself off Della's lap to run toward a tangle of bridles that hung down from a nail almost to the stall floor. Della turned her head away for a moment to speak to the stable boy, and then back again to see that Caroline had dropped the bridles and managed somehow to climb up on a platform more than twenty feet in the air, from one bale of hay to another, until she was perched far above the stable floor.

Della gasped and whirled to stand directly under her. "Caroline, how did you get up there so fast?" She turned to the little colored boy who gaped up at the child, no more help than Della was in that instant. "Run quick," she said to him, "and get Joseph to come get her down." Joseph was the handler, a strong boy of height enough to reach her with the ladder fast enough.

As the slave raced away to fetch him, she called out, "Caroline," keeping her voice calm, "don't move from there, darlin', not a whit." She glanced around to see if she could take the child's route up to her, but the bales of hay looked too perilous to bear her weight. The floor beneath Caroline was rickety board, half splintered in two places. If she fell or jumped and missed the hay, she'd fall through to the empty granary below or be pierced by the broken boards.

"Me!" Caroline crowed, her arms in the air with exultation. That was her most favorite word these days. "Me burr!"

"You are not a bird, Caroline, you cannot fly," Della said firmly, thinking she would surely switch that boy and Joseph, too, if they didn't hurry—and with that, Caroline called out a single cry, "Me, Mama!" and sailed off confidently into the air.

There was no time to think, no time to move, Della simply put out her arms and caught the child clumsily, breaking her fall and tumbling both of them to the floor heavily. Caroline then yelped in fear and surprise, but she clung to Della with a fixed grip, and all Della could think of was, she called to me, she said Mama and jumped to me, trusting that I would catch her. And I caught her. She hugged Caroline very tight and scolded her all the way back to the house. But from that day on, she ceased looking for another woman in her face.

🌾 🌾 🌾

Time passed slowly, it seemed, after the turbulence of the war years. Even the seasons seemed to crawl down the river with the torpidity of turtles long in hibernation. Most of a decade slid by, and the Cape Fear Valley settled into a somnolence that little seemed able to disturb. Even the War of 1812 with Britain scarcely ruffled North Carolina's long, stagnant hibernation. The years of tumult were over for good. The sun rose and shone on fertile fields, crops went to market for good prices, folks married, birthed, and died with the cycles of seasons, and the outside world troubled them not at all.

In fact, the outside world had trouble getting in. While the bowsprits of tall ships towered over Boston's waterfront and Manhattan's countinghouses, and Georgian houses of the wealthy surveyed the Delaware, and the James River was clogged with vessels, the Cape of Fear, battleground of the Atlantic, stood guard over the shipping lanes to Wilmington and kept them inhospitable to captains of trade.

The shoals and shallows of New Inlet and Frying Pan were passable for small schooners, brigs, and privateers, but the skippers of larger transatlantic ships feared venturing close when they could see, peering over the side of their ships, the sandy bottoms roiled by strong currents.

And the roads were just as haphazard. Cross Creek was the hub of five roads, and none of them was dependable. Some were mere widened trails pocked with mud holes and stumps. When the routes passed through a longleaf pine forest, there was the hazard of dead trees, boxed for turpentine and left standing. Summer storms sent them crashing across the road and unlucky carriages. One poor traveler from New York said he was forced to crawl along a slippery log over swampland while his slave swam the horses over, and another sojourner who was lost on horseback in a pine wilderness struck a flint to see the way and spent the rest of the night fighting off wolves who came close to investigate.

Trade recovered quickly after the war years, and Wilmington had products the outside world wanted—lumber, staves, shingles, naval stores, tobacco, and rice—but everything had to be transported by pirogue and raft. It was a system guaranteed to keep North Carolina surviving but asleep.

Four families in New Hanover County owned more than ten thousand acres each, and the majority held more than four hundred acres each. Wilmington was a pleasant river town, but it looked like it might never achieve its destiny as a great American port.

Della had gradually added to acreage round Deepwater, picking up small parcels when she could at auction, hacking back the swamp growth to make room for more tobacco bit by bit, buying more slaves when prices were up and refusing to sell when prices dropped until, finally, she was mistress of one of the largest, most successful plantations on the river.

"And it's no accident either," she confided to Caroline as they rode out over the fields together. Caroline had a good seat on her bay pony for a ten-year-old, though she tended to pull on the horse's mouth overmuch. "See that section of tall oronoko over yonder?"

"Mother, Gemma is being *impossible* today!" Caroline retorted, yanking again on the pony's reins.

"Caroline, I've told you before, if you're going to argue with your horse, you'll always lose so long as you're on her back. On her back, you persuade. On the ground before her nose, is when you do the arguing. Now, that oronoko leaf over there is the best we grow at Deepwater. Rolfe's leaf is good enough for most of them, and hardly any other planter on the river wanted to touch it, said it was too prone to bugs and dry scale, but we babied it along, and now see how it's tall as your father? We'll clear more from those ten acres than we will from more'n forty acres—"

"Mother, I can feel my hands beginning to freckle," Caroline grumbled. "How much longer do we have to ride these rows?"

Della turned and glared at her daughter, but Caroline was so busy fussing with her bonnet that she did not even see the look. "Someday, Caroline, this will all be yours. If you don't learn how to take care of it, some man will come in and do it for you. And take it away from you in the process."

"I don't give a fig for oronoco or Ralph's or any other kind of leaf!" Caroline snapped. "Papa says its unwomanly to care so much about the fields and the coloreds and—and so much about money!" She turned her pert face away, frowning furiously.

"Oh he does, does he?" Della asked archly. "Well, you can tell Papa next time he mentions the subject that I have to care about all this and the money, too, else we'll lose it all to someone else who cares more. That's the way of the world, chicken, the one who cares the most keeps the most."

Caroline rolled her eyes. "Mother, you always talk like you're writing things down."

Della started to snap back at her but then she subsided, hurt to the quick. Caroline was a smart girl, a pretty girl, but she had been difficult most of her life. Della loved her, but often she did not like her very much. She suspected that her daughter felt the same way about her. She said nothing more that afternoon, but that evening she said to Bathsheba, "I think it might be time for Caroline to go away from here for a spell. There's an excellent boarding school in Bath for young ladies. She could go abroad, of course, but I doubt her father would hear of it—"

"I misdoubt he'll hear o' dis idea too," Bathsheba said.

"He spoils her," Della said, rather peevishly.

"Somebody got to," the slave replied gently.

"What do you mean by that?" Della snapped at her. "I give that child the best money can buy, and you see how she takes care of her things—clothes strewn about her room like they're just so much flotsam, books left out on the veranda to get all mildewed; dolls—those beautiful dolls I brought her from Charleston!—she takes them out in the stable and forgets them in the hay. I swear, Sheba, she doesn't deserve such nice things. She deserves a good whipping half the time, and her father won't raise his voice to her, much less his hand—"

"He love her," she said simply. "Dat be all she really need."

"And I don't? I'm trying to teach her how to stand up for herself, how to run a proper plantation someday, how to be independent and strong so that some man won't take advantage of her and make her miserable."

"Her papa don' make her misery. Might be, if she find a man most like him, she be happy enough."

Della jerked out of her boudoir seat and snatched her hair out of Bathsheba's soothing hands. "I don't know why I listen to you, Sheba, you don't know two sticks about raising a child, and you haven't the vaguest idea what a woman in this age must do to protect herself." She turned and glared at the slave, for the moment seeing only her color. She was ashamed, in that instant, for having confided in her so many times as though she were almost an equal. "I'll deal with her father in my own way, Sheba, and Caroline will thank me for this when she's older. She'll leave for the academy at Bath inside the week. Go tell Bess to start getting her things ready."

"Yes'm," Sheba murmured. But she did not drop her eyes at Della's stare.

"What are you gawking at? Get going."

Sheba did not move.

Della was suddenly exhausted, and she sank down again in her chair. "Sheba, I'm not myself today. I'm sorry."

The slave smiled lovingly and lightly touched Della on her head. In that moment, Della saw that she had grown older also, that her hands were wrinkled with work and age, that her face was no longer smooth and unlined. She looked in the mirror and saw that the two of them had grown middle-aged together. Bathsheba said, "You do your best, Miz Della. Raisin' a girl-chile ain' easy, even if she your own blood. Some proper schoolin' won' hurt Miz Caroline none."

Della put her head down on her arms and began to weep quietly. She wanted Caroline gone . . . and she wanted Caroline never to leave her side for a day of her life. She kept crying softly as Bathsheba crept out and closed the door behind her gently. In a few moments, Della raised her head and looked again in the glass. Repairing her eyes, she looked closely at herself for the second time in the past few moments.

Almost fifty, she said like a dull chime in her head over and over. Strands of gray she covered with a black coffee rinse, many fine lines she camouflaged with powder—she had stooped to rouging her cheeks for extra vivacity a few years before and now could not do without. Her body was still firm, her throat relatively unlined. But it was when she gazed at Caroline that she saw true beauty, unalloyed by any cosmetics, undamaged by time. It made her feel protective and tender toward the child . . . and also sad for her own changes.

Caroline was becoming increasingly headstrong. Without some discipline, the sort of training a good academy for girls could provide, she would be unruly and unmanageable as a green filly soon. Della knew she had neither the patience nor the strength for the sort of confrontation that was brewing with Caroline. She preferred a known adversary: Phillip.

She found him in his study, going over the crop books. To her surprise and pleasure, he looked up with a warm smile when she walked in and beckoned her closer. He put one arm round her hip and drew her into his body. "These profits are the best we've shown in five years, Della," he said. "That oronoco was a stroke of genius. I must say, you make me very proud of you."

She flushed with startled pleasure. He rarely commented on her contribution to the plantation's prosperity, much less praised her so effusively. She leaned into his body and fondled his hair. It, too, was turning gray. She looked down into his face. Her handsome Phillip was becoming what she used to think of as "a distinguished gentleman," when she was a girl. Too old to dance with but too young to need a young lady to bring him a glass of punch. "I'm glad you're pleased," she murmured happily. "We need to discuss something, dear, and if you're almost through here, I think now would be a good time."

She felt him stiffen slightly. Anytime she approached him in that way, he grew wary. Perhaps every husband did. She went on as casually as she could manage. "You know that Caroline is reaching that age when she should be receiving more training than I can provide. She's growing so quickly—she's really almost a young woman now, not a child anymore. I think we should give some serious thought to her education."

"Indeed?" he said, and his voice lost some of its earlier warmth. "It sounds as though you already have."

"Yes," she went on bravely, "and I think the best opportunity for her would be the female academy at Bath. They have an excellent reputation, and many of the best families send their daughters there."

Phillip was silent. Watchful.

"We could send her abroad, of course, but she is likely too young for that."

"She's too young for Bath, as well."

Della shook her head. "You don't see her as clearly as you might, Phillip. She is not a child, truly. And"—here she faltered for a moment, but then decided to bluster ahead with the truth—"she's becoming difficult. I can't manage her anymore."

A rueful smile. "I see. This is the real fuel for this fire, then. You want her gone."

"I don't want her gone, I want her to be a lovely woman with a fine potential. Something I think she'd better develop under the tutelage—"

"Of a pack of strict old nuns with hands like leather and hearts full of sour grapes."

Della laughed then, suddenly, for his scowl looked so fierce and determined. "Ah, love, if you don't think Bath is a good idea, then *you* think of something for her. I'm telling you, the girl is running roughshod over me and Bess and Sheba and everybody else in the house, including you. But if you want to raise a hellion, have at it."

He softened visibly at her laugh. "No," he said, shaking his head, "I can't handle her either." He smiled grudgingly. "Do you know what she said to me when I asked her why she was riding astride the other day?"

"I can imagine," she said, grinning.

"Well, I couldn't. She told me she chose to ride her pony in that fashion because it felt better."

Della laughed. "What did you say?"

"I blushed, I believe. Before my own daughter. I blushed and stammered and could not think of a suitable retort." He rolled his eyes. "And she's not even of age yet. You're right. The nuns for the child. Bath is as good as any, I suppose. Have you spoken with her?"

"I thought you should do that."

"Oh, I see! You dole out the sentence, and I'm the executioner."

"She won't see it that way, if you're clever. Make it sound like a grand adventure, Phillip. You can do it." She stroked his shoulders coaxingly. "If anybody can."

That night they went together to Caroline's room, for Phillip would not tell the child of their decision without Della present. As always when Della entered Caroline's chamber, she was almost intimidated by its profusion of lace, crinoline, toys, books, the trappings of a young girl who had been denied little. Something rather distasteful about it, Della thought, like a banquet table groaning with too many rich desserts. Caroline was on her bed, playing with a sumptuously dressed doll half as tall as herself, plaiting the long, golden curls with solicitude.

"Papa!" she cried delightedly when she saw Phillip, brushing past Della to throw herself in his arms. "I haven't seen you for days and days and days!"

He nuzzled her fondly and laughed. "Scarcely that long, I should think. Didn't we just have lunch together yesterday?"

She pulled a delicate pout from out of the pocket of her pink cheeks. "You're always gone, Papa. I think you should spend more time at home. Mama, don't you think so, too?"

Della appraised he daughter kindly. She was a lovely child, but there was something that did not quite ring true in her voice. A small sadness, perhaps. A secrecy. "Absolutely, dear. And if you can get your papa to stay home more, then you're a better woman than I."

Phillip picked her up and took her to sit in the window seat next to him. He took her hand in his and said, "Caroline, how are you doing on your lessons with Master Powell?"

Master Powell, the roving instructor for many of the plantation children, taught the rudiments of English grammar, spelling, and arithmetic to some half-dozen pupils up and down the river. He was a Quaker, a solemn man with barely enough schooling to keep a step ahead of his students, but he was the best the plantation owners could find.

Caroline frowned. "Has he told you bad things about me?"

Phillip raised his brows. "Could he have?"

Caroline rolled her eyes, looking everywhere but at her father. "He's a boring man, Father, and he scolds me on my sums every time he sees me, but I don't think he knows them much better than I do."

Phillip patted her hand gently, and Della did her best not to glare at them both. "Well, perhaps Master Powell is not a very good teacher, pet, certainly not as good as you deserve. What would you think to a grand school that would be not only a fine education but also a great adventure?"

Caroline instantly looked at Della suspiciously. "In Wilmington?"

Della only smiled innocently, letting Phillip do the talking.

"There's no school in Wilmington that will do, pet, not for a girl with your intelligence. No, we were thinking actually of the academy for young women in Bath."

Caroline's eyes widened. "You want to send me away? All the way to Bath? And I wouldn't come home at all?"

Phillip hurried to explain. "No, no, of course you'd come home on holidays and whenever the academy has sabbaticals for the students, and we would come up and visit whenever you wished—"

"But you're sending me away," Caroline said flatly.

"Only if you want to go," her father said firmly. "We think it would be wonderful for you, Caroline, but if you don't wish it, we can perhaps think of something else—"

Della spoke up then, unable to keep silent longer. "There really isn't anything else, dear. There's no decent school closer than Bath, and you need more training than Master Powell and I can provide. You are becoming a young lady now, Caroline, and your behavior must come to reflect that."

"It's you, then, who wants to send me away," Caroline murmured. "Not Father."

Della cast a pained look to Phillip, silently pleading with him to intercede.

"We both think it's a good idea, Caroline," Phillip said solemnly.

He sounded sincere, looked committed to the idea, but Caroline gazed at him for a heartbeat and then away, her mouth skeptical. "If I were her real daughter, she wouldn't send me away."

Della's heart fell. "That's not so, Caroline," she said sadly. "You *are* my real daughter."

"No," the child murmured. "I never have been."

"No matter who gave you birth, I am your mother," Della continued as though she had not spoken, "and I want what is best for you. You need more than I can give you now. The female academy at Bath is a fine school, many of the best families send their daughters there—"

"It's because I'm so stubborn," Caroline said. "So headstrong, you said."

Della bowed her head. She could not face the child. "You know we have been having our scrapes, lately. But that's not the reason—"

"All right then, I'll go," Caroline said suddenly, her face sober. "I want to. I'll go at once."

Phillip glanced at Della, alarmed. "Well, there's no reason to rush this decision," he began.

"No, I agree," the child insisted. "It's best." Her head was high, her chin firm. "How soon can I leave?"

Della sank down on Caroline's bed, dismayed and silent. Where did this stubbornness come from? Why was Caroline so defiant, almost to the point of self-destruction? Della wanted to weep with despair in that moment. Had she been such a horrible example of womanhood that Caroline had so little softness in her? Had she loved her so badly that she was ruined for her lifetime?

They had agreed early on to always be truthful with her, and when she asked the inevitable questions about where she came from, Della had gently told her what facts she could. That Caroline was born to another woman and her father, a woman who long since went away, leaving her behind because she could not care for her. That Della and her father took her and cared for her because they loved her. When she asked why she had no brothers or sisters, Della said only that God had not blessed them with more than one child, but one child was enough. She had tried to love Caroline with all she could give, but she was not the kind of woman to dote on a baby past all reason. Often, it was easier to let the nurse take her, lift her, bathe her, feed her, and sometimes the day got away with little time for play. But she loved her as much as she could. And she had tried, for all these years, to never let Caroline know when she could not.

Now Phillip tried to embrace his daughter, but she sprang to her feet with a bright fixed smile on her face. "No, really, it'll be good, it's a fine idea. I'll go away to Bath, I'll get a good education, and I'll learn how to be a proper lady. A grand adventure, you said, Father. That's what it will be. Have you already made the arrangements?"

"No, of course not," Phillip said dismally. "We wanted to discuss it with you first, Caroline."

"Ah. Well, we agree then," she said, very evenly. "It will be a good opportunity for me, I'm sure. Now if you don't mind," she said with the air of a girl much older, "I'd really like to be by myself for a bit. I'll have to make a list of what to take and what to leave behind, won't I? Or will I be able to take everything?"

"Not everything," Della said softly. "You will be sharing a room with another young lady, and space will be limited. The nuns ask that you bring only a few treasures and no more than three frocks."

"Three?" Caroline's face fell, but her voice did not alter. "Well. If all the other young ladies bring only three, then I must too, I suppose." She thought for a moment. "I am not Catholic. Will the nuns punish me for that as well?"

"Of course not," Phillip said quickly. "They will welcome you as they do all willing students."

Caroline glanced at Della and then away. As though she could not bear to see her mother's face. "Well, that's good then. Now, if you'll both excuse me." She stood up expectantly, and Della had the strangest feeling that she was going to formally usher her parents out of her room like a woman in her own parlor.

Della and Phillip moved to the door, discomfited but unable to think of another thing to say. He stopped once and turned to speak, but Caroline waved him away. "Don't worry, Father, I'm fine, truly. This will be a good plan, and we'll all be happier for it."

Dismissed, they went out of her chamber and closed the door quietly behind them. Della murmured, "The child is more confused than I suspected."

Phillip glared at her fiercely. "You have broken her heart," he hissed. "And you made me do the thing, for God's sake!" He

stalked away, leaving Della bereft and shaken in the corridor, leaning against Caroline's stolidly closed door.

🔥 🔥 🔥

And so, their daughter went away. Phillip and Della took her to
Bath, laden with gifts and packages, most of which they knew the
nuns would confiscate for sharing with some of the less endowed
students. Della made a small ceremony out of placing her gold
filigree locket round her daughter's neck. "Aunt Tess gave this to
me when I was born, for good luck. She had it all her life, and
probably her mother before her wore it. Now, it's your turn to
keep it safe and for it to keep you safe, too."

Caroline smiled politely and tucked it within her bodice. She
kept a smile throughout most of the journey, not even weeping as
they made their farewells. With many promises to come to fetch
her for the holidays, Della and Phillip embraced her, keeping a
good show of solidarity in their decision. But once they were back
home again, the empty rooms and hallways of Deepwater seemed
to Della to be a muffled rebuke.

For three nights after Caroline's departure, Phillip did not visit
Della's bed. He found excuses to be away from the table for meals,
and he scarcely passed her in the house to speak to in the daylight
hours. Della ached with sadness and resentment, but she did not
approach him. What could she say, even if he might listen? The
child was gone. She was only partly sorry. She could not deny
those truths.

On the fourth night, Phillip opened her door and came to sit
alongside her on the bed. She put down her book and turned to
face him, half prepared for the worst. To her surprise, he bent
down and held her, pillowing his head on her bosom. "I miss her,"
he whispered.

"I know," she murmured.

"I miss you, too."

She felt the old familiar tenderness well up in her, and this time,
she did not fight it away. She held him tightly, and he pulled up
beside her, embracing her fully and sliding her under his body. The
tenderness flamed in her to a heat of strong desire, as though she
had been in hibernation for months. Somehow just the knowledge

that they were essentially alone in the house, with no child down the hall to call or to care for, made her feel freer than she had in a long while. And yet she could not say it to him, could not let him see how light she felt with Caroline gone.

And then he whispered, "You were right to send her away."

Startled, she pulled back and looked in his face. "I was?"

He kissed her deeply, lingering on her mouth as he used to when it seemed he could not savor her enough. "It was time. Ten years with a child is enough."

She was shocked by his candor, but she felt in that moment closer to him than she had in so long—as though the two of them shared a state of sin. It was wrong to feel such about one's child, she knew, and if any other parents felt that way, they certainly never would say it aloud. But she was so grateful that he had expressed her own feelings that she clung to him, almost burrowing into his chest and arms as though for shelter from her own ambivalence. He understood without her speaking, and he drew her then inexorably into the old, new, familiar, and yet somehow always strange maelstrom of desire between them.

🌿　🌿　🌿

The letters Della received from Severn began to dwindle quickly that spring, and her cousin's normally meticulous penmanship had faltered to a barely legible scrawl. Severn was past seventy, and though she had kept her youthfulness longer than most women her age, of a sudden, her years seemed to have caught up with her at last.

Severn hardly left her bed at all now, for her hips pained her to walk, and her heart galloped, she said, like a runaway horse at the least exertion. Usually Della took her some fresh apples or peaches from Deepwater's orchards, but lately Severn had trouble chewing the fruit, so instead she took a newspaper from Boston to read aloud to her. Severn's eyesight was failing, but she had never lost her interest in politics, local or otherwise.

The second week in April, Della made her usual monthly visit to find Severn much weaker than she expected. She showed no enthusiasm for Mary Ann's lemon cake, and even more surprising, no glee at the paper's report of Napoleon's antics across the continent. Della sat on the side of her bed and held her cousin's hand, alarmed at how small, white, and weak it seemed in her own. She chatted easily about Caroline's latest letter, the small gossip she had heard at a supper party the week before, and the atrocious prices of Brussels lace this season, compared with that which was coming in from the Spanish islands, when Severn squeezed her hand softly, and she fell into silence.

"You are good to come," Severn said softly. Her voice sounded small as a girl's.

"Well, of course I come," Della said soothingly.

"Many don't anymore." Severn smoothed the coverlet absently with her other hand. "I don't expect to see another summer, you know."

Startled by Severn's candor, Della laughed nervously. "Don't be silly, you'll likely outlive me, the way Caroline's turning me gray. She's driving the nuns crazy with her rebellions, of course, and my worst fear is that they'll send her back to us."

"Do you regret not having children of your own?" Severn asked wistfully.

Della thought for a moment. "I don't know. I did, once, think that if I couldn't have a child, I would die of emptiness. Then Caroline came to us, and I often wondered why I wished for such a thing. But I love her, despite her defiance and her disobedience and—" she hesitated. "Despite it all, I guess. I mostly think of her as mine. And Phillip loves her."

"Does he love you as well?"

Della considered her answer carefully. Severn had never asked her personal questions before. Indeed, they had rarely spoken of such things. Della wondered, sometimes, if Severn shared anything of her heart with anyone. "I think so," she finally said. "He does now, I believe."

"Did you ever tell him of your estate?"

"Never."

"But you bought lands adjoining Deepwater. How did you keep it from him?"

"I manage the accounts and have for years. He knows we added to the plantation; he doesn't know it was my money that did it."

"But the deed? The taxes?"

"In my name. I found a solicitor willing to accommodate my wishes. I paid the taxes, so he never had need to know—"

"So that if you divorce, your land will encircle his," Severn finished quietly.

"Yes," Della said firmly, lifting her head. She listened carefully to Severn's voice for criticism. There seemed to be none. "But we will not divorce. I will be with him until one of us breathes his last." Della smiled ruefully. "You never liked him, all these years."

Severn answered with the honesty of the aged. "No, I never did. But I have to say, I had little use for men in general. He wasn't much better or worse than the lot of them."

"I always wondered about that. Why did you never marry?"

Severn shrugged gently. "Never trusted one enough to bind myself to him for life. My own father was as good as they come, and even he was a rogue, as you know."

"No," Della said carefully, "I didn't know that."

"Well, he was," Severn said shortly. "And my dear mother never knew it. But *I* did."

"What, exactly, did you know of Father Dobbs?" Della made herself keep her voice level, unconcerned.

Severn looked up at her with angry, hooded eyes. "I knew your mother well, Della. Believe me, I wasn't as blind as my mother. If my father wasn't your father, he certainly could have been."

Della made an instant decision. She gave it no rehearsal in her mind or heart. "You're wrong, Severn. I've known of your suspicions for years, and Tess knew of them, too. But you're wrong. Father Dobbs was not my father. All these years, you've tortured yourself—tortured your mother and me, too—with nothing but a fantasy. My father was faithless, no doubt, but my mother was not. My father lived and died in Charleston, and *your* father was a decent man who deserves an apology, even in the grave, after all these years of your suspicions."

"How can you be so sure?" Severn asked weakly. She seemed almost unhappy to hear Della's denial.

"Because," Della went on without hesitation, "I received several letters from my father in his lifetime. One before he died, in fact, when he spoke of my mother with some nostalgia and regretted the fact that we had never been able to meet." It was a lie, but a graceful one, Della thought. This nonsense had gone on long enough.

Severn appraised her cousin carefully. "Is that the truth?"

"Of course it is," Della said firmly. "So if you go a maiden to your grave because of some imagined affront by your father with my mother, you've missed a good many kisses for nothing, my dear. I suggest you hop right out of that bed and make up for lost time."

Severn smiled ruefully. "I haven't missed that many," she said. "And I don't know if I believe you still, but it hardly matters anymore. Likely, I did what I did because I wanted to. We all do, finally."

The two cousins sat in silence for a moment, Della still holding Severn's hand. The only sound in the room was the delicate chime of the mantel clock.

"I remember you so well as a child," Severn finally said. "You were beautiful even then."

Della said nothing.

"And I could not abide it. Especially after my Caroline was taken."

"I know," Della said.

"But we had some jolly times together, did we not?" the old woman asked plaintively. "I remember how you used to skip rather than walk. And sing rather than talk. You were such an imp, Della. Such a . . ." she faltered. "So much life." She sighed. "I used to think you sucked it from those who loved you, somehow. From me. But that wasn't so. You took it from the air you breathed."

"Tell me, dear," Della asked gently, "did you ever fall in love? I mean, really and truly?"

"I thought I had once," Severn whispered. "Stephen Gage. And for a bit, I thought he was mine. But I would not have him then, and he would not have me later." She smiled faintly. Ruefully. "I seem to have been always out of time in my life, somehow."

Another long silence.

Finally Severn murmured, "You know, I don't have many regrets in my life, really. Mostly, I did as I pleased."

"Then you've been luckier than many of us," Della said softly.

"But one. One sore regret. I never had a child. I never truly wanted a husband, but I did want a child."

Della squeezed her hand. For years, it had seemed to her that Severn was scarcely a woman at all. She was somehow not connected to the life of women, not part of the whole scheme of marriage and babies and houses and husbands. Almost genderless, she was instead a woman of ideas, politics, and committees. A woman to draft a resolution for rebellion, not a receipt for the kitchen.

Della had never pitied Severn before. Now, just for an instant, she saw how lonely her life had been. She also, in that moment, understood how the aching annoyances, unwieldy complications, and chafing responsibilities of a husband and child made for a life rich and full and real. She felt used in every sense of the word, sometimes even used up past all endurance. But Severn's fate was more terrible in its hollowness, for scarcely having been used at all.

Della left her cousin feeling as though she had somehow been given another inheritance. Another mother had given her a legacy of sorts—not money, this time, but a certain revelation.

She sat alongside Bathsheba in silence as the carriage rocked along back to Deepwater, and the faces of women she had known well floated before her in mute procession. She realized that like Severn, she, too, had felt disconnected since Caroline was away. As though, without a child to care for, she was somehow cut adrift from the web of women and their lives. She had placed her locket around Caroline's neck, the locket that had come to her from Tess, from Leah Hancock before her, she supposed, and likely another set of mother's hands, daughter's hands, before that. And though she was not superstitious about such a silly trinket—she did not, after all, believe that whatever luck she might have in her life came from a gold chain and a filigree bauble—still, she had to admit that Caroline's absence, together with the missing talisman around her neck, did make her feel separate from her life in some essential way. Disconnected from a legacy of women whose voices she needed to hear.

She vowed, when she got home, to write to Caroline as soon as she put off her bonnet. Not another day should go by with her daughter not hearing her voice, however distant, and feeling her love, however imperfect.

🌿 🌿 🌿

Caroline had been in Bath for five years that spring. Della counted the seasons now more than the years. She was near sixty, and she did not know how many seasons she could anticipate of fine health and contentment. Deepwater was prospering, Caroline appeared to be growing into a young woman of excellent potential, although the nuns still complained of her headstrong ways, and the best leaf now dominated the fields. Della and Phillip were comfortable together at last, and the rare tumult between them seemed more to keep them in practice than because they had any real hope of gaining ground on the other.

Della was a wealthy woman of no small repute in the county. Severn had passed three years before, leaving few women still alive who had had a hand in the revolution. Della was one of the last, and younger women all over the state sometimes wrote to her asking of her memories, remarking on her courage. Her youthful scandals had not followed her into dignified dotage—or if they had, no one had the nerve to speak of them—and she was much sought after as guest of honor at various charity functions and glittering supper parties.

She often reflected these days as she rode the fields, her veil billowing about her face with careless disregard for what the sun might do to her skin, that life was indeed very good after all. She had all the comfort she needed, enough companionship to keep her from loneliness, and work to do to fill her hours with satisfaction. All the passions that seemed so vital to her years before, the dramas that assumed life-and-death importance were now, thankfully, amusing memories.

Bathsheba was her sole trial, at least today. She sighed as she dismounted, handing the reins to the groom. The old slave had fallen off the veranda steps the year before and injured her hip. Though she mended, she found the stairs to Della's compartments more and more torturous until now, finally, she could scarcely get up them unaided. Most of the time the young wench, Sophy, her replacement, had to lend an arm so that Sheba could even make it to the landing upright.

Della fussed at the old slave, telling her to stay down in the kitchen, but Sheba would not be set aside, she said, like a dry milch cow. She insisted on combing Della's hair herself, even though her eyesight could not tell a curl from a rat's nest, and Della usually had to redo the better part of it herself when Sheba wasn't looking.

Della would have thought that at her age, she would be unconcerned with such things as the latest fashion in coiffures, but she found her interest in her appearance unabated after all these years. She still looked to see if men noticed her entrance into a room, and she did not hesitate to display a generous décolletage if she thought the gown and the occasion warranted it. Indeed, she thought often, it's just as well my daughter is not here to model herself after me. She is better off with the nuns.

That spring, Phillip seemed to have found some new source of energy. He was up earlier than usual, making his rounds over Deepwater by noon, and up to his study poring over his journals, his account books, and his maps of the Carolinas, a study that kept him busy for hours at a time. Also, he had a new roan stallion just in from Charleston, a sleek and powerful hunter that made him feel a dozen years younger just to sit him.

That afternoon, however, Della waited supper on him until she was quite cross with hunger. Noon came and went, then one by the clock, and finally half past. She sent Joseph down to the stable to fetch him, but the slave came back empty-handed. "Boy say massa go down to the river on de new roan," he said mournfully.

"Did you go find him?"

"I cain' go dat far, Miz Della, not wid dis misery in my legs, you know."

She snatched her bonnet off the banister and flounced out of the house, muttering to herself. By the time she got to the stable, she was hopping mad. "Must I do everything myself on this place?" she asked Will, the groom. "Go and find your master, boy, and tell him to get himself home quick. Take the bay, she will likely follow that roan without a touch of the bridle."

The groom hurried to mount the little bay pony and scuttled out of the stable fast, looking back over his shoulder at Della, who stood swiping at her skirts with her bonnet. Back at the house, she sat down at the table and ate an entire helping of mashed potatoes with butter to calm herself. Time passed, and still Phillip did not come. She was about ready to go out on the veranda again when she heard the rustle and scuff of hurrying bare feet on the steps, and the groom burst into the dining room, his face all ashen with sweat. "Miz Della!" he urged. "You best come quick an' bring your physic kit, Massa Phillip fall off dat roan!"

She grabbed her medical kit from the closet and raced to the stables with the groom right behind her, mounted her mare, and made the boy lead her to the back pasture where it ran into deep woods by the swamp. She found Phillip facedown in the brush, his collar split by his fall, his brow bloodied and white as his linen. Furious with herself, with him, with any God who could allow such a travesty, she did her best to staunch his wound and bind him, then shouted at the groom until together, they were able to put her husband across the nervously dancing mare. Della rode the slave's pony back to the big house, leading her mare as carefully as she could so as not to jostle Phillip any more than necessary.

By the time Joseph and Moses were able to get Phillip to his bed, he was partly conscious, but he looked about the room as though he had never seen it before. The injury to his head had an ominous depression round the wound, as though he had suffered a strong blow to the skull. The roan still had not returned to the stable, and Della privately vowed she'd sell the stallion at auction cheap if he ever came home again. She sat up with Phillip through the night, listening for his string of babbled words to make some sort of sense. By the time the doctor arrived the next morning, her husband had lapsed back into unconsciousness again, and Della's nerves were strung tight as Moses' fiddle.

The doctor was an old gentleman from Wilmington who only came out to Deepwater when Della's own skills were exhausted. He examined Phillip's head with light, trembling fingers. Della saw that the man's palsy was worse than the last time he'd visited, and she felt her impatience rise. But she kept her tongue as he listened to her husband's heart, lifted his closed eyelids, felt for his pulse, and palpated his temples. He finally sat down beside Della on the chaise, his face solemn and his eyes downcast.

"I cannot give you much hope, Madam Gage," he said quietly. "It's quite likely he will not regain consciousness."

Della reeled back as though he had struck her. "My God, what are you saying?" she cried. "He simply fell from his horse!"

The doctor shook his head. "Likely, he was kicked, madam, by the shape and indentation of his bruise. He might have been killed instantly. It's a blessing he's still alive at all."

"A blessing," she murmured, not even aware of what she said. She rose with shaky knees and went to Phillip's side, taking up his hand. "And there is nothing you can do?"

"So long as he remains in this state, no. Should he awaken, perhaps I can relieve the pressure on his skull with bleeding—"

She sank down beside her husband, weeping over his hand. It was so cool and limp in her own! She reached out and tentatively touched his brow, running her finger over the whitened depression on his temple with a numb horror. She felt as if he must surely sense her presence, feel her touch, as though his eyes would flutter open instantly, and he would speak.

A low groan came from him then, and the doctor moved to her side, watching for any other sign. Phillip's chest rose and fell once, twice, a soft gurgle of reluctant air rushed from his lips as though something heavy sat on his chest—and without another sound or motion, he died.

She knew in the instant that he was gone. It was as if his body emptied suddenly, like a bladder drained of water, yet there was no perceptible change. Simply one minute he was there, and the next minute he was not. She set down his hand carefully, watching his face. She half expected him to move, his chest to rise once more and startle her, but he was silent. Motionless. Whatever had been her husband was no longer in the room.

"I'm sorry," the doctor said gently. "Master Gage is dead."

"I know," she said softly.

They sat for what seemed an eternity, staring at him silently. Della felt as dazed as though she herself had lived, been wounded, and had died, all in those long quiet moments.

"Is there someone to help you prepare him?" the doctor finally asked.

He was trying hard to be solicitous, but Della suddenly could not bear his presence. "Yes," she said, nodding, "we will be fine. Please file the necessary notices with the county. I can take care of him myself."

The doctor looked perplexed. "You are certain? I have a woman I call for this sort of thing—"

"No," she said firmly. "I thank you. But no." She was scarcely aware of his departure and Bathsheba's entrance, so fixed on Phillip's face was she. She stared at him as though he might somehow be able to communicate to her the great mystery of their lives together, their love, and what it all meant after all. When Bathsheba touched her gently on the shoulder, she turned and murmured, "Oh, Sheba. He's dead."

"Yes, Miz Della."

"And I barely spoke to him this morning."

The slave kept her hand on Della's arm.

"I didn't love him, Sheba."

"I know," the slave said softly. "But he love you. And you make him happy sometime."

She sank to the chair beside Phillip, now unable to look at him another moment. Weeping, she covered her face with her hands. "Caroline's going to be destroyed! And what will I do? I have nothing now," she cried softly, the pain building to a keen edge. "I am truly alone at last!"

Bathsheba came to stand beside her, holding her and rocking her back and forth as one might a small, bewildered child. "You never been alone, Miz Della, an' you won't never be. Dat de sort o' woman you are."

But Della hardly heard her. She rocked and wept for her daughter, for her husband, for the years between them wasted and gone, for the body she would never feel again, the passion long since spent and still missed—for forty years of her life as Mistress Gage of Deepwater.

🌿 🌿 🌿

For several years after Phillip's death, Della did her best to keep away from Deepwater. She traveled extensively over the continent, through the capitals of Europe, spending money as though she had only just realized she was a wealthy woman. She sent home boxes of dresses and trinkets for Caroline, sumptuous petticoats and soft cashmere blankets for Bathsheba, and a hundred trifling gifts for a host of friends. But finally, the sights of the continent paled, and she longed to be home again, riding the rows of green leaf in the sun.

She had no more returned than Caroline begged to go, having graduated from the academy at last with a mediocre record and a collective sigh of relief from the beleaguered nuns. Her father's death, his funeral, his absence had been so difficult for her that Della could not refuse her. She packed her off with a Charleston governess and a list of introductions for a season abroad. "After all," she confided to Bathsheba, "it did me a world of good. It'll cheer her up and likely make her appreciate home even more, travel always does that."

And then Della settled back into the responsibilities of Deepwater, but now with a distinct difference. The plantation was hers, to do with as she pleased. She no longer had to make even a semblance of consulting with anyone else about its management, and she found that her satisfaction in the lands' fertility and beauty increased tenfold now that it was hers alone.

She was more busy than she had been in years. She did not decline a single invitation; she never stayed in bed past six o'clock in the morning. A friend exclaimed, upon seeing Della at the Charter Ball in a gown she'd brought back from France, "My God, you're a hummingbird these days, my dear!"

"Why, whatever do you mean?" Della asked, quite pleased.

"Tiny, gaudy in color, fast as light, and absolutely fearless, is what I mean. Wherever did you get that cunning hat?"

Della thought of that remark later as she slipped into bed and decided that she would take it as a compliment, however it was intended. Even the word "gaudy" did not affront her. Let them see me coming, she told herself, and if they want a brown wren, let them invite someone else.

The seasons passed, and she found she longed for Phillip very little. She missed being married and the pictures that made in her mind, the convenience of the wedded state, but she no longer looked for him at the table, listened for his step in the hall, nor felt for his leg with her foot in the bed at night. Indeed, even when he had been alive, she did not yearn for him in his absence. Now that he had slept in the graveyard behind the guest quarters for a half-dozen years, it was as though he had always been there.

It was a cold drizzling day in October when Della heard the sound of approaching hoofbeats and a fast carriage coming down Deepwater Road. She looked up from her book and slid her slippered feet out from under the throw toward the fire. "Blast it," she murmured to Bathsheba who was nodding beside her in the chaise. "Who would come out on such a dreary afternoon?"

Bathsheba cleared her throat as though she emerged from the grave rather than from a nap and went to the window. "Some young miss gettin' out," she said, "an' she got her nigger with her. Must be gettin' colder, dey wrapped up in cloaks to de chin."

"Damn," Della muttered, pulling her shawl about her shoulders and struggling up from the depths of her chair. "I wish people would just keep themselves to home until spring comes round again." But she hurried reluctantly to the door, Bathsheba limping along behind her. Before they could knock, Della opened the door wide and was amazed to see the Charleston governess climbing the veranda steps, shaking the rain off her bonnet. Behind her, a young black wench carried a bundle close to her breast. In that moment, Della's mind flashed an ancient memory: the arrival that afternoon of another black wench, carrying a bundled Caroline up these same steps.

"What in the world?" she called out to the woman. "You're supposed to be in Paris, I believe, Mistress Lafonse. Where is Caroline?"

"She is still in Paris," the woman said mournfully, her eyes downcast as she swept into the house.

"Then what are you doing here?" Della asked angrily, ready to fly at her for forgetting her responsibility.

In answer, the young governess reached and took the bundle from the black wench and handed it to Della with great weariness. "I'm bringing to you your granddaughter, Madam Gage."

Astonished, Della opened the blanket and saw there a tiny infant girl. Dressed in fine swaddling linen, she had round her neck the gold locket Della had given to Caroline the day of her departure to the academy at Bath.

"Here's Caroline's letter to you, madam," Mistress Lafonse was saying. "Might we take a seat in your parlor? It is such a nasty day today."

Numb and amazed, Della walked with the silent bundle to the parlor, gestured the woman to a chair, and bade Bathsheba take the wench to the kitchen for warming. She gently laid the sleeping child on the chair beside her and opened Caroline's letter with unsteady fingers.

"My dear mother," the letter began, "I hope this finds you well and in good spirits. As you had hoped, I find the continent much to my liking, and I have met a good many fine people and seen many interesting things. But Paris is no place for a child, and I am not in a position to care for Laurel at this time. I know you will see to her well-being until I come for her. Her father and I plan to return after we finish our tour of the Alps—"

"She is married!" Della wailed, clutching the letter and turning to the governess with dismay.

"Six months ago," she said pointedly. "I could not stop her, nor would she allow me to send word to you of any kind."

"How could you have allowed such recklessness!" Della stood, shouting at the woman. "Your sole responsibility was to chaperone Caroline and see to her education abroad!"

The woman sighed painfully. "Madam, I have been virtually a prisoner in a Paris hotel room for several months. She met this man, she refused my advice or guidance, and together they kept me helpless between them. She took my funds, she made certain I did nothing without her knowledge, and she was with child and married before I could have a say in anything." She looked up at Della with fatigue and resentment. "Your daughter, madam, is a willful and headstrong young woman. She requires a stronger hand than mine to subdue her. I did my best." She gestured to the infant. "You see the outcome."

Della sank back in her chair, stunned and aghast. She took up the letter once more. "I have married an Italian nobleman, Mother, a man of excellent family and prospects. Antonio and I are blissful, and we look forward to collecting our darling Laurel in a few months, just as soon as his family sorts out the details of his holdings," the letter went on.

Della snorted skeptically. "She says he's an Italian duke or something."

"He's a scoundrel, madam." Mistress Lafonse sighed. "He has some small estate, I believe, but his primary assets are his black hair and his dark eyes, so far as I can tell. I expect he will make her supremely unhappy in time."

"But they are truly married?" Della asked.

"I saw the banns posted myself."

Della turned and stared at the tiny infant, still bundled against the cold. She leaned down and unloosed the swaddling, smoothing the tendrils of dark hair on its brow into place. The child did not stir. "Do you have an address for my daughter at least?"

"Only where they were planning to go next. I doubt they're there now."

Della scanned the rest of the letter hurriedly. "She does not say when she plans to return."

"No," the governess said. "She does not." She stood abruptly and brushed at her dampened skirt. "Well, madam, I have discharged my duty as I promised, and I take my leave of you now. I am deeply ashamed that I was not able to keep your daughter from her fate"—here, Mistress Lafonse looked more angry than aggrieved—"but as I said, I did my best. I was no match for the two of them."

Before Della could respond properly, the young woman stepped to the door and called for her wench. "I hope," she said as she went out the door, "that you can take some comfort from the child. She seems to be fine and healthy, with a warm spirit."

"How old is she?" Della managed to ask.

"Only three months, the poor little thing," the governess said sorrowfully as she opened the door to her carriage. "She'll likely be a beauty, at any rate."

The carriage pulled around and back down the road, and Della turned, dazed, to see that Bathsheba was holding the child against her broad bosom.

"My God, Sheba, whatever will we do with it?" she asked fearfully.

"We raise it up, Miz Della," the old woman said patiently. "Dat's de only choice we got." She looked down at the baby who was beginning to stir. "An' de only chance *she* got, likely."

Della sank to the veranda steps, heedless of the rain and the cold, holding her head in her hands. "This is impossible. I cannot do this," she murmured. "I am an old woman."

"Me, too." Bathsheba sighed. "Come in from de rain, Miz Della, you catch your death."

Obediently, Della got up and wandered in after Sheba, dazed and talking half to herself. "How in the world could this have happened? She's not old enough—she hasn't been *gone* long enough to wreak this much havoc on herself and the world!" Then she was struck dumb by the irony of it. The scene was so much like the night Phillip brought Caroline herself home, even to the seeming vast indifference of the child itself, that she was thrust back into the past, for the moment unable to speak or move.

But the cold seeped into her quickly, and the child whimpered as well. Inside the house, Della followed Bathsheba up the stairs, the old slave moving painfully as best she could with her burden. They took the baby to Caroline's old room and set her on the bed. The child watched them both solemnly as though she understood for the first time that her fate rested in their hands.

"She's a pretty thing," Della said tiredly, unwrapping the blanket about her limbs. "Look, she's very like Caroline was when she was this tiny. The same hands, the same feet. Her legs mottle up just like hers did, too. But that dark hair! And so much of it. Caroline's was light and fine at her age—"

"Likely dat her pa," Bathsheba said.

Della grimaced at the thought. "Well, run go tell Bess she's got another one to nurse."

Bathsheba rolled her eyes at the mention of her running anywhere at all. "Likely, 'nother one to raise."

"Don't say that. Caroline's going to come get this child, Sheba, or I'll know the reason why. I'm too old to face this again!"

The old slave chuckled to herself, shaking her head and heading down to alert the household that a child was among them once more. Della took up the baby and went to the window seat, letting the gray light fall on her silken head. She fingered the locket round the baby's neck and then took it off. "Not that you don't need the luck, Laurel," she murmured to the infant.

The child's eyes followed her carefully, the smallest of smiles playing about her perfect pink lips. Della dangled the chain down to where the child could just reach it, watching the tiny hand struggle to catch the gleaming gold in the light. Together, they sat thus in the window seat, murmuring back and forth to each other like two ageless souls, as twilight dimmed the horizon and turned the fields to a darker shadow.

Part Three

❦ ❦ ❦

1850—1875

"This is the age of High Pressure.
Men eat faster, drink faster, talk
faster than they did in our younger
days and in order to be consistent in
all points, they die faster. It is to
be feared that the invention of the
telegraph will give an additional
go-ahead impulse to humanity, equal to
that imparted by the rush of steam.
If so, Progress only knows where we
shall land."

Raleigh *Register*, 1850

G ood times had come to the river at last. Cane, cotton, and tobacco stood tall along the water, and markets clamored for all
the Carolinas could harvest. The little town of Cross Creek had
grown to three thousand hearty souls and named itself Fayetteville. Fine-
frocked ladies and waistcoated gentlemen rode the hundred-foot river
monster, the new white steamboat that plied the Cape Fear from Wilmington to Fayetteville in the remarkable time of twelve hours. At the
blast of the steamboat's whistle, the docks were filled with whites and
blacks alike, cheering and waving frantically at the smoking miracle.

The planters profited enormously, of course, by this new mode of river
transport, but the backcountry farmers still struggled with pathways
through the swamp and impassable roads in poor weather, spending half
the value of a crop to get it to market. Isolation was still North Carolina's
blessing and curse.

Blacks, who were the majority in the coastal cities, were both free and
slave, but after they lost the right to vote in 1835, many freedmen were
stolen right out of their homes and sold into slavery. Across the border in
Virginia, Nat Turner led slaves in rebellion, murdering fifty whites in
one night. Planters all over the South tightened slave codes in retaliation.

The Underground Railroad, which had started to shelter fugitive
slaves as early as 1830, now became more organized. Free-soil Party
members, women's antislavery societies, and religious groups like the
Quakers delivered more than two thousand slaves from the Cape Fear
region alone.

Word spread from plantation to plantation along the river, first by whispers in the dark slave quarters at night, finally with more daring, spoken of aloud in the tobacco rows in broad daylight. There was a railroad to freedom, just follow the North Star.

🌱 🌱 🌱

Laurel waited in the buggy, shivering despite the close, hot night. She pulled her thin shawl about her shoulders and willed even her breath to be still, that she might hear the speakers more clearly from within the meeting place of the Friends.

The Friends. That was what David called them, naturally, but they scarcely seemed friendly, no matter how they bowed politely to her outside services each Sunday. Quakers, the rest of the world called them and to Laurel, they would always be exactly that: quaking at the least little glower from God.

She could hear the murmurs from within the little house where the Friends met and if she closed her eyes, she could picture the scene well enough. David had taken her to every Sunday meeting for a month, and she still felt like a rank outsider. Likely always would.

Women on one side, men on the other, even the little children separated by gender as though they, too, might have unholy thoughts if allowed to congregate too close. The aching silence of it! No hymns, no praying aloud, and not much of a sermon either. Just the silence of two-dozen hearts beating, eyes closed relentlessly, presumably communing with Jehovah. An occasional murmur, a cough, the rustle of garments and sighs of tortured children. These Quakers made her little Presbyterian church seem like the liveliest place north of Charleston.

But she could not deny the power of the place, leastways in David's soul. He had been visibly trembling when he left her in the buggy to go within, and she felt a sharp stab of pity for him and resentment that they should judge him so.

Shunning. It was an ugly word, an even uglier idea. They preferred the word "disownment," but it all meant the same. That a good man like David Lassiter should be stood up and made to justify his choice—justify her!—simply because she was not of them. If he was shunned, pious Quakers could not receive favors from him or any sort of commerce, could neither buy nor sell with him, could not even eat at the same table with him. It was enough to make her think to snatch up the whip, turn the horses, and race the buggy back to Deepwater with never a fare-thee-well.

But she calmed herself and remembered his words the night before. "Don't be afraid, dear. Thee must simply stand before them and speak from thy heart. If they will not take thee in, they'll have to put me out."

"And will you be able to stand that?" she had whispered, afraid for him even then. He was holding her, sitting together on the chaise on the porch at Deepwater, and the moonlight was a bath of lovely brightness over the fields.

For answer, he had only kissed her softly. His way of telling her to ask no more hard questions.

The horse started suddenly, and a dark figure approached the buggy. "They wish to speak with thee now," David said in the shadows.

Laurel took his hand and climbed down. Now she trembled, too. But she straightened her back with a will and followed him into the place of Friends.

Within, it was bright and hotter still, the crowded hard benches leg to leg, men and women separated by a narrow aisle, and a simple pulpit at the front of the room. A man rose and gestured to her kindly. "Will thee sit or stand, mistress?"

Laurel felt David's hand on her shoulder, a quick squeeze of encouragement, and she raised her chin. "I will stand, thank you." She strode to the podium and stood behind it, gripping the sides of the wood for courage.

"David Lassiter wishes to take thee for wife," the man said gravely.

No preamble, no social manners at all, Laurel thought stiffly. She recognized the speaker now, the same man who helped keep the buggies in proper formation at Sunday meeting lest one bang against another. These Quakers liked a slow God well enough, but they preferred their horses fast. She dropped her head before the congregation, unsure if an answer was required.

"Our ways require us to keep to those who believe as we do," the man continued, "and our discipline demands that we may not marry out of the Society. David Lassiter has said that thee be willing to become one of us, if allowed, is that so?"

"Yes," she said, as clearly as she could manage.

"Then I must ask thee some questions, if thee agree, as to questions of faith."

"I agree," she said softly, still keeping her eyes low.

"Please give your name, mistress."

Though everyone here surely knows it, she thought. "Laurel Gage Rossetti. But I use my mother's maiden name alone. Laurel Gage."

"Your father is deceased?"

"And my mother as well. I was raised by my grandmother, Della Gage, in my mother's absence, and then by a cousin in Charleston. At my seniority, I received Deepwater plantation as sole heir to my grandmother's estate. But much of it has been sold off now, of course . . ." Her voice dropped away to a murmur, suddenly aware she had spoken too freely.

"Thee was raised in which faith?"

"Presbyterian. In Charleston. By my cousin—" she faltered.

"Thee has never married?"

She flushed. At her age, nearly thirty, she was as spinster as a woman could get and still be upright. But she straightened up again and met the man's gaze squarely. David was the same age, after all. "Never." Laurel felt the imperceptible shifting of weight down the rows of women on the right side of the room, and she gripped the pulpit a little more firmly. She felt like an empty jar: childless, husbandless, useless. Suddenly, her simple gray frock with the edging of lace about the collar and cuffs seemed impossibly garish and in such poor taste as to damn her with its ruffles alone.

"Does thee believe in the Lord God Jehovah?" The speaker's voice had strengthened at that last word, booming about the four walls like a bullfrog.

"I do," she said quickly.

"And in His disciples and their words in the Bible?"

"I do."

"And in His son, Jesus Christ?"

"Yes."

A pause. The man glanced around him as though for support and then went on. "It is forbidden to use profane language or intoxicating liquor. Will thee agree to abide by these banns?"

"I will."

"And to dress in the plain manner as God requires, rejecting all unnecessary ornamentation?"

"Yes." Laurel thought of the gold filigree locket she wore always under her bodice and was glad that God had not given these Quakers the ability to read minds any more than hearts. She would not take it off, not even for David. The slight buzz of a fly immediately to her right made her wonder idly what a fly was doing out after dark. It's the heat, her mind wagged at her playfully, the heat, the heat—and then she snapped back to attention, for the congregation had shifted position slightly again as though the room itself had tilted.

The man with the questions waited expectantly. Laurel sought David's eyes in a panic, but he was looking down grimly at the floor. "Will you repeat the question?" she asked faintly.

"I asked, mistress," the man said gently, "if thee will willingly set free those souls thee holds in bondage."

"My slaves?" Laurel asked blankly.

"Thee cannot be in our Society and hold men in bondage."

Laurel looked again to David, this time in bewilderment. She took a deep breath. "Mister Lassiter told me this could be accomplished over time. I am willing to hire workers to replace them, yes, but I cannot set free a dozen slaves on the morrow, sir, not and expect to take my crop to market. Surely the Friends can see the reasonableness of—"

"There is nothing reasonable about keeping men enslaved, mistress, and God does not care for thy crop."

She was silent at that.

"Thee must emancipate all thy people in bondage. Will thee do so?"

"I will," she whispered, picturing old Miles, who had been with her grandmother before she died, and Bessie, who taught her to make lemon cake when she was too short to see to the oven. Where would they go and how would they live, if not at Deepwater? Through most of her youth, she heard them singing in the fields, working close together, the driver starting a song with a drum beat, the slaves chanting their slow, monotonous song, mellow and liquid. They worked so easily, it seemed, with their gaily turbaned heads bent low, graceful in their movements, their bare dark arms like the pulse of oars in the water. The memory of her grandmother, Miss Della they called her even in her most ancient years, still making her rounds to the weaving house, to the smoke house to count the hams and the sides of bacon, doling out the quinine to those of her folks with bone fever and chills, mullein and onion soup for the coughs, sulphur and lard for the itch, and sugar pills for the old ones who simply wanted a little extra attention. And then her grandmother was gone, and she made the rounds herself, for her own people.

Just let me get through this, she told herself. David and I will do what we have to do, but let me simply satisfy them and escape. Let me marry the man I love!

"And thee must turn the soil to something other than tobacco."

She gasped. David turned with a start at this as well.

"Thee will be forbidden commerce in the noxious weed, mistress. Neither can thee use the stuff thyself."

"I do not," she said, stammering in confusion, "but I was not told—"

David stepped forward, his brow lowered and his voice hoarse with anger. "Many Friends plant tobacco!"

"It is a new discipline," the man said matter-of-factly. "Those who are now in the Society will be asked to winnow down their fields from tobacco to another crop. Those who are new to our faith will be asked to bring no sin among us."

Winnowed down, Laurel thought, that's exactly how I feel in the moment. She hesitated. It was one thing to gradually replace slave labor with paid workers, difficult enough to imagine making a profit on the leaf with wages to pay, it was quite another to turn over the soil and begin again with a whole new crop. Perhaps, over time, the loss would not be killing, but to do so in one planting season would be ruinous!

David suddenly moved to the pulpit beside her, and she was struck to silence by his nearness. "We shall take our leave of you, Friends," he said, his voice quavering. "I hereby disown myself."

Gasps came from those seated before them, and several men half rose to protest, as others found their voices and began to speak. But the questioner held up his hand for silence. "Thee will marry this woman, then?"

"Will thee accept her among you?" David countered with his own question.

The man actually looked saddened, Laurel thought in the moment, dazed and silent next to David. "We cannot. Not unless she satisfies the disciplines."

"She will not," David said firmly. "Nor will I any longer." And with that, he took her hand and gently led her from the room, the only sound the soft rustle of her gray skirts on the wooden floor. As they mounted the buggy, Laurel half expected someone to rush from the meeting place, to plead with them to stop, to reconsider. But the night was as silent as the bottom of the sea, and David clucked to the horses and drove on.

They rode together wordless, their shoulders touching with each jolt of the buggy, lost in separate thoughts. Laurel felt a despair of angry resentment and horrible guilt that David would have to give up so much to have her. And fear. Fear that he might not be willing to marry her after all. Or worse. That he would marry and live to regret it—regret her—after the newness of them together had worn away. Finally she ventured to speak. "You did not know about the new—discipline, then?"

He snorted. "Who could keep up with them all?"

His obvious anger quelled her. She squeezed her hands tightly together. Now, if he wished, she must let him go. She must relieve him of his promises to her. It was the only decent thing to do. A man could not be expected to give up so much for a woman, no, not even for love. David's only other family was in Pennsylvania, a brother and his parents. He had come to the Carolinas hoping for cheap land and an easier life, and the Friends in the Valley had helped him, given him work, a promise of some sort of future. Quaker daughters needed husbands, too, and she wondered how much of that need larded the disciplines they imposed. David would now be bereft. All he had was her. Likely, it wasn't enough.

And all she had was him, truth be told. She had suitors aplenty in the early years, but they did not suit her, not enough to bind herself to them for a lifetime. Deepwater, even with only a hundred acres left to her after taxes and bad management had dwindled it down, still took all her time just to keep it running. Two years before, she knew she could no longer afford an overseer, not for only a dozen slaves and a hundred acres. Now Deepwater supported her. Or she supported Deepwater. She could never quite be sure which was which. But one thing was certain, it had left her precious little time for courtship.

And she was no longer fresh, had never, in fact, been as lovely as her mother and grandmother before her. So when David Lassiter came along, offering to do carpentry and blacksmith work, offering, too, a shy smile and an almost-handsome countenance, she had suddenly taken stock of her life and invited him to stay.

And now, she must let him go again and let go of her dreams as well. But she would survive, she knew. Somehow. If she had learned nothing else from Deepwater she had learned this truth: everything changes. The key was to remember that.

The buggy turned now down the rutted road to the river, and as it jolted slightly, David reached out and took one of her hands in his, holding on tightly. Tears welled in Laurel's eyes. He was a good man.

"If thee hasn't changed thy mind," he said quietly, "I'll post the banns tomorrow. We can be wed in a week."

Laurel sobbed once, gasping in relief, tucking her head against his shoulder as though in refuge, speechless. She could only nod her head gratefully. They rode in silence down the rutted path to Deepwater, the fields on both sides bathed in white light. At the veranda to the old house, David tied the buggy and reached up to help her down. She went into his arms, clinging to his neck, holding him fast against her for a long, aching moment. "Are you sure, my love?" she asked. "You won't hate me for everything you're giving up?"

In answer, he took her hand and led her to the steps, pulling her down alongside him. "What am I giving up? A bunch of fools who take the words of God and twist them to their own ends. I did without them long enough, I can do without them now." He turned to her and embraced her. "But I cannot do without thee, Laurel."

She held him so tightly that she could scarcely breathe, did not wish to, almost wished to die in that moment in his arms. When he finally released her she murmured, "I may have been happier some other time in my life, but I can't think of when it was."

The high sound of some slave's laughter came to them then on the breeze from the quarters, like an exotic bird from the jungle.

"Thee has to set them free," David said. "I can disown myself from the Society, but not from the laws of God. It is an evil thing that I cannot abide, this bondage of a man against his will."

She nodded sadly. "But must I do so all at once? It will take some time, you know, to find workers—"

"Set them free and pay them as thee would any other labor."

She frowned. "I can't do that. You don't understand, they are used to doing very little for their food and a roof over their heads.

I can set them free, I can pay them well enough, but they will not work for me once they're free, not worth near what I'd have to pay them. They've been petted and spoiled for too many years. I should sell them."

"Thee cannot sell them and satisfy God. Thee will still be trafficking in human souls. Thee must emancipate them and hire others to take their place, if they will not work."

She thought for a moment. Now was not the time to dicker. Not with David and not with God. She needed them both too much. "But all at once?"

"Half before we wed," he said firmly, "and the other half by the end of harvest."

She frowned. He had said he wanted to be married within the week. How could she sell six slaves and hire workers in a week? Another delay! And harvest was only a month away. Not much time to find a dozen able-bodied pickers—but she put away her fear and resentment at David's obdurate stance, and she kept her voice even. "Will you help me?"

"Of course," he said. "And once the slaves are gone, we shall do what we can to free others."

She turned to stare at him in the moonlight. Who was this man, after all? Was she so eager to marry that she would bind herself to this stranger—this outsider—forever? In that moment it occurred to her that some people are really meant to live together forever and others simply do not want to be alone. She wondered which they were.

"Thee has heard of the Underground Railroad," he continued calmly.

"Of course," she murmured. Who had not? She vaguely knew, too, that some Quakers in the North were involved in spiriting slaves into Canada or New York or elsewhere where they might escape, but she knew no one who had lost a slave to such a group, no one who knew anyone who would do such a thing, and almost did not wish to know another single word about the subject. "Anyone caught helping a runaway can be fined. And arrested, I've heard. I think it's something like a thousand dollars—"

"The Fugitive Slave Act," David said sardonically. "A hundred lashes for any slave caught trying to escape and a branding on the hand. But hundreds make it anyway, and it is our duty to help them."

"How?" she asked faintly. She was almost afraid to hear his answer.

"We will shelter them at Deepwater until we can get them on board ships headed upriver to Fayetteville. From there, others will take them to Goldsboro. Friends there will get them north."

"You know Quakers in Fayetteville and Goldsboro who are part of this railroad?" She was amazed and aghast. What other secrets did his heart harbor?

"Friends in Goldsboro. We'll have to find sympathetic parties in Fayetteville." He seemed deep in thought, already thinking about the task ahead as though it were decided.

Laurel fought down her confusion and panic. It was one thing to emancipate her dozen slaves, folks who had been with her for a lifetime, some even who had been with her grandmother before she was born, it was quite another to turn Deepwater into a refuge for fugitives from all over the Carolinas. "But, David," she began, "it's a terribly dangerous undertaking, don't you think? If we are caught, they can take everything." She took a deep breath. "They can take Deepwater." To her, it wasn't necessary to mention the fines, the possible jail sentence. The loss of her land was surely the most awful deterrent of all.

"Thee can't live without taking risks," David said stolidly. "And we will live by the word of God, no matter the risks."

In the moment, she feared him so much that she hated him. But she feared losing him even more. It seemed to her that the most pious people she had known, those who seemed to know what God wanted for them and for everybody else, were also some of the most selfish. They rarely thought about anyone else and what they might need, for thinking about God and His needs and how they might best serve Him. "What about our family?" she asked, almost wearily. "I want to have children."

He took her hand and smiled. "So do I. Thee will have the most beautiful children, Laurel. And they will come into a world where slavery is known as the evil it is. We will teach them the truth by example."

"Like Jesus," she said softly, only half aware of the irony of what she said.

He turned to her, exultant. "Exactly." And he hugged her hard, jubilant in his victory.

And Laurel, fast within his embrace, thought to herself, I do love this man, and I will love him for the rest of my life. Likely, I will love him even after I'm dead. But sometimes it is rather hard to like him much, after all.

🌿 🌿 🌿

The same week Laurel discovered she was pregnant was the week that Winston showed up at their door, begging for shelter. A large black man, almost blue in the moonlight, he stood half in, half out of shadow on the veranda, his hat in his hand. Laurel stayed away from the door, holding the lamp, and his words were so fearful and muffled, she had to ask David to repeat them once the man was inside.

"He's from Atkinson," David said quietly.

That was nearly ten miles to the north, Laurel thought quickly, why did he not keep going in that direction?

"I hear 'dis a safe house," the slave said, still not lifting his head off his chest.

"And so it is," David said quickly, pulling the man inside and toward the kitchen. "Has thee eaten?"

Laurel followed along, her head in a whirl. When she saw her husband and the black man standing alongside the cooking table, the contrast between their two heads was so startling that she almost backed out again.

David was saying, "Thee must stay in the shed out back, there's a small room above the barn that no one goes in except myself. I will bring thee food and water every night, once the workers have left the fields. When we can find passage, thee will go upriver to Fayetteville, and from there, overland to Goldsboro. Friends will see thee safely to the North and freedom."

Thank God, Laurel thought, they had no more slaves at Deepwater. It was one less piece of property to be taken by the sheriff if they were arrested.

"Freedom," the slave murmured. "I got to go how far to find dat?"

David patted his shoulder awkwardly. "Maybe as far as Canada, maybe out west, depends on where seems most safe in the moment. It will be a long, hard row to hoe, but be brave and strong, and thee will be a free man. Has thee ever run away before?"

The black man nodded. "Massa cotch me in de swamp. De dogs tree me."

"And he punished thee for that?"

For answer, the slave pulled down his shirt to expose his back. Laurel gasped at the withered, corded flesh there, more tree bark than skin. It looked as though the man had been beaten nigh to death.

David's voice was now stiff with anger. "Has thee a family as well?"

"Dey all been sold. My wife an' boy, both go cross the river last winter. I ain' seen 'em since. Time for me to go agin, I figure, ain' got no more to lose. Dis time, if he cotch me, I kill him."

Laurel felt a cold anger grow in her heart for the cruelty of such a master, that he would create such a dangerous despair in any man, and for the moment, she was very proud to be married to a man who would dare to do something about such injustice. But then she recalled the life she carried within her, and fear overcame her again. She set the lamp down on the table and leaned against the wall, feeling almost faint.

David glanced at her. "Thee should go back up to bed, Laurel. I can manage this alone."

She shook her head adamantly. "I want to stay."

"Sorry for de trouble, missus," the black man said to her shyly.

"Why did you run away?" she asked him, sinking down in the rocker by the hearth, trying to make some sense of this.

"Because slavery degrades a man's soul," David said, glancing at her with some annoyance.

"Yes, of course," she said patiently, "but he must have his own tale to tell." She stood and moved the lamp closer so that she might see into his eyes. "Why exactly did you run away?"

"My massa a bad man, missus," he said hoarsely, almost as if he were ashamed.

"In what way was he bad?" she continued, despite David's glance of warning to her to stop.

"He get wrathful, an' he throw a chair, or he tie us up in de smokehouse for a whippin'. An' when he finish, he make a fire out o' de stems o' tobacco, an' he smoke a man near to death."

"Did he do that to you?" she asked relentlessly.

In answer, the man held out his wide, huge hands. His palms were red and smooth as river clay, with nary a line on them. "He

make me bend an' put my hands in de fire, so as to teach me not
to run," he said gently. "I cain' hardly bend 'em now."

"But what did you do to deserve such punishment?"

"Laurel—!" David said in protest.

She turned to him earnestly. "No, David, I want to understand
this. Did the man steal something? Did he refuse to work? Did he
act insolent? There must have been something he did to deserve
punishment, there's always another side to the story."

"I rip m' trousers," he said mournfully. "I cotch 'em on a nail,
an' dey rip down an' he got to get me new, an' dey wasted. So he
beat me, so's I recollect to take more care nex' time."

"I see," Laurel said softly. "He beat you for a pair of trousers."

"Which were not worth a dollar," David said indignantly.
"And now that he ran, his life is forfeit if he's caught. Has thee
heard enough?"

"Yes," she said meekly. Laurel sat down carefully in the rocker
by the hearth and watched the two men with a sense of detached
wonder. How many other slaves were, at this moment, either on
the run or planning their escape? David said more than a hundred
ran off from the county every year, and the numbers were growing,
not dwindling. That meant that somewhere, some other woman
likely stood in her kitchen and heard such a tale, some other
woman listened to her man make plans which, if discovered, would
imperil their lives forever. She wondered if other women listened
with more fortitude than she did.

David grabbed the old quilts stored above the pantry and ushered Winston out into the night, admonishing him to be silent. The
warning was unnecessary. The moment the slave saw the door open
to the darkness outside, he seemed to shrink in stature, to become
smaller and mute as a cowering animal. Looking about him in
terror, he scuttled after David toward the barn, hunched over like
a jungle ape, his white eyes flashing in the light from the kitchen
window. She waited and watched from the window for a long
moment.

Finally, David reappeared out of the shadows and came back
inside, dropping the bar on the door behind him. He embraced her
fervently, pulling her against him with a passion. "So now it has
begun," he said into her hair. "God sees what we do this night."

Later as Laurel lay beside her husband, she pondered his words.
She gazed over at David, sprawled alongside. He was so very dear,

she thought, almost reaching out to stroke his hair. But she did not. He was a light sleeper and did not like to be touched once asleep.

He had been unusually ardent tonight, she realized, with a hidden current of fierceness running through his embraces that she had not sensed before. Almost as though the anger he felt at slavery somehow was translated into a protest of flesh against flesh, the outcry of pushing aside boundaries even between their two bodies and entering her as though striking back at something he could never actually touch.

She remembered the first time they had been together, their wedding night. They were married at her own church, since his had abandoned them. The Presbyterian ceremony was brief; the guests were few. Some distant cousins on her side from Wilmington and Brunswick town, a few close friends, and the farmer's family David had lodged with since his arrival in the county were all who attended. They adjourned to the inn close by the church after the wedding to share a toast of cider and cheese pie, and then they turned the buggy back to Deepwater, as though it were any other day.

But the night was surely a revelation. Laurel knew the rudiments of a man and a woman together, of course, for despite the bluenoses at the Wake Forest Female Seminary, knowledge of the marital act was smuggled in along with forbidden lip rouge and rationed caramels. But she soon discovered that much of what she knew was wrong, and most of what she expected was not nearly as repugnant as what she'd been led to believe.

She was afraid the first moment she saw David standing at the foot of her bed in his nightshirt. He was suddenly taller and broader than he had been before. A stranger. But she held out her hand to him and when he took it, much of her fear dissolved. And when he embraced her completely for the first time with his flesh against hers, at once commanding and hesitant, she was filled with gratitude and joy.

She felt her heart open to him, and her body followed naturally, like water flowed to the open sea. There was little pain as had been whispered among the girls at night, no sense of invasion, only a liquid feeling of heat and dissolution of the edges of her skin, so that she could hear his heart beating within her own chest.

Afterward, shy and gleeful with each other, they talked of familiar things, like the crop and the house and the shoddy team of

Farmer Miles, as though to root themselves once more in who they were. But they knew they were changed forever, and they were infinitely grateful for the alteration, eager to shed their old lives, their old selves, and take on the future together.

Now Laurel lay in silence, no longer afraid. She knew in her soul that David was just a man, no more holy, no more wise than the best of them, likely not as clever as many. But she also knew that he would lay down his life for her and their child, without hesitation or regret. And that alone, she told herself, was enough to deserve her unquestioning loyalty. If he wanted to funnel half the slaves of the county through their barn to freedom, then she would stand alongside him for whatever fate would bring.

She mounded her hands on her still-flat belly. Within, she carried the beginning of their family, the fruition of a dream she had carried within her heart for more years than she could remember. She could recall feeling jealous of the slaves who seemed to so easily grow rounded each summer with child, deliver their healthy babes, and sling them about their hips, never separated from them even in the fields. What a joy, she had thought, it must be to feel so important to someone.

She said a quiet prayer to God to protect them, if that was His will, and she curled alongside David to sleep.

🌿 🌿 🌿

In 1852, the tobacco market was down again precipitously. Since it was less profitable to run hired hands over the rows than it had been to use slaves, Laurel and David found themselves needing to labor right alongside their crew to bring the leaf in for a profit, and even that was smaller than the year before by a quarter.

In late February or March, they sowed seeds in flats, and closely watched them, covering them with straw during cold snaps, uncovering them for sun. The seedlings were transplanted in April by hand, more than ten thousand to an acre. When the plants shot up, they were wormed, pruned, hoed and weeded until they were wide and tall with outstretched leaves and crowns of white flowers. Harvested in August, the lower leaves were stripped and piled on row sleds, dragged to the sheds, and bunched to hang from the gooseneck hooks on drying poles for six weeks or more. Cured, the leaves were packed then in hogsheads and rolled to the dock for shipping to Wilmington. That left three months of the year to deal with fences, new fields, firewood, and the thousand other chores that kept Deepwater running.

They worked until they could not stand upright without pain, and still their profits were meager. Laurel sat up many nights with the account books, trying to see a way to cut corners one more time. The baby was due any day now, according to the midwife. She leaned back in her grandmother's chair, a leather-bound refuge she had kept even when she had sold so many other things, and she slipped a hand between the chair and her lower back to ease the strain there.

David came in, carrying the lamp. "Thee will be exhausted," he said, setting it on the wide desk before her. He leaned down and embraced her shoulders, and she let her head nestle against him. "Prices will pick up soon," he comforted her. "They can't stay this low forever."

"They can go lower still," she said morosely. "Every time the politicians talk about abolishing slavery, the planters scurry to buy up slaves and get them in the fields before it's too late. Then the next season, we've got a bumper crop and bottomed-out prices, and I can't match a man who gets his crop harvested without paying wages to do it."

"Well, when they finally do end slavery forever, thee will be way ahead of the rest of them. They'll be scurrying for hands, and thine will already be in the fields."

She stood, pushing away the books in frustration. "I'm sick to death of worry. Seems all my life, I've been thinking about Deepwater and what's best to do with it. Most times, I feel like this land owns me instead of the other way around."

"Well then stop worrying. We'll do what's necessary, and we'll do it together, and what we cannot do, God will." He bent down and kissed her lightly, pulling back and looking at her as a grimace passed over her mouth. "What is it?"

"My back." She winced. "It's been aching all day." She started to rise with his help, but then a pain shot through her abdomen and her legs, and she half crumpled against him.

"Laurel?" He put both arms around her to support her more firmly.

She gasped at the internal sense of slippage she felt within her. "I think the baby's coming," she moaned softly. "Oh God," she whimpered. "I'm not ready!"

"Yes, thee is ready, dear, don't be afraid. I'll go for the midwife."

"Don't leave me!" she cried out, clutching him. In that moment, her water broke and Laurel was no longer able to stand. David lifted her up as easily as though she were a child herself and hurried up the stairs, murmuring, "I will send Tom for her then, he can take the bay—"

Tom was the crew foreman who lived in the largest of shacks that used to house the slaves; the bay was David's favorite mare. She started to protest, but then another pain hit her, and she could do nothing but cry out and clench his shoulder hard, arching her back and fighting his hold.

David put her to bed, easing her clothing off her as gently as he could. He disappeared only long enough to send Tom for the midwife and put water on to boil, and then he was back again at her side. By then, she was half weeping with fear. She could hear him murmuring prayers as he hurried to do her bidding, gathering linens, pulling the slop pot over closer to the bed, lighting another lamp, and moving always with the slow, methodical gestures of a man who feared nothing at all. The contrast angered her all at once, and she shrieked at him then in her pain, "For God's sakes, David, leave that and come and help me!"

He came to her side instantly and took her hand. "What would thee have me do?" he asked kindly, almost smiling at her.

The look on his face, the ridiculousness of his question made her laugh all at once and blew away her anger as quickly as a candle in a summer breeze. Suddenly, she was not afraid. "Why have this baby, of course," she groaned, gripping his hands tightly. "I believe I've changed my mind."

When the midwife arrived, David and Laurel were still holding hands, alternating between hard groans and rueful laughter, as they worked together to bring the child closer to birth. Shocked at their irreverence, she elbowed David aside, deftly manipulated Laurel into position, and had little to do but catch the child as it came forth into the light.

Laurel laughed again, this time with triumph and joy, as the midwife held up her son for her to see. "You're made for birthing, mistress," she said reluctantly. "The first one scarcely ever comes this easy—"

David took his son from the woman's arms and nestled him alongside his mother's breast. "They'll all come this easy," he said firmly to Laurel, ignoring the midwife now, "for God loves thee even more than I do."

Laurel could see the indignation on the midwife's face as David quickly paid her fee and bustled her out the door, and she thought for an instant, wistfully, that it might have been nice to have been petted and fussed over a bit, perhaps combed and washed as the woman would have done, for indeed, despite David's sure words, the birth was bloody, difficult work. But she let him have his way. David had sure opinions on everything, he was almost always right, and it was hardly ever worth challenging them. She settled back with a sigh, beaming down at her new son. She felt more whole, more powerful than she ever had in her life. No matter what might come, she was now a mother. They were a family at last.

🌿 🌿 🌿

More and more fugitives came creeping to Deepwater in the night now, and Laurel counted twenty-six who had been refuged, slipped aboard northbound ships to Fayetteville, and out again from their lives as silently as they came in. They were not the only "station," she knew, and she wondered about the secrets kept in cellars, attics, and barns all over the South.

Which neighbors were her allies? Which her adversaries? There was a secret language they used, words that were at once ludicrous and dangerous: a "station" was a safe house on the "principle line" or the road north on the Underground Railroad. The papers warned that those who sheltered slaves were nothing but criminals, but more and more slaves were running away every day, and they were more desperate, more determined than ever to be hidden out at Deepwater until they could be smuggled aboard northbound sternwheelers to freedom.

War was coming as surely as the spring, and people talked of little else. Five years before, Laurel could remember it was possible to argue against slavery in public. There used to be a Negro Sunday school upriver, and the Manumission Society in Wilmington had more than a hundred members. Even the occasional editorial questioned the defensibility of slavery. But no more. The more scared the planters became, the more the shackles tightened.

Bills circulated in the Carolina Legislature to forbid conversation between mulattoes and Free Negroes, to ban all education of slaves, and to stop the meetings of the emancipation societies. Some passed, some did not, but the talk grew more inflammatory with every passing month. Often Laurel was tempted to raise the question to David of taking their boy, Bill, and following many of the Friends north to Indiana, a free state that was unlikely to suffer the chaos of war. But she could not leave Deepwater. And then when her second child, a daughter, was born, emigration was impossible. Perhaps war would pass them over after all.

One night, a young black woman came to the door with a child strapped to her breast. She was covered in tattered shawls and blankets, her body shapeless under the remnants of what once must have been decent clothing. When Laurel met her with the lamp, she murmured, "Please, missus, is dis de safe house?" She all but collapsed in Laurel's arms as she let her in.

But when David approached, the slave drew back again in fear, glancing to the safety of the dark outside the door. "Thee need not be afraid," he said gently to her. "Thee has found the right place."

"You a preacher man?" the woman asked suspiciously, still keeping herself between David and the door.

"He's a man of God, girl, and he will not hurt you," Laurel said, leading her inside to the kitchen, grateful that William and Seleta, her new little girl, were both asleep upstairs. "Is your child well enough to travel?"

The woman looked at the chair in the kitchen but then sank to the corner of the floor instead. Unwrapping the blanket, she put the baby to suck. "She well enough. If she not, she die wid me, an' dat better den wid de marster."

Laurel glanced at the door as David entered, bearing in his arms a bundle of clean, dry linen for the woman and the child. She was relieved to see that William was not with him. The child was too young to hear these tales of the fugitives, she thought, but if he were awake when one knocked—sometimes even if he were not—David might wake him and encourage him to come and listen. And then he would tell the boy, "Life is hard, and thee must do your best for God." Often, he reminded Bill that God was watching everything he did. Too often, Laurel thought, but she did not interfere. William was truly his father's boy, long and lanky even as a baby, with little of the rounded softness she yearned for and much of David's sober manner.

Seleta, though, was her mother's child. Beautiful skin as soft as a pink camelia, perfect flat ears, eyes as blue as the distant horizon of the Cape Fear, and eager for all the hugs and kisses that William now disdained. Three years apart, the two might have come from different fathers altogether. Seleta would have wept at the woman's plight, perhaps, but William would have harkened to his father's words. More than harkened. Hung on them.

Yes, she agreed that life was hard. But did he have to hear of it in his own mother's kitchen?

Then she asked the slave the question she always asked, "Why did you run away?"

"I scared o' de dogs," the woman said, bowing her head so low that her voice was muffled in the child's hair.

"The dogs chased you?" David asked, almost avidly.

She shook her head. "Not me, sir. Dey cotch Jim in de swamp. De first time he run, marster whip him nigh to death. An' de second time, he brung him back an' tie him good in the quarter so's all could see. An' den he set de dogs on him." She faltered, and her voice fell to a whisper. "De tear his belly an' his face, an' he die under der jaws. His mama stood an' watch him die."

David's voice was angry. "He set the dogs on a man, and they ripped him to death. God will punish your master in His own time, woman, and thee is right to run from such cruelty."

Laurel was filled with a gentle, prodding horror. "Was Jim your brother?"

"He my husband." The woman sighed, her voice flat and broken. "Marster say he sell him south so he run. Now, he run no more. But I run wid dis baby, an' I find freedom or I die. Ain' no more for me back dere, anyhow."

Laurel went to the woman and gathered her up, bundling her into the clean linen, draping another blanket about her shoulders. "God go with you and your baby," she said faintly as David led the woman out and away. Then she sank back into the chair. It seemed to her in that moment that no place in the world was more ugly than her own land, her own state. She wondered that she could look a single neighbor in the eye again. She went up the stairs to Seleta's room.

The child slept soundly. Without waking her, Laurel picked her up and held her carefully against her heart, listening to the steady sound of life coming from Seleta's own chest, hearing her moist murmur. Comforted, then, Laurel set her back in her bed and went back downstairs. David would wish to speak to her of how he would get the woman and child to safety, and he would be disappointed if she were not waiting to hear him.

🌿 🌿 🌿

And so the refugees came and went again, and with each one, Laurel knew disaster came closer. She heard folks talk in Wilmington of a book an Eastern woman had written, *Uncle Tom's Cabin*, about a slave escaping with her baby only to die, and there was something about bloodhounds in it as well. She shuddered when she thought of the young woman who suckled her baby and then went on. No one on the Cape Fear claimed to have read the book, yet most everyone could quote some of the more damning passages. Planters were irate, and newspapermen wrote that the Stowe woman best keep her wicked ideas and slanderous tongue north of the state line.

The 1860 election seemed less a polling of the people's choice than a stand for survival. There was no more dispute in the papers about the moral or ethical problems of slavery: any differences between coastal planters and Piedmont farmers were forgotten in their truce to defend themselves against the more dangerous assault from the North.

Yet few voices called for secession. North Carolina voted to stay in the Union, and legislators went to the new Confederate government to try to quell the rising rebellion. When Union gunboats fired on Fort Sumter, even when Lincoln called for troops to suppress the Southern "insurrection," the state was still divided. It took North Carolina more than five weeks after war was declared to decide to join her neighbors, and when the state finally seceded, it was last to join the Confederacy except for Tennessee.

Meanwhile, the flood of refugees to Deepwater dwindled to a trickle, but those who came were more haunted, more determined than ever to escape their bondage. Laurel picked a special place in the near woods behind Deepwater and told the children that if they saw a soldier or any man carrying a gun, they were to run to their hiding place and wait for her to find them. "No matter what," Laurel told her children, "run and don't look back. Wait for me, and I'll come get you when it's safe."

Often now she looked out back for Seleta and William to find them gone off, hand in hand, to "hide out" in the woods, as Bill called it, for the excitement of pretending that the soldiers had come at last.

❦ ❦ ❦

Perched on a goldenrod stem, the large orange and black butterfly slowly moved its wings in and out, as though testing the breeze, a movement like a snake's tongue to taste molecules on the air. The monarch, called *Danaus plexippus* by scholars as the only butterfly that migrates north and south like the birds, was known to every child on the Cape Fear as the "big orange" and watched with fascination by William each spring whenever he saw one.

But he could not know that the monarch butterfly he watched at the edge of the kitchen garden was readying herself for one of the most amazing journeys any creature on earth would experience. She would not survive it, but her offspring would survive, and their offspring as well, and ultimately, her genetic memory housed in a different monarch might well visit that same goldenrod in the spring of the following year.

For now, however, the monarch flexed her wings and took off in the air over Deepwater, heading north and west, following the river beneath her as a pathway, over Raleigh. She had never made the trip before, and she had no idea where she was headed. She knew only that she must fly.

Finally, after a week of travel with stops only to take brief sips of nectar from spring flowers, she landed on a milkweek plant at the edge of a southern Virginia tobacco field. There were other monarchs hovering around the milkweed patch, males who quickly vied for her attention. She selected one, mated, and landed on a piece of the plant that was vacant. She had flown more than two hundred miles.

Inspecting the milkweed and finding it satisfactory, she turned over a leaf and laid more than four hundred pale green, bullet-shaped eggs, glued in place with secretions from her abdomen. Then, fluttering with exhaustion, she rested on a lower leaf, her wings beating very slowly. In a few days, she was dead under the milkweed. Around her, in the milkweed patch, were the bodies of other monarchs, male and female, their wings as tattered from their flight as hers.

Ten days later, the monarch's offspring emerged from their eggs as green caterpillars with black heads and a singular obsession for milkweed. Swarming over the plant, they quickly ate their weight, shed their skins, and ate their weight again until within two weeks, they were full-grown in their larval stage. One in particular grew restless early, found a suitable twig, and hung itself upside down for a day without eating. Within hours, it convulsed, split itself open between the eyes, and emerged from its own skin a jade green, shining casket of a chrysalis, spotted with gold dots, and hanging by a thin, black stem.

If William could have looked closely at this chrysalis, he would have seen that though it looked like a burial casket, in fact it was a cradle after all. The walls became thin and transparent over the next few days and within, the growing wings of the new monarch inside became visible. At some silent signal, the butterfly burst forth, expanded its folded wings, and sailed away on the first puff of air that would carry it north.

Again, this butterfly, just like its parent, traveled over land it had never seen before, finding landmarks it could only know in its cells, making its few hundred miles and then mating, laying its eggs, and dying. The offspring of the second generation followed its parents' patterns, and with each successive birthing and dying, the monarchs penetrated farther and farther north until they crossed the border into Canada, as far as the Hudson Bay by the end of the summer months there.

At this northern latitude, the nights were tinged with crispness, and autumn was short. Few flowers were available to feed the butterflies that arrived by the thousands. And so they gathered together for what was surely one of the most amazing migrations endured by any creature: they turned now to the south and flew all the way back across the continent again, over land they had never seen before, crossing as much as two thousand miles in a few months.

Sometimes they flew in flocks like birds, other times they flew singly, as lonely travelers over forests and mountains, cities and meadows, down across the Appalachians, always during the daylight hours, enduring storms, winds, and exhaustion. Few birds bothered them, for they gave off a bad odor and taste and even were poisonous to some species. In fact, so effective was the monarch's coloring as a deterrent, that a mimicking species, the viceroy, flew safely through the air as well on the monarch's reputation.

The offspring of the monarchs of Deepwater hurried over the mountains as snow approached, heading for the place in the south across the Mexican border where they wintered. Here, at an elevation of more than nine thousand feet, they clung to the fir trees in masses so dense that the branches bowed with their weight. There they hibernated through the coldest months.

As spring began to come to the Mexican mountains they stirred, flashed their wings, and took off again to the north, wending their way over forests and farmland until they finally arrived, a very few of them, back at the kitchen garden at Deepwater.

🌿 🌿 🌿

Laurel discovered she was pregnant again in the spring of that year of 1860, and she was overjoyed and overcome all at once. She had wanted another child, wondered if she could conceive again at her age, but to bring another child into a world that was so obviously going crazy on all sides seemed foolish at best and dangerous if the worst came to pass.

Nonetheless, as the months of her expectancy passed, Laurel put aside her concern and readied to embrace the child as thoroughly as she had William and Seleta.

Seleta was growing to be an active, vigorous child, with a sensitive nature and little of the somber demeanor that marked her brother and her father. Often, Laurel came upon her playing with the children of the hands, and she was usually in the lead, directing a pack of intrepid souls out of one adventure and into another. Even the older children let her boss them, Laurel noticed, for she did it with a sunny smile and an eager enthusiasm for whatever idea enchanted her in the moment.

Seleta was "catching," David said with a smile. And Laurel envied her daughter what seemed to be boundless optimism and curiosity about anything that touched her heart or her hands.

Now that her children were old enough to understand the concept of sin, a concept that David did not hesitate to explain to them whenever the opportunity arose, Laurel was glad that she no longer owned slaves. It was difficult to make Deepwater prosper with hired hands, indeed it was sometimes hard to see if they could hold onto the land at all with the threat of war and the blockade of Wilmington looming. But it would have been harder still to explain to her son and her daughter that their mother "owned" people and had to coerce them to obey.

Now that she had children of her own, she writhed in guilty memory of trespasses against decency she had committed when she kept slaves. She had never allowed them to go to meeting, for example, to speak of God. Everyone knew that the slaves planned insurrections when they got religion. At least she never whipped them. She once heard the master at Orton plantation say, "If I catch you servin' God, I'll whip you good. You ain't got no time to serve God. I bought you to serve me!"

She was ashamed now to think that she had stood by and listened to such evil. It was something she could never have told David in a hundred years.

She knew that slaves were hiding out in the swamps up and down the river, some likely were round the marshes near Deepwater, too scared to come in for refuge. Some of the fugitives said that children had been born, bred, and died there, a whole generation living on what they could kill or gather to survive. Regularly the patrollers went into the woods with dogs and guns, and when they found a runaway, they shot him if he would not stop. But some of them would rather be shot than taken again.

An old Negro chant drifted through her mind often these days, one she heard them sing before she knew its significance. "Steal away, steal away, steal away to Jesus, I hain't got long to stay here, oh steal away home."

She could remember when she bought a woman without taking her ten-year-old boy with her. At the time, it seemed natural enough, for the lad looked likely, and the two together would have cost more than she was prepared to pay. Now, she wondered if she would face that woman again in eternity.

One refugee's story in particular haunted her, especially now that she had children of her own. He told her that he had only been in America three years and could quite clearly recall his capture in Africa.

"More'n twenty people were taken from my village that day," he said in a somber, cultivated voice, with little of the melting sibilance of the West Indies slave. "Three children so young they still at their mothers' breasts. When we got to the ship, they put us in irons round the leg, and the man with the irons took the children from the mothers' hands and threw them over the side of the ship into the water. Two of the women leaped over after their children and sank out of sight, for the irons on their legs. One drowned; the other was pulled out by some men in a boat. A third woman who could not leap, being already chained to the man next to her, fought to get loose and broke her arm. She died later of a fever. The woman who was rescued from the water threw herself overboard one night whilst we were at sea, when they let us walk the decks for the air."

Laurel masked her expressions of horror as the man told his tale, but that night in bed, she pictured the scene as it must have been over and over, wondering what she would have done in such a circumstance. If she were enslaved, and her child thrown overboard, would she have followed it into the sea?

And then she realized the leap of the mind she had taken. She could now imagine herself like those women—slave women—as though there were indeed a common link between them of humanity. Five years before, she could scarcely have imagined such a thing.

She turned and looked at David. He was so sure of his God. He was so sure of most things, in fact. There was a certain comfort in living with a man so sure of himself and his place in the world and also a certain . . . confinement.

She sighed and closed her eyes, peaceful in her mind. It was the confinement of a warm bed, a strong set of arms around her, the kind of confinement she could appreciate. A song hummed through her head like a kind of benediction, the old slave song she had heard them sing out in the fields before she sold them all. "T'bacca, give me a lil' t'bacca, missus, for I's goin' to Jesus today."

Folks she had known, some of them, longer than she had known David. Three of them were too old to sell, really, and she all but gave them away just so they could stay with the younger, stronger hands. She wondered where they were now. If they were safe, dry, and fed.

Old memories flooded her. Christmas day at dawn, as soon as the blinds were opened, they'd flock to the porch calling, "Chris'-mas gif! Chris'mas gif!" for their shirts, calico, dolls, and fruit. And the way they always knew when a storm was coming. They'd watch the sky: green-yellow at the horizon, ugly black cloud banks, the river dark and waiting, growing rough at the edges, all of it meant a hard wind. As the air grew still and heavy and the horses and cows turned their backs to the river, like as not one of them would say to her, "De devil gettin' ready to blow a big breath!" And they were always right.

She never expected to see a one of them again, and that made her sad. "Massa sleeps in the feather bed," they used to sing, "Nigger sleeps on the floor. When we get to heaven there'll be slaves no more . . ."

🌿 🌿 🌿

Laurel's third child was born the day after South Carolina announced secession. She cradled the beautifully made boy joy-ously, knowing he would likely be her last. She wondered what else might be coming to an end all round her.

Because David was a known abolitionist, they had become more and more isolated from their friends and neighbors. Though no one actually knew that runaways were welcome at Deepwater, Laurel could see suspicion in the eyes of those few who still greeted her on her visits to Wilmington. The very fact that they kept no slaves on their land was reason enough, many felt, to shun them.

Tempers were high along the Cape Fear, and anxious eyes looked for gunboats in the bay at anytime. If Wilmington became the target of a Federal assault, the entire state would strangle on its blockaded crops. Meanwhile, the slaves sensed war coming as clearly as their masters and, understanding clearly that their own freedom was at issue, they instinctively did what they could to stymie production. It was not unusual these days to drive the buggy downriver past the larger plantations and see lines of slaves leaning on their hoes or meandering about the fields with a single irate overseer shouting at them to get back to work. Once they began to lose their fear, they were frightening.

To celebrate the birth of little Levi, David decided to take the family to a local camp meeting, something he would have shunned in less parlous days. But now he said, with chaos looming on all sides, any chance at all to hear the word of God was not to be missed. There was a gathering of Methodists in Miller's Grove just about ten miles north, and on a hot day in August, David packed the buggy with blankets, loaded Laurel's food baskets aboard, and tucked the children in the back for the journey.

Since the Great Revival twenty years before, smaller versions of revivals were common all over the state, usually attracting hundreds of folks for hymns and prayers and general good socializing. Laurel was amazed that David would take it into his head to attend such a gathering, and she felt it likely the Friends would not have approved. But she didn't question her good fortune: she was anxious to get away from Deepwater for a few days, and the children were eager for the adventure.

As they neared Miller's Grove, a large clearing ringed by live oaks beside a chattering stream, the roads to the meeting place were thronged with travelers. Buggies, carts, wagons, the meanest sorts of conveyances and smart-looking coaches all crowded together as they approached the open-air arbor that was the Methodist camp meeting. They parked the buggy, unhitched the horses, and turned them into a fenced field with the rest of the stock, and then began to walk the rest of the way, as they could get no closer for the crowds.

Laurel carried Levi in her arms, David kept Bill and Seleta's hands tightly in his own, and the press of people grew more bustling the closer they got to the grove. Families walking together, young couples arm in arm, children running to and fro among the moving feet, like a small city they all went the same direction. Tents lined the road, temporary shacks where women had hung out their kettles and laundry on lines and crude cooking hooks over open fires. Everyone seemed happy enough, Laurel saw quickly, to forsake their usual comforts for the conviviality of the spirit.

David lead them to the place in the grove where the preaching arbor stood, an open-sided shelter lined with rough benches for the congregation. A pine pulpit on a low platform stood watch over the wooden pews, and children ran among them shrieking and playing their games. Bill and Seleta began to tug at their father's hand to escape, but he held them fast, calling to a man who seemed to be in charge. After a brief discussion and the quick exchange of a two-dollar piece, the man led them to a shelter at the far side of the camp. It was a rough log shack with a hard-clay floor and a rickety porch, but it looked like a palace to Laurel after she'd contemplated setting up housekeeping in a tent with two children and a suckling infant.

In no time, David and the children had stowed their few belongings, and Bill and Seleta were set free to romp with whatever playmates they could find. Laurel pulled out the cabin's lone rocker to the rough porch to sit with Levi and watch the world go by. David strode off with a businesslike air to discover the schedule for preaching.

It seemed to Laurel that everyone in the county must be there: young and old, rich and poor, even some black faces sprinkled among the white. Women called to one another back and forth from their tents and porches; a young girl swept the porch of her family's rough lean-to in her best dress, returning the smile of a young lad who kept strolling proudly by her in a pair of new, too-large boots. Church folks scurried about looking important, their heads together in conference, their hands clasped behind their backs as though to stiffen them further.

Laurel was suddenly unreasonably glad to be there among them all. She had few enough callers in the early days; now no one rode down the long drive from the river road at all. She felt wondrously free and light to be among a pack of folks for a few days who did not care that she was the mistress of Deepwater, who did not know that her husband was a disowned Quaker, that her now-meager fields were worked by hired hands, and that her barn hid more than two-dozen runaway slaves in the last fortnight. She said a quick prayer of her own that the pulpit be too crowded to allow David a turn at the preaching, so that they might simply enjoy the fellowship without being branded first-off a Quaker family.

In no time, one of the women on a nearby porch sauntered over and called to her. Laurel beckoned her to come up, and she sprawled on the porch steps, spreading her skirts about her as though to sun them, chatting and exclaiming about Levi's perfect little face pillowed on Laurel's breast.

"Is this your first meetin'?" she asked happily.

"Yes," Laurel said, feeling almost shy. "My husband wanted the children to see it—"

"My lands, yes, it's quite a treat for the young'uns!" she went on. "My man's a regular, loves to come an' watch the preachers, even gets a bit of the Word hisself when he gets in his cups. My name's Dorothy Beale, from over Groveton way?"

"Laurel Lassiter, from the Valley. Do you have children?"

"Six little beggers, Lord knows where they've got to now, I scarcely see them 'tween meals once we lay up the tent. How many you got besides the one?"

Laurel beamed. "Two more besides, they're off running already."

Dorothy laughed and slapped at her leg where a mosquito was feasting. "That's one of the best blessings of these revivals, you don't see the young'uns from dawn till dark." She looked out over the grove at the people moving to and fro. "This year's a mite different, looks to me. Less coloreds, for one. More folks walkin' 'stead of drivin', too. Times is hard, an' getting harder."

"I was surprised to see any slaves at all, what with war coming and all," Laurel ventured.

"Shoot, that don' keep 'em away. The coloreds love the meeting, an' lots of masters nearby let them come so's to keep 'em happy, I guess. They get altogether at the edge of the grove an' all the slaves that died durin' the year, they preach them a funeral that day. They build a preachin' spot out o' brush an' twigs, an' we give 'em a bit o' this an' that, an' they cook it up and everybody takes supper, an' they come for miles around. An' then when the singin' starts, they join in fast enough, that part they love the most. Coloreds an' whites, slaves an' freemen, we get the slave traders an' the slave hunters an' the masters an' the elders, saints an' sinners all, they sing along big as the Lord, an' the grove just rings with it. 'Tis a sight to see."

"I imagine," Laurel said wonderingly.

"An' then the courtin' starts!" Dorothy said gleefully.

"Courting?" Laurel frowned. David would not be happy to hear of this.

"My lands, yes, the meetin' is a regular matin' ground! Why I met my own man here more'n ten years ago! I was walkin' with my ma an' pa, an' I had my brogan shoes over my shoulder an' had my dresses an' my pantalets tied up with a string to keep 'em from gettin' dusty in the road. I let my dress an' pantalets down an' put on my shoes when I got in sight o' the grove, but not before ol' Beale got a good sight o' me!" She laughed gaily. "We were wed before the year was out, an' ain' missed a meetin' since. These Methodists, they ain' like the Baptists, they put on a good show with fine dancin' most every night." She glanced over across the grove at her fire, and cried out, "Oh, there's Beale now, I got to go," and skipping off the porch, she called out, "You come round an' take supper with us, hear? My man loves to see the newcomers an' preach the Word awhile!"

Laurel smiled and waved back, trying to picture David and "ol' Beale" with their heads together conferring on the Bible. Shaking her head ruefully, she put Levi down on the cot in the shack, tucked the bug netting round his head, and set off to see for herself what the meeting was all about.

She came to the edge of the clearing where the tables were being set up for supper. Making a quick reminder to herself to bring back her two pies and the beef roast they brought, she marveled at the spread of food before her: every sort of meat and pie and pastry and corn dish a person might imagine, rows of melons, piles of peaches, tomatoes and squash, beans and beets, fried chicken by the platter, whole roasted game birds and fowl, and custards in bowls big enough to drown a dog.

A man dressed in a black frock coat and hat, much like Lincoln, stood at the side of the table and importuned passersby with warnings. "I am grieved!" he shouted to any who would stop and listen. "I am grieved to the heart to see so much labor and parade about eatables! So much extravagance! The Lord does not smile on waste and frivolity, and I think we might do without pound cake, preserves, and pastries when we pray to the heavens! The poor soul is little regarded before such a banquet of excess!" but people scarcely listened. Children pushed by him, reaching for whatever they might snatch from the table before maternal hands could fend them off, and women still kept coming, bringing out their covered baskets and platters. Laurel hurried back to the shack, snatched up Levi and her contributions to the bounty, and hurried back to find that most of the folks were gathering before the tables now to eat.

She found David and Seleta quick enough, Bill raced up to them just about the time they had their picnic blanket spread on the ground, and the bounty began to disappear from the tables much faster than it had been laid.

Once supper was finished and the dishes cleared off, the people began to gather at the arbor, moving up in family groups, clusters of young folks, and the black faces hovering near the rear. Women and children quickly filled the pews, and the men crouched or stood at the end of the benches under the overhanging eaves. The noise quieted some, but still an occasional baby cried, a child shrieked, and the murmur of the adults rose and fell like a soft sea as the preachers got up and down off the rostrum to speak. They talked of God, of eternity, of the judgment to come, sometimes shouting, sometimes imploring in almost a whispered prayer for the listeners to heed the promises of the Lord and His Son. The orators seemed to get more and more passionate, as though there was a reason to their order, until finally the last preacher took the pulpit, and a reverent silence settled over the people.

"He's the best o' the lot," a woman next to Laurel murmured, shifting herself in her seat and leaning forward in anticipation.

"Aye!" the preacher roared, and the whole congregation breathed out a collective, "Amen!"

"Aye! Ye are come as to a holiday, I see about me! Once more, ye come, bedecked in tinsel and costly raiment!"

Laurel looked about her in confusion. Few here wore anything finer than clean, simple frocks and trousers, but likely it was the best they had to show for most of them.

"I see before me the pride of beauty and youth!" the preacher trumpeted, and young girls in the first few rows blushed and turned away. "I see the middle-aged, the hoary hairs and decrepit limbs of age! Crowding each other aside in your haste down the beaten road! Hurrying to death and judgment!"

Laurel glanced at David who leaned against one of the rough pillars holding up the roof. He was frowning, but he was listening intently. Bill had already slipped outside the confines of his father's arm and was glancing to a boy next to him, teasing no doubt. Seleta sat spellbound next to her, taking in the preacher's words with wide-eyed wonder.

"Oh, fools and blindmen! Slow-worms, battening upon the

damps and filth of this vile earth! Hugging your muck rakes while the Glorious One proffers you the Crown of Life!"

"Mama, what's a muck rake?" Seleta whispered.

"I'm not sure," Laurel said, bewildered. "Whatever it is, he makes it sound evil enough."

By now, many of the congregation were in tears; Laurel looked to one side and an elderly woman with a straw hat was wiping her eyes silently. The fat woman in the row before her was sobbing openly. One old man cried out exultantly, "That's preaching!" and the crowd murmured "Amen!" with heartfelt unison. The fat woman in front of Laurel stopped sobbing abruptly and broke into "He Is My Rock," and the crowd was now swept along in the words and chorus as the preacher exhorted them to "come home" and "be washed in the Blood of the Lamb!"

There were shouts of thanksgiving and hallelujah as believers and sinners made their way to the front of the arbor, knelt in a line before the pulpit. The ministers came down from the makeshift stage to shake hands and pat shoulders, some of them weeping as copiously as those who knelt before them.

Seleta stood to see over the shoulders better, moving slightly toward the kneeling people, and David called to her, his voice carrying across the crowded room, "Seleta, sit thee down." She sat abruptly, as though the hand of God Himself had touched her. Laurel stared at David curiously. He was no longer leaning casually against the pillar that held up the arbor roof but had moved farther away from the gathering as though to somehow divorce himself from the proceedings.

Now at the front of the room, several of the faithful began to convulse and jerk in a frenzy, trembling and falling against one another as though in a faint, many of them weeping loudly in the extremes of emotion. One man in the corner, down on his knees before the pulpit, was barking sharply like a dog.

Laurel stood up and took Seleta by the hand. "I think it's time for us to go now," she said gently, leading the child out of the rows and to the back of the gathering. David joined her, William at his side. The two children were strangely quiet, as though they had seen something that would mark them for life.

David put his arm around Laurel's shoulder, but his face was dark with scorn and something else—it looked very like bewilderment to her. They walked past the fiddle players who were tuning up for the evening's dancing, past the clusters of old men smoking their pipes with their heads together jarring over the events of the world, past the small bands of children who had escaped the arbor and were running together in whooping troops through the meeting ground, drunk with the shadows and the night air.

David put the children to bed on the rough cots inside, and Laurel took up Levi for his final nursing, rocking silently on the porch. When her husband walked out again into the lamplight, she glanced at him to see if there was a change in his mood. He took a seat next to her, his head leaning against her knee while the baby slept peacefully at her breast.

"That was one of the ugliest scenes of human frailty I believe I've ever seen," he said softly. "I have to say I had not expected it to be this way. Not at all. Or I'd never have come."

"What did you expect?" she asked, her eyes closed, the rocker creaking gently.

"A lot more preaching and a lot less barking," he said gloomily.

She could not stifle a chuckle. "I thought Seleta was going to go up and pet the man," she finally said when she could. "Never in all my born days."

"Does thee think God means His people to act such fools?" he asked. She could hear the pain in his voice, the sincere bewilderment.

"I think," she said slowly, measuring her words, "that God likely loves all manner of fools, so long as they're doing their best to love Him back."

He thought about that for a moment. The sounds of the fiddles and the guitars now came clearly to them from the arbor. The dancing had begun. Laurel tapped her foot softly to the music, picturing the swirl of color and heat that would be the folks easing their hearts and their tensions in the stomp of the music. "Thee likes people more than I do, I guess," he said at last. "I find it hard to suffer such antics. And I am dreadfully sorry I brought my children to witness them."

"I'm not," Laurel said calmly. "It won't be the first time they see grown folks in a passion about something, and I can think of far worse things to be in a fit about than the word of the Lord."

"They were drunk with it," he said scornfully.

"Yes," she agreed, shaking her head with amusement. "But for a minute, they put aside their cares, strangers stood alongside each other like brothers and sisters, and they felt important to God. I guess that's worth something, after all."

He stretched and reached for the baby, cradling him as naturally as Laurel did. She smiled down at him happily. Nothing made her love her more than when he was loving one of their children.

"We'll leave in the morning," he said to the night air as much as to her.

She sighed, letting her disappointment show.

"Thee can't wish to stay at this circus," he said sternly.

"I can't recall the last time I got to just sit and visit with another woman." She closed her eyes again. "The only children Bill and Seleta ever see work in their own fields."

"I'm sorry that the evil of slavery has kept wrong-thinking neighbors from visiting," he said soberly, "but I cannot let my children stay in such a place, among such people."

"Yes," she murmured. "I know. We'll leave in the morning."

He handed Levi back to her wordlessly and rose to walk off into the darkness toward the stock pen. She knew that he was as good as his word. The horses would be ready; they would leave at daybreak. It would be the last time he would ever take such a chance again, likely. She felt so tired all of a sudden. She rose with Levi and went inside, snuffing out the lamp. Even a rough cot would be a comfort tonight.

🌿 🌿 🌿

During one of the coldest weeks in January 1861, a rumor raced like fire through the Cape Fear Valley that an armed Federal gunboat was on its way to Fort Caswell to capture the mouth of the river and thus most of the state. What was left of the militia, the Cape Fear Minutemen, gathered together with a few shotguns and pistols and a hurried cache of provisions, boarded a rickety schooner, and sailed downriver to meet the United States troops. They went to the door of Sergeant James Reilly at Fort Johnston at four o'clock in the morning and demanded the keys to the armory. They then crossed the Elizabeth River to pound on Fort Caswell's door, taking its cache of munitions.

Having seized both the forts that guarded the Cape Fear, they sat down and celebrated with a keg of rum from a nearby keep.

When Governor Ellis heard the next day that both forts were occupied by a group of armed, drunken men, albeit Patriots, he sent a regiment of state militia to restore the forts to federal control. The Minutemen sheepishly gave back the forts, but news of their adventure swept the state and fed the idea that, indeed, local control of arms and defense might well be ridiculously easy. As more and more states seceded, rational men began to ask themselves: why not North Carolina?

Laurel was nursing Levi the night David came home with the news that secession was imminent and that both forts had been taken and then released again. He had been in Wilmington meeting with their factor, trying to get a better price for their leaf though it was quite possible that no tobacco at all would be able to leave port once war began in earnest.

He came up and threw himself down on the bed, and she could feel the fatigue in him even from across the room. He turned on his side to watch his son at her breast, cradling his cheek on his arm. "I think he's the prettiest of the three," David said. "Thee makes the prettiest babies in the valley, I believe."

She beamed at him. "Pray to God that they have your brain."

"Not a thing wrong with their mother's." He watched Levi as though he were seeing him after a long absence. In fact, they had been so dreadfully busy this season, so harried by the threat of war, that he had little time for his youngest son. "Now that he's cutting teeth, shouldn't thee wean him? Seleta was off the nipple by now."

"This one's on his own schedule," she murmured, sitting him up.

"He hasn't started to talk at all, has he? Seleta said a score of words by now, and even Bill could say Mama and Papa."

In answer, Laurel turned Levi to face his father and playfully jounced the baby. "Tell him you'll talk when you're good and ready, and soon enough he'll be begging you to be still like he does your big sister."

Levi smiled peacefully as always, swiveling his eyes around the room, focusing on nothing. His dark hair and dark blue eyes against the perfect features made him seem almost more angel than child.

David frowned and sat up on the bed, moving closer. He took Levi's hands and pulled him upright into the patty-cake position. Playfully, he tapped his hands together and sang the rhyme to him, but Levi did not respond. He gazed someplace over David's shoulder.

"It's the lamp," Laurel said. "He's always been fascinated with light."

David followed the direction of his son's gaze and saw that indeed, the child was staring at the light with rapt concentration. He moved so as to block the baby's stare and still Levi did not blink. His stare did not waver, though he could not see the light. He did not move to meet his father's eyes, or stare at his hands, or glance back to his mother. No response at all.

Laurel's smile faded now. "What is it?"

David patted the boy's cheek lightly and spoke to him, calling him gently and teasing him. Only gradually, finally, did Levi turn his attention to his father, and then again, the beatific smile. "He lives in his own little world," David murmured. "He's not like the other two."

"What do you mean? Are you saying you think something's wrong with him?"

David said nothing. He took the boy from his mother's lap and sat him on the bed. "He's almost a year. He seems a good deal slower than Bill and Seleta, is all. I never really noticed it before, and I should have. Thee hasn't noticed?"

She dropped her head. "I guess, some. Certainly, he's not as bright as Seleta. Maybe not even as quick as William. But I can't say I've seen anything to say for certain that something's wrong with him. Every baby's different, and he's still so young."

"He hasn't tried to walk once, has he?" David turned again to Levi and made patterns with his fingers enticingly before the child's face, well within his grasp. Levi did not reach for them or crow or even show much interest other than to glance once and away. The pattern on the coverlet caught his attention briefly, then he turned away from that as well and searched the room for something else to stare at, his hands moving restlessly as if under someone else's control.

David murmured gently, "Why have thee not told me how backward the child is? Thee must have seen that he's not like the other two." To his surprise, Laurel began to weep softly.

"I hoped," she said, "that I was wrong. That he would catch up all of a sudden."

"Has he pulled himself to a stand at all?"

"He crawls a bit. But he seems to show no interest."

They looked in Levi's face then together, and David whispered, "He shows no interest in anything at all."

"That's not true," Laurel protested. "He takes the nipple eagerly and smiles at me!"

"An animal would do as much," David said. "Look into his eyes. What does thee see there?"

Laurel took up the baby into her arms again and stared into his face. Her mouth contorted in pain. "I see a beautiful baby!"

"He is no longer a baby, he's a child." He hesitated for a long moment, wondering how to ask such a question. "Does thee—does thee see a soul in his eyes?"

She looked again into Levi's eyes. He did not focus on her face; his eyes roamed haphazardly about the ceiling. She closed her eyes in pain and put the child back on the bed.

"Does thee see a spark of intelligence? A sense of himself? Does he know where he begins and the wall ends?" David picked up his son and held him high up over his head. The baby gave a little chortle of glee at the movement, but he made no effort to communicate in any other way. It might as well have been the wind that lifted him as his father's hands.

Laurel felt a great calm befall her, as though a hand had settled on her shoulder, a hand of comfort and healing. "You are saying he's an idiot, then." Her voice betrayed no emotion at all.

David turned and stared at her. "That is the ugliest word I have ever heard thee say in all our marriage." He put the baby down on the bed. Levi promptly rolled over and crooned quietly to himself. "Thee must have suspected something was wrong. What did thee think to call it, if thee ever said it aloud?"

She snatched the baby up again and held him. "I did not think to judge him so soon. I thought to let God make of Levi what He would in His own time."

"And so He shall," David said mournfully. "But in the meantime, it is we who must come to grips with what he is not and likely will never be. The child is not just slow, Laurel. The child's mind is . . . disordered. Nothing shines from his eyes except that which comes from the lamp." He sat down heavily, his shoulders slumped in despair.

"How can you say this so quickly? You barely know him!"

"I know what I see. And what I don't see," he murmured.

"Well then, a doctor. We'll get a doctor immediately."

"No doctor can give him what God did not."

"We certainly shall not give up on him so easily!"

His mouth turned down in an effort to control his pain. "Nothing about this is easy, Laurel. Nor will it be in the years to come."

Laurel wiped her eyes, no longer weeping. She felt the strength come back into her heart. She knew now she must be stronger than her husband, stronger even than sadness. This was what women did, she knew instinctively, when no one else could. They held the children close and went on to whatever lay ahead.

"Well, whatever we choose to call it between ourselves, we must never let the others hear the word," she said. "Levi is our child, he is their brother. He will be as loved, as wanted in this family as Seleta, as William, as any other child we might have in the future. God has a plan for Levi, I am certain. And it is not for us to question that plan."

To her amazement, her husband put a hand to his eyes and she could see the water there. He was half ashamed of his tears, turning aside so that she could not see his face. "Our son is an idiot. Thee said the word first. But others will say it soon enough." His voice was choked, his shoulders quaking. "But that is not the most terrible burden. It's his eyes. There is nothing in them. God has forsaken him!"

She sat down beside David and pulled his hand away from his face roughly. "Never say that to me again. God has not forsaken Levi and He has not forsaken you. That's why you weep, not for him but for yourself. Don't you dare weep! This child has as much of a soul as you, as much as me, and perhaps more than most. But that remains to be seen. Where is your faith? How can you give up on your own son so fast?"

David turned to her and held her, held Levi, too, between them. For a long moment, he said nothing, and Laurel could feel his pain gradually fade enough for him to speak. "Forgive me," he whispered. "Thee is stronger than I am."

"Well, perhaps I have had more time to accustom myself to the fact," she murmured. "I guess I have wondered about it for a good while. And then I stopped wondering. I suppose I have known in my heart for months." She patted her husband's face lightly. In that moment, she felt such a tenderness for him. For all his strength, he was in many ways not as firm in his faith as she was.

Her faith was simpler: she just believed that somehow everything would work out for the best. "There is nothing to forgive," she murmured.

They sat together holding Levi in silence. Laurel watched the tiny motes of dust move through the slant of sunlight in the room as though they were on water rather than air. She herself felt underwater . . . or wrapped in the most muffled of all cocoons. She wondered if she would have felt pain if pricked with a pin. Numb and dumb and wondering, her mind chanted softly like a hymn. Like Levi will be all of his life, perhaps.

Finally David said, "Should we send him away?"

She looked up, amazed. "To where?"

He gestured helplessly. "To some sort of—place for unfortunates. To a home."

"You mean an asylum?" Now her anger rose again at him. How could they sit so close, holding the child together, and have their thoughts be so far apart? Was marriage always so bewildering? "Of course not. He is our son, and we will give him the proper care and a good life, just as we will Bill and Seleta and any other children we have." Her voice brooked no opposition.

"We will not have others," David said, a little too quickly.

"Why do you say that? It's unlikely, I suppose, but it may still happen. Some my age are made mothers—"

"No." David looked away from her. There was no mistaking the set of that jaw. "Thee was too old the last time. No more."

She felt a place in her go cold to him, and it frightened her more than any other thing that had passed between them. And yet he did not even know it, she marveled. "Do you mean because of Levi and whatever sort of affliction he has? But we don't know enough about his future to say such a thing, and we certainly can't know if another child would be similarly afflicted. Bill and Seleta are perfectly normal children!"

"No. God has turned away from us, Laurel. Away from me. I am rebuked by the Lord. It began when I took thee for wife, perhaps, I don't know. But I have felt it for years."

She stared at him in cold wonder. Her youngest son was disordered, no doubt, and that was tragedy enough. But his father suffered from an affliction even more damaging, she could see that plainly now. David could not abide imperfection. He could not forgive it, either in her, his children, himself, or the world at large.

Most of all, he could not forgive it in God. "God is not in the business, I think, of rebuking," she said. "Certainly not through the affliction of an innocent child. And you are a good man, David. This has nothing to do with you!"

"I am prideful," he said mournfully. "And arrogant. Arrogant and stiff and I—" here he faltered. "Sometimes I actually hate my fellow man."

That one shocked her. "Well," she said finally, "I guess we all do at times. And yet you do great good with your life. I cannot accept that any God I could love would bend a child's mind to disorder simply to teach you a lesson." She stopped short of saying that, in fact, the very concept seemed to her the height of arrogance in itself.

David handed her Levi and rose to his feet. "Thee has more faith at times than I, Laurel. We'll do our best for the child, of course, and unless it becomes impossible, we will care for him ourselves. All our lives, likely, and someone will have to do it after we are gone. But don't speak to me of any more children. I'll not give God another chance to test me in this way." And with that, he went from the room.

Laurel sat and rocked little Levi as dusk settled over the fields, darkening the room. She looked out over the river as a wedge of ducks flew past and a blue heron waded out on the bank. From the woods, she could smell the faint odor of bracken and damp leaves, a rich dark fragrance of fecund earth. The promise of a fertile spring. A fertility she would not know again. She knew that she would never feel the same about anything from this day forward. Ever after, she would mark time as that which came before and that which came after the day she allowed herself to know that her last child, her most beautiful Levi, was damaged forever. And with the dream of his perfection, he took a piece of her marriage, something of his father's faith in himself and his God, and a part of her happiness forever.

🌱 🌱 🌱

The Wilmington papers carried many messages like the following one that summer:

$300 Reward! Ran away, bright mulatto girl named Linda, 21 years of age. Five feet four inches, dark eyes, black hair inclined to curl but can be made straight. Has a decay spot on front tooth. Can read and write and in all probability will try to make it to the Free States. All persons are forbidden, under penalty of law, to harbor or employ said slave. $150 will be given to whoever takes her in the state, and $300 if taken out of state and delivered to me or lodged in jail.

Dr. Flint

Only a few such runaways ever made it to Deepwater or any other "station" on the Underground Railroad. Plunging into the Great Dismal Swamp at the north end of the state, many tried to make it through the morass to what they supposed was freedom on the other side. Unfortunately, only Virginia lay on the other side, as entrenched a slave state as that they had escaped.

But into the swamps they went, and one in particular, the Linda of the advertisement above, ventured into the edge of the swamp alone, leaving her three children behind, hoping to gain freedom and the funds to buy them out of slavery when she could.

Linda came from a plantation near the old town of Bath, and her master chased her with a pack of hounds past the edge of the Dismal, pushing her deeper and deeper into the swamp than she had wanted to go, just as dusk came on the slow waters.

The night was hot, and the olive-brown snake lay on a twisted cypress log, half in, half out of the brown water. It was a heavy-bodied female, largely patternless, with a brown cheek stripe on the side of her head. Her eyes had vertical pupils like the cat's-eyes they most resembled, the eyes of a pit viper.

She was a four-foot cottonmouth. Some folks called her a moccasin or a trap jaw, for she did not bite and then drop like a rattlesnake, but held on with grim determination after her lethal injection. This August was her first to bear young. She had birthed ten seven-inch, strongly patterned versions of herself and her mate, a smaller cottonmouth long-since gone from this part of the swamp. She bore her litter alive and paid them little mind after their birth except to guard their nest, a place they vacated quickly enough. She was three years old and would likely produce more than a dozen snakes every other year.

But this year, she had laid claim to a lowland pond that stretched over four acres of the Great Dismal, warning off other moccasins from what she had determined would be her territory. An irascible snake compared to many of her reptile cousins, she was more willing to stand her ground and fight than flee. Like most predators, she slept half the day and hunted at night.

Now she lay in the water, gathering her energy for a kill. She had hunted the last two nights but had taken little. Tonight, she would search for a large kill, and then she would not move from her log for as much as a week again. A night bird called mournfully from the top of the cypresses that overhung her pond, but she did not stir. The stinging bugs hovered in dense clouds over the water, but they did not light on her scales. She waited, growing more alert by the moment.

A splashing came from the far corner of her pond, but she could not hear it because she was as deaf as any other snake to sound traveling over the air. However, she was exquisitely sensitive to every vibration of water or earth, and the facial pit on the side of her cheek could sense the warmth of prey many feet away. The splashing told her that something large had entered the water, far too large to be prey and likely large enough to be threat.

In some dim recess of her brain, she knew that her young had long ago departed, but her instincts kept her close to the nest still. The idea of its possible disturbance made her fearful and angry all at once. She swiveled slowly on the log, moving slightly deeper into the water for protection. She would not run unless she had to, and then only to save her life.

If she could have heard, she would have noticed that the calls of the crows overhead, disturbed in their nesting, had changed to new alarm cries that were unusual for this piece of the swamp. They told it all over the pond that man had entered their territory, but the cottonmouth lacked the warning that the rabbit, the raccoon, and the bear might have deciphered. She knew only that the water was disturbed.

The water grew more agitated, and then she saw movement coming closer, a large, dark shape half in, half out of the water, struggling through the dense brush at the side of the pond. She tested the air for clues to the threat with her long forked tongue, taking the particles back into her Jacobson's organ, the scent translator above her jaw. It was not bear, though it was large enough to be so; it was not deer, though the legs were long and thin.

The snake reared back and coiled tightly on her log to protect her body, enraged of a sudden at the chaos she sensed coming toward her, and she gaped her mouth wide open in her characteristic threat. Her mouth flashed white in the darkness, as strong a signal of danger as any in the swamp, but she sensed no hesitation in the oncoming intruder. The water was roiled now, and as the threat came near, she struck viciously out at a limb, aiming high up toward the middle of the body, and clamped her jaws deep in the strangely smooth flesh, determined to drive it away or die in the attempt.

Linda shrieked in agony and terror, snatching at the long, black snake that had suddenly stabbed her in the darkness, unable to see anything but a writhing shape, to feel the burning of the poison pump swiftly into her thigh, where she had pulled up her skirt to try to keep it out of the water. She lunged out of the shallows, screaming and tearing at the cottonmouth, yanking it out of her leg and hurling it against a low-hanging tree.

The cottonmouth felt a sharp pain as her body lashed the cypress, her spine snapped in two places, and she fell to the brush. There, contorting in dumb agony, making smaller and smaller circles in the mud, she finally lay still. By dawn, the ants would find her.

Linda fell to the ground screaming and weeping now, her limbs already growing hot and numb all at once. She tore at the bite on her leg, trying to rend the flesh, to reach it to suck at the venom, grabbing handfuls of mud to slap on the wound, but she knew it was no use. Even as she struggled, she could feel her heart constrict in her chest, her breath come more thickly, her eyes begin to swim and blur. The pain was intense; the terror worse than she had ever felt even when the master came on her in the night and made her submit. She fell back on her side and wrapped her head in her hands, hoping that she would meet God very soon.

It was likely the only wish she ever had that was granted.

🌿 🌿 🌿

War slammed into the Carolinas with the force of a hurricane in the summer of 1861 when Lincoln sent Union gunboats to bottle up Charleston harbor. Men all over North Carolina were called to duty, and many rushed to support the cause of freedom for the South. Many more, mostly small farmers in the Piedmont and mountain regions, swore they'd never lift a gun to protect "the rich man's niggers." Those who enlisted were told, and believed, that the the war would last for only six months. Recruiting officers predicted that they'd be able to mop up with a pocket handkerchief all the blood that Carolinians would shed.

One Southern gentleman quoted in the Raleigh newspaper, noting that all of his friends could hunt and ride and fight better than any Yankee he ever met, boasted that Southerners "could whip the Yankees with cornstalks." Reminded of this after the end of the war he then soberly added, "But they wouldn't fight with cornstalks."

Carolina troops immediately took control of Fort Macon on Bogue Sound, Fort Caswell, and Fort Johnston. A company of the Charlotte Grays seized the Federal Mint in that city and two days later, captured the U.S. Arsenal at Fayetteville. Now the Carolina soldiers had forty thousand weapons, money, and ample troops flocked to the Confederate flag. Horses for the cavalry were bought in Kentucky and herded in droves through the mountain passes; saddles and harnesses were commissioned in New Orleans and rushed to Raleigh by rail. Training camps were set up in a dozen spots over the state, and word went out all over the region for churches to send their bells to foundries to be made into cannons.

Many Quakers left the state for points farther west to escape both the ravages of war and conscription, and wagons full of folks who Laurel had once hoped to live among trundled past Deepwater upriver all the early months of the summer. David spent a week more morose than she had ever seen him, unable to lift his hand to a thing around the place. She knew he was in a crisis with his conscience, and she watched him carefully to see what he might do.

One night at table, William asked him if he would go to war to fight the Yankees, and David replied, "What does thee know of this war, son?"

"I know the Yankees want to try to run us," the boy said stoutly, "and we won't let them. They want to try to tell us what to do with our own property!"

The boy had a good mind, not quite as quick as Seleta, but sound and logical. He was no more prone to emotional outbursts than his father. Laurel knew, by his words, that he'd been getting his information from the hands.

"And what property is that?" David asked gently.

"Our land and our railroads and our slaves," Bill said. " 'Course we don't have any slaves, and it's wrong to keep them, but no Yankee should come down here and tell us what to do with them."

Seleta watched her brother and her father quietly. She glanced at her mother. Laurel shook her head minutely to warn Seleta to keep silent.

"And so thee thinks," David was saying, his voice still calm, "that we should go to war to protect our property?"

"I think we got to," Bill said firmly.

"Even if the property is other human beings, against the word of God?"

Here, William stopped and considered. Finally he said clearly, "I think it's wrong to own other men, Pa, and I think it's wrong to go someplace and tell the folks there how to live. But if the Yankees come here and try to take away what's ours and tell us what to do, I think we got to fight them."

"Fighting, too, is against the word of God, William," David said sadly. "So to answer thy question, no, I will not fight the Yankees, nor will I fight my neighbors. I will stay on my land and I will pray that the war will end swiftly."

Seleta spoke up now, despite Laurel's warning glance. "But what if they come to Deepwater, Father? Will thee protect us then?"

Obviously, William was not the only one who had been listening when others spoke of war. A long silence hovered over them like a bad kitchen odor, and both children watched their father with tense faces.

"I will do what I can to keep thee from harm, of course," David said steadfastely, "but I will not take up arms against my fellow man."

"Not even if he's taking up arms 'gainst thee?" Bill cried out anxiously.

"I will pray to God to keep us safe," David said, bowing his head. "And now I think we should say a prayer to keep hatred out of the hearts of our neighbors and good sense in their mouths. People sometimes talk themselves into war, and such talk is as bad as the battles themselves in God's eyes. William, will thee lead us?''

Bill cast huge eyes at Laurel and back again at his father. Laurel tried to placate her son with a glance, but he knew what he had heard and no amount of maternal soothing was going to alter his father's words. He set his chin, looking alarmingly like David himself, and clenched his hands together in what were more fists than supplicative gestures to God. "Almighty Father," he said, his voice high and frightened, "We pray that war will pass us by, but if it does not, I pray that Thee will send my father the strength to do his duty."

"William!" David erupted in anger, "leave the table this minute!"

White-faced, their son got up and rushed from the room. Seleta rose swiftly and ran after him, already weeping in confusion. Laurel looked at David sadly. "It will be impossible to keep the children from knowing what goes on all about them. And I suppose they must come to their own conclusions about what is right and wrong."

David stared at her indignantly. "I have always disagreed with thee about that. There *is* an ultimate right and an ultimate wrong, it is not always open to discussion or consensus. Owning other human beings is wrong. Fighting our fellow man is wrong. The opinions of a hundred sages will not sway me nor will the judgments of my family. So long as they live under my roof, they will accept the word of God!" The unspoken, "And so will *thee!*" rang in her ears silently.

Laurel bowed her head in despair. "Sometimes I think it is men like you who start wars, David, whether you stay around to fight them or not. Men of principle. Men who will not yield ground. Men who cannot compromise." She sighed and raised her head. "But, of course, we have no choice. We have lived by your beliefs for a decade now, we won't jump ship when the storm comes. Will you go to William?"

David shook his head. "Let the boy think on this awhile. He'll come around. And when he does, I will accept his apology."

Laurel rose and left him there at the table. "Well, I'll see to Seleta at least. All she wants is to feel safe, and I don't think that's too much to ask."

Later that night, Laurel crept to William's bed and stood gazing down at him quietly. Next to him in the trundle bed, little Levi slept on, undisturbed. Likely, the chaos and terror of war would sweep by Levi without his notice as did most everything else in his life. But William would be changed forever. More even than Seleta, probably, William would be tempered by the furnace of war, for that was the way of war and men, no matter their ages. How could she help him in the coming months?

She bent down and looked closer at Levi. Now of course they knew beyond a doubt that he was never going to be completely normal. In other, crueler times, he would have been called an idiot. Some would still brand him so, she guessed. But she would never accept David's assessment that the boy had no soul. She could see it in his eyes, sometimes, like slow, spring sun. It would be so good, she thought to herself, if human beings could learn to appreciate and love each other as they did other things in nature . . . like a sunset. One could watch the changing sky and marvel at the beauty without trying to change or control it. Yet we cannot watch the unfolding of a human being without trying to alter the course of the soul to better suit our needs. In that way, Levi's affliction was truly a hidden blessing, for it might teach them all—David not the least of them—that there were things they could not alter, which were a waste of time to judge good or ill, for they simply were and would always be. They could not change Levi in any way, they could only love him.

William's trousers stood in the corner, so stiff with tobacco gum that they barely creased at the knees. She bent to gaze at her eldest son. Despite his efforts to protect himself by applying a thick layer of dirt to his hands, his wrists were completely naked of hair. The tobacco gum pulled every hair off, leaving them bare and reddened.

She touched him lightly on his head, the hair there springy and coarse, thick like his father's. To her surprise, his eyes opened as though he had been awake for some time. "What?" he mumbled sleepily.

"Nothing, Billy," she said softly. "I just wanted to see if you were well."

He stared at her, still waking up. He rose on one elbow. "Mother, will war come truly?"

Ah, that children should have to ask such questions! Her heart twisted with shame for being part of a world that ran itself in such a brutal manner. "I don't know," she whispered. "But you mustn't worry about it. We'll be fine, no matter what comes."

"Father is angry at me," he murmured sadly.

She nodded. "But he loves you anyway. Are you mad at him, too?"

Her son thought for a moment. "Yes." He looked up at her in bewilderment. "I'm mad at him for not fighting."

"But he's doing what he thinks is right, Billy. It's probably not a fair thing to be mad at someone for doing that. Is it maybe that you're mad at him for not being like the fathers of your friends?"

He thought for another moment and then sighed. "Maybe. Mother, is Father a coward?"

"What's a coward?" she asked him softly.

"Someone who's afraid to fight." The twist of his mouth told her how painful it was for her son to say such a thing.

"Do you think your father is afraid to fight?"

He looked miserable. "I don't know."

She sat down on his bed and took his hand in hers. "Well, I don't think your father is afraid of much of anything. Do you know why? Because I've seen him do some very brave things, like help other men escape their chains, and stand up to people who tried to tell him what to do, and go out in the fields every day and work in the sun and the rain, no matter how he felt inside, so that his family could have what we need. So I don't believe your father is a coward. I believe he is a Patriot. Do you know what that word means?"

Bill shook his head.

"A Patriot is someone who does what they think is best for their country, even if that something is hard for them to do. Do you think you would have to be brave to be a Patriot?"

Billy's eyes began to widen. "Yes," he whispered. "Like General George Washington?"

"Yes. Your father is a Patriot, and he believes this country is more important than the right of a man to have slaves. So he made a hard choice. And that is a brave thing to do also. Do you understand?"

Bill leaned over and hugged her hard. "I'm sleepy now," he said.

"Good. Have pleasant dreams," Laurel told him, leaving the

room. Outside the door, she leaned back against it, closing her eyes in her second prayer of the evening. She prayed to God that she could come to believe in David's courage in the same way Billy would. For all of their sakes.

🔥 🔥 🔥

As the war began, Wilmington sat poised to defend the Carolinas, the most important port on the coast of two key Southern states. The city's wharves were crowded with coastal schooners and transatlantic ships, and the hills above the Cape Fear were decorated with the homes of the county's best families: the Ashes, the Waddells, Moores, Sprunts, and McNeills, veterans of the Revolution and harvesters of its spoils.

Just before the war, churches in the city were varied and well attended, and the theater pulled in large audiences for sophisticated musicales and light opera. Once Lincoln called for troops, however, blockaders became Wilmington's only heroes. Now, foreign sailors, gamblers, and opportunists crowded the streets, and even those native-born who had the courage to venture out were garbed in Confederate gray. Ladies did not venture out at all. Wilmington was overnight turned into a town of privateers, a port existing for the single purpose of running sleek, fast ships through the Federal fleet that lay off New Inlet and Frying PanShoals. Cotton fetched three cents a pound in the states and close to a dollar a pound in Liverpool. No port in the South changed faces so fast.

Speculators fought over prices; drunken sailors fought each other, and the women quietly withdrew to upriver homes and plantations. Fort Fisher guarded one entry to the river; Fort Caswell guarded the other. To have two entrances widely spaced and protected by forts made the Lower Cape Fear the South's most easily defended harbor. When Lincoln announced a total blockade of the Confederate's harbors, General Lee turned to Wilmington to provide the bulk of munitions, coffee, and drugs it would take to run the war.

Then yellow fever hit Wilmington like a grass fire, brought into port on the steamer Kate out of Nassau. In New Orleans, the disease was a well-known adversary, but no one had ever seen a case in Wilmington before. They burned tar to sweeten the air, and the clouds of noxious fumes hung over the city hills for weeks. The editor of the Journal complained that he could drive down the main street of town at noon and see no other vehicle save the doctor's buggy or a hearse. More than four hundred people died before the cold weather set in and checked the plague. In October, the remaining townspeople sadly compared notes as to which neighbors had died of the fever and which had fallen at Sharpsburg.

With the native Wilmingtonians weakened by fever and war, the new folk took up dominance. Tens of millions of gold were pouring into port, brought by blockade runners and only partially sent along to General Lee, and yet even those partial transfusions were keeping the armies of Lee and Joe Johnston in the field. Bachelors jointly rented the elegant big houses on the hills, and the opera house was filled with bawdy songs and Negro minstrel acts. And then the Federals began the total bombardment of the Lower Cape Fear with more than six hundred guns to Fort Fisher's forty-four.

The fighting was bloody and inevitable: Confederate dead and wounded were laid out in rows within the roofless walls of St. Philip's Church. For the first time, the Lower Cape Fear was open to the enemy, and in February, the full might of the Union navy rolled up the river, obliterating what it could along the way. Blockade-running days were over, and hunger would soon follow.

🌿 🌿 🌿

The news came to Deepwater ahead of the Union ships in a flurry of hysteria and a racket of jumbled wagons, carts, and buggies hurrying upriver out of Wilmington. Dozens of slaves walked alongside the tide of vehicles, some of them wandering through the plantations as though they were animals caught in the light of a hunter's torch. To Laurel's surprise, they were no less frightened of the Yankee invasion than their masters.

David came in from the fields, his face a study in consternation. He called them together over the table to tell them the news. Levi, as always, sat on his right side, smiling happily at the familiar faces round him, talking quietly to himself. Now four, he could understand much of what was said to him and even answer back in simple sentences. But Laurel knew that Levi's mind would never grow much past where Seleta was now at nine, and likely not even reach her cleverness.

David said it right out with no preamble. "Wilmington has fallen to the Union. I heard it this morning."

"Folks are running away," Bill said solemnly. "Will the soldiers chase them?"

"There may be no soldiers at all, son. Right now, they're running away from the ships, is all."

"Will we evacuate, too?" Seleta asked.

The whole table turned to her in wonder. "Where did thee hear that word?" David asked.

Seleta flushed slightly, almost smiling a bit in her pride. "I read it in my history. Will we, Father?"

He shook his head. "Not unless we have no choice. The bondsmen will need our help more than ever now, and it will be easier than ever to get them north to free states with the Yankees controlling the river. Our duty is to keep the railroad running, to keep ourselves safe, and our fields producing." He glanced at Bill. "We will do our duty."

Laurel asked, "What do you hear of casualties?" And then she could have bitten her lip, for Seleta burst into tears suddenly, her thin veneer of calm broken through at last. "Ah, darling," Laurel crooned, leaning over and hugging her daughter. "I'm sorry, it will be all right, I doubt the soldiers will trouble with Deepwater much."

"That's likely correct," David said, his voice held in check by supreme control, Laurel could tell. "We have no slaves, we farm only tobacco, and the only foodstuffs we have will not tempt them overmuch. The Yankees are civilized men, thee will see. They are here to liberate this land from the scorch of slavery, and when they discover how we have aided them, they'll not trouble us."

But Seleta did not look convinced. She tried to staunch her tears, but her mouth trembled out of control. Laurel reached for her and murmured what words of comfort she could.

"Folks say they'll burn everything, and the places closest to the river'll go first," Bill murmured.

"They won't burn Deepwater," David said firmly.

"How will you keep them from doing it?" his son asked him. The question hung between them silently with palpable shape.

Without thinking, David said, "We will fly a Union flag from the top of the roof. Or perhaps down at the dock where it can be clearly seen from the river—" At the shocked looks from his family, he stuttered to silence.

"That is impossible," Laurel said softly. " 'Twould be better to leave this place forever than to do such a thing."

David glanced at the indignant set of his son's jaw, at the horrified glance of his daughter and said quickly, "Well, I suppose thee is right as usual, Mother. No Union flag. But we will send messages somehow to the Union fleet to tell them that here a family stays who is loyal to the abolitionist cause." He smiled ruefully. "May we agree on that at least?"

Seleta rose abruptly from her seat at the table and fled the room. Laurel put out her hand and stopped David from rising. "Let her go. She's too upset to hear reason now. Give her some time to get over her fear."

"She better learn to live with it," Bill said solemnly. "We all best, because now our worst nightmares are here for certain."

🌿 🌿 🌿

The following night, the Yankee gunboats reached plantations downriver and blasted them into charred fragments of their former glory. A few were demolished; others were not molested, and no one could say why one was saved, another destroyed. Families who chose to stay on the river moved out of their homes and into small outbuildings, hoping that the shells would be directed where they were not.

Rumors flew upriver, and some said that if the master of the house pledged loyalty to the Union and promised to free his slaves, then the plantation would be left unscathed. Others said that if such an oath were given, that master's neighbors would tear his house down around his treasonous ears themselves. Still others doubted that any Union captain had the authority to accept such a promise and that they were simply toying with the defenseless farmers, trying to impress the South with their power and willingness to use it.

Men all over the county quickly left for war. The Cape Fear Minutemen, a local troop organized and enlarged after the taking of Fort Macon and Fort Caswell, swelled to more than a thousand, and they all took the Wilmington–Weldon railroad to Raleigh to the training camp to learn to be soldiers. Cheered and paraded through the streets of Wilmington, the would-be gallants left, and those who stayed behind were made to wonder if they were lesser men. Meanwhile, the evacuations continued.

Night and day, the carriages trundled past until Laurel felt certain the entire city of Wilmington, all the villages surrounding it, and every house along the river must be emptied as last year's wasps nests. The railroad, said to be the lifeline of the Confederacy since Wilmington was providing more supplies to General Lee than any other Southern port, was so crowded with military shipments that passengers were refused space. Every buggy in the city, it was said, was commandeered, and those who had scarcely walked a mile in their lives were now forced to march for hours.

Slaves from abandoned plantations wandered freely now, some of them staying with relations on other places, others going to the nearest open door. Kitchen gardens were stripped by thieving, hungry refugees, and any old shack or lean-to was likely to house some poor, confused wanderer.

Two nights after the news came that a nearby plantation was shelled, a young man came to Deepwater after nightfall, and he pounded loudly on the door as though he had faced the Devil himself and was no longer afraid of anything a mere master's house could hold. David went to the door with an air of concern, for the usual refugees who knocked were so timid that their scratchings could scarcely be heard. Laurel stood well back with the lamp, having shooed Bill and Seleta up the stairs out of the way.

It was a slave from Orton, a nearby plantation, the closest thing they had to a neighbor to the south that was still standing. Even Laurel recognized the man, a mulatto hand of about twenty years whom the master of Orton had been grooming as a trainer for his hunting ponies.

David welcomed the man courteously, but Laurel could see the wariness in his body. It was entirely possible that the master of Orton himself had sent the man to spy, under guise of requesting refuge. It was not the first time the possiblity had occurred to her, now that she no longer knew who was friend and who was foe.

"This the place fur runaways?" the man asked belligerently.

David took some time before he answered. "This is a house of peaceful Friends," he said. "We take no part in conflict, and we make welcome all who come to our door."

Laurel could see he was going to make the man ask for what he wanted, and the man was loath to ask for anything. She stepped nearer to him, so close that she could smell the sweat of fear. In that moment, she knew he was as panicked as any of them. "Come into the kitchen," she said, "and take some comfort by the fire. I have some fresh coffee boiling."

" 'Druther have buttermilk," the slave said sulkily. "You got some o' that?"

Laurel laughed ruefully. This slave had already learned to cover his fear with bravado. He would make a good freedman. "You are from Orton, are you not?" she asked, leading him to a seat and handing him the buttermilk jug and a cup. He quickly poured and downed a cup, pouring a second one with scarcely a pause. "I believe I've seen you out at the stables."

"I de head man wid' de brutes," he said scornfully. "De brute in charge o' de brutes." He glared at her. "But I got a name, same's any man." He glanced up as David came in with a bundle of blankets, a change of clothing, and a pair of old shoes. "I be Rufus."

"Why are you running away?" Laurel asked.

"Did thee hear the Yankees have taken Wilmington?" David asked. "Freedom may well be at hand—"

"Cain' come too soon for me, suh," Rufus said. "I ain' waitin' 'nother minute."

"Were you ill-treated?" Laurel asked. She could not say why she had to know the answer to that question from every fugitive, she only knew she had to ask.

Rufus sighed mightily and spoke as though he stood a good many years and miles away from where he was in the moment. "My woman be de servin' gal for missus. She stand behind her an' reach her de salt an' syrup an' stuff she call for. She cain' read or nuthin', but she a smart woman, an' her daddy be able to spell an' read, an' he goin' to teach our young'uns once dey come."

"Why didn't he teach his own daughter to read?" David asked.

"She sold to 'nother master when she but a little gal, an' only lately come back to Orton. I see her an' I jump the broomstick wid' her last spring."

Laurel smiled to herself. The slaves so needed some sort of ritual to formalize their weddings, births, and deaths that they had invented their own custom of "jumping the broomstick" with their intended bride to signify their intentions to live together as man and wife.

"Anyhow, she stand behind ol' missus one night, an' ol' massa be wrathful, jus' fit to be tied, he in such a evil mood. Was ravin' 'bout the crops, an' taxes, an' the triflin' niggers he got to feed, an' say, 'I gonna sell 'em, I swear fo' Christ, I gonna sell 'em South sure as I sit here.' An' ol' missus ask which ones he gonna sell, an' tell him to spell it out so my woman don' hear. Massa spell out R-U-F-U-S an' G-A-B-E. 'Course my woman stood there, not bat any eye, an' makin' believe she stone deaf like always, but she was packin' dem letters up in her head, an' soon's as she finish de dishes, she run quick to her daddy an' say 'em to him just like massa say, an' he say, quietlike, 'Dat Gabe an' Rufus.' So I lit out. Nex' mornin', massa come an' see I be gone, an' he got to cussin' an' ravin' so he took sick. He say missus go to town an' tell de sheriff, but she say she not settin' foot off de land wid all de Yankees about—"

"How does thee know all this?" David asked, "if thee escaped?"

"I come back to lie wid my woman," he said simply, not bothering to soften his words for Laurel's benefit. "I come back each night, but she tell me to go on now, an' save myself, 'cause massa soon be well an' when he is, he goin' be righteous wrathful for sure. So I goin' north. I buy her for myself soon's as I get my stash save up."

"You don't need to purchase her," Laurel said, "she'll be free soon enough, and so will you. You might want to consider being patient a while longer, with freedom so near at hand."

Rufus snorted scornfully. "I 'preciate dat word, missus, but de Yankees ain' God, an' it goin' to take more den a few gunboats to make my massa an' all o' de white folks give us up. I take my chance now, 'fore he send me someplace where I never get loose. My woman goin' to birth our son soon, an' he be free or I be dead tryin'."

"Thee is right, of course," David said, glancing at Laurel as if to ask why she would suggest otherwise. "Thee has been patient long enough."

David took the man out to the barn then, for the usual questioning process. He interviewed each refugee carefully now: was he or she smart enough, strong enough, and committed enough to make the trek to freedom? Where before, he might have accepted most any runaway, now David would not take in any slave who ventured a knock at the door. "We have to be sure they won't bolt under pressure," he said, "and maybe imperil the whole system and hundreds more who will come behind them."

There was more, she knew, that he did not say. A new law had passed in North Carolina that punished slave insurrection with death. The sentence included any man who helped a slave to freedom.

Laurel watched as the young man walked away into the darkness, the broad strength of his shoulders impressive even at a distance. He seemed to her, in that moment, to embody all the covert, repressed energy and anger of an entire race of men. Not a chance in hell, she thought, that Rufus would be taken alive.

And likely, not a chance in hell that he would see his woman and son again either.

❦ ❦ ❦

Laurel took stock of their provisions daily now, for meal and salt were low, and bacon would not last until the shoats were fat enough to slaughter. She said nothing to David about it and only vowed to cut whatever corners she could, to manage a bit more efficiently, and hope that soon something would happen and God would provide for them.

The few papers they could get were from Raleigh and Richmond and the stories they told did nothing to encourage her that the war would pass them without harm. Thirteen North Carolina counties were under Union control, along with all their crops, naval stores, and weapons. New Bern, Plymouth, Morehead City, Beaufort, Edenton, and Elizabeth City were all lost, and Goldsboro looked like the next target for the Yankee troops.

Worse than the mere facts of the occupation was the word that trickled down from refugees and travelers through the region. One man stopped on his way south to Charleston and took a meager supper with them in exchange for some fresh news.

"New Bern looks like the Mongols swept through, madam," he said dolefully. "Nothing's standing for a twenty-mile radius of the town. And outside, when you come on a farm still standing, the buzzards hover over everything like Satan's own. Dead horses, cows, chickens—they killed everything they could catch. The walls of the houses are scribbled on and hacked with sword cuts, and the writing—" He stopped at David's warning look. "Well, 'tis of a mean nature, madam, you can rest assured. If folks could see what the Yankees have done to that good land, they'd hate the name of Lincoln and his legions through all eternity. It just goes to show what a godless foe we're up against."

David scowled and ended supper that night as swiftly as he decently could, ushering the man to a cot in one of the least comfortable rooms in the house. Laurel knew why. Her husband hated to hear ill of those who were supposed to be bringing salvation. He could not abide the fact that the Yankees might not be all good, all righteous, but prey to the same weaknesses and evils of any other troop of men bent on a mission of destruction.

Laurel began hiding what food she could keep from the refugees and the scavengers, tying up small packets of meal and packing pork in barrels. It might go sour or it might save their lives. She also practiced with Seleta and Bill where they were to go and hide if the bummers came through, the deserters and vagabonds who seemed to trail ahead of and behind the troops, both Confederate and Union.

Seleta had become afraid of different parts of Deepwater, places where she might have played easily with no fear a few months before. She would not go close to the woods, the tall rows of corn, or the edges of the swamp. But Laurel had a new hiding place for them, deeper in the swamp, and she was firm that all three children should be disciplined to use it. As Laurel led Bill and Seleta to her chosen hiding place under a large bee tree, Seleta grasped her arm and shrank back from a trek that was a mere adventure a year before.

"There's nothing in the swamp that will hurt you," Laurel said, though she felt the inadequacy of her words even as she spoke them. "And Yankees won't go into the swamp nearly as quick as they will the woods."

"Then they're not as stupid as folks say," Seleta said, shivering and glancing about her up to the thick cypress trees and moss that hung down almost to their shoulders.

"We should be refugeeing with the rest of them," Bill sulked. "There's no reason to stand around to shake their hands as they come up the veranda and set fire to the place, no matter what Father says."

Laurel ignored them both and brought them to a huge live oak in the middle of a small patch of ground, edged by a murky pond. "If the Yankees come, and we get separated for any reason, I want you each to run for this bee tree as fast as you can run. Don't look back and don't wait for the other one. We'll bring some provisions and hide them here, some blankets and a lamp, and I'll tell your father where we'll be."

"What about Levi?" Bill asked.

"I'll get to him. Remember now, this is our new place, forget the old one—"

"How long must we wait?" Seleta asked, looking around fearfully. "What if it gets dark?"

"It may well," Laurel said firmly, "but you must keep faith that we'll all meet here and stay where you can be found. If it gets dark, simply make a nest for yourself under a brush nearby and don't move."

"And don't make a fire," Bill said stoutly, now caught up in the spirit of the plan.

"No fire. 'Twould only give away your hiding place. And you must tell no one about our place, not even your friends." She let her voice grow as somber as she felt. "This is not a game anymore. This new hiding place is to be our secret, and you may tell no one."

"Because the Yankees might get them and torture them to make them tell," Bill nodded.

"No." Laurel sighed. "The Yankees aren't given to torture of innocent civilians, I'm sure. You're not to tell because we cannot be sure who is our friend and who our foe these days."

"Because of Father," Bill said with a flash of indignation.

Laurel took her son by the arm firmly and pulled him around sharply to face her. The abrupt and unfamiliar anger in her gesture startled both children, and they froze. "You will not say such a thing again," she said to her son, fixing him with her eyes. "Do you understand me?"

Her son nodded, his eyes wide.

"Your father is a man of principle, and he lives by a code few others would abide. Whether you agree with his beliefs or not, whether I agree with them, does not change the fact that your father is a good man who has the courage to stand up for goodness in a world where there's too little of it for all of us." She paused, letting go of William's arms a little. Her voice softened. "It isn't easy to be your father."

Seleta murmured, "It isn't easy, sometimes, to be our father's children either."

Laurel reached out and pulled her daughter to her, holding both her children in a long, firm hug. "Nothing's easy these days, chickens. But we have a home, we have each other, and we have much to be thankful for, I'd say. Now let's talk about Levi. Who will be responsible for seeing that he is safely brought here?"

William glanced at Seleta for corroboration and then said, "We both will."

Laurel shook her head. "That won't do. One may grab him and run for the hiding place and then the other one will hunt for him and waste precious time. Someone needs to be responsible for Levi, and it should be only one of you."

"Then I'll do it," Bill said. "I can run fastest, and he tags along with me more than with 'Leta anyway."

"You are not to leave him then," Laurel said. "No matter what happens, son, you cannot leave him behind. Do you understand?"

"Yes, Mother. I won't leave him."

Laurel sighed and turned again toward the house, holding both her children's hands in hers. "Well then, that's settled. And we can all sleep a little easier knowing that we have a plan, at least. If the Yankees come, that is. They may not trouble Deepwater a whit. Your father seems to think they'll—"

"Father's wrong," Bill said calmly. "They'll trouble us a good whit, I'd say, and soon."

Laurel, surprised, turned and stared at him for an instant. The voice and attitude was that of a young man, not a boy. When had her son grown so poised and mature, right beneath her nose? And then Bill nonchalantly stopped and yanked a spur of dandelions off their stalks, blew their fuzz away, and tossed the remainder at his sister, looking for all the world like a twelve-year-old boy once more. Laurel smiled in relief. Nothing was changing *that* fast, at any rate.

🌿 🌿 🌿

That night as she told David about the hiding place and plans to keep the children secure, she was once more surprised. To her amazement, her husband was angered by the very idea that such a decision had been made, and without his approval. They were in bed, and he had withdrawn to the very edge on his side, turning to face her, his voice cold in the darkness.

"If I wanted to run and hide from the Yankees, I would have done so along with the rest of the rebels on the river. We have nothing to fear from them!"

"How can you say such a thing?" Laurel asked. "They have shelled half the houses on the river, they've laid waste to New Bern and thirteen other cities all around us!"

"I trust that the Lord can see the difference between them and us, and so can General McClellan. When he comes down the road to Deepwater, I want to meet the man with my family by my side, proud to make deliverance welcome on our lands."

"Oh for pity's sake, David," she moaned, "it's all very well and good to put your trust in God, but I cannot place such unwavering faith in Yankee soldiers. They're only men, and fighting men at that! Who knows what sorts of lusts may come on them in the heat of battle? I won't risk my children to that faith!"

"Then it's not much of a faith, Laurel. What if Abraham had said the same thing to God? No, the children will stand alongside us both and face whatever comes. There is more danger for them alone, in the swamp, than there ever will be on their own front stoop—"

"Facing five hundred Yankee guns!" Laurel sat up, her mouth set as stiffly as her spine. "I'm sorry, David, but I cannot agree. Seleta is too young and fair to provide such a temptation, and Levi—I cannot imagine what such a sight might do to his poor mind. If you must sacrifice a child to your principles, then it must be William, but the other two will be gone the moment I see a single Bluecoat. And if anything happens to my firstborn son, I shall never forgive you *or* your God."

David stared at her in the darkness, a great sadness coming over his face. "I never would have believed thee could say such a thing," he finally said softly. "That thee could defy me in this way. And over an issue of faith."

She put a hand on his shoulder to gentle her words. " 'Tis not about faith, David. 'Tis about facts. The facts are that when the Yankees come, they'll know little and care less about how many bondsmen you have personally refuged and helped to freedom. They won't know or care that you're a man of principle, they'll only know that you have land, food, and other things they'll want. Seleta must not be one of them."

Seeing she was strong in her convictions, David slumped down next to her, draping one arm across her lap. Heaving a sigh, he was quiet for a good while. "The war will change so many things," he said.

"It already has," she agreed.

"I suppose thee will now become like the women of Boston and New York and begin to demand the vote. Thee will want emancipation just like the Negroes."

She chuckled lightly. "And Free Love. Don't forget that."

He laughed and squeezed her waist. "I have seen little that's free about love, married or otherwise," he said ruefully. He leaned up and kissed her gently. "But I would gladly pay the price all over again."

She slid down into his arms, opening her mouth under his. The practiced feel of his lips upon hers drew from her the same response it always did, a deep sense of warm belonging, as though she were coming home after a long absence.

The next morning, Laurel stood at the window watching Levi play on the grass under the back window. He was running after a small butterfly that ambled in circles just a foot above the clover, and the boy ran in the same witless circles that the butterfly drew in the air. He was still the most beautiful child she had ever seen. Watching him was a fine blend of pride and grief, joy and the deepest sorrow she had ever known. She tapped on the glass to get his attention. He looked behind him, straight above him, down at his feet, and all around without turning toward the source of the sound. She leaned down and threw the window open, calling his name. Even with the clear sound of her voice to follow, it still took Levi more than a few moments to find her and focus, smiling broadly, at her face.

"Child, did you have your breakfast yet?" she called.

He nodded happily.

"You did? What did you eat?" She often wondered if Levi needed to eat anything but air, so weightless did he seem on the earth. Cassie, the cook, got annoyed with him easily and shooed him away when she'd let the others get underfoot. Laurel wondered if he would be fed at all if she did not keep track.

Levi thought for a moment, his brow furrowed in concentration. Then he beamed in victory. "Milk!" he cried up to her.

"Is that all?"

He nodded jubilantly.

She slammed down the window and hurried to the kitchen. "Cassie, did you feed Levi breakfast this morning?"

"Yes'm," Cassie drawled. Not yet eight o'clock and she was already weary, at least in her voice. She turned around from the fire and put her hands on her hips as if expecting a challenge.

"What did he eat?"

"Don' know what he et, missus, but I put plenty on dat boy's plate."

"He says he had milk."

She shrugged. "He got 'pone an' grits, like de other two. Dat dere's his plate." She gestured to a pile of dirty dishes still in the scouring pan.

Laurel took up a plate and saw that, indeed, it had the remnants of corn pone and grits on it, likely a decent meal for the boy. She sighed and set it down again. "I guess milk is the last thing he had, and that's all he remembers now. It's hard to know what he means sometimes."

Cassie shook her head scornfully. "He don' mean nothin'. But I feed him good, 'gardless."

Laurel patted the cook on the shoulder by way of apology for doubting her and went on outside to where Levi still cavorted in the sunny clover. "Levi, where's Billy?"

The boy looked around, confused.

"Where's Billy, Levi? Did you see him today?"

Levi looked all around as though to spy his older brother, but as he pivoted, he stopped, frozen in his movements, focused on what was coming down the road toward the house. A cloud of moving dust with a distant clanking of metal and jingling of spurs. The soldiers were here at last!

Laurel stood stock-still with Levi's hand in her own, watching chaos approach. Several dozen men were on horseback, some leading the troops, some riding alongside, and the dust from the horses' hooves roiled almost up to the animals' bellies. The foot soldiers marched in long ranks, their muskets on their shoulders—she could not make out the color of the uniform from this distance, and she put one hand to her eyes to shade them from the sun, the better to see—and then a flag fluttered into view, held by one of the cavalry to the rear. A dark field with light stripes and stars—a United States flag!

"Yankees," she whispered, horrified. Where was David? Seleta? Every plan she had made, every contingency she had thought of now went right out of her head, and she turned in a panic, clutching Levi's hand, calling, "Yankees! Yankees!" as she ran with the boy back into the house. She burst into the kitchen, hollered to Cassie and put her into a tizzy, and then looked out the window once more. They were closer still, and then she saw David hurrying to the house from the fields. Bill was running from another direction, and Seleta was still no where to be seen.

Levi began to scream, understanding at last that something was badly amiss. Laurel rushed to the stairs and shouted up for her daughter, but there was no answer. Praying she had already made her way to the hiding place, Laurel turned to see David pushing Bill into the house ahead of him and turning to take his stand on the porch. Bill rushed in, she pushed Levi toward him, shouted, "Get to the bee tree and wait for me!" and yanked the door open to stand alongside her husband.

David turned and shouted at her, "Stay with the children!" but she ignored him. She knew that if the Yankees were to be persuaded that Deepwater was no threat to the Union, she would have to show them that a family lived here, a woman with children, with no slaves, a plain life with few luxuries worth taking. She turned and called out, "Cassie! Cassie, come out here!"

Cassie stuck her head out the door, the whites of her eyes showing like the hind end of a terrified deer. "I ain' comin' near no Yankees!" and she slammed the door again.

By this time, the leaders of the division had halted the troops a good ways from the house, put them at rest, and proceeded ahead to stop several yards from the porch. One man dismounted and strode up briskly, saluting David as he stopped before him. Laurel gripped her hands together to keep them from visibly shaking, but she knew her voice, if she were called upon to speak, would betray her fear. She could see no obvious sign of dread in her husband's stance.

"Sir," the Yankee said loudly, "I would address the master of this place."

"Thee is addressing him."

"Sergeant Jordan, sir, United States Army."

"Thee is welcome here," David said calmly. "Deepwater farm has no master, however, for we have no slaves. We are a family of Friends, and we take no sides in this conflict."

"Quakers?" The sergeant peered behind David the better to take in a view of Laurel, who kept close to the side of the porch. She dropped her eyes and pulled her bonnet forward, struck mute. But then, she pushed herself to leave the shadows of the porch and go forward to stand closer to David.

"We have little to spare, but we will share that little with you," she said reluctantly. She glanced around at a noise behind her to see Cassie peering out the window, pressed against the glass as though the curtains might hide her ample body from view.

"Are you secessionists?"

"We take no sides," David repeated.

"Are you abolitionists, then?"

Her husband hesitated. "We abhor slavery, sir. We have refuged bondsmen and women who have sought to escape it. But we take no sides."

"Ha!" shouted the sergeant in sudden, derisive delight. "You take no sides, eh? I'm certain your neighbors see your point of view exactly, sir."

David gave him a thin smile. "Thee surely has heard of the position of the Friends before?"

"Ah, yes," the man said, shaking his head, "I've surely seen my share of Quakers. Now," he looked about him appraisingly, "Who is that within?" He pointed at the moving curtain and put one hand on his pistol at his belt.

"Cassie, come out!" David called firmly.

An answering wail of terror came from within.

Laurel whirled and opened the door, grabbed the woman's arm, and dragged her out on the porch. "The sergeant needs to see that you are not armed," she hissed at Cassie, pulling her forward out of the shade.

"Who are you?" the sergeant asked Cassie directly, stepping closer.

"Cassie, suh," she cried out with a squeak.

"Are you a slave, woman? This man says he don't own none."

She shook her head indignantly, suddenly finding her true voice, the tone that thundered at Billy whenever he snitched something from the kitchen behind her back. "I be free as you, suh," she said. "No man own me!"

The sergeant smiled ruefully as he gazed her bulk up and down. "I can see that now, ma'am." He turned back to David. "We'll be bivouacking in your fields, sir, and we'll require what provisions you can spare, as well as fresh water."

"Since we are not rebels, will thee give me a receipt for what foodstuffs thee takes? I understand that those loyal to the Union cause may apply to the United States government for repayment."

Laurel all but goggled at her husband's boldness.

The sergeant frowned. "I'm sorry, sir. That rule applies only to those provisions taken from the Free States, not from those who have seceded. You may not be rebels, but you live on rebel soil and whatever comes from that soil is rightfully United States property." He saluted one more time, turned on his heel, and went back to his horse. Laurel drew closer to David and they watched together as a phalanx of mounted men gathered about the sergeant, orders were given, and the men dispersed over the lower fields of Deepwater like so many blue locust.

"Ah my God, it has come at last," David said.

Laurel listened carefully to the tone of his voice, and it seemed to her there was almost a sense of triumph, a thrill of anticipation there that chilled her. She thought then suddenly of Seleta, of the boys hidden and wondering in fear at the bee tree, and she whirled from him, raced through the house, and hurried into the swamp to find them.

To Laurel's vast relief, she found all three children huddled under the bee tree, trails of Spanish moss hiding them from view. Seleta was holding Levi on her lap, weaving strands of the moss together to make hair for a small doll she had made of twigs and ribbon. Bill was curled up next to them, dozing in the shade. Levi spied her, shouting out "Mama!" happily, ignoring Seleta's hush.

"Have the Yankees gone?" Bill sat up straight as a poker, now wide-awake and ready to run.

"No, they're still there, but you can come back to the house, and we'll sneak upstairs. Seleta, I don't want you to be seen outdoors. Where were you when you saw them?"

"In the pole beans. I was coming up with the pan when I heard Cassie say, 'For Gawd!' and I ran round to see, then I ran straight here without stopping."

"Good girl."

"Are they going to burn us out?" Bill asked anxiously.

"No, no, they're only going to stop for a bit and eat and then go on. Your father told them we were loyal to the Union, and Cassie told them she wasn't a slave—"

Seleta laughed. "I bet she did!"

Laurel joined her laughter and gathered her brood together, herding them back toward the house. "The plan worked well, and that's good. Think of this as a rehearsal, children. Next time you see uniforms of any stripe, do exactly as you've done today."

Seleta's smile wavered then. "The next ones might not be so civilized," she murmured.

Laurel's heart twisted in her breast that her daughter should have to know such an apprehension, that she must live in a world where men might not be, indeed, civilized enough to leave intact a girl still in short skirts, no matter what the political sympathies of her parents.

The Yankee troops gradually spread out over the land that night and the next day, until there was hardly a place Laurel could look that did not have a small tent, a fire, a line with drying clothes, a stack of muskets leaning against each other. She thanked God a hundred times a day that Deepwater's crop was not something edible; as it was, she knew they had stripped the equivalent of ten rows for pocket tobacco. The corn was gone, every apple and peach and plum from the trees, the kitchen garden was pillaged, and her chickens were plundered by half. The sergeant formally commandeered two pigs, but left the shoats to fatten. She ventured out the second day to find the potato hills dug out as though by a man-size woodchuck, and she rushed back into the house weeping.

"Never mind," David consoled her. "We'll get by. The army needs it more than we do."

"How can you say such a thing?" Laurel wept angrily. "They have but to march another five miles, and they can clean out the next farmer! We have to stay here and starve!"

"We'll not starve," he soothed her, patting her shoulder. "God will provide for us handsomely, He always has."

There was little she could say to that, of course; there never was an answer to faith but more faith. And she accomplished nothing, she knew, by damaging his confidence. But she began to watch the soldiers with a fine-edged if mute resentment. When she heard them laugh and sing, when the fiddles and the pipes began each night, she begrudged them every moment of pleasure. They might be the ones on the side of righteousness, but there was nothing righteous about their bellies and their thieving hands.

Seleta spent a good deal of time in her room, and when Laurel went to her, she often found her on her knees. "Are you asking God to take them away?"

"I'm asking Him to help me understand," Seleta murmured. "Why should men wish to fight and kill each other for such a thing as slavery?" she beseeched Laurel. "Women would never do such a thing. Don't you think so, Mother?"

"Well, of course, they will tell you that it is not for slavery alone. They'll say it's for the cause of freedom, for states' rights, for the duty to save the Union, for a hundred reasons that somehow, taken all together, make them want to go to war. But I have sometimes thought they must go to war regardless, and they must work to find reasons to do so every so often, just to make them feel alive."

"It makes me feel dead, just to see them here," Seleta said.

Laurel went to her and embraced her. "They will be gone soon, God willing."

That night, Bill came racing into the house with his face inflamed with anger, rushed past his father, and straight to the closet where David stored his hunting rifles. He snatched a rifle, grabbed some shells, and stopped, panting, when his father called out, "Whoa, Billy! What is thee going to shoot?"

"A Yankee, if I have to!" Billy shouted at his father. "They're ripping up the barn and setting it afire!"

David took Bill by the shoulder and slid the rifle from his grip, as Laurel and Seleta came from the kitchen to see what the ruckus was about. "Slow down, son," he said, "and tell me what thee means."

"They tore up the fences, they got one side of the shed down, and when I told them to stop, they just laughed and kept on piling it on their fires!"

"And does thee think a boy with a gun will stop them?"

"Well, a *man* with a gun might!" Bill raged at David. "You take it, then, and make them stop!"

David shook his head slowly and led his son to the table, pushing him gently in a seat, placing the rifle on the table between them. "We are people of God, and we raise arms against no man, whatever his offense. If they burn down the whole farm, we will not defend ourselves with weapons, but with reason. If they will not listen to reason, then we will ask God to forgive them their blindness."

Bill began to weep with frustration. "But they're burning everything!"

"Just some posts and wood, son, that's all it is. It can be replaced easy enough. If they need the wood to cook their food, let them take it."

"Likely, it's our food they're cooking," Laurel said quietly.

David turned and glowered at her, but he spoke only to his son. "Thee must learn a lesson about goodness, son. It is easy to live according to God's word when thee is not beset by trouble. But it is when trouble comes that God's word will most comfort us. Any man can be good when times are good. Can thee be good when times are bad?"

"But how can we stop them?"

"I can go and speak to their commander. If anyone can stop them, then he is the man to do so, I think. And thee can come with me. If thee wants to tell him what thee thinks of his men and their conduct, thee can do so." He waited for a moment to let Bill think of what he had just said. Then, gently, "Are thee ready, son?"

Bill nodded and stood up, taking his father's hand. Together, the two of them went out the door, down the porch, and out the road in the dark toward the campfires, while Laurel and Seleta watched from the window.

It was a long while before they finally returned. Laurel saw them coming from the upstairs window seat in her room. She waited, listening as David saw Bill to his bed, heard the murmur of father and son together, waited until David finally came into the room and closed the door.

"What did they say?"

"The captain said they would likely only be two more nights. He apologized for the wood, but he said they could not risk foraging afield."

"So they're going to continue to take what they need."

David sighed. "At least Bill got to hear the man say the words himself."

Laurel turned back to the window. Out in the darkness, she

could see the scattered fires, the tents, the dark shapes of men hunkered over food, cards, their fiddles—all of them strangers with alien ideals and foreign ways. "What is it all for?" she asked softly. "Why are these strangers on our land? Why are *we* here, for that matter?"

David sank down beside her on the window seat. "Times like this, it's hard to remember. But I think we're here for the reason I told Bill. Just to add to the total sum of human goodness, if we can. Goodness needs replenishment, just like the land. Evil saps it, like weeds. And sometimes it seems that goodness is no longer something to be proud of. No longer respectable. Especially," he said, looking out over the troops in the dark, "in these days of hell on earth. So we'll do what we can to keep it going, at least in this house."

She leaned against him, comforted. At least for the time.

🌿 🌿 🌿

The Yankees left in a far less orderly fashion than they arrived. Rumors came to Deepwater of fighting just north along the Black River. Hands said they'd heard that Sherman's army was coming through, then that the rebels had pushed him back and that Lee's army was moving down from Virginia. The hysteria was wild, the news so varied that it was impossible to know what to believe or expect. But in a flurry of noise and seeming chaos, the Yankees packed their tents, threw their cookpots in the wagons, scattered their fires, and assembled to move out.

David had Levi out in the fields that morning, trying to teach him how to tie the tobacco bunches to the wagon. Each week, he attempted to teach Levi one simple task. Sometimes, Levi was able to learn what it was his father wanted; other tasks were beyond him, no matter how patiently David tried over and over to show him.

Levi's attention was all the more scattered by the presence of the Yankees at the fringes of his horizon. The numbers of men frightened him; the uniforms both lured and repelled him all at once. Laurel could understand that dual response, for she felt it as well.

But it was the horses that most of all sent Levi into a jittering panic. Though he was used to horses, indeed had seen them all his life around Deepwater, he had never seen more than a few at any one time. To see two dozen or more of the beasts all at once, penned in the makeshift corral the Yankees had roped off in the far field, or to hear them call and snort to one another, sent Levi into levels of confusion that he normally was able to surmount. It had gotten so that David would not work Levi on the same side of the house where the horses were tethered, for it was no use to try to get him to listen, his eyes were always fearfully turned to the noises and movements of the horses.

Now as the troops began to move and the horses, catching the excitement, grew more agitated, David was glad he had Levi around back of the fields. But the boy heard the horses regardless, and his body tensed, his eyes wandered to the source of the noise. "Soldier horses," he murmured to his father. "Soldier horses are mad."

"They're not mad," David said gently, "the soldiers are leaving now, and the horses are getting ready. Now, Levi, try to tie this one by thyself," and he handed a cluster of tobacco leaves to his son.

But Levi dropped them on the ground, looking up at his father with stricken eyes. "Soldier horses are leaving?"

David realized then that the fascination was stronger than the fear in Levi. He took him by the hand. "Yes, they're leaving now, and that's a good thing. We want them to go so that we can have our fields back and our food for ourselves. Thee wants to see the horses leaving?"

Levi took his father's hand and tugged hard in the direction of the Yankee tents, pulling him around the house and out into the open road. As they stood there watching, a team of horses was being moved into position before one of the larger supply wagons. Six horses, three handlers, each pulling two animals forward to bully and cajole them into place within their traces. Levi was moaning to himself at the sight of the horses, holding his hands down as though with an effort, as if he wished to run and embrace the horses or fend them away, David could not say which. "Soldier horses!" he said excitedly every minute or so, and David nodded quietly to him, keeping one hand firmly on his shoulder.

Then a mounted soldier hurried by, his horse brushing swiftly by the two last wagon horses as they waited their turn to be positioned. In a second, one of the horses broke, then the second horse, and both of them whirled and snorted, turned and whinnied in confusion, bumping against the tethered horses, making them jolt the wagon and jar it sideways. The driver snatched up his whip and laid it on the nearest horse, hollering to the animal to stand, and that horse broke, reared, and sent the two loose horses into a gallop. They came pounding down the road toward the house, David saw them coming and tried to yank on Levi's arm to pull him aside, up on the porch. Levi slid his arm out of David's hand and stood in the road as the two horses thundered to him, raised his hands in the air jubilantly, and screamed as loud as he could with what seemed to David to be a strange mix of terror and joy. David shouted his name in horror, tried to reach him, but the two horses were on him, separated on either side of the boy like the Red Sea, and then careened past, snorting and crying out in panic, crashing into the far fence to the side of the house.

David reached Levi and swept him into his arms, his face contorted in fear. The child was weeping in exultation, as though God Himself had just brushed his cheek. "You fool!" his father cried. "You might have got killed!"

Laurel touched him on the shoulder, having come out in time to see the near-disaster, and he turned to her, burying their son between them.

"Mama, soldier horses!" Levi shouted at her, turning to point to where the handlers were trying to get the two horses calmed and collected together, one of them limping badly, the other snorting and dancing as though ready for battle.

"I see them, son," she said as calmly as she could. "Why did you run in their way?"

Levi's focus blurred for a moment, and she could tell he was not seeing her. His face softened in a sort of memory, and he murmured, "Levi go with horses. Levi go, too."

She held him tightly against his father. "Levi's not going anywhere," David said, his voice still broken. "Levi stay with Mama and Papa."

Later, as they put the boy to bed, Laurel whispered to her husband, "You did not 'thee' him in the fear of the moment."

"What?" David asked, closing the door softly.

"You said 'you fool, you might have got killed.' "

He shook his head. "If thee says so. I don't know what I said."

"In the moment of terror, you forgot yourself," she said, smiling at him kindly. "Almost as if you forgot God as well."

"Well, I suppose that goes to show that my faith can leave me for a time," he said ruefully. "It rests lightly on my shoulders."

She patted his arm. "I am certain God understands such a lapse. But don't call him a fool ever again." She looked up at him earnestly. "Not ever."

He put his arm around her and led her to the quiet of their room.

❦ ❦ ❦

As the war continued and the Confederacy grew more desperate, David's position of neutrality became increasingly difficult to maintain. Agents for the Southern army were prowling the county, combing out draft resisters and deserters, and religious principles were no longer sufficient reason to keep them at bay.

In Tyrell County, the papers said, a detachment of Confederate cavalry went to a half-dozen farms and commandeered at gunpoint every horse they could find. Some of the animals were actually unhitched from plows out in the fields while their owners looked on in helpless indignation. When a few farmers dared to protest, they were thrown in jail by their own countrymen, the very men who had stolen the horses.

In Cherokee County, farther north, a squad of Confederate soldiers rounded up a group of overage citizens, some of them past sixty years, chained them together like criminals, and marched them more than a hundred miles to Atlanta. There, they were offered the choice of prison or enlistment.

Laurel convinced David finally that he should do as the children were doing: at the first sight of a uniform—any uniform—he was to drop whatever he was doing and hurry for the hiding place in the swamp.

But hiding out could not defend Deepwater from the ravages of war. In the spring of 1863, when Laurel was trying to see how the family could get by with so few workers and stock animals, the news came from Richmond, the Confederacy capital, that all farmers in the state would have to turn over ten percent of all produce—potatoes, corn, rice, beans, bacon, hides, everything—to agents of the Confederacy for taxes.

She went over the books for the last two years since the war began, and David found her at them late in the night, her head in her hand.

"How bad will it be?" he asked.

"Nigh to impossible," she said. "We've sold all we can sell, what's left that they haven't taken. We've been living off less than fifteen percent of what we produce and selling the rest. We don't have any reserves left. If we have to give them ten percent, we'll starve. It's as simple as that."

"What if we put more land to plow?"

"How will we farm it? We don't have the hands we need now, and you're in the fields from morning to night. Even the children do nothing but work these days, and still we are barely able to make it."

"We'll have to put in more corn, then," he said calmly. "We'll take out ten acres of leaf and put in corn, and we'll eat, at least."

"And we'll move the stock to the swamp," she said firmly. "Every chicken but a few, every pig but one or two, just to make it look credible. But all the rest will go to the swamp. The army will simply have to do without my shoats."

He shook his head. "We've never not paid our taxes," he said. "I don't mean to start thieving from the government, Laurel."

"This isn't a government," she snapped at him, "it's a gang of hoodlums. There's no law in Carolina, and no one to stand up to them unless we do it ourselves!" She ran her hand through her hair, wondering in one corner of her mind if this latest trouble would add yet more gray to her black. "I want to be loyal, just as much as you do, but loyal to what? The Confederates are as bad or worse than the Yankees, and none of them care what destruction they leave in their wake. When this is all over—and I pray to God that will be soon!—what will be left of this county for the survivors? Not much, I fear!"

He had listened to her carefully, his face changing little. When she finished, he turned away, glancing about the small library as though he had not seen it for a long while. "So I am to hide out at the bee tree like a young boy? With the chickens and the pigs?"

"What will happen to this family if you are taken by the agents against your will? It's happening, you know, and not all that many miles away. Do you think that you alone will be left untouched by war? As it is, we're barely managing, but we're better off than many. If they take you away, we'll lose this place to taxes, because I can't do more than I'm doing now!"

She thought of all the changes they'd endured since the war came to the Cape Fear. No coffee, no salt, and sugar was as rare as gold. Thank God for the river, and the fish, turtles, and fowl it provided, but since the Yankee took the cows, they'd had no beef, no milk, and no tallow. They'd taken the last of the kitchen garden, and the peach trees and cherries were stripped of fruit. And now they were low on cornmeal; she was mixing it with pea-meal to stretch it, and if she couldn't swap for some soon, she had no idea what she would do.

She began to tick off her fingers. "Bacon was a dollar a pound last year, now it's up to more than five. Corn's going for twenty dollars a bushel, up from five, and a barrel of flour right now, if you can get it, is more than one hundred and twenty-five dollars."

He looked shocked. "It was thirty-five just a few months ago."

"That's what I'm telling you. If you did the books, you'd see it as clearly as I do. We cannot go on like this much longer, but if they take you away, we cannot survive even the winter."

David bowed his head before her despair. "All right," he murmured, "I'll hide out with the children in the swamp, if that's what thee wants."

"It's not what I want," she said, sighing wearily, "it's what must be done. Pride is a luxury we can no longer afford."

"And honor, too?" He rose and left her then, bent over the books.

She put her head down on her arms and for the first time in her married life, regretted that she had chosen a husband whose rigid codes of right and wrong had brought them to this sorry place. They should have refugeed much earlier, but he insisted that he had a duty to keep the Underground Railroad open for those who might need it. They should have left once war broke out, maybe journeyed farther north where there were more Friends to join together. Safety in numbers, surely. The slight he was served so many years ago when he decided to marry her no longer mattered—or should matter. And yet they still lived their lives essentially in isolation . . . all because of David's stubborn pride.

It seemed to her that God did not intend man to be so stiff-necked, no, not with his neighbors, with his wife, or with himself. And what was this doing to his children? Bill went through each day alternately angry and fearful. Seleta rarely left her room except to work her rows; what sort of future could she have here and now? And Levi: the mere start of dust down the road made him babble and jump about, convinced that soldiers and their horses were upon them again.

Laurel slammed the books shut with a sense of finality. It was clear that she must make more of the decisions for the family. David was blinded by his faith and his pride, and could not be depended upon to do what was best for all of them anymore. Somehow, either by persuasion or by coercion, she must keep them safe, whether he saw the sense of it or not.

🌱 🌱 🌱

A new storm rolled through the Carolinas with the name of General William Techumseh Sherman. His reputation flew ahead of him in print and gossip, and those remaining planters in the Valley spoke of little else but his coming.

Laurel and David poured over the accounts in whatever papers they could find, often a week or two old, at the kitchen table after the children were asleep. Usually the news sheets had been so badly handled that whole sections were missing, and it took the two of them, heads together, to piece together the sense of what they were reading.

"They liken him to a thunderhead of locusts," Laurel murmured, as she read a Raleigh paper David had been able to get from a passing wagon.

"Satan Incarnate," David muttered as he read another account from a Wilmington journal, with fresh news from Atlanta. "Tecumseh, the bloody-handed," he read aloud. "The horrors visited upon Georgia are already legend. North Carolina must arm herself to resist a plague more potent than the Black Death, more destructive than the onslaught of Attila the Hun," David finished, his voice somber and measured.

"What did he do in Georgia?" Laurel asked. "Do you find any details in your pages? These I'm reading sound as though it's already common knowledge and need not be discussed again—"

David read on quickly, silently, and then put the pages down. "Burning, pillaging, looting. I guess it's not Sherman so much as his foraging parties. They scout out from Sherman's flanks, two or three days' ride from the main columns. And so, of course, they're not really under any real supervision by the officers. I suspect they do as they please."

Laurel's eyes widened in horror. "Where is Sherman now?"

David scanned quickly through the rest of his pages. "He's already done for Charleston. He's moving north, up the seaboard."

Laurel had by then found a passage that related the same information, and she read aloud, "Leaving a howling waste in his wake."

"Yes," David murmured. "We've been lucky so far. The only troops we've seen have been more or less civilized. We've lost stock and provisions to them—"

"But not our lives," Laurel finished for him. "Not our home."

"They say he'll cross the border from South Carolina by the end of February."

"That's only a week away!" she said, dismayed. "Are there no Confederate troops to stop him?"

"Joe Johnston's moving south, they say, to meet Sherman and beat him if he can, but there's not a soldier in the state who's not north with Lee in Virginia."

"So we're to face him unprotected."

David took one of her hands in his. "There's nothing new in that, dearheart. We've been protected by nobody but God since this whole mess began. I guess He'll do against Sherman as well as Old Joe can do, or better."

"Somehow," she said sadly, "that's not much consolation. David, I think we should send the children away. At least Levi and Seleta. If Sherman is coming up the river, I don't want them here to see it."

"And where should we send them?" David asked gently.

Of course, Laurel had no answer. There was no answer to give. There was no place safe in the entire South, no trains running for fleeing civilians, no safe refuge even if they could find a wagon and someone to take them. No hope whatsoever. As Laurel ran through the scant possibilities in her mind, she wanted to raise out of her chair and slap David's questioning glance right off his face. He should have seen this coming. Now Sherman was on them, and there would be nothing but prayers to turn him aside.

"If I could dig a hole deep enough," she finally answered, with a voice heavy as her heart, "I would hide them in the bowels of the earth itself. But since I cannot, they must meet Sherman and his hoard alongside you and me. And God help us all."

"He will," David said swiftly. He dropped his head to his hands in prayer.

Laurel watched him for a few moments in silence. She simply could not bow her head along with him one more time. She rose and walked away, leaving him alone in the lamplight.

🌱 🌱 🌱

News came that Sherman had burned Columbia, South Carolina, to rubble. The "bummers," as local people called those foraging parties of Sherman, found a large store of liquor in the city, set fire to bales of cotton and then lost control of the flames. Hundreds of men looted and torched in a drunken spree, and by morning, the capital of the state was nothing but ashes. As Sherman's army marched out of the city the next morning, those remaining inhabitants lined the streets, booing, hissing, and cursing the general and his troops. Sherman never looked back.

His next target was Cheraw, just south of the North Carolina border. Anyone who could read or who had access to gossip heard by two days later that the border had been breached, and Sherman was on Tarheel soil. A letter from one old man in Cheraw was passed from hand to hand until it reached Raleigh, where it was published in papers all over the state.

Laurel read it when she knew she would have a few moments of privacy, and David would not see her response. "There was no place, no chamber, no truck, drawer, desk, garret, closet or cellar that was private to their unholy eyes," the letter said of Sherman's men. "Their rude hands spared nothing but our lives. Squad after squad tramped through the halls and rooms of our home day and night. They killed every chicken, goose, turkey, calf, even down to the dogs. They carried off wagons, horses, broke our buggy, wheelbarrows, garden tools, axes, hatchets, hammers, and burned all the fences. Our smokehouse and pantry were stripped bare, they took every garment of clothing from women and children alike, not even sparing the napkins of infants, blankets, sheets, and every quilt in the house. Anything they did not need, they tore to pieces right before our eyes."

Laurel set down the paper and wiped her eyes, which were wet in sympathy for the poor, unknown victim of such atrocity. She turned to a more recent account of Sherman's movements to read that he was advancing toward the Cape Fear from the south, burning vast acres of pine forests before him as he came.

She set down the paper and rushed to the attic to where she had hidden her small trunk of valuables. Nothing that would interest a looter, surely, even the ravenous scavengers of Techumseh Sherman. Small packets of hair from each child; Bill's first pair of shoes, carefully wrapped in linen. Seleta's first hair ribbons and a lace gown Levi had worn at his first birthday. A few old letters from her grandmother, Della Gage, an old ball gown that her mother had worn in Italy a lifetime ago . . . and the deed to Deepwater.

She fingered the locket at her neck. She had never taken it off, not even when the Yankees came to the door. Should she hide it now? It was the only valuable she had, and she doubted anyone else would ever find it worth the trouble. She slipped it back inside her bodice. It gave her a sense of serenity to feel it there, as always, nestled against her skin like a mother's hand. A source of secret strength. She would not take it off, no, not even for Sherman.

She opened the trunk and stared at the trinkets from her life. Each item meant something to her; little of it would matter to anyone else. And yet to lose it all would be to somehow lose her past. Her children's past. She pulled the trunk to the edge of the attic door and sat on it, thinking where she could hide it that the damn Yankees would never find it. She remembered the most recent story about Sherman. The details of it told more about the man than she cared to know.

He had marched into Fayetteville, and word spread rapidly that the general's first target would be the town's textile mills, the only source of employment for most of the city and hundreds of people around it. Members of the town council and the owner of the largest mill went to Sherman's tent with their hats in their hands, begging him to leave the mills intact. The region was already starving, they pointed out, and no one would lift a hand to stop him from taking anything else he wanted. But would he simply leave the only thing that kept Fayetteville from desolation?

The way Laurel heard the story, Sherman heard the men out without uttering a single word, his face set like granite. Then he quietly growled, "Gentlemen, niggers and cotton caused this war, and I wish them both in hell. On Wednesday, these mills will be blown up. Good morning."

She could expect no quarter, no, not from such a man. Not even for the hair of her children. She opened the trunk and took out the items, carefully arranging them on the floor in order of importance. Rummaging in the attic stores, she found three old tins with tight-fitting lids. She transferred everything she could fit into the tins, lining one of them with the deed, and carried them outside to the back arbor. After a moment's reconsideration, she opened a tin, took off her locket and slid it gently inside the packet that held Levi's first baby hair. She felt naked as a fish without it. There, under the wisteria tree, she dug a hole and buried all that she wanted to save. When she was finished, she leaned against her shovel and looked back at the house. If there were a way to bury her home, she'd keep digging, even if the effort killed her.

If only it were that easy to hide her children. If they could be sealed in tin and buried under the scuppernong vines, she'd do it in a minute. And then let Sherman come and do his worst.

ᘘ   ᘘ   ᘘ

The valley of the Cape Fear had known the two most destructive armies of the nation's two most horrific wars: Cornwallis in 1781 and Sherman in 1865. Both generals chose this region, up and down the river, to decide the military questions of the hours.

Sherman's plan was to sweep through North Carolina and join up with Grant to defeat Lee once and for all in Richmond. The general felt sure that his devastation of the countryside on his way, however, was accomplishing almost as much for the Union cause as his arrival would on the field of battle. He knew that the reports of his destruction of the region were causing hundreds of Confederate soldiers to desert to try and protect their families and properties. And when he found them on the road, he did his best to punish them for their rebel choice and also for their desertion.

Punishment was something Sherman was inordinately good at meting out. After the destruction of Fayetteville, the general paused for a moment, considering the proper strategic move. Northeast was Goldsboro, a rebellious city with a full arsenal and a working mint. A tempting target on the way to Raleigh. To the southeast was Wilmington, the only deepwater port for the whole Southern coastline. A singular arrival decided Sherman's plan.

On the Sunday morning of Sherman's four-day stay at Fayette-ville, the army tug, *Davidson*, sent up from Wilmington, blew a triumphant whistle at the Cape Fear landing. Sherman's army rushed to the docks to pick up the first mail they'd seen since Charleston. But more important, it was clear that the Union forces still had control of the river and Wilmington, too. No real sense in going over already-won ground. Sherman consulted his maps and turned his forces north—away from the river, away from what was left of Deepwater plantation.

But he sent downriver in his stead the "tail" that had been following him since Atlanta: more than twenty thousand slaves who had dropped their hoes and picked up whatever they could carry to join Sherman's march out of the South to freedom. These twenty thousand "useless mouths" had pestered Sherman for a month. Now, he organized them into a separate column, gave them a small military escort, and turned them southeast to Wilmington.

The refugee column gave every appearance of the Israelites leaving Egypt, but without a Moses to lead them. Whatever horses, mules, dogs, cows, old family carriages, wheelbarrows, and carts they had been able to find or steal, they had dragged along, filled with bedding, cookpots, chickens, and babies. One family walked along, led by an old Negro man mounted on a mule. To the sides of the mule were attached pockets made of old tent flaps, a dozen strapped to the mule on both sides, and in each pocket was a black baby, all woolly hair and bright eyes. Some of the mules could barely be seen for their passengers.

The first refugees trickled in one morning while Laurel and Seleta were hanging up wash on the back line. The troops had taken most of the rope, so they had made something to hang the clothes on out of dried wisteria vines. Actually, Seleta said, it worked better than the old rope and sagged less in the middle. She had her mouth full of clothespins, trying to use as few as possible on Bill's breeches, for those were another scarcity at Deepwater. She cried out and pointed up the road, and Laurel followed her hand to see what was coming.

Another cloud of dust, not so high this time thanks to the late rains. Laurel shaded her eyes and braced herself for what was trouble, no matter which side was coming. "Get to the swamp," she said to Seleta. "Where are Levi and Billy?"

"I don't know, Mama," Seleta said, dropping her pins and shoving the clothes in the hamper. As she turned to obey and run toward the hiding place, she took a last look at the people approaching and shouted, "Mama, it's not soldiers. It's niggers!"

"Don't say that!" Laurel said, shocked. She had heard the word come out of her son's mouth but never from Seleta. She turned to see a long wavering column of black faces coming down the road to Deepwater, leading rickety horses, pushing and pulling some of the shakiest conveyances she had ever seen. "Oh Lord," Laurel whispered. "Here's another plague on our house."

"What are they doing?" Seleta murmured, coming closer. All thoughts of running were now out of her head. "Where are the soldiers?"

"There are a few there, I see," Laurel said, squinting across the moving line of people. "I guess they're bringing them back to their owners? Did North Carolina win the war?"

Seleta walked a bit closer, danced actually, in what was the first semblance of almost glee that Laurel had seen from her in the years since the war began. She was struck in the moment by how lovely her daughter was, how gracefully she had grown—and a jarring pain of remorse that her growing years had been so bleak and full of hardship. So many things I wanted for her! Laurel's heart whispered, so much I should have been able to give!

"Look, Mother!" Seleta laughed. "It's the darkies all come home again! The war must be over! We won't have to work anymore!"

David came hurrying from the fields then, with Bill and Levi by his side. He was looking back over his shoulder in agitation, and now behind him Laurel could see that indeed the flood of people down the road was like a long tail of a dragon, dark and undulating and a-rumble with noise. Two squads of cavalry flanked the long, clanking column, flying United States flags.

"What does this mean?" Laurel asked him as he came up to her, took Seleta by the shoulders, and pulled them all up to the safety of the porch.

"It means trouble, thee can count on that," David said nervously. "There must be close to a thousand of them."

"And they're all free," Bill said scornfully. "Same rights as a white man, but half the sense."

"Those soldiers can't possibly control them all," Laurel said, suddenly realizing the peril they represented. "Seleta, take Levi in the house." The boy was capering out at the edge of the steps, close to running up the road to meet the black parade. "Keep him out of sight and you, too. Until we see what this means."

"I can tell you what this means," Bill said sourly. "Every leaf that's near-ready will be stripped, everything that looks as though it could be eaten will be. We'll be living on swamp mud—"

"Bill," David said firmly, "that's enough. At least we have a roof over our heads, these poor souls have nothing. Once they leave, we'll still be better off than most—"

"Who's going to make them leave?" Bill asked.

And there was no time for David's response, for the ranks were now so close that the sheer clamor of their coming made speech all but impossible. To the rear, Laurel could see that the people were already fanning out over the fields as though they planned to set up camp for a millennium. Laurel knew that a quarter-crop would likely be damaged beyond salvage.

The officer greeted David with a halfhearted salute. "Good day, sir," he said with a clipped, Northern accent. "We are transporting refugee freedmen and their families back to their homes or to wherever else they may wish to settle. Do you own this land?"

"We do," David said.

"Well, we have the authority to parcel out half of it to these folks to farm as they see fit. If you cooperate, we will attempt to take as little of your ploughed fields as necessary."

David almost reeled back in shock. Laurel moved closer to him, touching him gently on the back to give him strength. "How is such a thing possible?" he asked. "This is our land!"

"I understand that, sir," the officer said calmly, "but they likely did more to make it productive than you did—"

"We owned no slaves!" David protested. "We helped many of them to escape to the North and freedom! We are Quakers!"

The officer gazed at David silently, weighing his words. "Dissenters. I suppose that must be taken in your favor, then. How much land do you own?"

"Less than a hundred acres," Laurel spoke up swiftly. "We once had more, but we lost it. And a quarter of that's fallow."

The officer turned and looked out over the fields that were now dotted with clusters of black folks with their wagons, their carts, their children. Already, cook fires had been started, and men were foraging at the edge of the woods and the swamp for firewood. "There's nothing in my orders that says I have to give up standing crops to these mules, so whatever fallow acres you have, you might show me where they run," he said quietly. "Since you are Quakers, we'll try to move them down the road."

"There are so many of them," David said in horror.

"Less than half we started with," the officer replied. "In places farther upriver, we left enough to take over whatever we found vacant—or with nobody left to care for it. Whole plantations parceled out and houses, too, so consider yourself fortunate in that sense." He grinned. "If the rebels ever come home, they'll find niggers in their upstairs bedrooms, I wager."

David shook his head. "I cannot believe that the United States government would allow such a thing."

"Right now, General Tecumseh Sherman is the government in these parts, and so far as he's concerned, rebels have no rights at all. But Quakers might be something else again."

"Is Sherman coming here?" David asked.

"No, sir, you're lucky on that score. He's turned north to Richmond. You got only his leavings to worry you."

"But this is a free land," Laurel murmured. "You fought a war to make it free for all people. Is it now the white folk who are to be enslaved?"

The man chuckled genially. "Eloquently put, madam. One of the softest reprimands I've heard since we've been on the road with this lot. As to your enslavement, I'm afraid I can't answer that question. I guess what you do with what's left is up to you. At least you'll answer to no master—"

"None save God," David said.

The officer looked him up and down appraisingly. "Aye, well that's true, I suppose. We'll all answer that call soon enough. But in the meantime, sir, I have a pack of niggers to dispose of, and I mean to do it as fast as I can. If you'll come with me and show me which of your fields you'd least mind giving up, I'll try to accommodate you. You've got one hundred—we'll take fifty and parcel it out to five families."

"But we don't have fifty acres of land to spare!" David protested.

"Those are my orders, sir," the officer said.

"Ten acres of fallow land for each? They'll scarcely be able to live," Laurel said. "What happens when they discover that?"

The man shrugged, brisk now and impatient to be on his way. "That's not my problem, madam, nor yours. I got my orders to give the land to them, but I don't mean to plough it for them, too."

"But it's *our* land," Laurel said again, understanding even as she spoke that it meant nothing. "It was my grandmother's land before me."

"By law, all occupied territory belongs to the conquering nation, madam. That's the rule of war. This land now belongs to the United States government. I suggest you appeal to President Lincoln, if you think you have a case." He doffed his cap politely, the interview obviously over. "I wish you good day."

The officer and his mounted guard wheeled away, back into the eddy and flow of the black folks all about him. Some of them stood stupidly, gazing over the big house of Deepwater as though they were in a dream. Others ignored the white folks and went about their business setting up camp, calling to one another, hurrying to and fro with foodstuffs and firewood as though they were building a small city.

"This isn't fair," David said sadly. "We don't deserve to be treated as one with slave owners, rebels, and soldiers against the Union. Half our land!"

Laurel could not speak. When she thought of all the years she had spent trying to keep the place together, all the rows of tobacco she had picked, bundled, carted to the drying shed, all the nights of poring over the books, trying to make the figures come out to a profit. The sacrifices she had made, the things she had done without—that her children had done without!—that the taxes might be paid, that the land might be saved—and now, it would be handed over, nearly half of it, as well as hand over half of her life—to strange black faces who would forever after be their neighbors. It was too deep a wound for tears.

"You better go with him," she said, her voice quavering. "He means to do the dividing now, and it will be our last chance to have a say in where we stand." She turned without another word to her husband and walked into the house. She passed the children without a sound, trailing one hand up the banister as if it were her only tie to the earth. Seleta stared at her, stricken; Bill started to speak and then closed his mouth. Even Levi stood silently, respectfully, as she passed by them and up to the silent sanctuary of her room.

Laurel lay on the bed carefully, her hands folded on her stomach, her elbows tightly to her sides, closing her eyes as though waiting for death. For her, losing half of Deepwater, half of the land she had held on to so long, the land her grandmother, Della Gage, had fought to hold through the revolutionary war, was indeed very like dying. It felt to her as though a piece of her body had been given away to strangers, never to be her own again. She held her hands still, refusing to pray to God.

"If it is Thy will," she murmured again and again, but the words brought her no peace of mind. "If it is Thy will, then I will submit." But no part of her heart agreed to the submission. No part of her soul wished well on those black folk who would take away her land with no more right to it than a band of roving gypsies. She did not wish for mercy, only justice.

After a long while of silence, when she could hear no comfort from God anywhere in her breast, she rose and went to the window to stare down on the fields below. Now the officer and his men were riding about the land, David was with them, she could see. He walked, because they had had no mount at Deepwater since the last set of troops came through. All about them, black folk thronged and gawked, like flocks of dark guinea hens running to and fro under their feet.

A flood of distaste filled her mouth, the bile of hatred. The first hate she had felt for such people, the same people she had risked everything for so many times, helping them to freedom. This was her repayment for her charity. This was what high principles led to after all was said and done: they might get to keep some of the better fields, but half of it was gone, no matter how many times she had fed some refugee in her kitchen.

She put a weary hand to her eyes, but they were dry with bitter despair. Whatever dreams she might have had for Seleta now were dissolved. There would be nothing extra, not ever in their lives. They could not afford to send her away to be educated or to provide her with anything frivolous or gay. She would likely marry some poor Quaker farmer's son, be expecting their first child inside the year, and grow old very quickly indeed. Old at twenty without ever having known the joy of childhood or girlhood, the heady delight of being young and lovely.

And Bill. He would inherit such a paltry amount of land now, even if they were able to keep it all. And that was a mighty big if, the way taxes were likely to rise after the war. Someone would have to pay for all the carnage, destruction, and waste. And it wouldn't be the Yankees. He would work harder than his father before him and for less.

And little Levi. They would carry the burden of him for all of their days with little hope that they would ever be able to afford the kind of training or help he might need. If it were possible for him to learn a trade, they could now not afford to apprentice him to a kindly master. He would likely be lost in the wilderness of his poor mind forever. All because the Yankees decided that the niggers should have free land.

Niggers. She hated the word in her mouth, but her mind could call them nothing else now. No more principles of sanctity and charity to protect them. They were just like white people. There were fine, decent whites, and there were rascals, riffraff, and no-count scum. In the same way, there were freedmen, men of color, Negroes—and then, there were niggers.

A trickle of remorse slipped under her hands and wormed its way into her breast at the word she rolled around in her mind. Niggers. Were they only niggers because they had nothing? Because they followed the Yankees blindly like a pack of dogs? Or were they niggers because they were going to take something away from her that had been hers all of her life?

She rolled to her side and began to weep with fear and self-loathing. The thought of losing half of Deepwater was so painful, so wrenching to her that she could feel nothing but anger. But it was helpless anger, without a target, for even as she wept she knew that it was not their fault that they had nothing. They had to eat somehow, and her land was no more sacrosanct than any other.

Laurel wept until there was nothing left inside her but dry, gasping hiccoughs. And when she began to quiet, she heard a small scratching noise outside her door. "Come in," she whispered, half hoping that her words were too weary to be heard.

Levi inched his head around the bedroom door and stared in at her. "Mama, you sick?" he asked softly.

She opened her arms and beckoned him forward. He ran hap-

pily to her and snuggled in under one arm, nestling close to her as
he could, one cheek resting on her chin. She could smell the
good-boy smell of him, the smell of earth and water and sunshine
mixed with a sharp, sour smell of the man he would someday
become. "I'm not sick," she said. "I'm sad."

"Because the niggers gonna take our land?"

She drew back and looked at him in amazement. "How did you
know that?"

"Billy said it. Said we gonna have to give it to the niggers now,
'cause of Papa."

"Don't say 'nigger'," she said automatically, "it's ignorant and
cruel."

"Billy said it."

"Well, Billy's wrong to say it, and you can tell him so next time
you hear him."

Levi chuckled at the notion that he could tell Billy anything at
all and be heard. But then he sobered when she did not join his
laughter. "Is Papa gonna give the—the Nee-grows—is he gonna give
them our land?"

"Papa's not going to give it to them," she said wearily, "they're
going to take it. The soldiers are going to give it to them. And that's
why I'm sad."

"Are they going to take it away?" he asked her, his eyes wide
and full of wonder.

She smiled ruefully. "No. No, they can't take it away, son. Even
Yankee soldiers can't do that."

He frowned in bewilderment. "Can we still walk on it?"

"I suppose."

"An' play on it, if we don't hurt the plants?" Levi had been
drilled at an early age that he might go among the crop anywhere
he liked, but he could do no damage to any growing thing there. As
the son of a farmer, feeble or not, it was by necessity his first
lesson.

"Yes, I suppose you can do that, too," she murmured, not
really listening to him anymore. "But we won't be able to plant on
it and work it as our own. No corn, no tobacco."

"Will we be poor?"

Once again she looked at him, surprised. It was really rather
wonderful that he had somehow learned the concept of poor and
not-poor, all by himself. Perhaps his mind was not so dim after all.

"No, we won't be poor," she said firmly. "But we won't have so much as we did before."

"Will we have enough?" he asked.

And with his final question, a sort of peace settled over her. God did, indeed, sometimes send His messages by odd conduits: a burning bush, a dove, and through the questions of a boy who would always be a child.

"Yes," she said finally. "We will have enough." She held him more tightly. "And so will they for once, I suppose. We'll have less than we used to, and they'll have more than they used to, and somehow I guess it'll all work out the way it should." She held him for long moments silently, savoring the closeness. Levi seemed content simply to rest in her arms, something his more restless brother would scarcely ever do. Finally she asked, "What else did Billy say?"

"Oh ho!" Levi crowed happily. "Billy is stupid!"

She smiled. "Why is he stupid?"

"He said, Papa should shoot the soldiers and make them dead."

"Why is that stupid?"

He shrugged eloquently. "More just come. Papa can't shoot them all."

She thought for a moment. There was a wisdom here, something she was loath to let go. "Levi," she finally asked him, "why does Billy blame Papa, do you think?"

He looked at her narrowly, suspecting a trick question. When he saw that she was serious, he subsided into her arms again and relaxed. "I don't know."

She waited patiently. "Can you guess?"

He struggled with something and then said, "Because Papa loves God more than us?"

She took a deep breath. "Do you think that's true?"

He wriggled out of her arms now, impatient with her questions and the effort it took to answer them. "Mama, don't be sad!" he said gleefully, tugging at her arms to pull her to an upright position. "Let's go tell Billy he's stupid!" And he began to laugh and caper about the room at the thought of it. She allowed herself to be pulled along, out the door and down the stairs, for it was certain no more good was going to come of wishing for death, alone on her bed.

The soldiers moved out three days later, taking nearly a thousand refugee blacks with them, and leaving behind a plantation stripped of nearly everything edible or useful. All inside the big house was left untouched, but anything outside its walls was fair game. Even the wisteria clothesline had been whisked away in the night by a pair of needy hands.

In their wake, the soldiers left five black families parceled out on ten acres each. They immediately set up housekeeping with their few, pitiful belongings, borrowing back and forth from one another and digging at the ground earnestly, laying out seed and watering it by hand with buckets brought up from the river. Working until too dark to see, they carried rocks from the woods to carefully plot out the boundaries of their fields, the two men of adjoining families standing together, head to head, to agree on which belonged to whom.

On the third night of the army's departure from Deepwater, a fire somehow started in the kitchen. Before Laurel and David could get the children out safely, it had engulfed the whole cook area and dining room. Outside, huddled together with only their nightclothes about them, they watched in horror as the flames quickly leaped to the upper story, ran along the gallery, and began to eat at the bedrooms.

From across the fields, the black folks came running, bearing buckets and shovels. Shouting to one another, they pumped the well, attacked the flames with hoes and picks and old blankets, and raced into the rooms they could enter, carrying out whatever they could pick up to save.

At first, Laurel stood frozen in horror, watching her house riddled with fire faster than she could seem to move her legs and arms to stop it. Then a woman bumped her as she paused to set down a porcelain vase at her feet. "Here, missus," she said hastily, "der's two more where dat come from," and she raced back inside to fetch them.

Her voice galvanized Laurel to action, and she joined David and Bill and Seleta, carrying buckets of water, pulling out what she could save, and stomping at the embers that flew out hungrily, trying for the porch, the parlor, the whole left side of the house.

By dawn, they stood exhausted, surveying what was left of Deepwater. One whole side of the house was gone, including the kitchen and the dining room. The stairs would need to be rebuilt, the ballroom was ruined, and the study with her grandmother's books was nothing but blackened timbers. What remained was Seleta's bedroom, largely untouched, and their own bedroom. Bill's room could be repaired; Levi's was smoke-damaged, but livable.

At least half of the house was gone, so far as Laurel could see. Something almost mathematically correct in that, she told herself in a daze. Half of the land; half of the house. The black men who had brought their families to help salvage what they could, touched their hats to her and mumbled their courtesies and regrets before leading their families away again. She thanked them for their help without being aware of what she said.

They slept fitfully outside the porch on the stiff grass, in what blankets and pillows they'd been able to salvage from the destruction. As the dawn came to Deepwater, Laurel rose and left David and the children sleeping on the ground. She walked up the steps of the porch, avoiding the areas that were charred and still smoking.

Amazingly, the fragrant rose that climbed the railing still clung in places. She touched a blossom gently. She supposed the rose was a good example to her to look up and smile at the sun and go on with life. But then roses had no memory.

She walked into the entry hall of the house, the same hall she had greeted visitors in a thousand times, the same hall her own grandmother had stood in, dressed in long ball gowns. She moved to the parlor, to the stairs, and up the stairs as though in a dream. The boards creaked under her heels in protest, as though the house had endured more than it could survive. Even her steps seemed more than it could bear. She entered the room where she and David had slept for more than a decade. The bed where her children had been born was smoke-damaged and filthy, but standing. She sat down on it gently, as though it, too, might disintegrate beneath her weight.

But she did not cry. There were no more tears left inside her. Deepwater would never, she knew, feel the same to her again. They would rebuild, of course, they would go on and do what they could with what was left. But she would never feel safe again in her life.

❦ ❦ ❦

A vixen lived on the edge of the tobacco fields of Deepwater, a small doglike red fox, who would have been known, had she a name, as Vulpes. She was a rusty-red color with snow-white under-belly, chin, and throat, a graceful creature with agile paws and quick eyes. Her singular feature, that which distinguished her from lesser gray foxes in the county—and that also, unfortunately, made her more visible to hunters and their guns—was her red, bushy tail, tipped with white. She was often hunted for her tail alone, for it was considered a handsome item to hang over a mantel or from the top rail of a flashy carriage.

This particular vixen had carved out a small territory for herself at the edge of the tobacco rows and the beginnings of the swamp. It was edged on one side by a large male who wandered over half the river, on the other side by another, older female who would not tolerate trespass. The young vixen, therefore, had much to do to keep herself well fed. Fortunately, her ears were keen, her pounce quick and deadly. When she had her first litter, fathered by the male fox to the south, she needed everything he brought in his hunting forays to keep herself and her kits alive.

Now in late autumn, she noticed new alterations to her terri-tory, and these changes made her even more wary than usual. The kits had been gone from her for a month or more, each of the five down a different trail. In a year, she would scarcely recognize them as her own blood. But their dispersal left her feeling anxious and restless all at once. And the new buildings of the men on her land did not make her any more content.

She saw them building, these dark men and women who had come and spread over the fields like so many vermin. Food was scarce enough these days. Where she could recall good feasts from the stands of corn, the berries, the fallen apples and cherries from the trees, these had not been so easy to find all summer. The men ate them before they fell to the ground; the corn was gone before it was ripe. For months, she had been forced to find much of her food in the swamp or from the river: frogs, crickets, beetles, and crayfish now filled her belly, though these were not her preferred meals.

Even the field mice were more scarce. And now, with so many

more people building their dens on the land, she knew that she would find winter even more hard than it had been the season before.

The fox knew man well, for she had lived on the edges of his fields for all of her life. She knew to keep from his sight, to hunt only at night, to dig her burrow under the protecting roots of a tree rather than in the open, for the man would chase her and kill her if he could. And if he did not, his dogs would.

She was wily for her age and clever when the dogs chased her. She knew to run on top of the hedges that bracketed the fields, running, jumping, leaping with incredible lightness over a mass of brush that was dense as a fence, sinking in but never touching the ground, leaving her scent and the hounds far behind.

She knew she should keep away, but there was something about these new buildings that drew the vixen closer. They had a different odor to them, one of the fields and the dirt. Few lights were in the openings, and the women who came and went from the doorways never threw scraps of food out on the ground. She saw no dogs among these people, and that made her more curious still.

One night, the vixen came quite close to the edge of the land where a new house was standing. She stood in the dark, just outside the pool of light from the window, and she sniffed the air appreciatively. The rich smell of bacon cooking wafted out to her, and her mouth watered despite her nervousness. It had been four days since she had meat, save frogs and beetles. She whined and kneaded the ground with her paws softly, unable to pull herself away from the intoxicating odor.

A noise from within, the door opened, and the vixen shrank back into the shadows. She waited. Perhaps the people would throw something out into the dirt. But the door closed again, and nothing came her way. She circled the house reluctantly, knowing that she should put distance between herself and this new thing on her land, but unable to do so because of the lure of the smell of cooking.

At the rear of the house, she discovered a new smell, one she vaguely recalled from seasons past. She stopped and listened. From within a small wooden cage, she could hear the distinctive sounds of chickens settling for the night. The small complaints, warbles, and clucks that were part of several hens jostling for space, fluffing out their feathers, and tucking their bills under their wings for sleep. She froze.

It had been so long since she had eaten chicken, she almost ran from the possiblity in fear. But she was hungry, and the bacon odor maddened her. She investigated the cage carefully. Wood on top, wood all round, save for one side of the cage that had wooden bars for ventilation. Two rope handles, one on each end. She could not see how to get it open. She knew that if she took the time to gnaw through the side bars, the chickens would wake, squawk, and call to the people within. She sat on her haunches quietly and appraised the situation. Then, she nudged the cage carefully with her nose, assessing it as much as she dared.

The three chickens within were sleeping now and silent. But that silence would be short-lived the moment she attempted to release them. She carefully climbed up on the top of the cage, easing her weight so that it did not move. She sniffed it at every joint and potential weak place. One hen murmured at the tiniest of movement, but then was still again.

The fox hopped off the small crate and looked carefully at the ground all around the house. It was packed smooth as glass from the people's feet, without grass or brush. She made her decision in a second. She took one of the rope handles in her teeth and pulled, testing it for give. Not a sound from inside. She put her full weight into the rope and pulled it, using her back feet and claws for traction. The box slid easily over the smooth ground, with nary a bump. The vixen pulled it farther now, straining and keeping both eyes on the house. A chicken inside clucked once, sleepily, and she instantly stopped. When all was silent again, she pulled slowly once more.

Inch by inch, she patiently pulled, stopping for breath sometimes, stopping to regain her footing another. In a little while, she had pulled the chicken crate more than two dozen feet from the house. A bit more, and she reached the edge of the light and into the darkness. Now, the ground was slightly rougher, and she paused to assess her situation. She could pull the crate in one of two directions: she chose the one with the least resistance. In another quarter hour, she had the crate a full sixty feet from the house in deep shadow.

Now she grew impatient, for the smell of the chickens was strong in her nostrils, and the smell of bacon was diminished. She pulled a little faster, and the crate jostled. A chicken squawked loudly, waking the others. In a second, all three birds screeched in fright, the door to the cabin opened, and she saw men coming out into the light. She did not hesitate. She leaped on the crate, crashed it open with her jaws, and yanked a chicken up and out by the neck. As the men rushed forward toward the sound of the hysterical fowl, the fox ran into the swamp, holding the chicken high and firm by its now broken and flopping head.

Back in her den, she feasted with a rare sense of victory. Perhaps these new people flooding her land with their buildings might bring something with them of value after all.

❧ ❧ ❧

And so the war was over at last. News of General Lee's surrender filtered down to Deepwater, and peace came over the valley that spring of 1865, bringing a sense of blessed relief.

The spring came on unseasonably hot, and folks were already scratchy about conditions caused, they said now, by unscrupulous leaders, ambitious generals, and fools at every level. Now, they just wanted to live their lives and plant their fields and see their children grow.

Laurel was no longer surprised each morning when she went out to the kitchen garden behind the house and saw the distant outlines of five small cabins. Finally it was no longer new that others lived on her land. She and David, after a spell of hibernation within what was left of their walls, had extended a hand of friendship to the newcomers. They could do little else, seeing that the usurpers were determined to be good neighbors. Now they lent tools back and forth, their children had made tentative inroads and compacts of friendship, and the wives spoke to each other genially when they were within hailing distance.

The war had changed so much that these changes seemed small in comparison.

Seleta was twelve now, a blossoming young woman with coltish legs and unruly auburn hair that always threatened to burst forth from the ribbons she used to subdue it. She had a shine to her, even from a distance, which seemed to lure others into her sphere. Probably the most intelligent child of the family, Seleta kept more secrets than most. Though Laurel felt closer to her than any other in the house, she knew there were places in Seleta's heart where she would not recognize the terrain, dark and shadowed spots where Seleta allowed no trespass. She loved her daughter most of all, though she tried never to show it.

Bill was, at fifteen, a young man now. Ripened early by the war, the soldiers, the fire—and the conflict he still felt about his father— he was stolid as an old ox, with little of Seleta's sparkle. Like his father, Bill was obsessed by order and the right way to do things. It was both their special talent and their flaw that they believed, both of them but often in disagreement, that there was always one correct mode of action in any given situation and it was their responsibility both to do that thing and to impart the knowledge to others. Consequently, they were both hard to love. Laurel loved them anyway. But she kept a place in her heart apart from them, for she had learned early on that they were capable of inflicting pain in the name of righteousness.

And then there was Levi. Still the most beautiful child for miles around, the boy's mind had likely grown all it was going to for this lifetime. He had some of Seleta's sparkle and none of Bill's stolidness. What he did have, all his own, was a way of seeing that others did not, and often could not understand. Laurel had come to have more respect for God's ways and mysteries by watching Levi, and for that, she would be grateful to her son for all of her days. Levi could look at something and tell the truth about it. Few children and almost no adults could do so as honestly, as gently as Levi could.

The children had reached their own pecking order, of course, as children will. Because of Levi, it had not changed as they grew older. Bill was the nominal boss; Seleta was often the one who, by example, decided what they would or would not do, and Levi loved them without condition. Thus loved, they were able to love each other just a bit more, too.

David somehow was on the fringe of the family though he was, nominally, the one who made all the decisions. The children and Laurel deferred to him, but it was as though there were an underground current of real life in whose dominion her power was inviolate and his was titular.

The big house was no more, at least in the way she would always remember it in her mind's eye. They had repaired what they could, restored what little they could manage, but lumber was scarce, paint was plentiful but only in gray or brown, and nails were as hard to get as needles for the first year after the war was over. They salvaged nails from the charred embers, dismantled some parts of the house and reassembled others, until they were able to live in what used to be splendor. A kitchen, three bedrooms, and the porch turned into a small sitting room was all that was left of Deepwater.

Laurel considered herself fortunate, however, when she saw the way others were living. One afternoon when they were too tired of chores to do another thing, David hitched their lone mule to their only wagon and drove her down the road toward Wilmington, stopping along the river to see what had become of their neighbors.

The Hanover house was gone, with only blackened chimneys to show where the huge home had stood. Even the two giant live oaks that used to flank the house were bent and gnarled, bereft of leaves, as though they intended to stand guard, tortured sentinels, for the rest of eternity. The fields were high with dry weeds, scattered with crows and rutted by what looked to be an army of wagons and horses. Obviously, the Yankees had stopped here as well. "Or perhaps the rebels," David said moodily. "Either one did no good, far as I can tell."

The Blockson house was half destroyed, leaning sadly to one side as if pushed over by a giant hand. From the road, they could see laundry strung on the porch, a dozen black folks moving in and out with perfect ease as though they'd been there for a generation. Not a white face in sight.

The third and fourth houses were no better, and Laurel grew too saddened to go further. But David was restless and wanted to drive, anywhere, she supposed, rather than back to the endless cycle of work and make-do that was Deepwater.

At the last house, they saw that it was in better condition than most, and there was some evidence that people were living there still. He turned down the road and drove the mule along the river. Laurel looked out over the water, soothed by the sameness of the Cape Fear. The river flowed endlessly, unperturbed, unruffled by the vagaries of men and their madnesses. Of all she could see, the Cape Fear alone seemed unchanged.

The house they approached had never been particularly grand, indeed, the Charles family who had bought it right before the war and restored it had little extra cash at the time and, likely, less once the conflict began. They were a large family of five daughters, and Laurel had heard that they'd been sent north to relatives before the first Union ship arrived in Wilmington.

They pulled up before the house, and David called loudly. Laurel's throat was tight with sadness, and she almost hoped no one would answer. The house was standing, but deep gouges had been cut in the wood by sabers, vulgar writings stained the walls, the wooden porches were splintered and scarred by hoofs, and every glass was broken. It was like looking at a once-proud woman who had been used badly by savage hands.

A man came round the corner at David's call, watching them suspiciously from a distance. "What y'all want?" he shouted.

"We're neighbors!" Laurel called out, hoping that a woman's voice would bring forth a woman in answer.

And indeed, a woman came now to the door. "Is that the Quakers from upriver?" she asked, shading her eyes with one hand.

"Yes, ma'am," Laurel said eagerly, jumping down from the wagon. "You weren't burned out!"

"Were you?" the man asked, still wary. His eyes said, not another pair of scavengers, we've got little enough to spare—

"Some," David said reassuringly, "but we're better off than many. About half the house is still there, and that's enough for us right now. We don't come to beg from thee, just to visit."

Laurel was already up on the porch, taking the woman's hand. "Our children are well, are yours?"

She embraced Laurel spontaneously. "Lord, if well means no husbands and no hope of them, I suppose they're well enough. Come in, come in! Tell us what y'all 've seen!"

They sat for several hours, with no more refreshment offered than cool water and the talk of folks who had been through what they'd been through and more. The Union troops had used the house and grounds as a headquarters for much of the first two years of the war, and it had only escaped worse damage because, fortuitously, Sophia Charles had an uncle in Boston who was dear friends with the Yankee commander. It had been to that Bostonian relation that the five Charles daughters had gone as soon as the conflict began.

And it was from Boston that they received what news they could, filtered down through the Yankee commanders to the colonel who held their house. They told Laurel and David that Sherman had ravaged most of the state, and that General Joe Johnston was all that stood between him and complete devastation in the final months of the war. Sherman had burned out and bow-tied nearly half the rails in the Carolinas and Georgia, and it was a wonder Lee was able to hold out as long as he did. "The man is a national treasure," Sophia Charles said solemnly, "a saint. And will be remembered as such."

Women and children had to beg for meals at the Union commissaries in Fayetteville, they told them, and in other towns where no food was available, the streets were deserted and silent as ghost towns. The stories the Charleses related told of guns that fired all night long, smoking houses and outbuildings, fathers bayoneted to give up the locations of hidden jewels and provisions, sick sisters lying abed who had the pillows ripped from under their heads by jeering men, soldiers breaking into fenced fields and houses like so many mad cattle, ripping and tearing and rending for the sheer sake of destruction.

And finally, they said, the armies reached Goldsboro, the once-peaceful little city now the scene of the last great battle. The streets were already knee-deep in mud from the incessant lines of horses, wagons, gun carriages, and ambulances. At night, campfires circled the city like a tightening noose, drums rattled day and night, and men were so nervous that they paced the streets through the night, unable to sleep. Citizens of Goldsboro had been living on corn bread, spring onions, a few turnips, amd some scraggly greens they took out of the woods. By the end of April, more than a hundred thousand troops crowded the town and the outskirts, and there was little food to be had for any Southern soldier.

Meanwhile, Sophia said, she had it from her uncle that Jefferson Davis knew Richmond was going to fall right after Goldsboro, for he had a telegram from General Lee saying his defensive lines had been ravaged beyond saving. Davis sent his wife Varina and their children south to Charlotte for safety.

"And, of course, the minute Varina Davis arrived, the whole town knew the war was lost. Had to be, if the president was sending his own out of harm's way. You know, her house wasn't ready for her yet, and she had to wait in the boxcar while they tried to find a bed for her to sleep in! And all the while, deserters and scalawags stood outside her car and cursed her and her husband to her face!"

Sophia shook her head in disgust. "As though the poor woman had a hand in what her husband did."

The Charles family suffered through the war, but at least their daughters were safe enough. The house was damaged, but not destroyed. "They camped all over the fields, in every building, and every room in the house had a dozen men in it, day and night," Sophia said mournfully. "The walls are standing, but the soul of the house is gone forever."

David shook his head ruefully. "From what we've seen, the soul of the whole state is gone forever, if it ever had one—"

"Sir," their host said coldly, "the soul of the South is very much alive in North Carolina. And in this house."

There was a frozen silence at the table, and the women glanced at each other, stricken.

"I believe you were a dissenter during the conflict, is that right?" the man asked.

"All members of the Society of Friends chose not to cooperate with either side," David said. "Thee knew we were Quakers when thee asked us to come in."

"That's right," Sophia said gently, with a pleading note to her husband. "They're likely our only neighbors left."

Laurel waited with stilled breath. A great sadness had settled over her the moment Mr. Charles spoke in that tone—the tone of dismissal she had heard so many other times since her marriage to David. Quakers. As though they carried a contagion of some sort, always strangers even in their own country. She lifted her eyes and gazed at Mrs. Charles, saying farewell in her mind.

But Mr. Charles leaned back in his chair and sighed heavily. "It's been a bad few years. I guess we all got to understand each other better than we have. Maybe if I knew then what I know now, I'd have been a dissenter myself."

Sophia Charles beamed, touched her husband's hand in a brief flash of love—Laurel liked her instantly for that touch—and went on regaling them with stories of the war and the gossip they'd heard as though the moment of rejection had never happened.

That night, as they drove the wagon slowly back home over the rutted road, Laurel took David's arm and held it closely. She felt a great love for him in that moment and more: a respect that after all this turmoil, he still stood by his principles, however much they cost him.

"I think we should start a school," he said suddenly, his voice like a low-toned bell in the night. "A school for Negroes and whites alike. There's too much ignorance in this world."

Startled, she took a moment to answer. "Both races? All together?"

"Especially in this county," he continued as though he had not heard her. "We'll get a teacher. A Yankee teacher. The valley will be crawling with them soon, thee will see. And one of them will want a job teaching. For what we can charge for each student, our own children can go for free and we'll still make some money in the bargain."

The war had not changed him, she could see that now. He would continue to stand by his principles no matter how altered their circumstances. The Underground Railroad was no more; now he would push the black folks to freedom with learning instead.

She watched the night go by as they drove along the river. The moon was huge and amber in the water. Still as glass the river seemed to be, as if she could walk across it as surely as she could walk on the earth itself. Such a deceptive beauty, she thought. She had stood on the banks before and been tempted to swim out as far as she could until she could swim no more and then let the river take her away, float her into oblivion and peace.

Let him talk and dream. He must do it to live, she saw that now. Her only peace came from letting him do as he would, from turning away if she could, gazing where he gazed if she must, but keeping a piece of her heart intact and fenced against him. For at bottom, he did not cherish her as he cherished his ideals. And he never would.

She watched the river in silence as he spoke on of his plans. He did not need her to comment, scarcely needed her to listen at all. She had somehow grown up in the past years, through the war, the birth of her children. No, she saw it now. It was the birth of Levi that had changed her. Wakened her from the dream of perfection.

The earth is the Lord's, and the fullness thereof, the world and they that dwell therein. The old phrases from her first prayers belled often in her mind now, when she needed comfort.

David never seemed to need comfort. His idea of perfection comforted him plenty. He could not love Levi, could not love anything or anyone so imperfect. Levi's birth had wounded him someplace deep inside, whereas it had set her free.

She no longer needed perfection to love, if she ever had. She no longer needed to be good to love herself. She knew she would be forgiven, no matter what.

🌿 🌿 🌿

Four months after they wrote to the Boston papers advertising for a teacher, Holden Turner's letter came to them, a Yankee teacher with a willingness to "bring the privileges of learning to black, benighted souls." In the same spirit that his Bostonian ancestors had gone to the Sandwich Islands to bring civilization to the natives, he was eager, he said, to bring the same light to the South.

Laurel swallowed her indignation sufficiently to shake the man's hand when David brought him back from the Wilmington station. He arrived at suppertime, and she welcomed him to their table, relieved that with the children present she would likely not have to carry much of the conversation herself.

He was a slight individual, with little of the weight David carried about his shoulders and upper body. Wiry and agile, he moved quickly and his eyes went everywhere at once with avid curiosity. His thinning black hair sloped back from his high temples and ended in a small queue at the base of his neck.

Bill asked him first, of course. "That the current rage up north?" he gestured to Mr. Turner's braid with his fork.

"Thee must excuse my son," David said with a warning glance at Bill. "We see few outsiders here."

"That'll change soon enough," the Yankee said genially. "This county'll be crawling with carpetbaggers in due time but no, boy, to answer your impertinent question, my queue is my own preference, not the common vogue." He pinned Bill with his gaze. "It bother you?"

"No, sir," Bill mumbled, glancing at his mother.

"Mister Turner," Laurel asked then, to spare the boy, "are the trains back to their regular schedules? We had wondered if you would be delayed en route by repairs."

"No ma'am," he said, his accent clipped and harsh after the soft stretch of that word she had heard most of her life, "they're not back to regular schedules and likely will not be for a year or more. Sherman's destruction was every bit as vehement as we'd heard in

Boston. There's scarcely a five-mile length of track left intact. I took a carriage for twenty miles at one station and a wagon for ten at another. I got lucky out of Fayetteville and caught an eastbound farmer with room on a dray and a decent mule, or I'd have been another two days traveling, no doubt. I note that you do not use the Biblical nominative; are you not Quaker as well?"

She frowned in puzzlement. "Sir?"

"Thee, thou, thy or thine, the archaic nominative case, likely from the middle English in origin. I had thought that Quakers only wed their own."

"What does thee know of the Friends?" David asked.

"Very little, I will admit," Turner said. "There are Quakers in Boston, to be sure, but I've never had them in my classes. Usually, they keep to themselves. But, of course, times are changing and I suppose Quakers will change with the rest of us."

"I would doubt that," David said soberly. "Mrs. Lassiter shares our faith but chooses to speak in her own way. Has thee ever taught Negroes before, Mister Turner?"

Seleta glanced up at the newcomer at that question, the first interest she had shown since he took his seat. Laurel looked at her face, surprised to see no small contempt there, ill-camouflaged.

"Never. But I look forward to it. There is some speculation that the brain of the black man is unable to process information as a white man's brain does, and I mean to discover if that bears truth. If it does, I shall write a book about it." He grinned. "If it does not, I shall likely write a book about that as well."

"You are going to write a book about us and sell it to Northerners?" Seleta asked then. "A book about your adventures in the Southern wilderness?"

He smiled at her gently. "You sound affronted, Miss Seleta, and I certainly intended no such thing. No, I am not going to write about you and your family, only about the Negroes I have the fortune to teach. That is why I came. For them. In Boston, some well-intentioned people think that the black man should be offered passage back to Africa, claiming that he can never assimilate into America. I hope to prove them wrong." He held her gaze until she returned his smile.

As the conversation went on then around her, Laurel watched this Holden Turner carefully. There was something about him she did not trust. Something that seemed to know too well how to manipulate people's feelings too easily. And then he turned his attentions to Levi, who had sat quietly throughout the conversation as he always did, eating methodically and then building small designs of whatever food he did not want on his plate. When she could, Laurel liked to give him more than he would eat, simply to give him something to do that would keep him happy and with them for a few more moments at the table.

"So my good fellow," Turner said to Levi, "Do you know your letters?"

Laurel glared at the man, but his attention was focused on Levi. He seemed not to notice the ominous silence at the table. Bill began to speak, glanced at his father, and thought better of it.

The teacher softened his tone and leaned down so that he was closer to Levi, eye to eye. "Would you like to read, boy? Like your brother and sister?"

"Yessir," Levi murmured, as in a daze. He was riveted on the Yankee's cravat, a red and black tie of ruinous brilliance.

"You shouldn't make promises you can't keep," Seleta said clearly, bravely.

"I do not, miss, I assure you," the Yankee replied.

🌿 🌿 🌿

David's dream of a school for white children and black children alike soon foundered, despite Holden Turner's enthusiasm. The black children flocked to his classes, held first in the old smokehouse and then, for want of room, in a small cabin made special for him by their fathers on the edge of Deepwater land. Indeed, their mothers and fathers came, too, at least long enough to learn their letters and see their children hold a primer for the first time. But no white families would send their children to sit alongside black students, even if the only other school available to them was in Brunswick, more than twenty miles downriver.

In fact, truth be known, it was more important these days to white families to have every able body out in the fields harvesting what crops could be brought to market than to have them learning to read and write. But there were more healthy black males than there were white males in the valley, and Negroes knew their sons and daughters must learn how to read to keep freedom from being taken from them again. So they came by the dozens to the one-room schoolhouse and sat outside in the dust and heat when the chairs were all taken. They came, and paid the small coin required for Master Turner's keep, even when it was murmured along the river that those who did would be punished for it.

Prices for tobacco went sky-high after the war, for many men who hadn't had the habit before battle, had it after. David was able to get twenty cents a pound for what crop he could produce, more than twice the asking price for the same leaf before the war. Durham and Winston, tiny towns before the Northern aggression, began to grow with the sale of tobacco. David once had to send all his crop to Virginia to the nearest auction house; now houses sprang up in Milton and Henderson and others soon followed. North Carolina had a new crop that made cotton look pallid in its wake.

Holden Turner lived in a cabin next to the little schoolhouse now, built for him by the families who cropped Deepwater land. Laurel would always think of it that way, she knew: Deepwater land. No matter what the deed said, no matter who walked the earth and tilled the soil, it was Deepwater. And, therefore, somehow it was still hers.

And yet it was good to have neighbors, whatever color their skin. To them, Deepwater was still "the big house," however diminished it may be. And she was still its mistress.

Times had eased since the war, and with tobacco so high, it was not difficult to get good hands. Now she walked over fields that were worked to their fullest, and by someone else rather than herself and her children.

One day she stood out in the fields with Levi, his hand in hers, the two of them murmuring together over the waist-high crop and the peculiar beetles crawling at the base of the leaves. They were harmless enough, a staple of any tobacco field. They damaged some leaves, but not enough to worry the farmer unless drought hit the fields heavy. But Levi loved their hard green carapaces and liked to handle them gently the way an old woman will finger her best pearls.

She looked up to see Holden coming toward them across the field.

"Mister coming," Levi said to her matter-of-fact.

He might not understand much but he missed little, she

thought. "Yes. Master Turner. Your teacher," she said. So far, Holden had been able to acquaint Levi with his letters, but only by daily drilling and constant reminders. The child could not seem to keep the shapes and sounds in his head more than a day or two at a time. But the man was relentless in his patience. No matter how many times he showed Levi a lesson, he never seemed to grow scratchy with the effort.

She looked up as he approached and waved. "David's in town," she said. "I expect him back by nightfall."

"I know," Holden said, "it's you I wish to speak with anyway, Laurel."

He had taken to calling her by her given name within a month of his arrival. Somehow, it seemed unfriendly not to allow it. Yet each time she heard her name in his mouth, it jolted her slightly. For almost two decades, he was the only man besides her husband who had called her Laurel. The sun was high, and she squinted at him, wishing she had brought her bonnet.

"A, B, C!" Levi called to him as he came up, laughing and reaching for Holden's hand.

"Absolutely correct, my good man," he said to Levi, brushing his hair fondly. "You'll have them all in no time. And then, the world will open for you like an oyster!"

Laurel chuckled at his enthusiasm. "It's good to see him so eager to learn."

"Every mind is eager, if given half a chance. Now, Laurel, tell me, are you a competent seamstress?"

She cocked an eye at him curiously. "Have you mending that needs doing?"

"No, no," he said, grinning, "I've students who need teaching, and I don't know one end of a needle from the other. The girls need some simple instruction in homemaking, sewing being one of several skills they should be taught. Most of their mothers never learned themselves, and now that they're not getting their clothes from their masters, they need to make them go as far as they can. Will you come and show them basic stitches?"

"Of course," she said, not watching his eyes. "I have more time now since we put on two more hands. Seleta could come as well, she does lovely fancy work—"

"Fancy work won't do," he said quickly. "Seleta is welcome if she wants to help me lead the little ones through their primers, but mostly I want a woman's hand at the helm here."

She hesitated a moment. Levi tugged at her hand. "Come to school, Mama," he said. "School is fun."

Holden laughed aloud. "A true scholar."

"Well. I suppose your father will not mind a morning or two," she said slowly.

"I thought David was a grand supporter of education for the Negro," Holden said.

She looked up at him sharply, suspecting a barb. She could see none in his eyes, but he appraised her closely, as always. "He does," she said shortly, "but he also is a grand supporter of wives taking care of their own families first."

"A noble cause, I'm sure," he said, bowing briefly.

She could see no obvious insincerity in his posture, sense none in his tone. She let it go. "I'll be there tomorrow morning. Needle in hand." She took Levi's shoulder as though to go.

"Let him stay with me for a bit?" He put his hand on Levi's shoulder, brushing her own.

She leaned down to Levi and kissed his cheek. "Don't stand out in this sun too long." She picked up her skirts and headed for the house without looking back at the two of them. Something about the exchange with Holden Turner had unsettled her, but she could not say exactly what that might be. Certainly she could not fault his affection for Levi or his commitment to his students. Nor was it improper of him to ask his favor. But his manner was so—so Yankee!

She sighed and brushed her hair from her forehead. It was too warm for early spring. She must allow him his differences, she reminded herself. They are the conquerors, we are the conquered. We must adjust to their manners, not the other way around.

On the other hand, she smiled wryly, the man is an employee at bottom. Nothing more, nothing less. On my land and at my husband's whim.

🌱 🌱 🌱

That night she casually mentioned to David her intention to join the students at Master Turner's school, expecting that he would praise her for her contribution. To her surprise, he frowned and turned away, suddenly quite busy at the account books, something he did now more and more.

"What is it?" she asked, a little nettled.

"Thee does not have enough to do here in our own house, thee must parade thyself before Master Turner's students?"

"Parade myself?" she asked, bewildered. "I'm only going to teach them to sew."

"And take some pride in it, no doubt."

Ah. The old Quaker voice of sin, she saw quickly. As David aged, he was growing more and more like the elders she had scorned so many years ago for their narrow vision and narrower tolerances. She absently fingered the locket at her throat, grateful that he had never tried to force her to remove it as vanity. "I scarcely think," she said calmly, "that teaching a handful of Negro girls their stitches will require God's forgiveness. Nor should it require your permission, actually."

He raised his brows so high that they threatened to shove his hair back to the middle of his head. "That tone is unbecoming, Laurel," he said sternly, "and unlike thy usual manner. I believe thee has been talking overmuch to Mister Turner."

"Why do you say that?"

"Because he is the only male for ten miles who thinks that women who speak their mind are the better for it!" He stood up and shut the account books with a slam. "If thee has decided what thee will do, no matter my word on it, then do not ask me at all." He walked out of the room, leaving her breathless with what she would have said if she had the courage. Or the temper.

She sat down at the books and put her chin in her hands. Such a fuss over nothing, she sighed. So typical these days. They had been perfect partners when true calamity threatened, but now that things were easier, they found it difficult to pull together in their traces. Well, she had promised both Holden and Levi that she would help the students, and she would do exactly that. David would simply have to adjust to the idea.

The next morning she walked to Turner's small cabin, carrying her sewing basket. As she walked, she hummed an old tune to herself that comforted her. "The old church bell will peal with joy, hurrah, hurrah, to welcome home our darling boy, hurrah, hurrah! The village lads and lasses say with roses they will strew the way,

and we'll all feel gay when Johnny comes marching home . . ."
Somehow the tune always made her think of Levi. Her boy who
would never come marching home, not in the way he should. She
put the thoughts aside. They were such old wounds, they should
scarcely hurt her at all anymore.

As she neared the two cabins out at the edge of Deepwater
lands, one that housed Turner and one that sheltered his classes,
she could hear the buzz of many voices, the call of his own loud
above the others. "Class!" he was calling. "What is the answer now
to this sum! Anyone call it out!" And a flurry of voices answered
his call, unintelligible in their noise. "That's right!" she heard him
say to someone as she went up the rickety steps. "Very good,
Jonah!"

She stepped inside the schoolroom, suddenly, inexplicably shy.
Holden did not see her for an instant; his back was to the door and
he was leaning over a student's slate. The class fell instantly silent.
She looked around and saw a few of the children she recognized,
but many more of them were strangers to her. Some of them were
grown men, almost, so tall and dark they looked crowded together
on the narrow benches with the smaller children.

Holden turned then and said, "Ah! Class, we have a very important visitor today!"

The little girl closest to Laurel stood up, smiled shyly, and took
her hand as though to comfort both of them at once.

"What does she have in that basket?" Holden asked the students.

"Sewin'!" a young woman called out.

"Supper!" shouted a little boy. The children around him
smirked appreciatively but they kept a respectful silence.

"Magic," Turner said solemnly. "The simple magic of needle
and thread, people. The magic of being able to mend your own
clothing and even make new for yourselves when the old wears
out."

The class was as hushed as though he had just announced she
were going to bring the dead back to life. In no time, he had her
seated before a row of five young girls, one as young as six, the
oldest nigh to twenty, her few needles parceled out, the thread cut
and tied, and heads bowed close to see what she could show them
with her deft hands.

His control of the class amazed her. As she sat back and

watched the girls try to duplicate what she did, she saw that he had the younger boys huddled over a book, deciphering the pages, and the older ones at the front of the room with their slates, chalking sums. All around him was a swirl of soft voices, but he always seemed to hear what each was asking, firing answers back and forth like volleys of shot. It was not like the quiet, disciplined classrooms she had seen nor at all what she expected. But there was an excitement here that she admired.

When she was finished with an hour of instruction, the girls had learned the most basic skill, a running stitch that would hold two edges of cloth together. The class was dismissed, and Holden walked her out the door across the field.

They strolled for a while in silence, Holden carrying her sewing basket. He had already praised her and thanked her profusely before the class, and she had stood, blushing slightly, to their eager applause. It felt strange enough to be in such a place, before such children—but to be applauded by them as though she had somehow performed a trick for their amusement! She was not at all sure how she felt about it. She could imagine what David would have said if he had seen her.

The fields were green and thriving, however smaller to her eye they seemed. She could still picture them easily enough with Yankee soldiers littered over them.

He interrupted her reverie. "My class tells me that they're the lucky ones," he murmured.

"I can imagine," she said.

He glanced at her. "I wonder if you can, truly. If any of us can. They say that freedom did not come to them, it only visited for a while. Most of them got nothing but the news they were at liberty."

"Some of them," she replied tartly, "got a sight more than that."

"That's true enough. But most of them got nothing. No place to go, nothing to eat, nothing to wear—freedom is just another sort of slavery to most of them. Some of them went begging back to their masters for shelter and food, willing to work for nothing but what he was pleased to give them. We did a terrible thing, freeing these people with no plans to help them past their freedom."

"Well, we're doing something at least. A few of them'll know how to hold a needle."

He smiled. "You're a good woman, Laurel. You've had your

own heartaches, but you keep your own counsel. Don't you ever get so weary of it all that you don't want to go on?"

She sighed. The sun was low and fiery on the edge of the land. "Sometimes."

"What do you do when you get like that?"

"I work a little harder. Weep." She smiled softly. "Go and ask Levi for a hug. He can hug away the wearies, sometimes."

"I imagine he can, at that." He walked for a few moments in silence. "I would hate to come upon you, weeping."

She glanced at him. "Why?"

She sensed him struggling for an answer, something he rarely seemed to need to do. "Because I would want to try and make it better somehow."

She did not raise her eyes to him.

"I would want," he said gently, "to hold you. And, of course, I could not. So I would rather not see you weeping at all."

Never in her life had someone other than David attempted to make love to her, yet Laurel had no doubt that this was exactly what was happening. Her mind warned her, stridently and swiftly, to freeze the man with a well-chosen rebuke or silent glare. But she could not bring herself to raise her eyes to his. They were close to the house now, and she turned to take her basket from him.

"Laurel—" he hesitated

"Please," she said quietly, "not another word. I cannot bear it."

He flushed but he did not turn away. "Is it such a sin, then, to care for you?" he murmured.

She walked away from him.

"Will you come again to teach the girls?" When she did not answer he called her name, and then she turned to him and waited. "Please, Laurel. Don't punish them because of me."

She thought of that. "I will come," she said. "I will bring Seleta with me."

He bowed to her, a small gesture of appeasement. "Whatever you wish."

He left her there within sight of the house, and she watched him walk away. The man had courage, that much was plain. And a certain dignity, whatever his grotesque Northern ways. There was youth in his stride and the set of his shoulders, and she wondered briefly what it might be like to be held in those arms. But then she cast those thoughts aside and strode quickly up the porch, into the safety of her house.

❧ ❧ ❧

Holden Turner's school for freed slaves had been open less than a month, and it was already the talk of the county. Several times a week, hateful letters came to Deepwater addressed to "The Quaker Nigger" or "Yankee Nigger Teacher." David seemed to take an almost bitter pride in being, once more, a problem for his neighbors because of his principles. After the first few letters, shocking and ugly in the extreme, Laurel did her best not to see them. Seleta and Bill had chosen, of their own accord, to attend the services at the new Friends meeting house upriver. It was one place where their father's ideals did not doom them to instant outcast status. Each Sunday, Bill hitched up the wagon and drove his sister to meeting, both of them clean and sober in a mantle of grown-up righteousness.

David would have preferred, of course, that they shun the Quakers as he had been shunned so long ago, but Laurel was simply pleased they had found friends and fellowship.

In fact, the night she heard the horses coming down the road to the house, she thought perhaps it was a group of Bill's new friends come to call at last. But they were moving too fast, too many of them, she realized with a start of fear.

David went out on the porch to meet them, and she stood behind him in the doorway, holding the light until he took it from her and sent her inside. She watched from the window as four riders circled her husband, dressed in white hoods and carrying rifles. "Where's the nigger teacher!" one of them hollered, his horse snorting and dancing dangerously close to the porch steps.

"Over there," David said plainly, pointing toward the far light from Holden's cabin.

The leader guffawed, "Thank 'ee, preacher! Not a man to waste powder in a losin' fight, I see!"

They turned their mounts and rode more leisurely toward the cluster of dark shapes that was the little schoolhouse and Holden's cabin. Laurel ran to his side. "Why did you tell them?" she cried, staring after them in apprehension.

"What was I to say? 'I don't know'? They would have burned us out just for meanness and still found him within the hour."

Without a word, Laurel picked up her skirts and ran across the field toward the cabins, David fast behind her. She faintly heard Levi call out to her, but she did not stop nor slow her headlong race out into the darkness. David could not run so fast as she, carrying the lantern, and she reached the cabin by cutting across the fields just as the horses came by the more circuitous path.

Holden had heard them coming, and he met the men before the cabin, his rifle in his arms. Every light in the cabin was ablaze, as though to frighten away the demons of hell. "What do you men want?" he asked, cordially enough.

The leader, the same rough voice who had accosted her husband on the porch, leaned down and reached for a bullwhip he had tied to his saddle. "We come to teach a Yankee some respect for the way we do things down here," he drawled, slow and evil like a coiling snake.

"The way you do things down here has changed, sir," Holden said evenly. "Mister Lincoln, Mister Sherman, and yes even Mister Robert E. Lee have seen to that." He picked up a rifle at his feet and gestured to David behind her. It was clear he expected him to take it up.

David stood his ground, unwilling to step forward and touch the weapon. "You men have no business here," he said to the riders, but even to Laurel, his voice seemed impotent and hollow.

One of the men laughed derisively. "A Yankee nigger-lover and a Quaker coward. You're right, preacher, it does seem rather a waste of our time."

Holden raised the rifle to his shoulder swiftly and held it pointed at the last man who spoke. "Get out of here, or I'll shoot you down like rabid dogs."

A man swore and drew his pistol, his horse nervously danced and shied, and Levi broke into the center of the men, looking around eagerly and reaching out to touch the nearest mount. Laurel screamed then, and Holden pulled his rifle down from his shoulder, his face full of fear for the first time. "Levi!" she called to her son, but he seemed oblivious to his danger, darting among the horses to touch them high on their flanks, their necks, as he was wont to do, his hands moving like hungry flies. David was strangely frozen, horrified and yet unable to do anything to stop his son. One of the riders struck at Levi awkwardly as his horse danced and circled, cursing the boy. "Get off, you idiot! What's wrong with him!"

"A Yankee, a coward, and a fool," the leader said, leaning down and cuffing Levi away, "that just figures, don't it?"

As Levi yelped and jumped out of the way of the man's next slap, Holden jerked the rifle to his shoulder again and fired it at the man's horse, catching the animal full in the flanks. The horse screamed, reared, and threw the man off, stumbling away, his back leg dragging and bleeding. Another rider took aim at Holden and fired his pistol, but his aim went wide, the bullet thumping into the side of the schoolhouse like the crack of a sheet on the line in the wind. In a flurry of movement, the horseless rider, hoodless now, too, reached up an arm to a comrade, was pulled onto the back of the horse. Levi was hollering "Mama! Papa!" in a frantic, desperate confusion, and Holden stood poised to shoot again once the boy ran out of range. But the riders whirled their horses and galloped away, leaving the lone horse to neigh piteously a few dozen yards away, still trying to drag its ruined hindquarters to join its comrades. Holden stepped off the veranda of the schoolhouse, his mouth set and hard. Without hesitation, he took aim at the horse's skull and fired, silencing the animal instantly. Levi shrieked once, awfully, as though he himself had taken the shot, and Laurel ran to the boy, hiding his face inside her arms.

"I don't know that thee had to kill the animal," David said then quietly, the first thing he had said almost since the fracas began.

"Then you don't know much," Holden said angrily. "What did you want to do, pray over him until he came to his senses?"

Laurel stopped and turned, facing her husband and Holden Turner, her whimpering son shielded in her arms. "Stop it, both of you," she said. "David, come tend to your son."

But her husband stood his ground, defiantly glaring at the Yankee teacher. "Thee can tend to him well enough."

Something erupted in Laurel then, a contemptuous rage that shook her deeply, an anger that she could only guess had been growing, stealthy and toxic, for too many years. "Oh, now you're brave enough, I see. To stand up to the only man who stood between us and those animals. Now that the danger is driven off!" She turned and stalked back across the fields, herding Levi before her, ignoring David's shocked and furious face behind her.

Laurel could not have said, looking back, when it happened that she began to desire Holden Turner. It seemed to her that desire had been dead in her for such a long time that it should have come as an immediate and recognizable shock to her system, a flood of feeling she could measure and say, "Here. Exactly here is when it began." And yet she could not. Her desire for him grew gradually but surely, as water seeps into arid earth in all directions at once, moistening her body, lubricating her mind, and making her feel like a piece of ripe fruit, heavy and full of nectar. All without her permission or acknowledgment.

But not, she told herself ruefully, without culpability.

For weeks after the incident with the night riders, she watched the man, looking for weakness. It seemed to her that she had never known a male so untroubled by ambivalent thoughts. He knew exactly how he felt about all issues, all peoples, all principles, but he did not carry that righteousness like an armor about him, as David did. She could find no flaw in him, the longer she looked. And she looked longer and longer these days.

At night, she began to find her sleep troubled by guilt and a sense that something was coming fast, barreling toward her like the Wilmington–Raleigh locomotive. Something that was still under control, still within reason, but that would shortly be off the tracks and running wild. She had no will to stop it, it seemed. Without wanting to, without being able to stop her mind from turning it over and over, she began to compare David to Holden in a hundred small ways.

At first, she tried to stack the deck against Holden by considering only those qualities—and weighting them heavily—which she knew David would best him in: his piousness, his sense of commitment, his good sense with the crops and the stock. But her mind hectored at her, whispering that David's piousness was self-serving, that Holden's sense of commitment had never really been tested, and that the teacher was better with minds than David was with tobacco.

She rolled away from David on those nights, trying to put space between them, to find some refuge where she could feel free of taint. But no such space existed, certainly not in the bed they shared.

And then the day finally came when she let Holden see her looking at him, could no longer pretend that he was only some strange Yankee with odd ideas and a set of cool, blue eyes that had witnessed things she did not care to see.

It was a long, slow afternoon in June, one of the hottest months on the river since the war was over. Too hot to work the fields, too hot to sit indoors and do sums over a slate. Not a student had come today, nor did he expect any. Holden Turner sat on the porch in the deep shade, a book in his hand. When she approached, he looked up with obvious pleasure and beckoned her on the steps.

"Why, Miss Laurel," he said cordially, gently mocking the Southern tradition even as he saluted it, "you're looking mighty lovely today."

She smiled ruefully, knowing only too well how the heat made her heavy hair sag, her bonnet wilt, and her face flush unbecomingly. "And you're mighty fresh for such a scorcher," she said. She stopped, unable to think of a single other thing to say to the man. Drawing her eyes away, she leaned gently against the post of the house, gazing out over the fields. Bill and David had gone into Wilmington early, and she did not look for their wagon until dusk.

He waited for her to speak, rocking gently to and fro, his eyes on her.

"I wanted to thank you for working with Levi," she said finally. "I never thought the boy would learn to read." She added lightly, "Neither did his father." Still, he said nothing. "But you shamed us both for our lack of faith." She smiled softly. "And my son can read. It's truly a miracle. No matter what, for the rest of his life, he will always have that."

"No one could ever shame you," he said. "I can't imagine shame ever resting on your shoulders for a moment."

She looked at him fully then for the first time. "You'd be surprised," she murmured, frightened by her boldness.

"Would I?" He got up from the rocker and sat on the bench nearby, gesturing her to take his seat. "Come and tell me about it, then. I like to be surprised."

Almost in a trance, she stepped up on the veranda and took the chair, rocking slowly and still gazing at him. There was not a thing she could say. And she did not even know whether or not she wanted him to perceive this in her eyes. And yet some quiet, inner voice told her that she need say nothing. That he was only waiting for a sign of permission from her to tell her how he felt himself.

"Were you very young when you married?" he asked softly.

She shook her head. "I was almost an old maid."

"And was he your first?"

She sighed, closing her eyes and leaning back her head on the rocker. "My only." It was so hot, even here on the porch, she felt her bones melting into the chair.

"I wonder," he said then, so gently that she almost was not sure she heard him at all, "if he will be your last."

She opened her eyes and looked at him with some alarm. "Likely," she murmured. "I'm too old for such."

"You are not," he said. "No one ever is. You're a lovely woman, Laurel." He looked down, almost shyly. The first time she had seen such an emotion in him. "I have thought so from the first." Without another word, he reached out a single hand to her, palm up.

She stared at it for a long moment and then, without thinking past the end of her fingertips, she laid her hand in his. They sat thus in the shadows, holding hands, without speaking. And that was how it began.

Within a month, they were lovers. Within two, she was occasionally visiting him in his cabin on those evenings when David's business kept him overnight in Wilmington. The children thought she was helping him prepare lessons for the students, she supposed; she offered little explanation and they seemed to need none.

Bill and Seleta had their own lives now, their own friends, their own social activities that frequently took them away from Deepwater. Levi was in his own world, as always, and like as not he wiled away the evening with his bug collection or rearranging his array of colored stones he had painstakingly gathered along the river over the years.

No one seemed to notice her absence. No one seemed to need her at all. Each time she berated herself for her betrayal, for the monstrousness of a woman her age, of her circumstances, led to such behavior, she seemed impervious to her own assaults of conscience. Often she took Levi with her to visit Holden, careful never to let the boy see anything other than the most circumspect affection between them. Levi took Holden's increased presence in her life as he did everything else, with a smile and an embrace of unconditional acceptance.

But the times she shared with Holden Turner, secret and forbidden and filled with dark joy, began to be the fulcrum around which her days turned and her heart danced.

🌿 🌿 🌿

Reconstruction hung now over the Cape Fear Valley like a pall of smoke from the lumber mills that belched out board feet faster than ever before. Yankees had flooded Wilmington, and the sleepy agricultural region was fast becoming a manufacturing center for the Carolinas. Tobacco was the cash crop; merchants were the new power elite rather than plantation farmers. Indeed there were no more plantations, only small farmers who were alternately in debt to their land or the middlemen traders.

The yellow tobacco, known as "bright" or "fancy" leaf, had taken over cotton fields all over the Carolinas. Thin, sandy soil, exhausted by cotton and fodder crops, did well for the new tobacco, and farmers who thought they were ruined began to see hope. Farm land long thought infertile would grow the bright leaf, and prices rose accordingly.

A dot on the Old North State map became famous, thanks to a twist of fate at the end of the war. Not far from a whistle-stop village along the main rail line, commanders from both sides met to make peace. Meanwhile, their troops went foraging and found a little tobacco factory at Durham's Station owned by John Green.

Green could not stop the "sampling" of his wares by the troops, but being a philosophical man, he supposed that his loss was to be expected as a price of peace. The troops finally dispersed, and Durham slumbered again.

But then the letters began to come in from those soldiers, now civilians; to the mayor, the police chief, the railroad master, to anyone they could think of to address who might be able to help them find more of that excellent Durham smoking tobacco. The letters reached Green, he went back into production, and his leaf became known worldwide for its quality: Bull Durham. "Bull" was meant to symbolize the rural community that gave it birth, but polite gentlemen could scarcely use the term in mixed company. So for the first fifty years of its fame, John Green's to-

bacco was alternately called, "cow-brute" Durham or "seed-ox" Durham.

By 1870, Durham was a thriving city; Winston opened its own factory and, inside of a decade, North Carolina was the world's greatest source of tobacco. In 1884, the first cigarette machine was installed in the factory of W. Duke, Sons and Company at Durham, and it rolled out 120,000 cigarettes a day.

Meanwhile, the carpetbaggers gradually began to leave the Carolinas, and the Negroes began to filter back home. Those who stayed and those who returned swelled the ranks of poor, illiterate Negroes to nearly half the total population, and the Ku Klux Klan grew from a social club of six young Confederate veterans to a powerful and dangerous force for violence in the South. Their primary targets were schools for blacks and small communities who harbored Yankee teachers.

🌿 🌿 🌿

Laurel and Holden found times to be together now, as often as they dared. After the first fever of the flesh was somewhat mollified, it was still such a joy to be within sight of him that Laurel took more and more chances. Sometimes she prayed to God to help her keep away from him, to help her act her age, and on those days when she felt fortified, she would keep to the house, almost angry at him for the pain she suffered. But more often she told herself that such feelings were given to her for a reason: as arid ground needs working and rain, she thought, her body and soul needed one last touch and a final nourishment of love. Surely God would not let her feel so if it were a sin. How could such happiness be wrong?

And on those days, she told herself, she would give up anything, take any chance, just to be near him.

Over the months, she had taken to sleeping apart from David, often nodding over her journal entries or a book until she slept the night away in her chaise, the office light burning until dawn. Insomnia plagued her, and her limbs and spine felt restless, unable to find a comfortable place either alongside him or away from him. She walked out into the fields at night, along the path that led to the cabin where Holden slept. And finally, of course, she allowed herself to go within, sometimes spending part of the night with him for comfort.

She knew she was courting disaster, but one part of her heart urged it to come; anything rather than live out her life in the limbo she endured now.

On just such a night, she had visited Holden sometime after midnight for a few hours. It was an innocent-enough interlude, actually, for neither of them felt the need to do more than hold each other and talk over the lamp, their hands together across his small writing table.

Laurel heard the horses coming before he did, and her voice died away as she listened. "Hush," she said, gesturing him to silence. "Do you hear that?"

He went instantly still, his body suddenly alert. "Night riders," he said. "Coming fast."

"Oh Lord," she moaned, rising and going to the door, "I must get out of here." She snatched up her lamp, her shawl, and hurried to the door, but before she could reach the edge of the veranda, he pulled her back.

"It's too late," he said, pushing her back inside the cabin, "they'll catch you on the road."

They stood in horror and watched as the horses came on too fast to retreat, too fast to hide. Holden cursed and grabbed at her hand, trying to pull her back inside, but she was frozen. He snatched at his rifle, cocked it, and then whirled around as she screamed. The riders opened fire as they got within range, and the sudden volley of shots, echoing like thunder across the silent, dark fields, snapped Laurel out of her fear and galvanized her across the porch and back into the house, screeching in terror.

The hooded men were on them now, circling the house, yelling like demons from hell, brandishing their rifles and shooting into the air, the windows, the walls for sheer meanness. "Goddamn them, every one!" Holden shouted, pulling her under the table for scant refuge.

"Why didn't you shoot!" Laurel screamed.

"I was afraid for you!"

The totality of her circumstances was suddenly clear to her. "David," she said, "he'll know I'm here!"

"No doubt he already does!" Holden shouted, reaching up and firing out the window desperately. There was a crash on the porch and a thudding of hooves, the little cabin shook with the weight of the horse up the steps, and a blaze of fire shot up outside the window. Laurel screamed again, and Holden snatched her hand and the rifle and went for the door, keeping her behind him, his rifle to his shoulder. "Don't shoot!" he called out, "I've got a woman here!"

Loud, derisive laughter from the men outside, and the clatter of hooves and erratic pistol shots, and Holden bunched her by his shoulder, pushing them out on the veranda. Flames were eating at the side of the cabin now, leaping high into the night. Even the horses were hooded, their eyes glaring in the firelight like something monstrous from hell.

"You and the Quaker lady been praying together, teacher?" one of the riders shouted, and he put a pistol shot through the window, shattering the glass. "We plan to come back and visit right regular, till you close this whorehouse down!"

Laurel heard a high cry then, and she looked to the left of the cabin and saw to her horror that David and Levi were standing together. Levi was yelping to the horses, his father had one restraining hand on his shoulder. David's face was grim and pale. Clearly, he had seen it all. From a distance, Bill and Seleta were hurrying across the field, Seleta's shawl flapping about her shouders, her hair loose from sleep.

Holden lowered his rifle then. "Damn you, then, you win. Leave us in peace, and I'll close the school."

"We got your word on that, Yank?" one white hood hollered.

"Hell, we don't need his word," the leader said, laughing, "next time, we burn it down and hang him from the Quaker lady's apple tree." He whirled his horse around, "Let's go, boys!" And they galloped away.

Laurel saw that Seleta and Bill had stopped some distance from the cabin, had seen most of what had happened. David looked at her, and her heart froze. His face was hard, rigid with shock and contempt. He turned Levi away and walked quickly toward his other children, turning them back. None of them looked back at her.

Weeping, Laurel stumbled off the porch and followed them to the house, keeping many paces behind. She did not turn when Holden called to her, but left him to put out the fire as best he could, alone.

❦ ❦ ❦

By noon the following day, Laurel scarcely recognized her life anymore. The night had been filled with David's coldness, alternating with his rages. He had at first refused to speak and then would not stop saying again and again the words that split her heart with their stabbing hatred. "Faithless wife," was hard enough, "Godless fool," was nigh unbearable, but the worst, the words she would never forget as long as she lived were, "Not fit to be a mother even to an idiot!"

Bill sided with his father, turning a silent shoulder to her when she appeared at table the next morning. He loaded up the wagon with some small goods, packed a trunk, and told Seleta to tell her that he would be making his home at the Bartlett farm upriver toward Cross Creek. They had offered him a job that a week before had not beguiled him. Now he would take it, he said, and welcome. He would send the wagon back in a week, he said, but he would not live at Deepwater again.

Her daughter told her this with averted eyes and then fled to her room. Laurel took to her bed and stayed most of the day, hearing David go in and out of the house, moving things as though he, too, were going away.

Finally, in the late afternoon, he came to her. Some of the rage was gone from his face but little of the coldness. She sat in her window seat, staring out over the fields of Deepwater as he spoke, noticing as though for the first time how lifeless and old his voice sounded in her ears.

"I presume that Holden Turner will be going north as soon as a train will take him," he said. "There's nothing more for him to do here, after all."

She did not move her eyes from the fields. "I don't know. You gave him the cabin, remember."

"I gave him the cabin to teach. He won't be doing any more teaching."

"I don't know what he'll do," she said tonelessly.

"No. I suppose not. The question is what thee will do."

She turned and stared at him. "What do you mean?"

"I mean, thee cannot expect things to be as they were between us." He folded his arms as though he were bargaining with his agent over tobacco prices. "Where will thee live?"

She was mute with amazement.

"I suppose thee will live with him, wherever he goes."

"We—we hadn't discussed it," she faltered. "I didn't think—"

"That much is apparent." He stopped her short. "If thee will send him away, and promise to have no further contact with him, then thee can stay here at Deepwater. Otherwise, thee must pack up bags and get ready to follow him wherever his—many resources might take thee." The sarcasm in his voice was deep and scathing.

"Deepwater belongs to me," she finally managed. "You have no right—"

"I have every right," he said. "Even if the law did not give me the right, which it does, thy conduct has given me every right to send thee off."

She turned away in disgust. In that instant, everything about her husband repelled her.

"Laurel, will thee swear never to speak to him again?"

A long, steely moment. "I do not," she said, her voice low and vibrant with anger. "And further, I will not be driven from my home."

"Thy home!" he cawed at her. "Thee has defiled this house, our marriage, and thy children! Thine own son will not speak to thee!"

"Deepwater is mine," she said. "Leave me if you will, but I will not be driven away." She turned and glared at him. "Not by my son, not by you, and not by a passel of lawyers."

He pulled himself up stiffly and glared at her righteously. "Thee will not keep from him, then?"

"Perhaps," she said. "But I will not be bullied into it."

He turned and stalked out the door. She heard him slam into his room, pull trunks around the floor, and throw his coats into them, making as much noise as if he moved the entire kitchen's contents. She slept then, drifting in and out of memory and sadness, wondering what would happen to her now. When she woke, she was as weary as though she had been awake a fortnight.

David left the next morning without bidding her farewell. She watched him drive the carriage away with her two best horses. When she went down the stairs, Seleta was sitting on the veranda, bent and weeping, her shawl wrapped around her like an old woman.

"Father's gone," she managed. "First Billy and now Father. He says he won't be back so long as you are here." She put her hands over her face. "Mother, what have you done?"

Laurel sank heavily onto a chaise a few feet from her. She noticed that her daughter had, in her confusion, dropped the Quaker form of speech she used more and more these days. "I don't know," she murmured.

Seleta looked up angrily. "Well, what will we do now?"

Laurel shook her head. "I don't know," she repeated.

Seleta stood and shouted at her, perhaps the first time in her life that Laurel had heard her daughter raise her voice in that way, with that anger. "Do you ever think of anyone but yourself?" She turned and ran up the steps, but she stopped at the top and froze her mother with her final words. "I am so ashamed of you, I could die."

Laurel dragged herself up again to her room, wondering idly if perhaps now she would die herself, so old and broken and empty did she feel inside. Thoughts of Holden came to her unbidden, and each time she tried to despise him, but she could feel no rancor toward the man. In fact, as the evening wore on and the emptiness in her grew larger than she could bear, she wished she could go to him for comfort.

Two days later, Seleta still had not spoken to her. The house seemed unbearably large, for they had been able to avoid each other successfully for two days, only hearing the other's footsteps as she came and went for food or water or the necessary shed. Laurel wondered if David had felt this way when the Friends shunned him. No, she realized. Because he had her, so he was not outcast at all. Never was he alone, not as she was now. There had been no word from him, or from Billy.

And no word from Holden. The light in his cabin came and went with the dusk and the dawn, but she had not seen him on the road or in the fields. She tried to remember everything she had heard him say about his family: a brother somewhere outside Boston; a sister, too, was it Maine? New York? His parents were gone, a smallpox epidemic ten years ago. Where would he go? Would he stay in her fields forever?

There was a knocking at Laurel's door that broke into her reverie. A formal, light tapping, as though she were a guest in her own home. No one but Seleta would knock like that.

"Come in," she said, her heart beating suddenly fast.

Her daughter came into the room, hesitating at the threshold. Laurel was struck by her beauty in that moment. Seleta was becoming a young woman faster than green was coming back to the fields. She was taller now than Laurel, willowy and graceful in her movements. Her black hair, a legacy from her father, was drawn back sharply from her pale, oval face, as though she would not suffer any frivolousness, even from her own body. She put her hands behind her like a schoolgirl facing the master.

"Where's Levi?" Laurel asked her, a usual question in the household. She hoped to break the ice by keeping to the usual.

"Down in the cellar." She shrugged. It needed no further explanation. Levi had built himself a small city in the cellar, complete with buildings, docks, roads, and a tiny railroad. All made out of discarded rubbish, rocks, and whatever he could salvage from the barn and the outbuildings. He spent many hours there, engaged in happy, oblivious play.

Laurel gestured to the chaise alongside the window seat. "Sit down," she said gently. "I'm glad you've come."

But Seleta did not move. "Mother," she began painfully, "I've come to tell thee something."

Laurel waited, a calm, small smile still in place. No matter what, she told herself, no matter what, I will not weep.

"I'm leaving, too." Seleta let the air out of her lungs as though she had been holding it for half a lifetime. "I'm going to marry Bradley Chapman. He's posted the banns, and the wedding will be next Saturday."

Laurel felt as though she had bumped her head on an unseen obstacle in the dark; she all but felt her forehead for the wound. "Bradley Chapman?" She could not recall the name.

"Father knows him. He—he likes him, I think. We met at the Friends' meeting last winter. He has a farm in Ward's Corner." She took another deep breath and brought her hands around in front of her, clasped. "He's asked me to marry, and I'm going to do it."

"But you're only fifteen!"

Seleta's chin went up. "I'm old for fifteen, people say." Her voice stiffened. "I feel older than that, these days, that's for certain. But anyway, I'm marrying Bradley Chapman on Saturday."

Laurel stared at her daughter in wonder, willing herself to calm. "Tell me about your beau, Seleta," she finally managed to say.

"He's a widower," she said shortly. "Four children. His farm is one of the best in Ward's Corner, they say."

"They say. Who says?" Laurel asked.

"The Friends. I'll see it, soon enough."

Laurel went to Seleta then and, ignoring the stiffness of her body, took her hands and gently pulled her to the chaise beside her. "Four children? Seleta, you're just a child yourself. This is impossible."

Seleta sat, but she kept herself just out of reach of her mother's hands. She laughed shortly. "Nothing's impossible, Mother, I've learned that lesson for myself. He's a good man, and he's offered me a good life. I shall be quite content, I'm sure."

"How old is this Bradley Chapman?"

"Thirty-five, I believe."

Laurel closed her eyes. "He will be an old man or buried by the time you're my age, daughter. Please think this through. Retract your promise to him, your father will speak to him." She opened her eyes and touched Seleta's shoulder. "Please don't do this."

Seleta's face did not waver. "I will marry him Saturday next, Mother. Thee may attend, if thee chooses. Billy will be there, anyway."

Laurel rose now in frustration. "You will do no such thing. I've never heard such nonsense in my life. I will write to this man myself and tell him that he is denied your hand, that your father and I will never agree to such a match. Who is this man, to come in and extract such a promise from you without consulting your family? You're too young to know your own mind!"

"At what age *do* you know your own mind, Mother? Pray tell me, indeed." Seleta gazed up at her calmly, but there was a stern line of coldness in her face, her jaw, most remarkably like her father's. "If thee sends a letter to Mister Chapman, I shall send another, telling him of my great shame at your conduct. I shall tell him that thee has no more rights as my mother, and I will go to him and marry him in another county. I will never see thee again as long as I live."

"You can't mean this," Laurel said, tears starting in her eyes despite her best efforts to keep them dry.

Seleta stood now and went to the door. She turned, one small hand on the knob. Her back was straight as the wall. "I only came to tell thee out of courtesy, Mother. And to say that if thee chooses to attend, thee may. But I do not need your approval, and I do not seek it."

"But"—Laurel sobbed, grasping at something that might stop this disaster—"what about your father? What about Levi? Surely, you cannot leave your little brother—"

Seleta shook her head sadly. "My father will do as he will. He always has. And my little brother will make his own heaven and hell, I suppose. Just like the rest of us." She hesitated. "So. Will thee come, then?"

Laurel tried to gather herself, to collect her wits. "Of course," she said mechanically. "Of course, I will come, Seleta. If you are to be married, I will be there. I am your mother, after all."

"Yes," Seleta said sadly. "You are my mother, after all." And she went out the door, closing it quietly behind her.

🌿 🌿 🌿

Laurel and Seleta existed as polite ghosts together at Deepwater for the next few days, Laurel trying to think of a way to dissuade her daughter from the coming wedding, and yet certain in her heart that there was absolutely nothing she could say. Only Levi provided them with both distraction and occasional small joy that week. Laurel took some comfort in the apparent fact that he was undisturbed by his father's and brother's absence. They had been gone before on business; he simply assumed, Laurel guessed, that they would be back soon. The boy flitted from room to room, inside and outside, as usual, lost in his own play and thoughts, however simple they might be.

On the night before the wedding, Laurel went to Seleta's room. She knew that it was too late to stop the proceedings; her daughter was far too conscious of the opinions of others to abort a ritual once it had begun. But she hoped, at least, for some small reconciliation. Or perhaps simply a sign of affection.

She knocked, and Seleta's voice came out calm and clear, as though she'd been expecting her. Laurel went in to find her daughter combing her long, black hair before her vanity mirror. She was bare-shouldered, with a simple cotton shift over her slender body, and Laurel's throat thickened at the thought of that body sharing a man's bed before it should have known such pain and pleasure. And all the other darkness that came from such a sharing.

"Are you ready for tomorrow?" she asked, sitting down on the bed.

Seleta nodded to a small trunk in the corner. "I can send for the rest of my things later, I suppose. Whatever I don't have, he will get for me."

"Is that what he's promised?"

She did not answer.

Laurel stood the silence as long as she could, reminding herself that she, after all, was the mother. Not the other way around. Finally, she took the small parcel of tissue from her pocket and set it on the bed. "I have a wedding present for you," she said. "It's not a fortune, but it's very dear to me."

Seleta glanced up at the tissue. "Your grandmother's locket?"

Laurel smiled and nodded. "I always wanted you to have it." She picked it up gently. "It's about all I saved of the old Deepwater. All that's left of the old days, after the war."

Seleta kept combing her hair. "I've never seen thee take it off."

"No," Laurel mused. "I did when I thought Sherman was coming, but other than that it hasn't left me. It's all I have of my grandmother's. Your great-grandmother, Della Gage. It should go to you, now."

Seleta stood and took it from her and set it on the vanity. She sat back down and began to plait her hair for bed. "I thank thee, Mother." Nothing more.

"Will you wear it tomorrow?"

"Oh, no. It wouldn't be appropriate, I think. The Friends are very plain, as thee knows."

Laurel sighed. "Yes, I know." She stood up. "Well. I wanted you to have it, anyway." She bent and kissed the top of her daughter's head. "Do you have anything you'd like to talk about before tomorrow?"

Seleta gazed at her for a long moment. Finally, she sighed, "No. I guess not."

Laurel felt herself flush, though she tried to will her cheeks to register nothing but maternal concern. "Bradley Chapman has been married before, of course—"

Seleta turned away. "I'll be all right." She moved to the window almost aimlessly, as though the room were suddenly too small.

"Well, I'll leave you then," Laurel said, to spare them both. "Rest well."

As she stood on the outside of Seleta's closed door, she realized it might well be the last time she would ever say good night to her daughter. Certainly in this home, at Deepwater, at any rate. Certainly the last time she would wish her daughter good rest as a virgin. Things would never be the same for either of them again. The last time. And she had not even kissed her good night. With an aching heart and steps that felt they should belong to a woman twenty years her senior, Laurel went to her own room. Surely nothing more could happen before dawn.

The next afternoon, she drove Seleta in the second-best wagon to the little meeting house downriver where the Friends gathered. During the brief, simple ceremony, she and Levi stood at the front of the gathering, Seleta accepted Bradley Chapman as her husband. All during the wedding, Laurel looked for David, but he did not appear. Bill stood alongside his sister, looking ten years older and solemn as a judge. He greeted Laurel soberly, shook his little brother's hand, then took his place among the elders as though born to the stripe.

Laurel thought she would have to fight down tears through most of the ceremony, but to her surprise, her sadness seemed too deep for tears, too hopeless for weeping. Bradley Chapman seemed a gentleman, despite his plain Quaker clothes and his Lincoln beard. He regarded Laurel with somber demeanor, shaking her hand as though she were a stranger he never expected to see again in his life. His four children, a boy and three girls, trailed behind him closely, their eyes large and inquiring, inspecting Seleta carefully. Clearly they had never seen her before.

At the end of the ceremony, Chapman gently kissed Seleta on her cheek and then handed her to one of the women elders to be helped toward his wagon. It was only after she saw her daughter helped up, placed between the children in the back, and the wagon began to move away, that Laurel began to weep. People moved away from her quietly and off into their small groups as though they spoke a different language. Bill doffed his hat to her courteously and then climbed aboard his own wagon and drove off. Only Levi held her hand and stood alongside her, prattling with eager curiosity about all he had seen.

Laurel had never felt more empty and alone. She somehow

managed to get them both in the wagon, get it turned for home, and keep herself contained the while. Almost dizzy with her sense of loss, she scarcely heard Levi, but she answered him just often enough to keep him happy through the ride, and when they turned down the road to Deepwater, she drove the horses right past her own veranda, right past the barn, and on down the field road to the little cabin where Holden waited. Ignoring Levi's questions, she hitched the wagon to Holden's porch, and went inside, leaving the boy to follow if he would.

Holden sat on a chair inside, as though he had not moved for a week. When he saw her, he opened his arms. She went to him, sobbing then, and he took her to the small bed, closing the door behind them.

❦ ❦ ❦

The whistling swan stretched its great wings and sent its call over the waters of the river, warning intruders from its territory with its distinctive cry, a loud, quavering coo, more of a bay than a whistle. The large male had a black bill with two high yellow spots, black feet and black legs. His wings were snow-white, now tinged with the rose of the day's last light. His mate, a smaller female, sought the shallows, her usual resting place on the river inlet.

They were a breeding pair, mated for life, and they had just arrived in the Carolinas after an arduous flight from the river deltas of Canada's Northwest Territories. Together with more than fifty thousand of their species, they began in late September from the colder regions, flew more than thirteen hundred miles at a high altitude, and finally came to rest along the coast from Delaware to the Cape Fear River. An equal number of whistlers summered in the Arctic and went to California rivers and lakes for the fall and winter seasons.

This particular pair of swans had traveled together for more than five years. Each breeding season, they nested and reared their young. Each fall, they headed south. They knew where they were at all times, and they knew what they were to do.

Whistler, the male, was still not over his migratory restlessness. It came on him each spring and fall. In the spring, he felt as though all the rivers of the continent were suddenly flowing through him, around him, leaving him behind. He was most aggressive with neighboring males then, looking for a fight, eager to take on any intruder. He moved his mate from one marsh to another, nothing was good enough for him, and the newly warm spring air only made him more anxious. Finally, as though he heard a signal from faraway, he prodded her to fly north. They usually met up with a few thousand of their kind in the Chesapeake Bay and then together, in separate but linked flocks, they flew north to the Canadian nesting grounds.

In the fall, his restlessness was even more pronounced. Once again, he prodded his mate to join the others until finally, they took wing and flew back again, over the edge of the continent, following the rivers and coastline, until they settled for the cold months along the Cape Fear. Usually a dusky cygnet or two, their hatchlings from the season before, flew right between them over the long miles. In this way, the youngsters learned the route to and from the breeding grounds. After one round trip, they joined the other adolescents for two years before they took mates of their own.

Whistler could remember last season flying with six cygnets, the largest brood he and his mate had produced. It was an arduous journey, for they covered more than five hundred miles with only three stops—two short ones on the coast and a full night on a lake over the mountains. They flew nearly forty miles an hour, over three thousand feet up. But all six youngsters made it safely. Now, they were with other cygnets, wintering in the Chesapeake.

He turned his attentions to his mate, noticing with alarm as he approached her that her proud, slim neck was bowed. Normally, she held it straight and tall. He paddled to her side where she was feeding fitfully on marsh grass, as though she had little appetite. He nuzzled her gently with his bill, rubbing her along her back and long flight feathers, but she did not return his brief caress. Her indifference alarmed him more. He retreated to the bank, sat down with his wings folded carefully, and watched her.

Though Whistler could not comprehend the concept of monogamy, he did know that every breeding pair he recognized had always been together, except for those rare couplings that ended by death or some other trauma. Sometimes, rarely, swans might separate during a season to sample other feeding grounds, but they always found each other to make the long migration in pairs. That was the safest way; that was the only way he knew. His mate's indifference to his caress was unusual, but as he watched her, he realized that it was not new. She had been unresponsive during nesting that season, had even sharply billed him a few times as he last covered her to breed.

As he watched, he heard her murmur to herself, a warbled complaint that he could not remember hearing before. He rose off the marsh grass and approached her once more, trying to herd her into the shallows, as much for his own comfort as hers. She turned and hissed at him sharply then, and paddled off to another area of the marsh. He waited for her to return. When she did not, he followed her resolutely, once more coming close and prodding her with his bill to return to their territory.

This time, without warning, she spread her wings and ran over the water, rising swiftly and turning in a wide bank for the north. Within moments, she was hundreds of feet in the air, flying with determination away from him. Whistler called to her once, twice, and then took to wing himself, flapping as strongly as he could to catch her.

When he did reach her altitude, he stayed well back of her tail, confused and bewildered by her behavior. Never had she taken the initiative to fly before; always it was he who led them to forage areas. Her voice was loud and complaining, even as she flew, and she seemed to draw strength from her call, flying more than three hours without stopping.

When she finally banked and landed in a small lake close to the Appalachians, Whistler followed her into the water, still keeping well back from her punishing bill. She scolded him loudly, and then paid him no mind at all. Hungrily feeding, she kept her back to him, only occasionally calling out in reprimand. As they came to another, more protected area of the lake, they found a dozen other swans feeding in the shallows. She hurried to greet them, as though they were her own brood.

As was often the case, the swans accepted her cordially enough; there was plenty of forage for all. But when Whistler approached, the largest male ruffled his breast feathers, arched his great neck, and displayed a threat posture that kept Whistler well back from the flock and from his own mate. He called to her repeatedly, but she did not respond.

Dusk came finally, and the swans moved slowly to their resting area in the tall grasses. Whistler's mate joined them as though she had slept with these strangers for two seasons or more. Anxious and dejected, Whistler attempted one last time to join her, but she drove him off.

He paddled out to the deeper water and took wing over the mountains. He banked and turned, several times circling the lake where his mate remained, calling plaintively. She did not rise to meet him; she did not respond to his call.

Whistler slept that night alone in the shallows across the lake. Then, desolate, he took off with daylight and flew to the south, back to the only region he knew, the Cape Fear, where he waited for his mate to return.

☙ ☙ ☙

Now Levi and Laurel lived in the little cabin with Holden, and the big house of Deepwater sat empty and forlorn as an abandoned ballroom. She found it easier to live with few possessions around her, with little to remind her of her marriage, her youth, all the years she was that other woman. That woman who owned land, who worried about tobacco profits, who raised three children and slept alongside the same man for two decades.

The hands came and went, the foreman did his job as always, the crops were brought in, but the news was brought to the little cabin, not to the veranda of the big house. Levi divided his time between Holden's porch and the basement where he'd built his elaborate city, and never seemed to question where they slept or why. So long as he could be near those he loved, the world turned on its axis as equitably as ever.

That year, the sun seemed hotter than Laurel could remember. The tobacco did poorly, withering without rain when they needed it, scorching in unrelenting sun all summer. Somehow, she could not bring herself to care with the same passion she might have the year before. She needed little, she knew now, to survive. And someplace inside her was numbed to any feeling, including worry. Somehow, they would get by.

Holden turned his hand to managing the crop then, so they could let the foreman go and save his wages. He had little else to do, he said ruefully, now that his students had been frightened off by the Klan. In time, he reassured himself, the children would return. In time, perhaps, she might be able to pay him his wages again. But for now, they must do what they could to provide for each other and Levi, and so Holden learned in a hurry what he could about keeping the fields from turning to dust and blowing away in the wind.

Laurel had no word from David, not a single letter from Bill. She mourned them secretly, turning their faces over and over in her mind, but her heart was hardening as well. Most particularly, she could not forgive her son's judgment.

How dare he condemn her? she asked herself over and over. How could he forsake her? Had he been the one betrayed, after all? Was it he who lost a wife? No, she told herself, he abandoned his mother, he did not lose her. After all I've done for him, she murmured again and again, after all I've sacrificed for them all. To be left without a word, not even a scrap of paper that says he is well, he misses me, he misses his family.

He is too much his father, she decided then, scorning to mourn him further. I will not torture myself with thoughts of him anymore. But she noticed, when she looked in the glass, that her lips were drawn in a tight, compressed grimace of hurt and anger these days, even when she thought herself relaxed and at ease. She resolved once again, several times a day, to think of them no more, the father and son. Let them take whatever solace they could from strangers.

Seleta wrote once in a while. Not often, but at least she made the effort. She said she was well, Laurel noted, as she hungrily read the brief letters over and over, she said that often as though it were, after all, the most important thing. She also said that Bradley Chapman was a kind man, a good man, that his farm was quite profitable, and his children well mannered. She said that she had a woman to do for her in the kitchen, but that the big house kept her busy enough. She had a small garden, she said, and she had put in herbs.

She said nothing of love, but that was like Seleta. Private with her feelings, even as a child, Laurel wondered sometimes if she even knew what love was. She had seen little of it between her mother and father, had never been courted really, so far as Laurel could tell, and chose to align herself with people who seemed to deny that earthly love—at least the fleshly kind—existed or should be allowed to exist at all.

Friends. Laurel sniffed at the letter reproachfully. Laurel and her Mr. Chapman found staunch support with the Friends, she said, and they went to meeting with the children twice a week, no matter what. Friends, indeed. Laurel had never forgotten the scorching rebuke David endured because of her, clothed though it was in words of gentle concern, and then again the cold courtesy they extended at Seleta's wedding. But perhaps they knew of her shame. Perhaps they were right all along, she wondered. But then she put that thought out of her head. Let Seleta choose who she would to people her world, if it made her happy. At least she wrote occasionally. At least she was well.

Levi seemed to miss his sister even more than Laurel did. Sometimes, when she would go to the big house to find him, she would discover him in Seleta's room, sitting in one corner quietly. When she came upon him, he had something in his hand he was turning over and over. "What do you have, Levi?" she asked.

He smiled and opened his fist, trusting that she would not take it from him. It was a black button off one of Seleta's frocks; she recognized it the minute she saw it. One of Seleta's favorites, a simple, gray bombazine with black trim and black pearlized buttons. Likely she would miss it. "Dear, we should send that to Seleta," she said gently.

But then she thought that surely Mr. Chapman could buy her all the buttons she would ever need. That was the least he could do. And Levi asked for so little. "Never mind," she told him then, handing it back. "Seleta would want you to have it, I think."

He smiled and chuckled happily, and Laurel's eyes welled with tears, for no reason she could name.

🌿 🌿 🌿

Somehow, a year passed for them in that fashion. She would not have believed she could have survived such a year, but there she was. A second hot summer passed, a second season when the crop did poorly, and Laurel could think of few other ways to cut costs and raise profits. She could sell the big house, of course, but she did not dare, even if she could have brought herself to do it.

Though she had not heard word from David, she knew that he would defend his ownership of that house and land against all comers. No, the house must stand empty and forlorn, even if they were coming to ruin in the little cabin across the field.

Holden was a mighty comfort. There was that, at least. When she lost her confidence and dissolved to nervous frets and weeping over all she had lost, all she might lose still, he held her and loved her, and she grew calm and still again. Nothing, she told herself, was worth more than that.

She was out tending the small garden behind the cabin one afternoon, carrying water to the bean plants. The sun was so strong, they needed watering every day now, or she'd lose that crop, too. The wind was stiff and gusty, and the water she poured on the plants seemed to dry even as it melted into the ground.

Laurel stood and watched the trees whip erratically back and forth at the edge of the field, and she listened to the wind. There was an ominous note to it, a keening sound that she had heard only a few times before. Each time, that sound meant a hard storm coming upriver. She took up her bucket and hoe and hurried out to the field where Holden was working the crew that day. She found him at the wagon, helping to load the piles of sucker weeds they were digging.

Her heart ached for him in that moment. An educated man, a man meant for white shirts and the rapt attention of scholars, he was reduced to bossing a gang of hands round a dusty tobacco field. His hands were as calloused and rough now as David's. His neck was permanently burnt red from the sun.

The wind was whipping the weeds from the wagon, and the hands were beginning to scan the sky with bewilderment, wondering what was coming. Laurel went to Holden's side and took his arm. "The wind's getting bad," she said, "do you think a storm's coming?"

"How should I know?" he snapped at her. But then he took her arm and squeezed it in quick apology. "These damn suckers are taking what's left of the soil, and the leaves are withering faster than I can take them off." He scanned the sky. "The wind's rising fast."

"Where's Levi? I thought he was with you?"

"He wandered off an hour ago," Holden answered her, gesturing to a hand. "Get that bunch over there, and we'll quit for supper!"

"Suppertime!" sang out the field hand, a large black man with hands like pink ham sides, and the crew slowed and grouped about the wagon. Holden shook his head. "I know better," he said to her, taking her arm and leading her to the house. "Once you say suppertime, you better mean it."

The winds were stronger still, and Laurel scanned the sky with a worried frown. "This feels like a storm to me," she said. "Where's Levi?"

"Probably fussing with his little messes," Holden said, and they walked toward the big house. Once inside, the moan of the wind seemed more ominous and apparent. It was steady now, rather than gusty, and the walls creaked up and down as if a hundred mice scurried within.

"Levi!" Laurel called out when they were inside. "Answer Mama, Levi!"

They heard a scuffle under the stairs, and the boy's voice rang out obediently, "Here, Mama!"

"Come on home right away, son, I think a storm's coming," Laurel said.

"But come and see this, Mama!" Levi called, his voice pinwheeling away from them. He scampered to the basement door and clattered down before she could stop him. Laurel and Holden followed him down into the shadows, Laurel fussing at him all the way to come on up and home. But Levi was crouched over his "city" in the basement, the lamp shining down on the little avenues and thoroughfares he had made as though a yellow moon illuminated it.

"I found this in Papa's room," Levi was saying as they came next to him. "Can I keep it?" The boy had scavenged a small crystal viewing glass of David's, likely by rummaging about in his desk, a glass he used to look closely at tobacco leaves to test for resin. Levi had set the glass up at the edge of the "wharf" of his little town, and it looked exactly like a small lighthouse.

"You shouldn't get into Papa's desk," Laurel said, half sternly. "He would never have allowed that, you know."

"Yes, but he's gone," Levi said solemnly.

Laurel blinked at the baldness of the boy's statement.

"So can I keep it?"

"It sure makes a great lighthouse," Holden said. "You were very clever to see that, boy."

"As soon as I saw it!" Levi said, beaming.

Laurel said, "You can use it, but you cannot keep it. You remember the difference, Levi?"

"Yes, Mama," he said reluctantly. "If Papa wants it back, I have to give it."

"That's right. Do we have a deal?" It was an old game between them.

"A deal," Levi said, putting out his hand to shake on it, a necessary part of the ritual.

"Look at this," Holden said, pointing to a house Levi had built of pieces of cedar shingle, strips of horse leather, and thatches of straw. "I doubt I could do better myself."

They listened as Levi took them on a tour of his town, showing them what he had done, Holden asking how he had made this or that, Laurel exclaiming over the detail and precision of the boy's fantasy. Finally it was the rising moan of the wind that pulled their attention back again, when a broken branch hit smartly against the side of the house above their heads.

"Lord, it is a storm," Laurel said anxiously. "I knew it." She took Levi's hand to pull him up quickly. They hurried up the stairs and went to the door, but even before they wrenched it open, they could tell that outside was not where they wanted to be.

The fields were swept by the winds now, and the trees were bent far lower than she could remember seeing them. Debris flew through the air, and the branches of the willow flapped horizontal to the earth. It was difficult to be heard over the wind, nigh impossible to stand. They hurried back inside and slammed the door. "It's a hurricane!" she cried.

A mighty fist struck the front porch then, even as she shrieked and jumped, the sound of something heavy falling close to where they stood. "Down in the basement!" Holden shouted, herding them both before him.

Levi yelped, half in fear, half in excitement, as they trundled back down again, and the sounds of the storm grew as they listened. "Will the wind blow down my city?" Levi asked her as they descended, "Mama? Will it?"

"No, we'll be safe down here," she said distractedly. "Go and play for a bit, Levi, while Holden and I decide what we should do." When the boy was engrossed once more with his little buildings and flotsam, she murmured to Holden, "Do you think it's a hurricane?"

"How should I know such a thing? I've never been in one in my life. Do you have them often?"

"Not this far upriver. But I've heard in my grandmother's time—"

"Your benighted grandmother again. What difference does it make what you call it, a storm or a hurricane or a tempest or a tornado—it's fixing to pull the house down around our ears, whatever its name."

Laurel listened. She was leaning against the basement wall that ran up through the hallway, to the middle of the house. She wondered if any of her long-dead relations had sat thus, sheltered by the old timbers of Deepwater, while the winds raged outside. "I guess the only real danger is if the river rises."

Holden looked morose. "No, my dear, the real danger is that we'll lose a field full of standing tobacco."

"But so will every other planter on the river."

"Small consolation, that. Virginia, so far as I know, will still be standing. And still be selling leaf to what markets are left." He took her hand, but he did not look at her. "If we lose this crop, we'll be ruined, I fear."

Another terrific slam against the side of the house then, and the walls shuddered perceptibly. "Good thing your ancestors had the good sense to build it strong," he said.

"And well back from the river."

Holden and Laurel sat for the next few hours, hearing the wind attempt to wrestle Deepwater to the ground, but the house stood— at least the part they could see and touch. Levi looked up at them for reassurance often, particularly when the noise and rumpus from outside became, at one point, so loud that they could scarcely shout over it. But then he continued to play with an absorption that Laurel found phenomenal.

Most youngsters, she knew, would have been huddled next to their mothers, anxious and fearful. But Levi did not comprehend the danger, and so it passed over him with scarcely a ruffle of his hair. So long as she met his glance and smiled with reassurance, his world was undisturbed. How fortunate he is, she thought as she watched him play. God has blessed him more than most, though people will scorn him for his limitations all of his life.

Finally the winds began to diminish. Laurel guessed it must be close to nightfall by now. She was hungry and thirsty; she knew Levi must be as well, though he never complained.

He did look up at her at last, however, and said, "Mama, I have to go to the privy."

She doubted it was even still standing. "We can go out now, I think," she said to Holden. "Shall we try?"

They went upstairs cautiously, not knowing what to expect. The upstairs area was damaged, but largely intact. Windows were blown out, portières ripped out of the wall, debris and branches scattered over the rooms, and a large crack ran up one side of the huge brick fireplace in the dining room. But the walls had withstood the storm. Deepwater was safe. Upstairs, there was still more damage. Seleta's room was hit hardest, for it faced the river. All the windows were broken, the room clogged with leaves and branches, and part of one branch had caught the corner of her room, ripping it open. But it was mendable. Everything is eventually, Laurel thought. I suppose that's the lesson the storm teaches. We can't stop its destruction, we can only pick up the pieces and go on.

Outside, the damage was more complete. The fields were flattened and stripped, the barn sagged horribly on one side, the outbuildings looked as though they'd been set to by an evil giant child with a capricious grudge. Shoved this way and that, they leaned precariously into one another, and one building was half up on another, as though the mating urge had struck it during the winds.

They went to the cabin to find it utterly destroyed. Only a scattered pile of planks and jutting timbers lay where Holden's schoolroom once stood. "Well, what the night riders started, the wind finished," Holden said sadly, picking among the debris for his few belongings. "I guess we'll have to live in the big house now, like it or not."

"I like it," Levi said.

Holden glared at him for the first time Laurel could remember. "You would," he said shortly. But he left it at that.

And so they moved into Deepwater, after they repaired what they could and closed off what they could not. In time, they promised themselves, they would repair everything, restore it even to its former grandeur. They carefully did not speak of David or the possibility he might return. They did not mention Bill or Seleta or their former lives. They lived, as best they could, as though they had no past at all.

Only the present moment. And only, if they were fortunate, the future. In time, they told themselves, all would be right again.

But time was the one thing they finally did not have.

On a cold day the following winter, Holden came to Laurel and sat her down in the parlor, taking her hands in his. She knew instantly to be afraid, for Holden was not a parlor sort of man. But she kept herself still, hoping that perhaps his announcement would be a joyful one.

He took a deep breath as though he faced an endless pool of cold water. "Laurel, I'm leaving," he said. "I can't do this anymore. I'm not fit for farming—" He held up her hand to silence her protest. "Please hear me out before you speak. I'm not fit for farming, and I hate it. I'll never hate it any less, I think, even if I get better at it. I want to go back to Boston. I want to be among my own people again. I'll never feel comfortable in the South, so long as I live." He smiled ruefully. "I thought I could, but I was wrong. I just don't like much of anything about it, I find."

"Shall we come with you?" she asked, knowing even as she asked what the answer would be.

He squeezed her hands. "No, dear. I'd rather you not. I want to make a new start, and I don't mean to do it with a woman and child." He looked away. "That's churlish, I know, but I never promised you marriage."

"No," she admitted. "We never spoke of it, really."

He looked relieved. "I've got my plans, like any man," he said, "and even if they're a little vague, they're no less important to me. I never figured on getting stuck down here forever. Do you understand?"

She let go of his hands and stood up, roaming the room slowly as though seeing it for the first time. Where was the abject grief she should feel? The outrage? The terrible sense of loss? She felt sadness, of course, and some annoyance at him for being, finally, a weak and useless man. But also, she felt relief. Cleansed. Of course, she realized then, *I suppose I have always expected this on some level of my heart. Likely, I deserve it. It's fitting, after all, that I should be abandoned, after all I've abandoned.*

She turned to gaze at him: the man she once thought she loved, once was willing to give up everything simply for his touch. He made her weary just to look at him. "When will you go?" she said simply.

He let out his breath as if he'd been holding it since he first took her hands. "Soon. If you think you can manage."

She smiled, a movement of her lips her eyes did not share. "Oh, we can manage well enough. We always have."

He stood and embraced her then, a sweet and tender holding that would have, at other times, brought tears to her eyes. But she had no more tears to weep, it seemed, for her eyes stayed as dry and calm as her heart.

He left two days later, after making some haphazard arrangements for his travel and a hasty hiring of a field hand to be manager in his absence. She knew whatever he set up would likely need to be dismantled soon enough, but she let him do what he needed to do to allow himself to depart.

And depart, he did. Down the road, walking with a jaunty air and a carpetbag over his shoulder, not much different from the way he had come just a few years before, Levi skipping along at his side unconcernedly. Holden Turner was gone. She knew she would never see him again.

🌿 🌿 🌿

Laurel and Levi lived alone now, occupying a quarter of Deepwater's rooms. The rest of the house she kept closed up, for it was harder to keep it heated and cleaned by herself. It was also harder to face all that empty space than she would have ever supposed. The house began to seem to her like the chambers of her heart, empty and closed up and lifeless.

Levi was fast leaving behind his boyhood, too old to tag along after the hands, scampering for their leavings and chortling incomprehending at their teases. He needed schooling, but there was no one to do it. Needed discipline, but no father was there to take a hand. She did what she could with both, but she knew he was only getting taller, not growing up.

Deepwater took all her time and what wits she could bring to it. After the hurricane, tobacco prices jumped, but she had little left to sell. She told herself that it was just as well, for she could not have managed a bumper crop with half the hands and a new manager who needed as much training as Levi did. That year, they made enough to feed themselves, pay the taxes, and buy half the seed they needed for next season. If they had another poor year, she knew, they'd be unable to pay the taxes.

One night in November, as she put Levi to bed, he asked about his father. Curiously, he had not asked after David very often, as though somehow he understood that his departure was for a reason too dreadful to speak of any more than necessary. But tonight, it seemed it was necessary.

"Is Papa coming for Christmas?" he asked.

She sat down on the edge of his bed, taking time with her answer. "I don't know," she said finally. "But I wouldn't look for him, son."

He thought of this for a moment. "Is Papa ever coming home again?"

She could not meet his eyes. "You miss him, I know," she murmured. "I miss him, too."

Levi brightened. "We can go and find him, Mama. We can tell him we miss him, and he'll come home."

She smiled sadly. "I don't know where he is."

"Does Billy know where he is?"

"Likely, he does."

"Do you know where Billy is?"

She nodded.

He thought hard again. "Well. Then we can ask Billy where Papa is!" He was very proud of his logic.

Truth to tell, so was she. She touched his cheek. "Yes. We could write a letter to Billy and ask him. If he will write us a letter back again."

"Billy will write us. Why won't Billy write us?"

She looked away. "We'll see. Do you want to help me with the letter to Billy?"

"Yes!" he said, laughing. "I'll tell him about the 'cane, and my lighthouse, and Henry." Henry was a scruffy black-and-tan who had wandered in and stayed, now tethered firmly to Levi's heart. He was long-gaited and awkward as Levi, with the same open eyes.

She sighed. "Well, then. We'll write the letter together, and we'll see if Billy writes back. Yes," she said, her voice lower and doubting, "We'll see. But Levi, don't hope too hard. Sometimes people don't do what we think they will do."

He watched her carefully, and she could see him trying to fathom her feelings. "Mama, why are you so sad?"

She looked up at him. His eyes were so beautiful, so full of trust. She wanted to tell him the truth, as best she could. "I am sad because I made a bad choice. And when I did, I lost what I had. Did you ever have two things to choose from and you picked one, and it was the wrong one? And then you lost the other?"

He frowned, thinking very hard. "Yes," he said finally.

"Tell me."

"I was down at the river, looking for bottles." Levi knew to simply tell her this was to invite a reprimand, for he was not to go to the river alone. But broken bottles, particularly green or blue ones, were his passion. They made such perfect windows in the buildings of his little city. She said nothing. He saw that she was not going to speak, and he went on. "I was on this rock? And I had my catching tree"—a forked branch he had tied in a way so as to net passing bottles. She had seen it in his hands a hundred times—"and two bottles went by at the same time!" He told her solemnly, "Mama, that *never* happens. So I tried to get them both, but I couldn't, and the river was taking them, so I had to pick, and I caught the blue one and let the green one go."

"And was it the right one?" she asked, sensing the answer.

"No," he said mournfully, as though reliving the moment. "It was just the top, and not even a good blue. The green one got away."

She thought for a minute. "Did you keep the blue one, anyway?"

He shook his head. "I didn't want it after all. But I wished I got the green one."

"Well, then." She leaned down and kissed him lightly. "You know how Mama feels."

He looked bewildered. "Did you lose a bottle, too?"

"No. It was something else. I made the wrong choice, just like you did, and I lost what I wanted. Because I didn't know I wanted it."

"I don't understand." He rubbed his eyes, ready now for sleep.

"I know you don't, son," she said softly, easing him back onto the bed. "Life is an expensive business, finally. I understand that now. Maybe you'll never need to." She kissed him good night again and left him, the door ajar, the lamp burning as always.

❦ ❦ ❦

Laurel spent much of that winter watching Deepwater go into hibernation. It seemed to her that her own heart and body were mirroring the slow somnolent slide into lifelessness of the fields, the gradual decay of the big house itself, and the silent, watchful stance of the natural world.

Even the Cape Fear was diminished in this season, sluggish and shrunken on its banks, gray and cold, with the spring bustle of birds stilled and the peepers buried deep in the sheltering mud.

Laurel walked the river often now, alone and pensive, her mouth sometimes moving of its own volition in conversations she had never had but continued to rehearse. She spoke to David most, telling him over and over why she turned to Holden, defending herself, berating him, pleading with him to love her as he did once. And then, once aware that she was veering dangerously close to some state that approximated Levi's, she would turn resolutely back to the house and find something, anything, to occupy the long, cold days.

Normally, the winter months would be times to repair, refurbish, and ready the land and the buildings for the hubbub of spring. But there was no money to hire hands, and she could not mend the harnesses, haul the fence posts, or brace the sagging barn herself, so she could only watch as each storm took more and more from the house, from the land, and from what little she had left. Still there was no word from Bill. Only an occasional letter from Seleta, drifting in like a wayward sparrow. She was expecting her first child, she said, and her husband was pleased.

Laurel searched the lines for some semblance of her daughter, looking for her own exultation at her pregnancy, hoping she would speak of her feelings, hopes, or fears. But there was little there to indicate any more than courtesy. She was having a baby soon, and that was all. As though she had mentioned the fact to a distant relation instead of to her mother.

Levi was more secretive now, pushed by urges in his body he did not comprehend. He spent hours alone, out in the woods or the swamp, trundling back packets of treasures that he did not share with her but hurried to store or dismember or reassemble somehow into more treasures. When she hugged him, those times he would allow it, she felt his man-boy body gone, all angles and hard edges under her arms. He was not her child anymore.

Indeed, she thought, nothing belonged to her anymore and she belonged to no one. It was a realization at once freeing and frightening. It left her feeling deeply numb in the extremities and hollow in the heart. She almost feared to look in the glass these days, for the changes in her were showing now in her flesh. Her hair had gone partly gray, almost overnight it seemed. And it was not only the color that dismayed her, but the texture. No longer smooth and thick, her hair, where it was changed, was unruly, coarse, and lifeless. Her skin felt too big for her cheekbones, and it hung over the corners of her lips and her eyes.

What lay ahead? That question mantled her shoulders and haunted her dreams every waking and sleeping hour. For the first time in her life, she had no answers.

🌿 🌿 🌿

It was a February night, and Levi had already gone off to bed, tired from his foraging in the cold wind. She sat by the fire in the dining room, the only place they now kept warm through these months, the rest of the house being closed off as best they could. As she drowsed over her mending—a task that seemed endless these days with Levi's clothing—she heard the approach of a horse toward the veranda. She stopped still and listened, her heart beating suddenly too fast for comfort.

The pistol was upstairs. She listened hard, holding her breath. There was no noise in the house save the low hiss and snap of the flames. Only one rider, it seemed to her. A quiet, stealthy intruder. She rose, moving silently to the window. A shadow approached the house, but she could not make it out clearly. She went for the stairs, holding her breath and avoiding the creak on the floorboards. And then—a low knock at the door.

Laurel froze, her hand at her throat. She knew instantly who it was. She whirled and went to the door, flinging it open. David stood in the darkness, the light from the lamp shining on the curves of his face. He doffed his hat. "Evening, Laurel," he said.

She swung the door wider. "Come in," she said, suddenly eager and shy all at once. "You gave me a start."

"Sorry," he mumbled. He hesitated at the door as though he had never stepped over its threshold in his life.

"No, no," she rushed to reassure him, "I'm just a little unsteady these days." She took a deep breath and calmed herself with a will. She smiled at him. "Come in, David. I'm glad to see you again."

She led him to the chair by the fire. "Levi's in bed already, he's going to be so sorry he missed you." She brightened. "But, of course, you should wake him. He'd likely rather see you than sleep."

David made no comment to that. He took his seat and glanced around the room, his hat still in his hand as though he were a stranger.

"You look well, David," she said, lowering her voice as she would to a spooky horse.

"Thee also," he said.

She flushed, suddenly aware that she would have liked to know of his arrival, to smooth her hair, to put on a clean frock. But then, David had never noticed those things. Perhaps he had not changed in that. He looked older, she saw then. His face was tracked with pain and uncertainty. Her heart softened to him then, and she put out one hand and touched his shoulder. "I've missed you," she said simply.

His smile was more grimace than pleasure. "And I, thee," he said formally. "I know thee is alone now."

She pondered this. "I guess everyone knows my business these days."

He shrugged. "Everybody knows everybody's business." He hesitated. "I thought I'd come and see if thee is all right."

She lifted her chin. "No, I'm not all right, if truth be known."

He had nothing to say to that.

"Where have you been staying?" she asked.

"All sorts of places," he said. "First the drought and then the storms—" He shook his head ruefully. "Not much in the way of decent crops, up and down the river."

Now it was her turn to be silent. For surely he must know that whatever diminishment other places had suffered, Deepwater had suffered more. And he would not say where he'd been.

After a silence, he offered, "Billy took a wife. A Quaker girl down to Brunswick. They settled at the Carter place. He apprenticed to the smithy there."

"Bill is married," she said quietly. "And I did not even hear of it." She gazed at the fire. "What is she like?"

"A good girl. Not comely, but fit and amiable. She'll make him a good partner."

"Seleta's expecting a baby," she said. "Anytime now, if she hasn't had it already. Her new husband treats her well, she says."

David nodded. She could not tell if he had the news before her or not. She was jealous then, wishing that she could have told him something he did not know. "Will you take a bite to eat?" she offered. "I'll put coffee on."

"Just coffee," he murmured. "It's cold as Boston out there."

She flinched slightly at the mention of Boston, but she did not alter her stride. She busied herself in the kitchen, putting together a tray with cups and saucers. She parceled out the smallest bit of her scant sugar store, for she knew he'd take that as a sign of welcome. Just before she took the tray in, she added a sprig of berried holly for color.

He took the coffee without comment, watching her over the cup. She could tell he struggled with what he wanted to say. She determined to stay silent. Whatever made him come must have been strong enough to give him courage to speak it aloud.

Finally, he murmured, "I thought perhaps to stay the night."

She smiled softly at him. "I'm glad you thought of it."

"Like to spend some time with Levi." He frowned. "Seleta's room will be fine."

"Actually," she said, "it's not been fully repaired since the storm. If it were light, you could see the damage. The house is all but falling down upon our ears. I closed it off a few months back, and it's not fit for guests."

"I'm hardly a guest," he said soberly.

"It's not fit for you either," she said easily. "But you can see for yourself." She took a breath and consciously softened her smile. "You're welcome to share your old bed, David. That or the barn, I'm afraid." She cocked her head, almost coyly. " 'Tis a long ride for a berth in the barn."

He smiled back at her ruefully. "How does thee know how far a ride it was, thee doesn't know where I've been."

"Wherever you've been," she said, "it's a long ride back."

They sat in silence for a moment. David sighed and stretched. "Well. If thee does not mind then, I'll accept the offer."

She stood and led him up the stairs as though he had not climbed them a thousand times. She paused at Seleta's room, to give him a chance to see for himself what he would have to contend with inside. But he shrugged. "I'll take your word on it." She continued down the hall now, deliberately slowing her steps, wondering what she would do once he was in the room. But he only took the lamp from her hand and set it on the bedside table, as he always had. Turning his back to her, he sat down on the bed and removed his shoes. Without a word between them, they disrobed, back to back, and got into the bed together.

She did not touch him. She lay on her back, her hands on her breasts, feeling strangely like the first time they lay together after their wedding. She knew she would never sleep a wink.

After a time, he reached over and took one of her hands, drawing it down and clasping it firmly in his. She gently squeezed his hand, and the simple comfort of his touch brought tears to her eyes. Finally, he rolled on his side to face her, rolled her over on her side away from him, and pulled her against him like a spoon in a drawer. The easy way their bodies moved into their known places seemed to her a benediction from God.

She thought then of the different types of courage she had known in her life. In her men. Holden Turner had the courage to face a pack of night riders with his rifle and his bravado. Had the courage, too, to face the heartbreak of a child's mind in a young man's body and try to make it better if he could. But David had the courage to stand and till the soil day after day, never knowing if the crop would come or if it would profit him, to stick to it through good seasons and bad, no matter what.

There was a time when she would have needed to decide which courage was the better attribute for a man. She no longer felt the need to make that judgment.

With his head nestled against her, his arm across her body, the length of him pressed against the length of her, she knew then she could rest. She sighed deeply, his hand still embracing hers. Without a word between them, they slid into sleep.

Sometime in the night, she woke and he was embracing her with more fervor. As though in a dream, she felt his lovemaking, like a slow dance they had done a thousand times together. She remembered the taste of his mouth, a taste of hardness and warmth, as of earth that had the sun on it too long. He cupped her face like a chalice. It was somehow so familiar yet so new, and she gloried in him, in his pleasure in her, as wordlessly they joined in the darkness.

The next morning, he woke before her. She knew because she sensed him waiting for her to waken, even as she became conscious of her body again. It was still dark outside, but a thin ribbon of red rimmed the horizon. The sun—and Levi—would be up very soon.

"Never will understand why thee did what thee did to me," his voice said softly.

She froze. Completely undefended, she could not speak.

"Thee betrayed me," he said simply, his voice surprisingly light.

It lit a spark in her of anger. "You were gone from me far before I left you," she said then. Amazed at her own courage. For as she said the words, she knew they were true. "You turned into an old man. A cold man. The day you knew Levi was not perfect."

He lay silently.

She held her breath, unable to fathom his silence.

"I don't know if I can trust thee anymore," he said. "Perhaps we've so poisoned the water between us, neither of us can drink from it again."

"You're right," she said calmly. "You'll never love me in the same way again. I will never be perfect in your eyes again, if I ever was."

"Oh thee was perfect all right," he murmured. "Once. Long ago."

Her heart twisted painfully. Nonetheless, she kept her voice steady. And as she spoke, her heart became steady as well. "But you still love me," she said. "And one of the reasons you do is *because* of all we've done to each other. Because we've been through so much. Because we've passed through all of this together. You talk of trust," she murmured, taking his hand, "but think of this. You'll never go a whole lifetime without pain and disappointment. You will never be able to keep your illusions. What matters is this: at the moment when you were betrayed, when that person truly felt they were leaving you, how did they treat you? Did they still treat you with some tenderness and respect? *That's* trust, it seems to me. When they didn't have to love you anymore, did they still try to, as much as they were able?'' She turned and gazed at him honestly. "No, you'll never have us perfect again, David, if we ever were. But what you'll have instead will be burnished and hardened and battle-proven as this land. And that, to me, is a richer love. It's a real marriage.''

He sighed. He relinquished her hand. For long moments, he was silent. "Well. We could go back and forth, I'm sure. I did this, and thee did that, and who started it and who finished it. Like the chicken and the egg." He smiled in the shadows and she sensed it. "But even Sherman had to call a truce eventually. Maybe if Levi had been . . . normal."

"He's as normal as he needs to be," she said quickly.

"Or maybe if Mister Turner hadn't come along."

"Or maybe if you hadn't taken on the cause, any cause, no matter what your family wanted or needed."

"Aye," he said solemnly, "a score of weak, foolish, mean things we did to each other." He thought for a moment. "Well. I'm sorry," he said.

She turned to him, amazed. It seemed to her in that moment that it might well be the first time she had ever heard him speak those words.

"I am . . . sorry," he repeated, "for my share."

"And I am sorry for mine," she said softly. She reached out and took his hand.

"I came to see thee last night," he said, "because I needed to know that thee was well. Thee and . . . our son."

She waited. She knew there was more.

"But I stayed because I wanted thee."

She smiled and squeezed his hand.

"I wanted thee. I guess because we've passed through it all together."

"I know," she said softly. And she knew then that she would never be afraid again. Her worst fear had been realized. She was alone. No matter what she had done to keep from being alone, no matter how much she had compromised her happiness, her life itself to avoid it, she had still ended up alone. All her land, her energies, her cleverness, her children—none of it could stave off ending up alone. But what she knew also was that being alone was not so bad after all. It was survivable. It was even, at times, a triumph of spirit.

She had felt before that she had made one large error in her life and it had destroyed her. One false move. One wrong choice. But now she understood that in truth, there were no wrong choices at all. The choice to love elsewhere was not an error. It was merely another detour on her journey. Another place to say: here . . . here I choose to grow toward a different patch of sunlight. Here I choose to blossom in a new hue. Another opportunity to know her heart and hence, God. And she was the stronger for it. So was her marriage.

"I missed thee, Laurel," David murmured then. "I missed our life."

Suddenly, they heard a noise from across the hall. Levi was up and moving.

"I missed him, too," David said with a wry grin.

"Then go and tell him so," she urged, laughing happily. "And then come and tell me again."

She watched his long body rise from the bed as she had countless times in the twenty years they'd been together, and in that moment, she felt as though she had somehow birthed him and been parented by him as well. Perhaps, she thought then, with a rush of tenderness, that is what the vows meant after all.

🌿 🌿 🌿

David slid back into their lives as easily as the spring came up the river, each day easing the edges of coldness and winter, until finally it seemed that it had always been warm and he had always been there. Two months after he'd come, Levi was on the veranda whittling at a small piece of soft wood. He was making a chimney for one of his buildings with a knife his father had recently brought him back from Wilmington. Laurel was in the kitchen when she heard him holler.

She ran out in fear, thinking swiftly that no matter if David wanted to show the boy that he trusted him, perhaps giving him a knife was too much after all—

Levi was capering about a wagon drawing near the house. A small, tidy buggy, a man and a woman were coming closer. She strained to see, one hand over her eyes as she stepped from the porch shadows into the sun.

It was Seleta. Laurel broke into a run, not waiting for the buggy to stop, and as the man whoaed his horses, she reached up and embraced her daughter, nearly pulling her out of the seat. Seleta burst into tears and slid out of her seat into her mother's arms.

They stood there, together, rocking back and forth as though they were one woman, laughing and weeping on each other's necks, while Levi danced about them, alternately hugging first one, then the other. When Laurel finally relinquished her daughter, Seleta turned and shyly reached into the buggy behind the seat, pulling out a wrapped bundle from the basket. She opened the blanket and said, "She has your eyes, Mama."

Laurel gazed into the tiny, perfect face of her first grandchild, an infant girl with the blue eyes like the wide river.

"Her name is Laurel," Seleta said softly. "Because nothing else seemed to fit her so well."

Through a blur of joyful tears, Laurel took the baby in her arms and put her to her cheek, murmuring words of welcome and comfort. She felt something scratch her neck, and pulled back to see. The infant wore the gold filigree locket about her neck, hopelessly large on her, of course, and dangling low on her belly. She had managed to tangle it in her fist and she looked up at Laurel solemnly, not at all sure that she was going to tolerate this introduction.

"Welcome to Deepwater," Laurel said to her softly. "We've been waiting for you forever."

AUTHOR'S NOTE

Those who are students of Caroliniana will recognize, of course, the name of Laurel Chapman, Quaker educator, tireless advocate of Negro rights, and eloquent historian of the South. Stricken at an early age by polio, she nonetheless rolled her wheelchair into the classrooms of the University of North Carolina, onto lecterns all over the state, and even, eventually, into the halls of Congress. Her six children went on to strengthen her legacy, donating the largest part of her estate to the university in her name.

The Laurel Chapman wing of the university library carries her journals, copies of her best-known speeches, and her personal memorabilia. Next to her walking cane and her spectacles, in a large ornate glass case in the rotunda, rests a small gold locket on a delicate filigree chain. The gold has worn thin as paper, and no wonder. Only a magnifying glass can make out the locket's inscription: "The Year of Our Lord 1565."

BIBLIOGRAPHY

Prologue

Ashe, Samuel A. *History of North Carolina*, Vols. 1–2. Greensboro, NC: Charles Van Noppen Publishing, 1908.

Dean, Jim and Earley, Lawrence S., eds. *Wildlife in North Carolina*. Chapel Hill, NC: University of North Carolina Press, 1983.

Johnson, F. Roy. *The Lost Colony in Fact and Legend*. Murfreesboro, NC: Johnson Publishing Co., 1983.

Kupperman, Karen O. *Roanoke, The Abandoned Colony*, New York: Kowman and Allanheld Publishing, 1984.

Merrell, James H. *The Indians New World: Catawbas and Their Neighbors*. Chapel Hill, NC: University of North Carolina Press, 1989.

Powell, William S. *North Carolina Through Four Centuries*. Chapel Hill, NC: University of North Carolina Press, 1989.

Schoenbaum, Thomas J. *Islands, Capes & Sounds: The North Carolina Coast*. Winston-Salem, NC: John F. Blair Publishing, 1982.

Soller, David R. *Geology and Tectonic History of the Lower Cape Fear Valley*. Washington D.C.: U.S. Government Printing Office, 1988.

Sprint, James. *Chronicles of the Cape Fear River: Being Some Accounts of Historic Events*. Raleigh, NC: Edwards & Broughton, 1914.

Stick, David. *Roanoke Island: The Beginnings of English America*. Chapel Hill, NC: University of North Carolina Press, 1983.

Part One

Dowd, Alton. *Deep River*. Durham, NC: Moore Publishing Co, 1977.

Lee, Lawrence. *The Lower Cape Fear in Colonial Days*. Chapel Hill, NC: University of North Carolina Press, 1965.

Lefler, Hugh T. *Colonial North Carolina*. New York: Scribners & Sons, 1973.

Meyer, Duane. *The Highland Scots of North Carolina: 1732–1776*. Chapel Hill, NC: University of North Carolina Press, 1961.

Moore, Louis T. *Stories Old and New of the Cape Fear Region*. Wilmington, NC: Private Publisher, 1965.

Rankin, Hugh F. *Pirates of Colonial North Carolina*. Raleigh, NC: State Department of Archives and History, 1965.

Rights, Douglas T. *The American Indian in North Carolina*. Winston-Salem, NC: John F. Blair Publishing, 1957.

Ross, Malcolm H. *The Cape Fear*. New York: Holt, Rinehart, 1965.

Rucker, John. *North Carolina: A Portrait of Its Land and Its People*. Helena, MT: American Geographical Publishing, 1989.

Salley, Alexander S., Jr. *Narratives of Early Carolina*. New York: Scribners & Sons, 1911.

Thompson, Roy. *Before Liberty*, Lexington, NC: Piedmont Publishing Co, 1976.

Tunis, Edwin. *Colonial Living*. New York: Thomas R. Crowell & Co., 1957.

Wetmore, Ruth Y. *First on the Land: The North Carolina Indians*. Winston-Salem, NC: John F. Blair Publishing, 1975.

Part Two

Boorstin, Daniel J. *The Americans: The National Experience*. New York: Vintage, 1965.

Burney, Eugenia. *Colonial North Carolina*. New York: Thomas Nelson, 1975.

Caras, Roger A. *The Custer Wolf*. Lincoln, NB: University of Nebraska Press, 1966.

Caras, Roger A. *Monarch of Deadman Bay: Life and Death of a Kodiak Bear*. Lincoln, NB: University of Nebraska Press, 1969.

Caruthers, Rev. Ed. W. *Revolutionary Incidents and Sketches of Character in the Old North State*. Philadelphia, PA: Hayes & Zell, 1854.

Creecy, Richard B. *Grandfather and Tales of North Carolina*, Raleigh, NC: Edwards & Broughton, 1901.

Fitch, William E. *Some Neglected History of North Carolina*. New York: Neale Publishing Co, 1905.

Larkin, Jack. *The Reshaping of Everyday Life—1790–1840*. New York: Harper & Row, 1988.

Kane, Harnett T. *Gone Are The Days*. New York: Bonanza Books, 1989.

Michaux, Richard R. *Sketches of Life in North Carolina*, Culler, NC: W.C. Phillips, 1894.

Raper, Charles Lee. *Social Life in Colonial North Carolina*. Raleigh, NC: E.M. Uzzell & Co., 1903.

Troxler, Carole W. *The Loyalist Experience in North Carolina*. Raleigh, NC: North Carolina Department of Cultural Resources, 1976.

Watson, Harry L. *An Independent People: The Way We Lived in North Carolina, 1770–1820*. Chapel Hill, NC: University of North Carolina Press, 1983.

Williamson, Hugh. *The History of North Carolina*. Chapel Hill, NC: North Carolina Press, 1973.

Part Three

Barret, John G. *Sherman's March Through the Carolinas*. Chapel Hill, NC: University of North Carolina Press, 1956.

Barret, John G. *The Civil War in North Carolina*. Chapel Hill, NC: University of North Carolina Press, 1963.

Blockson, Charles L. *The Underground Railroad*. New York: Berkley Books, 1987, 1989.

Brooks, Jerome E. *Green Leaf and Gold: Tobacco in North Carolina*. Raleigh, NC: Division of Archives & History, 1975.

Clayton, Thomas H. *Close to the Land: The Way We Lived In North Carolina, 1820–1870*. Chapel Hill, NC: University of North Carolina Press, 1983.

Devereaux, Margaret. *Plantation Sketches*. Cambridge, MA: Private Printing at the Riverside Press, 1906.

Fisher, Miles Mark. *Negro Slave Songs in the United States*. New York: Citadel Press, 1953.

Gates, Henry Louis, Jr. *The Classic Slave Narratives*. New York: Penguin Books, 1987.

Genovese, Eugene D. *Roll, Jordan, Roll: The World the Slaves Made*. New York: Vintage Books, 1972.

Haworth, Cecil E. *Deep River Friends*. Greensboro, NC: North Carolina Friends Society, 1985.

Hinshaw, Seth B. *Life in the Quaker Lane*. Greensboro, NC: North Carolina Friends Society, 1990.

Hinshaw, Seth B. *The Carolina Quaker Experience: 1665–1985*, Greensboro, NC: North Carolina Friends Society, 1984.

Hoehling, A.A. *Last Train From Atlanta*. Harrisburg, PA: Stackpole Books, 1958.

Holland, Irma Ragan. *Gone Glory*. Raleigh, NC: Private Publisher, 1986.

Johnson, G.G. *Antebellum North Carolina*. Chapel Hill, NC: University of North Carolina Press, 1937.

Jones, Virgil Carrington. *Gray Ghosts and Rebel Raiders*. St. Simons Island, GA: Mockingbird Books, 1956.

Lawson, John. *Lawsons History of North Carolina*. Richmond, VA: Garrett & Massie, 1956.

Lester, Julius. *To Be A Slave*. New York: Scholastic, 1968.

Oates, John A. *The Story of Fayetteville and the Upper Cape Fear*. Wadell, NC: Broadfoot Publishing Co., 1985.

Trotter, William R. *Bushwackers: The Civil War in North Carolina, The Mountains*. Winston-Salem, NC: John F. Blair Publishers, 1988.

Trotter, William R. *Ironclads and Columbiads: The Civil War in North Carolina, The Coast*. Winston-Salem, NC: John F. Blair Publishers, 1989.

Trotter, William R. *Silk Flags and Cold Steel: The Civil War In North Carolina, The Piedmont*. Winston-Salem, NC: John F. Blair Publishers, 1988.

Weeks, Stephen B. *Southern Quakers and Slavery*. Baltimore, MD: John Hopkins University Studies, 1896.

I am deeply grateful for the love and support of many people in my life, and without them this book would not have been possible. Ann LaFarge, my clever and committed editor; Roslyn Targ, my loyal and fierce agent; my family who always keeps my heart happy; certain very special friends who have listened uncomplainingly to my triumphs and defeats and who seem to stand always ready with heartfelt hugs, fellow writers in the hinterlands and elsewhere, and my husband, whose strong arms held me up through it all. But most of all, I am grateful for a new and tiny person in my life and heart—my enchanting daughter, Leah Justine. You, my angel, have taught me more about life and love in a year than I've understood in a lifetime.